From quiet beginnings, without any 'discovery' except by the great reading public itself, Frances Parkinson Keyes has grown to be one of the most popular and best-loved women writers in the world. Her books appear simultaneously in half a dozen languages and she appeals to those millions of people who demand a good story with rich and varied background. *Vail d'Alvery* is the story of the heir to Belle Heloise, stately plantation house on the banks of the Mississippi. *Vail d'Alvery* continues the saga of the aristocratic Southern family begun in *The River Road*.

Frances Parkinson Keyes

Vail d'Alvery

CORGI BOOKS
TRANSWORLD PUBLISHERS LTD
A National General Company

VAIL D'ALVERY

A CORGI BOOK 552 08416 6

Originally published in Great Britain
by Eyre & Spottiswoode (Publishers) Ltd.

PRINTING HISTORY

Eyre & Spottiswoode edition published 1947
Corgi edition published 1970

This book is a sequel to *The River Road*, and most
of the characters who figured in that book reappear, after
a lapse of years, in *Vail d'Alvery*.

This book is set in 9-10½ pt. Plantin

Corgi Books are published by
Transworld Publishers Ltd.,
Bashley Road, London, N.W.10.

Made and printed in Great Britain by
Cox & Wyman Ltd., London, Reading, and Fakenham

CONTENTS

' "Bloody Monday" brought one of the most frenzied scenes in Louisiana. . . . records.'

Harnett Kane: *Louisiana Hayride*.

Vail d'Alvery

PART ONE

'Bloody Monday'

(March 1929)

CHAPTER ONE

'I OUGHT to have known better than to have let your husband exhaust himself like this, Mrs. Tremaine. I can't tell you how sorry I am.'

'Oh please, Mr. Gayland, don't give it another thought! He'll be all right in the morning. I'm sure he will. And it isn't your fault anyway.'

'But it is. We didn't get in from the Club until nearly three! He can't have had more than two or three hours' sleep! I shouldn't have planned a guinea hunt the day after the dance – especially for a guest who'd spent the previous day climbing all over the sugar mill and riding through the fields. Your husband came down here for a vacation. He didn't come for an endurance test!'

Roger Gayland, the personable manager of the Central Santa Catalina, lifted his wine glass and hastily tossed off a drink. He was genuinely concerned about this extraordinary guest who had excused himself from the dinner table when the meal had progressed no further than mango cup and black bean soup, on the plea of extreme fatigue. A number of extra guests had come in by truck car from neighbouring centrals, the women in pretty filmy dresses, the men in white linens; the evening promised to be a festive one, with bridge and dancing later on. Meanwhile, the table, decorated with scarlet hibiscus blossoms, floating in a silver bowl among small lighted candles which floated too, was beautiful to behold; and the dinner itself was worthy of the best efforts which Anunciate, the Gaylands' mountainous and inspired cook, could put forth. Pargo almondine, roast sucking pig and guanabana ice cream were all scheduled to follow the mango cup and the black bean soup; and the only peer Anunciata had in the preparation of these typical Cuban delicacies was the head chef of the Jockey Club in Havana. Gayland had felt, with reason, that Sylvestre Tremaine was bound to be impressed with such a feast, and to compare it favourably with the one at which they had met. And here he was, fading out of the picture, before the colours in it were even set, so to speak!

The Tremaines were new acquaintances of the Gaylands. The capable manager and his pretty wife, Laura, were extremely popular with the American colony in Havana, and the last time they had gone into town, they had been introduced to the vacationists from Louisiana at a dinner which Sidney Wade, a member of the Consular Staff, and himself a Louisianian, was giving for them in one of the elaborate private dining rooms of the Club. The Tremaines were themselves the owners of a fine sugar plantation on the Mississippi River, Wade had told Gayland – at least it had once been a very fine plantation, though he was afraid Sylvestre Tremaine had let it run down since taking nominal charge of it, when he married Regine Hathaway. Sylvestre was an Orleanian who did not know anything about sugar then and had never learned anything since, though somewhat belatedly he seemed interested in trying. Gervais d'Alvery, the owner of Belle Heloise, the next place from the Tremaines' on the River Road, had made quite a name for himself through some successful experiments with Java cane; it really had begun to look as if the sick industry of the South were about to revive, largely through his efforts. At all events, Tremaine's pride had been pricked by the sudden *réclame* of Belle Heloise, which Hathaway might have had just as well, since soil and climatic conditions were identical on the two plantations. The Hathaway fortune, into which Tremaine had so advantageously married and which was in consequence available for investment, was far more substantial than the d'Alverys' and had nowhere nearly as many drains upon it. Therefore Tremaine had decided to look around himself, through the West Indies and Central America, to see if he could not find some adaptable improvements. That was why he and his wife had come to Cuba this year, instead of going to Europe. They were great travellers – possibly that was one of the reasons the plantation was not doing so well. Anyhow, they were going on later to Puerto Rico and Jamaica. Regine Tremaine was rather silly, but she was easy to look at. Sylvestre's mother and Sidney's had been friends all their lives. The Consul would greatly appreciate. . . .

Roger Gayland nodded understandingly over his liqueur and acted on the hint with promptitude. He hoped the Tremaines weren't going to hurry in and out of Havana, tourist style, he

12

said to Sylvestre, as the two sauntered side by side after dinner from the private dining-room to the private gambling rooms which adjoined it. They really ought to see something of Cuba, while they were about it. Of course it was as trite to say that the capital wasn't the country, here as anywhere – but it was also as true. The highway which Kaiser was building through the centre of the island was still only under construction, of course; but it was finished as far as Matanzas, and if the Tremaines did not have a car of their own with them, he, Gayland, would be delighted to send a company car for them. The central he managed, Santa Catalina, was just the other side of Matanzas, and they would pass a number of other pleasant places on the way, Central Soledad and Central Espana among them, where they could drop in and look around. The managers of nearly all of these places were Americans, and they were always delighted to see people from home. The Tremaines needn't be afraid of primitive living conditions – the *casa de viviendo* was really very comfortable. What did Mr. Tremaine think of the idea?

Sylvestre thought very well indeed of it, and said so, his handsome blue eyes fixed on the roulette wheel. It was very kind of Mr. Gayland to suggest it. Of course he would have to ask Regine, but he was sure she would be delighted. He felt more secure in saying this than he usually did, in making similar statements about his wife, who was becoming more and more captious with time. But she was genuinely enchanted with Havana – with their beautiful tiled suite overlooking the harbour, with the bars and shops and clubs, with the Consul's attentions. She had been effusive in her admiration of the private dining-room where they had just feasted – the distinctive drapes, the needlepoint chairs, the baroque glass, the wild orchids which formed the centre-piece. By the time she had drunk two Daiquiris and two Cuba Libres, she was giggling and gushing almost uncontrollably, and her enthusiasm had increased with each course. Later on, after she had consumed innumerable glasses of champagne flavoured with fresh pineaple, she would have consented to almost anything. Of course, by and by, when the effects of all these beverages were beginning to wear off, she might berate Sylvestre for draging her off into the country, when she was having a little fun at last and forgetting all her troubles. But he did not think so. He thought that life on a Cuban central would present enough novelties to keep her satisfied, for a few days at least. He glanced in her direction, decided that nothing would be gained by consulting her at this stage anyway, and agreeably accepting Gayland's invitation, concentrated again on the roulette wheel.

Regine put on the indicated show of outraged dignity because he had acted 'high-handedly' in neglecting to refer the matter to her; but as a matter of fact, she was as much pleased as Sylvestre by the Gaylands' proffer of hospitality, and hastened to pronounce every attribute of the central 'too romantic for words'. She applied this description to the double avenue of palms which in typical Cuban fashion led respectively to the sugar mill and to the manager's home, adding that a single alley of oaks, leading to a plantation house, would never seem adequate to her again. She applied it to the *casa de viviendo*, which was comfortable and rambling, with high ceilings, bare walls, tiled floors, and a succession of lofty rooms which all led into each other and into a central patio. She applied it to the carved mahogany furniture, made on the central by dexterous local carpenters, to the iron grill work ornamenting the long windows, and to the inlaid tables and trays, patterned of various native woods, which were scattered at random about the house. She applied it to the oxcarts used instead of mule teams to draw cane in from the fields, to the costumes worn by the different *comparsas* at the annual fancy dress ball of the employees in the central and to their performance of the danson, the conga, the rumba and other dances. Finally she applied it to the guinea hunt which had proved so exhausting to Sylvestre, but from which Regine had returned, after the better part of a day in the saddle, still as fresh as when she had started.

The strange part of it was, she now reminded her host, that Sylvestre had not seemed at all tired when they first came in. She recalled to Mr. Gayland that while they were in the patio for tea, Sylvestre had shown no signs of fatigue. Later, when they had gone back to their rooms, he had dawdled a long time over their mail, which had come in while they were out hunting, and she had been slightly surprised, because there really was not much of it. In fact, upon inquiry, he had told her there was no special news in it, just a letter from Sidney Wade, saying he had written to his mother that they and the Tremaines had met, and inclosing the letter she had sent in reply. She was very pleased at the renewal of the old family friendship, she wrote enthusiastically. Probably Sidney had forgotten, but she and Mrs. Tremaine had often made up picnic parties together when their children were small, spending the day with them 'over the Lake' or in the Pearl River woods. To refresh his memory, she was sending him a snapshot of Sylvestre that she had taken on one such occasion. Sidney had sent on the snapshot along with the letter, and Sylvestre, at Regine's request, had shown them both to her. She thought it was terrible, the way poor little boys had been dressed, twenty-five years ago, in those stiff piqué sailor suits that would stand alone, there was so much starch in them. The idea of taking children on a picnic in clothes like that. . . .

She had dismissed the snapshot, readily enough, after one glance at the white piqué suit. But Sylvestre had looked at it for so long that she finally asked him what he saw in the funny old thing, and he had put it back into the envelope, and said he thought he would take another shower. She had gone into her own room for a little nap, and when she went back to his, lo and behold! he was looking at the picture again. This time she thought he acted a little nervous. He glanced in a queer way from the picture to a bag that was standing in a corner, and then back at the picture again. She wasn't interested in either one, and she didn't see any reason why Sylvestre should be. Anyhow, it was dinner-time by then, and she could hear the other guests beginning to arrive. So she had told Sylvestre to come along and—

'You don't suppose he could have had a slight heart attack, do you?' Roger Gayland inquired, at least managing to get in a word edgewise, and speaking with genuine anxiety.

'Goodness no! there's nothing the matter with Sylvestre's heart. He's never done anything to strain it.'

'I'd feel easier if you'd let me call a doctor. We've got a very good one, right here on the central.'

She shook her head and effectively put an end to the argument by turning to the man on her other side and beginning a long breathless story with no particular point. In the end, Roger Gayland prevailed – 'spoiling everyone's evening for nothing!' as Regine pettishly put it. The slim, suave young Cuban medico could find nothing the matter with Mr. Tremaine beyond fatigue and indications of slight nervousness. He prescribed a sedative, said there was no reason why Mr. Tremaine could not continue his journey, and bowed his unctuous way out. . . .

Regine and Sylvestre had not shared a room, from choice, for some time, and one of the aspects of their visit to Santa Catalina especially pleasing to Regine was the spaciousness of the apartments which had been assigned to them. She went to bed, after her disappointing evening, without speaking to her husband, and the next morning she had finished her coffee and cuddled down for one more snooze, when he came into the room, fully dressed, and looking considerably more purposeful than was his wont.

'Good morning,' he said. 'Do let me thank you for all the tender care you gave me last night. I don't suppose there's one man in a hundred with such a solicitous wife.'

'Oh, for goodness sake! I knew there was nothing the matter with you. That silly little doctor said so himself, didn't he? I don't know just what kind of an act you were trying to put on, but whatever it was, it was a damn poor one, if you ask me. And I might remind you for the 'steenth time, that I don't care very much for your brand of irony, especially the first thing in the morning.'

'I'm delighted to hear you're not worried about me. Because if you were you might not think I was able to travel, and then we'd be held up here for several days. But that silly little doctor, in whom you have so much confidence, said that I could, you know. And I'm going to. I've been quite busy on the telephone while you've been asleep. I find we can get passage back to New Orleans on the *Heredia,* sailing tonight. Wade's been very helpful about the reservations and Gayland's kindly offered to drive us into town himself. We can have one more dinner at the Jockey Club before we leave, if you like.'

'You must be stark raving crazy! Why, the Gaylands invited us for two weeks and we've only been here four days! Besides, we've got passage from Santiago to Kingston on the nineteenth.'

'You mean we did have. I've cancelled it. We're going straight back to Louisiana. I've been recalled by very urgent business.'

'You dirty liar! You never did a stroke of work in your life! You've invented this just to spite me. You saw I was having a little fun at last, and you made up your mind it shouldn't keep up. If you're going back to New Orleans tonight you can go alone.'

'I can't think of any arrangement that would suit me better. I'll call Wade and tell him I don't need the *suite de luxe* after all, that any old kind of a cabin will be right. Shall I tell Gayland you'd like to stay here? Or will you come along back to the Sevile Biltmore?'

In the end, of course, she went with him, mutinous, sullen and abnormally silent. He made no effort to conciliate her, and throughout the trip they hardly spoke to each other, except in public. Shortly before they landed, however, Regine remembered that her jewellery, which as usual had been left with the purser for safe-keeping, had not been reclaimed and that Sylvestre had the receipt for it. She tried the door between their cabins, and, to her amazement and indignation, found it locked. Banging on it, she angrily demanded admittance.

'What do you mean, locking me out like that? Let me in this minute, you louse!'

'I'm busy right now. What do you want?'

'I want to get in. Never mind whatever else I want.'

Sylvestre made no reply, but Regine could hear a faint noise that sounded as if he were handling something that rustled. Mystified now, and increasingly provoked, she began to bang on the door.

'If you don't let me in this minute, I'll go to the purser and have him break open the door.'

'I advise you not to do that. I think you'd find you'd made a great mistake. Especially as by the time you got him here, he'd find the door unlocked. I'll be ready to open it very shortly.'

Regine, still raging, was now aware that her rage was futile. The mysterious sound of rustling continued for a few minutes longer, then stopped abruptly. Sylvestre opened the door and confronted her calmly.

'What can I do for you?' he inquired with cold politeness.

'You can refrain from locking your door in the future. After all, I'm your wife.'

'I don't have any chance to forget that, worse luck.'

'And incidentally, you can go and get my jewellery out of the safe. I hadn't thought of making the purser a present of it.'

'I have it here for you. I got it the first thing this morning. I didn't need to be reminded of that either.'

His tone implied that her relationship to him was comparable in significance to some trifling commission. She snatched at the leather box which he ceremoniously handed to her and flounced out of the cabin, slamming the much discussed door after her. They did not see each other again until it was time to go on deck, and Regine, watching her husband like a cat for some sign to explain his extraordinary behaviour, noticed that he moved with a strange stiffness utterly unlike his usual easy grace. He continued to walk in this way while they passed through the customs and went on to his parents' house. But this was one of the places where separate rooms had never been offered them, and where both had hesitated to suggest such an arrangement; the great connubial guest chamber, gloomily furnished in marble-topped black walnut, assigned to them in the Tremaines' old-fashioned house on Esplanade, did not even have a private bath-room, and without giving grave offence, they could not go on to Hathaway before the next day. For the next twenty-four hours, they were condemned to intimacy. Having accepted this fact, Sylvestre was placed in a position where he was automatically obliged to satisfy at least part of Regine's curiosity.

'Look here,' he said, as his mother's retreating footsteps assured him that she was on her way downstairs, 'I've got to let you in on a secret, because I can't help myself. But if you breathe a word of it to anybody, I'll choke you.'

'I'm not interested in your stupid secrets. I don't care whether you tell me or not.'

'Well, you seemed to, a short while back. Anyway, it doesn't happen to be the sort of secret you have to tell. It's the sort where seeing is believing.'

Without saying anything further, Sylvestre began to unfasten his trousers. Regine, watching him with reluctant curiosity, saw in amazement, as these slipped to the floor, that Sylvestre's legs, from his knees almost to his ankles, were encased with stalks of sugar cane. He sat down on the sofa, and began to detach these, sighing with relief.

'I can tell you I've been pretty darn uncomfortable for the last few hours,' he said. 'Not that I suppose it matters to you. But I couldn't have gone around with those things strapped to my legs, the rest of the day, to save my skin. Now listen. You know all the hullabaloo Gervais has created by getting that Java cane started at Belle Heloise and on to the market. Not that any of the credit is actually due to him, of course. It was all Fabian's idea. But birds can fly and so can I. There were some wonderful varieties of cane at Santa Catalina, kinds that have never been tried out in this country. I didn't see any reason why Gervais should beat me out at a game that two can play, and I didn't see any reason, either, why I should lose time by letting my find pass through two or three years' test at a Government Experiment Station. So I just picked a few stalks of cane that afternoon we were out in the fields, while you were raving over the oxen, and brought them into the house with me. Neither you nor anyone else took the slightest notice while I did it. I put the cane in my bag and got it to Havana all right that way. But of course I couldn't leave it there, for those snooping customs officials to find when they went rummaging through my luggage and report me to the agricultural authorities. So I strapped the stalks to my legs. I know plenty of people who smuggle liquor in this way, and that gave me the idea.'

He paused, long enough to add weight to his next words. By some miracle, Regine, unwillingly fascinated, for once did not interrupt him.

'I've been pretty careful to keep quiet about all this, so far, because I didn't propose to have you babbling to someone aboard ship, "*in strictest confidence*", what your smart husband had done. I thought at last I might actually have pulled off something you'd be proud of, or like to pretend you were, anyway. Now that we're through the customs and I haven't been reported, it doesn't matter so much whether you know. Anyhow, as I said, I couldn't have stood going around any longer with those things strapped to my legs. I had to take them off. And thanks to mother's quaint conviction that all married couples like to share a room, I had to let you see what I was doing.'

He drew on his trousers again, picked up the pieces of cane, and replaced them in the bag where they had previously been secreted, locking it and setting it down in a corner. Then he turned back to Regine, with a satisfied smile on his face.

'Well, that's that,' he said. 'I'll plant those stalks myself, to-morrow evening, right back of the house at Hathaway, where I can keep my eye on them. I'll beat Gervais at his own game yet.'

'And what about that old photograph you kept looking at? What's that got to do with this smart plot of yours?'

'I don't know what you mean.'

'Oh yes, you do. I mean that photograph of yourself, at the tender age of six or thereabouts, that Sidney Wade's mother sent him, and that you got all hot and bothered about.'

'I didn't get hot and bothered about it. As a matter of fact, I threw it away. I didn't even think it was worth keeping.'

'You acted as if you did when you first got it. You acted as if you were pretty excited about it, for some reason. I thought that was one of the mysteries you were going to explain.'

Regine's final remarks were addressed to a retreating figure. Sylvestre was already in the upper hall by the time she had finished speaking. He called back to her from the stairway.

'Some day that vivid imagination of yours is going to get you into trouble, Regine. Come on down as soon as you can, will you? Mother's signalling to me that dinner is ready.'

CHAPTER TWO

SYLVESTRE had lied to Regine so many times, about so many different things, that from an ethical point of view the small circumstance of having lied to her about the photograph did not trouble him in the least. However, he was concerned that she might either find it during some absence of his, no matter how securely he hid it, or catch him again in the act of inspecting it, and he was extremely reluctant to let her know he attached any special importance to it, or to have her wonder why.

Since the death of Mrs. Hathaway, Regine's mother, the second storey at Hathaway Hall had been entirely closed off. When they were there, Regine and Sylvestre occupied a suite on the ground floor in the ell, which was almost as large as the main part of the house, and which jutted out at right angles from this, back of the stairway. Both had two rooms and a bath to themselves, and with this spacious arrangement were very little in each other's way, even with their growing reluctance to be together. Sylvestre entered his wife's boudoir almost as seldom as he entered her bedroom; but she occasionally wandered into the apartment which he called his study, though he had never used it for anything which justified such a designation. Regine did not care for reading or sewing or any branch of housekeeping; neither did she care for gardening or outdoor sports. Therefore, from sheer boredom, she was restless. She was also innately curious and innately suspicious, and because of these traits, she watched her husband far more closely than a less inquisitive and more trustful wife would have dreamed of doing in her place. Sylvestre was acutely aware of both her attitude and her habits; this awareness served to make him doubly uneasy now.

He considered the possibility of embarking upon some chemical experiments, real or pretended, and reopening a suite of the closed chilly rooms on the second storey, which had never lost its air of emptiness and death, for this serious purpose. A laboratory could logically be locked against intrusion and accident, when it was left for the night; and the location of the one he visualized, at the end of a long uncarpeted stairway and upper hall, almost automatically precluded any noiseless approach to it. But if he spent most of his time in this remote second storey, he would not be able to watch the smuggled cane with the closeness he considered advisable. He had set it out himself, as he had told Regine he intended to do: but instead of putting it back of the house, according to his original plan, he planted it directly outside his study windows, clearing a small piece of ground on purpose to receive it, and fencing it in with wire. Reluctantly, he had told Grover Blood, the manager of Hathaway, how he had secured the alien stalks and what he hoped to do with them. He knew that Blood had always resented his presence at Hathaway, and cherished no desire to further his interests there: in his turn, he heartily disliked and distrusted his manager. But after all, he could not sit at his desk all the time, looking out of his study windows, and the Negroes on the place were all more accustomed to taking and heeding Blood's orders than his own. Besides, they too had always resented his presence, and they had never forgiven him for the explosion. Instinctively, they had laid the responsibility for this at his door, and Blood had not hesitated to throw out various hints in their presence about the 'bossman's' negligence, so that it had become the subject of widespread and continued gossip among them. They considered him directly responsible for the casualties resulting from it, and their hatred of him was the more intense because it was smothered. Sylvestre had overheard fragments of their talk from time to time, and although these were always quickly hushed in his presence, he knew that they constituted a menace to his authority. He watched for his manager, and when he saw Blood jogging past the house on his plantation pony, called him over to the newly planted patch.

'I'm trying a little experiment here, Blood,' he said with

elaborate carelessness. 'You might be interested in it too. That mound's planted with cane I brought back from Cuba with me!'

'Is that so?' Blood inquired, tonelessly. If he really did feel any interest in his superior's experiment, there was nothing in his voice to indicate this. He did not inquire how Sylvestre had managed to get the cane past the agricultural authorities, and he hardly glanced in the direction of the little patch. He simply sat on his horse, waiting for Sylvestre to go on.

'Yes,' Sylvestre proceeded, finding this harder than he had expected. 'I think I've got something there. I believe we may be able to start something at Hathaway Hall that'll turn the limelight away from those swelled-headed neighbours of ours, after awhile.'

Blood continued to sit on his horse without saying anything. Sylvestre went on more and more awkwardly.

'But of course we've got to get underway first. I wasn't able to bring a great deal. I don't need to tell you it's important that nothing should happen to those few stalks. Please give orders to the yard man to leave that corner alone. Of course, I'll tell him myself, but I want you to tell him too. And tell him and all the other hands that they've got to keep their kids away from the lawn around the Big House. The place is overrun with a pack of hoodlums most of the time. If they got in behind that wire and trampled that earth down there'd be hell to pay.'

'All right, Mr. Tremaine. I'll speak to Jonah and I'll give the children a talking to. Was there anything else?'

'No, there's nothing else right now.'

'Good evening, then.'

'Good evening.'

Sylvestre went back into the house feeling resentful as well as vaguely uneasy. There was not a little jealousy mingled with his distrust for his manager; he envied Blood both his unquestioned authority and his untrammelled existence at the rear of the plantation boarding house. Blood was the real master at Hathaway, indoors and out: men were afraid of him and women submitted to him. Phronsie, the 'high yellow' daughter of Jonah, the yard man, was one of several comely mulattresses on the place that Blood had ruthlessly taken; Jonah had never dared protest against his daughter's violation, and the girl, apparently, had accepted it without either struggle or shame. Many of the 'wild hoodlums' that Blood controlled so easily were his own children;

22

there was a harsh parental quality in the ease with which he handled them. And then there were the Renos, those beautiful savage sisters, 'fighting fierce' before the advances of every other man, but catering with the utmost compliance to Blood's sensuality. Once when Vina was leaving the boarding house, in a rage because Durice was threatening to supplant her, Sylvestre had come upon her unexpectedly as she was swinging through the grove at dusk, and he had tried to detain her. She had broken away from him, taunting him and reviling him, and then she had run like a deer straight back to her unhallowed and invaded hideaway. The memory of this meeting still made Sylvestre writhe. He had been unwise, to say the least, in trying to meddle with his manager's paramour. Probably she had told Blood about the encounter, and, if so, Blood must inevitably have despised him for his weakness, while resenting his trespassing. Either he should have left the girl alone altogether, or he should have gone ahead with what he tried to start.

He tried to excuse himself for the first mistake on the ground that the wild, graceful girl, running freely through the woods at dusk, with her long unbound hair streaming out behind her, had been a sight to rouse desire in any normal man. It was easier to do this than it was to find excuses for the second mistake. He told himself that his failure to take her was based on his reluctance to coerce her; but he knew that this was only partly true. If he had coveted her uncontrollably, he would have found a way to keep her, either by cajolery or by force; to his own chagrin, he found that he did not so covet her. Sometimes his senses were momentarily stirred and sometimes he succeeded in stimulating them; but neither sensation was lasting or overpowering. He had managed to sneak away to a few famous bagnios in the course of his European travels, and had derived temporary satisfaction from such experiences; but it was always shortlived. His marriage, as far as he was concerned, had been a fiasco from the beginning, though he had succeeded in meeting Regine's requirements as a bridegroom. He had managed to act with sufficient urgency at first to permit the tearful resistance and show of shocked surprise which he knew she would wish to enact; afterwards, with the sympathy and self-abasement to which she thought her altered state entitled her; and eventually with due appreciation for her sacrificial attitude towards his gross male nature. As a matter of fact, his desire for a child had long been his one incentive for approaching her, and lately she had begun to complain, not of his demands, but of his neglect, for his pretence of passion had worn thin. There was only one girl whom he really wanted to have and to hold and, through his own folly, he had lost her.

He went slowly up the stairs, after his tantalizing encounter with his manager, thinking neither of Grover Blood nor of Vina Reno, but of his first sweetheart Cresside d'Alvery. He was still thinking of her two hours later as he continued to sit in the bare room, which he visualized as a laboratory, and in which he had found at least temporary isolation. He had scarcely seen her since her marriage to her cousin Fabian d'Alvery, and it was not in the image of the tranquil and secure young matron, encompassed with loving-kindness, that he saw her now, but as the high-spirited, uncontrolled girl, straining to escape from a cheerless house and revolting against everything that represented an established and hateful order. But even this desperate mood had not been sufficiently strong to explain her impassioned surrender or to excuse the advantage he had taken of her inexperience and her recklessness. Her very sensitivity had been her undoing; she had been deeply devoted to him as well as madly in love with him; that was why she had scorned to question his trustworthiness or to count the cost of her prodigality.

The realization of what this had meant to her in disillusionment and in suffering had come to him with slow relentlessness, gathering force with time. Sylvestre had always been sensual and shallow, but he had never been deliberately vicious; Fabian was right in saying that Sylvestre had begun by labouring under the comfortable delusion that he and Cresside fitted naturally enough into the postwar scene, and that whatever they had said or done was merely a logical part of that picture. His first regrets after jilting her were largely selfish; he found Regine's frivolity, vapidity and sentimentality a sorry substitute for Cresside's blitheness, courage, and unquestioning love. It was not until he saw her stricken, on his wedding day, that sympathy was mingled with his mounting sense of frustration and unwilling bondage. Even then, he felt no special compunction for what he had done. He was appalled when he saw her lying broken in body, though still dauntless in spirit, on her great white bed after a bad fall from a ladder, where she had been perched while helping to decorate the White Ballroom for his wedding; and he had been

24

resentful because after he had taken her home, she would not let him stay with her in her extremity. But it did not occur to him that her accident was one for which he was either directly or indirectly responsible. It was not until he came upon her unexpectedly, in the hallway at Belle Heloise long afterwards, that he began to realize how completely her love had turned to loathing and to wonder why. Later on, each time she repulsed him, his bafflement, like his longing, increased almost unendurably, and he redoubled his efforts towards putting together the pieces of the puzzle which had so long foiled him. Now, at last, he thought he saw the complete pattern. What a fool, what a consummate fool he had been, not to realize from the beginning what had happened to Cresside, not to recognize a resemblance which now seemed to him so startling, not to know, instinctively, that he actually had begotten the son of whom he had long despaired!

It was all clear as day to him now. Of course Cresside had really fallen from the ladder, of course she had really hurt her back. But why? Regine 'Felt faint' every time it suited her purpose to do so; but Cresside had always been as scornful of such attacks as she was impervious to them; and then, without warning, she had fainted dead away. Sylvestre was an only child, and he had no close relatives and few intimate friends of his own age, so he had heard fewer intimate discussions of feminine symptoms than most young men. Even so, he knew the simple fact that sudden overpowering faintness was one of the first unmistakable signs of pregnancy. True, no one else had apparently given a thought to the possibility of some underlying reason for Cresside's disastrous vertigo – no one except her doctor, who must instantly have discovered the cause of it. But then, no one else suspected – or so he vehemently told himself – that he had become Cresside's lover two months earlier. He alone could have connected her collapse with that brief, secret interlude of passionate enchantment under the Easter moon.

If he had only done this as he stood looking down at her when she lay so small and helpless in her great white bed! Perhaps then it might not have been too late, perhaps he might still have had his only love and his only child! Some spark had passed between them as they gazed at each other; perhaps she had counted on him to guess what she would not tell him, perhaps if he had not failed her in divination as in everything else, she might have forgiven him after all. It was not until she turned away that she had said, 'This is your wedding day, Sylvestre. Regine will be waiting for you.' If he had only said first, 'Cresside, it's my wedding day, and it's yours too. It's you and I that belong to each other, not Regine and I. Her vanity will be hurt if I leave her, nothing else, so she'll get over it. Her love isn't a vital part of her, the way yours is of you. I don't deserve to have you forgive me, but can't you, out of that boundless love? I'm not much of a man, but I might be, if you'd help me to begin over again.' If he had only taken her tenderly in his arms and summarily sent for a priest, she might not have refused, point blank, to repeat her marriage vows after him. He remembered, and cringed at the memory, how she had said to him, that other time, 'It's just the same as if we were married, isn't it, Sylvestre? Because we're going to be, as soon as we can, because we love each other as much as if we were already.' And how he had answered, with his mouth and his breast on hers, 'Of course it's just the same. A few words mumbled by a priest don't make any difference, any more than a few words printed on a diploma.' She had not questioned his logic then, but afterwards – a long time afterwards – she had spoken of the matter again. She had said, 'It isn't just a few words, after all, is it, Sylvestre? It's what they stand for. In the marriage service and on the diploma too.'

Poor, reckless, loving, bewildered girl! Underneath all her flippancy and all her flouting, her confusion and her desire, the dependence on basic standards, the capacity for eventual straight thinking, were still there. That was why she might have relented at the eleventh hour. She had neither wanted nor expected to be a light-of-love; she had wanted and expected to be his wife. And certainly she would have been appalled at the thought of branding an innocent child. And he had left her, without a struggle, to expiate a sin that was less than half hers, to shield their son from the stigma that was his inescapable heritage.

The stratagem which had saved them both and blinded even the child's own father to the truth was, after all, relatively simple, Sylvestre now saw. Gervais' marriage to Meredith Randall and his sister's seduction had been almost simultaneous; their children, begotten and conceived at the same time, would normally be born at the same time too, and could easily pass as twins, and meanwhile, Cresside's injury was explanation enough for her seclusion. The doctor, of course, was utterly trustworthy, and up to the limits of their capacities, the servants were too. If ever there were a leak, it would almost certainly be accidental, and obviously, the d'Alverys had ceased to expect any such accident. If any of them had feared, in the first place, that he himself might guess that the boy they named Vail was his son, these fears must have long since been dulled by his own crass stupidity. The thought of Cresside as he had seen her standing on the stairs, the first time he had gone to Belle Heloise after his marriage. 'What do you think of the heir to all the d'Alverys?' she had asked him, holding up the beautiful blue-eyed, black-haired boy for him to look at. Such a superb bit of bravado could never have been staged without a complete sense of inviolability. Later, when he once startled her by coming on her suddenly at night, she had lost this sense; she had been afraid that by her defiance she had roused his suspicion. She had thought he had meant to question her about the child, to force the fact of its fatherhood from her. Women were much more conscious than men of procreation as a part of passion, perhaps because it was they who invariably proclaimed it to the world. He still had not thought of Vail as his son when he sought her out; he had thought only of her as his lost love, for the very sight of whom he yearned inexpressibly. In telling her that he had to see her, he had meant no more than that; it had really seemed to him that if he did not, his already empty and aimless life would be utterly unbearable.

It was at a festival celebrating the close of the grinding season that he had first become acutely aware of Vail. Hitherto he had subscribed, when he thought of it at all, to the unobservant masculine theory that all babies look alike. But during the lengthy periods when the three small d'Alverys were being paraded for the admiration of the guests he could not help noticing that they did not look in the least alike. It was natural that Philogene's countenance should be nondescript, since he was still an infant in arms, and therefore Sylvestre could not logically compare it to Vail's. But twins, even non-identical twins, usually bore at least a family resemblance to each other, and here were two as different as dawn from dusk. Not only in regard to colouring either; they were entirely dissimilar in both form and feature; and though both were admittedly fine physical specimens, Vail was the more advanced and the more provocative of the two. Sylvestre played with him until Dinah took him away, and for a long time afterwards he was haunted by the thought of it. But between the abrupt cessation of festivities at Hathaway Hall and his own frequent absences, he did not see the child again at close range for a long time and gradually he forgot about him.

The next encounter, when it came, was wholly unexpected. Sylvestre had stopped in at Tramonte's Fancy Grocery Store to get some of the antepasto for which this was increasingly famous, when he caught sight of two small black-haired boys, one of them evidently a few years older than the other. They were partially hidden by hanging strips of garlic and rows of beautiful cheeses, and seated at a table in the rear of the shop, with a lovely little blonde between them and a spotted spaniel at their feet. Both were absorbed in large platefuls of spumone and neither seemed to notice his presence; but after eyeing them attentively for a few minutes, Sylvestre walked back to the table.

'Hello!' he said, addressing the younger boy. 'Aren't you Vail d'Alvery? And isn't this pretty little girl your sister Sybelle?'

The pretty little girl smiled engagingly, showing small pearly teeth and delightful dimples. She nodded a friendly reply and then glanced down at her plate, archly rather than shyly. The little boy looked up, swallowing a spoonful of spumone before he answered. Something in the expression of his big blue eyes sent a strange shiver through Sylvestre.

'Yeah,' he said at last, unconcernedly. Then, as if eager to correct an oversight. Vail added, 'And this is Riccardo Tramonte. He's my best friend just now.'

The little Italian instantly slid from his seat and held out his hand politely. 'I'm glad to meet you, sir,' he said. 'Won't you sit down? I'll get some more spumone right away.'

'These damn Dagoes teach their children better manners than we do,' Sylvestre thought to himself resentfully. Aloud he said, 'Thanks very much, Riccardo. I'd like to, if I wouldn't be butting into your party. . . . Aren't you and Sybelle a long way from Belle Heloise, Vail, all by yourselves?'

'We're staying with Aunt Cresside. She always lets us come here and have spumone with Riccardo. He comes to have dinner with us first, except when he's in school.'

'I see. Well, that sounds like a very pleasant arrangement. Is this your dog or Riccardo's?'

'She's mine.'

'She's a very nice-looking little dog.'

'You bet she is. Uncle Fabian's dog, Belizaire, is her daddy. Uncle Fabian says none of Belizaire's puppies is ugly.'

'What's her name?'

'Maud.'

'Isn't that a rather queer name for a dog?'

'I don't think so. I think it's a swell name for a dog. Maud used to belong to Aunt Cresside. But when she went around the world she gave Maud to me. Belizaire stayed with us too.'

Vail put his partially emptied saucer down on the floor and Maud began to lap up the remains of the spumone with avidity. Riccardo, emerging from a door at the rear of the shop, again addressed Sylvestre with extreme politeness.

'This is Mr. Tremaine, isn't it?' he said. 'Mamma says, won't you come into the dining-room to eat your spumone? I'm sorry my father isn't home too. He's in Hammond, opening a new branch store.'

'How many branch stores has he now?'

'This'll make four. And he has six trucks. . . . Shall I tell mamma you'll come in, Mr. Tremaine?'

'Yes, if you and Sybelle and Vail will come with me.'

Riccardo picked up the saucer which Maud had effectually emptied, and held open the door at the rear of the store, ushering his guests into the kitchen beyond, where his mother Netta was waiting to welcome them. She was frankly forty, and as she had never made any effort to curb her enjoyment in macaroni, ravioli, gnocchi and other substantial foodstuffs, her figure was beginning to look full rather than rounded; in places her dark cloth dress seemed about to burst at the seams. But her beautiful brown eyes still gave distinction to her pleasant face, and her glossy black braids, still unflecked with white, formed a crown of glory for her well-shaped head. Moreover, the plainness and gracelessness of her clothes were almost startlingly relieved by the fine diamonds she was wearing, both in the long lobes of her pierced ears and on her roughened hands. She regarded all the children with a beaming expression and held out her arms to Sybelle, hugging her ecstatically, while Maud circled around them, barking in a joyous tone. Then, releasing the little girl, Netta put her arm affectionately around Vail's shoulder, while she nodded her greeting to Sylvestre.

'Howdado, Mr. Tremaine, howdado!' she said amiably. During the years while she had been gaining weight she had been losing her painful shyness, and her manner, though properly deferential to an important customer, was entirely self-possessed. 'Won't you come-a right along into the dinin' room, please? We goin to have-a leetla party, everythin' all-a ready. Verra nice you come-a too.'

She led the way, not without unmistakable pride, through a spotless kitchen, where, Sylvestre noticed in passing, the equipment was far more modern than at Hathaway Hall, to a dining-room furnished in golden oak, and hung with highly coloured lithographs of saints and martyrs surrounding a large framed crucifix. The religious note was accentuated by a similar gilt crucifix and some small plaster statuettes which stood on the mantelpiece, but slightly relieved by two large tinted photographs in oval frames, one of the ex-pedlar Luigi Tramonte incongruously clad in full dress so ill-fitting as to suggest rental, the other of Riccardo in a blue serge sailor suit, with a ribbon dangling from his hat. Netta had retained her predilection for paper flowers, and a multi-coloured bouquet of these ornamented the centre of the lace-covered table, which as usual was heavily laden, this time with small spicy cookies, covered with pink-and-white icing, little crescent-shaped pies filled with fluffy cream cheese, and numerous other delicacies which were new to Sylvestre, as well as the spumone and fig newtons with which he was already familiar. Sybelle clapped her hands with delight as she looked at the display, and then rushed back to Netta for another hug before wriggling into her seat.

'Oh, Mrs. Tramonte, you're the *nicest* lady! You've got my own favourite set of dishes out for me again! But why didn't you tell me we were having *viscotta* and *cassate* before I ate so much spumone in the store? You know they're my favourites! I won't have room for half as many as I want!'

'Now, now, you have-a plenty room, Sybelle. Mr. Tremaine, please, you sit-a here side-a Sybelle? We let-a leetla boys sit-a other side. What you want-a first? You ain-a had spumone yet at all, better you begin with-a that. Take-a leetla glass wine too. Luigi, he have-a good luck with his wine this year. Zinfandel grapes, they verra, verra nice for wine.'

She began to fill glasses and to heap plates, still conversing without self-consciousness or restraint. The two boys, stuffing themselves contentedly and slipping occasional titbits to Maud, who crouched expectantly beside them, did very little talking as the feast progressed; Riccardo occasionally contributed a brief remark, but Vail seemed completely indifferent to such amenities.

30

Sybelle answered sweetly and softly when Sylvestre spoke to her, but Netta, to whom she was obviously much attached, absorbed most of her attention; she rose repeatedly to embrace her hostess again, or to murmur words of affection and appreciation in Netta's willing ear. Sylvestre, liberated from conversational effort both by Sybelle's preoccupation and Netta's volubility, and more and more arrested by Vail, studied the child, who was seated directly opposite him, with increasing attention. Some time elapsed before Sybelle roused him from this scrutiny by making a startling request.

'I'll burst if I eat any more, Mrs. Tramonte, truly I will. Couldn't I play with the crucifix a little bit now?'

'Sure you can-a play with him all you want-a, Sybelle. Get-a the crucifix down from the mantle for Sybelle, Riccardo.'

Riccardo rose, and reaching for the gilt crucifix which stood between the statuettes, placed it proudly in front of Sybelle. Now that he could observe it more closely. Sylvestre saw the image was hung with various miniature utensils, representing the implements associated with the crucifixion – a sponge, a spear, a ladder, a lantern, a scourge, a hammer and so on – and that all these were detachable from the central figure and those which surrounded the cross. Gravely, Sybelle began to move these miniature utensils from one position to another, while Netta sat helpfully beside her, offering an occasional suggestion, and making small pious sounds under her breath. Vail had risen at the same time as Riccardo, and taking a sheriff's badge and a B-B gun from the sideboard, had gone into the living-room. Obviously, the crucifix did not hold his interest; but Riccardo continued to linger on the threshold, manipulating a lasso with considerable skill, and glancing every now and then towards Sybelle, as if to determine whether she were appreciating his performance. Sylvestre, after watching this by-play with amusement for some moments, thanked Netta for her bounteous hospitality, and excusing himself from the table, also went into the living-room and approached Vail, who had somewhat inconsistently added a belt, a bowie knife and a red bandana to his sheriff's badge, and was taking aim at various gaudy but otherwise inoffensive ornaments.

'What on earth are you doing, Vail?' Sylvestre inquired, more and more intrigued.

'Nothing,' Vail answered, once more allowing an interval to

elapse before saying anything at all. Riccardo again stepped into the breach.

'We're going to play stagecoach after awhile. Like in the movies. Vail's practising. Sybelle's the one who gets rescued. Mostly I'm the bandit chief and Vail's the sheriff. But sometimes Vail's the bandit and I'm Sybelle's father. Except when papa's here. When he's here, he acts too. He's grand.'

'I should think he might be. . . . I'd like very much to watch you two boys play stagecoach.'

Again he looked at Vail expectantly, and this time Riccardo waited for his friend to answer. The reply, when it finally came from the desired quarter, was anything but cordial.

'We're not going to play stagecoach right away. Sybelle always wants to play with the perfume bottles after she gets through playing with the crucifix.'

'The perfume bottles?'

Sylvestre was still looking at Vail, but as he was obviously uninterested in continuing the conversation, Riccardo was finally forced to do so.

'Yes, the bottles with the perfume mamma uses on her paper flowers. When they're most empty, she saves them for Sybelle. Then Sybelle fills them up with water, and goes around sprinkling things.'

'I see.'

'And next she dresses up in some old shawl of mamma's and some big old comb and fancy stuff like that.'

'I see,' Sylvestre said again, though this time he was not so sure that he did. Momentarily, he wondered if Gervais and Merry realized how much time the twins spent with the Tramontes when theoretically they were with Fabian and Cresside, and whether Sybelle's prattle had ever disclosed her status as Netta's petted darling and Riccardo's heroine of high adventure. But after all, it was none of his affair, and he was far more interested in Vail, who was certainly no prattler. He made another attempt to draw the little boy out.

'If you and Sybelle are going back to your Aunt Cresside's after you get through playing stagecoach, Vail, I'll be glad to wait for you and walk around to Somerulos Street with you.'

'We're not going back there. Aunt Cresside's coming here to get us after awhile. She's going to take us home in her new car that Uncle Fabian gave her. It's a knockout.'

Vail opened the door leading from the living-room into a small gallery, and with Maud at his heels, ran down the steps into the back yard, Riccardo, abandoning the lasso after one more backward glance at Sybelle, whose attention was still evenly divided between his mother and the crucifix, again made the appropriate gesture which Vail had neglected to supply.

'Do you want to come out too, Mr. Tremaine? You could look at the rabbits and the chickens. I take care of those. We've got a garden and an orchard.'

'What kind of an orchard?'

'Well, we've got a chestnut tree, cherry trees and fig trees. We have bay trees and Grand Dukes too.'

'I'll be glad to come with you. I had no idea there was so much land behind the house. That's a fine kitchen garden you've got. It looks as if you had nice neighbours too.'

Sylvestre's eyes wandered past the fruit trees and the coops and runs where the white chickens and brown rabbits were confined. He could see rows and rows of rich green vegetables rising above well-weeded ground and beyond them several neat well-located cottages. The entire scene was one of plenty and unostentatious prosperity.

'Yes. Those houses belong to papa. ... I think I'll feed my rabbits now, if you don't mind, before Vail and I play in our mine.'

'Your mine?'

'Yes, sir. We've got a mine over yonder behind the Grand Dukes. We keep our pretend treasure in it. That's fun.'

'I reckon it must be. I've never been much good at pretending I had something when I didn't. ... Vail's over there already, isn't he? I haven't seen him for the last few minutes.'

'Yes. Vail don't like to wait.'

'And do you boys let Sybelle dig for treasure with you?'

'Well, sometimes she comes and watches. We wouldn't let any old girl hang around, but it's different with Sybelle, because Vail's her twin. Anyway, she's not like those other old girls. She's all right to have around. And you could stay, too, if you want to.'

Sylvestre hesitated. He was terribly tempted to remain, to see what would happen if Cresside found him there talking to Vail when she arrived. In the end he dismissed the idea, partly because he was actually ashamed of it, and partly because Vail himself gave him so little encouragement to remain. Something about the little boy's attitude towards him seemed actually antagonistic. He rode out of town, obsessed with this thought, and with the strange notion that he had been looking at his own double, in miniature. It was absurd, he said to himself; no man knew what he really looked like: anyone could have black hair and blue eyes and a ruddy skin. But when he reached Hathaway Hall, he locked himself in his bathroom, and stood for a long time, staring at himself in his shaving mirror.

He went on telling himself it was absurd to imagine a resemblance, and then reflected on other resemblances which he had found or fancied. He had seen married couples who had grown to look like each other, especially after they had lived together a long time; he had seen adopted children who resembled their parents. But after all, such resemblances were largely those of expression. This was different. He wished he knew exactly what he had looked like when he was Vail's age. . . . And then, a few weeks later, he had found out.

It was fantastic that a faded old photograph, received from a comparative stranger on a remote Cuban central, should have clarified a mystery and explained an attraction which had baffled him for years. But it was also true. Sitting in the one broken, straight-backed chair which remained in the bare, second-storey room, Sylvestre took the snapshot from his pocket and scrutinized it carefully for the hundreth time. That was Vail's tousled black hair which his own mother had never successfully slicked into place, that was Vail's sturdy form undisguised by the stiff piqué suit, those were Vail's big clear eyes relentlessly staring into his own. 'The heir to all the d'Alverys' was actually his own heir, bone of his bone, flesh of his flesh, begotten under an Easter moon, born in a locked chamber on a bitter winter night. And he himself, during the secret travail of his child's mother, had been basking on the warm sands of the Riviera with the simpering fool he had chosen to marry in her stead!

It was too late to think of that now, he told himself bitterly, while still wincing at the thought, but a man did not have to act like a fool or cad for ever, merely because he had once played the part; he could profit by his past mistakes, he could retrieve his lost ground. . . . At least there was a well-established theory to that effect. But reviewing his own problems from a practical angle, Sylvestre saw no way in which he could solve them. How could he possibly prove that Vail was his son? The d'Alverys had safe-guarded the child and his mother at every turn. And granting for the sake of argument that he could prove it, what would the revelation of such a secret accomplish? Nothing except to tarnish the good name of the woman he loved and to stigmatize as a bastard the boy who could never belong to him. He could not marry Cresside now, he could not acknowledge and legitimatize Vail. He was doomed to stand helplessly aside, while another man encompassed his own lost love with tenderness and devotion, and his own child grew to manhood under a name that was not his.

Out of the chaos and resentment in his wretched mind, only one clear and comforting thought emerged; sooner or later Vail was bound to discover the truth, and conceivably, once this had happened, some chance encounter between father and son might bring about mutual acknowledgment of their relationship. Sylvestre realized that Vail adored Cresside; every reference the child made to her revealed the love and harmony between them. Consequently he would inevitably begin by despising the man who had brought such suffering and shame upon her, and – judging from Vail's conduct at the Tramontes' – there was apparently an instinctive antagonism to combat besides. Nevertheless, or so Sylvestre tried to tell himself with conviction, all close kinships had definite claims upon those bound together by ties of blood, and were possessed of hidden strength to enforce these; however reluctant Vail might be to admit that he knew Sylvestre was his father, eventually he might be persuaded or impelled to do so; once this had happened, Sylvestre was hopeful that he himself might extenuate his wrong doings, emphasize his repentance, and win his son's consent to occasional secret but intentional meetings. If he could do this much, he would try to be satisfied, since he knew only too well that it would be the utmost to which he could look forward. But even the admission of the hidden bond between them would in some measure assuage his broken spirit and alleviate the loneliness of his childless existence.

As he persistently dwelt on the idea that Vail would ultimately acknowledge their relationship, Sylvestre told himself that if the boy did not make the eventual discovery until he too had committed some hothead act of folly, he would judge him rather less harshly than if he still regarded him through the uncompromising eyes of a blameless youth. But this thought did not bring much consolation with it. In the first place, Sylvestre knew that he could not classify the seduction of Cresside tolerantly and simply as a hothead act of folly. It had been nothing of the sort. It had been a crime blasphemously committed in the name of love. In the second place, it did not in any way gratify him to think that Vail might inherit his weak traits instead of Cresside's strong character. He was proud because the boy looked like him, but he honestly hoped that the resemblance between them was only skin deep. In the third place, he felt he could not possess his soul in patience much longer; the sooner the showdown came, the better he would be pleased. Therefore, far from hoping that Vail's conduct would help to bring about a rapprochement between them, Sylvestre tried to conjure up ways through which, by his own present prowess, he could induce his son to think more leniently of his past sins. Any number of worthwhile men – so ran the specious argument he was preparing – began by frittering away their time, marrying for money, and living incontinently. But as they grew older and wiser they turned their talents to good account and became exemplary husbands and fathers. He would call upon Vail to observe the splendid rehabilitation of Hathaway Hall under his supervision – the rehabilitation which he had just begun by the introduction of the smuggled cane, and which his fond fancy already depicted as having reached remarkable heights by the time this imaginary conversation could take place. He would demonstrate his extraordinary patience and forbearance towards his tiresome and exasperating wife, and his blameless conduct as far as all other women were concerned. He would invite his son to come to him for the little favours which perhaps, under the circumstances, Vail would hesitate to ask of Gervais d'Alvery, but which he, Sylvestre, would be only too glad to grant, and with the little problems to which possibly Gervais did not have time nor inclination to listen. Of course, Gervais d'Alvery had always been a fine fellow, one of the best, and he had now become a very substantial citizen as well. But after all, he had a large family; he had to divide his attention among five children, which was very different from lavishing all his affection on one; and his existence was further complicated by his political duties, and by the financial worries which, though now greatly lessened, were still something of a burden. Sylvestre, on the other hand, with only the plantation to consider, had any amount of leisure and any amount of money, both of which were entirely at Vail's disposal.

I don't want your money. I don't want your advice. I don't want anything to do with you. Hathaway isn't yours, it's your wife's, and I don't want anything to do with her either. I don't want her wondering what's become of you, if you sneak off to see me on the sly, and finally ferreting out the reason you do it. I certainly don't want to go to her house. She was a false friend to my mother, just as you were a false lover. Suppose you are my father? Well, that's my hard luck. Suppose you would like to be with me? Well, that's yours. I can't help the fact that you got me. But I can keep away from you, most of the time, and I'm going to.

Sylvestre would gladly have given ten years of his worthless life if, after all his specious arguments, this did not still seem to him the inevitable retort. He tried to change it, or at least to soften it, as it came echoing back to thwart him and mock him, but without success. In imagination he continued to see the future Vail standing before him, ruddier and sturdier and older than the little boy at the Fancy Grocery Store, not only alien and antagonistic now, but accusing and condemning. . . .

Someone was coming up the uncarpeted stairway and down the long hall. The bare boards creaked under the advancing footsteps, and to Sylvestre there was something eerie about the sound; it was like the weird noise attributed to the uneasy ghosts which allegedly prowled through haunted houses at night. Annoyed with himself for entertaining such a nonsensical idea, Sylvestre slipped the snapshot back into his pocket, pushed the broken chair against the bare wall and went to the door. Regine met him on the threshold.

'What on earth are you doing up here all by yourself?'

'Just looking over the premises. I'm thinking of rigging up a laboratory here, if you wouldn't object.'

'What good would that do?'

'I might make chemical experiments here, the way Gervais d'Alvery does at Belle Heloise.'

'I thought it was that cane you brought in fastened to your legs that you meant to experiment with.'

'Well, there's no reason why I shouldn't do both, is there?'

'No, except I don't see how you can keep your eye on that cane if you stay up here much.'

This was exactly what Sylvestre himself had feared, while endeavouring to dismiss his anxiety as absurd. But he answered sneeringly.

'You didn't expect me to sit and watch it all day, out of my study window, did you?'

'It might not be a bad plan, if you really want to keep an eye on it.'

'I've put a fence around it. I've told Blood that Jonah's to let it alone and that the kids are to stay out of the yard from now on.'

'Well, evidently Blood hasn't hurried about relaying your orders. Anyway, one of Phronsie's children has climbed over your silly little fence and is squatting down there in the dirt, picking the eyes out of the stalks. I just thought maybe you'd like to know.'

Instead of simpering, as usual, Regine spoke with malicious triumph. Sylvestre pushed past her, and swearing under his breath, tore down the stairs and out of doors. A plump little pickaninny, dressed in calico, was seated squarely in the middle of the new plot with a small spade beside her, her beribboned head bent over an obviously congenial task: she was digging her small blue nails deep into the tender young stalks which she had just uprooted and plucking from them the tiny eyes which formed the seed for future shoots. Sylvestre swooped down and slapped her hands hard. Then he picked her up and shook her with all his force. Her head was bobbing back and forth on her shoulders and her eyes bulging from their sockets when he finally set her down.

'You come along with me,' he commanded. 'I'm going to take you straight to your mother and tell her to whip you to within an inch of your life, you devilish little brat!'

'Ah ain't done nothin', Mr. Tremaine,' the child whimpered, trying to draw away from him. 'Ah was jes' playin' in de yawd wid my spade lak Ah allus does.'

'Well, you're not to play in the yard any more, you hear? If you do, I'll whip you myself, and it won't be within an inch of your life, either. I'll sure enough kill you. Come on now, you can't get away from me. You needn't think you can.'

The child's whimper had risen to a wail by the time they had reached Jonah's cabin, where his two daughters, Phronsie and Meme, also lived with their respective broods. It was one of the pleasantest and tidiest on the plantation. Flowers bloomed profusely in its tiny yard, clean clothes flapped perpetually from a line hung between two chinaberry trees beside it, and only one harmless old feist wandered aimlessly among the fluttering fowl which surrounded it. The children playing on the small gallery were well-dressed and looked well-fed; no doubt Blood saw to it that they should be. Sylvestre thought savagely, recoiling from the unwelcome thought, which had just struck him, that the little girl he was dragging after him was probably his manager's daughter as well as Phronsie's. However, the realization of this did not prevent him from speaking harshly to the child's mother, when she lifted the hanging cloth from the open doorway and came out on the gallery.

'Frail this little hellion till she remembers to keep her damn paws off the plants in my garden,' he commanded harshly.

Phronsie regarded him thoughtfully before answering. She was neat-looking herself, like her children, and she was extremely pretty besides. Her figure was slight and graceful, and her skin was golden rather than brown. Both her neck, which was completely bare, and her arms, which were bare to the elbow, looked firm and warm against her thin white dress. She looked more like some of the lovely East Indians whom Sylvestre had seen during the course of his travels than like a Louisiana Negress. The children on the gallery came crowding up to her, and she caressed them, smiling while she hushed them. Her composure was complete. Resentfully, Sylvestre recognized the fact that he could not frighten her or even hurry her.

'Ah sho' sorry she been bad, Mr. Tremaine,' Phronsie said at last. None of the Negroes had ever paid him the compliment of calling him Mr. Sylvestre; they liked to show that, after all these years, they still considered him an outsider. 'Most generally, Minta she's a right good little girl. What you been doin', honey, to worry de bossman?' Phronsie went on, in her gentle pleasant voice.

'She's been digging up my new cane,' Sylvestre said vehemently. This time Phronsie answered so quickly that her reply was almost an interruption.

'Mus' be a misconviction somewheres. Ah doesn't ever let my young 'uns go out to de fields, Mr. Tremaine.'

'I didn't say anything about the fields. This is a very special kind of cane. I planted it in the yard myself, right by the Big House. I told Mr. Blood that the children were to be kept away from there, and that Jonah wasn't to do any weeding around there either. Mr. Blood promised me he'd see that my orders were carried out straight off. And the first thing I know, here's this brat of yours right in the middle of my patch, destroying my seeds.'

'Ah sho' is sorry, Mr. Tremaine,' Phronsie said again. 'Minta's sorry too, ain't you, sugar? She ain't gwine do it no mo', Ah promises you dat. But you has to excuse her dis time, please, suh.'

Phronsie smiled down at her little daughter and stroked the child's hair reassuringly. Minta had finally succeeded in wriggling out of Sylvestre's grasp and was clinging to her mother, regarding her accuser with frightened and reproachful eyes. She was even lighter than Phronsie. Sylvestre noticed, now that he had a good look at her; and, quickened to the consciousness of such things, he saw, or fancied he saw, a marked resemblance to Blood's gross countenance in her small features. Curse it, he would never get anywhere, with this lay of the land! He muttered something that was still wrathful and that was meant to be threatening as well, and then he strode off, bent on hurrying back to his desecrated cane and finding out how much damage had actually been done. In his haste, he almost ran into Jonah's other daughter, Meme, who was advancing towards the cabin with a large basket on her head, and was either unable or unwilling to change her course when she saw him coming. Meme had the sense of perfect balance which enabled her to carry such burdens with grace and ease and she walked freely and firmly but she was several shades darker than her half-sister, and she had none of Phronsie's inescapable charm. Blood had never bothered her, and she had been genuinely devoted to her husband, the poor Negro who had died from burns after an explosion which had always been blamed on Sylvestre's carelessness, and to the two children who had been instantly killed while happily carrying their father his lunch. Now she was pathetically loyal to the memory of all three. She still wore the dingy black in which she had persistently draped her spare frame from the beginning, and she seemed to take no comfort in her remaining children, who were left in the care of their aunt while she worked at the boarding house. She never smiled and seldom spoke, but she brooded perpetually, and little by little a sinister expression had crept into her lacklustre eyes. When she finally glanced in Sylvestre's direction, the look she gave him was one of such thinly veiled hatred that he veered away from it, and hurried on without saying anything to her except good evening. He had meant, when he went to the cabin, to speak sharply to Jonah as well as to Phronsie. But somehow Phronsie had thwarted him, and now Meme had upset him. He would not have put it past her to connive with Amen, the rising 'medicine man' who had begun life as the d'Alvery's yard boy, and 'put a conjure' on Hathaway. Of course there was nothing in these silly tricks and primitive beliefs. Nevertheless, he had not liked the look of the funny little bundle of string, feathers, and miscellaneous rubbish which he had found on the gallery that morning. . . .

He was relieved, on approaching the new cane patch, to find that the damage wrought by Minta was, after all, relatively slight. Most of the eyes were gone from the two stalks which she had dug up, but the others were undisturbed and intact; he could still count on plenty of seed with which to carry on his experiment. He replaced the earth and smoothed it down again with mingled hopefulness and relief, when Blood came up and spoke to him with unaccustomed civility.

'Phronsie's just been over to the boarding house to see me, Mr. Tremaine. She's very sorry for the accident, and so am I. In a way, I feel to blame for it. I did speak to Jonah, right after I saw you early this evening, and cautioned him about letting the mound alone. And I've put the fear of the Lord into most of the kids already. But I hadn't got around to Phronsie's and Meme's. I meant to go over to the cabin later on. . . . I told Phronsie you're right, that Minta ought to be switched. But she's so frightened already from the shaking and scolding you gave her that I really don't believe it's necessary. I don't believe you could bribe her to go near that cane patch again.'

Sylvestre noticed that the manager did not say, 'Minta will have to be switched', only 'Minta ought to be switched'. But he decided that after all it was better not to press the point. Doubtless Blood was correct in saying that he himself had already given the brat a wholesome lesson.

'Well, I hope you're right,' he said shortly. 'Still, I don't intend getting another scare like that. You'll have to put two or three of the older boys to watching that mound in shifts, during the daytime. I don't suppose there's any danger that one of the kids will walk in his sleep and start digging up the cane by moonlight, so there'll be no need of keeping up the watch at night. But I can't sit and stare at the patch out of my study window all day.'

This was the second time he had said that now, he realized, and the thought had been running persistently in his head before he put it into words. At this rate he would be going off his base pretty soon, over a half-dozen stalks of stolen and smuggled cane. And yet, of course, it was not the half-dozen stalks of cane themselves that counted; it was what they represented, what they might mean to him in the future. Cresside had reminded him how much some trivial thing could mean, long ago in the moonlight. *'It isn't just a few words, after all, is it, Sylvestre? It's what they stand for. In the marriage service and on the diploma too.'* Those stalks of cane represented the ultimate triumph which was to help him redeem his past sins in his son's eyes. He did not intend to let anything happen to them. Not even if he actually must sit and watch the place where they were planted out of the study window. . . .

'You sure can't, Mr. Tremaine,' he heard Blood say in a conciliatory way. 'Don't you worry about that, though. I'll get hold of a couple of trustworthy boys. I'll attend to everything. I'm just as interested as you are in having this experiment succeed and taking those stuck-ups at Belle Heloise down a few pegs. Well, good evening again.' The manager walked away, his self-assurance obviously restored. He was apparently well satisfied – almost too well satisfied, his employer thought – with the interview, and Sylvestre resented the ease with which it had been carried off by his manager; but after a final survey of the cane patch, he partially dismissed it from his mind and walked slowly up the curving stone steps that led to the gallery and across this to the house. It had been an unusually warm day, and probably that was the reason his head had felt hot all afternoon – that and the fact that the cursed brat and her smooth-spoken slut of a mother and her old black witch of an aunt had all got under his skin. When it came to that, not only his head felt hot. He felt hot all over. But he could fix that. He would go in and take a shower. It was almost dinner-time anyway.

He went into his study, looked out of the window at the mound, and walked on to his bedroom. He had been a fool to wear a tweed suit on a day like that, whatever the calendar said. He would get into Shantung or seersucker straight away. He took off the offending coat, the creation of a famous London tailor, and hung it over a chair. Next he unbuttoned his vest, laying his watch and chain on the table beside him. Then he decided to take one more look at the faded old photograph before he got into the shower. He reached into the pocket where he always kept it and it was not there.

CHAPTER THREE

HE stood perfectly still, the perspiration with which he was dripping changing to cold sweat. He was bathed in it, as he had been only once or twice before in his life, when he was recovering from a long illness but still very weak; it produced a sensation of debility so extreme as to verge on helplessness, and this time it was accompanied by a feeling of great constriction. His heart was no longer in the right place, but mid-way down his throat, and his hands were numb. He tried to reach for his handkerchief, to mop off the worst of the sweat, and at first his fingers merely twitched, refusing to function. He went through a period of ineffectual misery which seemed to him endless, while the lump in his throat continued to grow larger and larger. At last, however, he succeeded in wiping his face and rummaging through his pockets. But afterwards the cold sweat poured out of him more profusely than ever. The search was futile. The photograph was nowhere to be found.

He slipped hurriedly into his clothes again, trying to figure out, while he did so, where and when he could have lost it and how he was going to recover it. He certainly thought he had put it back into his pocket when he heard Regine coming along the uncarpeted hall; but he had done this so hastily that the picture might conceivably have fallen out because it was not far enough in. He groped his way upstairs again, peering around him as he went. It was getting dark and there were only a few inadequate lights on the second storey. It was hard to see anything in the dusk, and there was an eerie quality to the dimness and emptiness just as there had been to the sound of Regine's footsteps when she came over the bare floor. He jumped when he heard her calling to him now from below.

'Sylvestre! Where on earth are you?'

'I'm upstairs. What do you want?'

'Dinner's ready. Micah's looked everywhere for you. Why did you go upstairs *again*, for heaven's sake?'

For the first time, he felt bitterly sorry that he had lied to her about the picture. If he had only refrained from telling her he had torn it up, he could say, quite casually, that he had mislaid it, and that, as Mrs. Wade wanted it back again, he was hunting for it so that he could send it off. Of course, that would not explain why he had attached enough importance to it himself to carry it around in his pocket for ten days; but at least it would not be nearly as awkward as to confess that he had never destroyed it, and to try to justify his falsehood. Under the circumstances, his safest course lay in saying nothing at all, at least for the present, and throughout dinner he maintained a stubborn silence in the face of Regine's persistent curiosity. He could not eat, but he managed to sit still until she had finished; then he walked out on to the gallery and down the steps leading into the yard, while Regine continued to pursue him with her fretful questions.

'Why don't you speak to me? Where are you going now?'

'I haven't anything special to say to you. I've got to go out for a few minutes. I won't be long.'

'But *why* do you have to go out?'

'Good God, Regine, do you want an explanation every time I walk across the yard?'

He strode away, increasingly angry not only with Regine but with himself. He did not see why on earth he had put the photograph in a small leather travelling frame by itself, instead of among the papers and notes in his billfold. If he could have said he dropped his wallet, and set everyone searching for that, the chances were at least even that when and if it were found, it would be returned to him unmolested. But the little picture frame was a single one with an open face; the first person who looked at it might easily see the same resemblance that he had. To be sure, Regine had not done so, but then she had barely glanced

44

at it, and she had been more intrigued by the queer clothes than by the child's features depicted in it, which was typical of her. If she saw it again, however, she would inspect it more closely, searching for the clue to her husband's interest, and very likely she would discover this. She had seen Vail almost as often as he had, which was not very frequently, to be sure, but enough for her to put two and two together, once her suspicions were aroused. As for Blood, he had probably seen a good deal of the little boy. The d'Alvery children rode their ponies on the levee, visited the family tomb in the cemetery, played with the little piccaninnies from the quarters, and ranged freely up and down the River Road. Considering the proximity of the two plantations, the common interests of the two and the surface friendliness between Lézine Sance, the overseer at Belle Heloise, and the manager at Hathaway, it was inevitable that Blood should have run into Vail over and over again. Besides, after the explosion, while the Hathaway cane was taken to Belle Heloise for grinding, Blood had been there every day, and doubtless the little d'Alverys haunted the sugar house, after the habit of their kind. Probably Blood had already noticed the tell-tale likeness; probably he was only waiting for the chance to put his conjectures to the best use. The photograph would give him just such a chance. As for the Negroes, they seemed to have a sixth sense about such things anyway. Phronsie, whose child he had just manhandled; Meme, who held him accountable for the hideous death of both her husband and children, had far more reason than Blood to wish him ill; if their suspicions were backed by evidence, they might make deadly use of it.

Sylvestre had taken a flashlight with him when he went out, but, conscious that Regine was watching him from the gallery, he did not dare to use it. He scuffled along the grass, cursing the inadequate starlight. As he approached Jonah's cabin, he began to move more cautiously; lights shone from within it and he could hear sounds that seemed to come from the gallery, even before he could see the outline of figures; someone was crooning a lullaby and someone was strumming a banjo. Probably Phronsie was singing to Minta to soothe the child after her fright and Jonah was playing the accompaniment. It was quite possible that Blood had gone back there; Sylvestre remembered that the manager had said he intended to visit the cabin that evening anyway, even before the disturbance created by Minta. He always did these things brazenly, so secure in his place as 'head beater' that he was indifferent to the scandals he constantly created. And Durice Reno was too fearful of the menace personified by Deéte to risk losing him to her sister, as Vina had lost him to her, through a tempestuous display of jealousy.

When Sylvestre came close enough to the cabin to see, though still indistinctly, that four persons were seated on the gallery, he stopped; and while he hesitated about going on, he heard a car drive into the allee, and saw its lights go off in front of the stone stairway. Apparently he and Regine had callers; if he did not put in an appearance presently she would begin to call him, thus proclaiming the fact that he was prowling about the grounds for some unexplained purpose. Feeling more thwarted than ever, he went slowly back to the Big House, still scuffling as he went. He realized now that he could not find the photograph that night, that he would have to try again in the morning, and meanwhile someone else might come upon it accidentally. Fortunately, Regine was a late riser, and thanks to the arrangement of their rooms, she would be none the wiser if he were up and about by daybreak. He was generally a late riser also, and his appearance on the grounds at an early hour would inevitably be a source of surprise to the servants. But that much of a chance he would have to take. He must find the photograph. He must – he must – he must. . . .

The urgency of this possessed him. He was still terribly hot, still intermittently bathed in that awful cold sweat, and his head had begun to ache too, so badly that it stupefied him. The loss of the photograph was still all too clear in his torpid mind; but he took in only the general drift of conversation. His callers were two old friends from New Orleans, Ray Tucker, now a member of the legislature, and Bert Snell, an habitual hanger-on, and both were in a state of extreme excitement. Apparently the House of Representatives had been a scene of wildest disorder that day. The Speaker, John Fournet, had ignored the demand of Representative Cecil Morgan of Caddo to speak on a point of personal privilege. Morgan had stayed on his feet, shouting, 'I have in my hand an affidavit that the Governor has tried to procure the assassination of a member of this House!' and the Speaker had ordered the Sergeant-at-Arms to seat Morgan. But three of his fellow-members had formed a human barrier around him, and the entire legion of Long sycophants and paid goons had not been able to shout him down. Amidst the outcry, however, Fournet had recognized the ostensible motion of Cleveland Frugé, one of Long's floor leaders, to adjourn. This would have meant the end of the special session, blocking any effort to impeach Long. Fournet had made out that he was putting the motion, and opened the voting machine, and without regard to the plain fact that no real vote was being recorded, had declared the House adjourned. Thereupon a free-for-all fight had developed, which reached unimaginable proportions. Representative Sayes' forehead was laid open, while other legislators piled on top of each other in the bull-ring yelling and swearing. . . .

'The worst nigger brawl you ever saw couldn't compare with it,' Tucker declared, with an enthusiasm which he evidently expected his host to share. Sylvestre, who had not heard more than half of the dreadful details, tried to put some show of interest into his reply.

'It must have been some fight. How did it end?'

'Well, in the end Mason Spencer called a voice roll and it stood seventy-two to six against adjournment. Huey's in for impeachment now, sure as shooting. By the way I suppose you realize that no one's worked harder for it than that next-door neighbour of yours, Gervais d'Alvery. He and Huey never did get along, and ever since that Standard Oil tax came up they've been fit to tie. D'Alvery hasn't lost a chance to get in his licks. I wouldn't like to be in his shoes if Huey ever gets out of this hole.'

'Gervais is usually able to look after himself pretty well.'

'He'll sure as hell get a chance to fix Huey's clock if the House puts in an impeachment resolution tomorrow, like they say they're going to do. Huey'll be tried by the Senate, and Gervais has one damn big vote there now.'

'Can't people talk about anyone but Long in Louisiana nowadays?' Sylvestre burst out irritably.

'He'll do big stuff unless they impeach him,' Snell replied. 'If that happens, you won't be hearing of him so much. We only thought you'd like to hear the news. Looks like nobody's going to bed in Baton Rouge tonight. The whole town's standing around in the middle of Third Street till yet, and the newspapermen have already christened the day "Bloody Monday"; the moon's red all right and it's my guess this is only the beginning of trouble. But if you want to talk about something else . . . Where have you been keeping yourself?'

47

'Well, we've only just got back from Cuba. We've travelled a good deal lately, you know. And when I'm home the plantation keeps me pretty busy.'

Even to Sylvestre this sounded inane. The plantation had never kept him busy, and Tucker must be aware of this; everyone knew that Grover Blood was the real master of Hathaway. But Sylvestre could not think of anything else to say. His headache was getting worse; his temples were throbbing now, and another wave of cold sweat had drenched him. He wished Tucker and Snell would go home and leave him in peace, so that he could hunt for the photograph again. No. damn it, he couldn't hunt for the photograph again until daylight, but he could lie quietly in the dark trying to figure out where he had dropped it. Of course, before he went to bed he would look out of the window and make sure the Cuban cane was still all right. He had almost forgotten about the cane in his worry about the photograph. Almost, but not quite. If Tucker and Snell would only go. . . .

'Well, we better be pushing along,' Tucker said at last, tardily sensing a lack of cordiality. 'There's likely something fresh astirring in old Red Stick by this time. . . . But why don't you come in to Izzy's some night and have a snack with me and some of the boys? We've got a good crowd – you ought to get in with it.' He shook hands, looking at his abstracted host more attentively than before. 'You're O.K. these days, aren't you, Sylvestre?' he inquired, with a touch of solicitude. 'I mean, you're feeling all right? You look sort of peaked to me.'

'Of course he's all right,' Regine interposed, answering for him. She did not have a headache, but she too had found the conversation hard to follow, besides being deadly dull. Her distaste for the discussion of any political question amounted almost to a mania, and her contention that all men in public office were either boors or crooks had so far successfully separated her husband from many of his youthful cronies. She did not propose to let the garrulous Mr. Tucker and his vulgar associate, Mr. Snell, get the idea they were welcome at Hathaway Hall, thus late in the day. She hoped they had seen the significance of her failure to offer them drinks. 'He is dreadfully busy, though,' she went on coyly. 'I know you've all got the habit of thinking that Gervais d'Alvery's the only planter on the River Road, who ever accomplishes anything, but you're wrong. If it wasn't a deep dark secret, I could tell you something—'

Somehow Sylvestre succeeded in shutting her off, by leading the way into the hall and talking himself, more volubly than at any previous point in the evening, as he attempted to usher the callers out. But the door into the White Ballroom was open, and as they went past it Tucker asked if Snell, who had never been at Hathaway Hall before, could have a look at it. Sylvestre obligingly lighted the gas, revealing the vast apartment in all its glacial splendour, and the two visitors stepped inside on the slippery floor.

'Nothing to touch it, anywhere around here,' Tucker remarked with gratifying admiration. 'Don't use it much though, do you?'

'No, just for weddings and funerals. We've had one of each in the last ten years, that's all.'

'Maybe you're about due for one or the other again, then,' Snell remarked jocosely. Regine, who had quickly rejoined the group, looked at him with unconcealed contempt.

'I'm afraid I don't think that's very amusing, Mr. Snell,' she said freezingly. 'Besides, my husband seems to forget that when I was a girl we often had balls in this room and that I made my début in it. I'm very proud of it and I have a great deal of sentiment about it. We have forty rooms in this house and the White Ballroom's my favourite. Mr. Tucker's right in saying there's nothing around here to touch it. So of course, we don't use it indiscriminately. We keep it for occasions of real importance.'

'Well, you'd call weddings and funerals important, wouldn't you now, Mrs. Tremaine?'

The impossible creature seemed bent on being offensive to her. She turned and walked back to the living-room without another word, holding her head very high. When Sylvestre returned there himself, a few minutes later, he confronted her with unconcealed rage.

'You sure were the gracious lady throughout that conversation,' he said furiously. 'I haven't got so many friends left – you might at least be civil when one of them bothers to look me up. And that doesn't mean you need to go around shooting off your mouth, either. Do you happen to remember that I said you weren't to tell, or even to hint, about that little experiment of mine?'

'Oh yes! I remember all right! But I reckon I can speak if I want to. . . . I didn't tell anything, anyway.'

'You would have, if I hadn't shut you up. And you may find I'll do it more forcibly next time.'

'Is that so? Well, you listen to me, Sylvestre Tremaine. . . .'

She followed him into his room, still haranguing him, and she did not leave him until he had told her, three times, for God's sake to clear out, each time speaking more roughly than before. He extinguished the gas, went over to the window, and looked down at the mound where his cane was planted. The starlight was brighter now, and he could see it clearly. If only it did not look so much like a grave! he thought, with an involuntary shudder; a place where hopes were buried, not revived. The involuntary comparison depressed him, and the depression only deepened when he forgot the cane again in his concern about the photograph. His temples were still throbbing, and when he pressed his cold, wet hands against them, instead of relieving the pain, this made it worse. Tucker must be right. He probably did look peaked; he certainly felt like hell. He'd hardly ever been ill in his life, and of course he wasn't ill now; just the same, something must be wrong. If he could only find that photograph, he'd feel better. If he could only be sure no one else had found it. . . .

He woke to find himself sitting on the sofa, still fully dressed. He went and looked at the mound again, and then he relighted the gas. It was two o'clock in the morning, four hours to go before daylight. He got out of his clothes and took the shower which he had abandoned in the afternoon; but it required such an effort to do this that he did not even try to dry himself. He lay down on his bed, naked and exhausted, and fell into another stupor, which was troubled by dreams this time. He was searching, searching everywhere for the photograph, but he could not find it. And he was looking for it in such strange places – all the places where he and Cresside had been together. First the night club called the Willows and the levee and the cypress grove where they had been when they were in love with each other. Then the hallway where she had turned on him with such loathing and the cemetery where she had told him she would not marry him if he were the last man left on earth. He kept begging her, in these dreadful dreams, to help him with his search, and she kept scornfully declining to do so. And after all, he could not blame her for that, since of course she would not wish to be confronted with the likeness that would help him to prove Vail was his son as well as hers. But he pleaded with her, and finally tried to catch her, and when he did that she disappeared and everything was dark and he had to search blindly and alone. . . .

At last he woke again, and this time his head was clearer, though it still hurt him unmercifully. Daylight was just filtering into the room, and he jumped up, remembering that there was not a moment to be lost, that he must find the missing photograph at once. He pulled on his shirt and trousers, discovering that this required an effort too; however, his sense of urgency drove him forward and presently he forgot his weakness. He did not put on his shoes, but this was only because he knew he could move more noiselessly without them; if he did not find the photograph on the stairs, or on the second storey, he would come back for them before he went outdoors.

He went up the stairs one at a time, panting, and scanning every inch of the floor space. He was relieved to find that he could move so noiselessly, that his painful progress was not marked by any of those eerie sounds he had heard the evening before. He stopped for breath, when he reached the second storey, and wiped the sweat from his face with his shirt. Then he crept along again, still carefully scanning the floor. At last reaching the room at the far end of the hall which was his destination, he saw, with some surprise, that the door was slightly ajar. He could have sworn that he had closed it the night before as carefully as if some priceless treasure might be hidden there – as he now knew that indeed it might be. But the latches on old doors were unreliable; often you thought they had caught firmly, only to discover afterwards that they had sprung open again. With no fresh feeling of concern, he leaned against the jamb, resting for a moment before he swung it wide. Then he cried out in fear and in fury. Regine, clad in a white dressing-gown, was standing in the centre of the bare room, an evil expression on her beautiful face.

CHAPTER FOUR

FOR a moment he stared at her stupidly, too dumbfounded to believe his eyes. Then he sprang towards her, clutching her arm. 'What are you doing here?' he demanded roughly.

'The same thing you're doing here, I reckon. Haven't I got as much right here as you have? After all, this is my house.'

Ordinarily he would have made a stinging retort to her last statement. This time he did not even hear it.

'What do you mean by the same thing I'm doing here?' he demanded, still more roughly.

'Oh, I know you think I'm a simpleton, but at least I'm not a congenital idiot! I realized when you came back here last evening there must be some special reason for it. Of course I didn't know what the reason was, but I thought perhaps you were hunting for something you'd lost and were worrying about. When you went scuffling around outdoors afterwards I was pretty sure that was it. I was pretty sure you hadn't found it, too, because you acted mighty jumpy all the time those men were calling. So I figured you'd come back to look for it just as soon as it was light again. I guessed right too, didn't I? But you see your poor silly little wife had the same idea. And she got here first.'

'And what good do you think that did you?'

'Plenty, maybe. . . . Let go my arm, Sylvestre! you're hurting me.'

'I'll hurt you a lot worse if you don't answer my question this minute.'

'Oh, I'm not afraid! You wouldn't dare!'

She laughed, and at the taunting sound, his last remnant of self-control deserted him. His head had been throbbing before; it was pounding now. But his thoughts, which for a long time had been so confused, were suddenly clear, and his strength, which had streamed away from him, came surging back. At all costs, he must find out how much Regine knew or guessed, and then he must silence her. It would be easy enough to discover whether she had the photograph, for she was obviously wearing nothing but a nightgown under her sheer negligée, and she had only soft heelless slippers on her stockingless feet; there was no way in which she could conceal anything about her person. But she might conceivably have hidden the photograph somewhere else, if she had been upstairs long enough, though it would take some ingenuity to do it, in such a barren place; and the action, on the face of it, would seem pointless. Her instinct would naturally be to take her booty away with her.

Moving with inescapable swiftness, Sylvestre released his hold on her arm, but immediately seized both her hands, pinning them in one of his. She strained away from him, screaming, but her struggle and her outcry were both ineffectual; he was far stronger than she was, and there was no one else within hearing. All the servants slept out: and tardily remembering that they would not come on duty for two hours yet, and that consequently there was no chance of rescue, Regine next tried vainly to bite her assailant, while he rummaged in the pockets of her dressing-gown, shook it free from its fastenings, and finally stripped it off her. Then, forcing her to the floor and dropping on one knee, he tore off her slippers and shook these. She was trying to kick now as well as to bite, but he continued to dodge as he ran his questing hand over her again and again, from head to foot. There was nothing whatsoever on her beautiful body but the filmy nightgown. It was futile to search any longer.

Sylvestre took hold of her feet with his free hand, gripping them as reluctantly as her hands. Pinioned like this, she could not struggle against him. He leaned over her and spoke to her savagely.

'Tell me what you've done up here, you hellcat!'

'Don't you wish you knew, you damn brute!'

'I'm giving you one more chance.'

'What do you mean, one more chance? You can't keep me here forever.'

'No, but I can kill you, and I will if you don't answer me.'

From the moment that he seized her, Regine had been furious, and her rage had mounted with his violence. But until this moment she had not been frightened. Sylvestre's manhandling, though it bruised her body and outraged her dignity, had not really shaken her sense of fundamental security. She had always possessed the stronger will of the two, and she had bent him to this, when and as she wished; over and over again, she had made him pay for the slightest show of resistance, and all the time he was searching her she had been sustained by the vindictive thought that she would take rich revenge for this insulting treatment. Now there was something about his flushed, distorted face that sent a shiver through her. She had never before seen that menacing look in his gorgeous blue eyes, or that rigid expression on his weak, handsome mouth. Instinctively, she shrank away from him, bracing herself against the floor.

'I haven't done anything. I'd only just come here myself when you got here.'

'You lying little bitch! You were gloating, not five minutes ago because you'd got here first.'

'It was just a bluff, Sylvestre, truly it was. I didn't really have anything to gloat over. I was provoked with you because you wouldn't tell me what you were doing up here or why you went out last night. It's natural for any woman to be curious about her husband, especially when he acts the way you do, shutting up like a clam and streaking off by himself all the time.'

The sharp bravado had all gone from her voice. It had sunk to a dragging whine, but it did not appease the frenzied man who was holding her down. Gripping her hands and feet more firmly than ever, he bellowed at her.

'What in hell did you imagine I was looking for?'

'I didn't know. But I really did think you'd lost something. I wanted to find out what it was.'

'Well, what did you find out?'

'I didn't find out anything, Sylvestre. I realize now it was all a mistake, that you haven't lost anything, and that you weren't hunting for anything. I'm sorry I've made all this fuss. I won't ever do it again.'

'You're damn right you won't. You won't ever have the chance.'

The look on his face was not merely menacing any more, it was actually murderous. And he was no longer crouching beside her. With one of his swift, unpredictable movements, he had released her feet and sprung on top of her, so that he could keep her prostrate while straddling her body and still have both hands free. These hands suddenly became abnormally strong, and they were moving rapidly towards her throat. Regine's whimper rose to a scream again.

'Oh, don't – don't – don't! I'll do anything you say, but don't treat me like this! I can't bear being hurt so; I can't stand—'

'If you don't tell me what you've done with that photograph, I'll strangle you. I give you two minutes to decide. One of them's almost gone already.'

The clarity of his thoughts had long since been swallowed up in frantic determination; the pounding in his head had become a tumult, the confusion in his mind a chaos. At first he had realized he must not give himself away by referring to the photograph until he was certain Regine either possessed it or knew its whereabouts. He had adroitly avoided any mention of it. Now he had completely forgotten the necessity of such precaution in the

54

deadliness of his purpose. He was impelled to force Regine to speak or to silence her for ever. His lapse was his undoing. Regine's wits were sharpened by desperation, and the wording of his threat indicated a last chance of escape. It did not take her two seconds to seize upon it.

'I'll show you, Sylvestre, if you'll let me up.'

'No, you won't. You'll tell me, lying right where you are.'

'But you can't go and get it while you're holding me down like this. And I don't think I can explain exactly. I wedged it in – oh, it's terribly complicated. You know it isn't easy to hide anything in a bare room like this, Sylvestre.'

It had suddenly dawned upon her that perhaps fear and rage did not wholly account for her husband's horrible behaviour. His skin had a mottled, poisonous look and madness was mingled with the menace in his eyes. She remembered his collapse at Central Catalina, the increasing strangeness and secretiveness of his conduct ever since. The fainting fit which the Cuban medico had dismissed so lightly might have been the first sign of some serious derangement after all; probably Sylvestre was feverish and delirious now and such symptoms might account for a great deal. The possibility did not rouse the slightest sympathy for him, but it did suggest that cunning and patience might work wonders. When she saw him looking around, vainly trying to locate a possible hiding place, and felt his hold on her slacken slightly, she was doubly confident that her guess might mean her salvation. But after a moment's hesitation, he disappointed her.

'You'll have to explain. And if you don't lie still while I'm looking. I'll come back and knock you down again. I'll knock you *out*. I'm going to be sure you've told me the truth before I let you go. I know what a damn liar you are.'

'Oh, Sylvestre, how can you be so cruel to me! I won't try to get away, I won't lie to you. But—'

'I said, two minutes. I think they're about up.'

His transfigured hands were creeping closer to her throat. She screamed again.

'I put it back of the mantelpiece when I heard you coming. There's a little crack between the shelf and the wall.'

Jumping up, he rushed across the room to the fireplace and saw that at least part of what Regine had said was true: the mantel did not fit closely to the side of the room; it was conceivable that a small thin picture might have been slipped between the marble and the wall; but there was nothing in sight. He turned furiously back to Regine.

'You *are* lying to me! The crack's there, but the picture isn't.'

'It must have fallen down inside. You can see that the crack's big. Maybe you can pull the shelf away farther, if you try.'

He grasped the heavy mantelpiece with both hands and tugged at it. But apparently the crack was an old one, for the shelf seemed securely settled in its present condition. Its immobility maddened him still further. He tried to shake it, stopping every now and then to see if the crack had widened and to glance in the direction of Regine to make sure she had not moved. When he saw that she was still prostrate and motionless and that he had made no impression whatsoever on the crack, he attacked the mantel with redoubled fury, and presently, when he stopped shaking it, this was only to glare at it with increasing intensity. Realizing that his attention was at last thoroughly diverted, Regine cautiously raised herself to a sitting position. Then, watching him closely as she did so, she silently got up, and putting one bare foot softly before the other, began to tiptoe across the floor.

She had almost reached the middle of the room when the marble shelf suddenly gave way, falling forward with a loud crash amidst chunks of cement and clouds of pulverized plaster; and as Sylvestre sprang over the wreckage, and bent down to examine the yawning space behind it, Regine saw her chance to slip through the door, which was still ajar. In another minute she would have gained the hallway and with it her freedom; with so good a start she could have outrun her captor, even if he had missed her then. But a puff of wind, wafted through the open window, blew the door to just as she reached it. Startled by the sound, Sylvestre looked up, and the next instant he had pounced upon her.

'So you thought you'd get away! Well, you can think again! And I shan't let you off so easy this time. This time you'll really get what's coming to you!'

He tried, without success, to throw her as he had done before. She had managed to get her hands behind her before he reached her, and without holding these in his grip it was harder to force her down. He grasped her around the waist and shoulders, grappling with her, but she managed to keep her footing. All he could do was to force her further and further backwards, until they were nearly to the window which he had so carelessly left

56

open the evening before. Then as he pressed her against the sill he gave her a quick shove. With one last terrible scream, she toppled over and fell.

Sylvestre watched her hurtling through the air and heard the thud of her body on the ground, his befuddled brain clearing again. Then everything was still. He had not really meant to kill her, only to frighten her into telling what she knew and what she had done. But if the fall had broken her neck, as he believed from the stillness it must have, he would not be sorry. No matter how little she knew, it was too much. He realized now the fatal mistake he had made in asking her what she had done with the photograph. If she had not known before that the photograph was in existence, she knew it afterwards, and, out of revenge for his abuse, she would have been spurred on to make vicious use of her knowledge. Only death could silence her effectively, and therefore he hoped she was dead. In a minute he must go and make sure. Meanwhile, he must think out his wisest course of action. He had no mind to hang for murder. And he still had not found the photograph.

He left the window, picked up the fallen dressing-gown and slippers, and looked carefully around the room. It was still completely empty, except for the broken chair and the rubbish on the floor by the fireplace. He went over to the mantel and examined it with the utmost attention. The photograph was not there, and it could not possibly be hidden anywhere else. So Regine had made up the story about slipping it between the mantel and the wall, lying to the last as she had lied from the beginning and as he had always lied to her! Involuntarily, he thought of an old German saying which Cresside, who was surprisingly good at languages, had often quoted to him: 'Zwishen uns sei Wahrheit' – let truth be between us two. There would have been truth between him and Cresside if he had only allowed it, for she, at least, had passionately desired it; there had never been either the will or the attempt for it between him and Regine. But he could not blame her for this last lie. All the responsibility for that lay at his door. He had terrified her and enraged her, and then, while he was frantic with fury himself, he had given away the secret which he could not trust with her. She had slyly taken advantage of him, and now she had paid for this with her life.

Holding the dressing-gown over his arm and the slippers in his hand, he went out of the room – purposely leaving the door ajar this time – down the stairs and through his apartments to Regine's, which were back of the ones he occupied. There was a bay window in her bedroom, similar to the one in his study; he had always hated these inappropriate Victorian excrescences on an ante-bellum house, and again a strange thought crossed his mind: he would be able to have them removed now, restoring the original lines of the building. He would not be a browbeaten husband any longer, but a proud landowner in his own right. He looked out of the bay window and saw Regine lying on the ground beside the main part of the house from which the ell they occupied jutted at right angles. He did not go outside, for, though it was very dry, he did not intend to take the risk that his footprints might show in the soft ground. Moreover, though the quarters and all the outbuildings were on the other side of the Big House and at considerable distance from it, he did not intend to have some stray Negro, passing by on a chance errand, catch sight of him bending over his dead wife's body. For he was positive now that she was dead. She had not stirred since he had looked down on her from upstairs.

He folded the dressing-gown, laying it across the foot of her empty bed, and placed her slippers neatly beside it on the floor. Then he went back to his own room and walked over to the bay window there. The mound beneath it was undisturbed, and it no longer suggested a grave to him. Instead he seemed to see the tender stalks which he had planted pushing up from it and quivering slightly in the soft breeze, their colour clear and beautiful, like the colour of jade. Sylvestre considered the mirage with relief and satisfaction, telling himself that his cane was safe and thriving, and that in due time he and his son would together enjoy the fruits of his enterprise, undisturbed by any alien presence.

But first he must find the photograph, first he must explain Regine's death, first he must get rid of this damned headache and these damned sweats. It was hard to decide with which of these attempts to begin, especially as his strength was streaming away from him again. But he believed that in spite of his returning confusion he had finally thought out the best course to pursue. He took off his shirt and trousers, put on his pyjamas, and went back to bed, lying there quietly until he heard Micah, the butler, and Jinny, the cook, stirring about in the kitchen. Then he reached for the old-fashioned bell pull which hung under the canopy, and tugged it hard three times. This gave Micah's special signal, and though the butler had never served his master with that special type of alacrity which betokened genuine respect and admiration, he appeared with reasonable promptitude. As he opened the door, Sylvestre spoke to him querulously.

'Where in hell have you been all this time?' he said. 'Hereafter one of you niggers has got to sleep in the house, so I can get hold of you if I want anything. As it is, I might die before any of you came around – you're later and later all the time getting to work. I've been sick as a dog all night. I tried to call Mrs. Tremaine and I couldn't make her hear me. Then I tried to get up and walk across the floor and I fainted. It was all I could do to get back into bed. Tell Mr. Blood to send someone into town for Dr. Champagne straight off. I believe I'm a dangerously ill man.'

CHAPTER FIVE

ACTUALLY, Sylvestre did not believe anything of the sort. But Dr. Champagne had hardly looked at him when he made the same observation mentally.

The physician's arrival at his patient's bedside had been greatly delayed, and he reached it in the state of much perturbation. He was a man full of years and wisdom, and his long and varied experience as family physician to half the countryside and coroner of the parish had made him almost impervious to surprise and shock. He knew that something must be radically wrong when he found Phronsie standing at the entrance to Hathaway, with the unmistakable air of being stationed there to waylay him; but he naturally assumed that the message she had been told to give him concerned Sylvestre. He was speedily informed of his error.

'Please, doctor. Mister Blood say, will you come round to de side ob de house, back ob de ell, befo' you goes in to see Mr. Tremaine? Dey's been a mighty bad accident dere.'

'What kind of an accident, Phronsie?'

'Miss Regine, she's a-layin' on de ground, right outside de dinin'-room. Looks lak she done fall out ob de window upstairs.'

'Hasn't she told you herself how she got hurt?'

'No suh, she ain't said nothin'. Looks lak she cain't.'

'You mean she's too badly hurt to talk?'

'Yas suh, dat's what Ah means. Looks lak she done broke her neck.'

'You're not trying to tell me you think she's dead?'

'Yas suh, Ah is. Mister Blood, he say, wasn't none of us to tetch her till you get here.'

Dr. Champagne opened the door of his car and motioned Phronsie in beside him. As usual she looked tidy, calm and lovely; neither her voice nor her manner betrayed the slightest agitation. The physician had occasionally observed Negroes who seemed to gloat over a catastrophe, when their affections were not involved; but usually, in the case of close connection with a tragedy like the present one, they grieved openly and sincerely. Phronsie's composure struck him as abnormal. He continued to ask questions as he drove rapidly up the allee.

'You've spoken twice about Mr. Blood. What about Mr. Tremaine? Is he too ill to take charge?'

'Yas suh. Us done tol' him about Miss Regine layin' on de ground with her neck broke and he don't do nothin' but thrash around in de bed, and say he wish he had broke neck hisself, 'stead of a splittin' head. Don't seem lak he takes nothin' in. Leastways, Mr. Blood, he thought—'

'Who found Miss Regine? How long ago did all this happen?'

'Micah, he jes' natcherly happened to look out ob de dinin'-room window when he was a-passin' through dere. He say he don't know what made him. He'd been through de dinin'-room three-four time already dis mornin', without seein' nothin'. Mr. Tremaine, he done ring his bell to tell Micah to have Mr. Blood send for you, and den he ring agin to ax had Mr. Blood sent, and Micah, he hadn't never looked out ob de window, goin' back and fo'th to Mr. Tremaine's room. But bimeby he jes' natcherly—'

'And then he called Mr. Blood immediately?'

'No suh, he done called Jinny de firstes'. She come and she see Miss Regine layin' on de ground with her neck broke and she scream and scream—'

Dr. Champagne decided that, in her own quiet, collected way, Phronsie was gloating after all. At all events, it was clear that she could not be hurried in acquainting him with the complete sequence of events, and they had already reached the Big House. He parked his car in the driveway, picked up his bag and hurried around to the side of the building, Phronsie following close behind him.

Before he saw anyone else, the sound of voices reached him. For the most part these were awestruck and subdued, with only an occasional shrill or strident note. Strangely enough, no one seemed to be sobbing. As he rounded the ell he came upon a cluster of Negroes, encircling a spot which they effectually concealed, and so absorbed in gazing at it, and in muttering to each other, that only two or three of them glanced in his direction as he approached. But Blood had obviously been watching for him. The manager, who was standing a little apart, talking with the Chief Engineer and one or two other men whom Dr. Champagne did not recognize, detached himself from this group and came forward hurriedly.

'I'm sure glad to see you, doctor,' he said earnestly. 'This is bad business.'

'Very bad. I must hear all you know about it as soon as possible. But I've got to get to Mrs. Tremaine first. Stand back, boys.'

With Blood at his side, he pushed his way through the circle and knelt down beside the lifeless figure on the ground. The Negroes watched him fixedly, but the murmur around him suddenly ceased, to be followed by a deep hush; not one of the onlookers stirred or spoke while his expert hands performed their grim task. Regine was lying as she had fallen, in a crumpled heap, and in his determination that nothing should be done until the arrival of the doctor, Blood had not even covered her. The lovely body, the long soft hair, the flawless face, were all concealed; but the eyes were staring, the posture grotesque, and rigor mortis had already set in. The Negroes shuddered as they gazed at her. It was only a moment before Dr. Champagne looked up, speaking with stern authority.

'She's been dead several hours,' he said. 'You did right not to move her, Blood, until I got here. But I want to get her into the house now. Fetch me a sheet and something we can use for a stretcher. And send one of your boys for the sheriff – he'll have

61

to be in on this too. The others better go on about their work now.'

Murmuring again, the Negroes began to move away, many of them with backward glances. Blood, having given the requisite orders, remained with the doctor, awaiting the arrival of the stretcher and the sheet. Without further questioning, he began to volunteer additional information.

'I couldn't help this ghastly delay, doctor. Micah didn't discover the accident until after Bart had started to town for you.'

'Phronsie told me that much. And that he and Jinny just stood and screamed at first. Perhaps you'll go on from there.'

'They tried to get Mr. Tremaine up, and they couldn't. Then they went over to the other side of the house and yelled till they made Jonah hear them. He came for me. Micah was afraid to stay here without Jinny, and Jinny was afraid to stay without him; so neither of them would come. They were scared stiff as it was, what with a raving maniac in the house and a corpse on the ground outside. I got here as fast as I could. There wasn't any doubt in my mind that Mrs. Tremaine was dead, from the moment I looked at her, though, of course, I don't know enough about such things to guess how long before that she'd been killed. But she was cold when I touched her, so I reckoned it was quite some time. I'm glad I did the right thing, not moving her. It seemed sort of heathenish, leaving her there on the ground. But I figured that until a coroner—'

'As I said before, you did right. But as you said before, this is a bad business. And we're still a long way from the bottom of it. I'll be thankful when the sheriff gets here. . . . Well, here come the boys. Let's get this part over with, anyway.'

Leaning over, he lifted the dead woman himself, laid her gently down on the shutter which served as a stretcher, and covered her carefully with the sheet which the men had brought. He had never cared for Regine Hathaway, as he had cared for Cresside d'Alvery; but, after all, he had brought her into the world, as he had all the children in the great houses along the River Road, and he had always retained the feeling of intimacy with her and responsibility for her typical of old-fashioned family physicians towards their lifelong patients. It was appalling to him that she should have met an untimely death in such a horrible way. He walked silently beside the stretcher, with a heavy heart and a troubled mind, and when the small procession reached her room he again lifted her up, and placed her carefully in her own bed with the same gentleness which he had shown in laying her on the shutter. Then he dismissed the two bearers and turned again to Blood.

'There's nothing more either of us can do here at the moment. Of course, nothing should be disturbed in the bedroom until Mason's seen it. But somebody ought to stay here. What about Phronsie? She seems a good deal more intelligent and collected than Jinny.'

'She is. I'll get her straight off. I told her to wait in the kitchen to see if she was wanted.'

'Good. I'll tell her what little I have to say, and then I'll go in to see Mr. Tremaine. I'd rather you didn't leave the house either, Blood, until Mr. Mason's been here. You can stay in the library and let me know when he arrives, if I'm still with Mr. Tremaine then.'

Sylvestre was apparently unaware of the physician's presence for some moments after Dr. Champagne had entered his room. He was lying on his back with his eyes shut, breathing heavily, and he neither moved nor looked up when Dr. Champagne spoke to him softly and laid a quiet hand on his shoulder. His face was terribly flushed, his skin hot to the touch through his sleeve. The doctor spoke to him a second time, and a third. At last he rolled over, 'thrashing about the bed', as Phronsie had said, for a few minutes, and afterwards muttering something unintelligible under his breath while he stared at the doctor. Then he closed his eyes again and relapsed into immobility and silence.

The doctor felt his pulse, which was racing, and took his temperature, which was a hundred and four. Sylvestre made no resistance while his wrist was held and the thermometer was placed under his arm, but he did not rouse again either, and he seemed equally oblivious of the stethoscope's passage over his chest and of the thumping administered to his abdomen. Having examined him as thoroughly as possible under the circumstances, Dr. Champagne regarded him gravely and at some length; then he went back to the library and spoke to Blood, who was sitting on the sofa with a half-emptied glass of whisky in his hand.

'Better lay off that for a while yet,' he advised. He had often been called on to treat the manager during one of Blood's periods of abandonment to corn and chloroform, and he had no delusions about what would happen once Blood was really started on a drinking bout. 'We've got a very sick man here. You'll have to send another boy to town to bring out a nurse. But I can't wait for her to get here to have help with him. I need it right away. Is there anyone on the place who could give it to me?'

'No one but Phronsie and Durice. You've seen for yourself what both of them can do, when I'm having one of my spells. But I don't have to tell you Phronsie can't be in two places at once. And I don't know how you'd feel about having Durice at the Big House.'

The manager did not speak either defensively or apologetically; he simply made a statement of fact, and, to the doctor's relief, his voice was clear and steady as he did so. Evidently the half-emptied glass of whisky in his hand was his first, and he had set it down without argument at the doctor's suggestion. 'I'll get another boy on his way straight off,' he said, rising. 'And I'll send Durice over at the same time, if you say so.'

'Send her, by all means. Mr. Tremaine mustn't be left alone for a minute. I'll stay in there with him until Mr. Mason gets here. Then I'll probably have to leave long enough to go over the ground with him. Tell Micah to watch for the sheriff while you're out on your errands. He ought to be able to do that much without having the heebie-jeebies.'

The doctor walked back to the threshold of Regine's room, observed Phronsie sitting quietly and respectfully at the bedside, and himself returned to Sylvestre's, where Durice, looking strangely subdued, presently joined him. He gave her a few simple instructions, telling her to call him instantly if the patient should rouse, and then he went hurriedly upstairs, passing quickly through a succession of great empty rooms and not stopping until he came to the one at the rear, with the open window and the fallen mantelpiece. Even here there was nothing to detain him, because neither of these provided a fresh clue to the mystery; he had already seen, from the outside, that the window was open, and the heap of rubbish on the floor had no conceivable connection with Regine's death. After an absence of only a few minutes he returned to the sick-room and sat down, considering the different aspects of the baffling situation while he continued to watch his unconscious patient, and trying to focus his attention on the living rather than on the dead for a moment. He regretted that he lacked the necessary equipment for a blood test, but he did not feel at all sure that even if he could have made it, this would have helped him to recognize Sylvestre's symptoms. He remembered that the Tremaines had just returned from Cuba, and that they had been travelling extensively through the West Indies and Central America before that; it was entirely possible that Sylvestre had picked up some obscure tropical disease which was known only by hearsay to most general practitioners in Louisiana, and which he himself had never treated. Probably he decided that as soon as he got back to town he would telephone New Orleans, and summon a specialist for consultation: he felt increasingly sure, as he continued to watch the sick man, that there was no time to be lost in pursuing such a course. But he could not start back to town immediately; he must await the arrival of Mason. He began to worry about several other patients whom he had not seen yet that morning, to whom he had not even telephoned, and to whom he could not telephone from this isolated place. There was an old man with double pneumonia, a young girl whose appendix had burst before he could operate. They were both as badly off as Tremaine. . . .

'Please suh, Mister Mason done come. He done look aroun' outside already, and say ain't nobody to leave de place. He tell me to find out where does you want he should go nex'?'

'I'll come right away. I want him to go straight to Miss Regine's room with me.'

Dr. Champagne rose with a sigh of relief. He and Mason were fast friends, though their mutual acquaintances had always been somewhat puzzled by the congeniality. The doctor, who was paunchy, stooped and careworn, came of a distinguished family, and might have made a great name for himself as a specialist in a large city if he had not honestly preferred a general practice among his own people. The sheriff, young, slim and alert, was a product of 'catfish town's' worst slums. He had climbed rapidly through his own efforts to his present position of prominence and responsibility, and he was ambitious to go farther. His entire record was creditable to him, and the fact that he had kept his office clear of graft had won him the regard of the community. Since he was likeable as well as honest and able, he got on well with almost everyone; but the elderly physician was one of his few intimates. They not only trusted and respected each other; they were extremely fond of each other. Dr. Champagne felt as if part of the heavy burden he was trying to carry was already lifted by Mason's mere presence. He greeted his friend in much the same way that he himself had been greeted by Blood, while they shook hands gravely.

'I'm thankful you're here at last. We've got an ugly situation on our hands.'

'Suicide?'

'I'm afraid so. Of course, maybe it's just a hideous accident. But what would Regine be doing upstairs at daybreak unless she went there with suicide in mind? The second storey isn't used, never had been since her mother's death. And even if she went up there, why should she perch on a window-sill and topple off it?'

'She wouldn't. I think I'd dismiss the comparatively comfortable theory of an accident. But would she have any motive for suicide?'

'None that I know of. But obviously her neck was broken by a fall from that open window.'

'Evidently, but not obviously. You haven't thought of murder?'

'I've thought of it, of course, but I couldn't account for that either. Who would go upstairs looking for Regine at such an hour in the morning – even suppose someone wanted to murder her, and I don't see why anyone should? She wasn't overburdened with sense and she could be pretty tiresome, but she wasn't the sort to stir up violent enmity.'

'You say the second storey hasn't been used for years. Have you been up there this morning?'

'Yes, I've just come from there.'

'Well, suppose you go again. Suppose we go together. By the way, the coloured boy who came in to get me – Bart, I believe his name is – says Tremaine himself hasn't appeared at all so far. Claims he can't get out of bed.'

'That's correct. He's unconscious. He's a very sick man.'

'You sure of that?'

'Of course I'm sure of that. I assume you want to see him for yourself, though. Come on in.'

They went back to Sylvestre's room together. He was still lying on his back, still breathing stertorously, his face mottled, his body inert. Mason, who was by no means squeamish, underwent an overpowering feeling of revulsion as he looked at him. Turning away from the bedside, he beckoned the doctor to follow him into the hall.

'I reckon he's out of the picture all right. Anyway, he and his wife were on pretty good terms, weren't they, as far as you know?'

'Yes, pretty good. I wouldn't have called them an unusually devoted couple, but they seemed to get along as well as most married couples I've come across.'

Mason nodded, smiling a little grimly. Like the doctor, he had suffered his disillusionments on that score, and no longer took them too seriously. 'You don't suspect the manager or any of the sugar house staff, I suppose?' he asked. 'When Blood's drunk there's no telling what he'll do, and the mechanics at a mill take their tone from the man who runs it.'

'I know that, but Blood's cold sober this morning, and I don't need to tell you that except when he's on one of his tears, he's as level-headed as they come. Besides, it's all to his interest to have Regine live; as long as she was the owner and nominally in control, he could do what he pleased; she never interfered with him, and neither did her mother before her. He always has resented Sylvestre's presence, though; I know that. I'd be a good deal more suspicious if he'd been the one to fall out of the window. Well, that's beyond the point. Blood's shown remarkably good sense and good management about everything and the men under him are all a pretty good sort right now – there was a thorough house cleaning among the staff members after the explosion. I wish he'd got rid of his women too, but I'll say this for him, he knows how to handle them. He had Phronsie waiting at the gate for me and she's watching Regine now. You've just seen Durice for yourself.'

'Yes, and she still looks more like a whore than a ministering angel to me,' Mason remarked, his smile growing even grimmer. He leaned against the newel post of the stairway and spoke reflectively. 'However, that's not saying she looks like a murderess. And I'll grant that Phronsie's quite remarkable in her way. I think we can dismiss the women on the place. None of them would have had the physical strength to drag Mrs. Tremaine all the way upstairs and down a long corridor, let alone to pitch her out of the window. But a man might have. And it isn't just a mill that takes its tone from a manager; it's the whole plantation. The hands on this place haven't got too good a name either.

67

I've been sent for more than once to settle rows of one kind or another, and some of them have been pretty ugly.'

'I know that too, but I haven't the slightest reason to think this accident was the result of any kind of a row. None of those you've been called to settle was connected with the Big House in any way – I don't know a place where that's more remote, in every sense, from the quarters.' He drew up a chair and sat down. Apparently Mason, who was young and strong, did not mind standing indefinitely; but he himself was beginning to feel his age, and the incidents of the morning had affected him, personally, far more deeply than they had the sheriff. If they were to go on talking this thing over, he would have to get off his feet. 'We can check and see if there was any sort of a disturbance here last night, but even if there were, that wouldn't prove anything to me,' he went on.

'No, it wouldn't prove anything, but it might indicate something. And there could have been a murder without a row. I just mentioned rows to remind you of Hathaway's general character.'

'I don't need reminding. I've been called out here too, after those rows were over, to patch up the rioters. And I'll admit murder may have been done this morning. I told you before that I would. But supposing a man could have been able to drag Mrs. Tremaine upstairs when a woman wouldn't, why should he? It doesn't stand to reason, when it would have been so much easier to get rid of her some other way.'

'No reason except that a fall from a window would look more like an accident. But if I know anything at all about Mrs. Tremaine, she would have fought like a tiger if she'd been attacked. Any signs that she had been?'

'Of course there were some bruises. But not more than could have been caused by her fall.'

'What about her clothes?'

'She didn't have anything on but a nightdress. That wasn't either torn or stained. Her dressing-gown was folded across the foot of her bed and her slippers were on the floor beside it, just as if they'd been neatly placed there by the maid who got her mistress's things ready for the night.'

'I may be getting you all wrong, Doctor, but everything you say sounds to me as if you weren't very eager to have me push my inquiries. How about it?'

68

The doctor did not give a direct answer. Instead he spoke as if he were thinking out loud. 'Of course I want justice done,' he said slowly. 'But I don't want to get some poor nigger in trouble by casting suspicion on him when I'm convinced he's never been near the house. I've seen too much harm come from charges of that sort. And I don't want to stir up a family scandal either. I've also seen too many of those. It's my honest belief that Regine Tremaine committed suicide, though I don't know why in the world she should have. And of course there's just the thousandth chance that she may have been a sleep walker, though I never heard that she was. In that case her self-destruction, wouldn't necessarily have been deliberate.'

'In other words, you don't want her death laid to anyone else's door?'

The doctor brought out his direct answer at last. 'No, I don't, Mason. I'll go further than that – I'll say I hope very much you'll feel you can report that her death was accidental.'

They exchanged a long look of mutual understanding. Then the sheriff turned away, jingling his watch chain.

'Well, if that's the way you feel about it, I reckon I shall too, in the end,' he said reflectively. 'But as a matter of form, I'll have to talk to Blood and at least two or three of the other men and go over the premises pretty thoroughly. And of course, I've got to take a look at Mrs. Tremaine.'

Retracing the steps the doctor had already taken, they went up the stairs and down the long corridor together into the room at the rear. At the sight of the fallen mantelpiece, a gleam of fresh interest came into Mason's observant eyes.

'What about this, Doctor?'

'Well, what about it?'

'Marble mantelpieces don't fall down by themselves, do they?'

'No, but we don't know how long since that one fell down. And I can't see any connection between a fallen mantelpiece and a suicide or a murder – at least, not this time. Regine hadn't been hit with a heavy slab – there'd be marks of it if she had, and there weren't.'

'Just the same, I'm going to question the Negroes. Bound to, on the face of that. I'll begin with the house servants.'

Micah and Jimmy were still cowering in the kitchen; they had not dared to creep away to their own cabin, and neither could anything have persuaded them to go into the front of the

Big House. When the doctor and the sheriff approached them, they looked at each other instead of at their callers, and their expressions were stubborn as well as terrified. Evidently they had taken some sort of council together, and decided on a course of action in case they were hard-pressed at any point. Mason spoke to them reassuringly.

'Don't look so frightened. I haven't come to arrest you. I only want to ask you a few questions.'

'Us doesn't know nothin', Mr. Mason, sir. Ain't no use to ask us no questions.'

'You can tell me which of you does the sweeping in this house, can't you?'

'Us helps each other, Mr. Mason, sir. Us doesn't never try to do it alone. It's a mighty big house to sweep, you can see dat.'

'Yes, I can see that. . . . Well, if you help each other, then you both ought to be able to tell me why neither of you cleaned up that mess on the second floor the last time you were sweeping up there.'

Again the two servants exchanged glances. 'Us ain't seen no mess on de second floor. Us don't know what you means by dat mess,' they said almost simultaneously.

'All right. Then perhaps you can tell me how long it is since you've swept up there.'

'Us disremembers, exactly, Mr. Mason. Mought be some time back, mought be jes' a few weeks.'

'I'm sure Mrs. Tremaine must have been particular about having the house kept clean. I'm sure you must have had some regular day for sweeping.'

'No suh, us hasn't, not since Mis' Hathaway done died. Mis' Hathaway, she done make us clean de whole house good every Friday. But po', po' Miss Regine, don't seem lak she ever cared wuz de house clean or not. She lak'd everything round her person nice and pretty, clothes and sheets and de lak ob dat, but she didn't care nothin' 'bout no ole empty second storey, no *suh*! Oh po', po' Miss Regine! Ain't ever gwine hab nothin' pretty round her no mo', after she be's laid in de grabe.'

As if controlled by unseen springs, the Negroes both suddenly sat down on either side of the kitchen table. Jinny, putting her apron over her head, began to wail, while Micah ejaculated, 'Save us, please, Lord!' at intervals which he apparently judged to be appropriate. Mason, addressing them somewhat more severely than before, said they had better try to search their memories, as he might want to question them again. Then he turned to Dr. Champagne, the grim smile twisting his lips again as he started across the room.

'That's like what my wife calls trying to sew with no knot in her thread,' he remarked. 'Just the same, I think that fireplace has some connection with this business and I've got to go on trying to find out what it is. I believe I'll go over to the boarding house next.'

'Please, sir, I think Mr. Tremaine's waking up. He may be just talking in his sleep, but anyway he's muttering to himself, so I thought I'd better let you know. You told me to come for you if he roused.'

Durice Reno was standing in the doorway, her bearing alert, her expression self-important. The doctor barked out a brief word of commendation, but neither he nor the sheriff stopped to question her; they hurried away together while she stood looking after them with a quizzical expression in her mocking green eyes and a half smile on her full red lips. Micah and Jinny, cutting their lamentations short, rushed upon her.

'What he done say, Miss Durice?'

'Plenty. But I ain't telling what. Leastwise not now. I can't stop to talk to no niggers. I got to get back to my patient, ain't I?'

The house servants had always treated her with the unique type of contempt reserved by Negroes for the persons whom they considered poor white trash. This was her chance to take revenge. She sauntered slowly away, shrugging off their importunities, and re-entering the sick-room on tiptoe. Dr. Champagne, who was slightly deaf, and who was already bending over the bed, did not look up. But Mason, who was standing near him, wheeled around and spoke to her sharply.

'That'll be all for the moment, Durice. I'll call you if you're needed.'

She turned reluctantly, debating whether she might possibly see or hear something more if she lingered near the keyhole; but the sheriff's manner did not encourage her to do this. She decided that he was quite capable of flinging the door open at any moment, and that if he did so, and found her there, he might deal with her harshly. He was no doddering old softie, like the doctor, as she knew from previous unpleasant experience. She went on to the library, where she picked up a movie magazine, and began to turn its pages in languid interest. Nothing that had ever happened in Hollywood could compare, in her opinion, with what was happening at Hathaway right now. . . .

Her suspicions in regard to the sheriff were quite correct; he made sure that no eavesdropping was taking place before he returned to the bedside. But the doctor had momentarily forgotten the very existence of Durice, for the first word he caught when he leaned over Sylvestre had been 'Cresside'. It was mumbled indistinctly, and it was followed by a long interval of silence; but eventually it was repeated as part of an incoherent sentence. The doctor, startled by this unexpected and ominous reversion to a long-buried secret, took Sylvestre's hand and tried to speak soothingly.

'Cresside isn't here, Sylvestre. She's never been here, you know. You mean Regine, don't you?'

'No, I don't mean Regine. I mean Cresside. I want to speak to Cresside d'Alvery.'

His voice was suddenly firm and forceful. He opened his eyes and looked at the doctor, his dull gaze clearing.

'If she isn't here, you'd better send for her. There's something I want to tell her.'

'Very well, I'll send for her. But just in case she can't come, suppose you tell me what you wanted to say to her. I'll be glad to give her the message.'

'Why in hell should I tell you? What are you doing in my room?'

'This is Doctor Champagne, Sylvestre. You know me; I'm an old friend of yours. I'm in your room because you're sick, and because I hope I can help you to get better. You can tell me anything you'd like to have Cresside know. I'm an old friend of hers too.'

He had often found that if he spoke to a delirious person as if the man were rational, it helped him to become so. He hoped that this might happen now, and he also hoped that he might be able to divert Sylvestre's thoughts and words into some other channel. He glanced towards the sheriff, but Mason was still standing near the door, watching the entrance while listening intently to everything that was being said; the doctor could not catch his eye and signal to him that he too could be spared for a few minutes.

Dr. Champagne had no reason to suppose that Mason had ever possessed the slightest inkling, until this minute, that Cresside d'Alvery and Sylvestre Tremaine had ever been anything but agreeable and casual acquaintances. If Sylvestre could only be sidetracked, Cresside's secret might still be guarded and others might be disclosed. He tried a new approach.

'Did you want to tell her Regine had been hurt? Of course she'd want to know that, they were such old friends. I'll see to it that she does. She'll be very sorry.'

Sylvestre gave a short guttural laugh, ending in a snort. The sound was ugly and unnatural. But his answer showed that he had understood the question.

'No, I wanted to tell her that Regine couldn't hurt her. You can tell her that if you like yourself, since you're such an old family friend. You can tell her I fixed Regine so she can't do any more mischief. She's done plenty already. But I've put a stop to that.'

'How, Sylvestre?'

'Why, I pushed her out of the window! I don't mind telling that to an old family friend. She lied to me and I put a stop to her lying. The only trouble is, I didn't find where her cache was first. I tried hard enough. She said it was behind the mantelpiece, so I tore that down. But there wasn't anything there. The damned dirty lying little bitch—'

He became increasingly profane and increasingly incoherent. For a few moments the doctor continued to question him, patiently and adroitly. But the effort was futile. Sylvestre had relapsed into his coma. There was a long silence. Then Mason crossed the room quietly and stood beside the doctor's chair, putting his hand over the back of it.

'Well, that's that,' he said briefly. 'At least, you don't think he was just raving, do you?'

'He was raving, but I think he was telling the truth too. I think he did kill his wife. I think he imagined she knew something or had something that might injure someone else, and in his fevered state—'

'Then he could have got out of bed, early this morning? He wasn't too sick after all?'

'He must have been, by all the standards we know how to set. But sometimes a man with a deadly purpose has a strange spurt of strength.'

'It won't last though, will it? He's going to die, isn't he?'

'I don't know what to say. I might be mistaken again. I told you before he couldn't have gone upstairs. But he did. He tore down a heavy mantelpiece and pitched a strong, active young woman out of the window. However, if I weren't afraid of guessing wrong again, I'd say he couldn't live till night.'

'I reckon you won't guess wrong again. I reckon one of the reasons you guessed wrong before was because you wanted to. We all do that sometimes. . . . No need for me to send in my report straight off. We can wait twenty-four hours and see what happens. If he does die . . . That was Mrs. Fabian d'Alvery he was talking about, wasn't it? She's a fine woman, one of the best. And Fabian's always been a mighty good friend of mine. If Tremaine dies . . . Well, I still don't see why we couldn't report an accidental death. Hell, it's some kind of an accident, isn't it, however you fall from out of a window? I'll just forget about the boarding house and the quarters, for the present anyway. I'd better push along to town and see if I can get that nurse of yours on her way out here, so that you can get on to your other patients. I suppose you'd like to have me drop in at the undertaker's, too? Anything else I can do?'

The doctor appeared to ponder. 'Relations aren't any too cordial between Hathaway and Belle Heloise,' he said finally. 'All the same, the d'Alverys and the Tremaines used to be pretty good friends and they're still near neighbours. If we could get Merry d'Alvery over here, it would help a lot. I've seen her before in an emergency, and she's good. Anyway, I think it would be just as well if you took time to go over and have a short talk with Gervais about what's happened. He'll be getting some kind of news through the Negro grape-vine, and he'd better have a straight story.'

'Right. It won't take me five minutes to run over there. Perhaps I could even bring Mrs. d'Alvery back with me.'

As the sheriff went out of the front door, he noticed that a long spray of white flowers had already been attached to it. The gallery was empty, but at the foot of the curving stone stairway a little girl with cream-coloured skin and neat braids was standing, clinging to the wrought-iron railing. She looked up at Mason expectantly.

'Hab Mr. Tremaine done died?' she asked.

74

'No. Mrs. Tremaine died, I'm sorry to say. But Mr. Tremaine's very ill. You mustn't make a noise.'

'Ah ain't gwine to make no noise. Mr. Tremaine, he can't get out ob de bed, can he?'

'He sure can't. I just told you, he's very ill.'

Mason got into his car and started for Belle Heloise, intent on reaching there as quickly as possible. Half-way down the driveway, he encountered a tall, spare Negress, dressed in rusty black, so deeply engaged in conversation with a Negro whom Mason recognized as Amen, the 'medicine man' of the River Road, that she did not even hear the approach of the car. Mason tooted his horn, and Amen seized her by the arm before she looked up, startled, and jumped out of the way. Ordinarily, the sheriff would have stopped to speak to the pair, but for the moment he was in too much of a hurry because of other matters that seemed to him more pressing. At the entrance, he met Merry, turning into it, and put on his brakes abruptly.

'I was just coming after you,' he said with relief. 'Dr. Champagne hoped you'd be willing to come, and that Captain d'Alvery would be willing to have you.'

'I want to do anything I can. Gervais isn't home, but I know he'd feel the same way about it. He started in to town early, on account of this fight at the Capitol – an impeachment resolution's being introduced in the House some time today and the Senate is in session too. Of course, he hadn't heard, before he left, that there was trouble at Hathaway. But Sance went over to see Blood about something, and came straight back to me. And the quarters are humming with all sorts of blood-curdling rumours already. I hope the facts aren't quite so bad.'

'I'm afraid they are. But I'll leave the doctor to give you his version of them. I've got to get in town as soon as I can. I'm thankful you're here to stand by, Mrs. d'Alvery.'

He wheeled his car around and disappeared at top speed up the River Road; Merry went on towards the Big House. She too saw Meme and Amen talking together; but, like Mason, she was in too much of a hurry to stop, so she did not hear what they were saying to each other.

'Ah ain't never ax yo' to put no conjure on Miss Regine, Amen. Yo' done wrong.'

'Ah never did put no conjure on Miss Regine, Meme. Ah done put it on Mr. Tremaine, jes' lak you say.'

'But Mr. Tremaine, he ain't dead. Onliest thing 'bout him, he be's sick.'

'He's gwine to be worse, you mark my words, Meme. Dat conjure Ah put on him, Ah ain't never know it to fail. De white folks, day gwine to say he died ob a fever. But Ah knows better. Don't yo' hear dat death bird a-singin' in de tree? Death birds don't sing for pussons dat's daid already. Dey sings for pussons dat gwine die.'

'Effin it works, how much Ah got to pay yo' fo' your conjure? Ah's poor, yo' knows dat.'

'Ain't got to pay me no money at all. Jes' got to let me keep dat little ol' picture yo' showed me, what yo' done pick up on de path side ob your cabin.'

'Pooh! Dat's easy.'

'Sho' it's easy. Well, looks lak we'd better not stay here too long a-talkin'. Yo' be's pickin' some mo' flowers, Meme. Gwine to need 'em pretty soon for a double funeral.'

They parted, both well satisfied with their talk. Meme went on slowly up the allee and joined her little niece, Minta, who was still standing in an attitude of expectancy on the stone stairway.

'Hab Mr. Tremaine done died yet?' she asked, even more eagerly than she had asked the same question of Mason.

'No, honey chile. But he's mighty sick lak.'

'He couldn't get out ob de bed and cotch me, then, could he?'

'No, sugar, he couldn't cotch you now.'

Meme walked on towards the garden, and presently her arms were filled with beautiful white flowers, Minta, after wandering up and down the garden paths for a few moments, turned back. Presently she was squatting down, contentedly, on top of the mound under Sylvestre's study window, spading up the stalks of cane which were left in it, and picking the eyes from them, one by one.

She was still sitting there, humming contentedly to herself, when Merry came to the window, half an hour later, and pulled down the shades.

CHAPTER SIX

MRS. HATHAWAY had never invited her nieces, the Misses Wilhelmina and Gwendolen Murdock, to Hathaway Hall. She had always regarded her elder sister's marriage to a Pittsburg industrialist as a *mésalliance*, and no visits were exchanged between the two families from the time it took place. The marriage culminated in a divorce, which, if anything, made a bad matter seem worse, for Mrs. Hathaway held equally rigid views on both subjects; and these views had not changed when Mrs. Murdock died, leaving two grown daughters. They wired their aunt, asking if she and Regine would not attend their mother's funeral; but the reply was an uncompromising refusal. Several years later, when her own mother died, Regine made no corresponding gesture; she had never been aware of her cousins as individuals, and she saw no reason why she should belatedly burden herself with their presence. But after the double tragedy at Hathaway, Dr. Champagne, acting on Fabian's advice, himself wired to the Murdocks, and they arrived in time for the spectacular ceremonies in the White Ballroom. Afterwards they naturally lingered on for a few days, to recover from the fatigue of their hurried journey and the strain of the funeral rites; and before the question of their return to Pittsburg could be pressed, they had clearly established their relationship, secured a judgment fixing the amount of their inheritance tax, and been duly recognized as legal collateral heirs of Regine Hathaway Tremaine, deceased.

Merry had hastened to offer the hospitality of Belle Heloise to the strangers on their arrival, but they had declined this, preferring to make their headquarters at Hathaway Hall from the beginning. Apparently they were excited rather than appalled by the gruesome aspects of the situation. Miss Mittie, with her usual bluntness, observed that they were having the time of their lives, shuddering, and other spectators of their extraordinary behaviour were inclined to agree with her. They appeared at the funeral robed in heavy mourning, and they continued to wear this while receiving the callers who came to Hathaway in the course of the next few weeks with mingled motives of condolence, curiosity and congratulation. Everyone was agreed that even the most conservative Creoles in the community had never appeared swathed in so much crêpe, or equipped with so many sable accessories. But when their faces were unshielded by black-bordered handkerchiefs, the sisters' expressions, especially in moments of relaxation, were smug rather than sorrowful, and everything about their bearing suggested satisfied security. Inevitably they were the subject of much discussion.

'I believe they're getting the first sure enough thrill they've ever had,' Gervais remarked to Fabian, voicing much the same sentiment Miss Mittie had expressed. 'It's a toss-up which they're enjoying most – the murder mystery or the fabulous good fortune of inheriting a white-pillared ante-bellum mansion. There's no doubt that they *have* inherited it, I suppose?'

'Not the slightest, that I can see. Regine was an only child, and her parents, her grandparents and her aunt are all dead. These cousins are the nearest relatives.'

'Then there's nothing to prevent them from settling right down here, if they want to?'

'I don't know of anything. Louisiana isn't one of those states that has long delays before an heir can be sent into possession. There's no fixed period to prevent the immediate recognition of any heir-at-law. You must have known that.'

'Yes, I reckon I did, but I was still hoping there might be a catch somewhere. Well, I suppose we may as well get ready to recognize them as neighbours too. But it sure hurts. I think we're about due for a little better luck along those lines. The River Road seems to be picking up about every kind of specimen you can think of these days.'

For once, it was the male contingent which did most of the talking at first in the d'Alvery family. Cresside had gone to the double funeral with Fabian, and afterwards had made the one requisite call on the newcomers and issued the one requisite invitation to them, calmly and courteously. Then she had retired from the scene without causing curiosity or comment because she did no more. After all, she no longer lived on the River Road; the Murdocks were not her immediate neighbours and she was not bound to them by any ties of long-established friendship. The circumstances had been entirely different at the time of Mrs. Hathaway's death, for then Merry's advanced pregnancy had prevented her from performing the customary friendly services at a time of bereavement. But on this occasion she had taken charge of arrangements so promptly and efficiently that neither Cresside's presence nor her mother's had been indicated over any protracted period. Madame d'Alvery had also called with proper formality, and had intimated that in due course an invitation to dinner would be forthcoming. She had not actually extended it at the moment, but her call was returned so promptly, and with such an air of expectancy, that she set the following Sunday. The Murdocks came early, stayed late and talked volubly, their sprightly expressions and assured bearing more than ever at variance with their gloomy clothes. As they started to leave, they said they would expect the d'Alverys to have Sunday dinner with them, just as soon as they could get that great big house of theirs in some kind of presentable shape. It was still in a terrible condition. They had never in all their lives seen so much dirt and such mountains of rubbish. It was a disgrace to let things get in such a condition. And on top of everything, they were having servant troubles. . . .

Madame d'Alvery, who had never experienced servant troubles and who did not consider them either a genteel or an interesting topic of conversation, begged her visitors, rather coolly, not to think of making the slightest superfluous effort. She understood that of course they would wish to reorganize Hathaway Hall in accordance with their own tastes and needs, and she realized that this would take time. She appreciated their courtesy, but perhaps she should tell them immediately that she never dined out, except occasionally at her married daughter's house, when there were no other guests; she was sure they would understand, and excuse her from coming to theirs. As for Gervais, Sunday was the only day in which he had leisure to share with his wife and children, and after Mass, he always devoted it to them; so naturally Merry never left the plantation either, under those circumstances. The Murdocks postponed their departure to expostulate, and as an interminable argument seemed to be impending, Madame d'Alvery begged them to excuse her, saying that the unfortunate state of her health made her dependent on a siesta, and mounted the stairs without a backward glance.

Half an hour later, Merry came upstairs, looking tired herself, and sat down beside her mother-in-law's couch. She wanted to be sure Madame Mère was all right, she said, before going back to the *garçonnière*; she was afraid the experience of entertaining the Murdocks had been very exhausting. Worse than exhausting, Madame d'Alvery declared; it had been extremely painful. She was ready to assert that such obnoxious persons had never previously sat at meat in the dining room of Belle Heloise, except, of course, during the Yankee occupation. . . .

'Perhaps the River Road's due for another Yankee occupation of a different kind,' Merry said wearily. 'With Charles Boylston at Hackberry and now these Murdocks at Hathaway—'

'*Chère*, I beg you not to mention Charles Boylston and these Murdocks in the same breath. Charles is a gentleman, even if he is a Yankee and a Protestant – indeed, I have always heard that a great many persons of comparative culture reside in Boston. I do not know anything whatsoever about Pittsburg, except that it is very smoky and that steel is manufactured there. I believe I can understand now why my poor friend Mrs. Hathaway felt her sister's marriage so keenly, though at the time I was inclined to think she was unnecessarily harsh. I have always contended that even a *mésalliance* should be accepted with dignity by an offended family. After all, once it is a *fait accompli,* the new members are absorbed with those already established, and often they improve very much. But I can see that unfortunately nothing of the kind happened in this case.'

Merry knew that her mother-in-law was not deliberately malicious in referring indirectly to another case where the outcome had given unexpected satisfaction; but she could not think of any response which might not either indicate some personal resentment of Madame d'Alvery's position, or admit the premise that her marriage to Gervais had been a *mésalliance*. Very wisely she was silent, waiting for her mother-in-law to continue. She did not have to wait long.

'Such clothes!' Madame d'Alvery exclaimed. 'I am not referring to the fact that the Misses Murdock have gone into mourning for their cousin, which is in itself, of course, entirely proper. I am referring to the lack of restrained elegance in the garments themselves and the lack of *savoir faire* with which these are put on. I am persuaded that these women have never worn handsome black themselves before this time, or even seen it becomingly worn. Nor can I believe for a minute that this excessive show of grief is sincere. Why should it be? They had never met Regine in their lives. . . . No, I believe they have heard that

Creoles habitually make much of mourning, and that they are striving to impress us by their inept imitation of our ways.'

'I think you're probably right,' Merry remarked, feeling it was safe, this time, to agree with her mother-in-law.

'But it is not only their clothes that are so appalling! It is their voices! It is their manners! It is everything about them!'

'I didn't like them very well myself, and I don't think Gervais did either.'

'Certainly you did not like them very well yourself. How could you? And how could Gervais? I hate to say anything like this, even to you, my dear Merry; but still I feel forced to ask if you did not remark what was most shocking of all, and that was their conversation. When they were not talking about Hathaway Hall as if they wished to impress us that they had always been used to an equally elaborate establishment, they were talking about the male sex. Evidently they have mistaken the cool courtesy Charles has shown them for deep personal interest – or rather they have not really mistaken it. They have deliberately misinterpreted it.'

'I'm afraid they have,' Merry admitted. 'I'd noticed that too, Madame Mère. At least it seemed as if I did. But I thought perhaps I was doing them an injustice. I hoped so anyway. ... It's funny, isn't it, the way they both look rather like Regine, without being at all pretty? She was mighty pretty; no one could deny that.'

'Yes, she was pretty, but she was without character and that showed in her face. That is what shows in theirs also, constituting a kind of resemblance. And it is impossible to do women of that type an injustice, especially women of that type who have reached a certain age and who are still unmarried,' Madame d'Alvery retorted with feeling. 'It would be bad enough if they had confined their gushing remarks to Charles. But the inclusion of Grover Blood in their conversation, as if he were an intimate, is so unpardonable an indelicacy that it is also incredible.'

Again Merry was silent. The Murdocks' interest in their manager, and their unblushing expression of this, had shocked her quite as much as it had her mother-in-law; but the underlying reasons for this were somewhat different. It was inconceivable to Madame d'Alvery that the châtelaine of a plantation, at least theoretically a gentlewoman, should consider or treat her manager familiarly, whatever his reputation. To Merry, more conscious of a changing social order and herself a product of the proletariat, their lack of delicacy was indicated not by their liberal attitude in this respect but in their willingness to consort with a notorious loose liver. A man equally corrupt but more subtle might easily have kept his true character a secret, for a time at least, from newcomers; but Grover Blood had acted with his usual effrontery and openly pursued his usual dissipated course since the coming of the Murdocks. He had begun to drink the day of the funeral, and his disgraceful carousal had lasted almost a week, creating far more scandal than any of his previous debauches. In the midst of it he had fulfilled his long-standing threat of supplanting Durice Reno with her younger sister Deéte, doing so under circumstances even more lurid than those under which he had supplanted Vina with Durice; and Deéte was now brazenly installed in the seraglio at the rear of the boarding-house and boasting of her triumph without shame. The Murdocks could not possibly have been unaware of their manager's disreputable behaviour, since they must have seen evidences of his intoxication with their own eyes, and since Durice had rent the air with her screams before she had been brutally silenced and evicted. Yet he was hardly sober enough to stand before they made him welcome at their table, and they were now frequently seen in his company.

Merry was still sitting beside her mother-in-law, turning all this over in her troubled mind, when Vail came in to ask, did she know it was six o'clock and wasn't she going to read aloud that evening? She left immediately with him for the *garçonnière*, where the younger children were waiting for her; and though she continued to think about the newcomers with misgivings, she did not mention them again to her mother-in-law and Madame d'Alvery did not bring up the subject either. Several weeks elapsed before she saw the Murdocks again, and when their next meeting took place she was inclined to feel sorry for them rather than critical of them. Wilhelmina, the elder of the two sisters, came over to Belle Heloise to say that Gwendolen had been ill for some days and that she had become deeply depressed; they would both be more grateful than they could say if Mrs. d'Alvery would drop in to see her for a few minutes. Merry, whose sympathies were easily roused, and whose conscience smote her because she had neglected a sick neighbour, volunteered to drive back with Miss Wilhelmina immediately, and her offer was eagerly accepted. She found the invalid still in bed, but propped up with pillows and obviously glad of company; and, sitting down between the two sisters, she listened to their joint lament, and tried to put in an occasional word.

Plantation life, it seemed, was by no means all that their first fond fancy had pictured it; they had not dreamed that the mere mechanics of living would be so difficult. In the first place, the servants were slovenly and stupid; the Misses Murdock did not for the life of them see how their aunt and their cousin had ever put up with them. After the first week they themselves had decided to dismiss Micah and Jinny and replace them with well-trained, hard-working substitutes; they had been informed, before they started for Louisiana, that it was as easy as anything to get niggers to work for you down there. One of their friends, who had spent some time in the Deep South herself, had actually said that all anyone had to do was to stand on the levee and shout and the darkies would come running. But they had discovered, to their sorrow, that this was far from being the case; they would be obliged to keep Micah and Jinny after all, or have nobody in the house at all. And since the servants knew this as well as they did, and were also deeply resentful of the unsuccessful effort to oust them, these worthless creatures were now slacker than ever and insolent as well. Miss Wilhelmina had even had hard work to persuade Micah to serve afternoon tea. . . .

'You know, I don't believe he ever did it before,' Merry said consolingly. 'You probably wouldn't have had so much trouble if you'd suggested coffee. And I'm afraid your friend must have been thinking of the "good old times" when she told you about standing on the levee and shouting; it isn't all that easy any more. So far we've been very fortunate at Belle Heloise, but I don't know how long we shall be. We can see quite a difference in the new generation that's just coming up. For instance, Amen, who was the yard boy when I was married, thinks he's much too good for that job now, though his father, Selah, is very proud of being our butler. And Lethe, the younger children's nurse, can't be compared with Dinah, who took care of both my husband and his sister when they were little and came to me when the twins were born. I don't think we ought to blame them too much. I think they're groping for something they haven't found yet, that they don't know how to find, and we haven't helped them much, I'm afraid. . . . I imagine there's a little extra difficulty at Hathaway too, because some of the Negroes around here are afraid of the place, or pretend to be. You know how superstitious they are, and when a double death occurs under rather strange circumstances ... Well, of course I'd be glad to have a little talk with Micah and Jinny myself if you'd like to have me. I take it for granted you offered them higher wages than Regine was paying them – they always expect that from Yan – from Northerners. I know Charles Boylston was up against the same thing that you are, but I was able to straighten that out, so perhaps I can help you too. ... Is there anything else I can do for you?'

They would be no end grateful if she would speak to Micah and Jinny, the sisters hastened to assure her, and they were sure she could help them in other ways too. The plumbing kept getting out of order, and it seemed to be practically impossible to get anyone to come out from town and fix it; perhaps she knew of somebody? The cistern was not anywhere nearly large enough, either; it had not run dry yet, but it showed signs of doing so, and Micah had assured them, as if he were really rather pleased than otherwise about it, that very frequently it did; then it would be necessary to 'switch over' to the well water, which turned everything it touched brick red.

'All our linen will be ruined,' moaned Miss Wilhelmina, 'our beautiful embroidered linen! And I suppose we shall look like Indians when we get out of the tub! Micah says that when the cistern runs dry he has to tote all the water for dish washing from the old sugar basins out back, and that he doesn't know whether he'll be able, this year, he's got Arthuritis so bad. That's what he calls it, Arthuritis. Jinny is complaining too. She says every time she raises her arms it gives her such a swimming in the head that she feels faint. She says she's sure she's coming down with heart trouble, and that if she does she'll have to get a lot more rest than she's having now. As if she wasn't loafing most of the time as it is!'

'The cistern won't run dry as long as the spring rains keep up,' Merry assured them, deciding it was better not to resume the subject of Micah and Jinny. 'I'm afraid if there's a drought this summer you may find the water situation quite a problem, though. We all do. But every time I ruin a towel or get out of a tub looking like an Indian I see something that makes up for it. Don't you? I'm sure there isn't any place in the world, for instance, where the flowers and the trees and the birds are as beautiful as they are on the River Road. I'd miss those a lot more, if I didn't live where I could see them all the time, than I do a little water once in a while.'

The Misses Murdock were not able to look at it just that way; an abundant water supply was simply one of the commodities which was taken for granted in civilized communities like Pittsburg. So, incidentally, were mail delivery and telephone service. They had never even inquired beforehand whether they would have these; and then to find, on the very outskirts of the state capital, within a few miles of the state university too . . .

'Gervais feels just the same way about all that as you do,' Merry told them. 'He's working on it too, but I don't know whether he'll get very far. You see, he isn't on the best of terms with the present administration, and that makes quite a lot of difference – more than it ought to. About the road too. I know that's in terribly bad shape. I've never seen the sandboils worse than they are this year.'

The road was indeed in bad shape, the Misses Murdock agreed vehemently – so bad that it discouraged visitors from coming to Hathaway and that they found it very hard to drive over themselves. This meant that they got out very little, for so far they had not been able to secure a satisfactory chauffeur. Neither Jonah nor Micah had ever driven a car, which was another unpleasant surprise; they had taken it for granted that every handyman about a place could drive nowadays. And it appeared that none of the other Negroes could be spared from the fields just then, which seemed to them a queer way of running a big place. They would have thought that surely one – but they had talked and talked to Mr. Blood about this and it had done no good. And he was too busy to take them any place himself. Their first impression was that he would prove very obliging, but they were sorry to say . . .

'Work is very heavy on a plantation, almost all the year around,' Merry reminded them. 'When you've lived on one a while, you'll realize that, and you'll get used to the isolation. In fact, you'll like it.' She did not want to discuss Mr. Blood or the lack of visitors at Hathaway Hall. She thought the less said about the manager the better, under any circumstances, and she was very much afraid that the Murdocks had not made a sufficiently favourable impression to encourage a continuation of visits, now that the first curiosity of the countryside had been assuaged. 'We don't have a chauffeur either,' she went on. 'And

I don't drive to town very often myself. I'm not an especially good driver, because I learned too late, so I don't enjoy it; and then of course five small children keep me pretty busy! But I do go sometimes. I'll be glad to stop by for you and take you with me the next time. And I'll try to be more neighbourly. I feel terrible to think I've neglected you while you've been sick, Miss Gwendolen. I hope you won't be again, but if you are you must let me know straight off. . . . Dr. Champagne has taken good care of you, though, hasn't he? He's the soul of faithfulness – the roads are never too bad for him to get through to his patients! I don't see how he does it always, but he does.'

Dr. Champagne had been out only once, Miss Gwendolen said, bridling a little. He had not seemed to grasp the gravity of the case, and, in any event, both she and her sister were agreed that he evidently had not kept abreast of the times. They preferred a more up-to-date physician. To do Dr. Champagne justice, he *had* seemed to grasp this phase of the situation, and had recommended a young practitioner named Dr. Leonard Manners. Dr. Manners was exactly the right type: he had such a pleasing personality! He was so gentle and sympathetic! but unfortunately his services were in such great demand that he could not get out on the River Road every day. The Murdocks were not surprised at his popularity; but it did make things hard for them, because, with the servants so slack and everything – well, it had been a trying period. They were beginning to feel doubtful whether they could continue to live at Hathaway Hall after all. . . .

'Oh, you mustn't feel that way about it,' Merry said in genuine distress. Nothing that had occurred in the course of the call had caused her to like the Murdocks any better than she had before; but she was concerned because their first favourable impressions had not lasted and because she herself had done nothing to make these more enduring. 'You'll get used to all the little inconveniences, really you will. I know, because I did myself. You'll feel, after a while, that nothing could induce you to live anywhere else.'

'Possibly we might, Mrs. d'Alvery, if there were anything to offset the little inconveniences, as you call them. In our case, birds and trees and flowers aren't enough, as they seem to be for you. You see, we've always been used to a very delightful and sophisticated society in Pittsburg, and nothing ever happens on the River Road. . . .'

'When she said that, I had hard work not to laugh,' Merry remarked, in telling Gervais about the call afterwards. 'Here they are living in a house where there'd been a mysterious suicide before they got there, and since they've arrived their manager's driven one girl off the place and taken on another, creating a scandal all over the countryside. I wouldn't call that so uneventful, would you?'

'Not exactly. But I don't think your new-found friends were completely candid when they complained that nothing ever happened on the River Road. I think what they really meant was nothing has happened the way they wanted it to.'

'What do you think they wanted to have happen, Gervais?'

'They want to get married,' Gervais said bluntly. 'Do you think they'd worry all that much about the plumbing and the cistern and the telephone if they had someone making up to them? They told you themselves they'd feel differently if they had anything to offset these little inconveniences. Their white-pillared ante-bellum house doesn't mean a thing to them unless it can be coupled with romance with a capital R – quite aside from the fact that they've reached the age where they'd be a little anxious and eager anyway. I should think you could have guessed that, from the way they talked and acted, that Sunday they were here to dinner. I'm sure *maman* did.'

'Yes, I know she did. She spoke to me about it then. But I think maybe you and she are a little too hard on them, Gervais. I think—'

'No matter what you think, I know. They came down here to get married, because they hadn't succeeded in Pittsburg and they felt maybe they'd have better luck in a new field. They were ready to go to almost any lengths in their hunting too. Of course Charles would have been the perfect answer to their maiden prayers. But Charles saw through them just as well as I did – he's about to start off on another trip, did I tell you? He's getting so he's away almost as much as the Tremaines used to be – I'm not sure how much of this is flight and how much is just growing restlessness – he wanted to get married too, you may remember, but certainly not to anyone like the Murdock sisters—'

'You're exaggerating, Gervais. He couldn't marry the Murdock *sisters* very well, if he did want to, now could he?'

'All right, all right. As I've said to you a good many times before, don't be so literal!' He did not speak irritably, in the way he so often did when he made this accusation, but laughingly and teasingly, putting his arm around her and drawing her close to him. 'Either one of the sisters. There's not much choice between them, when it comes to that. If he had, he wouldn't have run into any of the difficulties and delays that I did.'

'Difficulties and delays! I married you the very day you asked me!'

'The very day I asked you for about the 'steenth time! Well, we won't go into that. What I was saying was that poor Charles had to run so that he wouldn't get knock-out drops in his coffee when he was making a neighbourly call, and wake up to find himself in such a compromising position! – and place! – that, being a gentleman, there'd be nothing he could do except make straight for the minister's.'

'Which sister do you think would have given him knock-out drops and dragged him off to her room?' Merry inquired, finally entering into his lightness of mood.

'I think they'd have flipped a coin. Or maybe they'd have fought it out, tooth and toenail, to the death, leaving the spoils to the survivor. Because it's certain that they've both been after him. And it's also certain that now they'll do the next best thing, as they see it. Unless this young doctor they're trying to get into their clutches comes across, they'll both go out for Blood, and I'm not making a bad pun either.'

'Gervais! You shouldn't joke over a thing like that!'

'I'm not joking any more. I'm in deadly earnest. And I shouldn't wonder if Blood fell for it in the end.'

'Why, that would be horrible – for a nice woman to marry a man like that!'

'Honey, I don't see why you go on thinking they're nice women. They're horrible women. It would serve them right – either of them right – if Blood did consent to a marriage.'

'But, Gervais, have you heard what the Negroes are whispering about Blood now?'

'You mean that when Durice wouldn't go, he took a whip to her? Yes, I've heard, and I think it's probably true. But I don't think that would stop either Wilhelmina or Gwendolen. Some women actually get a thrill out of a man's cruelty. Look here, you're getting all white around the gills. You can't even stand hearing about anything of that kind, and Franchot's just like you that way, do you know it? We've got to get him over it somehow – it won't do for a boy to be squeamish. Sometimes I've thought – but never mind about that now. And let's forget about those next-door neighbours of ours for a while and think about ourselves instead. I might go so far as to make love to you if you'll give me the chance. I haven't in quite a while. I mean, you haven't. . . .'

This conversation left Merry still more troubled than the one with her mother-in-law. The Murdocks reminded her of her promise to take them into town when she next went herself, and she kept it; but she did so unhappily, and after that she made excuses, both to herself and to them, about going in again, and similar excuses about visiting them: her family seemed to take up all her time: she had never found housekeeping so hard; she was not feeling very well for some reason. . . . Miss Gwendolen recovered from her illness, and both sisters came frequently, on their own initiative, to the *garçonnière*. They were never invited to dine at the Big House again, and Madame d'Alvery and Gervais avoided them pointedly; but Merry continued to suffer their presence, and, once in a great while, to return their visits. No one else went to Hathaway now, no one else sympathized with the strangers' isolation and disillusionment. She knew that if she deserted them, they would be utterly alone, and her kind heart contracted at the thought of such desolation. . . .

Then, late in August, she received a letter, delivered by a smirking Negro, which filled her with fresh consternation.

'DEAR MRS. D'ALVERY,

'I am writing to tell you that Mr. Grover Blood and I were married very quietly this morning, and that by the time this letter reaches you we will already have left Hathaway on our honeymoon. I would have asked you to be a witness at our wedding, but I realized that I would only embarrass you by doing this, because of course I know from the way they have acted that your mother-in-law and your husband have both tried to keep you from being my friend. I feel that they have been very unjust and unkind, though perhaps I should not say this to you; but so has my sister, as far as that goes. She was not present at my wedding either, and she is now packing to go back to Pittsburg for good. No doubt you will hear from her soon too, telling you her side of the story, for she thinks she has one, though I don't. I am glad she is leaving, as she has shown that she is utterly unfitted for plantation life and there would have been no peace while she was around; but of course I could not put her out as long as she was co-owner of Hathaway, and I have had a time with her. Fortunately I have enough money from my mother's estate to buy out her interest in the plantation, and I shall do so immediately. I expect to be very happy now that I am married to the man of my choice, and I hope that when I return from Hot Springs you will resume the visits which have always meant a great deal to me – that is, if you can do so without having your mother-in-law and your husband make you uncomfortable about them. You might tell them for me that my husband's background is just as good as any of the River families', and they had better recognize this, for I intend to have them. It is not his fault that his parents lost their place during Reconstruction and that he has had to earn his living on other people's plantations. Lots of splendid men have done just the same thing without having to contend with all the prejudice that he has; but from now on he will have everything he wants, for I have plenty of money to show the world, which I shall do. The time will come when Hathaway will be recognized as the finest plantation on the River Road; of course it should have been long ago, but evidently no one had enough spirit to make it. I have, as everybody will soon find out, and in my future position of prominence, I shall not forget that you were nice to me when I came here as a bereaved stranger and did not treat me like the dirt under your feet.

'Yours with affection and appreciation,

'WILHELMINA MURDOCK BLOOD.'

News of the fresh upheaval at Hathaway had already reached Gervais when he came in to dinner. Merry interrupted his vehement arraignment of everyone and everything on the place by showing him the letter she had received.

'I still feel sorry for the poor woman,' she persisted. 'I feel sorry because she's been so unhappy here, because she realized no one liked her, that she didn't fit in. I feel sorry she's married that horrible man in desperation. Perhaps if we'd all been a little more hospitable to her she wouldn't have done it, because she wouldn't have been lonely. Now she's got nothing but misery to look forward to. She's quarrelled with her only sister, and presently her husband will begin to abuse her, and she'll be a hundred times worse off than she ever was before. That letter's the most pathetic mixture of bravado and resentment and gratitude that I ever read.'

'Good God, we didn't *ask* her to come down here, did we? I'll bet she never would have left Pittsburg if she hadn't been just as "isolated" there as she was here – that kind of a woman never has any friends no matter where she lives. You may be able to work up some pathos out of the situation, but it's more than I can. I don't want you going over there, Merry, you hear? You've no call to help a thwarted angry old maid you hardly know pack her trunks while you listen to her lamentation, and you certainly haven't any call to welcome back the bride and groom. Christ, when I think of that man Blood lording it at Hathaway! Not because he was the manager, mind you. Now if it were Seaver who'd made a rich marriage, I'd say good luck to him. But Blood's just as low as they come.'

'I know he is, Gervais, and I understand how you feel. All the same, I'm going to help Miss Gwendolen get off. Just think how humiliated and abandoned the poor woman must feel, all alone in that big house, except for those sullen servants! Getting ready to go back to the place she left so triumphantly, thinking she had such a bright future! I won't be making a social visit, Gervais – you might object if I were, but I won't be. I'll be performing an ordinary act of Christian charity.'

Gervais continued to vociferate, but Merry quietly persisted in the face of his opposition; she had done this from the beginning, when a matter of principle was involved, and though Gervais could make such a course doubly hard for her, and usually did, he could not swerve her from it. She spent the greater part of the next two days at Hathaway Hall doing everything she could to ease the departure of Miss Gwendolen, who was first hysterical, then vituperative, and finally overwhelmed by the course of events. At last Merry took the wretched woman to the station and saw her comfortably installed in a Pullman seat which she herself had taken pains to secure. As the train pulled out, Miss Gwendolen pressed her face to the window for one last look at her only friend. Then she covered her eyes with her black-bordered handkerchief. She had resumed her heavy mourning for her departure, and Merry's last impression, like her first, was of a grief-stricken figure.

The newly married couple were absent for several weeks, for the wedding trip was extended to include New York, Washington and several fashionable resorts. During the interval Merry continued to go periodically to Hathaway Hall, supervising the servants and cajoling them into getting it swept and garnished against the return of the bride and groom. She did not let her charitable impulses carry her so far as to welcome them in person on the occasion of their home-coming; but she did see that everything was in perfect order, that the house was decorated with flowers and that the ice box was well stocked with food. It was hard for her to do all this, not only because of Gervais' continued opposition and her mother-in-law's expressed disapproval, but in the face of the antagonism which her presence roused at Hathaway itself. Merry had never before been conscious of ill-will among any of the Negroes, but she was conscious of it now; she knew they felt she was 'siding' with the woman they all hated and regarded as an interloper, more than ever now that this outsider had married their own substitute for a 'bossman'. They blamed Wilhelmina Murdock, not Grover Blood, for the marriage, and they blamed Merry for giving it countenance. The same feeling pervaded the factory and the boarding house. Deéte Reno had not been dispossessed from her quarters, and it was freely predicted that Blood would go on spending most of his time there. Deéte heard the predictions with satisfaction, and smiled evilly to herself. . . .

The day after the honeymooners' return, Merry received a second letter from Wilhelmina, delivered, like the first, by a smirking Negro, and this time tied to a small package. The bride was very much touched at the evidence of Mrs. d'Alvery's thoughtfulness which had greeted her on her return. She had thought of Mrs. d'Alvery too, in the course of her trip, and had brought her a little present which she was sending herewith. She hoped Mrs. d'Alvery would like it, and that they would be seeing each other very soon. The bride had bought quantities of new clothes, too, which she would like to show Mrs. d'Alvery, and instituted various changes on which she was eager to get Mrs. d'Alvery's opinion – or now that they were to be neighbours for keeps, might she say Merry's? And she was, always, most affectionately . . .

Merry opened the small package with misgivings, to find a diamond wrist watch embedded among layers of soft cotton in a satin-lined box. Her misgivings mounted as she recognized its value. Gervais would certainly protest against her acceptance of such a gift, and yet she could not return it without giving grave offence. She was beginning to see more and more involvements as a result of her single-hearted kindness, and, momentarily, she almost wished that she had followed Gervais' advice and left the Murdocks severely alone. But at the same time she knew that she could not, conscientiously, have acted otherwise than she had. When Cresside came out to Belle Heloise, later in the day, she confided her perplexities to her sister-in-law, finding her, as usual, a ready and sympathetic listener. But on this occasion, though Cresside was ready to lend all possible support, she was not as encouraging as usual.

'The whole thing's a mess. If Blood would only run straight, or something like straight, it might iron out, after a fashion – not that he and his bride would ever be accepted by the people they'd like to have for friends, but they wouldn't be completely ostracized by everyone. Of course he won't run straight, though. And you know as well as I do by this time, Merry, that the River families will stand for a lot from their own black sheep, but they won't put up with much from outsiders. Wilhelmina's goofy and Blood's rotten. You could try from now till doomsday, and you still couldn't make *maman* and Gervais feel any different about them. I know you meant to do the right thing, but you're just letting yourself in for more and more trouble. You see for yourself how it works out.'

'You don't think I ought to go there at all?'

'I know it's mighty awkward all round, Merry. Heaven knows you've had enough trouble with Hathaway already, trying to walk a tightrope all the time Sylvestre and Regine were there. And that was nothing to what you're up against this go-round. I'm beginning to think the Negroes are right, that the place does have some kind of a curse on it. Well, since you've gone as far as you have, I believe that if I were you I would call once – in the daytime, when Blood's sure to be out in the fields. I'll go with you, if you like. And I should think you'd have to keep the watch. Suppose I ask Fabian about it, though. You don't have to tell Gervais you've got it, this very day, do you?'

'No-o,' Merry said, so doubtfully that Cresside knew that even this temporary concealment would distress her; and in the end it was agreed that Merry should tell him while Cresside was still there, so that she would not have to bear the brunt of his displeasure alone. As usual, Fabian was helpful in pouring oil on the troubled waters. He did think that perhaps Merry had leaned over backwards in her efforts to be nice to people who did not deserve it, but after all that was her way, and a good way, if you took your religion literally, like she did. Certainly she would have to keep the watch, but in thanking Mrs. Blood for it she had better try to discourage further gifts and further obligations. And certainly she should call once, in the daytime, as Cresside had suggested. He felt sure that the call would be returned in the same way. Personally, he did not think that Blood would try to push anything, from a social standpoint; he was too shrewd for that. When he was sober, there wasn't a shrewder man anywhere around. If he would only stay sober . . .

Taken by and large, Fabian's conclusions were a good deal like his wife's, and their temperate views of the situation seemed to be justified, at least for the moment. Nothing untoward occurred in the course of the call which Merry and Cresside made together. The bride, who was beautifully dressed, received them with effusion and insisted on showing them her trousseau and her newly appointed apartments. She was obviously extremely conscious, and smugly so, of her marital state, and made numerous intimate references to 'Grover'; but she gave vent to no resentful comments on the general attitude of the countryside, and uttered no threats concerning the future. Tea was elegantly served by an imported maid who had been added to the household staff, and when the calls were returned, as they were after a suitable interval, Mrs. Blood's new Rolls Royce was driven by an English chauffeur, impeccably uniformed. She appeared at church in the same style, and other evidences of lavish living became apparent day by day. Arnold Fletcher, the same architect who had precipitated Gervais' financial difficulties, was called into consultation at Hathaway Hall, together with an outstanding interior decorator and an outstanding landscape gardener. Presently the place was swarming with workmen; the huge white façade glistened with fresh paint, the neglected grounds resumed a semblance of their original formality. In so far as she could fulfil her purpose in making Hathaway the finest place on the River Road by spending money upon it, the new Mrs. Blood was doing so. All the outward and visible signs of supremacy were there; only the inward and spiritual grace was lacking.

Nevertheless, as the autumn passed, the splendour in which the bride lived became less and less solitary. Though Cresside and Merry did not call a second time, other visitors came more and more frequently to Hathaway. Wilhelmina actually appeared at the *garçonnière* one afternoon with the triumphant announcement that the Governor had been to her house the night before.

'He came after the servants had left for the night,' she went on to say. 'And he had his bodyguard with him. My, but they're a lot of huskies, aren't they? The Governor pounded on the door with that loaded cane they say he always carries. I thought the house was coming down! Grover got a pistol out of the dresser drawer, before he went to let them in – of course he didn't know who was there. Of course I didn't either, and at first I tried to keep him from going downstairs. But he doesn't know fear. He told me not to be silly and went straight along, and I was so frightened that I just cowered under the bedclothes, shuddering. Then I heard Grover saying, "Why, come right in, Governor – this *is* an honour!" And next I heard Mr. Long asking for whisky.'

'You don't mean to say you thought it was an honour to have Huey Long come to your house in the middle of the night, battering down the front door and demanding whisky!' Merry exclaimed.

'Well, after all, Merry, you know the Governorship's a great office in any State. I was wondering whether I oughtn't to get up and dress, so that I could welcome Mr. Long myself. But when Grover came back to our room for the keys to the cupboard where we keep most of our whisky, he told me to stay where I was. Then he muttered something about not getting out any of the old stock; that Long was so drunk already he wouldn't know the difference, whatever was served. But right after he went back to the living-room I heard the Governor roaring, "Christ, this must be what you use for your own toots, Blood! I don't water my drinks with chloroform to take away the taste. I want some of your real stuff, and I want it god damn quick!"'

'And you still felt his visit was an honour?'

'Well, I do think he expresses himself rather crudely, but he has force, and personally I greatly admire force in a man. Next I heard him saying, "I'll bet you I can smell out something better than this myself!" and he started to the wing where the down-stairs bedrooms are. We've never slept there because—'

'I shouldn't think you would.'

'But I always keep them in perfect order. I'll say this for my-self, I'm a model housekeeper, even if I do have those lazy niggers to contend with all the time. Pretty soon I heard a shout and a crash. It seems Mr. Long went right up to the first bed he came to and pulled down the mosquito bar. Grover told me afterwards that he said, "Jesus, no one sleeps under those things any more! No one but a" – well, I can't say the two words he used – "like you. I'll bet you've got something or somebody hidden in that bed, you . . ." '

'I know what the words are, Wilhelmina, but I don't like to hear them, so I'm glad you didn't repeat them. I'm glad he didn't find anything after all that vulgar commotion, too.'

'Well, of course there wasn't any *one* hidden in the bed,' Wilhelmina said, a trifle sharply. 'But Grover *had* put some of our finest whisky under the mattress on account òf the servants. The Governor acted as if he thought it was a great joke, finding it. The men all went back to the living-room after that, and sat around for hours.'

'Drinking?'

'Well, naturally Grover had to drink with the Governor,' Wil-helmina retorted, speaking sharply again. 'But Mr. Long never lets any of the bodyguards touch a drop, anyway. He stopped shout-ing and storming after he got what he wanted, and grew more and more genial. He says he knows he can find a place for a man like Grover, that my husband could be very valuable. And if he gets an official position . . .'

It was quite clear that Wilhelmina Blood was thrilled and gratified by this episode, that she did consider even such an in-trusion an honour when instigated by the Chief Executive of the State, and that the prospect of being affiliated with the all-powerful Long machine impressed her greatly. Pending this ad-vancement, she began to make club connections as well as church connections, and her generosity, in both directions, was con-spicuous. To be sure, the bridegroom did not appear in the increasingly pleasing picture, and the captious might have com-plained that there was something wrong with it for this reason. On the other hand, he created no fresh scandal. If he continued to visit the boarding-house and the quarters, he did so after dark, and with none of his former bravado. If he drank, he did so in extreme moderation. The grinding season began auspiciously, with a full crew in the fields and excellent organization in the factory. Sance, who had managed to maintain amicable relations with Blood throughout the crucial period since the manager's marriage, as he had on many less critical occasions, brought favourable reports to Belle Heloise of the situation at Hathaway. There was a lot of new machinery at last; there was a fine crop coming along; Blood was handling everything just right. There wasn't a better man, in his line, anywhere in the Sugar Parishes. What if he did carry on? What if he did know on which side his bread was buttered? Hell, that was his affair. He knew his job. . . .

Gervais listened, grudgingly, to his overseer's praise. Then, late one Sunday night, Sance came to the *garçonnière*, and told a terrible story, white to the lips. . . .

Merry knew that catastrophe had befallen as soon as she heard the overseer's knock. She got out of bed and wrapped a dressing-gown about her. Then she waited, shivering, until Gervais came back into their room, shutting the door behind him as if he were trying to close it on some kind of horror. He took hold of her shoulders, gripping them hard, and tried twice, unsuccessfully, to speak to her.

'Tell me quickly, Gervais, what's happened? Has one of the children—?'

'No, the children are all right. All the family. All our people. It's at Hathaway.'

'What's at Hathaway?'

'Another accident. The explosion wasn't anything compared to this. Or the suicide. They've got Blood away, they've had to; he'd have been torn to pieces if they hadn't. It won't be safe for his wife to stay either. You'll have to help her now. I shan't try to stop you this time.'

'Of course you won't. You wouldn't have before, if you'd understood how I felt, or how much she needed me. But you haven't told me yet, Gervais—'

'It's so ghastly I don't know how to tell you. It's always so hard for you to listen to horrors.'

'It is hard. But if it's something I ought to know, I'd rather hear it from you, Gervais, than anyone else. Please tell me.'

'Blood went on another tear Saturday night. The servants say it started with words at the Big House. Blood and his wife quarrelled.'

'Yes, Gervais. I know you were afraid they would some time. Go on.'

'So he left her and went to the boarding-house. Deéte's still there. At least, she was still there—'

'Yes, yes, Gervais. Go on.'

'They drank and drank, almost all night. They shouted out loud that they were celebrating their reunion. Everyone in the boarding-house heard them. There's no mystery about what happened this time.'

'What did happen?'

'Suddenly he turned on her and drove her out. Cruelly, the way he had Durice. He told her to go and get Durice. He said he wanted her sister back again, that he was tired of her. And at last she started. She was so drunk she didn't know where she was going. He was so drunk he didn't know anything had happened after she left. No one thought it was queer she didn't come back. Everyone thought she'd slunk home, like both her sisters before her.'

'Where had she gone, Gervais?'

'She'd wandered out to the mill yard and climbed into the carrier.'

'But she couldn't have, Gervais. A dozen people would have seen her and stopped her. She couldn't have climbed into the carrier when it was going, anyway.'

'It wasn't going. That's what I'm trying to tell you. At Hathaway they shut down the mill Saturday night to clean it and don't start it up again until Sunday night. There's no one around outside except the watchman after it's closed. He wasn't anywhere near the carrier when she climbed into it, dead drunk. She was still drunk when it started again.'

'Gervais, you're not trying to tell me—'

'Yes, I am; that's just what I'm trying to tell you. The crusher feeder saw her when she came over the top, but he couldn't stop the carrier then. She was ground to pulp, right before his eyes—'

Suddenly he realized that she could not stand any more. She was shaking all over, and the horror which he had made her visualize was reflected in her eyes as she stared at him. Then with a sharp intake of breath she buried her face on his shoulder. He put his arm around her and bent his head to touch hers.

'There,' he said. 'There. Don't, Merry.' His voice was quiet and gentle, as if he was speaking to one of the children. 'It's a hell of a world, some ways, and horrible things happen in it now and then. Take it easy for a few minutes – you'll feel better if you do. But as soon as you can pull yourself together I want to take you to Hathaway.'

'I couldn't go. I wouldn't be any use this time.'

'Yes, you would. You're needed badly, and you've always told me that being needed meant more to a woman than anything in the world except being loved. Didn't you mean it?'

'Yes, when I said it. But—'

'This is the time to prove it, then. Because it's the only time you'll have a chance, as far as Wilhelmina Blood's concerned.' He waited a minute and then he spoke with inescapable finality. 'If you don't help her now, you never can,' he said slowly. 'She can't stay on the River Road after this. It's the end for her at Hathaway.'

'For I the Lord thy God am a jealous God, visiting the iniquity of the fathers upon the children.'

Exodus xx. 5.

PART TWO

'Visited on the Children'

(Summer 1930)

CHAPTER SEVEN

FOR the first few years of his life Belle Heloise was Vail d'Alvery's world, and to him it seemed perfect and complete.

In this world were shady groves, where you could play hide-and-seek, and wide stretches of open lawn, where you could race with your brothers and sisters; a garden that was always bright with flowers waiting to be picked for Mummy and *grand'-mère* and Aunt Cresside; a big friendly house, with a sweet-smelling kitchen where someone was always making good things for you to eat when you were hungry, and a big bedroom where it was always still and dark, when you were tired and needed to go to sleep.

The house was filled with kind people, white and black both, who wanted little boys to be happy, and the Small Yard was alive with kindly creatures too. Nostar, Vail's pony, was the largest and most important of these. Vail had thought beforehand that he wanted to have a pony with a white star on its forehead; but when it arrived at Belle Heloise, as a present from Uncle Fabian and Aunt Cresside, though it was the most wonderful pony Vail could imagine, it was jet black all over. So Vail named it Nostar. Sybelle, Vail's twin, had a pony too, named Twinkle, because that name went so well with Nostar. They rode all over the Small Yard and the levee together, and, when Daddy went with them, over the headland too. Phil, who was eleven months younger than Sybelle and Vail, did not have a pony yet. When he went with them he still rode with Daddy, on the front of the saddle.

Next to Nostar and Twinkle, Maud and her families were the most cherished adjuncts to Vail's out-of-doors world. The families were new and different every year, and there were always a few days of heartbreak when the beautiful puppies were given away. But Maud, another present from Aunt Cresside and Uncle Fabian, was Vail's very own. Mummy and Daddy had both promised him faithfully that she would never be taken away, and the certainty of this was his greatest comfort when the puppies went. Maud was a lovely little spotted spaniel with great pleading eyes, who followed Vail wherever he went and slept on his bed at night. She had only one bad habit: sometimes she chased the white ducks which waddled back and forth at will through the Small Yard, fluttering up, once in a while, to perch on the rims of the old open sugar kettles now used as garden ornaments, or to paddle through the rain water with which these were filled. Once she had killed two of the golden ducklings that mysteriously appeared one morning, waddling after a proud mother duck, and then Daddy had made Vail whip her, and had actually said something about sending her away after all if she did not do better. But she had done better, and the heavy load which weighted down Vail's heart at the thought of life without Maud was lifted again.

In addition to the ponies and the dogs and the ducks, there were all sorts of little wild creatures that helped to people Vail's world. There were little brown cottontails which went leaping through the garden to the grove, so fast that Maud could not catch them, and squirrels which scampered down the boughs of one tree and up the branches of another. There were carpenter bees that Vail loved to shoot with his air rifle, lying on his back for hours at a time in the sunlight, watching the bees at their work of boring the wooden framework of the gallery, and aiming at them just as they plunged into the holes they had made. There were funny little lizards which changed their colour from green when they were on the grass to brown when they were on the garden path. Once in a while there was a snake too. Vail almost stepped on one, zigzagging over the stone steps leading into the patio, when he went to let Maud out the last thing at night, one time when her puppies were very young indeed and needed her all the time. He had shrunk back, frightened for a moment, but he knew he must take care of Maud, whatever happened, so he had gone out of another door, and when he came back the snake had disappeared. Afterwards he told Aunt Cresside about it, because he felt he had to tell someone, and Daddy did not like to have anyone even speak of snakes. Aunt Cresside had praised Vail and said he had done just right, that snakes nearly always slithered away if you left them alone, and that he must not let them or anything else spoil his world, which was so beautiful. He promised her he would not, and he never had, after that.

Besides riding horseback on the levee, Vail and Sybelle spent a great deal of time sliding down it. A levee slide was made of two or three barrel staves with flat pieces of wood nailed at each end, and at each corner of the footpiece a string, tied to use like a rein. The twins sat solidly on one end of the slide and put their feet firmly on the other, grasping the strings and guiding the slide with these; and before they started down the levee bank they greased the underside of the staves to make them good and slippery. Vail did not believe that the coasting up north which Miss Mittie, their teacher, told them so much about could compare with levee-sliding for fun. It was the most fun of anything they did, especially when Vail and Sybelle sat on the same slide, as they liked to, though each had one.

A great deal of Vail's time was spent playing games. One of those he liked best was played in the autumn, when he and Sybelle and Phil all helped to pick the pecans in the grove and spread them out in the sun to dry. Even Joyeuse and Franchot, their younger sister and brother, tried to pick pecans and join in games almost as soon as they could toddle. Vail would pick up double handfuls of the nuts and say: 'Old horse, old horse, who wants to ride him?' The other children all tried to be the first to shout: 'I'll ride him!' Next Vail would ask: 'How many miles?' Phil usually made the mistake of saying a great many; it was Phil's way to talk big about everything. Then he would lose because he had to pay Vail the difference in pecans between the number he had guessed and the number Vail actually held. Sybelle did better. She considered carefully, tipping her golden head first to one side and then to the other while she talked; she also watched the size of the pecans and compared these to the size of Vail's hands. So very often she won. Then she held the pecans while the other children guessed. Of course, Joyeuse and Franchot did not know much about counting; they were just as likely to say ten as three. But they liked to play and Vail liked to have them.

They all played other games, too, like 'Jack in the Bush' and 'I'll Cut Him Down' and 'How Many Licks?'; and Vail and Sybelle helped with the plums in the summer-time, just as they did with the pecans in the fall, gathering the plums as soon as these turned yellow and learning how to ripen them in meal. They learned a great many useful things like that, little by little, so that they would know how to take care of Belle Heloise themselves some day, when Mummy and Daddy were old, the way *grand'-mère* was now, and did not want to be worried any longer; and from the Negroes they learned all sorts of sayings and stories, which were fun listening to, whether they were really true or not. For instance, Selah told Vail that if he would hold a penny in his hand while the New Year's whistles were blowing he would have plenty of money for the next twelve months, but that if he wanted sure enough greenback money he must also eat cabbage and hogshead and black-eyed peas for dinner New Year's Day. Amen told him that the yellow butterflies which came winging over the levee by the hundred, early in the spring, turned into shrimp by and by, and that it was really butterflies they were getting when they crossed the batture to empty the boxes which had been tied to stakes in the river shallows near the bank. And Dinah told him that the reason the lightning bugs could gleam in the darkness was because they made their homes in the 'sparkfire wood' which was scattered through the swamps, and could draw on its hidden flames whenever they wished. She said that the lightning bugs stored up fragments of these flames in their own bodies, and released these as they wished, by pushing their bodies out while they flew. She also said that the children must not stay out too late in the evening, or wander too far from the Big House, because, if they did, the lightning bugs would lead them astray into briar patches; she could tell many a tall tale of disobedient children who had been so misled. Miss Mittie, who called lightning bugs fireflies, the way people did up North, said this was all stuff and nonsense, and Vail was inclined to listen to her instead of Dinah, because he liked to stay out after dark. When he stole out and stood beside the levee at night it was hard for him to tell sometimes where the ridge of this ended and the skyline began, and which were fireflies and which stars against the velvety blackness. But it delighted him to try, and he learned a lot that way about the sights and sounds and smells of the country at night. Apparently the fireflies retreated to their homes in the 'sparkfire wood' and stayed there all winter, for he never saw them then; but they came out in the early spring, at the same time that the wayside hedges were sweet with honeysuckle and blue iris and spider lilies began to bloom along the River Road. He picked bunches of these flowers to take back to Dinah for peace-offerings, so that she would not scold him for staying out later or threaten him with a briar patch; and then she was placated and told him more stories, about the roadside flowers and how they got their names, and he learned all that too.

Of course there were sure enough lessons too, out of books, which were bothering sometimes, though they did not actually spoil anything. But most of the lessons were not *too* bothering except during the first drowsy spring days. And Miss Mittie, who seemed to know how children felt about these, did not keep Sybelle and Vail and Phil in the old schoolhouse very long at a time when it began to be warm and sunshiny and inviting outdoors. She got them to their desks early in the morning, but when she saw their eyes straying from their primers to the open windows where the wasps were buzzing she said, there, that was enough, they could make up for lost time some rainy day. And off they went to ride the ponies and romp with Maud and do all the other wonderful things that were beckoning them outdoors.

Often Miss Mittie came with them. Once Aunt Cresside had shown her how, she tied pieces of meat on strings at the end of short poles, and day after day sat patiently for hours while they trotted up and down the banks of the big drainage ditch back of the house to catch crawfish. Sybelle or Phil would carefully lift one of the short poles to raise the bit of meat to which several crawfish clung with fatal greed, and Vail would scoop them into his net, which he then emptied into a big bucket. (The crawfish and the tempting sunshiny weather came at about the same time.)

Miss Mittie also helped the children to harness the big black grasshoppers which came along later in the year, and which everyone except Miss Mittie called devil horses, because they had first been brought to Louisiana in the horse feed of the Yankee soldiers who had made so much trouble at Belle Heloise before most of them were buried in the graveyard beyond Angus Holt's garden. Miss Mittie, who had begun life as a Yankee herself, could not be expected to feel the same way about the devil horses as the rest of them did; but the children overlooked this because she was so helpful in the matter of harnessing.

The harnesses were made of thread, and the carts the devil horses drew were made of match-boxes, and the stables where they lived were made of shoe-boxes. Miss Mittie helped make all these things, after Aunt Cresside had shown her how, and explained that when she was a little girl she and Daddy had driven devil horses themselves. She told the children that they had also gathered driftwood for the Christmas bonfires on the levee, and hunted quail eggs on the ditchbanks along the rough roads, when their father drove over the headland in his top buggy, taking Daddy and Aunt Cresside with him; then afterwards the quail eggs were hatched under the hens in the chicken-house. Vail and Sybelle gathered driftwood too, and learned to mix it with roseau reeds and pile it around tall central poles which were placed on the levee just before Christmas; and then on Christmas Eve they went up there to help light these piles and to listen to the crackling of the roseau, which sounded exactly like the fireworks they set off on the Fourth of July. So it was really like having two celebrations in one. And they hunted quail eggs once in a while themselves, but not very often, because Daddy did not usually drive a buggy when he went over the headland. Usually he rode horseback, taking Phil in front of him on the saddle. But sometimes, when Mummy said she would like to see the stand of cane too, Amen got out the old surrey and they all piled into it. That gave the children their chance to hunt quail eggs, and very good fun it was too.

Once Vail asked *grand'mère* if she had done all those wonderful things when she was a little girl, and she said no, because she had no one to play with, and it was not much fun levee-sliding or picking up pecans, or fishing in the ditch, or driving devil horses, or hunting for quail eggs alone. But Vail had plenty of people to play with. Sybelle and Phil were both fine playmates, and Joyeuse and Franchot were pretty good too, and would do better still when they grew a little bigger. They were there to play with all the time, and other playmates were there off and on, among them Barry and Nellie Pereira, who came up from New Orleans with their father and mother every now and then, to stay at the Big House. Still another was Riccardo Tramonte, whose father had a magnificent store right near the ferry, and a whole fleet of motor trucks besides, which carried provisions all over the State, supplying smaller stores which he owned also. Vail liked Riccardo even better than he liked Barry and Nellie, though Daddy and Mummy did not seem to like him so well. They never invited him and his father to stay to dinner, much less to spend several days, the way they asked the Pereiras. This was puzzling to Vail, because if he had been allowed to have his way he would have asked Riccardo to Belle Heloise every Sunday. Riccardo could not have come other days in any case, because he went to a big school, where he was already in the fifth grade, and on Saturdays he played games, not just marbles and pitch and toss, but important games like baseball. In the summertime he went travelling, down the River to New Orleans, and all over the State in his father's trucks. One summer he actually went to Italy to see his grandparents, and brought back some coral beads for Sybelle and a Sorrento paper cutter for Vail. (Mummy would never let Sybelle wear the beads, though they were ever so pretty, but Vail kept the paper cutter in his desk and used it all the time). Riccardo was three years older than Vail, and it was Vail's greatest ambition to be like him in every way. Sybelle agreed with Vail about Riccardo; she also thought he was very wonderful, and she was always delighted to see him when he came to Belle Heloise. But then Sybelle agreed with Vail about almost everything. Lou Ida said it was because he was her 'litter brother'. Litter brothers always meant more to their sisters than ordinary brothers, like Phil and Franchot, or so Lou Ida said, anyway.

Besides the Pereiras and Riccardo, of course, there was also Frances Belle, Aunt Cresside's little girl, who came to Belle Heloise almost every other day. She would be a fine playmate too when she got a little bigger. She was a very nice little girl though she was not quite as pretty as Sybelle. Vail was sure no one else was as pretty as Sybelle. She had beautiful blonde curls and blue eyes and the softest, pinkest cheeks in the whole world. Phil and Franchot and Joyeuse had brown hair and brown eyes and clear pale skin. Vail's cheeks were very red and his hair was jet black and his eyes were blue, not a soft sky blue like Sybelle's, but a deeper, brighter colour. They were big, except when he squinted them up, which he did sometimes when he could not see very well. He could see the print in his primer all right, but in some of the books Daddy kept at his office the print was very small, and when Vail tried to read it he squinted up his eyes.

Vail and Sybelle had almost finished their primers now, and soon they would have first readers, which had pretty big print too, though not quite as large as it was in the primers. Miss Mittie had the first readers put away in her desk already, waiting for them, and they were very excited about this. Every now and then they asked her to lift the lid so they could see the readers, which had beautiful red covers and which were tucked away in a corner beside Miss Mittie's pencil box. Phil had not got very far in his primer yet; he would always rather play than study, not just on warm sunshiny days, but any time, Miss Mittie tried to scold Phil because he was so lazy, but no one ever scolded Phil much, and Daddy did not even try. Daddy had taught them all their letters, on the plantation bell, before they began with their primers in the schoolhouse, and when Sybelle and Vail did especially well he let them ring the bell afterwards. But he let Phil ring the bell whether Phil did well or not. He even let Phil blow the whistle when grinding was over.

One day, just before the end of grinding, Vail and Sybelle and Phil all managed to get into the purgery together when no one was watching. There were big barrels of *vincanne* in the purgery, ready to serve to the hands as soon as the final whistle blew; but the children had never had any, though Phil had teased and teased for a taste. Phil seemed to think – and Vail and Sybelle agreed with him – that *vincanne* was probably just as good as *cuite*, which was mighty good indeed; when it was cooked up high it was as good as pull candy. The *vincanne* was disappointing after all, and Uncle Fabian, who came out with Aunt Cresside and Frances Belle and found them all three very sick and sleepy feeling in the purgery, said something about stolen fruit not being the sweetest after all. Uncle Fabian spoke pretty sternly to them for sneaking into the purgery and for stealing the *vincanne*. No one had thought of looking for them there until he did, and Mummy and Aunt Cresside were frightened because they were so sick; and Uncle Fabian said, and meant it, that they ought to be ashamed of themselves for making their Mummy and their Aunt Cresside so unhappy. Daddy scolded Vail and Sybelle a little, but he did not scold Phil at all. He said he thought it was funny to see the little tyke tipsy.

They never went back to the purgery, because they really were sorry – at least, Sybelle and Vail were – that they had made Mummy and Aunt Cresside unhappy, and, anyway, there were lots of other places in the mill that were more interesting than the purgery. One of these was a small square room on the pan floor where a Negro named Cato spent endless hours shovelling sugar and singing spirituals as he shovelled. Cato was an enormous man, whose coal-black body, bare to the waist, was always glistening with sweat. He wore white cotton pants, with a pocket on each side, and from these pockets hung huge handkerchiefs, one bright red and the other bright blue. He took these out of his pockets from time to time and wiped the sweat from his brow and his body, but it came right back again in little shining beads. The rest of the time he shovelled sugar, which was piled so high that it looked like a big snowdrift, or so Miss Mittie said. Of course, the children themselves had never seen a snowdrift, but she had shown them some pictures of these in a geography book they were going to study by and by, and they agreed with her. Miss Mittie also had a glass paperweight, representing a snow scene. If you turned it upside down, and then put it right side up again, little glittering flakes would fall from the top of the paperweight on the tiny houses and trees underneath it, and presently everything would be white and sparkling. The children loved the paperweight, which Miss Mittie had brought with her from Salem, Massachusetts, to Baton Rouge, Louisiana, many years before, but it was not big enough to remind them in any way of the endless piles of sugar which Cato shovelled. Daddy told them that this was crystal sugar, and that it kept going down a shaft that led from the small square room to the granulators, which would complete the process of making it into the beautiful white sugar for which Belle Heloise was famous. Daddy used pretty long words sometimes.

The children never tired of watching Cato, or Betsy Ann, the little old white mule that went round and round outside the sugar house, her traces fastened to a long pole, her bridle to a slender wooden crossbar attached to this. She propelled a little mill which a sample boy fed with cane from carts and which extracted juice from the cane stalks. Daddy explained to the children that the cane ground by Betsy Ann's mill was not the cane they raised at Belle Heloise; this went directly into the carrier from other carts. It was cane brought to Belle Heloise by planters who lived elsewhere, and who were paid according to its sucrose content. The juice from the cane for Betsy Ann's mill was kept apart from the other juice and taken to the laboratory for testing. In this way Daddy could always be sure that the other planters were getting just what they should for their cane.

'Betsy Ann represents the first step in the chemical analysis of the cane,' Daddy said, using big words again. The children nodded, their eyes on Betsy Ann, who was still faithfully and patiently going round and round. Her labours seemed as endless as Cato's.

Vail remembered the first time he had ever noticed Betsy Ann especially, because it was then he had asked Daddy if that little white mule was the one the men called Minnie. Vail had heard the men saying that Minnie was a very fine mule, with plenty of body, and he thought this must be the one they were talking about, because it would seem to him that she would need plenty of body to turn the mill so endlessly. But Daddy had laughed, saying no indeed, Minnie was the best mule they had, worth lots and lots of money, and she had to be kept for work in the fields. Vail must watch, the last day of grinding, for the gayest cart that came in and its lead mule. That would be Minnie and her cart, because the men took more pains with these, and had more pride in them than in any others. Betsy Ann was just a poor old broken-down mule who couldn't do anything harder than turn the little mill.

'That looks hard to me, though,' Vail said pityingly, still thinking how endless Betsy Ann's labours were.

'But it isn't – not nearly as hard as the work Minnie does. . . . Look, Vail, you'll probably be a planter yourself when you grow up, and of course Philogene will. It isn't too soon for you to begin to learn about mules, to recognize good ones and poor ones. They're very important on a plantation; they represent a big investment.'

There Daddy went, using long words again. But Vail was really interested, and he tried to look as if he understood.

'Don't ever forget how much the mules mean to the men who handle them,' Daddy continued. 'Once you've given a pair to one man, don't ever try to shift and give it to another. There's likely to be a killing if you do. There was a killing at Hathaway, just last week, because Mr. Tremaine took a pair away from his man Jam and gave them to another man named Kish. He didn't know any better.' Daddy spoke with scorn, and Vail, who somehow had never cared much for Mr. Tremaine, nodded with real understanding this time. He was sorry a man had been killed, partly because he was naturally kind-hearted, and partly because he knew that the Negroes at Hathaway had no graveyard of their own, as they did at Belle Heloise. Even the few who strayed from the plantation came back to be buried, and he wondered what the poor people at Hathaway did when they died, since there was no proper place for them to go afterwards. He would have liked to interrupt and ask Daddy, but Daddy did not like to be interrupted. 'Mr. Tremaine says a mule's just a hybrid with no pride of ancestry or hope of posterity,' he went on, using such long words now that Vail could hardly follow him. 'He's a great one to talk about that. . . . Well, he's lost a man, and it served him right. I don't want you losing any men or any mules either, Vail. I want you to feel responsible for them. And another thing: that responsibility means taking care of the mules when they're old. Of course, it costs something to feed them, and money's more important to a good many planters than anything else. I hope it won't be to you. I hope you will feel the mules have earned their right to a comfortable old age. At Belle Heloise we've always felt it was even worse to send a mule away from a plantation where she'd lived a long time than to shift her from one driver to another. I've seen a mighty tough overseer beg a planter, with tears in his eyes, not to sell the old mules who'd outlived their usefulness. . . . See here, you look as if you were ready to cry yourself. There's nothing to cry about. I'm not going to sell any mules, and I'm sure you're not either. Run along and find Sybelle. You know about Minnie and Betsy Ann now, and which is worth the most. By this time next week I expect you to know the name of every mule on Belle Heloise, and the name of every driver.'

He did not do quite as well as that, for there were a great many mules on Belle Heloise, dozens and dozens of them, or so it seemed to Vail. But he learned to know quite a number of them and he learned which were teamed together: Fuzzie and Florence, Martha and Mary, Clara and Agnes, Sarah and Sophie. He noticed that these were all ladies' names and asked about that. Then he learned that on Belle Heloise, as on the best plantations, only mare mules were used. Of course, at Hathaway it was different. Mr. Blood used horse mules, such as Floydie and Major, Sam and Bill. He learned which men handled the mules too: Roden, Monk, Temps, Orange, Neeley. He learned that four mules were attentively driven with one line in the fields, but that when only two, in tandem, were attached to the empty cars which had previously brought cane to the carrier on the plantation railroad they were hardly guided at all. After an 'empty' was unloaded near the mill it was detached from the miniature train, and a Negro snapped the chain of his tandem hitch to it. Next the mules hauled it around a sharp V curve to the other side of the mill. At first the car seemed heavy and the long iron chain attached to it was taut. But as the pull progressed the chain slack-ened. Then the driver told the mules to go on, and he himself draped his legs around the long iron chain and went to sleep. He did not need to watch the mules, because they knew the way as well as he did, and the sharp curve did not bother them at all. They took it at an easy gait, and the driver continued to sleep until the 'empty' had rounded the factory and reached the place where it was picked up to go out into the fields again.

All this was intriguing to Vail. He did not stand hour after hour in the dusty sunshine, patiently watching the carriers come in, as Merry had stood that autumn before the birth of Philogene; he scampered about from one part of the plantation to another. But every now and then he stopped long enough to see something of special interest, and soon there was almost no process on the plantation with which he was not familiar, no aspect which did not stimulate him or satisfy him. He knew that the reason dirt was brought from the batture and put in the bottom of the furnaces was because this would keep the bagasse from sticking. He knew that the purpose of lime was to make the impurities in the raw juice settle, so that these could be removed from the rest, and that blackstrap molasses, the leavings of sugar-making, was fit only for cattle. He knew that the little magnifier which he sometimes saw Dupu using was provided so that the sugar boiler could watch the grains in the syrup and get exactly the right amount, and he also knew that the old man really preferred to use his fingers for testing, and that he often did so on the sly. He loved to listen to the men singing inside the factory, to the sound of the engines growing louder and louder as he went up the sugar-house road and skirted the mill pond, and to the trip of the automatic which measured the exact weight of each bag, as the finished sugar poured down from the granulators into the open bags standing on the sugar scales. He loved to stick his fingers into these bags, hurrying to get as many tastes as he wanted before the bags were sewed across the top to close them, and trundled away to the vast storage warehouse or to the freight cars drawn up on a track behind the mill, waiting to take Belle Heloise sugar away. He loved to see the black chimneys looming up against a blue sky that had little fleecy white clouds racing across it, and the still golden sunsets behind the moving branches of the shadowy trees. He loved to watch the great bonfires of burning shucks and rubbish and the flaming radiance which transfigured the façade of the sugar house after nightfall, with the dark derricks etched against it in bold relief. He was very conscious of colours, and once he asked Aunt Cresside if she had ever noticed the way the sky changed, over the stack, just at sunrise. It was queer pinky blue at first, then lemon yellow, then orange, then a flaming red slowly spreading beyond the stack at either side, all across the horizon. Aunt Cresside said no, she never had seen all that, but she would like to, and she would come out to Belle Heloise the very next morning on purpose. So they stood for a long time together watching these wonderful colour changes in the sky. It was a very happy morning for him, because, though he loved to stand before the stack at sunrise by himself, he found it gave him even more joy when Aunt Cresside was there with him.

But best of all he loved to ride on the funny little engines which pulled the open cane cars through the fields at Belle Heloise to the sugar factory. In a general way the men spoke of these engines as the 'dummies', but they all had special names of their own besides. There was a very old dummy named LUCIEN ESTRADE, and two newer ones, a PHILO-ENE D'ALVERY and a MEREDITH D'ALVERY. Vail thought it would be fine if there were one named CRESSIDE D'ALVERY, too, for Aunt Cresside and another ISABELLE D'ALVERY, for *grand'-mère*, and he told Daddy so. But Daddy said they could not afford to have any more dummies just now, and that Vail had better be satisfied with three, which was as many as there were at Hackberry Lodge and more than there were at Hathaway.

Of course he was satisfied, Vail answered hastily, clambering up the steps of the dummy and pulling Sybelle up after him, before Daddy could change his mind about letting them have their promised ride. They had wanted very much to get on at this special hoist because it was the farthest from the scale house, and that would mean the longest possible ride. But John, the engineer, and Joe, the fireman, had been muttering about the heavy load they had already, and saying maybe it wasn't the best time for the chilluns to ride the dummy. John and Joe had both succeeded their fathers in the positions of trust which they now held, and they were both training young relatives – John his eldest son, Joe his younger nephew – to succeed them by and by. Meanwhile they knew they could not be too careful.

Once he and Sybelle were actually aboard the dummy, however, Vail knew that John would not put them off. He would tell them to stand back from the boiler, braced against the tender, and he would try to speak very severely. But if they begged him he would let Sybelle ring the bell and Vail blow the whistle just before the dummy started, and this was almost as much of a privilege as it was to ring François Estrade's great plantation bell or to blow the mighty whistle at the mill when grinding ended. So Sybelle tugged at the bell pull with all her might and main, and Vail blew as hard as ever he could, and then they were off, leaving Daddy behind at the hoist, sitting on his horse, with Phil in front of him on the saddle.

Another bell they liked to ring was the one on the *John D. Grace*. That was even more of an adventure than ringing the bell on the dummy, because it involved a much more exciting excursion. The *John D. Grace* did not stop at Belle Heloise very often, and neither did any other steamer, though in the wonderful old days, which they persuaded *grand'mère* to tell them about sometimes, all the beautiful side wheelers had stopped there regularly, both for passengers and for sugar. But when the *John D. Grace* did stop nowadays Vail and Sybelle were sometimes allowed to go aboard, in charge of Miss Mittie, and ride down the River as far as Gardere Landing, where Daddy met them with the car or Selah with the old surrey, to take them back to Belle Heloise over the River Road. And meantime they always had steamboat hash in the saloon, which tasted so much better than anything Lou Ida cooked, and went up into the pilot house to help steer the boat, and blow the whistle and ring the bell. The captain was a very kind man, always joking and laughing, and they found out that the pilot, though he did not say much, was kind too inside.

Lézine Sance, the overseer on the plantation, was another very kind man, and on rainy days, when they could not play outdoors, Vail and Sybelle loved to go after school to the house near the quarters where Lézine lived with his mother, a funny old lady with hardly any teeth, who always wore a white cap and who did not speak much English. Their house was one of the first buildings ever put up at Belle Heloise and was unlike any other on the place, though there were many similar to it farther down the River Road, around St. Gabriel and Geismar and Union. The children found this house fascinating. Its walls were made of adobe, formed from a mixture of mud and moss and supported by hand-hewn timbers placed crosswise. Construction of this kind was called *briqueté entre poteaux* and was very sturdy and lasting. The walls in the front-room, which was Madame Sance's special pride and joy, were tinted dusty pink, and her best furniture was arranged neatly all around them – the commode and the armoire and the four-poster she had brought there as a bride, when she married Lézine's father. The bare floor was made of wide planks kept very clean, and two old rockers, with a low wooden bench between them, were always drawn up on either side of the hearth, whether the fire was lighted or not. When her housework and gardening were done, Madame Sance sat in one of the rockers and knitted, and every now and then Lézine came in from the fields and sat for a few minutes in the other. He was a very devoted son and took pains to keep his mother company in this way. The children sat on the low bench, side by side. Lézine told them how the crop was coming along, and Madame Sance told them stories about her girlhood in St. Gabriel, where she had lived with her parents and eleven brothers and sisters in another house that was *briqueté entre poteaux*. One of the reasons she had consented to marry Lézine's father was because he could promise her a home like the one she had always lived in; otherwise she might have hesitated to go so far away from her family – all of fifteen miles. According to her, life on the River Road was not half as exciting as it had been when she was young, and the purpose of most of her stories was to prove this. But to Vail it seemed very exciting indeed, and she was one of the persons who helped to make it so.

Madame Sance always offered the children coffee, asking them whether they would rather have it black or white, and they told her white, because they were not supposed to drink strong coffee yet, though they both liked it very much already if it had lots and lots of sugar in it. Dinah had begun to put a little coffee in their morning milk, about a teaspoonful to a cup, when they were four years old, and this had gradually been increased, though they still did not have the half-and-half mixture which Daddy and Mummy and *grand'mère* drank for breakfast, nor were they allowed to drink second and third and fourth cups, like their elders. The first time Madame Sance offered them coffee, as far as Vail could remember, she had not only asked whether they would like it black or white, which they understood, but also whether they would rather eat it or drink it, which they did not understand. Then they had watched her and discovered that she dipped large pieces of mish bread in her cup and sucked the coffee from these, and that this was what she called eating it. So after that they told her they would eat their coffee too.

Vail could sit contentedly for hours, listening to the stories Madame Sance told and 'eating' the coffee she gave him; but even she was not as fascinating to him as the tall, quiet Negro they called 'Honeybee' Crock. In the spring bees often swarmed at the side of the house over Angus Holt's garden; you could see them whirling through the air and hear them droning; then presently they began to get inside. *Grand'mère* was not afraid of them, the way Franchot was, but they annoyed her. She was wakened in the morning by the noise they made, and when she saw them circling round her room and hanging from the tester of her bed, she said it was time to send Amen for Honeybee Crock, who lived in a cabin a piece up the River Road. Then Honeybee Crock would hasten down in his model 'T' Ford and stand under the window of *grand'mère's* boudoir, beating on a dish-pan with one of Lou Ida's big kitchen spoons. Presently the bees would start flying out of *grand'mère's* window and swarm on one of the low-hanging limbs of the mimosa tree; Honeybee Crock said they did this partly because they liked the noise he made and partly because they liked him. When a large cluster had formed on the limb, Honeybee Crock stopped beating the pan and began to talk to the bees, whose droning became softer and softer. Then at last he took them in his bare hands and put them in a special hive which he always had with him and carried them away. They never stung him; they were glad to go with him. After that the bees did not bother *grand'mère* any more than a year; but Vail always waited and watched for the time when Honeybee Crock would come back again the next spring.

For a long, long time these people and these pleasures sufficed to make Vail d'Alvery's world perfect and complete. Then it began to enlarge, and at first this expanding sphere seemed just as beautiful and even more exciting than the smaller one had been.

Instead of seldom leaving the plantation, he began to go more and more often to town. One evening, shortly after his seventh birthday, he heard *grand'mère* telling Mummy and Daddy, rather severely, that he and Sybelle had now reached the age of reason, whatever that might mean, and that it was high time they had religious instruction, beyond the prayers she and Mummy had taught them and the Bible stories told them by Miss Mittie, 'a Protestant from Massachusetts', as *grand'mère* called her, in a queer tone of voice – why, Vail did not know. He could dimly remember that when he was very, very little a sour-faced priest named Father Martin had come regularly to Belle Heloise to hear *grand'mère* confess and celebrate Mass in her room; but later on, after she was not so puny any more, she often went to church in town and Father Martin's visits became more and more infrequent. When she suggested that he should begin coming regularly again, to teach Vail and Sybelle their catechism so that they could prepare for the Holy Communion, Vail did not think much of this plan; he remembered Father Martin as one of the few unappealing figures peopling his pleasant world. Therefore, he was very much pleased when Daddy said no, rather shortly, they would get the kids to town somehow for instruction, and soon after that Vail and Sybelle began to go to catechism classes at St. Agnes's.

The catechism classes themselves were not so much, Vail privately thought; but he did not say this, because he could see that Sybelle really enjoyed them, and because Daddy made such an effort to get them to town, in spite of all there was to do on the plantation in springtime, and because *grand'mère* was so gratified that Vail and Sybelle were being properly prepared, at last, for their first Holy Communion. But the trips into town which these classes involved were simply swell. They were made in the new Buick that Uncle Fabian and Aunt Cresside had given Daddy and Mummy for a Christmas present after the faithful old one had practically fallen to pieces; and when a catechism class was over, Vail and Sybelle always went to visit Uncle Fabian and Aunt Cresside, who took them back to Belle Heloise later on in their own car. By the time the period of instruction had passed, and the first Holy Communion had been duly celebrated – Sybelle looking like a little angel in her floating draperies, Vail very self-conscious in his stiff white suit – the visits to Somerulos Street had become a habit. So these went on and on during the next two years. And in the course of these visits, Vail and Sybelle did all sorts of things they had not done at Belle Heloise. They went to the movies. They went to Luigi Tramonte's Fancy Grocery Store. They went to the Capitol and saw Daddy sitting in the Senate Chamber.

All this was great fun and very exciting. But once in a while something happened that made Vail feel uncomfortable instead of joyous, and raised the first doubts in his mind about the perfection of his expanding world.

For instance, there was the time that Betsy Ann died. All through the grinding season she had gone patiently round and round outside the sugar house, her traces fastened to the long pole, her bridle to the wooden crossbar, propelling the little mill which a sample boy fed with cane stalks and which extracted the juice from these. She had never stopped until the final load was in. And then, when Monk went to unfasten her, she had fallen where she stood. Vail had been standing nearby, watching her until the last minute, as he always did, and hoping that Monk would let him lead her away to the mule shed. He hurried over to her and knelt down beside her.

'She's all tired out,' he said wrathfully. 'It's too hard for her, going round and round like that. I'm going to ask Daddy to give her something easier to do next year.'

'Won't be no need, Vail.' Monk had knelt down beside the little white mule too, and was touching her with understanding. 'She tired out all right. She through. Ah done hear, plenty times, 'bout mules and folkses too droppin' right in they tracks, but this here the onliest time Ah ever seed it.'

'What do you mean, she's through?'

'She's daid. Ain't you never see no daid mule lyin' on de groun' befo'?'

No, Vail had never seen a dead mule before, or any dead creature, to think of it as such, for the things you ate did not count, even those that men brought home when they went hunting. The sight was almost more than he could bear, for he had loved Betsy Ann and she had been a part of his life as far back as he could remember, so he stayed with her as long as they would let him, and when they came with a cart to take her away, he asked if she were being carried to the coloured cemetery, and if he couldn't go too and see the funeral. Aunt Cresside came along just then and explained that mules were not buried in cemeteries, and that it would be better for Vail not to try to stay with Betsy Ann any longer; and for the first time in his life he broke away from her and went up on the levee all alone except for Maud. He did not want even Aunt Cresside to stay with him during the first hours of grief over Betsy Ann. It was not that he was ashamed to have her see him crying. It was only that he had to be by himself for a while.

Then there was the time that Mr. Tremaine had come butting in at the Fancy Grocery Store, just when Vail and Sybelle and

Riccardo were having such a good time eating their spumone. If Mr. Tremaine had had any sense, he would have known they didn't want him hanging around. And still he stayed and stayed, asking tiresome questions, until Vail wished he could tell him just where to get off. Mr. Tremaine had spoiled the whole afternoon, butting in like that. Vail was glad when he heard Daddy telling Mummy, not long afterwards, that Mr. and Mrs. Tremaine had gone to Cuba, that very likely they'd be gone all spring. Daddy went on to say it was no wonder everything at Hathaway was going from bad to worse, and Vail gathered this was because no one looked after Hathaway properly, the way Daddy looked after Belle Heloise. But even then Vail was guiltily glad Mr. Tremaine had gone away. He did not want Mr. Tremaine hanging around, whatever happened at Hathaway.

Afterwards his feeling of guilt about Mr. Tremaine increased, and with it his feeling that everything was not right in his world. Because Mr. Tremaine did not stay long in Cuba, and just a few days after he returned to Hathaway he died, and people said it was because he had caught a bad tropical fever. At least, most people. Vail heard Amen talking to some of the other Negroes about it, and Amen said it wasn't nothing of the sort. But when they asked him, what then, he wouldn't tell. He started to, and then he saw Vail and stopped.

Of course it was not Vail's fault that Mr. Tremaine had gone to Cuba, he knew that. But he had been so glad to get rid of him that when Mr. Tremaine died it gave him a queer feeling in his stomach, even worse than when Deéte Reno was killed in the crusher a few months later. He would have supposed, beforehand, that if anyone had told him he would be rid of Mr. Tremaine for good, he would have said that was grand. And it was not grand. He tried to tell Aunt Cresside how he felt about it, and for the first time he found it hard to talk to Aunt Cresside. That was another thing that made him feel something was wrong. And for a long while he looked in the opposite direction every time he went past Hathaway Hall. He hated the sight of that big black empty house. He hated the thought of it. He hated everything that reminded him of Mr. Tremaine, and he had never hated anything or anyone before in his life. . . .

The following summer he came across someone else whom he hated. This was a queer little man who stood beside him back of the Senate rail when he and Sybelle went there with Aunt Cresside to watch Daddy, who was talking, with all the other men listening to him. The little man had small, sharp features, a thin pointed nose, and little rat ears that were set very close to his head. He had oily black hair which came down over his little rat ears, because he needed a hair cut, and he clutched a big umbrella all the time. He offered Vail some gum, which Vail declined, though ordinarily he would have accepted it with avidity; he was very fond of gum, but *grand'mère* considered the use of it an extremely vulgar habit, and none of the children at Belle Heloise were allowed to have any, out of respect for her views. Therefore they habitually welcomed every possible chance of getting it elsewhere. But Vail, who was not usually any more observant about such matters than other small boys, noticed that the little rat-like man had grimy fingernails and clammy-looking hands, and he shrank from putting anything in his mouth that such a repulsive creature had touched. The man gave a funny little laugh, which sounded to Vail something like a rat's squeal, when Vail refused the gum; and then he made one or two remarks under his breath, using very nasty words. Vail had heard some of the words before, in the sugar house and the quarters and the fields, but they had not sounded so bad in those places as they did here in the Senate Chamber, and he hoped very much that neither Aunt Cresside nor Sybelle would hear them. But evidently Aunt Cresside did hear them, for she glanced across Vail at the little rat-like man, and presently she said she thought perhaps they had better be going; she didn't believe anything more that was exciting would happen in the Senate that day.

The little rat-like man was still standing beside them, clutching his umbrella and muttering nasty words under his breath. When they reached the rotunda, Daddy joined them and said, hello there, he'd seen them going out, and how would they like to come across the hall to Chris's cigar stand for a coke. Or course they all said that would be grand, and it was. There was something about drinking a coke under the big stained-glass dome that made it taste better than it did at home. Vail and Sybelle made theirs last as long as they could, but finally Aunt Cresside said, for heaven's sake, hadn't they sucked the bottles long enough, and how about coming over to the house for a few minutes? And Daddy said swell; cokes were all right as far as they went, but they didn't go far with him. He could still top them off with mint juleps, and he would, whenever he had a chance. He had to see a man for a minute, and after that he'd be right over to Somerulos Street.

By the time he got there, Aunt Cresside had the juleps ready and some more cokes for Vail and Sybelle, and Uncle Fabian had just come in from his office, so Frances Belle had climbed up on his lap and was asking funny questions and was awfully cute. They were all having a grand time, and Vail was hoping that Daddy wouldn't think about going home for a long while yet, when Aunt Cresside began to ask questions herself.

'Gervais, have you ever noticed a queer little rat-like man, clutching an unbrella, in the crowd back of the Senate rail? He's been there every time that I have lately. He sat beside us today.'

'I reckon you must mean Sammy Mudge. Yes, I've seen him. He's always hanging around when Long's on the floor, or when anything's going on that Long wants to have watched.'

'He looks to me like a foul creature. What does he prove?'

'Well, he's on the payroll as a State Highway Policeman, but as far as I know he's never done anything but pass by twice a month and pick up his cheque.'

'He must do something the rest of his time.'

'I suppose he must, but I wouldn't know what it is. He's more or less of a mystery. You're not the first person who's been curious about him. Some people figure he's got a dagger in the handle of that umbrella he clutches all the time, but that's just a rumour. He's never been seen with Long, but there's probably some kind of a body buried between them.'

Vail did not like to hear about bodies being buried. He had heard a great deal of that kind of talk, when Mr. Tremaine died of the bad fever and Mrs. Tremaine fell out of the window and Deéte Reno was killed in the crusher; he hoped he would never hear any more. Involuntarily he wriggled a little in his seat, because of the queer feeling in his stomach. Daddy saw him and drew the wrong conclusion, which was something Daddy did more often than Aunt Cresside.

'These kids are getting restless, Cresside. You run them ragged, taking them here, there and everywhere. I wouldn't bother, if I were you. They can't understand what it's all about, over there at the Capitol. Why don't you just let them stay in the yard? Well, time I got them home now, anyway. I'll be seeing you. . . .'

Daddy did not say anything more about Sammy Mudge on

the way home, and Vail hesitated to say anything himself, because once Daddy dismissed a subject, he did not like to have someone bring it up again. But Vail kept thinking about the horrid little rat-like man, and a few days later, to his surprise and disgust, he saw him again, this time at Belle Heloise.

It was one of those pretty evenings when Miss Mittie was lenient about lessons and Vail had left the old schoolhouse early, and was on his way to the stable to saddle Nostar and Twinkle. Sybelle was not quite through with her sums, which she could not do as fast as he did his, but in a few minutes she was coming to meet him, and they were going up on the levee together. Vail was hurrying, so that he would have both ponies ready by the time she joined him, and he almost ran into Sammy Mudge, who was standing near the old brick stable, half hidden by the shrubbery clumped around the tall arched windows, and talking to Amen, who seemed to be much interested in what he was saying. They both jumped a little as Vail came running up, but Sammy Mudge spoke to him straight off in a way that was meant to be pleasant.

'Why, hello!' he said, grinning in a toothy sort of way. 'If it isn't the little fellow who doesn't like gum – unless he's changed his mind. If he has, I've still got plenty. We were just talking about you, sonny.'

'Hello,' Vail said curtly. He gathered that Sammy Mudge expected him to respond to this second suggestion about gum, and to inquire what the two men were saying about him; but, with characteristic stubbornness, he did neither. Instead he swung along towards the stable, intent on getting away from the 'foul creature', as Aunt Cresside had called him, and wondering why Amen should have anything to do with him.

'Say, sonny, what's your hurry? Come on back.'

Vail went on without turning. But when he reached the stable door he hesitated for a moment, and then, instead of going in, he ran across the back of the Small Yard to the *garçonnière*, where he found Merry sitting in the living-room with Franchot on the floor beside her, playing with his blocks. The little boy jumped up joyfully at the sight of the bigger one and flung two small, thin arms around Vail's waist. He had never been as husky as the other children, and stayed in the house more on that account.

'Come build houses for me, Vail. Build me a sugar mill, like the last time.'

'Sure I will, Franchot, after supper. I'm going riding with Sybelle right now, and I want to see Daddy first. . . . Has Daddy come in from the fields yet, Mummy?'

'Yes, dear, he's in the office.'

'Is he by himself or has he got men there?'

'I think he's alone. What's the matter, Vail?'

'Nothing. I just want to see him.'

Franchot sought, somewhat clamorously, to detain him, but after repeating his promise about the toy sugar mill, Vail freed himself and ran out again. Gervais, who was just leaving the office, waved a greeting to him.

'Hello there! Through school already?'

'Yeah. Sybelle and I are going up on the levee. . . . Daddy, do you remember that man we saw in the Senate, the one who holds the umbrella?'

'Sammy Mudge? Sure I do. What made you think of him?'

'He's out beside the stable, talking to Amen. He tried to stop me when I went by.'

'What do you mean, he tried to stop you?'

'Well, he said for me to come back. But I didn't want to talk to him. You didn't invite him out to Belle Heloise, did you, Daddy?'

'You're darned right I didn't. I'm glad you told me he's here, Vail. I'll have a word with Mr. Sammy Mudge myself. You go ahead and get ready for your ride.'

Again Vail hesitated at the stable door. Now that Daddy was there too, he did not want to get away. He wanted to know everything that happened, because it might be exciting. But he knew, from Daddy's expression, that this wasn't Daddy's idea, and he had learned from experience that it was a good thing to respect Daddy's ideas. However, the stable door was wide open and so were all the stable windows, because it was such a pretty evening, and as he saddled the ponies he could not help hearing what Daddy was saying to Sammy Mudge and Amen. He hoped and believed that Daddy would not mind this, because he was not eavesdropping on purpose. . . .

'Hello, Mudge. Quite a ways off your beat, aren't you?'

'I have to do my work on the Highway, you know, Captain d'Alvery.'

'Belle Heloise isn't a highway.'

'Well, I was inspecting the River Road. You know, well as I do it's got to be watched when the river's up.'

'First time I've known the Highway Commission to worry much about it. Anyway, the river's not up.'

'It's rising – at least, we got a report that it was due to rise. So the Engineer said for me to come out and have a look. I never knew when I left town that the water in my radiator was low. Must have sprung a leak or something. So I just dropped in to get her filled up. Nothing wrong with that, is there? And now your boy here's got me all fixed—'

'You'll be on your way again? Good. Sorry he gave you the trouble of walking all the way back to the stable. There's a pump right by the Big House.'

There was a brief silence, broken only by the sound of hurrying footsteps. Vail knew that Sammy Mudge must have scuttled off, leaving Amen alone with Daddy. Then he heard Daddy's voice again, even colder and sterner than it had been before.

'I didn't see any water-can either. I thought I'd let that pass, because I wanted to get rid of that rat more than I wanted to stand here listening to his lies any longer. But I think you better tell me why he really came here, Amen.'

'Ah doesn't know, suh, hones' Ah doesn't, Captain. Ah done give him his water already. Right out ob de pump too, jes' lak you say. De can is settin' right dare now, you can see it fo' yo' ownself. But after us done fill de radiator, Mr. Mudge, he say he never wuz to Belle Heloise befo', he lak to take a little walk aroun' de place—'

'You're darned right; he's never been to Belle Heloise before. What's more, he isn't coming here again. Better get that straight, Amen. Think you have?'

'Yes suh, Captain. Ah has it goo 'n' straight. But—'

'But that still doesn't explain why he should have wanted to take a little walk around the place. Or why you should have let him, without asking me first. Or why you should have been hiding in the bushes, whispering to him. Or why he should have tried to stop Vail.'

'Ah di'n' think you'd mind effin he took a little walk around de place, Captain, an' us wuzn't hidin' in no bushes, us wuz jes' restin' after de walk. An'—'

'Come clean, Amen. You can't put me off with that kind of talk. You'd better tell me what you've really been up to.'

Instead of answering directly, Amen began to whine in a different key. 'Must be some misconviction, suh. You allus suspicious Ah be's cuttin' up when Ah isn't, lak de time you fin' me and Creassy in de chicken house.'

'You're god-damned right I'm suspicious. I know you've got some of the niggers along the Road believing you're a conjure doctor, you no'count, trifling, nappy-headed fraud, and you've just about broken your daddy's heart, carrying on the way you have. There's never been a better man working on this place than Selah, and that's saying plenty, too. We've always had good people working for us at Belle Heloise. You're the only really sorry one I could name.'

'Captain, Ah swears to God—'

'You can stop right there, Amen. I never knew you to say you swore to God that you weren't getting ready to tell the damnedest lie you could think of. I told you I wanted to know what Sammy Mudge was doing on my place, and you know it. Quit stalling. You better come clean right now if you know what's good for you.'

'He come to git water, lak he say, and den we done took a little walk an' – oh please, suh, don't lay hold ob me dat away! Yo' hurts me, yo' hurts me bad! Ain't nothin' mo' Ah can say. Mr. Mudge he jes' axed me wuz yo' all good friends with Mr. Sylvestre and Miss Regine when dey wuz alive.'

'All right; we're getting somewhere now. I'll let go of you after you've told me the truth. What did you say when he asked you that?'

'Ah say, yo' wuzn't friends exactly, leastwise Ah disremembers ever seein' yo' all ever actin' lak yo' wuz friends. Ah done hear though, a long while back, things wuz different.'

'That what was different?'

'Dat yo' and Miss Regine wuz friends, but dat yo' didn't want to be friends no mo' 'count ob Miss Merry. An' dat Miss Regine she took on 'caise she wuz mad an' den she done stole Miss Cresside's beau away from her an' marry him.'

'You told Sammy Mudge all this dirty gossip about your own white folks?'

'No suh. Yes suh. Lea' go my arm, please, Captain, suh. Ah never mean no harm, Ah wuz jes passin' de time ob day, lak us duz sometimes—'

'Listen to me now, Amen, and get this good. I don't aim to say it again. If ever I hear of you talking to strangers about the d'Alverys or any of their kinfolks, or if ever I hear of you and that bastard Mudge even being seen together, I'm going to kill you. You wouldn't be able to run far enough or fast enough to get away from me. ... I ought to give you a hiding right now, but I'm afraid if I started I wouldn't stop till I did kill you sure enough. You know me, Amen. You know I'm not just making talk. Mind now, the next time there'll be no questions and no talk – just one awful dead nigger, and that'll be you.'

Again there was a sound of scurrying footsteps. Vail stood very still, a new kind of fear gripping at his heart. He had heard Daddy speak loudly and harshly a good many times when he did not understand what it was all about, but he had never before known him to say that he would kill anyone, and the threat gave Vail the same queer feeling in the pit of his stomach that had come there once or twice already, only now it was worse. He wanted to get out of the stable, and he wished Sybelle would hurry up and come, so they could go for their ride; her sums must have taken her longer than she expected. ...

At last he decided not to wait for her any longer, but to build the toy sugar mill for Franchot after all; Sybelle would come and look for him in the *garçonnière* anyway if she did not find him in the stable. He hitched Nostar and Twinkle in their stalls and started back across the yard, walking slowly, and glancing over his shoulder once or twice to see if Sybelle were coming after all. There was no one in sight, but pretty soon he heard sounds from the *garçonnière*: Daddy was still shouting, and Mummy was begging him to hush, the way she did when she was trying to soothe him. But this time Mummy sounded unhappy herself, which was very unlike her. She did not raise her voice, but still it did not sound the way it usually did.

'I know it's dreadful, Gervais, but please try to tell me about it quietly. I'm so afraid someone else will hear you.'

'There isn't anyone else around to hear me. Don't you suppose I know? And don't you suppose I know that if Amen told Mudge that much, he told him a lot more? Don't you suppose I know that rat is Long's stool pigeon? Don't you suppose I know he's been sent out here to dig up dirt?'

'Please, Gervais! Please be careful. And please don't be so upset. There's no dirt Mudge could dig up here now. There's nothing Amen knows.'

'No dirt? Nothing Amen knows? I'll bet there's nothing he doesn't know! There's been a leak somewhere, there always is.

Creassy's always known and Amen's wormed it out of her some way. He's told Mudge everything he knows, and Mudge hot-footed it back to Long with the news! I'll bet Long knows by now that Sylvestre Tremaine was Vail's father!'

CHAPTER EIGHT

SAMMY MUDGE left Belle Heloise exceedingly well pleased with himself and his achievements. To be sure, Captain d'Alvery's inopportune appearance had given him a few moments of acute uneasiness. But nothing had come of this after all, to Sammy's intense relief. Placing his umbrella carefully beside him on the seat, and settling back in his car with a good grip on the wheel, he prepared to enliven the long drive to Maringouin with a mental review of the recent successes which had followed a long series of failures.

This was by no means the first time that Sammy had been summoned to a secluded hide-out, deep in the swamps near Maringouin: a 'camp' to which Huey Long retired at intervals, ostensibly for mental relaxation and strenuous physical exercise. A few of his boon companions generally accompanied him to this sylvan retreat, which was reached by one of many obscure logging roads transecting the region, and it was presumably the society of these cronies which afforded him the mental relaxation: a wood pile in the rear of the house – a weather-beaten cabin rising on stilts above a relatively high piece of cleared ground – suggested the wherewithal for strenuous exercise. But Sammy Mudge had never found His Excellency engaged in making the chips fly. Instead it was his experience that after he had passed the armed guards who were stationed along the logging trail he would be met in front of the shack by Clovis, the wizened and toothless caretaker, with whom he would exchange a brief greeting. After that Clovis would disappear inside, where Huey was invariably ensconced, and announce the arrival and identity of the visitor. Sometimes this announcement met with an immediate response, and sometimes it was repeated over and over

again before it was acknowledged in any way; but the acknow-
ledgement, when it came, varied very little in form.

'All right, all right! Tell the son-of-a-bitch to wait.'

The interval which followed was generally a long one, and
Sammy Mudge became very tired before it was over. No one
ever asked him to sit down, and though he leaned on his faithful umbrella, this did not give him as much support as he might
have wished. No one ever offered him any refreshment either,
and he was always hungry and thirsty after his tiresome ride; a
bottle of beer and a sandwich, or even a coke and a cracker,
would have helped a lot, especially on those occasions when he
had failed in his appointed mission and knew he was in for a
dressing-down. Now that at last he had succeeded beyond his
fondest hopes in ferreting out the facts concerning a secret scandal, he did not need a stimulant as much as usual; but it was
hard for him to control his impatience as he stood leaning on
his umbrella and waiting for Long to appear. He was eager to tell
his story, produce his evidence, and receive his reward. . . .

He had begun to feel that he had passed the point of endurance when the Governor of Louisiana emerged from the shadow
of the doorway and crossed the narrow gallery of the shack,
scratching himself as he came. His appearance was even more biz-
arre than when he had first startled the State by his eccentricities,
and the insolence of his manner and bearing had become more
obvious with the years. His hair was tousled above an unshaven
face, and he wore nothing but pyjama pants and bedroom slippers, the scantiness of this attire accentuating the ungainliness
of his body. Without the slightest sign that he had even seen his
faithful henchman, he squatted down on the steps, called over his
shoulders for a cup of coffee, and then sat staring straight ahead
of him till Clovis brought it. Having consumed it, still with no
sign of recognition to Sammy, he called in the same loud tone of
voice for a cigar, and after getting this, sat chewing it without
lighting it for some minutes more. Then, without warning, he
turned and roared at Sammy Mudge.

'Find out anything?'

Sammy jumped and then swallowed hard, in his effort to collect himself quickly. But he did not allow his great moment to
escape him. He managed to answer promptly and adequately.

'Sure I found out something.'

'All right. What?'

'Well, d'Alvery's still mighty short of cash. He's paid off some of his notes, but there's a lot of 'em on call yet. They come to around a hundred and fifty thousand—'

'Jesus, what I got to contend with! Ain't every mortgage in this state recorded so any fool can go and look at it? Ain't I got a bank examiner with a tongue in his head? Every nigger on the River Road knows d'Alvery's hard up.'

'I just mentioned the money like in passing, Governor. I heard a lot of talk about that along with the rest, and so naturally—'

'What do you mean, the rest?'

'The rest I found out about the d'Alverys. While I was down on the River Road, inspectin', I run out of water for my radiator and—'

'I don't give a good god-damn about your radiator—'

'All right. . . . One of them twins at Belle Heloise ain't a twin.'

'What do you mean?'

'That boy ain't no twin of that girl and he ain't Gervais d'Alvery's boy.'

'Who you been talking to?'

'Well, I been talking to Durice Reno, that old blister of Blood's, for one. And I been talking to that conjure nigger they got on Belle Heloise. You see—'

Long jumped up, ran his hands impatiently through his tousled hair, threw his half-chewed cigar into a puddle, and sat down again. 'Listen! Will you for Christ's sake come to the point?' he shouted. 'So you've talked to some whores and some niggers and you can prove by them the d'Alverys took in a baby and raised it for one of theirs! You mean it was the Captain's kid by some other woman?'

Sammy smirked toothily. 'Better'n that, Governor. This is his sister's kid.'

'Why, you crazy weasel-head, his sister's married to Fabian d'Alvery. She'd be raising her own children if that were her boy. Anybody would know that much; anybody except maybe you.'

'No, Governor, it's like this: you take some time back she used to go with that guy Tremaine at Hathaway and she got hooked. So when the baby was born d'Alvery and his wife covered up for her account: it was born just about the same time as d'Alvery's little girl; they made off like Mrs. d'Alvery had had twins. But only one of the kids was hers; the other one, this boy, was his sister's.'

Long dropped his head between his shoulders and stared fixedly at the ratty little man as though trying to hypnotize him. Sammy shifted his umbrella nervously from one hand to the other and finally broke into speech. 'Honest, Governor,' he began placatingly. 'I'm telling you how—'

'Shut your damn fool face! Here I am working night and day trying to do something for the people of this State and I got to rely on dumb half-wits like you for what little help I need.' He suddenly straightened up like an uncoiled spring. 'If I have Joe and Tony take you out in the middle of that swamp and leave you there, you reckon you could ever find your way out? Well that's what I got a good mind to do.'

'But, Governor—'

'Don't you "but, Governor", me. What the hell are you trying to do, get me shot? Get me run out of Baton Rouge?'

'But look, Governor, I even brought you this snapshot I bought off that conjure nigger at Belle Heloise. It's a picture of this kid's daddy when he was a kid himself, and it's the spittin' image of that boy like he looks today excusing his clothes.'

'Give me that god-damn thing.' Long snatched at the photograph, tore it into fragments without looking at it, and threw the pieces at his retainer. 'You and your "I thoughts",' he snarled. 'I can send out in that swamp and get varmints that are smarter than you – yes, and that smell better. If there was any use explaining. . . . But what the hell! I could make more dough talking to the side of this house. If I don't have you killed, you think you got sense enough to keep your trap shut? Because one way or another it's going to be kept shut.'

'Sure, Governor, sure. I only tried to do what you wanted.'

'You better try to do what I don't want. Maybe you'll get it right that way. Get back to Baton Rouge and don't let me see you again till I send for you.' And as Sammy, crestfallen but obedient, started off, Long shouted, 'Wait,' and turned towards the shack. 'Got those things wrapped up, Clovis?'

A muffled but affirmative answer came from within. 'All right. Put 'em in a box and bring 'em out here,' Long directed. Then, turning to Mudge again, he went on: 'Couple of fish and a softshell turtle. Take 'em in to Joe King at the Heidelberg. Tell him to put 'em on ice for me. Think you've got sense enough not to get to Baton Rouge with a dead skunk instead of these catfish?'

'Sure, Governor, I'll take 'em right to the hotel.'

'And call up Oscar and Jesse and tell 'em I want to see 'em here first thing tomorrow morning.'

'I'll telephone straight off soon as I've given Mr. King the fish.'

The wizened caretaker had reappeared, carrying a long box, and handed it silently to Mudge, who stowed it away in the rear of the car. Sammy, somewhat cheered by this new evidence of trust, got in himself and leaned out of the window.

'So long, Governor. Count on me. I'll see to everything.'

He disappeared down the rough road between the watchful guards. Long looked after him, a quizzical expression on his pudgy face as he stood scratching himself luxuriously. Then he turned back into the house.

The details of this scene were, of course, unknown to Gervais. But his assumption that Mudge had 'hotfooted' it to Long became a certainty two days later, when he received a curt note summoning him to see the Governor the following morning at ten o'clock. He handed it to Merry on returning from the Capitol that evening and, lighting a cigarette, began to pace restlessly up and down the long room, awaiting her comment.

'He's sent for you before, hasn't he?'

'You know he has. I told you about the offer he made me.'

'Then mightn't he just want to make you another?'

'Merry, you're guileless, but you're not all that guileless. There isn't but one Lieutenant-Governorship and I've turned that down already. It would have meant a lot to me too, not just in itself, but a stepping-stone. I'd have jumped at it if I could have had it on the level. But there's nothing else he could offer me at the moment, even if he wanted to, and you may be damned sure he doesn't. This time he's got it in for me.'

She came up to him and put her hand tenderly on his arm. 'I wish you wouldn't take all this so hard, honey,' she said. 'It troubles me when I see you worried. What difference would it make if Long did have it in for you?'

'Plenty. You don't seem to realize, Merry, how much I care about going ahead, politically. Not just for my sake, either. For yours and the children's. I'd like to see you all in the Mansion, I'd like to take you all to Washington—'

'But I thought you loved Belle Heloise better than any place in the world. You said when you came back after the war that you never wanted to leave it again.'

'This isn't a case of what I love. It's a case of what I accomplish. And I just said, not only for myself—'

'I'm sure I'm happier at Belle Heloise than I would be in the Mansion or in Washington, Gervais. I'm sure the children are better off here too. It's a wonderful place for children. They're all thriving, they're all happy. . . . At least, they're nearly always well, they're nearly always lively. Of course, Franchot isn't quite as strong as the others, and I've been a little troubled about Vail these last few days. He hasn't seemed like himself.'

'I haven't noticed anything. What do you think's the matter?'

'Well, he's hardly talked at all, for one thing.'

'There's nothing unusual about that. Vail never talks much.'

'No, but he talks some, and when he's silent he's still companionable. This is different. He's acted as if he didn't want to talk to anybody. He hasn't eaten much either.'

'Probably needs a good dose of castor oil. Why don't you give it to him?'

'Because I don't think there's anything the matter with him physically; I think he's got something on his mind. Miss Mittie went back to the schoolhouse yesterday for something she'd forgotten and found him there poring over a dictionary. She's been trying for a long time to teach him to use one without the slightest success, so naturally she was startled at finding him absorbed like that, and, anyway, it isn't like him to stay indoors after school hours – he always wants to get out and run around, you know that. Miss Mittie asked him if she could help him find what he wanted, and he shut up the dictionary and went off without answering her. Later on I saw him riding on the levee, but he was alone – I never knew him to start off before without Sybelle, and she felt terribly. It was all I could do to comfort her. He won't play with the other children either, and you know how kind he's always been to them.'

'I still think castor oil's your answer. Vail's never tormented Joyeuse and Franchot, I'll say that for him; just the same, he's always been stubborn and contrary. Dose him and then leave him alone. He'll come around all right. Anyway, don't worry me about him just now. I've got enough on my mind as it is. . . . Another thing you don't seem to realize, Merry, is that this isn't just a case of losing out politically. It's a case of fighting probably blackmail and everything that goes with it. I've always told you we'd have to face the music some time. I reckon that time's now.'

'And you still think it wouldn't help to tell Fabian?'

'Tell Fabian? That Long's fixing to spread smut about Cresside?'

'Fabian might be able to stop him. He's pretty powerful, you know, after all, in his quiet way. At least, I should think it would be worth trying.'

'I don't. I know it's the last thing on earth I ought to try.'

As a matter of fact, he did not dismiss the suggestion quite as abruptly as his words and manner indicated. Lying sleepless beside Merry during the long night, he considered the question from every possible angle. But in the end he found that his viewpoint was the same as it had been in the beginning; and it was still unchanged the following morning when he met his cousin accidentally in the lobby of the Heidelberg hotel. Fabian, whose cynical outlook on life had been greatly tempered by his happy marriage and triumphant fatherhood, greeted Gervais with a genial grin.

'Hello there! What's your hurry? Come on into the coffee shop and tell me what's cooking at the Capitol while we snatch us a small black.'

'I'd like to, but I haven't got time.'

'What's the matter? The legislature doesn't meet till eleven, does it?'

'No, but I've been summoned to the clown prince's presence.'

'Where, at the State House?'

'No, in his highness' suite up on the tenth floor.'

'Better take him tribute in the form of strawberries and cream. They tell me he's a sucker for that.'

'It's an idea. I think I'd know just where to put 'em too. But I don't believe they'd do the trick this time.'

'What's it all about?'

Gervais shed his lightness of manner. 'I wish I could honestly say I didn't know,' he said rather ruefully. 'But I think I do. The way matters stand we're out to beat that bond issue scheme of Long's with its sixty-million-dollar slush fund. It squeezed through the House by one vote, but with Cyr on our side on the Senate, Pike Hall and Boone and John Caffery are all set to talk it to death in as fine a filibuster as ever was put over.'

'I know; everybody's talking about that on the streets.'

'Well, I think the crazy bastard is going to threaten to bring me around to his side.' Gervais lowered his voice. 'Believe it or not, he's already offered me the Lieutenant-Governorship in the next election. I bet John Fournet would give birth to a litter of goats if he knew it. But naturally I turned it down.'

'And now you figure it will be the straight iron fist with no velvet glove? What the hell could he possibly threaten you with?'

Gervais hesitated, thinking again of what Merry had said about Fabian and aware that his cousin suspected he had not spoken with complete candour. Then he shrugged his shoulders impatiently. 'Who knows what the maniac has in mind?' he muttered and turned hastily towards the elevator. 'See you in church,' he called back as he entered the cage and the mirrored doors slid shut.

A swart thick-shouldered man was pacing up and down the hall near a side door which shut off two rooms at the end of the corridor into a single suite. He gazed at Gervais impassively as he approached.

'All right, Joe. You can tell his Nibs I'm here,' Gervais informed him.

Without a change of expression, Joe turned and knocked on the door. It was opened by a muscular young man with close-cropped blond hair. He was coatless and thus exposed a well-filled shoulder holster. 'It's the Senator,' Joe announced.

'Yeah, sure,' agreed the guard. 'Come in here, Senator. The Governor's taking a bath. He'll be right out.'

This prediction was almost immediately verified as Long, wet and glistening, stepped from the bathroom on to the thick-piled rug of the parlour, towelling himself briskly. 'Sit down, Senator,' he urged. 'Hope you ain't as fussy as that Admiral who'd like to get me shot for treason because I never had nothing on but my pyjamas when he come up to see me.'

Gervais chuckled. 'No, I'm not fussy, Governor,' he assured his host, accepting the proffered chair.

'You know,' Long said, towelling himself more slowly. 'It's a funny thing. You take when I was a kid up in Winnfield, folks thought if you took one bath a week that was a-plenty. Now you got to bathe every day. No telling what they'll think up next.'

Gervais accepted this bit of social philosophy without attempting to elaborate on it. 'No use beating about the bush, Governor,' he said. 'You wanted to see me about something.'

'That's right,' agreed Long. He turned to face the bedroom. 'Murphy, bring me my socks and drawers,' he called.

'Well, here I am,' suggested Gervais.

'What I wanted to talk to you about was this programme of mine for helping everybody in this State. Now we give 'em the free school books, even though they went to the Supreme Court of the United States to try and stop me, and we got the good roads started, but we got to keep the work going. You know folks need jobs. I expect you've heard about that crash that Wall Street rigged up on the country. We pass this bond issue bill and that'll help everybody. It'll give us the roads, and the Lord knows that the people of this State need 'em, and building the roads will give jobs to people that ain't got 'em.'

'Governor, my mind's made up about that,' Gervais said unsmilingly. 'I haven't changed it since we talked the other day.'

Long who had put on and laced his shoes rose from his chair stamped his feet tentatively and called to the bedroom: 'Where the hell's my pants?' Then he turned to Gervais. 'You know there's more ways to kill a cat, Senator, besides choking it to death with cream cheese,' he said slowly.

'Meaning just what?' Gervais asked.

'Meaning I tried to show you how we could help each other, but you wouldn't listen. This time I'm telling you you better help me out on this bond issue bill.'

'Governor, are you threatenng me?'

'I most assuredly ain't. If I was a mind to threaten, there's a couple of stout boys with guns to back me up, so you don't need to bow your neck any.'

'Suppose you say in plain English just what you're after.'

'All right. What would you say if I was to tell you that I know plenty about what's been going on at that plantation of yours?'

Well, I knew that was it all the time, Gervais said to himself. *I knew it was coming and here it is. It's no surprise, so it oughtn't to be a shock either. But it is. A thing like this always hits you harder than you figure it's going to, when it finally comes, no matter how well prepared you think you are for it.* Aloud he only remarked stiffly: 'I'd say blackmail was a little out of line among the duties of a Governor.'

'Who's blackmailing anybody, d'Alvery? Listen, you're a silk stocking. I'm a country boy from Winn Parish. I got every big corporation in the State and every big newspaper and every crooked politician fighting me. The way that John Sullivan doublecrossed me, do you think I'm going to ask Emily Post what fork I should use when I'm fighting back? I got the common people of this State to study about. They're the ones trusting me. They're the ones crying for these roads and I aim to see them get 'em. You got one vote that I need. John Parker could get a vote out of you whenever he wanted to, just by talking to you. Well, I guess I ain't got his highbrow winning ways, the kind you take to, and when I offered to dicker with you the other day you wouldn't listen. So, if there's ary a way under the shining sun I can buy that vote out of you, or club it out, I aim to do it.'

'Do you really think, Governor Long, that you or anybody else on earth could bribe me or club me into doing something dishonest?'

'What's dishonest about giving poor people roads?'

'The dishonest part is handing you sixty million dollars that you'll use to line the pockets of your special friends, if not your own directly, for the control of every election in this state during the next ten years.'

Long suddenly chuckled. 'Do you for true think I'll take ten years to spend that dough?' he asked.

'Certainly not,' retorted Gervais. 'I was talking about the control – if somebody doesn't shoot you first.'

Long snorted. 'Somebody'll have to shoot it out with a lot of boys that'll be shooting back before he ever shoots me. But that ain't either here nor yonder. . . . Ever think of resigning from the Senate?'

'No, never.'

'Well, you might.'

'And if I don't?'

'Well, if you don't, and if you don't dicker either, some of the things I know about what's been going on at that high and mighty plantation of yours will be put to use. And before you say anything to that you might stop and think what it'll mean to you and all your kinnery.'

Gervais rose and crossed the room without replying. Then, with his hand on the doorknob, he turned. 'Sorry, Governor, no sale,' he said coldly. 'Pop your whip any time you choose. But don't forget that once you have popped it it'll be my turn.'

CHAPTER NINE

IN spite of Gervais' contention that nothing was the matter with Vail, Merry remained unconvinced. However, she was secretly almost as much disturbed over her husband's break with Long as he was himself, and the lesser anxiety was swallowed up in the greater one. She continued her efforts to tempt the little boy's appetite, and she gently reminded him several times that he was hurting the other children's feelings by his unreasonable refusal to play with them. But she did not make repeated attempts to draw him out, and, having won his confidence, to comfort him, as she would have done if she had been less anxiously absorbed. Vail, sensing her preoccupation without understanding the reason for it and increasingly hurt and perplexed, withdrew further and further into his protective shell.

Much of the conversation which he had so unfortunately overheard was still incomprehensible to him. But one fact stood out inescapably: Sylvestre Tremaine, whom he had always hated with all his might and main, was his father. The man whom he still habitually labelled as Daddy had said so, angrily and positively. It was obvious that he resented the relationship as much as Vail himself, but it was also obvious that he was sure of it. And automatically this not only meant that the man Vail called Daddy was not really his father after all, but that Sybelle was not his twin, Joyeuse was not his younger sister, Phil and Franchot were not his brothers and Mummy was not his mother.

All this was so staggering that at first he did not grope beyond it. But presently the question which was its inevitable sequel crossed his troubled mind: if Mummy was not his mother, who was? Certainly not Mrs. Tremaine, for if she had been he would have lived in that great blank house at Hathaway with her and her husband, instead of at Belle Heloise with Daddy and Mummy – that is, with the d'Alverys. But even if she were not, even if Mr. Tremaine had been married before to some lady who had died, it seemed strange to Vail that Mr. Tremaine had not insisted upon having him live there anyway. Vail knew that men wanted and expected to have their children live with them, at least in all the cases he could think of. There must have been some special reason why Mr. Tremaine did not want him. Or Mrs. Tremaine. He remembered the reluctant and often cruel stepmothers in the fairy stories he had read. That must have been it: his own mother had died, and Mr. Tremaine had not wanted him, or else Mr. Tremaine had been afraid that his new wife would be unkind to him; so they had fixed it up that he should live with the d'Alverys. Just the same, it was funny that Mr. Tremaine had never come to see him at Belle Heloise, and that he should be called Vail d'Alvery instead of Vail Tremaine. . . .

He was turning over these strange things in his mind, sitting all alone, except for Maud, on the River side of the levee, so that no one would see him from the Road, when, for no reason at all as far as he could see, he remembered something Amen had said: 'De d'Alverys ain't never forgive Miss Regine for stealin' Miss Cresside's beau.' After he remembered that, he kept on thinking about it. He had heard Daddy – there, it was no use, he couldn't call him anything else – and Uncle Fabian too teasing Aunt Cresside about Mr. Charles Boylston, who used to live at Hackberry, down the River Road, and who still came back there once in a while. When they teased her like that, they spoke of Mr. Boylston as her beau, and she did not seem to mind, though she did not joke about it the way they did. But they had never teased her about Mr. Tremaine, and now that Vail thought of it he remembered that the only time he had ever talked to her when she had not been glad to talk to him in return was the time he had brought up the subject of Mr. Tremaine. He was sure Amen must be mistaken. He did not believe Mr. Tremaine had ever been Aunt Cresside's beau. If he had been, Daddy and Uncle Fabian would have teased her about that too, once in a while, and she would have laughed when she listened, the way she did when they teased her about Mr. Charles Boylston.

Vail had practically convinced himself that Amen was mistaken, finding considerable comfort in the conclusion, when he remembered it was this very statement of Amen's which had made Daddy so furious that he began to talk about killing. And afterwards, when Daddy was talking to Mummy, he had said: 'Amen *knows*. There's nothing he doesn't know.' So it must have been true after all. Daddy was angry because Amen *knew* and because he told what he knew. And this was that Mr. Tremaine had once been Miss Cresside's beau and that Miss Regine had stolen him away from her. It wasn't a joke the way it was about Mr. Charles Boylston. It was a disgrace. People weren't supposed to joke about it; they weren't even supposed to know about it. He had always thought Aunt Cresside was the loveliest lady in the whole world, lovelier even than Mummy, and he knew that Uncle Fabian thought so too. Uncle Fabian had been her husband for a great many years, and another thing they joked about was the fact that it had taken her a long while to make up her mind to marry him. But some time, even before this, that hateful man, Mr. Tremaine, had been her beau. Daddy was so ashamed of this that he had threatened to kill Amen for speaking of this, and Aunt Cresside must be ashamed of it too, or she would not have refused to talk about Mr. Tremaine herself. . . .

Vail finally left the levee and walked slowly home with Maud at his heels, the puzzle still unsolved. It was supper-time already, and everybody else was at the table; he could hear voices coming from the dining-room as he approached the house, and without stopping to wash his hands he went through the pantry and slid silently into his seat. He fully expected to be scolded, as *grand'mère* was very particular about punctuality at meals, and it was one of those minor matters in which Daddy always sided with her against Mummy. But neither *grand'mère* nor Daddy said anything to him about his tardiness now or even appeared to notice his arrival. They were too busy talking with each other.

'I confess I was surprised at Mr. Goldenberg's call, Gervais. I have always thought he showed remarkable delicacy of perception in recognizing that your transactions with him were confined to business. It is strange that after all these years he should have come here to make a social call.'

'Do you remember the Sunday afternoon when that skunk Bisbee came out here to make a social call and what happened afterwards?'

'Yes, very well. But surely you do not imagine—'

Daddy laughed, but he did not sound as if he thought anything was funny.

'I don't visualize Goldenberg as a skunk, if that's what you mean. His stripe's different from Bisbee's and he's done the best he could for me. But I think he's probably been put in a damn awkward position himself. Probably he came here to tell me about it, hoping it would be a little easier all round than if he sent for me to come and see him. It would have been, too. I'm sorry I missed him.'

'What is this awkward position to which you refer, Gervais?'

'Well, I know that an examiner went to the Citizens National Bank this morning dead drunk and started a fearful row. After he'd spent an hour or so in general hell-raising, the President decided it was about time to telephone the Governor and find out what it all proved, as Cresside would say. He did find out.'

'Find out what?'

'That Huey wanted the bank to extend some of the notes it meant to call, and call some it meant to extend. He said, if it didn't, he'd have all the State funds on deposit there withdrawn. The Citizens National's in pretty good shape, as banks go these days. But it can't afford to lose those State funds.'

'And yours would be among the notes the Governor wanted called?'

'Not a doubt of it. He warned me he was getting ready to club a vote out of me, if he could. This is the first blow.'

'But what can you do to save the situation, Gervais, if your assumption is correct?'

'I can't tell you right now, *maman*. I don't know yet myself.'

Daddy's voice had begun to be edgy. He did not like to have *grand'mère*, or anyone else, ask him so many questions. Mummy, who had not said anything so far, spoke now and there was something the matter with her voice too. It did not sound edgy, but it sounded very unhappy.

'Mr. Goldenberg came over to the *garçonnière* after he left the Big House, Gervais. He talked to me too. I haven't had a chance to tell you.'

'Well, suppose you wait and tell me a little later on.'

Mummy opened her lips and closed them again without making any sound. *Grand'mère* spoke severely.

'Gervais, I should also like to hear what Mr. Goldenberg said to Merry.'

'All right. I didn't say you couldn't. But I don't think the table—'

'Selah will not come in again, Gervais, until I ring for him. And fortunately all of this is over the children's heads. . . . Vail, stop pushing the food around on your plate that way. Why don't you eat your supper properly?'

Grand'mère was not eating much supper herself, as far as Vail could see, and neither were Daddy and Mummy. He was tempted to say so, but decided it probably would be better not, so he took up his silver mug and tried to sip some milk. That was easier than gulping down rice and beans. Mummy looked from *grand'-mère* to Daddy as if she could not quite decide which one to mind, and then she went on and said what *grand'mère* wanted her to.

'He told me what you thought he'd come to tell you, Gervais. The Governor has threatened the bank, and Mr. Goldenberg can't do anything more as a director because the bank can't afford to lose those State funds. You guessed right about that. But Mr. Goldenberg told me something else too. He said he'd be glad to make you a personal loan. If he did that you could pay off the notes, couldn't you?'

'You mean he'd take over the mortgage himself?'

'That's what he'd have to do, isn't it? I didn't understand exactly how it would work out, but I knew he was trying to be kind and helpful. I knew—'

'And I can tell you what I know. I do understand how it would work out. The Goldenbergs would be the real owners of Belle Heloise instead of the d'Alverys. And if you ask me, that's the way the old Shylock meant to have it work out from the beginning!'

'Gervais, how can you be so unjust? He's distressed, really he is, about the bank. But he says—'

'I don't want to hear any more about what he says. I've heard too much already. And I'll tell you something else myself: if that wily old Levantine ever gets hold of Belle Heloise it'll be over my dead body!'

Daddy flung down his napkin and jumped up from the table. Mummy sat very still, and Vail could see that she was crying. *Grand'mère* sat very still too, but she held herself bolt upright, and there were no tears on her cheeks. She did not say anything until Daddy had stalked out of the room, and then she reached across the table and took Mummy's hand.

'You must not be so distressed, *chère,*' she said. 'And you must not reproach yourself, or let Gervais reproach you, for going to Mr. Goldenberg in the first place. Of course, he is not a person whom I should have expected to meet socially, in the old days. But I agree with you he had no ulterior motive in arranging the loan to begin with, and that his purpose in coming here today was kind.'

'Would you mind as much as Gervais, Madame Mère – having him take over the mortgage?'

'Yes. I should mind very much. I have kept hoping we could regain a clear title to Belle Heloise ourselves, and this arrangement would mean our shifting our obligation from an institution to an individual. Any possibility of alien possession is alarming to me, as you know, and this is not only a matter of family pride. There are the children to think of now. We must safeguard their future.'

Grand'mère glanced around the table, looking at them all in turn. She had apparently not paid them much attention before, but Vail knew she always noticed a good deal, whether she seemed to, or not. Franchot was half asleep already; he had pushed aside his bunny plate and was resting his chubby arms on the table and his tousled brown head on his arms. Joyeuse and Phil had finished too; they were surreptitiously playing cat's cradle behind the cloth. Sybelle was eating, quietly and daintily; her head was turned away from *grand'mère*, but Vail knew that she was listening as carefully as he was, and that later on, if he would give her the chance, she would talk to him about everything they had heard. . . .

'I do think of them,' Mummy was saying. She was not looking around, like *grand'mère*. Her eyes were still on her plate, and her voice still had that unhappy, strangled sound. 'I think of them all the time – at least when I'm not thinking of Gervais. I worry about them all the time too. Gervais thinks I never worry about anything, but that's because he's a man. I worry because there's so much I can't do for either him or the children, no matter how hard I try. Gervais needs a heap of money to pay his debts and keep this plantation running, and they're going to need a heap too for a good home and good education and a good start in the world. I know how important Belle Heloise is to them. The good home isn't any problem as long as we've got this, but it would be if we lost it. And even with it I don't see how on earth we're going to give so many of them all the advantages they ought to have.'

'Hush!' *grand'mère* said warningly. But it was too late. Vail had been so concerned, since he came in to supper, about Daddy and Mummy that he had forgotten all about himself for a few minutes. Now he remembered his own troubles again, and these began looming up before him, larger than ever. When *grand'mère* finally gave the signal to leave the table, and Sybelle asked eagerly what about playing jackstraws, he said, go ahead and play with Phil if she wanted to; he was going out and he did not want her tagging along either. But instead of going out he went up to his room and sat for a long time fingering the piggy bank that stood on his dresser, between the picture of Aunt Cresside, riding an elephant in Ceylon, and the battered brush and comb which he always neglected to use unless someone came along and made him.

For some time now Vail had been given an allowance of a dollar a week, and he had been taught, out of this sum, to save money for contributions in church, deposits in the piggy bank, and presents for the family and the servants; he had also been allowed to spend money from it on movies and candies and marbles and similar items. He had always been very proud of this allowance, and had managed it fairly well, keeping accounts in a little ruled book which Miss Mittie recognized as part of his equipment for satisfactory progress in arithmetic. Aside from planning how to use his allowance, he had never thought much about money. But he remembered that several times, no matter how carefully he planned, he had not had enough to get or do the things he wanted, and if Daddy advanced him small sums on such occasions it was always harder to balance his little ruled book afterwards, and in the end he had to go without more than in the beginning. So he understood that something like this was worrying Daddy and Mummy now. Daddy was troubled because he had spent more money than there really was on things he wanted, which evidently worked out badly for everyone, and Mummy was troubled because there would not be enough money to give so many children all the things they were going to want. She would not have needed so much if there had not been so many children. She had said so before *grand'mère* had hushed her up, and Vail could see for himself how that would work out. It must take a lot of money for five children, more than twice as much than if there had been only two children. And even if there were four instead of five, that would help some. It did not seem fair to him that Daddy and Mummy should have to keep on spending money on a boy who was not theirs after all, when they had two boys of their own, and two girls as well.

He kept thinking about this before he went to sleep that night, and afterwards he dreamed about it in a confused way. The next morning when he woke up he was not sure, at first, just how much he had heard at the supper table and how much he had dreamed, but he talked things over, very cautiously, with Sybelle, making her happy by seeking her out, of his own accord, for the first time in several days, and afterwards some things were clear to him, because Sybelle, who had listened to every word, just as he supposed, knew exactly what had been said at the table. But there were still other things which were not clear to him, and he kept on thinking about those. He could not see yet why he had always lived at Belle Heloise if Mr. Tremaine was his father; he could not understand why Aunt Cresside would not talk about Mr. Tremaine if he had been her beau, and why Daddy wanted to kill Amen for doing so; he could not guess who his mother had been. . . .

Sybelle had seemed so pleased because he had gone out of his way to find her, and had been so helpful about untangling dreams from things which had really happened, that finally he decided to seek her out a second time and see if she could help with these other problems too. He found her sitting under the mimosa tree in Angus Holt's garden, all dressed up clean for the evening in a white dress and white socks, the big bow on top of her golden head bobbing a little as she bent over a book in which she was apparently much absorbed. Vail thought he had never seen her look so nice, and it came over him that, though he had treated her badly these last few days, he loved her better than anyone else in the world except his Aunt Cresside. The realization that she was not his twin after all, or even his sister, smote him afresh.

'Hello there,' he said carelessly. 'Gee, you read lots, don't you? I wish I could read that much. I've got so many other things to do, I can't.'

'It's too bad,' Sybelle said understandingly. She did not dispute the greater demands which a boy would naturally have upon his time, but yielded the point with feminine tact and feminine graciousness. 'I wish you could read this, anyway,' she went on, eager to share her pleasure with him. 'It's grand. It isn't one of our own books that we got Christmas. It's a book I found in the library.'

She spoke somewhat smugly. The children were not supposed

to take books from the library without permission, and, as a matter of fact, not many books were casually left around there; most of them were kept in locked secretaries. Evidently Sybelle had 'put something over', on their elders, and felt pleased about it rather than guilty.

'What's the book about?' Vail inquired, without going into the ethics of the situation. He really did not care much, but he wanted to make up to Sybelle for treating her so badly, and he could see that she wanted to talk about the book.

'A foundling,' Sybelle said, still smugly. 'I adore stories about foundlings, don't you?'

'I don't know. What do you mean, foundlings?'

'Well, sometimes they're princes in disguise, of course. I like those best of all. But this one isn't. It's just about a poor little baby whose own father and mother didn't want it.'

'Why not?' Vail inquired, pricking up his ears. He had not dared to hope this would be so easy.

'Well, his father was a very wicked man who did something queer to his sweetheart.'

'What do you mean, something queer?'

'I don't just understand. But she was terribly ashamed of it anyway. And afterwards she had a baby and she didn't want anyone to know.'

There was a slight pause. Then Sybelle whispered a hesitant question.

'Vail, do you know how babies come?'

'Yes,' Vail answered abruptly, flushing as he did so and thinking about Maud.

'I wish you'd tell me.'

'Well, I won't.'

'All right, then, don't. But, anyway, I think what happened in this book – the queer thing, I mean – had something to do with the baby coming. Does something queer happen, Vail? You might tell me that much.'

'It isn't queer exactly. But—'

'Well, but Mummy and Daddy weren't ashamed of having babies, Vail. They were pleased. And Uncle Fabian and Aunt Cresside were pleased about Frances Belle. Terribly pleased. I think you're a meanie not to explain. And I think from something this book said that, whatever happens, it's all right if you're married, but if you're not . . . Listen, Vail.' Sybelle picked up the book and began to spell out loud. 'Do you know what i-l-l-e-g-i-t-i-m-a-t-e means? That's what this baby was. He wasn't just a foundling, he was an i-l-l-e-g-i-t-i-m-a-t-e child. In lots of places they call him a bastard too, and it seems to mean the same thing. I've heard the men on the place talk about bastards, especially black ones, haven't you, Vail? But I don't believe they meant the same thing that this book does. I never heard them say that a black bastard was an i-l-l-e— What's the matter, Vail?'

'Nothing. I've got lots to do, that's all. I can't stand here all day talking about some fool book you've read and waiting for you to spell out long words.'

'But, Vail, I thought you wanted to hear. I thought you said you wished you had more time to read yourself. I thought— Vail, please come back!'

Vail had wheeled suddenly away from her and was running through the garden towards the wicket gate that led to the Yankee cemetery. Sybelle threw down her book and ran after him, but the grass had not been cut that spring and it was tall and thick. She stumbled on some stones which were hidden by it and fell down, tearing her pretty white dress and barking her dimpled knees. When she got to her feet again, whimpering a little with pain, Vail had already crossed the cypress grove. Sybelle saw him plunging into the bushes beyond it, and after that she lost sight of him.

So she never knew that he had flung himself down on the grave shielded by the strange hybrid tree where flowering thorn and bitter fruit grew together, and that he was crying as if his heart would break.

CHAPTER TEN

WITHIN a few hours of its appearance, reports of the outrageous scene at the Citizens National Bank were spreading like wildfire through the capital and the State. Hardly a man came into Fabian d'Alvery's once that afternoon who talked about anything else. This was by no means the first evidence of the Governor's high-handed methods in punishing people who got in his way and rewarding his faithful followers; but it affected more men in each group, and it hit harder and closer than anything that had happened in Baton Rouge before. The city seethed with resentment, rage, fear and excitement.

When Fabian started home he was still undecided whether to mention the occurrence to Cresside immediately or to wait until she spoke of it to him of her own accord. It would not take her long to realize that her brother would be affected by the disgraceful contretemps; she had known about the loan from the beginning, and Gervais had never made the slightest secret of his enmity for Long. Fabian, who always liked to think things through before speaking of them to anyone, and who seldom acted with haste, finally decided to sleep on the matter, at least; if Cresside had said nothing by the time he left for the office next day he would broach the subject. Momentarily he had forgotten that they were to entertain out-of-town guests that evening, some agreeable people named Townsend whom they had met in the course of their travels, and who were now breaking a transcontinental trip in New Orleans. The Townsends had written ahead suggesting that they should come up to Baton Rouge on purpose to see the d'Alverys, and the response had taken the form of a cordial invitation. When he remembered this, Fabian realized that their friends would probably have arrived before he reached the house himself, and that the conversation would almost automatically be slanted towards past pleasures which they had all enjoyed together, and not towards some local fracas of which the less said the better to outsiders who might still be unaware of Lousiana's political disgrace.

His assumption proved correct. He found Cresside seated at ease on the garden terrace with the four Townsends grouped around her, listening lazily while her enthusiastic visitors recalled the details of a day they had all spent together in Cintra, and saying excitedly that none of the gardens they had seen there surpassed the d'Alverys' in charm. It was true that this had become increasingly beautiful with the years. Shortly before his marriage Fabian had bought two lots which adjoined his own, torn down the ramshackle little houses which had long been an eyesore to him, and surrounded the entire area with a high brick wall. Previously his shrubs and flowers had been planted in a haphazard manner, even his cherished camellias being stuck in here and there every which way. He had enjoyed working in his garden, and it had reflected fostering care, but it had been without orderly design. When he called in a landscape gardener to help him make it worthy of his bride's reception, the combination of this expert's knowledge with his own money and eagerness had worked wonders. Soon flagstone walks were bordered with bright-coloured flowers, shrubs were clumped for effectiveness, a lawn formed a wide, unbroken expanse of emerald green. At one end there was a lily pool, at the other a fountain rising above the statue of a smiling child, and in the centre a sundial recording the radiant hours. The enclosure became one of infinite harmony and peace.

Fabian had been amply rewarded by Cresside's appreciation of his efforts and his thoughtfulness. She quickly came to share his delight in his garden and to pass a great deal of time there; it was her preferred place for resting and reading, for playing with Frances Belle and Belizaire, for spending long quiet periods with her husband after his day's work was over. It was also her chosen centre for entertaining. When the camellias were at the height of their bloom, she gave small garden parties almost every week. Wearing an exquisite pastel-coloured dress and carrying a large shallow basket over her arm and a pair of long shears in her hand, she would lead her guests proudly from one beauty spot to another, and as they progressed she would clip the choicest blossoms that they passed and lay these tenderly in her basket. Later on, after coffee and drinks on the terrace, each of the guests was given a little flower-covered tray to take home, the different varieties carefully divided to produce the most charming effect – Alba plenas on one tray, Magnolia floras on another, pink perfections and purple dawns on others still. Fabian nearly always joined Cresside on these occasions, making the round of the garden with her and calling her attention to the perfect blooms that she had missed. He experienced a deep satisfaction from having her entertain in this way, so adequately and graciously, yet with such tranquillity and simplicity. He told her so, and, touched by his feeling about it and his way of expressing this, she created more and more occasions for hospitality of this type. Everyone in Baton Rouge considered it a compliment to be asked to one of Mrs. Fabian d'Alvery's garden parties, and invitations for house guests were eagerly sought and highly prized.

The camellias had been gone for months now, of course; their falling petals had made small circular carpets on the grass beneath the laden trees, some snowy, some rosy, some flaming. Cresside loved them better when they lay like that than at any other time, she said, though they were past the point of picking then, and there was an interval between parties before the azaleas were at their height; after those came successively the daffodils and iris, the roses and gardenias. In the interval she and Fabian kept the garden to themselves and their child and their dog, cherishing it more and more all the time. Later in the season, like this, only a few roses remained, and only the gladioli and zinnias were at their best; neither Fabian nor Cresside cared as much for these as they did for the earlier flowers. But the guests from the north had never seen such gladioli and such zinnias in the course of all their travels, and kept saying so. Besides, the grass was still like green velvet, and the pool was covered with lilies floating among their pads and the fountain trickled softly through the evening quietude. All these aspects of the garden enhanced its loveliness and deepened the peace with which it was permeated. Fabian could not bring himself to speak of crassness and calamity in such an atmosphere.

After they reached the dinner table he decided that this was not the time nor the place either. Carmelite had always been a superlative cook, but it had taken Cresside's guiding hand to supply a setting worthy of her masterpieces, and Cresside's piquant presence to add the final touch of charm to a feast. The lace-covered table was set with shining silver, fragile glass and precious porcelain; it was lighted with tall tapers and decorated with exquisite flowers; and as Fabian glanced across it at his wife he thought that she herself had never looked lovelier than she did that night. Without being beautiful, in the sense that Merry was beautiful, she created a greater effect of beauty. Fabian knew that this effect was only an illusion, but he also knew that it was the reflection of an inner radiance which was real. By encompassing Cresside with tenderness and devotion he had done far more than give her present happiness. He had made her feel that her security was impregnable; he had effaced the very memory of past pain and danger. The restless and riotous years, like the years of shame and suffering, were all behind her now. Her life was one of walled gardens and candle-lighted rooms, of quiet, well-ordered days and nights beautified by close communion with a man who loved her and whom she loved. . . .

The dinner progressed smoothly and delightfully, from the perfect soup with which it began to the perfect pudding with which it ended. The Townsends continued to recall the pleasant excursions which the d'Alverys had shared with them, and to express the hope that they might have similar experiences in the future. Why not? Fabian said, looking across the table again and seeing that the suggestion was pleasing to Cresside; they had not liked to leave their little girl for any length of time, so since her birth they had not travelled much. But presently she would be old enough to travel herself – oh, not around the world, perhaps, but certainly as far as Europe. He had been intending to look up those castles in Spain where the early de Alverez had lived before they crossed over into Southern France and became d'Alverys instead. Spain was a very pleasant place; for the matter of that, Southern France was a very pleasant place too. They could probably find a suitable villa in Pau where Frances Belle could be installed with a competent and trustworthy governess, and which he and Cresside could use as a centre for their side trips? He had always wanted to spend at least a week in Carcasonne, and to go from there to Nîmes and Arles and Avignon. Was that the sort of excursion the Townsends would enjoy too?

Exactly, they told him with enthusiasm; and after dinner was over and Frances Belle had come in to make her curtsy and say good night Fabian set up a tilt-top table and spread motor maps of Europe on it. When these were finally folded up and put away, everyone was astonished to find how late it was. A tray laden with soda siphons and excellent liquor was brought in and put down where the maps had been, and Cresside mixed the drinks which Fabian passed. But the Townsends did not linger over these. It had been a wonderful evening, they said, but if they did not go then they never would. Well, they'd keep in touch with the d'Alverys about the French trip – next summer ought to be the very time. Good night, good night. . . .

Carmelite and the house boy who had been added to the small but efficient domestic staff had already left for the night. Cresside and Fabian took the drinks and the ashtrays out to the neat, quiet kitchen themselves, gave the living-room the final touches which would leave it orderly for the morning, looked in on Frances Belle to see that she was sleeping quietly, made the rounds of the outside doors to make sure that these were locked.

But as they reached the one leading into the garden Cresside opened it again.

'Let's go out for a moment more, shall we? It's such a lovely night!'

They stepped out on the little terrace. The starlight was very soft and the tapering forms of the trees were reflected in dark shadows across the smooth lawn. Not only the fragrance of flowers, but all the subtle scents of summer were in the air. Cresside slid her hand into her husband's.

'You know what I've been thinking all evening, Fabian?'

'Sure. I'm the world's champion mind-reader.' He laughed and leaned over to kiss her hair. 'Don't encourage me to talk nonsense by doing it yourself. You know crystal-gazing isn't in my line. Tell me straight out.'

'I've been thinking that no one has the right to be as happy as I am.'

'Why not?'

'I don't know. Perhaps because there's so much misery in the world.'

'We all get our share of it some time,' Fabian said. Then, because he did not want any words of his to remind her about the share she had had, he added hastily: 'Don't forget that if you're all that happy you make me mighty happy too.'

'Do I really?'

'You know it, don't you?'

'I hope so. . . . Yes, I do know it.'

'And you really are all that happy?'

'Yes, really. You know that too, Fabian.'

'Because I built this garden for you and buy you Venetian glass and sapphire bracelets and plan trips for you?'

'Don't joke about it. You know those aren't the reasons.'

'I don't know anyone who can afford to joke about it any better than we can, do you, Cresside?'

'No. You're right. We can joke because we're so safe.'

For a long time after she had gone to sleep he lay thinking of what she had said, but no anxiety permeated his thoughts. He knew that he had made her happy, he knew that he had given her security. But still he was not satisfied. He wanted to make her happier still, he wanted to safeguard her still further. The instinct to please her and protect her had always been as strong within him as the instinct to possess her, and now it had become a driving force. For in his possession of her he himself had found not only great joy but complete fulfilment. By accepting his love and bearing his child she had vindicated his starved manhood. He could never sufficiently requite her.

She stirred slightly in her sleep, stretched out her arms and found his waiting to receive her. She seldom spoke at such moments; words were superfluous in the harmony that prevailed between them. But this time she began to murmur drowsily, her lips already against his.

'Fabian, I want to say something to you.'

'You can say anything you want to, darling. You know that.'

'No. This is hard.'

'Well, if it's hard—'

'But I want to. We've been mighty happy, Fabian, like we said this evening, but we could have been happier still.'

'I couldn't.'

'Yes, you could, and so could I. If I hadn't always put Vail first.'

Fabian did not answer. Cresside caught her breath, but the sigh did not end in a sob, as he was afraid it might. It ended in swift, tense speech.

'Even the night we were married I was thinking about him. I was worrying for fear he wasn't all right, that he wouldn't be unless I was at Belle Heloise to take care of him. Every time I thought of his asking for me and not finding me it nearly broke my heart. I missed him so it seemed as if I couldn't stand it. No matter where we went or what we did, I kept yearning for him. And you knew it. You can't deny it.'

'I shan't try to deny it, darling. But I never held that against you. I expected it. I knew it was bound to happen.'

'Perhaps you thought I'd feel like that for a little while. But I don't believe you thought it would last. I think you hoped that after a little while you'd come first. Didn't you?'

'Perhaps. Yes, I suppose I did. But I've never held that against you either, Cresside - that you couldn't put me before Vail. You've given me so much—'

'If I'd put you first, if you'd known you were first, you'd have let me have another child.'

'No, I wouldn't have, Cresside. I've told you, and I meant it, that I'd never let you suffer like that again. It isn't as if you

154

could have children the way Merry has them – a few hours of discomfort, a few minutes of pain, and then everything all over. I can't stand that long-drawn-out agony of months. I've reproached myself for letting you have Frances Belle – I knew what you'd been through with Vail. But I wanted a child of my own, and so I was selfish enough to let you give it to me. But I'm not selfish enough to let you do it again.'

'You wanted a *son* of your own. You haven't got him yet.'

'I'll never get him. I couldn't love any son more than I do Frances Belle.'

'How can you tell unless you have one?'

'We've been all over this before. Do we have to argue about it again, Cresside?'

'No. I don't want to argue with you about anything. I didn't start out to do that – I don't ever mean to. I only started out to tell you that you do come first now. You have for a long time. I wasn't sure you knew it. Did you?'

'No. I'd begun to hope so. But I wasn't sure.'

'I want you to be sure. I'm telling you so you will be. And there's something else I want to tell you, Fabian: I know now that you were right about Vail all the time, that he's better off where he is, without me. I've never owned up before that I'd changed my mind about that. And I've changed my mind about being too happy. I'm going to revel in my happiness from now on, because you say it makes you happy too. I want to do everything in the world I can for you, Fabian.'

Daylight was already filtering into the room when she fell asleep again. But Fabian did not go to sleep. He lay looking at her, his heart welling up with fresh tenderness and new determination.

'I'll keep her happy,' he vowed to himself. 'I'll keep her safe. If anyone ever tries to hurt her again I'll kill him, so help me God.'

CHAPTER ELEVEN

ONE of Cresside's hard-and-fast rules was about telephoning
Fabian at his office. The poor man had no time to himself, she
sometimes said gaily; his working hours belonged to his clients
and his leisure hours to her; but at least neither intruded on the
other. She made such a point of this non-intervention that any
departure from it was disquieting to Fabian; if his secretary told
him that Mrs. d'Alvery was on the wire, he leapt to the conclusion that Frances Belle had gone down with diphtheria or
that Carmelite had inadvertently set fire to the house. When he
picked up the receiver, the day after the Townsends' visit, in
response to his secretary's summons, it was with the knowledge
that something equally calamitous had happened.

'Is anyone in the private office right now, Fabian?'

'No. You can say whatever you want to and I'll try to answer.'

'I've just come from Belle Heloise. Gervais'd already gone to
town, because he's bound not to miss a moment in the Senate
Chamber, with this filibuster going on, come hell or high water.
But I gather he's pretty well shot to pieces. *Maman* and Merry
certainly are, anyway.'

'What's the matter?'

'All Gervais' notes have been called. Didn't you know? Merry
seemed to think you might.'

'I was afraid they would be, when I heard about the rumpus
at the bank yesterday. I meant to speak to you about it. But
there didn't seem to be a good chance yesterday evening – or
last night. And you were so sound asleep when I left this morning that I didn't want to disturb you.'

There was a brief silence. Fabian knew that momentarily Cresside's troubled mind had reverted to the pleasant evening with
their friends and to their own intimate hours of rich and rewarding communion. His thoughts had constantly wandered in
the same direction all the morning, and he had made no effort to
control them. He was glad to feel that Cresside was also dwelling
on their mutual happiness.

'I hadn't heard anything about the rumpus at the bank from anyone else,' she finally continued. 'The Townsends came early, and before that I was busy getting things ready. You know how it is.'

Fabian did know. He realized that the smoothness with which his pleasant household ran was due in no small measure to Cresside's skill and patient management, and that the degree of perfection, it had reached was by no means accidental. Cresside went out very little, and, though she was hospitable, she preferred to invite her guests at stated times, for definite occasions like her pleasant garden parties, than to have them dropping in at any and every hour of the day. In like measure, she did not call up her friends unless there was some special reason for it, and she discouraged idle chatter over the telephone on their part. 'Merry says Mr. Goldenberg went out to Belle Heloise yesterday afternoon and offered to take over the mortgage,' Cresside went on. 'She thought it was mighty decent of him, and I do too. But Gervais doesn't look at it that way, and *maman*'s taking it pretty hard too, though she's nicer about it than Gervais. She would be, of course.'

'Yes, of course. . . . You'd like me to see Gervais straight off, I suppose?'

'I'd like you to send some kind of message to him straight off, if you don't mind. And then go on out to Belle Heloise as soon as you can leave the office and stay until he gets home. Meanwhile you can talk to *maman* and Merry. At least, I'm taking it for granted you can. I'm taking it for granted there's something helpful you can say to them.'

'You bet there is. Don't worry about it, Cresside. Anything else?'

'Yes. There's something the matter with Vail too, Fabian. He hardly spoke to me and he got away from me as soon as he could. Merry says he's been acting up for about ten days now. But he seemed all right to me when I've seen him before.'

It was Fabian's turn to pause for a moment. So Vail's found out, he said to himself. Well, I always knew he was bound to, sooner or later, but I hoped it wouldn't be this soon. If only Cresside hasn't guessed that's what's the matter . . . and if only a lot of other people haven't found out too. . . . Aloud he said quietly: 'I wouldn't worry about that either. All kids have their off times, you know. I'll have a talk with him and find out what the trouble is. I reckon I can fix it up all right. I've got to meet a client at the Heidelberg for lunch, but I'll go out to Belle Heloise straight from the office, like you suggest. Don't wait supper for me.'

'I'll have a bite with Frances Belle when she has hers. Then I'll have another with you when you get home – in the garden.'

'Right. So long, honey. ... By the way, you're still happy, aren't you?'

'Yes, now that I've talked to you. That was all I wanted. I know everything's going to be all right now.'

Fabian hung up the receiver and reached for a pad of scratch paper. For a moment he sat drawing small geometrical designs on it. But only for a moment. Then he tore off the ornamented top sheet and wrote five words on the next one, which he slipped into an envelope addressed to Gervais.

'How much do you need?'

His departure for Belle Heloise was unavoidably delayed. It was late afternoon when he reached there, and the Big House was preternaturally quiet. Evidently Selah had gone out to the servants' quarters, for no one met Fabian at the door, and he wandered through the downstairs rooms without finding anyone. Then he went outdoors again and stood beside the wing where Madame d'Alvery's boudoir was located.

'Are you there, Tante Isabelle?' he called. 'May I come up?'

'If you please, Fabian. I was half expecting you.'

He found her, not enthroned, as usual, on her sofa, but sitting in a large Turkish chair by the window, looking down on Angus Holt's garden. She turned as he came in, and, though her dark eyes met his with their usual dauntlessness, he could see that her natural pallor had a grey tinge. He put his arm around her and kissed her.

'Why put in the half? You ought to have been wholly expecting me, after what you told Cresside this morning. You ought to have known I'd get here as soon as I could.'

'I hoped you would, Fabian. I sent Lucie away so that we could talk privately if you did. But I have ceased to expect very much of anyone.'

'Nonsense, Tante Isabelle. You know I'm bound to be around. Don't talk like a tragedy queen making her last great speech upstage before she kills herself. Talk to me like an affectionate mother-in-law. What were you looking at so hard when I came in?'

'The green rose. You know about the green rose, Fabian?'

'Yes, of course. But why were you staring at it so?'

'I was thinking, Fabian, that I should hate to have it tended with alien hands. It is so uniquely our own. I have never given even a slip of it away.'

Her own hands trembled a little as she spoke, though her voice was still firm. The so-called 'green' rose was one of such extreme delicacy that its translucent white petals reflected the verdure of its foliage and actually seemed tinged with this colour themselves. The parent plant had come from a Sevillian courtyard, and the same bride who had brought the Spanish statue to the house had planted this rose herself at Belle Heloise long before the advent of Angus Holt. In planning his garden, however, he had given it a place of honour, and the rose had always retained this. Madame d'Alvery was right in calling it unique; there was not another like it in any garden on either side of the River Road. It dominated the sago palms and palmettos, the false indigo and monkey grass, like a princess; even the camellias and Creole lilies looked stiff and common beside it, and the other roses lost their importance. Fabian knew that to Madame d'Alvery it was the symbol both of family tenacity and of family superiority. He did not minimize all that it meant to her.

'Well, I hope you never will,' he said, speaking more lightly than he felt. 'I sure don't see any reason why you should – unless, of course, you feel like giving slips of it to your granddaughters some day, so they can plant it in gardens of their own and carry on the tradition. I know I'd admire to have one in the Somerulos Street garden, as they say up north, but I understand how you feel about it. . . . Look, I sent Gervais a message this morning, and asked him how much he needed to get clear. Everything's fixed up, or going to be. If you're sitting here worrying for fear some lady friend of Long's is going to start cutting your green roses, or even that Mrs. Goldenberg's going to, you can stop right now. Incidentally, though, Mrs. Goldenberg's a mighty nice old lady, almost as nice as you are.'

'Do you mean to tell me that you have assumed the mortgage, Fabian?'

'Hell, no! I just paid off the notes, that's all. Gervais and I can straighten out the details later.'

Madame d'Alvery's hands were still trembling. Fabian drew up a chair beside her and took them in his own.

'Listen, Tante Isabelle,' he said, 'don't you start getting any false ideas about this. I didn't mind letting Gervais flounder along alone just so he didn't hurt anyone but himself while he was doing it. I'm afraid I didn't even mind so much as I should when he hurt Merry in the process. I figured she'd married him with her eyes open, for richer, for poorer, for better, for worse, and that she ought to be able to take what was coming to her. She has too. I hand it to her. She's taken it darn well; she's a good soldier. . . . I didn't mind so much whether he hurt you either. You were pretty hard on poor Uncle Philogene, and I figured it might be good for you to have a taste of your own medicine. Well, you are hard, but you're a good soldier too. I hand it to you as well as Merry. All of which is neither here nor there. The person I don't want to have hurt and don't intend to have hurt is Cresside. And it would hurt her like hell if she thought Vail wasn't going to stay on this place.'

Madame d'Alvery's hands had gradually ceased to tremble, but she did not try to speak. She continued to look at Fabian in silence, her gaze not only unflinching but intent.

'I haven't a son of my own,' Fabian went on. 'I don't expect to have one. So I've got to give Cresside's the place mine would have had.' Fabian had never before spoken of Vail to his mother-in-law as Cresside's son, but now he did so in a matter-of-fact way, as if the reference were one which was natural between them. 'That isn't too hard for me either,' he went on. 'Vail's a great kid – any man could be proud to have him for a son, or in place of a son. I'm going to see that he gets everything that's coming to him – at Belle Heloise and elsewhere. And incidentally I don't intend to let Gervais forget that for all practical purposes his white-headed boy, Phil, isn't the "heir to all the d'Alverys", as Cresside had the guts to call Vail, the very first time she showed him off. Gosh, if I hadn't been in love with her before then, I sure would have after that. And what she says stands. Where is the little tyke, by the way? I want to have a talk with him this evening too.'

'I have not seen him since dinner-time, Fabian. And he hardly spoke to anyone then. If you can get him to talk with you, it will be more than any one of us has been able to do, for a fortnight now.'

'And it hasn't occurred to any of you to wonder why?'

'Merry has worried about him. But she has been even more worried about Gervais. Surely, Fabian, you do not think – after all these years – after all our care—'

For the first time, fear leapt into her brave eyes. Instinctively, she tried to rise. Fabian put a detaining hand on her shoulder.

'Better let me try to find out first, Tante Isabelle,' he said gently. 'If he does know – and I'll bet my bottom dollar he does – then somebody else does too, besides the original conspirators. I'm also willing to bet that none of them gave the secret away. And whoever that somebody else is, I can probably deal with him better than you can, if you don't mind my saying so. But first I'm going to find Vail. Sit down again and go on looking at your garden rose in peace. No one else has got a prayer of picking it.'

Fabian waved to his mother-in-law from the doorway, with his old gay gesture, and went on through her bedroom to the upper hall, calling Vail as he did so. The chamber in front of Madame d'Alvery's, which had once been Cresside's, was now restored to its original state as a guest chamber; Henry Clay had always slept there when he visited Belle Heloise, Zachary Taylor, Judah P. Benjamin, and the host of other dead and gone celebrities. Now it had the *soigné* air of being kept in readiness for their worthy successors. The room across the hall from it, which had been Merry's bridal chamber, had been assigned to Sybelle, when it was judiciously decided that she and Vail were too big for joint occupancy of their original nursery directly behind it; but Vail had continued to sleep there. Receiving no response to his call, Fabian pushed open the shutter door and went in.

Some indefinable quality of the room's emptiness roused his suspicions. It was abnormally neat, for one thing. Like most small boys, Vail habitually scattered his possessions about and neglected to pick them up again. Now the room was completely uncluttered. Even the bureau was bare. Cresside's picture was gone from its place.

Fabian went back into the hall, closing the shutter door behind him, and walked thoughtfully down the stairs. He could hear Selah moving about in the dining-room, setting the table for supper, and enticing odours were stealing subtly from Lou Ida's kitchen. Fabian had originally intended to go to see Merry as well as Madame d'Alvery, but now he decided against it. He felt reasonably certain that all the children, except Vail, were with her in the *garçonnière*, as he knew that she conscientiously tried to read aloud to them for an hour every evening. He did not want to talk to her about the notes unless he could see her alone, and he did not want to risk rousing suspicions which were possibly still non-existent by asking questions about Vail. He decided to follow his hunch, and strike off down the River Road.

He had not gone more than two or three miles before he caught sight of the little figure for which he was watching. Vail was trudging along the road, carrying a small suitcase, which he kept shifting from hand to hand, as if it had already begun to seem very heavy. Maud was following at his heels, not leaping about him and snapping for bugs or nosing excitedly in the grass as she usually did, but dragging her feet reluctantly. Every now and then she stopped entirely, cringing and curling herself into a dejected crescent. When she did this Vail stopped too, setting down the suitcase and leaning over his dog to encourage her in a voice of false heartiness. Fabian watched him for a few moments without trying to catch up with him; then he quickened his pace, and, putting on his brakes, leaned out of the window and spoke casually and carelessly.

'Hello there, Vail! Looks like we're going in the same direction. Want a lift?'

Vail did not answer immediately, and Fabian did not try to hurry him. He waited as if it were quite natural for the boy to take his time.

'No, I reckon not,' Vail said at last. 'Me and Maud were just out for a walk.'

'I'd be glad of your company a piece down the road. I've got a long ride ahead of me, and I'll have to take most of it alone. You could have your walk with Maud, going back.'

Again Vail considered his answer at length. 'All right,' he said finally. 'If it would keep you from being lonesome . . .' Without explaining his small suitcase, he lifted it into the car, involuntarily sighing with relief as he did so. Then he signalled to Maud, who jumped up with her first sign of joy, and climbed in himself. Afterwards he sat staring straight ahead of him with the suitcase at his side and Maud in his lap.

'It's a nice evening to be out on the road,' Fabian remarked, after a considerable interval. 'Let me know if I'm taking you too far, though. You'll have quite a walk back.'

'You don't need to worry about that, Uncle Fabian.'

'I wasn't worrying. I was just calling your attention to it. I know it's hard sometimes to keep track of distances.'

'Yes. But maybe I ought to tell you, Uncle Fabian. I didn't mean to go back to Belle Heloise tonight.'

'I see. Well, I thought you might be spending the night with friends when I saw your suitcase. But afterwards, when you said you were just out for a walk with Maud—'

'That wasn't exactly true, Uncle Fabian. I took Maud with me because I figured she was mine and I had a right to her. Of course, Nostar's mine too, but I didn't know just how I'd take care of a pony. Now a dog like Maud doesn't take up any room. She sleeps with you.'

'That's right,' said Fabian encouragingly.

'And she eats the scraps off your plate.'

'Yes; but of course when she's going to have puppies she needs more than scraps and she oughtn't to get too tired, walking, either. It doesn't seem as if we could miss again. The new family's due in a few weeks, isn't it?'

'Ye-es,' Vail said doubtfully. He had temporarily forgotten the prospect of the new family and the possibility of the little black puppy for which Fabian had watched and waited so long. Obviously the reminder was not especially welcome.

'I won't let her walk too far at a time,' he said rather hurriedly. 'And I'll give her lots of scraps. Just the same, a dog isn't so much trouble as a pony. A pony's got to have a stall. And it's got to have oats.'

'That's right,' Fabian said again, without pressing the subject of the puppies.

'And I didn't know just where I was going to find the stall and the oats. I'm not going to spend the night with friends – at least, not that I know of. But I thought there'd be some place—'

'Yes, of course anyone along the Road would be glad to put you up. Except now that Hackberry's closed there aren't any houses very near. And naturally the folks would like to know where you were. They might worry if they didn't, don't you think? Not that you can't take care of yourself all right. They know that. It's just the way fathers and mothers have to worry, that's all.'

'Yes, but—'

The stubborn little mouth had begun to quiver. He waited till he stopped choking. Then he went doggedly on.

'But Daddy and Mummy aren't really my father and mother. Did you know that, Uncle Fabian?'

'Yes, Vail, I knew that. I've known it a long while. I knew you'd find it out some time too.'

'Well, so I don't think Daddy and Mummy would worry the same, do you, as if they were really my father and mother?'

'Yes, I think they would, I think they might even worry more. Because they're responsible for you to your real mother. They promised her they'd take good care of you, if she'd trust you to them and let you live with them. They persuaded her that she ought to – that is, they helped me to persuade her. I felt just the same way about it, you see. And if you went away, no telling where, they'd be afraid she'd think they hadn't taken good care of you or that they hadn't made you happy.'

Vail did not answer.

'She would too, you know,' Fabian went on. 'She trusted you to them because she thought it was best for you to live at Belle Heloise and best that everyone should think that they were really your father and mother. She'd be terribly upset if she found out you'd run away. She'd believe she'd made a mistake, after all.'

Vail still did not answer.

'It's this way, Vail: a long time ago someone made your mother very unhappy. So ever since then all the rest of us have tried to see that she wouldn't ever be unhappy again. We didn't think it was fair that she should be. I still don't think it's fair that she should be. And if she got upset about you – well, that would make her unhappier than anything else in the world, because she loves you more than anyone else in the world.'

Vail swallowed hard. 'I didn't know that,' he muttered. 'I thought maybe—' He stopped, partly because it was so hard to go on and partly because he did not know how to go on. Fabian finished his sentence for him.

'You thought maybe no one would care if you ran away?' he said. 'Why, you couldn't have, not if you'd really figured this thing out. I don't believe you even tried. If you had, you'd have known that everyone would have cared. For instance, poor little Sybelle's probably crying her eyes out this minute, wondering where you are. I'll tell you why I think you ran away. I think something happened at Belle Heloise that made you feel badly and you thought maybe you'd feel better somewhere else. Didn't

164

you? You were thinking mostly how you felt yourself, not how anyone else felt. Weren't you?'

'Gee, Uncle Fabian—'

'I said *mostly*. I know you thought there'd be a difference between real fathers and mothers and make-believe fathers and mothers, the way they'd worry, but just the same—'

'I reckon you're right, Uncle Fabian. I reckon I did think mostly if I could just get away—'

'We all think that once in a while, Vail. But we're always wrong about it when we do. The only way to make a hard thing any easier is to lick it. Not to run away from it. Once you've licked it, then it never seems so hard. The way for you to lick this feeling you've got is to go back to Belle Heloise and stay there. And if you want to do a really thorough job, you'll never let on what you found out, because it wouldn't do you any good and it would make everyone else feel worse. . . . How did you find out, by the way?'

'Well, Sammy Mudge came to see Amen. They were hiding in the bushes by the stable, whispering, when I went to saddle Nostar.'

'I see. So then—'

'So then they tried to make me stop, but I wouldn't. I went and told Daddy Sammy Mudge was there. And he was awful mad. He sent Sammy Mudge away, and then he gave Amen an awful bawling out for tattling on his own white folks. I heard because I'd gone back to the stable to finish saddling Nostar and Twinkle. I didn't listen on purpose. Sybelle and I were going for a ride.'

'Sure you didn't listen on purpose? And what happened next?'

'Next Daddy went back to the *garçonnière* to tell Mummy about it. He shouted at her, the way he does when he's mad. She tried to make him hush because she was afraid someone would hear him. I did hear him. Franchot had asked me to build blocks with him, and when Sybelle didn't come to the stable to go riding—'

'Yes?' Fabian said encouragingly.

'I went back to the *garçonnière* too. At least I started. And Daddy said Amen must know everything. He said Amen must know Mr. Tremaine was my father!'

It was no use. He could not help choking now, no matter how

hard he tried. He blurted out his final words between sobs, and then he tried to wipe his eyes and nose on his sleeve, before leaning over and burying his face on Maud's faithful little body.

'I hated him, Uncle Fabian,' he said in a smothered voice. 'I hated him worse than anyone I ever knew, except Sammy Mudge. The way Daddy hates snakes.'

Fabian brought the car quietly to a stop. 'Look here,' he said. 'There's no use getting farther and farther from Belle Heloise when we've got to get back there – the sooner the better too. But I want you to come up on the levee with me for a few minutes first. I think it'll be easier to have a good talk there than it is here, don't you? And I want to have a talk with you, Vail. I want to set you straight about two or three things before we start back.'

Without protest, Vail clambered out of the car. As he stumbled up the bank of the levee, he snuffled several times, and wiped his eyes and his nose on his sleeve again. But by the time he reached the ridge he had stopped. He sat down, drawing Maud into his lap once more, and stared at the river, as he had previously stared at the road.

'It's this way,' Fabian said, lowering himself clumsily to the ground beside Vail. 'I wanted to tell you I hated Sylvestre Tremaine too. I reckon we'd find that we felt the same way about lots of things, Vail, if we had a chance to talk them over. I hated him just the same way you do, the same way your Daddy hates snakes. That's a good way to put it, and you're not the first person to do it. There are some people who are a lot like snakes, and Sylvestre was one of them. Sammy Mudge is another. But Sylvestre Tremaine is dead. He can't do any more harm with his coils and his poison. And Sammy can't either. There are ways of taking the fangs out of snakes even while they're alive. Did you know that?'

'No,' Vail said, looking up with sudden interest.

'Well, there are. So forget about Tremaine and don't worry about Mudge. I know how you must feel having Tremaine for a father, but forget about that too. I don't know how you'd look at it, but I'd be mighty pleased if you'd try to pretend that I was your father. Just to yourself, I mean, and when you and I are together. Because, you see, I've always wished I were.'

'Gee, Uncle Fabian—'

'I've wished it for two reasons, Vail. First because I think you're a fine boy, because I'd be mighty proud to have a boy like you for my son. I've got the nicest little girl in the world, I wouldn't trade her for any boy I ever saw, but I'd have been awfully glad to have a boy too. Every man wants to have a son – you'll find out that for yourself some day. So let's pretend I have, and that it's you. Shall we? Good! let's shake on it.'

Vail extended a grubby little paw and Fabian shook it hard. Then he went on holding it.

'I'm going to talk to you now as if you were my son, Vail, and as if you were grown up. The second reason I wish you were mine for true is because I love your mother so much. When a man loves a lady a lot he wants her children to be his children too. He's sorry when they're not. So I'm sorry about that, and she is too. But it's grand for me to know that even if I couldn't be your father, you could have the loveliest lady in the whole world for your mother. ... Haven't you always thought your Aunt Cresside was the loveliest lady you ever knew?'

'Yes,' Vail muttered.

'Well, you thought right, because she is. And you know now that she's your real mother, don't you?'

'Yes.'

'You and I'll talk about all this again some time soon. You needn't be afraid to ask me anything you want to, and I think I can explain lots of things to you, so you'll feel better about them. I'll explain why Aunt Cresside didn't want you to know she was really your mother and why you mustn't ever let her know that you've found out. But now we've got to get back to Belle Heloise, where she wanted you to stay. And we've got to keep mum about this. Because it's our secret now. Right?'

'Yes, Uncle Fabian.'

'Good! Come along. Maybe you'd give me a hand while we're going down the bank. It's hard for me to manage alone, where the walking's rough. I'm going to count on you to help me over the rough places, Vail, when we're out together, after this.'

When Gervais swung into the driveway at Belle Heloise that night the Big House was already in darkness, but he saw that a light was burning in his office as well as in the *garçonnière*. He went first to his own living-room, where he found Merry waiting up for him.

'Fabian's still here,' she said, in answer to her husband's unspoken question. 'He said he wanted a word with you before he

167

went back to town. He's waiting for you in the office. Oh, Gervais, isn't it wonderful that he could help you – and that he did?'

'I can tell you that better when I know just how many strings there are attached to his *beau geste*. But I'll grant you it's reprieve, anyway.'

'You're not going to talk to Fabian like that about it, are you?'

'Don't worry. I didn't mean to imply the reprieve wasn't a godsend. I'm prepared to pay for it, in cash or in kind. I was only trying to tell you I knew I'd have to.'

He left her, crossed the narrow strip of lawn which divided the small twin buildings, and entered his outer office. This was dark and empty. But the door was open into the large inner room which Merry had made so characteristic of a luxurious library, and Fabian was sitting in a Morris chair beside the big desk.

'Hello,' he said, without getting up. 'How's the filibuster going?'

'Fine. There's not a chance of getting that bond issue bill through the Senate.'

'Even without your vote?'

'What are you driving at, Fabian?'

'You told me yourself, the other day, that, with Cyr on your side, Pike Hall and Boone and Caffery were all set to talk it to death. I should think they could talk just as well with you on the plantation as in the Chamber. Maybe better. And I don't believe any one of them would go back on his word.'

'I said, what are you driving at?'

'Just this: I think I know now what Long had up his sleeve when he sent for you the other day. Never mind now – it's too late to go into that tonight. We can take up the details some other time. I don't know how far he'd go, or how fast he'd move, to carry out any threats he may have made – personally I believe there are some limits to what he'd dare do. But he sure didn't lose any time getting his bank examiner to the Citizens National, and I think we'd better beat him to the draw before he tries anything else. I drafted a letter while I've been waiting for you. It's lying there on the desk. If you'll sign it I'll take it in with me tonight and see that it's delivered the first thing in the morning.'

Fabian nodded towards a single sheet of paper lying on the centre of the neat blotter. Gervais picked it up and read it through at a glance. Then he flung it down on the desk again.

'If you think I'm going to let that dirty son-of-a-bitch frighten me—'

'He's frightened you already, hasn't he?'

'Not into quitting. I'll fight him to the last gasp. If he gets licked on this, he's through. All I've got to do is to hang on to the end of the session and then—'

'Then, if he's licked, he'll start all over again and win out some other way. The time to stop him was ten years ago, and none of us had the guts, or the brains, to do it then. We may think we've got the guts now, but those won't do us much good without the brains, and we sure haven't got those. Maybe we can find some new way to fight him, but it'll take time to figure that out. And it's a sure thing we can't lick him the old way. You're through in politics, Gervais. You might just as well face it. But you've still got the plantation. At least, you can have it if you want it.'

'He suggested the same course you'd like to have me follow, and I told the dirty bastard I'd be damned first. I told him he could pop his gun whenever he wanted to, and that when he'd done that, then it would be my turn. Do you really suppose I'm going to let him think—'

'It's a long lane that has no turning. I'm not saying I don't hope you'll have a chance to get back at him yet, some day, that I won't help you every way I can. All I'm saying is I care a damn sight more for my wife's happiness and my own peace of mind than I do for your career.'

'You said yourself you didn't believe he'd dare—'

'I don't. But I'm not taking any chances. As I said before, you're through with politics, but you've still got the plantation. You don't owe me a red cent, Gervais. But I'm going to have your signature on that letter before I leave this room.'

The Governor of Louisiana, running through his morning mail, chuckled and turned to the only visitor he had at the moment, who happened to be one of his purchasing agents. 'Listen to this letter I got here from that lily-livered silk stocking Gervais d'Alvery,' he said. ' "I find that the interests of my plantation demand so much of my time under present conditions that I cannot also do justice to my duties as a Legislator. I therefore ask you to accept my resignation as Senator from the 20th Senatorial District, effective immediately." '

Long laid down the letter with a laugh. 'It's a funny thing

about d'Alvery,' he said. 'I was talking to him a few days back and kind of hinting we knew all about his many troubles, meaning I would maybe fix his clock so he'd lose his plantation, and lo and behold, he jumps up and makes a regular Little Rollo–Lord Fauntleroy speech thinking I meant something else. Never mind what right now – I might tell you some time later. But he needn't have worried. I might've taken a chance on him, but that crippled cousin of his, Fabian d'Alvery, is one man I don't fool with. He's mighty quick on the trigger, I've found that out already. Well, good riddance, that's all I can say. I have a hunch that things are going to start coming my way right soon.'

> . . . 'Little by little and stitch by stitch,
> The girl is put in her proper niche
> With all the virtues that we can draw
> For someone else's daughter-in-law.
> A girl to be kind to, a girl we're lucky in,
> A girl to marry some nice Kentuckian,
> Some Alabaman, some Carolinian –
> In fact, if you ask me for my opinion,
> There are lots of boys in the Northern sections,
> And some of them have quite good connections—'

From 'John Brown's Body,' by Stephen Vincent Benet.

PART THREE

'The Sweetest Story Ever Told'

(May 1936–December 1936)

CHAPTER ONE

'HELLO, Auntie! I heard Uncle Fabian had gone to Washington again, so I came by to see whether you and the kid wouldn't like to go to the Plaquemine Sugar Festival with me.'

'Why, hello, Vail! I think that's a grand idea! But are you sure we wouldn't be in the way? Isn't there someone else you'd rather take?'

'No, I'm sure there's no one else I'd rather take. You're still my best girl, Auntie. Come on.'

Vail put a stalwart arm around Cresside's slim waist, hugging her hard and kissing her soft cheek resoundingly. He had never gone through a period of self-consciousness about demonstrating affection; he embraced Sybelle and Joyeuse spontaneously and warmly, unembarrassed even when Gervais told him, somewhat derisively, that he was the only d'Alvery who had ever kissed his sister without being bribed or badgered into doing it. But he could afford to take the jibe good-naturedly, for his worst enemy could not have accused him of effeminacy. At sixteen he was already taller than either Fabian or Gervais, and so powerfully built that, lacking the typical weediness of adolescence, he would have looked like a man, except for his tousled black hair, the youthful glow of his skin, and the immaturity of his carriage and manner. He was an unusually striking and attractive boy, just as he had been an unusually striking and attractive baby; but he had not yet learned to carry his height or control his strength, and his clothes always looked outgrown, outworn, and unsuitable. Cresside ventured to smooth back one of the unruly locks which fell over his forehead, because she knew Vail would regard the gesture as caressing rather than critical; but she did not dare to straighten his flaming necktie or button his loosened shirt. He would have taken it from her, as he did so many things that he took from no one else; but she realized that he was touchy, that he did not like to have anyone fuss over him, and she refrained from presuming on his fondness.

173

'Your lessons for tomorrow are all done, I suppose?' she asked, turning towards her bedroom from the hall where they had been standing.

'You lie, Auntie. You don't suppose anything of the sort. But you're wrong. As a matter of fact they are done – for once,' Vail retorted. 'Where's the brat? Should I collect her while you're fetching your bonnet and shawl?'

'She's in the kitchen with Carmelite, making gingerbread men. She's getting to be a very enthusiastic little housewife. But she'll drop her cookie-cutter like a shot when she sees you. She doesn't hesitate to tell everyone – including your brothers and sisters, I'm sorry to say! – that you're her favourite cousin.'

Cresside smiled over her shoulder at Vail, who grinned in return, and went on into her bedroom. Though they were crowded in their little house on Somerulos Street, Fabian and Cresside were both attached to it, and had never seriously considered leaving it. They still slept in the square bedroom back of the library, with Frances Belle in the tiny one behind it, which had been created when part of the second ground-floor chamber was partitioned off into a bathroom. After she got bigger she could move to one of the two dormers, which were surprisingly pleasant – after she got bigger or after she was displaced by a little brother, Cresside sometimes added. But Fabian never mentioned the little brother, and he occasionally said, rather curtly for him, that Frances Belle would have to be a good deal bigger before he would consent to having her sleep upstairs.

Cresside sat down in front of her dressing table, applied fresh make-up discreetly, and fluffed out her dark hair under a blue hat. Her happy marriage had caused her to bloom. There had never been a rift between her and Fabian, or a cloud as large as a man's hand darkening their home; she had come to embody this harmony and tranquillity, and at thirty-five her face was softer, her figure more feminine than at eighteen. She had kept her slenderness and her style and she had no white hairs and no wrinkles. Vail often told her that people would really think she was his best girl instead of his aunt, while they were among strangers, if she did not develop a middle-aged spread or try out a henna rinse, and she was always secretly delighted when he teased her in this way. She had a few acquaintances on the west bank, but not many, and it pleased her to think she might be mistaken, if not for Vail's sweetheart, at least for an elder sister, at the Plaquemine

Sugar Festival. Taking off the blue hat, which she decided was a little old-fashioned, she slipped out of her dress too, and changed quickly into a fresh gay print that made her look younger than ever, and a flower-wreathed straw which matched it. When she went back to the hall which divided her bedroom and the library from the drawing-room and the dining-room, she found that Vail and Frances Belle had already gone out of the house and were waiting for her in the car. They called to her gaily, and she joined them.

All three could sit together in the front seat without crowding. Vail admittedly took up more than his share of the space, but Frances Belle was a slight, elfin child, prettier than her mother had been at the same age, but otherwise very much like her; she took up no room at all, to speak of, and Cresside took up very little, so that evened things up, Vail declared, hoisting himself in behind the wheel. He had not been driving a car long, and the only one available for his use was an old rattletrap which Gervais had discarded; but the boy handled it well and kept up a stream of high-spirited conversation as they drove along.

'This ought to be a good show today. You've heard the name they've given the pageant, haven't you?'

'I don't think I have, Vail. I haven't heard much of anything about the Cane Festival.'

' "The Sweetest Story Ever Told". Dad thinks that's silly, but I think it's keen.'

'Well, he would, you know, Vail. Humour has to be of a very high order to appeal to Gervais. But I agree with you. I think it's a good title for this particular kind of a pageant – it isn't designed primarily for the intelligentsia. Do you know anything about this sweet story?'

'Oh, it's supposed to trace the history of sugar from the time when this "was shrouded in the mists of antiquity" up to the "moment of its present high development". There'll be eleven floats. This pageant's in addition to the regular Festival parade, by the way. It's something new this year. ... The maids for the queen's court of honour are being chosen differently too.'

'Are they? In what way?'

'Well, you know last year and the year before they were sponsored by the different plantations, and named after them – Margaret Supple was Miss Catherine, Margaret Hecht, Miss Saint

175

Delphine, and so on. But this year the schools have been invited to select the maids.'

'Which schools?'

'Well, mostly high schools from the different parishes, but some academies too. I'm sorry Grand Coteau wasn't one of them. Sybelle ought to have stood a good chance of being picked for a maid, and she'd have got a great kick out of it.'

'Do you think Sybelle's happy at Grand Coteau, Vail? I wasn't happy at Convent – I was glad when I heard it had closed down.'

'You're darn right, she isn't happy. But that wasn't the big idea. You know the folks wanted to get her where she wouldn't run into Rick Tramonte. Daddy and Mummy could stop him from coming to the house, but they couldn't stop him from walking the levee. And when we took the victoria down to the batture for sand dances he always showed up. . . . Maybe you don't know it, but Sybelle's a riot when she dances in the moonlight.'

'I do know it. I've known for a long time she would be. Your Uncle Fabian predicted, years ago, that something like this would happen. I wasn't sure it had happened to Riccardo Tramonte, though. No one came right out and told me before why Sybelle was sent away to school.'

'Well, I reckon we can't blame it all on the batture. Sybelle and Rick made a getaway once, and of course that would have to be the night Dad took it into his head to come down on the beach. When he found out they'd gone to one of those bootleg shindigs at Hathaway he was fit to be tied. They'd never done it before and I don't believe they ever would have again. Neither of them runs with the "hotcha" gang that goes there. But they were bound to cut loose sooner or later, and they had a bad break, picking the time they did. Dad acted the heavy father – if anyone ever told him those went out with the war he didn't listen. But he couldn't very well lock Sybelle in her room and poke bread and water through a shutter door. So he thought Grand Coteau was the next best answer.'

Cresside did not reply immediately. She knew that Hathaway had succeeded the Willows as the popular 'hot spot' on the River Road, but she had never previously discussed the matter with Vail. Quite aside from her own personal feeling about it, there was something uncanny in the current vogue among riotous students for taking their own band and their own liquor to the deserted house, and dancing, by guttering candlelight, in the

White Ballroom from dusk to dawn. The abandoned plantation was posted and theoretically trespassers were prosecuted; but so far no serious attempt had been made to break up the outlawed parties which had begun when prohibition was still nominally in force and had continued to flourish since its repeal. The thought of her lovely young niece in such a setting, under such conditions, was appalling to Cresside, and she realized, more keenly than ever before, how her own rash conduct at the Willows must have affected her family. But she was wise enough not to voice any censure of either Sybelle or Riccardo to Vail. Instead she spoke gently, suppressing an involuntary sigh.

'Sybelle's awfully young, Vail, to be falling in love.'

'Aw, come clean, Auntie! You know being young isn't the lowdown on that. If she'd gone overboard for somebody like one of those Pereira boys, Dad would have said buh-less you, my chee-ild – I mean my children. But Rick won't ever be anything but a Dago pedlar's son to them. It don't matter his father's one of the richest men in Baton Rouge, even. Say, you got to go to some of the football games with me this fall, Auntie, and see him in action. He was the hottest sophomore full-back L.S.U. ever had, and made All-Southern.'

'I want to go to the football game, too,' piped up Frances Belle, speaking for the first time.

'Right. We'll all go to the football game, sugar. That is, if I'm here.'

'What do you mean, Vail, if you're here? I thought you told Fabian you didn't want to go to Princeton.'

'I did tell him so. Look, Auntie, I've been meaning to talk to you about this for quite a while. Wait till I steer Leaping Lena down the levee and on to the ferry. Then we can get out and stand in the bow.'

Cresside opened her lips and then pressed them together again. Because finances were admittedly still in a bad way at Belle Heloise, it had been natural for Fabian, as the rich relative of the family, to offer to help meet the expenses of Vail's education, and equally natural for him to suggest his own alma mater. However, Vail had stubbornly but gratefully declined. He never could make the grade at one of those swell Eastern colleges, he said, a little ruefully; he wasn't in their class. Now, with Uncle Fabian it was different, because he *was* in their class; and it was damned white of Uncle Fabian to suggest sending him. But he thought L.S.U. was more like it, for him. Phil would be ready for L.S.U. the same year he would, because Phil was smart, just the opposite from him. He thought probably they better stick together. That is, if he could manage to make the grade at all; his latest marks hadn't looked much like it. . . .

'Vail, I want a coke,' Frances Belle said shrilly, breaking in on Cresside's recollections.

'Sure you do. So do I. So do you, don't you, Auntie?'

'No, thanks, Vail. You and Frances Belle go get yours. I'll wait for you here.'

They had already come over the clattering gangplank, paid the collector, and swung into line with the other cars. Now they got out of theirs together, Frances Belle darting off towards the soft drink stand on the upper deck, with Vail in rapid pursuit, and Cresside walking slowly to the bow. Hunched up in front of her was the same wide-shouldered Negro she had first seen while crossing the river with Fabian sixteen years before. He looked almost exactly as he had then, except that he was thinner; bent over a horn in the making, he moved a shard of glass back and forth along the rounded surface, as though he were still engaged on the same task that had busied him then. She stopped and spoke to him.

'Good evening, Willie. Remember the first time I saw you on this ferry a long while ago, when I was with my cousin Fabian d'Alvery before we married? That was our little girl who went by just then.'

Ferryboat Bill looked up, grinning. 'Proud to see you again, Mis' d'Alvery. De Lord, think how de time go by! Don't seem possible you could have a gal-child big as de one I just see. De boy look fine, too. *She* got no beau already, have she?'

'Oh no! Why, she's only eleven. That was Vail d'Alvery.'

'Sure enough? Well, I still says I don't see where de time go to. Me – I's makin' blowin' horns till yet, like you sees. This here ram's horn done been sent me to fix up all de way from Afriky.'

He held it up so that she could get a better look at it. It was beautifully polished, and somehow it reminded her of the Shofar which she and Fabian had seen in a Synagogue at Jerusalem. She paused long enough to admire it, recalling with poignant happiness that joyous period in the Holy Land. Then she went on, with a pleasant good-bye, her anxious thoughts already reverting to

Vail. Was he unhappy at Belle Heloise, she asked herself wretchedly, and straining at the leash to escape? It certainly was not beyond the realm of possibility. She had been terribly unhappy there herself, and so had her father before her, Philogene because he never belonged to the place, and she because she never conformed to it. Perhaps Vail, who did not really belong or conform either, was beginning to be vaguely conscious of this, vaguely restless and rebellious. They must take up the question of Princeton again and not only for Vail's sake, but for Fabian's too. Fabian, with no son of his own, would be happy to have at least a foster-son there. . . .

'I didn't upset you, did I, Auntie? I didn't mean to. There's nothing to be upset about.' Vail had come back and was standing close beside her with his arm around her, just as Fabian had stood when they first crossed the ferry together. Other memories crowded in on Cresside, but she detached her mind from those centring on Fabian and listened intently to Vail. 'It's only that I've had a pip of a job offered me, and I think maybe I'd rather have that than go to college anywhere. Naturally, if I could help Phil I'd stay with him, like I was going to in the first place. But Phil needs me like a cat needs two tails. He's got so many friends that I've got to pry him loose from them all the time, or I'd never see him myself. Everybody likes Phil.'

'Everyone likes you, too, Vail. You've got lots of friends yourself.'

'Sure, I've got lots of friends. But it isn't the same. You know that just as well as I do, Auntie.'

'Who offered you this job, Vail? What kind of a job is it?'

'Mr. Pereira, the last time he came to Belle Heloise for the weekend. It's a job in his coffee importing house. He said twenty-five dollars a week to start, just as soon as I got through high school, and a steady raise every year. . . . Why, Auntie, what's the matter?'

Cresside had suddenly dropped her purse. As Vail retrieved it and gave it to her, she answered him with obvious effort.

'Nothing's the matter, really. I'm upset at this sudden idea of your not going to college. And it just so happens that a long time ago I knew a young man who went to work for the Pereiras and they didn't get along very well. Perhaps you wouldn't either.'

'I don't see why not. The Pereiras are grand guys. It must have been this fellow's own fault if he didn't get on with them. Who was he, anyway?'

'Perhaps it was his fault,' Cresside admitted, disregarding the last question. 'But, Vail, you've taken me completely by surprise. I never heard you say you were interested in learning the coffee business. I thought you were interested in being a sugar planter. I didn't dream you thought of leaving Belle Heloise – unless you went away to college, of course, but then you'd come back. I'd miss you very much if you went to New Orleans. It may be very selfish of me, but I can't help hoping you won't.'

'But, Auntie, I wouldn't be nearly so far away from you if I went to New Orleans as I would if I went to Princeton, and you never said a word about my doing that! I could come home from New Orleans week-ends, and I could see you then, couldn't I? Anyway, Belle Heloise is just bulging with boys. One more or less wouldn't make any difference. Honest now, do you think it would?'

'Of course it would,' Cresside said unconvincingly. 'It would make a difference to your family and it would make a difference on the plantation – you're needed on the plantation.'

'Auntie, Phil wants to stay on the plantation and Franchot wants to stay on the plantation. And some day we'll all want to get married and have families of our own. Do you think there'd be room for us all at Belle Heloise? Somebody would have to be the boss – and that wouldn't go so good with the others.'

'But you're the eldest. If anyone goes, it ought to be one of the others.'

'I don't see why, when they're interested in sugar and I'm not.'

'But you *are* interested in sugar. You wanted to come to this Festival today. You were more interested than any of the others. None of the others took the trouble to come. I don't believe they even thought of it.'

'No. But, you see—'

Cresside looked quickly up at Vail. He had been talking to her very earnestly, but now, to her astonishment, he looked a little sheepish. He seemed on the point of explaining something and then to be bashful about it. Nothing could have been more uncharacteristic of Vail. And as she looked at him again, Cresside saw that he himself had straightened the tie and buttoned the shirt which she with such difficulty had forborne from touching. His unruly hair had been neatly slicked into place, and as the

breeze from the river ruffled it slightly, he raised a preternaturally clean hand and smoothed it back.

'Why, Vail!' she exclaimed involuntarily. 'You didn't have any
special reason for wanting to come to the Festival, did you? I
mean, there wasn't any *special* person you thought you'd see
here? Or was there?'

'Vail, I want an Eskimo Pie,' piped Frances Belle. She had kept
quiet for a long time, during a tiresome conversation from which
she had been excluded, but now she could stand it no longer. She
seized his hand again, dragging him once more in the direction of
the soft drink stand and speaking to him urgently. 'If we don't
hurry we won't get it before the ferry lands,' she said. 'Come on,
please, Vail!'

They were on the road between Port Allen and Plaquemine
before Cresside got the answer to her question. Something had
deterred her from repeating it, and she had almost decided Vail
was determined to ignore it, when he broached the subject again,
of his own accord.

'You asked me a while back if there was any special reason why
I wanted to come to the Festival,' he said, with rather unconvincing nonchalance. 'Well, of course I always like to see the
Plaquemine–White Castle ball game at Athletic Park – they
have darn good teams for places that size. And I like to eat at
Breaux's Restaurant. That gumbo they have – Boy! That's
something.'

Cresside waited patiently for Vail to come to the point.

'And this year a big motorcade is coming up from St. John
Parish – all the cars with banners and stuff showing what planta-
tions and factories they come from. And the Governor and Mrs.
Noe are coming. I reckon they must be in Plaquemine already.
We're kind of late.'

As if he could hardly wait to see Governor and Mrs. Noe, both
highly familiar and completely unexciting spectacles in Baton
Rouge, Vail pressed his foot down on the accelerator and took a
firm grip on the wheel.

'Usually there are quite a lot of pretty girls there too,' he went
on, reverting to the tone of unconvincing nonchalance in which
he had begun. 'The maids sure do look right cute wearing their
gingham dresses and carrying their sugar-cane bouquets. Until
now they've been rather on the grown-up side, though – some of

them as old as twenty, I reckon. But now that there's been this idea of high school kids—'

'Is one of your school friends a maid in the Festival?' Cresside inquired guardedly.

'You mean from Baton Rouge? No one from the high school; there's a girl from St. Joseph's Academy and quite a few from the sororities at L.S.U. – but of course they're old,' Vail explained. 'Most of the smoothest ones come from other places, like Breaux Bridge and Abbeville and New Roads. There's a girl from New Roads that's a knockout. She's smart too. She's the winner of one of the prizes the committee offered for the best essays on sugar growing. Gosh, if I was as smart as that girl, I wouldn't have anything to worry about. I could go to Princeton, like you and Uncle Fabian want me to.'

'What is this girl's name?' Cresside inquired, still guardedly.

'Susannah. Most of the crowd call her Sue, though.'

'Susannah what?' asked Cresside, refraining from asking what crowd, though this was the first time she had heard of a crowd from New Road in connection with Vail.

'Susannah Prescott.'

'Any kin to the Baton Rouge Prescotts?'

'No. She's a damn Yankee,' Vail chuckled. 'Her folks come from somewhere in New England – Connecticut, I reckon. Or maybe it's Vermont. It doesn't matter – one of those little States,' Vail continued with Louisianian loftiness. 'They're some sort of kin to Charles Boylston. I thought he might have told you about them. I met them through him.'

'No, he hasn't told me about them. I haven't seen much of Charles Boylston lately.'

'Well, I've always thought he had a crush on you. I always thought Uncle Fabian cut him out,' remarked Vail, with the disconcerting penetration of the young. 'Not that I'm sorry, though. Uncle Fabian's worth a dozen Charles Boylstons. Some Yankees are nice, just the same.'

'Have the Prescotts bought a place in New Roads?' inquired Cresside, dropping the subject of Charles Boylston.

'Yes, one of those nice old houses near Parlange, facing False River. You must know the one I mean. It used to have a queer German-sounding name. But the Prescotts have changed it. They've renamed it Salome.'

'Salome!'

'Yes. That was the name of one of Sue's great-grandmothers. You wouldn't believe it, but she saw the name herself in some little country burying-ground where the Prescotts used to have their family lot. Salome Church, this lady's name was, and she married a man named Shadrach Prescott. Sue says she came near being named Salome herself. Her father wanted to, but her mother stood out against it.'

'I should think she might.'

'It makes a nice name for a place, don't you think?'

'Yes, I think it makes a nice name for a place.'

'Mr. and Mrs. Prescott want you to come and see them at Salome,' Vail announced. 'You and Uncle Fabian both, of course. I reckon you'll meet them today. They'll be coming to Plaquemine with Sue.' He slowed down and slipped one of his hands briefly into Cresside's. 'If they ask you to go to see them, you'll say yes, won't you, Auntie?' he asked, and his voice was no longer casual; instead there was a note of entreaty in it. 'Of course, I would have told Mom about Sue,' he said, 'except that she is so upset about Sybelle and Rick already. I knew she'd say I was too young too. . . . I oughtn't to have told you you were still my best girl, Auntie, because you're not any more. Sue's my best girl now – that is, I want her to be. The reason I want to get a job is so I can start earning money myself and be independent. And I wanted you to come to the Festival so that you could see her.'

'Vail, please stop at the drug store so we can get a banana split!' begged Frances Belle.

CHAPTER THIRTEEN

VAIL was right; they had been a little late in getting started. When Frances Belle demanded the banana split, he spoke impatiently to her for the first time.

'Good Lord, we haven't got time to go to a drug store now. It isn't half an hour since you had a coke and an Eskimo Pie. Those ought to hold you for a while. We've got to get this car parked somewhere, if we can find a place for it. The town's jam-packed full already.'

Frances Belle continued her clamour while Vail circled anxiously about, and Cresside tried to quiet her, with forced patience but without satisfactory results. She knew that her efforts would have been more successful if she could have concentrated on the fractious child instead of the impatient youth. But she was hardly conscious of what she said as she attempted to quiet her little daughter; in her distracted state it was all she could do to keep her voice under control. She had been so pleased because Vail thought of sharing his outing with her, so flattered that he kept up the joking pretence that anyone would take her for his best girl, so sure that she represented the paramount interst of his life; and, after all, he had not brought her to Plaquemine because he wanted her to have a good time; he had not come to watch the sports or listen to the speeches or associate with sugar planters. He had come because he wanted to see a pert little Yankee who was inappropriately established at New Roads, and he had brought his Aunt Cresside along so that she would make the suitable and gracious approach towards acceptance of this girl and her family. It was ridiculous, it was incredible. Vail was much too young to be serious about a sweetheart. Why, he was only a few years older than Frances Belle, who kept squirming around and shrilly demanding some form of food every few minutes! Vail's general behaviour was almost equally immature. And yet – and yet. . . . Startled as she was at the turn of events, she must not forget to be fair. He had not shut her away from an experience that was vital to him; he had asked her to share it, he wanted her to share it. He had not spoken of it to Merry, but he had revealed it to her. And he had not done anything discreditable, he had not shown himself untrustworthy in any way. This girl who had caught his fancy might be an outsider, but apparently she had background and breeding, she probably behaved herself; and Vail was courting her openly, not only willing but eager to have both her family and his witness his suit. Suddenly a great wave of relief engulfed her, sweeping away the haunting dread of years: that some day he would do what his father had done and be what his father had been. She looked towards him with eyes that were bright with tears, but they were tears of thanksgiving. . . .

'I reckon we can just squeeze in here,' Vail was saying in a voice of triumph, as he indicated a narrow alley which by some miracle had been overlooked. 'Come on, let's get going. I'm afraid we'll just have to stand anywhere we can find a place to see the parade. You don't mind, do you, Auntie? Afterwards I'll see that you get a good seat somewhere.' Oblivious of her inner turmoil, he was still concerned for her comfort. 'That's the L.S.U. Band you hear, Sugar,' he went on, speaking good-naturedly to Frances Belle again in spite of his haste. 'A hundred and sixty pieces they brought over. Makes you feel proud of the old home town, doesn't it, to think they can furnish all that many? It's heading the parade. The Drum Major's Llewellyn Williams. That white outfit of his pretty smooth, isn't it? – and he sure swings a wicked baton. We'll see the floats in a minute. Here, stand in front of me, both of you. I'm wide enough to keep off the crowd and tall enough to see right over you.'

The bystanders on the curb in front of the Hotel Silber had made room for them, and they wedged their way in between a tall raw-boned young farmer wearing a plaid shirt and a battered fedora, and a corpulent woman in rusty black, whom Cresside recognized, after a few minutes of trying to place her, as Mrs. Hartzberg the kindly neighbour who had befriended Max Stoetzner in his extremity. Presently they were chatting like long-lost friends, discussing, with enthusiasm, the details of the parade which was now progressing triumphantly down the street. Following the band and preceding the floats came a large contingent of plantation overseers, mounted on their sturdy cobs. These men, living the year round in the saddle, rode not only with the accustomed ease which might be taken for granted, but also with an effect of unity which would have done credit to any cavalry. Vail, who was an excellent horseman himself, gazed at them with mingled admiration and regret.

'Sance ought to be there,' he said in a voice of disappointment. 'He can ride with any of them. If Sybelle had been home she'd have got Dad to let him come. Sybelle can do almost anything with Dad – at least, she could until the hullabaloo about Riccardo. Now Phil's the white-haired boy. And he wasn't interested in this show, for some reason.' Vail followed the overseers with his eyes until they had turned the corner, clattering out of sight. By that time it was too late for him to get a good look at the first float, representing the creation of sugar by a celebrated magician at the request of an Indian Rajah. Frances Belle, greatly intrigued by the brilliant colours and fantastic costumes with which this float was embellished, and filled with curiosity as to their meaning, nudged him in the ribs, avid for information.

'What are those men doing there? Why do they wear clothes like that? What are they saying to each other?'

He tried to explain, but the first float had gone past before he succeeded; those portraying the successive introduction of sugar into China, Persia and Egypt were already lumbering past, and Frances Belle had begun to ask questions about these. The Crusaders appeared, establishing their sugar routes across the Mediterranean; Columbus, bringing it to Santo Domingo; Etienne de Bore, discovering modern granulating methods, and Frances Belle's curiosity was still unappeased. On the final float a group of Negro hands was gathered around a mammoth plantation bell. Obviously delighted at having become the centre of attraction, they grinned expansively, showing their dazzling white teeth and responding jovially to the applause of the crowd.

'Our hands belonged on that float too,' Vail said, turning from Frances Belle to Cresside and speaking in the same regretful way in which he had referred to Sance. Evidently the fact that Belle Heloise had not figured in this Festival was preying on his mind, and suddenly Cresside realized that this was because he would have been proud if the Prescotts could have seen it represented and been properly impressed with its importance and prestige. 'That bell doesn't begin to be as big as ours,' he went on. 'The inscription on it isn't so hot, either. I can't even make it out.' And then Cresside seemed to see her father standing by the great bronze bell, which was so eloquent a memorial to Thiac-Maignon, the Creole artisan who had cast it, and to hear the first Philogene drawling:

'*J pour joie, A pour amour, P pour passion, R pour ravir, T pour tempter, I pour ivresse, E pour extase – dis donc, Cresside, a tu compris?*'

She did understand now, but she had learned in a hard school, and when she was Vail's age she had not known at all. A fresh pang shot through her heart at the realization that he must learn it all too, and that such knowledge never came easily. She had been thinking of the Prescotts as interlopers on the Southern scene; now she saw that in the supercilious New England way they might consider Vail easy-going, ill-groomed and unscholarly. As a background, Belle Heloise did not loom as large as it once had; even its rightful heir would be no great match for a girl of wealth and position. And Vail was not its rightful heir. Though, of course, the Prescotts did not know that, must never find that out ...

'Let's drift over to the Knights of Columbus Home,' Vail proposed restlessly. 'That's where the queen and her ladies-in-waiting were supposed to watch the pageant. The rest of the bunch will most likely be somewhere around. Anyway, we can find out. I reckon we can get through the crowd now. Would you feel like trying, Auntie?'

'Of course I feel like trying it. I'm still a pretty good walker, you know, Vail, in spite of my advanced age, and the Home's only about a block away.'

'Advanced age, my foot! You don't look a day older than those coeds!'

He put his hand under her elbow and they 'drifted' along to the Knights of Columbus Home. But apparently they had delayed too long. The balcony was already deserted. Disappointed, but by no means disheartened, Vail suggested that they should go on.

'I reckon the only thing to do is to keep milling around until we find someone we know. There's going to be a concert on the Community Club grounds and the queen's parade is going to wind up there. Then the girls will go straight on to the ball. We're certain to see the Prescotts at the Community Club.'

'I'm hungry,' Frances Belle announced. 'I want my supper. I'm tired of walking around. Can't we have supper somewhere, Vail?'

'You must have tapeworm, kid. You don't do anything but eat,' Vail retorted. But he did not speak crossly. Instead he looked at Cresside inquiringly. 'It might not be such a bad idea, you know,' he said. 'We could go to Breaux's Restaurant and just sit there until it's time for the concert. Sit and eat too, of course. Other people might think of the same thing.'

The sidewalk was clearing now, and their progress was fairly rapid. Leading the way, Vail dove down three or four steps to a half-hidden entrance into a channel-like café with a lunch counter at one side of the narrow space. Beyond this counter the space widened somewhat, and tables were scattered about where, Vail explained, 'the twenty-five-cent lunches were served'. Here he paused, looking quickly around, and then hurried forward again towards still another section of the café divided from the 'twenty-five-cent tables' by a step and a railing. Almost immediately he turned to Cresside in triumph.

'Oh, Auntie, there they are now! Mr. and Mrs. Prescott, I mean! At the first fifty-cent table. . . . Why, how do you do, Mrs. Prescott? How do you do, sir? Mrs. Prescott, this is my Aunt Cresside, Mrs. Fabian d'Alvery. And this is my little cousin Frances Belle.'

His voice rang with pride as he presented them. Cresside acknowledged the presentation graciously, and Frances Belle, quickly remembering her manners, hastened to drop a quaint curtsy. In return they were greeted with cordial civility. She and her husband had just started their tea, Mrs. Prescott said; of course Mrs. d'Alvery and Vail and Frances Belle must join them. Only she knew they would rather have coffee. She hadn't lived in Louisiana long, but she had lived there long enough to know *that*! Extra chairs were quickly drawn up to the table, and the toast and fig preserves which had accompanied the tea were promptly supplemented by heartier fare. Frances Belle became speedily absorbed in a double sundae, and Cresside, drinking her coffee in slow sips, appraised the Prescotts with decreasing anxiety, perfectly well aware that they were likewise appraising her. They were gentlefolk, there was no doubt of that, even gentlefolk of considerable distinction – a little on the stiff side, perhaps, but that was understandable. Both were tall and slim and fair, with that subtle resemblance to each other which long and harmoniously married couples often attain; seeing them in a crowd, Cresside would have taken them for brother and sister rather than for husband and wife, and as she observed them more closely she saw, or fancied she saw, that they resembled Charles Boylston too. They were both courtly, if reserved, of manner, and they were both dressed in beautifully tailored clothes, more appropriate for city than plantation wear, in Cresside's opinion, but undeniably fashioned by a master hand. Mrs. Prescott was wearing no ornaments but her engagement ring and a brooch at her throat, but these jewels, like her clothes, were exceptionally handsome. Vail, though he spoke both to Mr. and Mrs. Prescott with more obvious respect than Cresside had ever seen him display towards his elders before, did not seem overpowered by them; indeed, he apparently knew them well enough already to be comparatively at ease with them.

'I've been looking around everywhere for Sue, sir. I thought she'd be at the Knights of Columbus Home.'

'No, only the queen's ladies-in-waiting and the two previous festival queens watched the parade from the balcony with her. All the other maids sat on a platform in front of the Catholic Church.'

'I wanted her and Auntie to meet each other. Do you know where she is now?'

'She's just gone to some friend's house to dress. You know the girls are wearing colonial costumes this year instead of gingham, and I imagine they're getting great fun out of it – I never knew a girl who didn't! But of course Sue must meet your aunt later on . . . You're staying for the ball, I hope, Mrs. d'Alvery?'

'I'm afraid that would mean keeping Frances Belle up too late,' Cresside began. Then, seeing Vail's expression of consternation, she added hastily, 'But I suppose that wouldn't hurt her, for once. Yes, we'd be glad to.'

'Then you'll see Sue in all her glory at the Community Club. Perhaps we can sit together. . . . We've been hoping, Mrs. d'Alvery, that something would bring you and your husband to New Roads. Don't you ever come over to False River?'

'We haven't been there in a long time. But we'd like very much to call on you. Is Sunday a good time? Fabian's in Washington today, but that's unusual. He's nearly always at home and at liberty on Sunday.'

Sunday was a *very* good day for them, Mrs. Prescott declared. Indeed, they were trying to continue their lifelong custom of making a feature of their Sunday breakfasts and asking their friends to share these, at noon instead of nine: that and the pitchers of fruit juice on the sideboard were the only innovations. They served baked beans, brown bread, codfish balls, apple sauce, doughnuts and coffee, just as they always had.

'It sounds wonderful,' Cresside murmured appropriately, not without some inner qualms concerning the codfish balls. But the Prescotts were playing up nobly, and for Vail's sake she was determined not to let them down. It presently transpired that they had served these Sunday delicacies not only in Boston, or thereabouts, as she had more or less taken for granted, but pretty much all over the world. Mr. Prescott had been for a long time in the American Foreign Service, though he had now retired and spent most of his time tinkering with inventions; he had served in such divergent points as Lisbon, Port-au-Prince, Cairo and Helsinki. Looking at them more closely, Cresside saw that both he and his wife were considerably older than she had at first supposed; Susannah must have been born when they were far past their youth. Was she an only child? Cresside wondered, remembering that Vail had not mentioned any brothers and sisters. Mrs. Prescott answered her unspoken question.

'Our one ewe lamb is taking to Louisiana like a duck to water,' she said. Then, laughing a little, she added, 'There I go, mixing metaphors again! My cousin Charles is always teasing me about that.' The conversation turned, naturally enough, to Charles Boylston, and Cresside and the Prescotts were still talking about him when Vail reminded them it was time they started to the concert.

The Community Club was on the same street, but it was several blocks away, near the locks, where Bayou Plaquemine flowed into the river. Frances Belle's footsteps were lagging before it was reached, and though she had ceased to clamour for food, she was obviously tired and sleepy. Cresside suggested that it would be better if she kept the little girl at the rear of the grounds, and urged the others to go forward without her; but it was soon obvious that the only seats left were in the back row of the roped-off space. The Prescotts and the d'Alverys sat down side by side and listened, with uniform politeness but varying absorption, to the performance of the State University Band.

The music was surprisingly good, and the band members made a gorgeous showing in their purple and gold uniforms. But in spite of her best efforts, Cresside's attention constantly wandered from them. She was watching the street for the first glimpse of the parade and straining her ears to catch the sound of the other band which would accompany it. Vail, she knew, was even more impatient, and he showed it. The Prescotts remained completely calm, applauding at all the proper intervals, their eyes fixed on the gold and purple uniforms. If it had been her daughter who was shortly to appear as a figure of fantasy, she could not have been so serene, Cresside thought, glancing down at the drowsy child nestling at her side. It would be only a few more years before Frances Belle would be as old as Susannah, taking part in festivals, going to balls, finding her first suitor. Her heart failing at the thought, Cresside pressed her little daughter more closely to her side. . . .

The band was playing 'The Stars and Stripes Forever', which was apparently its final selection, and the parade was coming at last. The strains for which Cresside had been listening became audible, faintly at first, but gradually growing louder and louder. The red flare of torches appeared in the distance, and presently the Negroes who carried them came into view, their white coats and white kerchiefs ruddy with flickering light. The Negroes were in high spirits; they sang and whistled, exchanging jokes with their cronies among the spectators, and occasionally interrupting their march to execute a few dance steps. In their wake the first float, golden and gleaming, swung into sight, drawn by four fine black horses, whose harnesses had been wrapped in gold cloth. In the centre of the float a masked girl, adorned with the jewels of a Carnival Queen, was shown stepping from the crystal circle of a hemisphere. She wore a golden crown and carried a golden sceptre, and two other girls, also gorgeously dressed, bore their golden train. The float moved slowly so that there would be time for the queen to bow and smile in every direction, acknowledging the applause of the crowd; but after it had passed the Community Club, the parade accelerated its pace. The light from the torches was fitful, bringing some of the floats into brief relief and obscuring others; Cresside's impression of the majority was confused. She saw Father Time encircled with girls dressed in pastel shades, all so young and pretty that they had no cause to fear him, and failed to catch the symbolism of the display. She saw a water wagon – one of the great barrels on wheels used in the cane fields – surrounded by laughing Negroes, as the plantation bell had been earlier in the day, and this seemed to her significant and appropriate. A horn of plenty trundled by, overflowing with animated sugar bags. Then a great sugar bowl, with a charming head peeping from it and others peeping around it, swung around it, swung into sight, and Vail clutched her arm excitedly.

'There's Sue! In the sugar bowl! Look, Auntie! Isn't she a knockout?'

Cresside murmured, 'Lovely, darling!' with convincing enthusiasm, but the float had gone on before she received more than a fleeting impression of shining silver and fair young faces; and after these had disappeared, Vail was no longer interested in the parade. He wanted to get into the hall before all the best seats were taken, as they had been at the outdoor concert. As it proved, he was right in urging his companions to hurry and in propelling the sleepy Frances Belle himself. The Community Club was packed already, and it took some manoeuvring to get a good look at the stage. This had been ornamented with a backdrop representing the façade of an ante-bellum plantation house, with a columned entrance and long French windows. Patches of young cane were scattered realistically over the foreground, and at one side, under a clump of trees, the queen – who had apparently been whisked in through a side door – was seated, still masked, on a large throne-like chair, her maids of honour hovering attentively near her. A string orchestra had been playing while the audience was gathering, but now a slight, kindly-looking man mounted the platform and held up his hand for silence.

'Ladies and gentlemen,' he said. 'It is a great pleasure and a great privilege for me, as the Mayor of this city, to welcome you to the third Louisiana Sugar Cane Festival. I think those of you who have attended our first two festivals will agree that this year Plaquemine has surpassed all its previous efforts. This evening you have beheld a representation of the sweetest story ever told. You must have thrilled, as I did, at the splendour of that magnificent historical pageant. And while its spell was still strong upon you, another parade has magically unwound before your wondering eyes – a parade led by the Queen of the Festival, enthroned on a golden float, and followed by other sumptuous floats proudly bearing as their burden the loveliest maids from every sugar parish in this State, come to do honour to our own.'

The Mayor paused to take breath and to await applause. Relieved on both scores, he continued with increasing fervour as he approached the climax of his peroration.

'But up to this moment, ladies and gentlemen, you have been denied the privilege of meeting these lovely young ladies. In the case of the Queen, even her identity has been withheld from you by means of a mask. In the case of the others, while you have been able to gaze on their charming countenances, you have not been informed of their names or the location of their homes or the educational institutions which have chosen them as representatives. It is now my proud prerogative to introduce to you this bevy of beauty, beginning, of course, with their Sovereign Lady. Queen Sucrosa III, I command that you unmask, revealing yourself to this gathering as none other than Miss Genevieve Kearney of New Roads!'

Again applause resounded, spontaneously this time. The Queen, accepting the Mayor's hand, stepped from her throne to acknowledge it; and as it went on and on, she made a graceful, deprecatory gesture, signifying that it was time to stop, and glanced towards her ladies-in-waiting as if to say it was their turn now. They were both Plaquemine girls, whom the Mayor had known from childhood, and at some length he traced their family background and cultural development and paid due tribute to their charms.

'At this rate, it will be midnight before we get to dance,' Vail muttered, creasing his yellow programme and uncreasing it again. 'The old geezer must be wound up. The introduction of the maids was supposed to start at nine-twenty and it's past that now.'

'Not much past, really,' Cresside told him in a whisper. 'I think the Mayor's almost through anyway. And he's enjoying himself so much! You shouldn't resent it if he rambles on a little. Besides, think how proud the families of those girls must be. They're drinking in every word he says.'

'Well, I'm not,' Vail said tersely. 'I want to see the maids have some kind of a chance. I want—'

'Hush, darling! He really is through with the ladies-in-waiting. Now he's signalling to someone else.'

A pretty girl had appeared from the wings and given her hand to the Mayor, who presented her to his audience as Miss Katherine LaCour, representing the Innis High School. She curtsied gracefully, crossed to the other side of the stage, and went down the runway, where she was met by a young man who had been patiently standing there for some moments, obviously awaiting some kind of a cue, and they took their places in a semicircle of reserved seats in the front of the hall. Before Miss LaCour and her escort had moved aside, the Mayor was introducing another maid, and another young man had stepped eagerly forward to escort her to the semicircle. The fourth time that this process was repeated, Vail stirred in his seat and half rose.

'What's the matter?' Cresside asked, still in a whisper.

'Nothing. I reckon it's time for me to be moving towards the stage, though. It'll be Sue's turn any minute now.'

He went carefully past her and the Prescotts, nodding and smiling a little self-consciously, and edged his way along the side of the hall, moving with his usual boyish awkwardness and holding his head with an air of assurance which Cresside felt certain must be assumed. He had said nothing about this part of the programme, which was evidently the prelude to some sort of a fancy dance, nothing about Susannah's selection of him as a partner. For it must have been a selection; this orderly progress could not be impromptu; it had obviously been planned with great care. If Vail had not been shy about disclosing the rôle which he was to play, he would have talked about it, as he had about other features of the Festival; and suddenly Cresside felt a pang of pity for him. It meant so much to him, this meeting with Susannah, and it might mean so little to her! Vail was young to be hurt. . . .

'Miss Lydia Dupuis of Breaux Bridge, representing the Cecilia High School,' the Mayor was saying. 'Miss Nancy Barker of Plaquemine, representing St. Basil's Academy. Miss Beulah Butte of Reserve, representing the Leon Godchaux High School . . . Miss Susannah Prescott of New Roads, representing St. Joseph's Convent. . . .'

Holding her breath, Cresside watched the wings for Susannah's entrance. She saw a slim girl who held herself very erect, and whose brown hair was parted smoothly in the middle. Her eyes were grey, her eyebrows and eyelashes almost black; they made a striking note of colour in her otherwise pale little face. She had a small straight nose and a firm but shapely chin. At first she gave the impression of being very demure; but when she smiled and acknowledged her introduction, she showed bewitching dimples and her lashes curled coquettishly down over her delicate cheeks. The curtsy she made was accomplished and graceful, and the colonial dress which she wore was obviously no festival costume, hastily put together for the occasion from sleazy material; it was made of rich cream-coloured grosgrain and trimmed with ivory-tinted lace. Cresside guessed that these warm shades might be the result of antiquity, that both dress and lace had once been snow-white and that they had served as the bridal finery for one of Susannah's great-grandmothers, perhaps the startlingly named Salome Church. But whoever its original owner, Susannah wore it well; the tight pointed bodice and plain elbow sleeves became her; the voluminous skirt made her trim waist look all the smaller. Only over the bosom it did not fit her; her ancestress must have been fuller breasted than she was, probably because Salome was older than Susannah when she wore it and had already lost Susannah's appealing immaturity. Even in colonial times, girls as young as Susannah did not marry. Or did they? Did they do it sometimes even now? Cresside looked at Susannah with fresh apprehension and reluctant admiration, as the girl walked slowly down the runway to meet Vail. After that, Cresside saw nothing clearly until the Royal Dance was in progress, and Vail and Sue were circling the hall among the other maids and men escorts.

They danced easily and well together, as if they had done it before and were accustomed to each other's ways. But there was far less appearance of abandon in their movements than in those of most couples on the floor. Many of these were already cheek to cheek; others were releasing each other to execute fancy steps, and then flinging themselves into their partners' arms again, more closely embraced than before. Vail's steps and Susannah's were in perfect unison, but he held her lightly, and she continuously gave the effect of insisting on her identity, rather than merging it with his. For the most part she danced in silence, her head slightly bent, and Cresside was more conscious of the girl's smooth brown hair and its white part than of her highbred little face. But every now and then she looked up with the arch expression for which Cresside was already beginning to watch, and said something which obviously pleased and amused Vail very much, for he threw back his head and laughed whenever she did so. Something about this carefree interchange of merriment struck Cresside as inexplicably poignant. She looked away from the dancers, belatedly turning her attention to the Prescotts.

'I understand now why Vail was so upset when I said perhaps we wouldn't stay for the dance. He's very fortunate to have your lovely little daughter for a partner. She's easily the most charming girl in the group.'

Briefly, and not too emphatically, Mr. and Mrs. Prescott disclaimed their right to the compliment, commenting favourably on Vail in return: he had so much vitality, and at the same time so much stability for a boy of his age; and he was almost outrageously good looking! That special combination of colouring – very black hair with bright blue eyes and ruddy cheeks – was most unusual. The Prescotts were eager to see his twin; they had heard that she was really a beauty.

'Yes, there's no doubt of that. But don't expect her to look like Vail. She's as fair as he is dark, and has wonderful blonde ringlets instead of a straight black mop like his. I don't know whether you remember Mary Pickford in her prime – well, Sybelle's a little that type. The younger children are delightful too, especially Philogene. He's generally considered the flower of the family. But I mustn't run on like this about my young relatives. . . .'

Her eyes wandered towards the floor again. All the girls, wearing their quaint coloured colonial costumes and dancing with a natural zest of youth and high spirits, made a pleasing picture. But she had spoken the truth when she said that Susannah was the most charming in the group. While Cresside looked at her with renewed intentness, half hopeful, half fearful of finding some flaw, the music came to a slow stop. Lingeringly Vail's arm began to slide from Susannah's waist, and, as if slightly intolerant of his procrastination, she freed herself, in the same light, easy way that she had danced, and started across the floor with Vail following her. When she reached the side, she faced Cresside with her bewitching smile, holding out a small shapely hand.

'I'm so glad you came to the Festival with Vail, Mrs. d'Alvery,' she said. Her voice was cool and pleasant, like her parents', and she spoke with complete poise. 'And is this Frances Belle? What a sweet little girl! No, please don't wake her!'

Susannah bent over the sleeping child, smoothing back a stray curl. 'I've been wishing I could meet the rest of Vail's family ever since he brought Phil to see me,' she went on, straightening up again. 'I hoped Phil would come to the Festival, but Vail says he wasn't interested. I'm afraid I didn't make much of an impression on him. But he did on me. I've kept telling mother and father that they might as well make up their minds that Phil's my fate, because I have. I'm going to wait for him to grow up.'

CHAPTER FOURTEEN

As the d'Alverys approached the little house on Somerulos Street after taking the last ferry, Cresside saw, with surprise, that the lights were on in the library and realized that Fabian must have come home unexpectedly. Her joy at the thought of seeing him was tinged with regret because she had not been there to welcome him, and she ran swiftly up the steps, leaving Vail to follow with Frances Belle in his arms. The little girl had slept soundly throughout the drive home, and she did not stir when Vail lifted her out of the car. Fabian opened the front door and greeted his family with mock reproof.

'Deserting me, are you, Cresside? Stealing your aunt, eh, Vail? What's the big idea?'

'The idea was to introduce me to Mr. and Mrs. Prescott of New Roads and their daughter Susannah,' Cresside answered with something of her old drollery. 'But the Plaquemine Sugar Festival was the medium for this auspicious presentation. We've seen two parades and a coronation and a ball, and we've listened to three bands. We're pretty much all in now, but we'll tell you about it tomorrow. Goodnight, Vail. Just shift Frances Belle over to her father, will you? I think I can get her undressed without waking her. Thanks for taking me to the show. I've had a swell time. And, by the way – I think Susannah's a grand girl.'

Muttering an incoherent word of appreciation, Vail kissed her good-night and sauntered down the walk. From the gallery Cresside watched him as he got back into the rattletrap car and slammed the undependable door so that it would shut. Then she waved to him a last time and went back into the house with her husband as Vail bucked off down the street. Consequently she did not see him turn the car around and start back into town instead of proceeding towards the River Road. He did not stop until he had almost reached the ferry again. Then he drew up at the little house behind the Fancy Grocery Store where Luigi and Netta, in spite of their mounting prosperity, had continued to live, and where they had taken it for granted that their only son would continue to live with them, instead of in barracks or at a fraternity house, while he attended the University. A few lights were still burning inside, and beyond the open window Vail could see Riccardo seated at a desk. He whistled, giving a special signal that had been understood between them for years. Riccardo immediately jumped up and came to the door.

'Hello there! What on earth are you doing out at this time of night?'

'Hello yourself! I've been to the Plaquemine Sugar Festival. What are you doing *up* at this time of night?'

'Studying. The finals are getting too darned close for comfort.'

'Hell, you should worry. You haven't got a mark below A minus all year.'

'I'm not worrying. But I don't want to get anything lower than that next year either. . . . I haven't been studying all evening, anyway. Just off and on. I've been reading that new book of John Gunther's, *Inside Europe*. It's keen. You ought to read it yourself, Vail, and find out what's going on over there. You haven't got the first idea.'

'I got plenty to do, just trying to keep track of what happens right on the plantation. Dad can't look after everything. . . . What else you been doing while I been out dancing?'

'Sounds sort of like the ant and the cricket, the way you put it. I've been listening to Paul Sullivan's broadcast. Do you know what? He's sure we're in for another war.'

'You're crazy with the heat. Or else he is. The last one was the war to end all wars.'

'That's what you think.'

'It's what everyone thinks, isn't it? I know that's why Dad went.'

'I reckon it's what everyone thought in 1916. I don't know that so many people think that way any more. What does your father say about the occupation of the Rhineland?'

'Nothing much. Something about how France and England could have stopped it between them, but maybe they didn't think it was all that important or they would have. He said a lot more about—'

It had been on the tip of Vail's tongue to say, 'About the Italian invasion of Ethiopia,' but he stopped just in time. Riccardo, either oblivious of the slip or pretending to be, swung open the screen door.

'Come on in, why don't you? If we're going to settle the future of the world we might as well do it sitting down.'

Vail did not wait to be asked a second time. There was nothing on earth he liked better than to stay up till all hours arguing with Riccardo on weighty matters which neither of them understood very well. When he did not return from an evening's outing it was assumed that he was spending the night on Somerulos Street. Occasionally this was the case, and, as no one ever brought up the question, he did not feel it necessary to disclose that far more frequently he was spending it at the Tramontes'.

'I could do with something to eat,' Riccardo announced, latching the screen door. 'How about you?'

'I sure could. I haven't had anything to speak of all day.'

'I thought they had good food over in Plaquemine.'

'Maybe they do somewheres. We couldn't find anything,' Vail declared shamelessly, forgetting how recently he had chided Frances Belle for her unbridled appetite.

'Well, we had a man-sized hunk of roast for dinner. Must be a lot left. Let's see, anyway. Don't make any more noise than you can help. Father has to get off to Lafayette around five tomorrow morning – I mean this morning. I don't want to wake him and mother.'

The two boys tiptoed to the immaculate kitchen and switched on the lights. The huge white refrigerator loomed enticingly before them. Opening it, they extracted the substantial remains of a twelve-pound beef roast, cut off thick slices, and made themselves bulky sandwiches. Reinforcing these with three-fourths of a chocolate layer cake, half of a dewberry pie, and two bottles of milk, they returned to Riccardo's bedroom and spread the feast on his desk in the midst of his books and papers.

'How was the dance?' Riccardo inquired, sitting down, his mouth full of sandwich.

'Swell. Aunt Cresside liked Sue a lot too. At least, she said so, and she's all set to be nice anyhow. The hitch will come with Mom and Dad and *grand'mère*. Especially *grand'-mère*.'

'How come?'

'I never knew it to fail. A fellow's family always says, why yes, of course she's a very nice girl, but still she isn't exactly the *sort* of girl that—'

Vail grinned, speaking in a mocking falsetto. Riccardo failed to return the grin.

'Anyway, they don't stop you from taking her to a dance. They can't, so long as her folks let her go. Now you take Sybelle and me, we can't even get to go to a dance together.'

'I know. It's a dog-gone shame.'

'I thought maybe I could take her to the junior prom this year. But I've just got a letter from her saying no soap.'

'Gee, I'm sorry, Rick. If it was my say-so, she'd go with you, you know that. Anyway, it's a cinch no one can keep you from taking her to the senior ball. You're sure to be Colonel of the

Corps next year, Rick, and if you choose Sybelle for Sponsor of the Regiment—'

'What do you mean, if? You know good and well I'd choose her. I chose her for one of the Battalion Sponsors this year, but all it got me was I had to choose over again – my big fat cousin Drina Montegino from New Orleans.'

'Just the same, I don't think even Mom and Dad would try to keep Sybelle from being Sponsor of the whole Regiment.' –

'I do. Besides, I may not have any say about it. There's nothing so certain about me being Colonel.'

'Well, you're a Major already, aren't you? If you·can get to be a Major when you're a junior I don't see any reason why you can't get to a Colonel when you're a senior.'

'You seem to overlook the little detail that there are four Majors and only one Colonel.'

This was so undeniably true that Vail did not attempt to deny it. Instead he devoted himself to the dewberry pie, having by this time devoured his share of the sandwiches.

'Anyhow, I've got one thing coming,' Riccardo said after a reflective pause. 'At least, I think I have. I'm almost sure father's going to give me a boat for a graduation present.'

'Gee, that's swell. What kind of a boat?'

'Well, naturally I want a Gar Wood. I don't know whether it'll be a light cruiser or just a speed boat.'

Vail whistled. The Fabian d'Alverys had always been extremely generous to him, but none of their gifts had begun to reach the proportions of a Gar Wood boat, nor did he know anyone besides Riccardo whose parents would have thought of giving graduation presents on such a scale. 'I should think a speed boat might hold you for a while, you lucky bum,' he said enviously.

'Yeah. But if I got a light cruiser, then you and I could maybe go up north and bring her down the river ourselves.'

'Say, that would be the cat's whiskers, wouldn't it? How long do you reckon it would take us to make the trip?'

'Oh, we ought to allow a couple of weeks. Might as well look around a little while we're about it. And maybe after we got the boat down here we could work it so as to take the girls out on it sometimes – Sue and Sybelle.'

'Yeah, maybe we could. Especially if we could get Aunt Cresside on our side.'

'You think your Aunt Cresside's tops, don't you?'

'You bet I do. There's nothing the matter with Mom, though, or your mother either.'

They went on talking about the new Gar Wood and all the uses to which she could be put while they finished up their food and undressed. There were two cots in Riccardo's room and one of them was always in readiness for Vail; he kept a pair of pyjamas under the pillow, an extra shirt in the bottom bureau drawer, and a toothbrush of his own in the bathroom. They gave him an extra feeling of 'homeyness', even when he neglected to use them, as he very frequently did; while a hidden package of razor blades was a still more beguiling features of his visits to the Tramontes. He had not as yet achieved a razor of his own, as his need for one was not yet urgent or even obvious; but he experimented with Riccardo's, once a week or so, to his own great satisfaction. Tonight, however, he suddenly felt very tired, so he dropped off his clothes and got on to his cot without a single superfluous motion. He was almost asleep when Riccardo, who was much more meticulous in his habits and therefore took longer to get to bed, spoke to him again.

'You know. I've been thinking, Vail. If there is a war, I'll get into it right away.'

'How do you figure that out?'

'Because when I graduate I'll be a reserve officer with a Lieutenant's commission. I won't have to wait for a draft or anything like that.'

'Hell's bells, Rick, you talk as if you *wanted* us to get into a war.'

'No, I don't want us to get into a war. But if we *do* get in—'

'Oh, for crying out loud! You've got war on the brain. You better stop listening to Paul Sullivan and reading John Gunther.'

'Well, you'd better read *something*. You'll forget how if you don't. Did you see Mussolini's statement about Ethiopia in the *Advocate*? Didn't that get a rise out of you? Because if it didn't it sure as hell should have.'

So Rick was ready to talk about Mussolini after all, and maybe he was right about another war, at that. If there really were one, of course Vail would want to go himself; he did not read books and listen to broadcasts, foretelling one, the way his friend did. But he had always been a ready listener to the accounts of Lucien Estrade's dramatic feats on Beauregard's staff and of the exploits in France which had led to the winning of Gervais' medals and the death of the two uncles for whom he himself had been named; he had always hoped that some time he himself could exceed their triumphs, and make the family even prouder of him. He had also seen numerous thrilling movies depicting the glories of war which had inspired him with the fancy of sharing these in the hero's rôle; and since he had met Susannah this idea had taken a firmer hold on him. It was gratifying to imagine her following his triumphs from afar, keeping his picture in uniform on her dresser, weeping when she saw his name in the casualty list, welcoming him on his well-decorated return with open arms. Vail dwelt on these pleasing pictures with renewed satisfaction driving down the River Road the evening after his excursion to Plaquemine. He was alone, for Philogene and Joyeuse had stayed in town to go to the movies with some of their own special cronies, and Franchot had been ailing the last few days. So there was no chaffing and chattering going on, and he could think things through by himself, as he had always liked to do. He believed that Rick was right about most things. Every time he went to the Tramontes' he firmly resolved that he would read more, that he would study harder, that he would strive to be more like his idol. But he was no sooner back on the plantation than this absorbed him again. He resented the hours that he was obliged to spend in school, without spending extra hours buried in books after he reached home. He did not want to study, even after it grew dark. It was one thing sitting up half the night, once a week or so, talking to Riccardo; but if he sat up late every night he was too sleepy mornings to get up at daybreak and ride out over the headland. And that was what he loved to do above everything else in the world. He might talk about going into Mr. Pereira's office to learn the coffee business, because he was flattered that he had been offered the job, and because he was not sorry to impress Aunt Cresside with its importance. He might even feel he had better accept it, because there were so many of them at Belle Heloise and because he would need more money than he could get at home, as his rightful share, if by any chance he should happen to want to get married some day. On the other hand, he might decide to go to Princeton after all. He did not really object to it because it was a highbrow Eastern college; he could make the grade if he tried, and reluctantly he admitted to himself that perhaps he ought to, on account of Sue. There could be no comparison between the eligibility of a suitor who had gone to Princeton and a suitor who had gone into the coffee business straight from high school. But in his heart of hearts he knew that he would never willingly leave Belle Heloise for any reason whatsoever, that it was almost as much a part of him as his hands and feet. All the aspects of it which had meant so much to him as a child meant even more to him now.

He was nearly home again, and something within him quickened at the realization of this; but as he approached the desolate expanses of Hathaway, he deliberately looked in the other direction. It was habit he had failed to outgrow. He himself had never been to any of the 'bootleg shindigs' which were responsible for Sybelle's banishment, and he shared the aversion which the local Negroes had for the place, though without superstition. It had never been inhabited or planted since the hideous accident which had caused Deéte Reno her life and banished Blood in order to save his skin. He was now managing a sugar factory in Mexico with conspicuous success, and Wilhelmina, who had long since divorced him, spent most of her time wandering aimlessly over the Continent from one watering place to another, much as the Tremaines had once wandered. The Negroes who had worked on the plantation had been only too glad to leave; some of them still lived in the scattered cabins along the Road, raising small patches of cane and vegetables themselves, or working at Belle Heloise when extra hands were required; others had moved into town, 'bettering themselves'. Micah and Jinny were profitably installed in the household of a Standard Oil magnate; Jonah was the janitor of a school; Meme ran a small café identified with the sign STRICTLY COLOURED. Phronsie had gone over to the West Side, where she had achieved a more ambitious establishment, more alluringly designated. Under the twinkling legend MISS PHRONSINA'S HOUSE OF JOY appeared the further caption COME IN AND PLEASURE YOURSELVES. There was evidence to indicate that this admonition had not gone unheeded. But Minta had been sent off to an excellent school, and from there she was going to a coloured college. Later on, she was going to be a teacher herself.

The deserted cabins at Hathaway were only part of the desolate scene which Vail so deliberately avoided. The looming façade of the Big House was no longer white and gleaming; it had taken on a greyish tinge, and though this was only from lack of paint, the result was eerie, especially in a dim light. The garden and lawns which had formerly been so elegantly patterned had long been overgrown with rank grass and weeds, and thickets were closing in on the once productive fields. Wilhelmina Blood had been trying for years to sell the place, but without success. There was no market any longer for houses and plantations of that size. A new order of things had brought about a different way of living, and the River Road had been shorn of its unique importance as a thoroughfare by the new airline highway, which cut straight across country, instead of following every bend of the Mississipi, and reduced the distance between Baton Rouge and New Orleans by nearly thirty miles. Besides, locally, nearly everyone except the riotous students shared Vail's feeling about Hathaway.

He continued to look at the levee now, until he had rounded the bend in the road which marked the boundary between Hathaway and Belle Heloise; then, joyously, he turned back to his own land. The hoe gang which had been cleaning the fields were just leaving these to go home, and the hands were singing as they swung away towards the quarters. The cane was already shading the rows, and Vail thought, with satisfaction, of the old saying that if the fields were green by the first of May the crop was assured. He knew that this saying was not infallible, that if the next months were so rainy that the hoe gang could not work regularly, the Johnson grass would get ahead of the men and there would be the devil to pay. But if this did not happen, and nothing else untoward occurred, the cane would be as high as the fourth bars of the old-fashioned fences by the Fourth of July. Then the crop really *would* be assured.

He hoped nothing would happen to it this year, for Dad's sake. Dad had been through a long siege of bad luck, and it was time he had something better coming to him. The plantation was a part of him too, and he suffered with it and throve with it, just as Vail did. Except for his family and his hunting, it was almost his only interest now. Vail had been too young, at the time of his foster-father's retirement from politics, to grasp many of its implications, but he did know that there had been a bitter disappointment connected with it, and that since then Dad had tried to make the plantation compensate for everything else. He was highly regarded, not only as the virtual saviour of the sugar industry in the State, but as a progressive planter who did not rest on his laurels but who continued to experiment in new methods and to improve old ones. He had met with marked success in both directions; frequently he was asked to deliver addresses and write articles on the cultivation of sugar cane, and he was also called into consultation at various agricultural experiment stations, including the one in Washington. Though all this gratified him, to a certain degree, he was not essentially a writer or a speaker, and he had wanted to go to Washington in a different capacity. His failure to do so had embittered him. He looked and acted older than he was, and it was only when he went hunting that he seemed to shed his cares and his age.

The year before he had gone, at Charles Boylston's invitation, on a hunting trip to Alaska, taking a train to Seattle and a boat to Juneau, before starting back into the hill country. Harvey Lawrason of Denham Springs, who came more and more frequently to Belle Heloise now that Hackberry Lodge was closed most of the time, had been his fellow-guest on this occasion, for Mr. Boylston never did things by halves, once he got started. He had even told Gervais he would be glad to invite one or two of their former political associates, if the Captain thought it would do any good. Charles thought it might; now that Huey Long was dead, politics were going to be different in Louisiana: for instance, there was Happy Sevier, who had always been a good friend of his: Happy was now a member of the legislature, and might very well become quite a power there. But Gervais smiled rather wryly, and replied that it was Charles's party, and that, of course, the host must do as he pleased. As far as he personally was concerned, however, he did not care about trying to get in touch with anyone who had not first made an attempt to get in touch with him. He thought they would have a much better time if only the three of them went, as originally planned. So it had been decided that way, and the expedition was a great success. Gervais had sent back numerous snapshots, showing himself with a formidable growth of beard, and standing proudly beside a Kodiak bear he had killed. The bear's head had been mounted and placed over the fireplace in his study, supplanting a family portrait, while the fur had been made into a rug to be put in front of the hearthstone. And Gervais had actually come home with the beard, even more bushy than it looked in the snapshots. Afterwards he had given a big party, inviting all the educators and sugar men who thought highly of him as a progressive planter, and for a time the atmosphere had been very jovial. But he had pointedly omitted from this gathering all acquaintances with political connections, and presently he had sunk back into his old bitter state.

Vail had been delighted that Dad had had this fine trip, and, with Sance to help him, had shouldered the responsibilities of the plantation in Gervais' absence, as he always did during the briefer periods when Gervais went to Washington and elsewhere. He did a very good job for a boy of his age; he was flattered at the confidence shown in him and tried to deserve it; but he could not help feeling sorry that the trips Dad took were so seldom the sort in which Mom could share. When Uncle Fabian went anywhere he took Aunt Cresside with him; sometimes Frances Belle went along and sometimes she was sent out to Belle Heloise while her father and mother were gone; but in any case, Aunt Cresside shared in all Uncle Fabian's pleasures and opportunities. Of course, Vail understood that Mom did not like hunting or sports of any kind, and that while Dad did not mind this, the way he minded that Franchot did not like them either, he nearly always chose a hunting trip when he went anywhere for pleasure, and this automatically debarred Mom from going too. Of course, Daddy could not take her to Europe and Hawaii and Peru, just like that, the way Uncle Fabian took Aunt Cresside; there was not money enough and there was the responsibility of too many children. But he could have taken her to Washington once in a while and to New Orleans fairly often. *Grand'mère* and Granny Randall and Miss Mittie could have looked after the family while he did that. Mom was only a little older than Aunt Cresside, maybe three or four years, but there were times when she looked almost as old as *grand'mère,* whose face did not have a line in it even yet, and whose figure was still her great pride. Mom loved her husband and her children and her home devotedly and she never complained because it did not ever seem to occur to Dad that she might have welcomed a few outside interests and diversions; but Vail felt they would have given her a great lift, and that she would have looked younger and felt gayer if she could have had them.

Before Sybelle had been sent away to Grand Coteau, on account of Riccardo, Vail had usually managed to have a ride with her on the levee after they got home from school; now he spent this period with Sance or Plauché, doing whatever was indicated at the season. After supper he generally played some kind of game with Joyeuse and the younger boys before he went reluctantly back to his books for an hour or two. The youngsters were all very good at games, and showed so plainly that they were pleased because he played with them that he was flattered by their outspoken gratitude and admiration. Besides, the games gave him a good excuse for putting off the lessons, and in his mind there was only one choice between the two.

On Saturdays and Sundays he spent even more of his free time with the youngsters. He taught them all to swim in the river and to ride on the levee; he took them fishing in the barrow pit and squirrel hunting in the woods back of the plantation – at least he taught them all to swim and to ride, and he took all of them except Franchot hunting and fishing. It made Franchot sick to see a fish squirming on the hook, and he cried the first time he saw a squirrel, which had been frisking and barking only a few minutes earlier, lying dead on the ground. The others all made fun of Franchot when this happened, but Vail had stood up for him. He was a good shot for his age, and he liked to go fishing as well as anyone; but he had not forgotten how he felt when Betsy Ann died, and he knew that in a sense Franchot loved all free wild creatures the same way he himself had loved Betsy Ann.

'Leave him alone!' Vail had said fiercely to the others, as they crowded around Franchot, jeering. 'If this isn't his idea of a good time, it isn't, that's all.' Vail took up the dead squirrel and tossed it away where Franchot would not see it. 'Come on, brat, let's you and me go home. There's lots else to do, beside squirrel hunting. I'd rather ride on the levee myself, any day. What say we go for a ride straight off?'

Vail had a real horse now, because he had outgrown Nostar; but Nostar was still alive and well, and though he was getting stiff and slow, Franchot rode him and loved him. Maud had died of a ripe old age several years earlier; but before she died she had produced not only the coal-black puppy which Uncle Fabian had wanted so long, but a replica of herself, which Vail loved almost as much as he had loved her, and which he named Maudie after her. He said that from now on there would be a Maudie at Belle Heloise, just as there was always a Minnie. The current Maudie went racing along the levee when Vail and Franchot rode there, nosing the ground and snapping for bugs, just as her mother had done before her. She was an integral part of the plantation too.

This last winter Vail had not spent as much time with the youngsters as before, first because he had taken on more responsibilities during the grinding season and afterwards because he had gone to New Roads on so many week-ends. Groups from the Baton Rouge high school frequently started out on a Friday evening over the fine paved highway now connecting Baton Rouge and New Roads and reaching Jim Jarreau's camp in time for supper. This supper consisted of perch, trout or *sac-à-lait* fried in deep fat along with little cornbread balls, called hush-puppies, and the girls and boys ate prodigiously of these homely delicacies. After supper there was always dancing in the adjacent pavilion, connected with the bar, sometimes to the music of the gaudily coloured juke box at one end of the hall, sometimes to the strains of a hillbilly band, imported for the occasion. Groups from the New Roads schools also came to these suppers and these dances, and it did not take long for the two 'crowds' to get together, especially as many Baton Rougeans had relatives living along False River and vice versa. Often the Bouanchauds or the Kearneys gave house parties, and then the 'gang' from Baton Rouge stayed over until Sunday for more dancing and for various kinds of sports.

The Saturday night dances were different from any others: whole families came to the 'night spots' from the surrounding countryside, some on foot, some in wagons, and some in broken-down cars. They were seldom seen seated around the tables, though occasionally they brought food with them; more often they got to dancing with the least possible delay, refreshing themselves from time to time with beer, which they drank direct from the bottles, standing at the bar or on the dance floor. Even nursing mothers found the exigencies of their condition no deterrent to their enjoyment; they carried their babies in their arms while they danced, and permitted them to feed at will. The babies were in no wise upset by this casual treatment either; they evidently drank in a love for dancing with their mothers' milk. As soon as they were able to toddle, they began to dance themselves, taking to it like ducks to water; and the older they grew, the more proficient they became. The patriarch of a family danced with his great-grand-children, and his wife knew all the latest steps. The high school groups did not mingle much with these family parties, but they liked to be in the same hall with them, vicariously sharing their pleasure; there was a general feeling that nothing was quite so much fun as the Saturday night dances on False River.

The young people also hunted on horseback during the winter week-ends, riding pinto ponies from Glenwood plantation, where they usually went for at least one meal with Trammel Harrison and his wife, who had been Miss Josie Glen. They fished off Lawrence Bizette's wharf, where chairs were provided for their comfort, and if the fish did not bite very well near the wharf, then they hired boats from Oliver Guillaume and went flyfishing or coasting. They went speed-boating too, as several of the local boys had craft of this kind, and it was exciting sport, especially by moonlight. On Sunday mornings many of them got up early and went to Father Savouré's little church at Lakeland, because he was their favourite priest; then they resumed their fishing and boating and hunting until it was time to start back over the new highway again. Very often as they went bucking along towards town they sang the song which was such a favourite among the local children that some of their elders who had not admired Huey Long said sarcastically it must be part of the school curriculum:

> 'They call him a crook, but he gave us free school book,
> Tell me what's the reason they shoot Huey Long?
>
> Huey Long in his grave, while we riding on his pave,
> Tell me what's the reason they shoot Huey Long?
>
> Huey Long's dead and gone, Louisiana left alone,
> Tell me what's the reason they shoot Huey Long?'

Vail sang this song along with the rest of the crowd, as he did 'You're the Top', 'The Music Goes Round and Round', 'Moon Over Miami' and numerous other favourites of the moment. Most of them he hummed or whistled at home too, but he was careful never to include 'What's the Reason They Shoot Huey Long?' in his solos. He knew that Dad hated the very mention of Huey Long's name, and that in some vague way the Kingfish had been responsible for his political disappointment and his subsequent bitterness. Vail did not have very much to say about the excursions to False River in any case; their significance to him soon centred around Susannah Prescott, and he was not ready to talk about her yet. He had not outgrown his childish habit of taciturnity, and none of his elders tried to force his confidence or restrict his freedom; it was taken for granted that he could come and go as he pleased, and that he would want to go more than he did when Sybelle was at home, because he missed her companionship. But until he told Cresside about Susannah, when they were on their way to the Plaquemine Sugar Festival, it had not occurred to any of them that he had already found another companion who meant even more to him.

Vail had first met Susannah at Jarreau's, and after that once or twice at the Triple Arch and the Island Queen; but her parents did not allow her as much latitude as most of the local girls were permitted. If she went to a fish supper with her friends, Mr. and Mrs. Prescott went too; although they sat at a separate table, they made their restraining presence felt just the same. They required their daughter to leave the Friday evening dances at ten-thirty, and they did not let her go to the Saturday dances at all, once they had seen the young mothers dancing and nursing their babies at the same time; moreover, they always took her home themselves. But at the Bouanchauds' house and at Glenwood she was not quite so strictly chaperoned, and Vail was everlastingly grateful to Miss Josie for giving him his long-sought chance to see Susannah alone.

He dwelt on this episode now as he swung into the driveway and came in sight of the Big House at Belle Heloise. Most of the crowd had assembled, as usual after Sunday dinner, in the huge chamber back of the parlour at Glenwood; it was the favourite gathering-place. But Susannah did not care for it. She did not make this too obvious, because she was too well-bred; just the same, she managed to convey the impression that she had never been accustomed to sitting in bedrooms in mixed groups, and that she would a little rather not. She lingered behind in the parlour, and Vail lingered too. Several of their fellow-guests called to them, but Miss Josie glanced at them and went on without them to the huge chamber, which was dominated by two enormous four-posters.

'They're having a good time where they are,' she said. 'Why not just leave them alone for a while?'

Susannah had seated herself on an old horsehair sofa, crossing her small feet in front of her and folding her slim hands in her lap. She did not say anything at all; she simply sat there, looking composed and contented and very, very pretty. Vail, who had never cared for noisy girls, found himself liking her better than ever when he found she did not immediately start in on the same pointless chatter. He seated himself at the opposite end of the sofa, feeling comfortable and contented too. The silence between them was not awkward; it was companionable. But eventually he was moved to break it.

'This is a nice place,' he said. 'I like to come here.'

'Yes. I do too.'

'You live in a pretty nice house yourself, don't you?'

'I think it's nice.'

'I'd like to see it some time, if I could.'

'I'm sure father and mother'd be very pleased if you'd care to come and call.'

'Sure enough? You think I could come this evening?'

'I don't know why not. I don't think they have any other engagement.'

'Maybe I could take you home. Then, if it was all right, I could come on in. Were you planning to go home with anyone special?'

'No. Just any way it happened.'

Mr. and Mrs. Prescott did not insist on taking their daughter home themselves after she had been to parties in private houses during the daytime. But in return for this concession it was understood she was to remain with a group. She did not 'date', she was not 'going with' anyone – in fact, Mr. and Mrs. Prescott considered both these expressions, and the practices they described, extremely vulgar.

'Do you think your father and mother would mind a lot if it would be with me? I mean, without anyone else along?'

Susannah raised her eyes and considered him carefully. This was not upsetting to Vail either. He preferred a girl who thought things over, the way he did, to one who jumped at the chance of going anywhere, any time, alone with a boy. Besides, she had beautiful eyes, and when she raised them he had a really good look at them; usually they were half hidden by her long black lashes.

'Don't you have to take some of the crowd back to Baton Rouge in your car?' she inquired at length. She had learned to speak of the 'crowd' since coming to New Roads, though she had never done so when she was going to the Winsor School in Boston.

'Yeah. But I'll have plenty of time to come back and get them. They'll be whooping it up for hours yet.'

A sudden burst of merriment from the bedroom served to confirm this statement. Susannah rose, smoothing down her skirt.

'All right. Let's go and tell Miss Josie good-bye straight off, shall we? Unless you'd like to stay longer, of course.'

A month or two earlier she would have said: 'Let's go and say good-bye to Mrs. Harrison now, shall we?' Vail was impressed with the progress he was making towards talking like a regular human being, and he thought her idea of immediate departure excellent. He hastened to the door at her side.

'I'll bring Leaping Lena right around,' he said enthusiastically. 'Thanks a lot, Susannah.'

That was all there had been to it, except, of course, the ride between Glenwood and Salome. This would have been wonderful if she had only sat beside him on the front seat of the old rattle-trap car, with her hands folded in her lap and her eyes veiled again. But that was not all there was to it. In order to say something, Vail had told Susannah about Maudie and asked whether she liked dogs too. After thrilling him beyond words merely by saying that she did and listening politely to his praise of Maudie, she had gone on to tell a very exciting story.

'I have a dog now too. I never had one before, but this German Police was on the place when we came, so mother let me keep him. His name's Major.'

'That's a nice name for a German Police.'

'Yes, I think so. He's a very gentle dog and he has a strange story. A wolf is in love with him.'

'A wolf! In love with a dog! I never heard of such a thing!'

'No. I never did either. Would you like to hear the strange story?'

'You bet I would.'

'Well, you see, Mr. McPherson, the man who owned Salome before we did, brought a wolf there that he had caught while he was hunting once in North Louisiana. It was a young lady wolf, a grey timber. He kept her caged at Salome for about two years. Then he decided to set her free again. She ran off into the woods, but every night she came back and stayed with Major. She does still.'

'Gee, I'd like to see her.'

'You can, some time. She never hurts anyone, but she's never been caught again either. She comes to see Major and then she runs off to the woods again. Mr. McPherson kept hounds too, and every once in a while after he set the wolf free he used to invite his friends to Salome – Voralberg its name was then – for a wolf hunt. Of course, he locked up Major beforehand, because, if he hadn't, Major would have tried to protect the wolf. But the men set the pack of hounds after her, and they followed themselves in cars from different points on the plantation. There are old cattle paths all around the place that have been made into good roads. Sometimes the chase lasted so long that they went as much as two hundred miles – not straight, of course, but in circles amounting to that much. But the wolf had so much more endurance than the hounds that finally she exhausted them and won out, and the very next night she would come back to Major again.'

'Does your father have wolf hunts too?'

'No. But Mr. McPherson kept on having them for five years, and still the wolf never stopped coming. But she's still very wild. She's never "softened" for anyone but Major. She's never had any cubs either.'

Vail was tremendously intrigued with this whole story, which he thought even much more exciting than the one about Romulus and Remus. He was also curious about the conduct of the wolf with the police dog when she was in heat, but he decided, rather quickly for him, that it would not be suitable to ask Susannah questions on such a subject or discuss it with her, at least until he knew her a little better. In any case, they were already turning into the driveway at Salome, and afterwards there was only time for a brief stilted call in the formal drawing-room before he had to go back to the crowd. At least, that was all there had been for that day. Since then he had been to Salome a number of times, and once Phil had gone with him. . . .

For a moment the image of Phil at Salome rose up to disturb Vail's happy memory. Phil had been instantly at home there, as he was every place. He had not minded the formality of the drawing-room, or the restraining presence of Mr. and Mrs. Prescott, or the precision of the service at supper, for which Susannah's parents, unbending for the first time, invited the two boys to remain. It was because of Phil, not because of Vail, they had done that. Vail had never made them laugh, the way Phil did; he had never asked them easy questions or told them funny stories. They had taken an instant liking to Phil, and that was clear enough; they had urged him to come to Salome whenever he felt like it. But Phil had neglected this golden opportunity, never going to Salome a second time. He had his own crowd, which preferred the Amite to False River; and the next week-end, when Vail, trying hard to be fair, asked him to come along, he said hell no, he had other fish to fry besides those you could get at Jarreau's. He did not so much as refer to the Prescotts' kindness.

So Vail had gone thankfully back to Salome by himself, and Susannah, after asking briefly for Phil, had amazed and delighted Vail by inviting him to be her escort at the Plaquemine Sugar Festival, for by that time she had written the prize-winning essay and had been chosen to represent St. Joseph's Academy. And now he had told Aunt Cresside and Rick Tramonte all about her, and was eager to tell Mom and Dad and *grand'mère* too. . . .

Maudie came bounding out to meet him as he put up his car in the shed, and continued to leap along beside him as he entered the Big House. It was nearly always quiet there in the early evening, when Mom was still in the *garçonnière* and Dad still in the fields and *grand'mère* resting, and there was something very pleasant about the abiding peacefulness. Today it was even quieter than usual, for with Phil and Joyeuse both in town and Franchot in bed there was no one around to make any noise. Vail was very sorry for Franchot, the poor kid was sick such a lot. He decided to go over to the *garçonnière* straight off and see if he could do anything to help pass the time for the little boy; but first he would get rid of his books – for a while, anyhow. He was on his way to his own room with them when *grand'mère* called him.

'Is that you, Vail? I should like to speak to you a minute before you go out again.'

He went willingly enough into the boudoir. His grandmother, who was, as usual, enthroned on her sofa, indicated the Turkish chair beside it.

'Did you have anything you meant to do just now, Vail?'

'I thought I'd see if Franchot would like to play checkers or something, that's all. Do you know how he's feeling?'

'He is better. Suppose you stay with me a few minutes first.'

'All right.'

Vail sat down in the Turkish chair and waited. He did not have to wait long.

'Your Aunt Cresside came out to dinner this noon, Vail. She told us that you had taken her to the Sugar Festival in Plaquemine yesterday.'

'Yes, I did. I thought she got quite a kick out of it too. Didn't she speak as if she'd had a good time?'

'She spoke of meeting a family named Prescott, from Boston, distantly kin to Charles Boylston and now living in New Roads.'

'Well, I thought she liked them too.'

'Apparently they are persons of some background, in their own way. I have always liked Mr. Charles Boylston, Vail; I believe you are aware of that. I see no reason for assuming in advance that I would not like his kinsfolk. But I am surprised you have never told us before of this new acquaintance, since apparently it is important to you.'

'I didn't know it would seem important to you, *grand'mère*. If I had I'd have been glad to tell you about it.'

'It is important to me also.'

'Well, there really isn't a lot to say. Except there's a girl I like, and I reckon Aunt Cresside's told you that already.'

'Yes. She told me this girl was very lovely to look at, that she carried herself and conducted herself with great dignity. I could see that she was most favourably impressed with everything about her, and I was inclined to be favourably impressed also, until your Aunt Cresside mentioned something she had said at the end of the evening which seemed to me rather lacking in restraint.'

Vail thought for a minute, trying to isolate one speech of Susannah's from all the others. 'You mean the joke about Phil?' he finally asked. 'Why, Aunt Cresside didn't take that seriously! She couldn't have. It didn't amount to anything. You mustn't take it seriously either, *grand'mère*.'

He rose and walked over to the window. He did not want to talk about Susannah any more just then, after all. He had been glad to until the subject of Phil had come up. He was slightly ashamed because he found this so irritating, but there it was.

'Just hearing about Susannah isn't enough,' he said. 'I want you to invite her over here – with her father and mother. I reckon Aunt Cresside's told you that too. She promised me she and Uncle Fabian would go over to New Roads for one of the Sunday breakfasts the Prescotts have, and then I thought we could ask them all to Belle Heloise for Sunday dinner. Let's wait and talk about Sue after that, shall we? I really have a lot to do right now.' He looked out of the window, and then he smiled, as if he had thought of something that pleased him. 'I'll tell you what, *grand'mère*,' he said. 'I'll bet you dollars to doughnuts that when you see her you'll say here's a girl at last, good enough for the green rose!'

CHAPTER FIFTEEN

THE indicated exchange of civilities between Belle Heloise and Salome began almost immediately.

The Sunday following the Sugar Festival, Fabian and Cresside called on the Prescotts, and the call was promptly returned. An exchange of invitations next ensued, with Cresside taking the lead by asking the Prescotts to a garden party, and at the garden party Gervais and Merry, Vail and Philogene were all present. Waiving formality, the Prescotts proceeded to invite all the d'Alverys to Sunday morning breakfast, even though Gervais and Merry had not yet called – a departure from precedent which, as far as the Prescotts were concerned, represented a real landmark. Only Madame d'Alvery and the younger childen were missing when the family delegation set out for New Roads to attend this time-honoured festivity; and a week later the two clans came together in full force, when the d'Alverys entertained the Prescotts at Belle Heloise.

By this time Sybelle, having returned from Grand Coteau, was home again for her summer vacation, and helped to welcome the guests. Charles Boylston, who had briefly reopened Hackberry Hall, was included in the Prescott group; and the Pereiras, who were week-ending at Belle Heloise, relieved the family atmosphere. The household servants, scenting a budding romance and revelling in the prospect, outdid themselves to impress the Yankees and the city people with the sumptuous fare and skilled service to which their own white folks were accustomed. The codfish balls and baked beans, the brown bread and apple sauce served by the Prescotts on their blue Canton ware were meagre indeed compared to the shrimp and oyster gumbo, the turkey and cornmeal dressing, the okra and rice and spoon bread, and the puff pudding which Lou Ida excitedly prepared and which Selah served with dignity on the Sèvres plates which had been painted to order for Evaline Estrade with the complete history of Evangeline. Madame d'Alvery, wearing all the ancestral jewels she still retained after fulfilling her votive offering, presided in regal fashion at the head of a table covered with old lace and set with ancient silver. Gervais, resuming his neglected rôle of genial host and expansive man of the world, played this again to perfection. Merry, wearing a new and becoming dress which Cresside had chosen for her, looked young and lovely again, and Cresside herself was, as usual, the personification of chic and charm. Fabian, almost as familiar as the Prescotts themselves with the distant parts of the globe where they had lived, conversed about these with understanding and ease, and the poise which Sybelle had acquired at her Convent school enhanced her artless graces. Mrs. Randall contrived to be unusually agreeable and Miss Mittie contributed several New England witticisms. Indeed, the only members of the family group who did not endeavour to create a favourable impression, and signally succeed in doing so, were Frances Belle and Philogene.

Frances Belle was restless. She did not like to sit for such a long time at the table, keeping still while a lot of grown-up people she did not know talked about a lot of things she did not understand. She wanted to jump up and run around, and she wanted to talk herself. Moreover, though she was fond of food, she did not want it all at one big meal like this, either; she wanted to have some of the things she liked best for dinner and the rest at intervals during the afternoon. Her instinct told her that Lou Ida would not want any chilluns running in and out of the kitchen after this feast was finished; she would want to go back to her own quarters and rest her feet and discuss the Prescotts with the other servants. Frances Belle also resented her separation from Vail. It was tacitly understood that she was always to sit beside him when she came to Belle Heloise, and here he was placed between Susannah Prescott and Nellie Pereira, while she herself was wedged in between Franchot and Barry Pereira. Franchot did not talk much because he was not feeling very well, and, though she knew she ought to be sorry for him on this account, she was feeling too sorry for herself to have much sympathy left over; and Barry Pereira never talked much to anyone except Joyeuse, who was sitting on his other side, telling how crazy she was about her chemistry course. Frances Belle grew more and more silent and sullen, and then she began to pout. Finally she got up from her seat and whispered first to her father and then to her mother, who looked at each other and said, all right, if *grand'-mère* was willing, she might be excused now. Mr. and Mrs. Prescott, who missed no detail of her behaviour, told each other afterwards that they simply could not understand why Mr. and Mrs. Fabian d'Alvery, who were such charming, cultured persons themselves, had not taught that horrid little girl better manners.

Philogene's conduct was even more reprehensible; he was worse than restless, he was rebellious. He had already made plans to go with his own crowd to Amite when he was informed that he was expected to be on hand for the Prescotts. At first he had flatly declined to do any such thing; it had taken an admonition from his father, much sterner than those Gervais usually gave Philogene, to bring him around; and though he had stayed at home, because he had been forced to, it was with the mutinous resolution that he would show that prim, stuck-up little Yankee Vail had such a crush on just what he thought of her anyway. Susannah, who had been secretly fearing that she would not have a chance to talk to him, was overjoyed to find that though Vail was on one side of her, Philogene was on the other. But her joy was short-lived; Philogene displayed none of the fascination which had so captivated her and her parents on the occasion of his one visit to Salome. He answered her in gruff monosyllables when she spoke to him, and spoke about nothing at all of his own accord; and as soon as dinner was over he mysteriously diappeared, and was seen no more for the rest of the evening.

When Mr. and Mrs. Prescott referred to him, in the course of the drive home, in the same disparaging way that they had spoken of Frances Belle, Susannah quickly defended him. She did not believe he was feeling well. Someone had told her Franchot was not, but she thought that was a mistake; she thought it must be Phil instead. He had given up other plans in order to be home that day; he had told her so himself. Well, he would not have done that unless he had meant to be pleasant, now would he? Yes, she did think Madame d'Alvery was a very fine-looking old lady. Yes, she did like both Mr. and Mrs. Fabian d'Alvery and Captain and Mrs. Gervais d'Alvery, and she did think Sybelle and Joyeuse and Franchot were all very nice. But she still liked Phil the best. She had told him she hoped he would come over to New Roads the next time Vail did, and he had said he wasn't sure, he thought he might be going to Amite, but he would come if he could. She believed he would come, and that the next time he would be feeling all right again.

While the Prescotts were discussing the d'Alverys, the d'Alverys were equally busy discussing the Prescotts. Sybelle told Vail, very sweetly, that she thought Sue was lovely and that she did not wonder he was crazy about her; but a minute later her lips began to tremble, and when he asked her cripes, what was the matter, she asked him if he didn't wonder she felt badly to think the whole family would break their necks, like this, to be nice to his girl and her family, when Riccardo and his parents were never asked to the house for so much as a cup of coffee, and when she hadn't got to go to the junior prom. Here she had been home just a few days, and Dad and *grand'mère* were already saying they thought it would be a good plan for her to make a nice long visit to their kin in New Orleans, and Mummy was not saying anything; so probably she would have to end up by going.

'I wish I could do something to help, Syb. You know I think Rick's a grand guy. You know I don't want you to go away. I've missed you like hell all winter.'

'You've gone over to New Roads nearly every week-end. I don't believe you missed me over there.'

'Yes, I did. That is, I knew it would have been even more fun if you'd have been along. Look, Syb, I'm going to try to work something. I'm going to see if we couldn't fix it so Rick could go along to New Roads the next time I do, and you too. You don't have to start making those visits right off, do you?'

Sybelle shook her head, her brimming eyes overflowing. 'It's no use, Vail. You know the Prescotts wouldn't invite Rick to their house either, and that's where you really want to go, when you talk about New Roads, isn't it? I'll just have to wait. But I can tell you one thing. I'll never look at anyone else, not if I live to be a thousand. And I can tell you another. Just as soon as I'm of age, I'm going to elope. Rick says now he won't let me, but maybe by that time he'll be just as whipped down as I am now!'

She sat down on the bench beside the refectory table and turned her head away, so that Vail would not see that she was crying, even though she realized that he knew it. Ordinarily he would have sat down beside her and tried to comfort her. But now, hearing approaching footsteps, he merely put a steadying hand on her shoulder and spoke in a warning voice.

'Hang on to yourself if you can, Syb. Someone's coming.'

As he spoke, the door from the hall into the patio was thrown open, and Mr. William Pereira came out, rubbing his hands together and smiling with an air of great heartiness. He had put on considerable weight with the years, and his phenomenal prosperity had increased his inherently cheerful outlook on life. At the moment he was replete with good food and good wine and he had found his fellow-guests excellent company. He could not have been in better humour.

'Well, well!' he said jovially. 'What are you doing, off here by yourselves? Not badgering your sister about her boy friend by any chance are you, Vail?'

'No, sir, we were just talking. I was telling her—'

'Don't you let him try to put anything over on you, young lady,' Billy Pereira persisted. 'You're in a position to give back as good as you get, these days. And this is the lad who tried to persuade me that the reason he wanted to go into the coffee business was because he wasn't interested in sugar! Well, now we know what he *is* interested in, don't we, Sybelle?'

'I reckon I didn't explain just right, sir. What I meant to say was—'

'Oh, I know what you meant to say and what you meant to keep up your sleeve, too! But the cat's out of the bag now all right. Well, I seem to be getting as much mixed on my metaphors as Mrs. Prescott does. . . . Have you noticed whether Sue's inherited that from her mother, Vail?'

'I don't think she has, Mr. Pereira. But anyhow—'

'Anyhow, it wouldn't matter if she had? Suits you right down to the ground, eh, just the way she is? Now I tell you what, Vail. It never does any harm to look around a bit. That's what I'd do if I were you. I wouldn't let this little Yankee have the satisfaction of knowing you'd fallen for her, hook, line and sinker. I'd keep her guessing. I'd let her worry. It's good for girls to worry. Why, look at Sybelle here, worrying her head off, and she was never prettier in her life!'

'If you don't mind my saying so, Mr. Pereira—'

'But I do mind. I'm giving you good advice and I'm telling you you ought to take it. Just the same, I'll say this too, Vail. Now that I really know what your interests are, I'll make you a better offer – thirty a week instead of twenty-five, whenever you care to start. Any young couple ought to be able to manage on thirty a week. You could, couldn't you, Sybelle, if you had the chance?'

There was seemingly no end to Mr. Pereira's joviality. Sybelle and Vail continued to writhe under it, while he went on and on. Meantime the 'small fry' had all gathered in the parlour around the old piano, and were singing vociferously to the accompaniment of Joyeuse:

> *'Va-il d'Alvery, so they say,*
> *Goes a-courtin' ev'ry day.*
> *Sword and pistol by his side,*
> *Susy Prescott for his bride!'*

The strains of this song, which none of the singers seemed to find it tedious to repeat, penetrated easily to the patio. Vail could feel his face flushing and his temper rising; if it had not been for Sybelle, he would probably have 'blown up'. But he did not want to risk adding to her discomfiture, and at last the ordeal ended. The small fry deserted the piano and rushed out into the yard for a game of croquet. The Pereiras announced that they must allow for a brief stop at Hackberry Hall on their way to New Orleans, and Charles Boylston departed to prepare for their coming. Cresside and Fabian went home too, deciding that was the best place for Frances Belle, who was still sulking. The members of that immediate family had the Big House to themselves again, and assembled in the library to enjoy a quiet evening and talk over the day.

'I like those people,' Merry said, unequivocally. 'I like them all. I'm glad we've met them. I hope they'll come to Belle Heloise very often.'

'That man Prescott's nobody's fool.' Gervais also spoke without hesitation. 'Vail, you said he was a retired diplomat, and I had an idea he was just sitting around on his hands these days. But it seems he tinkers with machinery all the time. He's had two or three inventions patented already. Now he thinks he's on the track of something that'll revolutionize cane cutting. I suppose it would be too much to hope that anything would come out all right in this wretched business—'

'The P.O.J. came out all right.'

'Yes, I grant you that, Merry. But with all these governmental restrictions on acreage and marketing that we've got now, we're almost back to where we were before we started those experiments. Just the same, it would help if we could solve some of our labour problems by machinery. That problem's bound to get worse instead of better. Those strikes they're having in France are just the forerunners of what we've got to expect here.'

'That child spoke excellent French,' Madame d'Alvery interposed. 'Her parents' was good, but hers is better – *vraiment, de l'académie!* I was interested in her account of the False River dances. They have evidently made quite an impression on her, and she describes them very well. I used to go to dances in New Roads occasionally when I was young, Gervais – more often than you and Cresside ever did, I think.'

'Did you, *maman*? I never heard you speak of it before.'

'Possibly not. . . . I also went once to a dance in a public hall in Back Brulé with your father shortly after we were married – Doiron's, I think the name of it was.'

'Tell us about it, *grand'mère*,' Sybelle urged, with genuine interest.

'Well, the hall was just a rough structure divided into two rooms, a large one for dancing and a small one where the children who were brought along could be put to sleep, some in beds and some on quilts spread out over the floor. In the larger room there were benches surrounding the wall where the older members of the community sat and watched the dances. The local girls were in *robes de style* made of flowered cretonne, identical as to cut but different as to design. They had all provided their escorts beforehand with enough material for blouses to match their dresses; hence it was easy to tell which young men and which young girls were interested in each other.'

'That's not so hard, ever,' muttered Vail, whose spirits were beginning to revive.

'A violin and an accordion furnished the music and the party opened with the Lancers,' Madame d'Alvery continued, without appearing to notice his interruption. 'Only those in costume were allowed to take part in this, though outsiders were welcome to look on and join in the subsequent figures. But of course my husband wished to participate in every dance, and knowing beforehand of this ruling, he had insisted that we go provided for it. So I had a very lovely *toile de Jouy* made on purpose for the occasion, and we danced with the others. I remember that the refreshments consisted only of Creole gumbo, baked sweet potatoes and black coffee – a rather extraordinary menu, but I must admit that it tasted good.'

'I'll bet it did,' Vail said, thinking of the gumbo at Breaux's restaurant in Plaquemine.

'My husband enjoyed it so much that he wanted to make up a party again the following summer. Of course it was impossible at any other time of the year.'

'Why, *grand'mère*?'

'Because such expeditions could be undertaken only when the dirt or plank roads were passable and it did not take too long to go with a horse and buggy – remember, we had no "pave" then and no automobiles. So we made our plans. But the next summer my poor little baby was only a few months old and I could not leave him. My husband suggested that I should take him, after the fashion of the Back Brulé women – which I gather is still the fashion in the countryside around False River.'

Madame d'Alvery paused in her recital and smiled. Her family, who had never before heard of the expedition she had just described and who had never known her to tell a story in this vein either, waited, with suppressed astonishment, for her to continue.

'It was the sort of jest he enjoyed,' she said. 'Indeed, I do not think he would have been in the least nonplussed if I had taken him at his word. But I could never unbend as he did. ... I lost my poor little baby shortly afterwards, and then of course I did not dance again, at Doiron's Hall or anywhere else. But I believe I still have that *toile de Jouy* dress put away somewhere, though I have not seen it in a long time. I shall ask Lucie to look for it. I recall that the pattern was made up of rose garlands and blue lovers' knots against a cream background. Possibly Susannah might be interested in seeing it or even wearing it, if costume dances are becoming general again. I believe, Merry, that it would compare favourably with the dress she wore in Plaquemine, from what Cresside told us of that.'

'I'm sure it would, Madame Mère. I'd like to see it myself.'

'Well, we will look it up. Susannah would set it off very well. She has been taught to stand and sit properly, which is something in this day and age. You really must speak to Joyeuse, *chère*. She sprawls over everything. When she sits with her knees spread apart and her toes turned in, as she does half the time now, it is almost more than I can bear. I suppose it is what comes of sending her to a public school. And does she have to wear socks and sneakers, except for sports? After all, she is thirteen now, and unless I am very much mistaken, Barry Pereira is beginning to be *épris* with her. It is ridiculous, but it appears to be true. If she is old enough to have a beau she is old enough to act like a young lady. Well, as I was saying – the little Prescott really does act like a lady. She even enters a room with grace, which in my experience is rare in the young. I notice that she does not wear socks and sneakers. I must say she is very suitably dressed. Very stylishly too. You may be sure everything she has comes from Paris.'

It was some hours later before Fabian and Cresside spoke about Susannah. They had gone to bed early, almost as soon as Frances Belle, for they were unaccountably tired, and Fabian had fallen asleep almost immediately. He woke to the realization that Cresside was also awake, and guessed that she had not slept at all. He reached out his arms and drew her towards him.

'Anything the matter, darling?' he asked gently. 'You're not worrying about Vail, are you?'

'Yes, I am.'

'But you knew this would happen some time.'

'Yes, some time. But not when he was only sixteen.'

'Most boys have crushes as young as that, Cresside. I know I did. Not that it got me anywhere.'

'That's what I'm worrying about, mostly. He's so young to be hurt.'

'There's no certainty that he will be, is there?'

'No, but I'm afraid he will. I'm afraid this isn't just a crush. I'm afraid it's the real thing. And I'm selfish, like most women. I'm not ready to lose him so soon. I didn't think I would.'

'Well, there's one person you'll never lose. You know that, Cresside. Doesn't it help at all?'

'Yes. I do know that. And it does help. A lot.'

She put her face close to his in the dark and kissed him. Then she lay very quiet in his arms. They were still around her, holding her and supporting her, when she finally went to sleep.

CHAPTER SIXTEEN

VAIL went to bed, the night after the momentous gathering of the clans, in a glow of happiness. The day had seemed perfect to him from beginning to end, and only one regret crossed his mind: he wished he had told his family about Susannah Prescott months sooner; as it was he had wasted a great deal of time which might have been far more profitably spent. But even this regret was short-lived. He was too elated over the satisfactory present to dwell with disappointment on the wasted past, especially as he foresaw an increasingly rosy future. Now that Susannah had come once to Belle Heloise, he was sure she would be coming right along; she would be there for the swimming and the fishing and the sand dances that summer, and in the fall for hunting. Sybelle would ask her to slumber parties, and they would sleep in the very next room to his, which was an exciting thought, just in itself; they would get to be close friends, the way girls did when they sat up whispering to each other half the night, and this would create another bond between him and Susannah. Of course, Sybelle would also go with him to New Roads, and he would find a way to get Rick there too, whatever Rick and Sybelle might say about it themselves. Suppose the Prescotts were just as unreasonable about pedlars' sons as the d'Alverys? Rick had managed the sand dances, and if he could do that he could certainly manage Jarreau's. . . .

In these rosy dreams Vail failed to consider the eventuality that, though Susannah did come to Belle Heloise several times during the early part of the summer, it was neither Sybelle's company nor Vail's for which she showed a marked partiality, but Phil's; and that, though the twins were frequently asked to Salome, Phil was always included in these invitations. Then in August Mrs. Prescott found that she could not stand the heat in Louisiana any longer, and departed for Bar Harbour, taking

Susannah with her; to make a bad matter worse, when she re-joined her husband in November, she left Susannah behind with Boston relatives, to resume her studies at the Winsor School. It appeared that Mrs. Prescott had been disappointed in local scholastic standards; she had also felt that possibly Susannah was going to more parties than were good for a girl of her age, and that it would be better for her to remain in the North most of the time until after her formal début at the Chilton Club. When that had taken place Mrs. Prescott would be delighted to have her daughter enjoy a carnival season in New Orleans, under the right auspices; indeed, she thought they might take a house there for part of one winter. At all events, Susannah would not forget how kind and cordial everyone in Baton Rouge and New Roads had been to her and would look forward to seeing her Louisiana friends again in due course of time. . . .

Vail accepted the first of his own disappointments fairly philo-sophically. He was as ready as anyone to admit Phil's superior attractions – the easy grace, the quick wit, the fluent speech, the laughing ways which he himself lacked. Phil had never gone through an awkward age, mentally or physically; he danced well, he talked well, he wore his clothes well. There was a harmony between his brown hair and his hazel eyes and his delicately tanned skin which was less striking but more pleasing than the violent contrasts in Vail's colouring; even more pleasing, many persons thought, than Sybelle's exquisite blondeness. Phil and Joyeuse looked and acted very much alike, and Franchot would have shared this beguiling resemblance if his sensitive little face had not been so thin and pointed and his bearing listless instead of gay. Vail could understand why Susannah should have found Phil better company in many ways, and he did not begrudge his brother her preference for sharing superficial pleasures with him; Vail felt that somewhere deep within her she must instinctively feel that he really counted to her for more in important respects, because she counted so tremendously to him, and that presently the superficial pleasures would not matter. He thought, since he knew beyond any shadow of a doubt that she was destined to be his sweetheart, she could not help finding it out too, sooner or later.

Phil's own attitude towards Susannah was responsible, in no small measure, for this absence of active jealousy. He soon ceased to avoid her or to treat her rudely, but he accepted her favours instead of seeking them, and there was a little condescension mingled with his carefree affability. If he and Susannah became separated from the others in the course of a sport which they all shared, such separations were either accidental or manoeuvred with great delicacy and adroitness by Susannah herself. Phil never instigated them. His attitude towards her was exactly like his attitude towards Nellie Pereira, and Nellie's methods were a little less subtle than Susannah's. Phil took the line of least resistance with girls, and, since Nellie made it more difficult to resist than Susannah, she saw more of him. And she was a very pretty girl too. Vail counted on Nellie to divert Phil more and more as time went on. This confidence helped to quiet the pangs which might otherwise have tormented him.

However, he found it much harder to reconcile himself to Susannah's indefinite removal from the scene. In her absence, the week-end outings to False River completely lost their allure for him, and even the diversions he had always most enjoyed at Belle Heloise began to seem dull, flat, stale and unprofitable. He came in for a good deal of teasing, which he took good-naturedly at first, but more and more touchily as time went on and Susannah did not even answer his letters. Fabian was the only person who succeeded in reasoning with him during this period, or even in persuading him to talk about his troubles.

'You know, I've always thought the only kind of a girl who was worth having was the kind that was hard to get,' Fabian said one day, apropos of nothing in particular, when the two were sitting on a log, resting during a dove hunt. 'It took me five years to persuade your Aunt Cresside to marry me. First I had to get her used to the general idea, and then I had to give her long breathing spaces between proposals. You just can't hurry that sort or badger them. It takes times and it takes tact to get them in the end. Your Aunt Cresside admits herself that if I'd tried to pull anything fast on her everything would have been all over.'

It had always been tacitly understood between them that they should refer to Cresside as Vail's aunt. This time the reference had other implications for the boy, in any case.

'Five years!' he exclaimed in outspoken dismay. 'What on earth did you do with yourself all that time? I should think you'd have gone nuts.'

'Not at all. I was too busy.'

'What doing?'

'Making money, for one thing,' Fabian said practically. 'I knew I'd need plenty if I had a family later on. I don't think your Aunt Cresside's ever gone without anything she wanted. I don't intend that she ever shall. Or Frances Belle either. But I had several other interests besides raking in shekels – my camellias, for instance, and Belizaire. And I did a lot of travelling in connection with my law practice. I learned to speak Spanish, and I met some very interesting people and saw some very beautiful sights.'

'Didn't you ever get low in *your* mind?'

'Lord, yes! Everyone gets low, every so often. And I didn't have anything definite to bank on for a long while. There wasn't any reason why I should have had – then or later, as far as that goes. You'd know that, just to look at me.'

Fabian had never referred to his deformity since the first day he had asked Vail to help him down the levee bank, and Vail seldom thought of it himself, unless it was directly called to his attention. Fabian had too many other attributes which were more arresting.

'All the same, I managed to hang on to a forlorn hope for two years,' he continued, smiling as if certain recollections of the period were not altogether unpleasant. 'And after that it wasn't so hard because the hope wasn't so forlorn. I'll admit the courtship seemed to me more like an endurance test than a romance, almost up to the last. But that was worth waiting for. And so were all the years we've had together since.'

He picked up a dry stick and poked reflectively among the fallen leaves, the happy smile of reminiscence deepening. Then he dropped the stick, brushed some stray twigs off his knees, and put his hand on Vail's shoulder to steady himself as he rose.

'Time we were getting back, I reckon,' he said. 'They'll be looking for you at the Big House and for me on Somerulos Street – seems pretty good to have supper waiting and someone glad to see you when you get in, doesn't it? Fact is, I think that's about the best part of the hunt. We might go out again next Sunday, though, unless you've got something better to do.'

'No. I haven't got anything better to do.'

'Well, for the love of Mike, don't talk about it in that tone of voice, even if you haven't. But look here, Vail, you're beginning to go stale on this place – it's time you got off it for a while. You'd better take a quick trip to Europe with us this summer.'

'Gee, that would be swell, Uncle Fabian, if Dad could spare me—'

'Of course he could during the slack season. We'll take a fast boat – might as well be the *Normandie* – and go wherever you say for a few weeks – France, England, Italy. Afterwards – see here, I don't want to run the subject of Princeton into the ground, but—'

'I've been meaning to tell you. I've decided to go after all – that is, if you still want me to and I can get in.'

'Of course I still want you to and of course you can get in – at least, you can if you really put your back to it and do some sure enough studying between now and next June. I even suggest that we cut down on all this Sunday hunting, much as I enjoy it – a good deal of work can be crammed into long week-ends, as your friend Rick could tell you. By the way, I was glad to hear that he got his Colonelcy. I thought he would. I'm picking that lad to go straight on and up. But don't forget I'm picking you to do the same.'

With his usual deliberation, Vail turned this conversation over in his mind before he began to act upon it. But not long after it took place his correspondence with Susannah changed in both volume and character. Instead of plying her continually with rambling and reproachful letters, he waited for one of her own brief and infrequent missives, and, after allowing a week or so to elapse, answered it in kind. He was working hard as hell, he told her, between school and grinding. His chemistry course was a caution, at least he thought so, though that brat Joyeuse simply ate up anything of the sort. She spent every Saturday fooling around the laboratory at the mill – at least, when she could get the head chemist to let her. He was at the mill till all hours himself, as they were mighty short-handed. He hadn't been over to New Roads in over a month, so he didn't have any news for her about the crowd. He hadn't even been hunting, because he was too busy week-ends. But his Dad was planning a squirrel hunt in the Atchafalaya swamp back at Port Allen to celebrate Phil's birthday, and of course he was going to take time out for that. The whole family was going, even Franchot, who hated hunting, as she knew. But Franchot wanted to please Phil, especially when Dad had gone to all this trouble, and Mr. Lawrason was coming over from Denham Springs too. Mr. Lawrason didn't go in much for squirrel hunting as a rule; he always wanted to use his dogs, so cat hunting was more in his line; but he was making an exception this time, on account of Phil's birthday. After that they would all be too busy in what spare time they had getting roseau reeds ready for the Christmas bonfires, so she mustn't be surprised if she didn't hear from him straight off again. He sent her his best. . . .

Susannah read this letter with more attention than she had given any he had sent her in some time, and answered it fairly promptly, for her. But several weeks went by before she heard from Vail again, and she had actually begun to watch for a letter. When it finally came, she found it contained only a few lines.

'DEAR SUE,

This is just to say I was glad to hear from you, and that I would have written sooner except that Franchot is very sick and I can't seem to think of anything to say but that, because it's all I've got on my mind. I wish to heaven we'd never gone on that damned birthday hunt, and I don't feel right now as if I would ever want to go hunting again, though I suppose some day I shall. I will tell you what happened later on, that is if you want to hear. Meanwhile you must not think it was Phil's fault or Dad's that everything went wrong, and you must excuse this measly little note.

Yours,
VAIL.'

The hunt to which Vail referred with such bitterness began under very pleasant and auspicious circumstances. Harvey Lawrason arrived at Belle Heloise on the eve of Philogene's birthday, bringing with him his trailerful of dogs, as if he hoped that the nature of the trip might be changed at the last moment. However, he took the announcement that the plans stood for a squirrel hunt with hearty good nature, and after an excellent supper, while everyone else sat around the fire listening to him, embarked on a series of typical tall tales. Gervais, who was in rare good humour, rallied him by saying these were not up to his usual standard, however.

'Which-I-God, a funny thing happened last week to a nigger I knew up in Tangipahoa Parish. Quit this nigger's name was. His ma named him that because it was the tenth to come along in twelve years and she figured it was quittin' time for her. But she had another one after all, and named him Golast, and he was. Well, sirs, as I started to say, this nigger Quit went out in the woods to chop, and his wife, Silky, toted his dinner out to him in a bucket, just like she always done. 'Bout the time he knew she was coming he drove his wedge into the top of an old block, and then he sat down on it himself to rest a mite while he waited for her. She see him settin' there when she come along, and he had a grin on his face too; she was a mighty good cook, and he always looked forward to them dinners she brought him. But when she hollered, "Hello, Quit!" he didn't answer her, and after she got up close to him she could see he was dead. The pressure of the wood in that block had drove the wedge up through his body, right where he sat.'

'You say this happened to a nigger you knew up in Tangipahoa Parish, Harvey?'

'Yes, sir, just this last week.'

'Well, it's a funny thing, but my father told me that same story, about a nigger down here on the River Road, when I wasn't more than five years old. I wouldn't go looking for any more stories in Tangipahoa if I were you, Harvey – they're stale. Fact is, I think that's one parish I'd steer clear of anyhow, if I were you. The men up there don't stand for any fooling, when it comes to their womenfolk. They shoot mighty quick. And with tastes like you've got—'

'Which-I-God, I got the same tastes as any man, ain't I? Only difference is—'

'If you're planning to get off at four in the morning, I think the children ought to start for bed early,' Merry said, rather hastily. Franchot was snuggled up on the sofa beside her, half asleep already, and she ran her hand lovingly through his hair. 'This little boy seems to be coming down with another cold,' she said. 'He's been sneezing all day. I believe he's a bit feverish now, too. I think perhaps he'd better not go after all.'

'But, Mummy, I want to.'

'You know, you don't like squirrel hunting much, honey. Remember that first time, when Vail brought you home—'

'Aw, I was just a baby then.' Franchot was wide awake again now, and hastening to defend himself. He spoke almost too eagerly. 'Course I like squirrel hunting – leastwise I'm going to, soon as I get used to it. Besides, this isn't just any old squirrel hunt, right on the plantation. It's a real trip, way over to the other side of Port Allen. And it's Phil's birthday party. Like he had a cake and everything, only different.'

'We're going to have a cake too, anyway, after everybody gets home. You could help me put the candles and the lettering on, if you stayed here.'

'Merry, it's no wonder that boy's a mollycoddle. You pamper him like nobody's business. Right at the very time when he's beginning to get over his silly willies about hunting.'

'There's a phobia of your own, Gervais, you've never got over.'

'Good God, Merry, are you trying to compare a natural antipathy for poisonous snakes with squeamishness about the mere sight of blood?'

'About needless killing? And calling it sport? Yes, I am.'

They were on the verge of one of those heated arguments which roused Gervais to quick and violent rage and transformed Merry's characteristically gentle and yielding attitude to one of stubborn resistance. Their love for each other was still strong and vital after all these years; but they had never achieved the complete harmony which existed between Fabian and Cresside, and a struggle of wills, like the one which was now beginning, completely disrupted the pleasant atmosphere. Vail, who was always acutely uncomfortable during such scenes, rose and edged over to Franchot, throwing a persuasive arm around his shoulder.

'You heard what Mom said about getting to bed, brat. Come on let's go. I thought maybe you'd sleep in my room tonight. Then one of us would be sure to wake up the other on time.'

'I thought Phil was going to sleep there.'

'Well, he is. But hell's bells, there's room for all three of us, isn't there?'

It was the first time Vail had made such a suggestion, and Franchot was thrilled at this admission into the fellowship of his older brothers. He was still more excited when he really did wake up first. He had been restless all night, partly with the fear that he would oversleep, and partly because his cold, which seemed to be getting worse, made him uncomfortable. But in his elation over the chance of rousing both Vail and Phil from their profound slumbers he forgot his aching head and sore throat; and when Vail asked him, during their hasty breakfast, how was the cold this morning, he said truthfully enough that he felt fine, he thought it was gone. Gervais, noticing his flushed cheeks, asked him the same question and received the same answer. Well, the flush was probably due to excitement, then, Gervais decided, not without reason; for Franchot's apparent exhilaration lasted during the drive to Port Allen and over the old logging roads behind it. The woods which the hunters soon entered were the dismal type of low cypress, where quantities of gaunt black 'knees' projected from pools of stagnant water and the scattered gum trees were already bare of leaves; and as the ground became increasingly soggy they got out of their cars and started to separate into groups of two. It had originally been Gervais' intention to keep Phil with him and send Franchot off with Vail; but, proud of the little boy's sudden staunchness, he made an abrupt change of plan.

'You tag along with me, son, and I'll show you some real sport. Before the day's over you'll forget you ever thought you didn't want to hunt. Listen, do you hear that bluejay? He's warning all the other creatures in the woods that someone's coming. We have to keep mighty quiet for a few minutes.'

There was a period of profound silence. Gervais stood with his arm around Franchot's shoulder, waiting. Then a flock of crows circled overhead, calling harshly and interrupting their flight to swoop down towards one tall tree after another.

'They've found an owl,' Gervais whispered to Franchot. 'He was asleep, but they waked him up. Now they're chasing him from tree to tree, pecking at him.'

'Will they hurt him?'

Gervais could feel Franchot flinching as the child asked the troubled question. He answered nonchalantly.

'Not to worry about. Just watch, Franchot, and I'll show you lots of other interesting things. You must keep your eyes open in the woods and your ears too. That's a Lord God you hear now.'

'A Lord God?'

'Yes, a very large woodpecker with a big topknot. You can't see him, though. He may be as much as half a mile away. He gets on a hollow stub in a swamp and raps away at it. "Log God" is the old English name for him. That's how come the coloured folks got it changed around to "Lord God". Some of them even call him "Papa Lord God"!'

Franchot listened attentively. Nothing about the deliberate beat of the woodpecker's rapping suggested pain, and the longer he stood still the longer the evil moment of killing could be postponed. Presently he heard another sound, this time one that was vaguely familiar.

'Isn't that a cat bird, Daddy?'

'No, it's a cat squirrel. I'm not surprised you thought it was a cat bird, though. They sound a lot alike. He must have seen some of the others in our party. We'll wait here a minute or two longer and give someone else a chance for the first shot.'

The delay added to Franchot's sense of reprieve, but he was chagrined at having mistaken the cat squirrel for a cat bird. He had often watched squirrels in the woods back of Belle Heloise and had learned a good deal about them. He knew that when they were feeding on cypress balls you could hear them a long way off, just as he had heard the woodpecker a few minutes before. He could even recognize two distinct sounds – the noise the squirrels made while they were gnawing the cypress balls with their teeth and the noise the pods made after these had been emptied of seeds by the squirrels and were dropping in a light patter on the dry leaves which covered the ground. He knew that after a squirrel had finished with one ball it would scamper to a limb from the crotch of the tree where it had been feeding and begin searching for another seed pod; and that after it had eaten all it wanted, if nothing happened to disturb it, then it would start playing with two or three squirrels. It would race round and round the trunk of the tree, flipping its bushy tail in the air, and sometimes it would even leap from one tree to another, which was still a prettier sight. On the other hand, if it caught sight of a human being, it gave three or four short, sharp barks close together, thereafter moving very quietly, to keep the tree between itself and its probable enemy, and then 'freezing'. Since Franchot knew all this, he felt he should also have known enough not to mistake a bird's note for a squirrel's bark. He was grateful to Gervais for making light of his error and eager to atone for it. So, instead of seeking further reprieve, he assented with apparent willingness when Gervais suggested it was time they were getting on with their hunt.

For some moments more they kept together, moving quietly forward. They heard two shots, close together, and then, after an interval, a third one farther off. The others were beginning to get their squirrels, Gervais remarked; possibly they had come across a wood duck too. But it was squirrels they were really out for this go-round. And it was about time for Franchot to start looking for them himself. How about this point for a stand? It looked pretty good to Daddy because there was a clear vision of the upper limbs all around. He was going farther on himself, but he would be within easy calling distance if Franchot wanted him – only of course no one shouted on a hunt unless there were a darn good reason for it. But he knew Franchot realized that. He would come back after a while, whether he were called or not. Meantime Franchot was on no account to leave his stand. If he wandered off he might get lost for true. Well, so long and good hunting!

Franchot did not voice any objection when Gervais suggested leaving him; but after his father had disappeared among the trees he was a little frightened by the stillness and the solitude. These woods were not like those back of the plantation, which he knew and loved so well; they were darker and more dismal, and their strangeness, as well as their gloominess, was disquieting. The crows had ceased their circling and cawing and the woodpecker no longer rapped against his hollow stub. No more shots rang out in the distance either. The silence was complete. But it was not a tranquil stillness; there was a queer tensity to it. Standing watchfully at the point of observation where his father had placed him, and conscientiously watching the upper branches for the squirrel he was expected to shoot, Franchot was conscious for the first time since early morning that his head was hot and his hands cold and that his throat was really very sore.

He was still gazing steadfastly at the trees when his attention was diverted by a strange sound in the distant underbrush. For a time he tried to disregard it, but as it continued, growing a little louder as if it were getting closer, he turned in the direction from which it seemed to be coming and peered with a feeling of mounting fright into the tangle of underbrush. At first he could see nothing; then he became dimly aware of moving branches and of a strange horned creature which was causing this motion. Something enormous and terrifying was unquestionably coming towards him. Franchot dug his feet more firmly into the ground, bit his trembling lips and fired.

The shadowy creature leaped into the air and then charged wildly forward, knocking against the trees which obstructed its path. Franchot dropped his shotgun and screamed. Then he shrank back towards the swamp, overwhelmed with shame and terror. The scream had been involuntary, and he was appalled because he had not managed to suppress it; he knew that while he might have shouted in an emergency the scream would be unforgivable; he had lost his last chance of proving he was not a sissy and a 'fraid cat. And he had no idea what to do next. He had promised not to leave the stand and he ought to keep his promise at least. But the strange wild creature was lunging nearer and nearer, still knocking against the trees as it came.

Another shot rang out and the great animal leapt up again and fell heavily to the ground. The next instant Franchot heard his father's voice calling to him.

'Stay where you are, Franchot. I'll be there straight off.'

'Yes, Daddy.'

He was shivering all over now, no longer with fright, but with the relief which was mingled with his shame and with the cold which was no longer confined to his hands and feet, but which had crept all over him, except to his hot head. He stood still until he caught sight of Gervais hurrying towards him, and then he could not wait any longer. He rushed forward and flung himself against his father.

'Steady there! What made you think you could kill a deer with squirrel shot?'

'I didn't know what it was. I never saw a live deer before, Daddy. I just fired, that's all.'

'You hit him in the eyes with your number six; the shot scattered and blinded him. That's why he thrashed around so. You needn't have been frightened – he couldn't see you and you could have kept out of his way. We must have disturbed him from his bed, moving around, so he started moving himself. But he's good and dead now. Come on and have a look at him.'

'I – I don't want to, Daddy.'

'Nonsense! Of course you want to. He's as fine a nine-point buck as I ever saw. I'll have his head mounted for you, just like I did the bear's I shot in Alaska. He's yours, you know. You really got him.'

'No, I didn't, Daddy. You got him. He's your deer.'

'I only finished him off for you – good thing I brought along a couple of buck shot shells just in case. . . . But I wouldn't have got him unless you'd blinded him first. I'm proud of you, son. I was nearly ten years older than you before I got my first buck and he wasn't nearly as fine as this. Not by a long shot.'

Gervais leaned his shotgun against a tree and fumbled for his hunting knife. When he had freed it from its sheath, he knelt down beside the buck, his face glowing with pleasure as he examined the mighty antlered head. Franchot watched him anxiously while he arched the great neck back and exposed his throat.

'What are you going to do now, Daddy?'

'I've got to cut his throat to bleed him. Afterwards I'll have to gut him too. But before that I'm going to "blood" you. Don't you know every hunter's blooded after he's killed his first deer?'

'But I didn't kill him; you killed him, Daddy! I wouldn't have killed a deer for anything. I said I'd try to kill a squirrel this once because it was Phil's birthday, but I never said—'

'Come on, son! You want Daddy to keep on being proud of you, don't you?' As he spoke Gervais plunged his knife into the angle below the deer's jaw and drew the sharp blade forward and down. A slow flood of dark crimson followed the steel, welling and bubbling out on the grass. He thrust his hand into the blood and jumped up. Franchot backed away from him.

'Don't touch me with that nasty stuff, please, Daddy!'

'Now, now, mighty hunter!' Gervais strode swiftly towards him and clamping the fingers of his left hand into the struggling boy's shoulder, smeared the blood across his forehead. With a sharp cry, Franchot flung his arm over his face to protect this, but Gervais thrust it laughingly aside and spread the evil-smelling liquid over the child's cheeks and neck and rubbed it into his hair.

'Now you're a sure enough hunter at last,' he said triumphantly. 'I was afraid we'd never make you into one, but you've gone and made yourself into one. . . . Stop that screaming, Franchot! Stop, I told you!'

He tried to take hold of Franchot again and to clap his hand over the child's mouth; but this time Franchot eluded his grasp and ran swiftly towards the swamp. When he reached this he leaned above it, dashing the stagnant water over his head. He was no longer screaming when Gervais caught up with him, but he was still sobbing, and he turned to his father with a look of loathing on his blood-streaked little face.

'Don't you touch me!' he cried. 'Don't you ever touch me again! I hate you! I hate you! I hate you!'

Suddenly he began to be sick, retching violently and vomiting into the stagnant water. Gervais, kneeling down again, tried to support him and to soothe him. But Franchot fought him off.

And then, without warning, he toppled over in a dead faint.

Everyone told Gervais afterwards that of course it was not his fault. Everyone, that is, except Merry.

He waited in vain to have her tell him, as everyone else did, that she knew he did not realize Franchot had such a bad cold; if he had, of course he would not have taken the child hunting in the first place. Of course he did not realize how much chilly swamp water had run down Franchot's back when he tried to wash the blood off; otherwise Gervais would have got him out of his drenched clothes. Of course he did not realize that the sight and smell of blood really did make the child sick; if he had, he would never have enforced the hideous ritual of 'blooding' . . . Merry could have said all this, for it would have been true. Instead, all she said was, while she sat by Franchot's bed, waiting for the doctor to come: 'I've always felt that he was more like me than any of the others. I couldn't have stood it either. I've stood a good deal, but I couldn't have stood that.'

She was very quiet, then and afterwards. She did not even say that if it had not taken so long to reach the doctor Franchot would have had a better chance. She never admitted that she was tired during the long days and nights of watching and nursing, of hoping and despairing, that followed the birthday party. She sat, dry-eyed and composed, at the funeral, and stood, still dry-eyed and composed, by the open grave. But when Gervais tried to put his arm around her to support her there, she drew away from him; and when he came into their room that evening she was still wearing the veiled hat that she had worn to the cemetery, and she looked up at him over an open suitcase.

'I was coming to tell you, in just a minute,' she said steadily. 'I'm going to spend the night with Cresside and Fabian. Perhaps several nights. I'm not sure what I'm going to do after that. Except that I'm not coming back here.'

'Merry, you're completely unstrung, you're completely shattered. No wonder, either. But you don't know what you're saying. You couldn't.'

'Yes, I could. I do. And I'm not unstrung. I'm not going to argue with you this time either, Gervais. But I'm going.'

'Merry, I've never needed you so much in my life as I need you now. You can't fail me now.'

'I never have before, have I, Gervais? You'll have to give me credit for standing by, without complaining, through thick and thin for nearly eighteen years.'

'I do, Merry. I never could have pulled through myself without you. I can't go along without you now, either.'

'You'll have to, Gervais.'

'You've got three other children of your own and a foster-child. They all need you too. They can't get along without you either.'

'Vail's almost a man now. He can look after himself and Phil, if you can't, and if Fabian and Cresside don't – but they will. Your mother can look after Sybelle and Joyeuse, at least until we can work out something better. I don't know why we've always treated her as if she were an old woman. She was under fifty when you came home from the war. She isn't old even yet. And she's strong as steel.'

'She didn't do such a good job of looking after Cresside, you may remember, Merry.'

'Well, my mother's here too. That is, I don't suppose you'll turn her out, even if I do go. Or Miss Mittie either. I think I've earned their keep.'

'Merry, how can you be so unjust? You know your mother's welcome, that she always will be, and Miss Mittie too. But they'll be lost without you; we all will. It's been you who's given us courage, who's given us hope, who's given us strength. Don't take all that from us now. We can't survive if you do.'

For a moment he had a faint hope that she might waver. Instead, she turned away from him without answering and continued to pack the open suitcase.

Vail had a very sweet letter from Susannah in answer to the one he wrote telling her that Franchot was ill and that he couldn't think of anything else. A few weeks later he had another, telling him she had just heard about Franchot's death, and that she wanted to let him know how very, very sorry she felt for him. If there were anything at all that she could do . . .

There was nothing that Susannah or anyone else could do for Vail just then. It was one of those times, of which Fabian had warned him before there would be many, when he had to fight his way through alone. It did not make it any easier for him to know that Gervais was fighting through it alone too.

239

NEITHER Fabian nor Cresside tried to reason with Merry or even to talk with her the night after Franchot's funeral, and they managed to make Frances Belle understand that Aunt Merry was very unhappy and very tired too, and that she must not be worried. The little girl was feeling very badly about Franchot herself, so she understood that part; but she did not see why Aunt Merry was coming to Somerulos Street for a rest, instead of just going to bed at the *garçonnière*. However, an unwonted firmness in her parents' manner warned her that it was not the time to disregard their suggestion, and the more she glanced at Aunt Merry on the ride back to town the more she realized that something dreadful must be the matter. Because Aunt Merry not only looked very sad and very tired; she had changed so much in all sorts of ways that she did not seem like the same person any more. She seemed like a total stranger.

After they got home, and Aunt Merry had gone to bed in one of the little dormer guest rooms, Frances Belle called her mother and talked to her about Franchot, and asked if Merry looked the way she did because he had died. Cresside said yes, and then she tried to add a reassuring note.

'I think perhaps Dr. Champagne will come to see Aunt Merry in the morning, darling, and give her something that will make her feel better. Perhaps she'll feel better anyway, after she's had a good sleep.'

'She didn't look as if she were sleepy to me, Mummy. She looked queer. Had she gone to sleep when you came downstairs?'

'No. But I hope she will pretty soon. I hope you will too. Goodnight, honey.'

'Mummy, I don't feel sleepy either. I feel sort of frightened. I wish you'd stay with me.'

'There's nothing to be frightened about, darling. But I'll stay with you if you want me to.'

Cresside lay down beside Frances Belle and gently stroked the little girl's head and back. For a long time Frances Belle tossed restlessly about, but little by little she was quieter, and finally her even breathing betrayed her drowsiness. Cresside waited until she was sure Frances Belle was sound asleep before she herself moved from the bed. Then she tiptoed back to her own room, where she knew Fabian would be waiting for her.

'Frances Belle's upset,' she told him in her troubled voice. 'We oughtn't to have taken her to the funeral. She's too young to see that sort of thing.'

'Is she upset over the funeral or is she upset over Merry?'

'Well, both, I suppose. I'm upset about Merry myself. Aren't you?'

'I'm concerned. But let's not worry too much until we see how she is in the morning. Things do have a way of working themselves out, if you give them a chance.'

'They take a long while sometimes. And this is so out of character. Merry's always faced everything like a good soldier before.'

'Perhaps that's why she can't face this. There's always a limit somewhere. But I confess I wouldn't have expected it of her either. . . . Well, as I said before, let's wait and see what happens in the morning.'

There had still been no sounds from the dormer bedroom when Fabian left for his office the next day, and both he and Cresside hesitated to run the risk of disturbing Merry if she were resting at last. However, at ten o'clock Cresside went upstairs with a tray and knocked on the door, so lightly that the rap could not possibly have roused Merry if she had still been sleeping. But she answered immediately.

'Come in. I'm not asleep.'

'Have you been awake long?'

'I'm not sure, I think so.'

'Well, why didn't you call me when you first waked up, Merry?'

'Why should I, when I didn't want anything?'

'Because of course you wanted something. You always want coffee as soon as you wake up.'

'You mean I always did. I don't anymore. But I'll drink some if you'd like to have me, Cresside.'

Merry sat up in bed and accepted the tray from her sister-in-law's hands, pouring out the coffee and drinking it clear, in slow, small sips. But she did not unfold the napkin in which the rolls were wrapped, or even appear to notice anything on the tray except the coffee, and presently she set the cup down.

'Thank you,' she said. 'Cresside, I've been thinking. . . . I believe I'll go and see Mr. Goldenberg.'

'Today?'

'Yes, today. I don't want to put it off. I'm afraid if I do I won't go, and I believe it's the best thing I *can* do.'

'I hoped you'd stay in bed today, Merry, and rest. I hoped you'd let me send for Dr. Champagne and ask him to give you a strong sedative. If you could have a good long sleep—'

'I don't want a good long sleep. I want to do something. I want to get things settled.'

'I know Mr. Goldenberg's always been a mighty good friend to you, Merry. But do you think that just now—'

'Yes, just now, more than ever.'

Cresside took the tray and turned towards the door. She was afraid that whatever she said might be wrong, and that therefore it was probably better to say nothing. At the same time she did not feel she could let her sister-in-law make the rash move which was evidently in her mind without at least trying to stop her. She set down the tray on a small table and went back towards the bed.

'Merry,' she said with great earnestness, 'I know what it's like to be desperately unhappy myself – you realize that, don't you? I know what it's like to feel trapped with despair, just the way you do now. I would have been trapped, too, if you hadn't helped me. Well, it's my turn now. You must let me help you. I believe I can, if you'll only give me a chance. I won't urge you to go back to Gervais if you feel you can't. I won't talk to you about your duty to your husband and your children. I won't try to stop you from seeing anyone you choose or doing anything you think best, if you'll just wait until you're physically and mentally fit to do it. But you're not now. You're a sick woman – very sick. I'll play fair with you. I won't send for Dr. Champagne unless you tell me I may. But I want you to play fair with yourself. You won't be doing it if you try to get out of bed and go downtown today.'

'I'm not sick. But I am desperate. I've got to find a way out of my despair. I can't do it lying in bed. And no one else can do it for me. Not even you, Cresside.'

'But you said Mr. Goldenberg—'

'I said I wanted to see him. That's all. And I'm going to.'

She pushed away the covering and swung her feet over the side of the bed. Cresside made one more effort.

'Then let me call him up and ask him to come here, Merry. It's a lovely mild day. You can sit on the terrace and talk to him. I promise I won't let anyone disturb you.'

'We've none of us ever invited Mr. Goldenberg to come and see us at home before, have we? I should say this was a mighty poor time to begin. Besides, I'd rather see him at the store. It would seem more natural to me. And this is a business call, anyway.'

'Well, would you let me call up and make sure he's there, and free? I'd hate to have you make the effort for nothing.'

'He's always there and he's always free, as far as I'm concerned. You don't suppose Hazel would try to keep me from seeing him, do you? She's still his secretary, you know. She had the good sense to keep her job after she married. Of course she never had any children.'

It was worse than useless to argue with Merry; Cresside saw that at last. She picked up the rejected breakfast tray and left the room, heavy-hearted.

Merry was right; she had no trouble in penetrating Mr. Goldenberg's private office. She was followed by curious glances as she went through the store, for her deep mourning made her conspicuous, and something in the expression of her pale, set face was also very arresting. However, if she were conscious of the attention she was receiving, she did not betray this. She seemed oblivious of the strangers who stared at her, and she barely acknowledged the greetings of acquaintances, but went steadily on to the little cubicle where Hazel was typing in her old easy, methodical way. Hazel was in the middle of a paragraph when Merry approached, and nodded without looking up, waiting for a good stopping-place before rising to greet the unidentified caller. That was a habit of long standing too, and heretofore Merry had always respected it. But this time she interrupted.

'Hazel,' she said impellingly, 'I want to see Mr. Goldenberg right away.'

Hazel jumped up so quickly that she struck the release on her machine and sent the carriage shooting across to the other side. 'Why, Merry!' she stammered. 'You frightened me! You're the last person in the world I expected to see!'

'I didn't mean to frighten you. Mr. Goldenberg's in, isn't he?'

'Yes, he's in. I'll let him know, straight off, that you're here. ... Merry, I want to tell you that I'm terribly, terribly sorry for you. I think it's the saddest thing I ever heard. I nearly cried my eyes out yesterday at that poor little boy's funeral. I wish there was something I could do for you.'

Hazel's sympathetic eyes filled with tears again. Merry looked at her without any sign of emotion.

'There is. You can tell Mr. Goldenberg I'm here,' she said briefly, and leaned over to straighten a paper.

Neither Mr. Goldenberg nor his office had changed in any noticeable respect since her last visit. He rose to greet her, gravely and quietly, and then he sat down again and regarded her, still gravely and quietly, with his shrewd, bloodshot eyes. He did not express any surprise at seeing her and he did not offer her condolences or ask her questions. He waited for her to say whatever she wanted to tell him, and meanwhile his gravity and quietude were reassuring to her, as they always had been. She did not feel hurried about speaking to him, and she looked around the office, taking in its familiar details, while she prepared to do so. The thermos jar, the bud vase and the picture of Mrs. Goldenberg were still in their accustomed places. Merry remembered now that Mrs. Goldenberg had died some time before, and wondered, fleetingly, if Gervais would keep her picture beside him for years after she was dead. No, of course not. Men did not cherish the pictures of women who left them, only the pictures of women who stood by until they died. She was not standing by, and unfortunately she was not going to die. It was Franchot who had died. ...

'Mr. Goldenberg, I've always found I could talk to you very candidly about everything that matters a great deal to me,' she finally heard herself saying. 'I came and told you when I wanted to get married. I came and told you when I was afraid we'd lose Belle Heloise unless you could help us keep it. Now I've come to tell you that I've left Belle Heloise and my husband.'

'I'm very sorry to hear that, Mrs. d'Alvery.'

'I knew you would be. But still I thought you'd understand, if I told you why, and I want to.'

'I shall certainly try. And when I said I was sorry, I did not mean for a moment to pass judgment. You realized that, I hope. I only meant it seemed a pity you should be disappointed in anything that meant as much to you as your marriage or your home. I should have said that of all the women I have ever known there was never one to whom both meant so much.'

'They meant everything. I was willing to give up everything else for them. At least I thought I was, a long time. I *did* give up a great deal.'

'I am sure you did. No woman could have done so much for her husband, or preserved her home, in the face of great difficulties, the way you did, without making tremendous sacrifices.'

'I did make tremendous sacrifices. I loved Gervais so much I sacrificed my pride and married him when I knew his mother would have done everything she could to keep me out of her house. Then over and over again I sacrificed my will and my judgment so that Gervais could have his own way. The few times I opposed him we quarrelled bitterly, and I dreaded those quarrels; so I avoided them as much as I could. Besides, I *wanted* him to have his way, even when it took him from me. It took him further and further all the time. I didn't realize it would, and I don't believe he did either. I've got to be just. At least, I've got to try.'

'I am sure you would never be anything else, Mrs. d'Alvery.'

'I don't know. I don't think it's right for a woman to talk like this about her husband to anyone. But I've got to talk to someone. I've kept still just as long as I could. I can't stand it any longer. I tried to talk to a priest, but I couldn't do that. You know I wasn't born a Catholic. I only' – she bit back the words – 'I only became one because I knew it would mean so much to Gervais that I convinced myself I believed what he did.' But she might just as well have said them, as far as Mr. Goldenberg was concerned. 'I can't seem to get much out of the confessional,' she went on lamely. 'It isn't that I mind the principle; I think that's wonderful. I looked forward at first to laying my problems before someone wise and righteous, in complete confidence and candour. But there's always a long line of people waiting in a church, every one of them in a hurry, and the priest seems to be in a hurry too. I can't pour out my soul when there's that sense of pressure and haste.'

'No, I can see that would be hard for you.'

'Of course this time a priest would have come to me. But I've been disappointed and thwarted so many times I couldn't risk it again. And I couldn't talk to Cresside, because she's one of the family. Naturally, it would be easier to talk to a woman than to a man, things being equal. But as it was—'

'You know I have always been very much honoured by your confidence. You know I'm very proud that you regard me as your friend.'

'I've got so few,' Merry said in a low voice. 'You see, all these years that I've lived at Belle Heloise I've hardly seen anyone but my family, and I've hardly been off the plantation. I went twice to New Orleans when I was first married, but that's about all. I didn't mind, for a long while. I didn't care whether I ever saw anyone except my husband and my children. Gervais and I were very close at first. Very – very happy. And he enjoyed everything we did together as much as I did. But while I was having children so fast, he got out of the habit of doing things with me. There wasn't money enough to do much anyway. And then gradually he got out of the habit of talking things over with me too, except the things that went wrong. Presently we weren't sharing anything except our troubles. No pleasures. No viewpoints. No ideas. Gervais expected me to make the best of the hard times, and I expected that too. But I didn't expect that after the novelty of marriage wore off he'd prefer to have all his good times without me. I didn't expect he'd find his only serious interest in politics and crops and his only diversion in hunting. I didn't expect he'd never ask what I wanted to do and where I wanted to go or what I thought or how I felt. I didn't expect that when I lost my lover I'd also lost my companion and my mainstay.'

As she went on speaking, her voice became increasingly unsteady. She paused, hoping to bring it back under control, and again Mr. Goldenberg waited quietly for her to go on.

'I heard Regine Hathaway say once that all a man wanted anyway was someone comfortable to sleep with,' Merry said at last. 'I flared up and told her that he wanted a great deal more than that, *in his wife*. I said if that was all he wanted he didn't

246

ask a girl to marry him, he didn't offer her his name and his home and his position, he didn't choose her for the mother of his children. I thought—'

'And you were right in thinking so. You say you want to be just to your husband, and I believe you. So in spite of your feeling that he has failed you, I beg you not to imagine—'

'I'm not imagining anything. I know that he wanted someone to keep his courage up, just as much as he wanted someone comfortable to sleep with. More, after a while. So I tried to do that. No one will ever know how hard I tried. And what happened in the end? He wasn't satisfied with having me sacrifice for him; he wanted to sacrifice the children too. He needed someone to bolster his courage all the time, and yet he called our poor little boy a coward. He drove that child to his death, badgering him and hounding him. If it had only been me instead . . .'

She bowed her head and for a long while she did not even make any attempt to go on. But this time Mr. Goldenberg reached over and took her hand firmly in his.

'You are being very unjust right now,' he said gently. 'When you recover from the shock of this terrible experience, you yourself will be the first to admit it. Captain d'Alvery loved that little boy just as much as you did. He wouldn't willingly or consciously have hurt him for the world. But every father tries to develop manliness in his son. That's what Captain d'Alvery thought he was doing – all he thought he was doing. Harvey Lawrason's been here to see me too, Mrs. d'Alvery. He's another good friend who talks to me confidentially. Perhaps you've never seen it, but there's a very tender side to Harvey's nature. He's completely shot to pieces himself over this. He says none of them had the slightest idea the child was sick before they started on that fatal hunt. And as for the "blooding", he's seen that done over and over again, and never knew a man to think of it as anything but another episode in a day's sport. He admitted it's pretty rough sometimes – said he'd seen a shirt torn right off a young hunter's back, and his whole body smeared with blood over and over again. And once the deer's entrails draped around the hunter's neck and its stomach put on his head for a cap—'

'On a child? A delicate, sensitive, twelve-year-old child?'

'Lawrason didn't say. No, I suppose not. Boys as young as that don't often shoot a deer – after all, Franchot only did it by accident. But your husband wasn't thinking of him as a delicate, sensitive, twelve-year-old child, Mrs. d'Alvery. He was thinking of him as the son he'd been afraid was going to grow up a milksop, who turned out to be a good sport and a fine shot after all. He was so proud of the boy that his pride swallowed up everything else. He didn't think straight and he didn't see straight. He'll never get over that as long as he lives. I'm so sorry for you that I can't find any words to tell you how sorry. But if you'll forgive me for saying so, I'm sorrier still for your husband.'

'Mr. Goldenberg, if I'd thought you'd say that to me—'

'I had to say it, because it's true, and some day you'll realize that too. But I know you can't do it now. No one could expect you to. And I want to do anything and everything I can to help you over this hard period. I've been trying to think how I could all the time we've been talking, but so far I haven't succeeded. Could you suggest anything yourself?'

'I'd be very grateful if you'd let me ask you one or two questions.'

'I wish you would, if that would help.'

'You've spoken to me about Harvey Lawrason; you've defended my husband yourself, and said that he did. But would you have done what Gervais did?'

'No. Probably not. But your husband belongs to a great Creole family and I'm only an emigrant Levantine who's made his own way in the world.'

So he calls himself a Levantine, Merry said to herself, surprised that her tragic thoughts could be diverted, even for a moment. *He isn't ashamed of it. Of course there's no reason why he should be, but I've always supposed he was. I'm sure Gervais thought so too.* Mr. Goldenberg went on talking while she pondered in amazement.

'I didn't say that sarcastically, Mrs. d'Alvery. And I wasn't trying to disparage great Creole families or extol poor Levantines, either. But every class and every race have the faults of their virtues as well as the virtues of their faults, their correlative weaknesses and strength. Prowess is an essential quality in men of your husband's breed; sensitivity isn't. It's the other way around in mine. But don't forget it was just that sort of essential quality which made you fall in love with him – prowess and vitality and magnetism and grace. You didn't fall in love with him because he was gentle and wise and subtle and long-

248

suffering. If you'd been looking for that in a man, you'd have fallen in love with Fabian d'Alvery instead of Gervais d'Alvery.'

'Both d'Alverys!'

'Ah, but Fabian isn't an Estrade too! His mother was a Lassiter, wholly unrelated to his father. She came of a very different strain. And Fabian's a cripple, not a physical paragon; a scholar, not a warrior. He's seen more and suffered more than Gervais ever did — or could. He's learned more — he's got a greater capacity for both suffering and learning. But, as I said before, none of that made you love him. The kind of man you were impelled to love was also the kind of man who wouldn't know how unhappy he was bound to make you or how cruel he'd almost inevitably be to a little boy who was more your child than his.'

'Then in spite of everything I've said, and the way you know I feel, you think I ought to go back to him?'

Mr. Goldenberg appeared to consider, and while he did so Merry realized, with mounting gratitude and in spite of her agitation, that they had been talking for a long time already and yet he had given no sign of preoccupation or haste, though he was an extremely busy man. If she could only have talked to a priest like this! ... She was grateful for Hazel too — there had been no inopportune telephone calls, no distracting taps on the door. Only a very zealous and a very efficient secretary could have guarded her employer and his visitor like this.

'Yes,' Mr. Goldenberg said at last. 'I do think you ought to go back to your husband. I'm afraid I may hurt your feelings again; nevertheless, I'm going to remind you that while you sacrificed a great deal for him, he's done a great deal for you too. He did offer you his name and his home and his position, he did choose you for the mother of his children. The name's ancient and honourable, the home's beautiful and historic, the position's not only secure but outstanding. Lots of people pretend to scoff at advantages of that sort; but the only persons who really take them casually, and who can afford to, are the ones who've always had them. You're very honest, Mrs. d'Alvery, so I'm sure you will be willing to admit you *hadn't* always had them.'

'Yes, I am. But—'

She almost added, 'I don't think they're really all that important.' But she could not do it because, as Mr. Goldenberg said, she was too honest to pretend. And she was also withheld by the sudden poignant realization that they were supremely important to him, and that the knowledge he himself could never obtain them, for all his wealth and his power, was bitter to him. 'Do you think that if a man gives a woman a great name to share and a handsome house to live in and a prominent social position to maintain, she ought not to expect anything more of him?' Merry inquired, substituting the question for the statement she had so nearly made.

'No. But I think they ought to go a long way in making her recognize her obligation to him,' Mr. Goldenberg answered imperturbably. 'Especially when he gives them to her gladly and proudly, as your husband has, and not grudgingly, as so many husbands do. And I think his personal conduct should also have great weight with her. As far as I am aware, Captain d'Alvery has never given you the slightest cause for complaint on this score. Gossip travels fast in a place like this. I should almost certainly have heard if he gambled recklessly or drank to excess, or if he humiliated you by improper conduct with any other woman.'

'No, he doesn't – he hasn't,' Merry said quickly.

'Well, then, human nature being what it is—' He broke off, looking at her with a smile which, oddly enough, had in it something of the whimsical quality of Fabian's. But it lasted only a moment. He shook his head and sighed. 'I wasn't trying to argue with you,' he said, almost sadly. 'I was only trying to make you see the whole picture, at least as I see it. And it seems fairly clear to me. But I know you won't go back to your husband in your present frame of mind. Perhaps you can't. Perhaps it seems like such an impossibility that it really is an impossibility. ... If it were feasible for you to do whatever you wanted, what would you choose to do, right now?'

'I'd go back to work. I'd like my old job with you. Of course I know I'm terribly out of practice, that I couldn't qualify for it any more. So please don't think I'm asking for it, indirectly. But it's what I'd like. I can't live up to the d'Alvery standard. I've tried and I've failed. I'm sorry, but I'm not as ashamed as I was before you made me see what those standards really are, the way you did just now.'

'You could get back into practice. You've done typing for your husband right along, haven't you?'

'Yes. I've always handled the correspondence and the accounts. He's never had a secretary since we've been married.'

'You mean he's never had a paid secretary. There, I shouldn't have said that. Well, there's no question that you could qualify, as far as ability goes. But I wouldn't take you back into this store, Mrs. d'Alvery.'

'You wouldn't? Not if I were really good enough?'

'No. Because I'm not going to be the one to give the whole parish the chance to say that a girl from St. Napoleon Street tried to cross the tracks to the River Road and couldn't make the grade after all.'

Merry flushed and bit her lip. Before she could frame an adequate retort. Mr. Goldenberg went on.

'But that doesn't mean I couldn't give you a position elsewhere, if you really want one, and I can see you're in earnest about that. Besides, you've convinced me that a complete change would probably be the best thing in the world for you. And it so happens I have a good many interests outside of Baton Rouge, though I don't say much about them here. As a matter of fact, I'm the principal stockholder in two very large New York stores. I'm in a position to add anyone I wish to the personnel in either. I'd be very glad to add you. But not in a secretarial capacity.'

'I couldn't qualify in any other capacity.'

'You're a very attractive woman, Mrs. d'Alvery. But if you'll forgive me for saying so, you're not nearly as attractive as you easily could be.' He looked at her, not unkindly but appraisingly, with his far-seeing eyes, and Merry, for the first time in years, felt acutely conscious of the lost trimness of her bearing, of her casual coiffure, and of her unmanicured hands. But almost immediately came the comforting realization that Mr. Goldenberg was right, that the effect of her figure would be very different in better-made clothes, that her neglected hair was still beautiful in itself, and that with a little care and attention her hands might be beautiful too; it was only because she had lost interest in her appearance when she thought Gervais did that this had ceased to be a credit to her. 'You were one of the loveliest girls I ever saw,' Mr. Goldenberg went on, impersonally. 'You could be just as lovely now, in a different way – not with that first elusive freshness which is never recaptured, but with the mellowness of maturity. If I'm not mistaken, you're still under forty. You could be almost irresistibly charming, if you cared to make the effort. I'd like very much to see you do it. ... Incidentally, how is your French?'

'Why, it's – it's fair. I didn't know much when I married, but I started talking it right away, with my mother-in-law, because I thought that was one thing I could do to please her, and she taught me a good deal. She's insisted all the children must grow up bilingual. She's taught them too. And we very often speak French at meals and read it aloud. . . . What makes you ask?'

'I was wondering whether a position on my Paris staff would interest you. The two New York stores I mentioned both have offices there, and we keep several representatives in France all the time, besides our seasonal buyers. We could easily use another.'

'You'd send me to Paris!'

Her voice was very like a sick child's who had suddenly been offered a sojourn in fairyland. Mr. Goldenburg did not fail to notice this. Nevertheless, he answered in a matter-of-fact way.

'I'd be very proud to have you in my Paris bureau. I think, after you'd learned the ropes, you might easily become its directress. The present one's over sixty, though she doesn't look it, and she's been saying for some time she wished we'd give her an assistant whom she could train to take her place, eventually. I believe you'd be the very person. That is, if you're sure you'd be happy so far from your family, in the long run.'

'But I've told you—'

'Yes, I know. I don't think you'd mind the separation from your husband – for the present. And it might be a good thing for both of you. But what about your children? Could you leave them?'

'Franchot was the one I couldn't have left,' Merry said, her eyes filling with tears again. Then she went on, at first using much the same words she had spoken to Gervais the evening before, but gradually changing her line of argument.

'Vail's almost a man. He's always been independent and self-sufficient. And Phil's his father's whiteheaded boy. Gervais can easily be father and mother both to him.'

'I wonder. Boys' mothers mean a great deal to them – often more than their mothers realize, I believe. Mine was the most powerful influence in my life, even more powerful than my wife. We came up together, the hard way. My father'd been killed in one of the Turkish massacres when I was a baby, so there were just the two of us, and part of the upward climb was pretty tough. By the time I married the way was easier. And ease isn't

252

what always keeps people close together, in spite of what you think now, Mrs. d'Alvery. Sometimes it is sharing troubles and hardships that counts for the most.'

Momentarily his eyes rested in thought on the framed photograph of his wife: then he glanced at Merry again, and this time his gaze was less impersonal than when he had told her, a few moments before, that she had been a very beautiful girl and that she might still be a very beautiful woman. Merry remembered the shrewd, shrivelled little old lady whom she had met when Mr. Goldenberg invited her into his office to see the Victory Loan Parade, and also the large, effulgent woman wearing satin and pearls and sables, and she understood why a man like him would have felt closer to his mother than to his wife. At the same time she wondered why the realization that Mr. Goldenberg was a tremendously wealthy widower should suddenly have made her vaguely uncomfortable, and why she was so conscious now under his glance when she had not been self-conscious at his words.

'I really don't think I mean all that much to Phil,' she said, a trifle hurriedly. 'Besides, he's self-sufficient too, in a different way. He's so popular that no one person means a great deal to him, not even in his family. Sybelle's different; but it's Vail she's dependent on, rather than me. As long as she has Vail, she's satisfied. And just now I think she and I might be better apart. There's been a little friction over her first suitor, and I think perhaps if we separated for a time. . . . She could visit me once in a while, couldn't she?'

'Certainly. Whenever you liked. Besides, you should come back to this country at least once a year, to keep in touch, anyway. And possibly you'd like to take your younger daughter with you. Joyeuse her name is, isn't it? That would be perfectly feasible, from my point of view.'

'Oh, Mr. Goldenberg, you've made everything seem so natural and easy – and *right*! I haven't words to tell you—'

'Don't try. You haven't asked *me* to tell *you* much of anything, by the way – what your salary would be, or your living conditions, or anything of that sort. Would you feel five thousand was fair to begin, with transatlantic passage furnished twice a year and some kind of an additional expense allowance for incidental travel and other items? I should think you could manage on that, but I'm not sure. You'd have to spend a good deal on clothes, especially at first.'

Again his eyes wandered over her appraisingly. But this time she was not embarrassed because she did not even notice the searching gaze.

'Manage on five thousand!' she gasped. 'With travel expenses besides! Why, Mr. Goldenberg, I've never had five *hundred* a year to spend on myself! If I had five thousand I could help at home too. I could—'

'You see, you're already beginning to think of helping at home,' he said, rather dryly. 'No, you shouldn't try to do that. You'll need to spend at least that much on yourself, if you're to fill the position I have in mind acceptably. You'll need not only good clothes; you'll need a suitable apartment, and a car, and efficient servants. You'll need to go about quite a little too, visiting picture galleries and museums and châteaux; a great many of the best fashion ideas have come from such sources. And then you'll have your young daughter with you. She'll need to go to a good school, to have travel advantages too. No, I don't think five thousand and expenses will be enough. I think you had better start with seventy-five hundred. And I'm sure you won't make the mistake of supposing for a moment that this offer is philanthropic. I'm expecting you to earn every cent of your salary. I'm confident that you're going to.'

He did not actually rise, but he made a slight movement which indicated to Merry that he would like to have her do so, that he considered the interview over. As she got to her feet, still too dazed for adequate speech, he made one more suggestion.

'You know now that you can get away any time you wish,' he said. 'You have the prospect of financial independence already. I believe that after a little while you'll find that your new interests and your provocative surroundings will help you to overcome your grief. So, if you will permit me to say so, I think you should try very hard not to do anything at present which you would regret afterwards. Under normal circumstances you have great self-control and great dignity. I know it will be hard for you to do what I am going to suggest, but I hope you will not find it impossible. I hope you will now go back to your sister-in-law's house and permit her to send for Dr. Champagne, as she wished to do earlier this morning. I feel sure he will prescribe a sedative and tell you to stay in bed for a few days. After you have had this much-needed relaxation, I think you should talk to him candidly, telling him much that you have told me, and I am convinced he will say you are desperately in need of a complete change and a long rest – in the sense that any release from strain is rest. Then you may tell him about my offer, and he will almost certainly advise you to accept it. After that, I think you should have an equally frank talk with your husband, and that you should ask Dr. Champagne to talk with him too. Captain d'Alvery may oppose the plan at first, but I do not believe he will do so for long. I think he will realize that if you stayed at Belle Heloise, in your present condition, you would soon have a very serious nervous breakdown – so serious that you might never recover from it. I am less sure that he will realize his only hope of getting you back lies in letting you go, but perhaps he will. At all events, I think you should stay quietly at Belle Heloise for a fortnight or so while you are making your preparations for departure. Don't let anyone outside the family get an impression of flight, or of rupture. If you follow my suggestion, it will be very simple to say, afterwards, that you have gone away for a rest cure, and, later on, that you developed interests, while abroad, which led to an independent career. So many women have these nowadays that you could do it too without causing any comment, provided you go about it in a way that seems logical, and provided the career is important enough and pursued far enough from home. I do not need to tell you that the executive director of a Paris office woud occupy a very different position, in the eyes of the world, from a stenographer in Goldenberg's store on Third Street. There would be no question, in the former instance, that you had been unable to cross the tracks. On the contrary, the general opinion would be that you had done it so successfully that you had been able to go much farther than the River Road.'

He held out his hand, and Merry took it mutely. She did not ask him how he happened to know she had already left Belle Heloise and had gone to Somerulos Street. At the moment it did not even occur to her to wonder.

'I have been assuming all this time that eventually you would want to come home for good,' Mr. Goldenberg said. 'I hope and believe you will. But if for any reason you decide, in the end, on a divorce, of course Paris is an excellent place to get one. Several very able lawyers are among my acquaintances there. I will see that you meet them socially at once, so that if you feel you need them professionally later on the way will already be paved for you. In fact, I can probably arrange an introduction in person. Mrs. Goldenberg and I always used to go to Paris every year. She bought all her clothes there, and I laid the foundation for the present office. Since her death I have not been back. But I have been thinking for some time that I ought to go regularly again.'

'Off we go, into the wild blue yonder,
Climbing high, into the sun.
Here they come, zooming to meet our thunder.
At 'em boys, give 'er the gun!
Down we dive, spouting our flame from under,
Off with one hell of a roar,
We live in fame or go down in flame;
Nothing'll stop the Army Air Corps!'
Taken from *The Army Air Corps*, by Major Robert Crawford.

PART FOUR

'Letters to Susannah'

(Spring 1937 – Autumn 1942)

CHAPTER EIGHTEEN

BELLE HELOISE,
May 26, 1937

DEAR SUE,

I was very pleased to get your letter telling me about your
school and everything and reminding me it was quite a while
since I had written you. I know it is but I did not feel much like
writing for a long time after Franchot died and Mom went away.
(I suppose you know she had a bad nervous breakdown and as
she couldn't seem to get well at home or in a sanatorium, Dr.
Champagne decided that perhaps a complete change would help
and she has gone to Europe, taking Joyeuse with her, which of
course leaves another hole, though we were all glad the kid could
have such a swell chance.) It's been pretty grim here at Belle
Heloise ever since, and I didn't go to New Roads or anywhere
else all winter, so I don't know what's been cooking. I have just
kept plugging along trying to get better marks than I have so far,
because I know if I don't I won't have a prayer of getting to
Princeton, which I have now decided to do if I can. I wish now I
hadn't gone to school for so long just to eat my lunch.

Last week my friend Riccardo Tramonte graduated from
L.S.U., so I broke down and went to the military commencement
and it was quite a show. Eighty-nine cadets got their Lieutenant's commission and Colonel Hill, the Commandant, administered the oath of allegiance to them after the graduation
ceremonies. There was the traditional flag raising which is always one of the main features of graduation morning and there
was also a regimental parade in the a.m. Then a review in the late
p.m. and of course the military parade award programme in the
gymnasium. Rick got the highest award of all, the L. Kemper
Williams sabre which is given annually to the best cadet officer.
Colonel Williams, who is past-president of the Reserve Officers
Association, presented the sabre in person. It is a knockout and I

got about the biggest thrill of my life when Rick accepted it from him. Syb went to the exercises and a concert in the Greek Theatre with me and took part in the dress parade, but *grand'mère* would not let her go to the senior dance, on account she is in mourning, even though she had been chosen Regimental Sponsor. At least *grand'mère* said mourning was the reason. Me, I can't see how it would have been any worse for her to wear a party dress than her sponsor's special uniform, or how it would do Franchot any good now to make Syb miserable, and that is what *grand'mère* did and Dad too, not to mention leaving Rick high and dry for the dance. I would not stand for it if I were in their place and I don't know how much longer they will either. She and Rick have thought a lot of each other ever since they were kids. Of course I realize everyone says that is just puppy love, but I think sometimes you can tell right from the start no matter what age you are. I reckon you can guess why I feel that way about it so I won't go into it all again.

Rick has gone abroad now, the lucky bum. The Tramontes invited me to go along and Uncle Fabian and Aunt Cresside invited me too but I figured I had better stick around here a while longer. I'll be gone soon enough anyway and the house seems pretty empty already to Sybelle without having anyone else lighting out of it.

To answer your question, Phil is fine. He has been pitching on the high school baseball team sponsored by the American Legion all spring and Baton Rouge has won games with Bogalusa, Hammond and Slidell, which gave us the District Championship, though we lost afterwards to New Orleans in the State Finals. Of course Phil went there to play and has been there twice besides to stay with the Pereiras who have shown him a tall time. They gave a dinner at the North Shore Club that he said was simply the cat's whiskers, boiled crabs and turtle soup and sheep's head salad and everything. *Grand'mère* doesn't seem to mind having Phil play around even if he is supposed to be in mourning.

Well, as I said before there is really no news so I will close. As ever

Your affectionate friend,

VAIL D'ALVERY

DEAR SUE,

Well, what do you know? I got into Princeton after all and I'm coming East around Sept. 1st, maybe a little sooner. Uncle Fabian and Aunt Cresside are planning a trip to New York and New England then and this time I have decided to accept their invitation and go along. That is the slack time on the plantation anyhow and besides a few weeks here one way or another won't make much difference when I'm going to be gone all winter and they will mean a lot to me. We thought we might take in Bar Harbour somewhere along the line as we shall be motoring. Will you please let me know how late you will be in Maine yourself and whether your family would have any objections if we turned up? Of course we would stay at a hotel and we do not want to put you out at all but gee it is nearly two years now since I have seen you and it would be swell if I could, at least I think so.

We had quite an epidemic of graduation in the family this spring because Phil got through high school too and Sybelle finished at Grand Coteau. Phil has decided to go to Tulane instead of L.S.U. as long as I'm not going to be there, at least he said that was the reason but I'm beginning to think the d'Alverys are mighty good at alibis. He has been itching to get away from the plantation for a long time and he is crazy about New Orleans so Tulane is a logical choice, though I should think he would rather go into the R.O.T.C. which is just starting up there than to take the regular college course, but naturally it's his business, not mine. I wouldn't be so sure the Pereiras wouldn't have something to do with it. What I mean is Mr. Pereira and Barry went there, not just that Nellie will be going to Newcomb next year. I think Dad is disappointed but he has been very decent about it as he is about most things. I don't think he's caught on yet that Phil isn't interested in sugar and I hope he won't for a long time. He's had a good many knockout blows as it is.

Sybelle is going to stay at home because *grand'mère* doesn't believe in college for girls and I don't believe Sybelle cared much about going anyway. *Grand'mère* and Dad both hope she can be a Maid at Carnival this next year, she would have stood a good chance of being Queen of Comus if Dad could have spent more time in New Orleans and kept in with his relatives and important friends, the way Uncle Fabian has. There won't be any question about Frances Belle when she comes along because Uncle Fabian and Aunt Cresside have an apartment at the Pontalba now and go down there a lot and Frances Belle is meeting everybody and everybody likes her. But Dad has never been able to afford to do anything like that and he has let all his best contacts slide except for the Pereiras and of course they have Nellie to look after first. He talked to me about it and said he was sorry about Sybelle, he had always hoped and expected she would be a Queen but somehow he had let the chance for it slip just like so many other things. I'm afraid he feels he has been a failure but there is no reason why he should really because he is a grand person. I told him I was sure Sybelle wouldn't care about being a Queen anyhow, and that was the truth because I don't think she will. All she cares about is marrying Rick and I reckon it is just as well he stayed abroad, that is if Dad and *grand'mère* are going to keep on along the same lines. Rick is studying for his Master's at the Sorbonne. Mr. and Mrs. Tramonte are so proud of him they can hardly see straight; of course they were always but this is just the cat's whiskers as far as they are concerned. I go to their house once in a while to spend the night just like I did when Rick was home, it gives them a chance to talk about him, of course I might add it gives me a chance too.

Well, let me know about Bar Harbour as soon as you can because it really would be swell if I could see you there as I said before.

With my best,

VAIL

BLAIR HALL,
PRINCETON UNIVERSITY

DEAR SUE,

Of course I was very much interested to get your letter saying you were going down to New Orleans for Mardi Gras. Yes, I do remember hearing your mother say she thought it would be a pleasant experience for you. Of course it is just my hard luck I won't be in Louisiana when you get there, but you will see Sybelle because she is going to spend three months with our Estrade cousins who live on Esplanade and take in the whole show. I think things are going to be all right for her, about being a Maid I mean, but naturally all that is supposed to be a deadly secret right up to the day of the ball.

I am surprised Phil didn't answer your letter, I reckon he's busy studying for his mid-years, or maybe as you say he never got it anyway, though just Tulane ought to reach him all right. His complete address is Kappa Alpha Fraternity House, Tulane University, New Orleans.

This is a grand place, wonderful teachers, a swell bunch of fellows, beautiful grounds and buildings. I wish you would come and see it, perhaps you will some day. I am majoring in American history, as that is what Uncle Fabian wanted me to do, and don't think I made any mistake. However, I may as well confess I seem to be getting a lot more out of the Civilian Air Pilot's Training for which I signed up right after I got here than I am anything else. I am by no means alone in this feeling, for the whole college is air-minded and there is a Flyers' Club where nobody talks about anything else. However, not knowing how much interested you are in subjects of that sort, if at all, I won't go into details about my course right now.

As ever,

VAIL

BELLE HELOISE,
September 4, 1939

DEAR SUE,

I would have written before but I have spent most of my time lately listening to the radio at the Tramontes' and expecting every minute to hear Rick say 'Well, what did I tell you?' but he hasn't. He sure left Europe in the nick of time, apparently the people who are caught over there haven't a notion of how or when they can get home. Rick was really itching to stay, so he wouldn't have minded if he'had got caught, but after all he has been gone a winter and two summers already and all this time his father has been counting the days until he would become a junior partner – the business is a big one now, mostly wholesale, and Mr. Tramonte's getting on in years, so he really does need help. Besides it looks an awful lot like Italy would go in with the Axis later and the Tramontes are going to take it mighty hard if that happens. Personally I think it's just as well none of them is in Naples right now because it's a cinch they'd have a tremendous row with their friends and family about Mussolini if they were.

Now that Rick is back in Baton Rouge to stay – unless we get into this war ourselves which he still says we will – there has got to be a showdown about having him at Belle Heloise and I'm going to have a try at thrashing the whole thing out with Dad and *grand'mère* after supper tonight. I have only got ten more days at home before I go back to college and naturally I want to see all I can of Rick during that time as I shan't get another chance until Christmas, and I don't propose to keep going to his house and never asking him to mine. Besides even if Dad and *grand'mère* won't consent to a formal engagement I want them to at least admit there's an 'understanding' between Rick and Syb, because there is, whether D. and G. like it or not. When you come right down to it there's not the slightest reason why S. and R. shouldn't get married straight off except the family is so mule-headed about it. Rick is getting a fine salary and earning it too and Syb has had plenty of chances now to find out whether there might be anyone she would like better and there isn't. Some ape is always bobbing up that she met when she was at Grand Coteau and the River Road gets blocked with cadets coming out from L.S.U., not to mention all the old fogies who gave her a whirl when she was in New Orleans last winter and want to keep on doing it. And they just aren't there as far as she's concerned. If a girl cared for me like she cares for Rick I'd be right in the seventh heaven. Of course I don't mean any old girl. I mean a very special girl and you know who.

In one way I'm sorry to have a showdown just now with Dad because he has had another big disappointment which he has taken rather hard. You know that the place next to ours, Hathaway Hall, has been vacant for a long time and has got terribly run down. Mrs. Grover Blood who owns it has been trying to sell it for ten years because there were lots of reasons why she didn't want to live there herself but neither did anyone else. Well, this summer a Mr. Trevers, a big shot from Monroe, got really interested in the place and made Mrs. Blood a good offer for it. Then he found out that the Sugar Act of '37 would prevent him from marketing anything but syrup and he wanted to market sugar – at least he could have marketed sugar from ten acres but what would that amount to when he would have had nearly 3,000 under cultivation? You see this fool law provides that only mills that were in operation when it was passed would be given the marketing quota and that this would be based on the amount produced then and as Hathaway had been closed down for nearly ten years, Mr. Trevers couldn't get any quota. So finally he got all hot and bothered and said he would have to withdraw his offer. Mrs. Blood took the case to court and Uncle Fabian did everything he could to help her, but there was no soap. She stayed with us while she was trying to make a go of things, and she and Dad kept talking evenings about what was the use, you couldn't win in the sugar business whatever you did. Then one of these junk agents came along right out of the blue and said there was a big demand for American machinery in Mexico and offered Mrs. Blood $50,000 for the machinery in the Hathaway mill and she took it. The machinery cost close to $350,000 so that meant a $300,000 loss but she said it was better than having the mill stand idle forever and she was sick of the whole thing anyway. All this week the wreckers have been tearing things up at Hathaway, and Dad has gone over there every day and watched them, and said well, that was the end of sugar raising at one more place on the River Road and as far as he could see he might as well let the wreckers come here and gut our mill too. Of course that was all nonsense because we were operating full blast in '37 and the only way we had been hurt by that law and the other one those ginks up in Washington passed two years ago and then repealed was that we had to plough under part of our cane and burn up some more. Naturally that was pretty bad but not bad enough to get us to the point where we would let some Mex who would sell sugar back in the U.S. at a big profit have our machinery for a song. If Dad had only gone to Congress like he should have I bet he could have stopped all this foolishness and he would have been a lot happier about everything. Mom was the only person who could talk Dad out of these moods he has now. She was always so cheerful and sure everything would turn out right in the end until she broke down all of a sudden. I guess she had just taken it too long. Now there is no one to fill her place with Dad or the rest of us as far as that goes. But we thank our lucky stars she didn't get caught in this European jam anyway. She has had a swell job in Paris for two years now which she has enjoyed very much, and it has been fine for Joyeuse too; but she had quite a lot of piled up leave so she decided to let her assistant go to the fall openings and spend her leave in Latin America. You see her work has to do with fashions and that sort of stuff and she thought it would be a good plan for her to see the native costumes in Peru, Bolivia, Guatemala, Mexico and what have you, to get new ideas. She had seen most of the picture galleries etc. in France which is another way she gets ideas, but not the ones in Italy, so she and Joyeuse went down to Naples, stopping along the way to look at pictures and finally took one of those high-toned Italian ships that go straight to the west coast of South America and landed in Valparaiso. Now that she's got there she naturally wants to make the most of it, especially as she can't do her job in Paris while this war is going on and wants to run things in New York till the shooting's over, once she gets organized for a good start.

Well, I hope I haven't bored you with all this talk about family matters and about sugar, but you see I feel as if you were one of the family, at least you know I wish you were and as far as the sugar's concerned I care a lot about that too and I'm going to be a planter no matter how many laws these ginks pass, or how many quotas they fix or how many acres they make us plough up and burn over. I never could be anything else, come hell or high water, and I shall hang on to Belle Heloise even if it is the last plantation to raise sugar on the River Road. I would rather die myself than have it gutted and deserted like Hathaway. Down deep in his heart I know Dad feels the same and maybe I can have some influence with him because we are the only two left with this feeling except *grand'mère* and it is different with an old lady than with a man. Maybe she thinks it isn't but I know it is. Phil has finally told Dad that he doesn't want to stay on the plantation which of course was another blow. He wants to go into business with Mr. Pereira instead. I thought of doing that myself for a while but it was not because I wanted to. It was because I thought maybe that would be the quickest way to make money. If I had a grand girl just waiting to marry me like Rick I might be thinking more about that, but as it is I'm not, and even if I were I know now I'd have to manage and so would my wife on what I could make at Belle Heloise because this is where I am going to stay.

As ever,
VAIL

BLAIR HALL,
PRINCETON UNIVERSITY,
May 28, 1941.

DEAR SUE,
I have just done something that seems mighty important to me

so I hope it will seem that way to you too. Anyway I want to tell you about it.

I think I wrote you I was very disappointed because I was not old enough to register in the draft fall, I thought it was tough luck to miss it by just a few months and I decided I would not wait for the second registration if I could help it. Ever since I came up here I have been hearing and seeing a lot that has made me feel Rick was right when he said we were bound to get into this war, though I couldn't see it while I was still on Belle Heloise. (Somehow the idea of war doesn't hit you very hard in a place like that, it always seems so peaceful, but when you get right down to it there was plenty going on there in my great-grandfather's time.) Rick was right when he said there was going to be one in Europe and I didn't believe him when he first told me that and now I realize my mistake. With Yugoslavia and Greece both conquered things are moving mighty fast and there's no telling which way they'll move next. Well anyway, yesterday when I read Roosevelt's proclamation announcing an unlimited state of National Emergency something snapped inside of me and I sent in an application for enlistment in the Army Air Corps as a flying cadet. Of course my civilian pilot's training is going to come in mighty handy now, as I've already taken two phases (primary and secondary) and have a total of nearly 90 hours in the air. So I'm not especially worried about the flying cadet examination and I'm hoping very much to get into action right away but I don't believe I'll have much chance of making one of the summer courses, it's so late already. If I don't I'll go home as soon as I've taken my physicals; I have to go into New York for those – 90 Church Street. Well I don't suppose the address makes any difference to you, but somehow even that's exciting to me.

As ever,

VAIL

P.S. – By the way, I don't think I wrote you before that Rick was called to active duty in Feb. He had received a notice from the War Dept. several months before saying he would be and asking if there were any reason why he would need a deferment. Of course there wasn't, and he reported to Camp Shelby at Hattiesburg, Mississippi. He's crazy about it there and naturally his letters make me even crazier than I was already to get going myself.

DEAR SUE,

Well, here I've been practically all summer, just as I was afraid I might be, and nothing much has happened so there has been no point in writing. I've been busy with the usual chores on the plantation and I've managed to get over to Hattiesburg several times to see Rick. Once I even managed to take Syb with me and Rick has been home for one short leave too. Of course Syb and I haunted the Tramontes' house while he was there, and Dad did not ask too many questions about what we did when we went into Baton Rouge evenings. We were supposed to be at Aunt Cresside's when we were not going to the movies or what have you, but I think he suspects we were actually at the Tramontes', and though he has never invited Rick out here himself, he hasn't kicked up too much row when I've asked Rick to stay to dinner or something on my own. Dad's calmed down all sorts of ways since Mom left and looks and acts lots older than he is, and I honestly believe if it wasn't for *grand'mère* he'd stop putting up a fight. But she eggs him on, every chance she gets. If she only knew it, she's making a big mistake, because it's the fact that Dad's seemed more ready to let nature take its course that's made Rick and Syb willing to let things slide a while longer hoping he'll see still more reason and give them the kind of wedding and send-off they really want. But every time *grand'mère* gets up on her ear, they think maybe they'd better take the shortest cut out of all this nonsense, which of course they could do perfectly well.

I've been hoping that the next time I wrote I could tell you Mom had come home, because it didn't seem like she could stay in Latin America forever, and anyone would think two years would be plenty to learn all there is to know about quaint costumes and things like that. She has been back to the United States once and her route was right through New Orleans, but she didn't get a stopover to come home. I think that was just the last straw as far as Dad was concerned, because when it happened he had to stop pretending she wasn't well enough to come and face the fact she didn't want to come. He'd kidded himself along just as far as he could. She did invite Syb and Phil to visit her in New York and they both went and had a grand time. I went in from Princeton too, once or twice – it was term time for me while she was there, though Phil was having vacation from Tulane – and she took me out on the town too. We went to all the best shows and restaurants etc. Mr. Goldenberg who owns the big department store on Third Street in Baton Rouge was there one evening too and was also very nice to me. He happened to be in New York on business. I don't know whether you know he owns two big stores in New York too, and that these maintained the Paris bureau Mom directed till the war broke out. Not that there's any reason why you should. Anyway he dropped in to see Mom and we all went to see *Lady in the Dark* and to the Oak Room at the Plaza afterwards. Mr. Goldenberg didn't seem to have any trouble getting reservations. Mom had a suite at the Gotham and she was looking like a million dollars. I never realized before what a knockout she was or at least could be. She has an office in Rockefeller Centre and a big staff and it's all mighty smooth. And she certainly isn't sick any more though there wasn't anything put on about that when Dr. Champagne said she was. She was good and sick for a while. But not for nearly as long as Dad tried to think. I don't mean he wanted her to be sick, I only mean ... Well, I reckon I'm getting all balled up and I'd better stop trying to explain. But anyway, what I'm slowly getting at is, this summer Joyeuse wrote she was all fed up with Latin America and wanted to come home. She said Mom didn't need her any more than a cat needed two tails, and was Dad willing she should take the next plane she could get a seat on. Of course Dad cabled her he was and we all went down to meet her. I'm sure he thought right up to the last moment that when Joyeuse got off that plane Mom would get off too, that they were planning to surprise him. And then Joyeuse got off alone after all. She is just as smart as paint, you'd never recognize her as the leggy little somebody she was when you last saw her. She's only 18, but she seems older than Syb in lots of ways and has she got a line, in three languages at that! She's going right into the junior class at the University, can you beat it? I had no idea they taught so much at those foreign schools as she's managed to pick up. She's planning to major in chemistry and physics and to spend all her evenings and week-ends in the laboratory at the sugar house as soon as grinding begins. I think Barry Pereira has different ideas about the way it would be nice for her to spend her week-ends, but that's neither here nor there. He hasn't got the field to himself by any means though. I think poor Dad is in a daze with so many boy friends cluttering up the scene, but I'll say this for Joyeuse, she knows how to handle them all mighty well, I reckon she learned more languages in the course of her travels, and she gets no end of airmail letters from all over the place, addressed in big bold masculine hands. Well, I should worry about Joyeuse. Syb's the one I've got on my mind.

Speaking of Barry Pereira, he got a great kick out of his R.O.T.C. training and is all fixed up now with a commission of Ensign in the Naval Reserve, so he's in the same sort of position that Rick is, generally speaking, in case we get into the war – ready to jump right into the fight the minute it starts. And here I am still waiting around to hear from that application of mine.

I gave Phil your message and he said to give you his best too. Of course he'll have to register early next year and I suppose he'll be drafted right after that. I still don't see why he didn't go into the R.O.T.C. when he had such a good chance at Tulane, and he still doesn't see it my way, in spite of Barry Pereira and everything and we've stopped talking about it because we both seem to get hot under the collar when we try.

Well, I reckon this is all the family news for the present and I've written you again as if you really were one of the family and will repeat I wish this were true. You've told me you wanted to think it over and I've tried not to hurry you, to give you all the time you needed, but don't you honestly feel you've thought it over enough now? Couldn't you possibly say yes and let me come to see you before I start back to College?

Honey, if you only could, it would mean everything in the world to me.

Yours ever,
VAIL

BLAIR HALL,
PRINCETON UNIVERSITY,
November 2, 1941

DEAR SUE,

Well I seem to be off to a flying start at last and I don't mean to make a bad pun either.

As you know I was pretty discouraged not hearing a word all summer or for two months after I got back here. But yesterday evening I got a notice from the War Dept. telling me my application had been accepted and instructing me to report immedirarely to the recruiting officer at the P.O. Building in Trenton. Of course I hot-footed it in the first thing this a.m. and my orders are to start immediately for primary school at Cimarron Field, Oklahoma City, so please address your next letter there. I understand I'll be there until Jan. and get sent on to Enid, Oklahoma, for basic training which comes next – that is if I can make the grade. I also understand they don't allow cadets much time out for writing love letters but you can bet I do love you and that I shall never stop trying to get you to marry me whether I keep on saying so every few days or not. There is no time to enlarge on that now either though as I have to pack.

Yours ever,
VAIL

CIMARRON FIELD,
OKLA,
January 5, 1942

DEAR SUE,

This is only to say hello and to wish you a good year coming up. The schedule here is mighty stiff, just as I expected, and there isn't much time for letter writing. However, since you say you'd like a description of the place, here goes!

This field is about 25 miles out of the City located on very flat plains. The buildings are quite attractive – white frame construction decorated inside with a scheme inspired by the Indian tribes around here. We sleep in double-deck bunks and the food is super. There's a huge stone fireplace in the recreation room with Indian relics all around it which would be a grand place to spend hours of ease if we had any. The flying field is sod-covered with a wind tee separating the right and left traffic patterns in the centre. These are the main items that occur to me right now though I suppose I could think up a lot more if I had the time. Maybe they'll suggest some questions to you and if they do I'll gladly answer them, probably from Enid as I expect to be pushing off for there pretty soon now unless there's some sort of a last minute slip-up.

I have had a note from Dad saying that he and Harvey Lawrason and Charles Boylston have all written to the War Department for questionnaires to fill out. I didn't see it – I don't get much time for reading either – but it seems there was a general notice in the papers asking men who had served as officers in the

First World War to do this if they felt inclined. Dad had already written offering his services and had got a polite acknowledgment, nothing else; but now he hopes the questionnaire may lead to something. I wouldn't be surprised to see him get into active service yet before Phil does, or me either, and all I can say is, more power to him. I like to see the old boy showing some spirit again. It's the first time he has in a long while but now he's like an old fire horse rearing to go again.

Well, time's up, so I must sign off, with my best as always,

VAIL

TELEGRAM

ENID,
OKLA,
March 15, 1942

MISS SUSANNAH PRESCOTT,
NEW ROADS, LOUISIANA.

MADE THE GRADE ALL RIGHT. LEAVING IMMEDIATELY FOR ADVANCED SINGLE ENGINE TRAINING AT LAKE CHARLES. SORRY NOT TO SEE YOU EN ROUTE BUT SHOULD HAVE BETTER LUCK DURING NEXT TWO MONTHS AS I SHALL BE MUCH NEARER YOU. MY BEST AS ALWAYS.

VAIL

GERSTNER FIELD,
LAKE CHARLES, LA,
April 3, 1942

DEAR SUE,

I was ever so pleased to know you got the note that was attached to the handkerchief-sized parachute I released when I went over Salome on my last navigation flight. I jazzed the throttle and waggled my wings too, but I knew there wasn't much chance you'd realize who it was, since I couldn't let you know beforehand I was coming and ask you to be on the lookout. It was a grand flight, the best I've had so far. It was such a clear day that visibility was really unlimited and of course I was delighted to see the cane coming up to such a good stand. False River was beautiful from upstairs and Salome stood out so plainly I almost felt as if I could reach down and touch it or you. I wish I could have.

Realizing it was so uncertain whether you'd get the little note, I didn't put three things in it that I wanted especially to say. The first is that I can't tell you how glad I am you're back in Louisiana at last. I began to think you were going to stay in Boston the rest of your life and of course I couldn't help wondering whether there might not be some special attraction keeping you there. Secondly, I've got some good news: I get one week-end off while I am here and this next one's it. Of course I'm heading straight to Belle Heloise and by the time you get this or very soon after your mother'll be having one from *grand'mère* asking if you won't all come over and spend Sunday with us. And please remember that we mean it and that we want you the worst way.

Third I'm going to ask if you won't come to my graduation on the 20th of May. Uncle Fabian and Aunt Cresside are coming and bringing Frances Belle and Dad is bringing Sybelle and Joyeuse. It's even possible that *grand'mère* may come, so you see you'd have plenty of chaperons – worse luck, but I know your father and mother still go in for those in a big way. Of course if you like I will ask them too and I really think they might find it rather interesting because the school here is going to put on quite a show when its first graduate cadets finish training and get their wings. I'm tickled pink to be in this first class. Just a year ago this place was a rice patch out in the country; now it is a fine flying field with any number of red-roofed, grey-shingled buildings, streets, planes, officers and enlisted men who keep it humming day and night. It makes you realize we do things in a big way in the U.S.A. – even in the South, whatever you Yankees say, once we get going and have a reason for it! Well, I won't write any more details because I hope you'll soon be seeing it yourself. Let me know when you're coming and how many so I can make reservations at the Majestic.

As ever,
VAIL

P.S. – Yes, Phil was drafted all right and sent to Camp Beauregard for processing. Now he's at Fort Bragg, near Fayetteville, North Carolina. You're right: I don't see why you don't hear from him direct. Rick's still at Shelby but doesn't think it'll be long now. Gosh, I wish he and Syb could have got married before he pushed off. I don't need to add I hope I can. Harvey Lawrason has got another questionnaire from the War Dept., more complete than the one that came in first after he and Dad and Charles Boylston all wrote in January. So he has answered it and is eagerly awaiting developments. He went over to Belle Heloise to tell the family about it, incidentally regaling them with his usual tall tales. This time he told one about a man who lived up near Denham Springs, and who had said he hoped there wouldn't be any mourning at his funeral; instead he wanted his friends to get together and celebrate in a big way. Well, according to Harvey, he died, and the celebration took place just as he wanted. But all the guests, including the officiating clergyman, got so high that the next day no one could remember where they'd buried the corpse and they haven't found him yet. I wish I'd been around myself to hear good old Harvey telling this story and saying Which-I-God every few minutes. There's no one tells a story just like Harvey does or such stories either.

Dad and Charles haven't had a second questionnaire yet, but Charles heard that a procurement officer for the Army Air Corps was to be in New Orleans on his way East from Dallas, so Charles went down to see this man and Dad went at the same time and tendered his services to the Commanding Officer at the Port of Embarkation. So they are also eagerly waiting to see what happens next.

> ARMY AIR FORCE
> AERIAL GUNNERY SCHOOL,
> HARLINGEN,
> TEXAS,
> *August* 1, 1942

DEAR SUE,

Of course I was interested to hear that you had stopped off at Fayetteville to see Phil on your way North, and I agree with you that your parents have made a lot of progress towards a more enlightened viewpoint about chaperons and am glad you could take advantage of it. Just the same I'd like to have got the good of this change of heart myself and I sure was disappointed that you didn't get to Lake Charles. You see, I'd counted on having you pin my wings on for me, and though I was glad to have Aunt Cresside do it, if you couldn't, still it wasn't quite the same. Most of the fellows had their girls pin their wings on after the exercises but there was one quite interesting exception to this: Colonel Schauffler, who made the graduating address, pinned his own wings, which he had won 25 years before, on his son, who was one of my classmates, and who is now here at Harlingen too. The Colonel made a good speech, telling us we had been fortunate in having the preparation we needed to go out into the world and fight and now we were the best trained men, not only in the U.S.A., but in the world. He 'reminisced' as he called it, a little, and said that when he was training he was in the air only two hours before he got his licence, and that General Billy Mitchell, who did so much to make it possible for us to get our flight training, was up less than that. Even when Col. S. made his first flight over the German lines in 1917, he had been up only 12 hours. I know we're lucky in having so much better preparation all around, but at that I wish it didn't take quite so long to get into action for I sure am rearing to go. However, there are rumours that next year the course is going to be a lot longer, so I suppose that instead of griping I ought to thank my lucky stars that I got in when I did.

To get back to the graduation, it was held in Recreation Hall and was mighty impressive. The Chaplain who delivered the invocation called it the first milestone of the post and invited us to pause there. After that he got going on the Pilgrim Fathers and I didn't quite see the connection or follow him very well, but I'm sure you would have. The stage looked swell, all fixed up with flowers and plants, and we marched across it to receive our wings and personal congratulations from Col. S. to the tune of war planes overhead, so it was all very military as well as very festive. Col. S. also presented the class with a song which he and his daughter wrote, so you see he was quite the big shot of the occasion. The name of the song is 'Happy Landings Army Air Force' and it was printed on a large white drawing board where we could all see it, and illustrated too. The hall was chock-full of the pilots' families and friends and I sure was glad to have so many of my people there. I think they got quite a kick out of it too, especially Aunt Cresside. Dad got a snapshot of her taken while she was pinning on my wings which I am enclosing just in case you'd be interested. Of course I never told her I really meant you to do it. I missed Mom too, so things weren't quite perfect, I don't suppose they ever are. I don't know though – that very afternoon one of my classmates, Marion Henderson, was married in the Post Chapel. His girl and her mother had both come down from North Carolina, his father assisted the Chaplain in performing the ceremony and his mother and brother were there too. I reckon he thought things were about perfect, I know I would have in his place.

I was unexpectedly sent to Matagorda to finish my gunnery practice; now I have been shipped down here as tow-target pilot and don't know how long I'll have to stay before I get across. Rick made it all right, not long after I last wrote – left San Francisco as a First Lieutenant in his Infantry Division and is now 'somewhere in the Pacific', the lucky bum! Charles Boylston has started on his way too as he was ordered to report to Harding Field for physicals two weeks ago, then commissioned Captain in the Air Force straight from civilian life and sent to Miami. (His service in the First World War was in Infantry, but that doesn't seem to matter!) He had just 9 days at Hackberry before starting off, but Seaver has really run their things for years and done it mighty well, so that doesn't matter so much. Harvey is foaming at the mouth because he has got no further than a 3rd questionnaire, this time from the procurement officer in New Orleans, and according to Dad arrived there breathing fire and brimstone over the delay which he doesn't like any better than I do; but I think he'll be getting somewhere pretty soon. Dad has been in New Orleans himself for two months now, on duty at the Port of Embarkation with the rank of Captain, but has applied for transfer to the School of Military Government at the University of Virginia, as he thinks the course there might lead to something for which he is better fitted. I don't know just what will happen to the cane crop this year with neither of us at Belle Heloise and a lot of the hands gone too, for the draft has caught up with some of the Negroes and others have left to take big paying jobs in town. However, Sance is still on the job though he's getting pretty old now and I know he will do the best he can and Uncle Fabian has given me one of your father's harvesters for a combination birthday and Christmas present, which of course is going to make a huge difference too.

My duties as tow-target pilot here consist almost entirely of flying an AT-6 equipped with a reel on which cable is wound to pull up the flat flag-like tow-target. An enlisted tow-reel operator rides in the rear seat of the airplane and it is his job to attach the tow-targets and play out the cable through a hole in the bottom of the fuselage. The work is apt to be rather monotonous as it consists of flying from the field to the gunnery ranges which parallel the Texas coast north from Brownsville – a distance of approximately 50 miles. After we reach the gunnery ranges we fly at a specified altitude from one end of them to the other, then turn around and fly back again. The training missions are accomplished by a group of 4 airplanes, one two-target airplane and 3 firing airplanes, flying in formation as far as the gunnery range; than the tow-target plane starts up the range, playing out 6 or 7 hundred feet of cable to which the flag-target is attached and one of the firing airplanes makes passes at the target. In all cases the firing is towards the open water. Each of the gunners is using ammunition that is distinguished from the other gunners' by paint applied to the nose of each bullet before it has had a chance to dry completely, so when it passes through the cloth target a coloured ring, red, green, blue, or what have you is left on the flag-target. When all the firing planes have completed their mission, the tow plane returns to the home base, releasing the target over the base where it is retrieved by a ground crew.

Well, that's enough shop for today!

As ever
VAIL

HARDING FIELD,
December 10, 1942

DEAR SUE,

This is Phil's twenty-first birthday and I sure wish we were together for it because he is already overseas, the lucky stiff. Somewhere in Northern Ireland, I think, but of course all we have is his A.P.O. number. If you thought my letters sounded discouraged before, I don't know what you will think now. I was sure I was going to get across after Harlingen, especially as I asked for overseas duty, but when my orders came through – well, just look at the top of this page and you'll see that it has taken me 13 months of the hardest kind of training to get as far as home. Of course, it's nice in a way to be near the folks and I can run out to Belle Heloise every evening, but I should hate like hell to have to tell my grandchildren one of these days that I fought the battle of the Heidelberg Baroque Room. Right now I'm taking what is called an indoctrination unit course along with about 600 others. I'm not going to explain that. It wouldn't interest you, and the less I talk or think about it, the better I feel.

I haven't the faintest idea how long they'll keep me here; probably until I trip over my long white whiskers.

Phil isn't the only one who's made it overseas. Believe it or not,

Charles Boylston after O.T.S. at Harrisburg for training in Combat Intelligence, is now somewhere in England with the Eighth Air Force. I bet even Harvey Lawrason beats me across. He's in Dallas now waiting for assignment – a Captain in the Military Police. I have a hunch he may get the snappiest berth of all. With the kind of luck he usually has I'd be an ace by this time. And what do you know? He got the time off to get married before he went to Texas and the wedding was at Belle Heloise! Everyone thought he was a confirmed bachelor though there was a pretty little widow in Baton Rouge he liked a lot and used to come over from Denham Springs to see. She lived in one of the Pentagon Building apartments and of course they're nice but they're mighty small, and she didn't have any kin, so *grand'mère* crashed through and offered her the parlour at Belle Heloise for the ceremony. Syb wrote it was a very pretty little wedding and Dad got up from New Orleans and gave the bride away. Since then Mrs. Lawrason has been in Dallas near her husband though she is coming back to Baton Rouge when he goes overseas. Gosh, some people have all the luck! *Grand'mère* is all set to keep on being nice to her though they never knew each other before. War does make a lot of difference in some people's feelings and I can't understand why it hasn't yet in Mom's. She is located in New York now for the duration and is doing awfully well, that is, financially. She writes to all of us except Dad and *grand'mère* and she would like very much to have either or both of the girls come and live with her but it just so happens they prefer to stay at Belle Heloise. Syb is working at the local headquarters of the Red Cross and Joyeuse is doing a swell job on the plantation and still making good enough marks to get by at the University. She is really running the laboratory as we do not have a graduate chemist left there now. The one we did have has gone to Dupont, and though the younger man who was working under him has stood by and is very capable and intelligent, he does not even have a high school education. Two women, wives of men who are working in the mill, who are high school graduates, are helping him, and doing the best they can too, but Joyeuse has taken charge of the whole outfit and they were thankful enough to have her. The others all work on eight-hour shifts, but she just ploughs right along, night, day, any old time. I don't see how she stands it, but she seems to thrive on it. (Incidentally we haven't even got any sample boys left any more;

sample girls have taken their place too!) All this is rather rough on her various boy friends, especially Barry, whose ship gets into New Orleans every now and then and who would naturally like to have her come down there while it is in port. But she says there will be plenty of time for all that, meaning I suppose dates, after the war is over, which shows she isn't very hard hit yet. Just as well, two in one family are enough even if they weren't as far gone as Syb and I both are.

To go back to Joyeuse for a moment. I don't know whether I ever told you she can run a tractor as well as any man I ever saw and I wouldn't put it past her to go straight out into the fields if the labour shortage gets any worse. The new harvester is working like a breeze, the crop will get in, and it's a good one.

As ever,
VAIL

P.S. – Don't you think you could make it over here for just one week-end at Christmas-time?

HARDING FIELD,
July 1, 1943

DEAR SUE,

What do you know? Rick has been in Fiji! he has sent Syb some trinkets from Suva and she and I have both had long letters from him. Syb didn't show me hers – just read parts of it to me – which didn't surprise me much! But I think you'll be interested so I'm copying down parts of mine.

'Word came through today that we are permitted to say where we have been this last year and since this is the case I might tell you a little about it. Most of my time we spent in the bush but I got in to Suva three times and stayed at the Grand Pacific Hotel (!) which is reserved for officers only and where the servants are Indians. While there, was able to get a little beer and a good deal of Scotch whisky which is about all they drink over here owing to the British influence.'

Well, from there Rick goes on to tell about some marriage customs among the Fijis which I reckon I better not repeat to you as I don't know just how they would strike you though I thought they were very interesting. If you think you'd like to hear them let me know and I'll put them in my next letter. After describing these quaint customs Rick goes on to rave about the

279

beauties of the island, which, however, apparently didn't make up for the discomforts, as he says: 'Our biggest problem was encountered on patrols and routes into the interior and hell is a small word for the hardships of jungle country. At one time I stayed wet for 10 days. All of my equipment including soap, extra socks and what little else I carried were soaked during the first two hours. There is nothing harder than to have to lie down in a pool of water on a chilly night in wet clothes and try to get enough sleep to keep you plugging along the next day. When I finally emerged into civilization, such as it was, my shoes were in shreds and my clothes in ribbons. That was when I took five days' leave in Suva. I had so much water in my system that all the liquor I drank did no good – the water neutralized it. But some of the dinners with the English resembled heaven. To go to their lantern-lit wood houses and eat off china at a table with cloth on it and have cold beer in the evening was anything but hard to take.'

There was a lot more and I just ate it up but I've got to remember you've hardly met Rick and that you can't be expected to care what's happening to him the way I do, and besides he's only one of several who're having exciting experiences. Dad graduated from the School of Military Government at Charlottesville late in May, right up close to the top of his class, and was sent at once to Algiers for final indoctrination and training, alongside British outfits. Charles Boylston is 'somewhere in Scotland', apparently at some air station. Harvey Lawrason has been in Rio and is now apparently in Bombay, but from his necessarily vague letters his wife gathers this is just a way-station to some even more exciting place. Everybody but me seems to get sent to exciting places.

I have finished the indoctrination course I mentioned in writing before, and am now one of 80 left here out of the original 600 who took it, the others all having been divided elsewhere, but of course I couldn't be one of those. However, if I can't be overseas I'm glad to be near home, and at least the work isn't monotonous any longer, quite the contrary. I have now begun to have first-hand experience flying P-47s in formation flights over Lake Pontchartrain. The last one I was in was not such a success as far as I was concerned. The weather closed in, one of those fogs boiling up from the Gulf, so I headed towards Lake Maurepas and started to follow up the Mississippi but got lost because the visibility was so bad. Finally I was led home by a combat returnee pilot who was out scouting the weather. Now I've been put up for questioning because I left the flight, and can only hope the quality of mercy won't be too much strained in my case.

As ever,

Vail

Belle Heloise,
September 18, 1943

Dear Sue,

The next date line will probably be the stockade at Camp Livingston where I will be awaiting execution for having mutinied. I don't know just how much longer I can take the battle of Third Street. I've about made up my mind to push one of our stone lions off his pedestal and take his place as being more of a contribution to the war effort than anything they've got me doing now. You've heard about our lions, haven't you? Nobody knows where they came from or how they got there. The day after Harding Field was opened, there they were. Incidentally, a cow was found in the swimming pool at the same time. Nobody knows how she got there either, but they got her out. She's probably gone the way of all hamburger stands by now, as she was real; but the stone lions have stayed on. They say that any time a virgin walks between them those lions roar. However, there's never been any kick about the noise. One of them has lost his lower jaw, though, so maybe he tried to roar once.

Otherwise it's the same old routine that I've written to you till you must be as sick of it as I am. Our squadron of P-47s is the hottest one in the entire Air Force. Maybe that's why they're keeping us here. Any time we get to Europe and Fatso Goering hears about it, the Luftwaffe will quit and the war will be over.

Phil is in England and no doubt has got hot and cold running girls in every shire. He's griping because his outfit missed the North African show, Sicily, Italy and all the rest of the good clean innocent fun in the Mediterranean. He should be in my shoes; then he'd really have something to gripe about.

As ever,

Vail

DEAREST SUE,

Well they've come through at last – of course I mean the overseas orders. I've had final physicals, made my last will and testament and now I'm getting 10 days' leave. After that I'm to report to the staging area and receive my equipment down to the last shoestring and razor blade. Then I'll be on my way almost any moment.

So this won't be a long letter. It's just to tell you the news and ask you again if you won't marry me. Not whether you'll think it over, this time. Whether you won't do it, straight off. We could crowd a lot of happiness into 10 days, honey, if you would. I know there wouldn't be time for the kind of wedding you'd like to have. But does that matter such a lot, at least, if you care? You could wear that dress of your great-grandmother's that you wore at Plaquemine, couldn't you? And everyone would help you get ready. It ought not to take so long at that. Please try hard to say yes, and say it quick. Because of course 10 days are quite a lot, but we've got to make every one of them count. Please, Sue. Please, darling. If you only knew how much I love you and how hard I'd try to make you happy I'm sure you would.

As ever,
VAIL

'We are fighting in the quarrel of civilization against barbarism, of liberty against tyranny. Germany has become a menace to the whole world. She is the most dangerous enemy of liberty now existing. She has shown herself utterly ruthless, treacherous, and brutal. When I use these words, I use them with scientific precision.'

THEODORE ROOSEVELT: Speech in Oyster Bay, L.I.,
April, 1917

Or

'The right is more precious than peace, and we shall fight for the things which we have always carried nearest our hearts – for

democracy, for the right of those who submit to authority to have a voice in their own governments, for the rights and liberties of small nations, for a universal dominion of right by such a concert of free peoples as shall bring peace and safety to all nations and make the world itself at last free.'

WOODROW WILSON: *Address to Congress,*
April 2, 1917

PART FIVE

'*Hail the Conquering Hero*'

(Autumn 1943 – Autumn 1944)

CHAPTER NINETEEN

'THIS is the next best thing, isn't it, Vail?'

'Yes, it's the next best thing. But you know it wasn't the next best thing I wanted. It was the very best.'

'Hush! I'm afraid someone will hear you!'

'What difference would that make? I don't care if the whole world hears me. It's true. Don't you think, Sue, that even now – I've still got three more days. We could get married tomorrow. We could—'

'I said, please hush, Vail! People are staring at us.'

'Let's get out of here, then, and go some place where they can't.'

He rose, pushing back his chair abruptly and signalling to their waiter. They had dined at the Court of the Two Sisters and stayed on for dancing afterwards. Between every dance Vail had proposed again, lightly and casually at first, more and more urgently as the evening wore on. Susannah was thankful he had suggested leaving at last. She had been on the point of doing so a dozen times herself, but she was trying hard to help Vail get all the pleasure he could out of these last days, and she did not want to suppress him or rebuke him, if she could help it. Now she had almost reached the breaking-point.

She had answered his last desperate letter very gently. She wished she could say yes, she told him. He must not think it was because she would miss a big wedding if she married him straight off; she knew things like that did not matter when you really cared. But that was the trouble. She didn't really care – at least, not enough to marry him. She thought the world of him and all of that. And he mustn't blame her father and mother. She had told them about his letter, and they had both said they would be willing. They were very fond of him too. It was just that she didn't love him the way he wanted. And it wouldn't be fair to marry him when she didn't. But if there were anything else she could do . . .

Vail had gone to Cresside and Fabian, after hearing from Susannah, and they had immediately invited the girl to spend a week with them at their apartment in New Orleans. She had accepted by return mail and had joined them there the following day. As there were only three bedrooms at the d'Alverys' apartment in the Pontalba, he took a room at the Monteleone and he had slept there for a few hours each night; the rest of the time he had spent with Susannah, who consented readily to every outing he suggested and proved herself a consistently adaptable and delightful companion. They had made the harbour tour on the *President* and returned to drink coffee at the French Market. They had dined in a private room at Antoine's and taken in the floor show at the Roosevelt. They had wandered through the French Quarter, window shopping as they went, and ended up at Pat O'Brien's after having their fortunes read in tea-leaves. They had gone to the Fisherman's Mass at Our Lady Star of the Sea. And now they had been dancing, closely embraced, all the evening. But there had been no other close embraces, nor even a light exchange of kisses and an occasional lingering handclasp. Vail knew that if he started to kiss Susannah the kisses would soon cease to be light, because that kind would not satisfy him, and she knew it too. Through forbearance on his part and tact on hers they had managed, so far, to keep their association merry and casual. Now Susannah realized that it could not be kept like that any longer.

The interested eyes which had already made her uncomfortable followed them as they moved across the floor and left the restaurant. Now that he had outgrown his early awkwardness and brought his unruly locks under control, Vail had become an exceedingly handsome young man; his colour was as striking as ever and he wore his uniform with dash as well as with distinction. Unhappily, Susannah realized there was not a girl among those who were watching them, unless in love with someone else, who would not jump at the chance of being with Vail. Because vanity was not among her failings, she did not consider the correlative probability that there was not a fancy-free youth in the restaurant who would not have been equally glad to squire her. Just as Vail had outgrown his awkwardness, she had outgrown her slight stiffness. Her flawless features had become softer and sweeter; she had infinite grace of bearing; everything about her was charming. Meeting an unusually bold glance, she flushed a little, bending her head and veiling her eyes in her old shy way. Vail caught the presumptuous look, glared at the offender, and held open the door for her.

'I reckon it was just about time we left,' he said, reverting to the light and easy way of speaking which he had managed to maintain until that evening. 'You were attracting altogether too much attention, Sue. All those stares had nothing to do with my inopportune proposals; they were wholly the result of your fascination. ... All right, we'll skip it. Where do you want to go next?'

'I suppose I might suggest that you take me home.'

'You might, but I hope you won't. I reminded you a few minutes ago that I had three days more. Now I'll remind you that's all I've got. You don't expect me to waste one of my evenings in the Pontalba Building, do you?'

'We could sit on the gallery. It's plenty warm.'

'We could at that. It's not a bad idea of yours, Sue. I don't see why neither of us thought of it before.'

Susannah made no direct reply. The d'Alverys' gallery was comfortably and attractively equipped with rattan furniture and potted plants; Cresside had managed to give it the same gracious atmosphere which characterized her walled garden on Somerulos Street, greatly as the two places differed in every other respect; but she had also screened it so effectively from the adjacent galleries that she had given it great privacy too. Susannah had deliberately avoided so intimate a setting for a *tête-à-tête*. Now she knew that the time had come for her to seek it because she could no longer postpone the moment of talking to Vail with great candour.

They went quietly through the paved vestibule and up the bare curving steps to the apartment. Shaded lamps still gave a subdued glow to the patio and drawing-room, but the bedroom doors were closed, and the pleasant stillness suggested that no one had waited up for them. They went out on the gallery and through the delicate tracery of its ironwork looked down on Jackson Square. The old-fashioned street lamps shone brightly above their dark standards and the façade of the Cathedral caught some of their radiance and reflected it. Otherwise the square was in soft darkness. The Cathedral clock struck midnight, and the notes vibrated and trailed off into silence. Then nothing happened to disturb this. Vail came closer to Susannah and put his arm around her.

'Sue!' he said imploringly.

'Yes, I want to talk to you, Vail. Let's sit down, shall we?'

She freed herself gently, but when he tried to take her hand, after they were seated, she did not repulse him. She spoke to him with great earnestness, however.

'I've got to tell you, Vail, why I can't marry you; why you must stop asking me to. I hoped I wouldn't have to, but after tonight I know—'

'You don't have to tell me anything you don't want to. There's nothing you could tell me anyway that would change my mind. I haven't changed it in all these years, have I?'

'No. But you will now. I don't love you, Vail; I've kept telling you that all along and you wouldn't listen. Perhaps you'll listen if I tell you I belong to someone else.'

'No, I shan't. Because if you were engaged to someone else you wouldn't be out here with me. You wouldn't have been running around with me all this week. You couldn't play any man a dirty trick like that. You haven't got it in you.'

'I didn't say I was *engaged* to anyone else, Vail.'

'Well, good Lord, you're not trying to tell me you're *married*, are you?'

He laughed lightly, and leaned over to give her the kiss she had so long managed to evade. She drew away from him.

'Yes, I am. That's just what I'm trying to tell you. I'm secretly married. I've been secretly married for nearly a year.'

'I don't think much of your joke, Sue.'

'It isn't a joke. It's gospel truth.'

'You couldn't be married. No one would marry you and keep it a secret. No one would want to.'

'My – my husband did, Vail. He wouldn't marry me unless I promised to keep it a secret. And – and I wanted him so much I didn't care what terms I married him on, just so I could do it.'

'The dirty, thieving blackguard! The miserable sneak! The—'

'Oh, Vail, stop – please stop! You mustn't talk about him like that! I'm – I'm married to Phil.'

The soft stillness of the night had suddenly become electrified; instead of uniting them, it tore them violently apart. Vail dropped Susannah's hand and leapt to his feet.

'You're – you're married to Phil!' he said hoarsely. 'You've been married to him for nearly a year. No, you're not; you couldn't be; No Army chaplain would marry you secretly and no civilian priest either. Even if there were, you couldn't keep it a secret. If you went off together and registered at a hotel, someone would be sure to find out about it. Besides, you'd be using Phil's name now, you'd be getting part of his pay, you'd be living at Belle Heloise while he was gone, waiting for him to come back—'

'Vail, you don't understand. We were married by a Justice of the Peace. Phil – persuaded him not to let anyone know.'

'You mean he bribed this damn rascal not to record the marriage?'

'Vail, please don't talk about it like that. It wasn't Phil's fault. It was mine.'

'You'll have hard work making me believe that, Sue.'

'But it was. You see, Phil knew I was in love with him. I don't mean he thought perhaps I might be, from the way I – from the way I ran after him. Because I did run after him. You know that. You've seen me do it, over and over again. But I mean I told him so too. Of course I shouldn't have, but I did. And the last time I went up to Fort Bragg he said, hell if I felt that way about it, maybe we better get in a week-end together before he was sent overseas.'

So that's what he did, Vail said to himself. *I reckon that's what Aunt Cresside has always been afraid I'd do some time. I reckon she's dreaded that she'd find out, sooner or later, I was the same sort of blackguard my father was. And instead, it was Phil who did it. Phil, who'd always been the white-headed boy of the family. Phil, who's the overseas hero now, winning medals while I got stuck at one training camp after another. Well, he may be all that, but he's a dirty bastard just the same. He took Sue off to some filthy cat-house and registered under a false name and laid her. No, I'm getting this all mixed up. Phil's an officer and a gentleman; I'm the bastard. But I wouldn't have done what Phil'd done. I've always loved Sue too much to mess around with whores, and Phil'd treated Sue as if she were a whore herself. My sweetheart, who was going to be my wife. God damn him to hell! . . .*

'Vail, you don't understand even yet.' Sue was speaking in a voice of desperate pleading. But she was not pleading for herself, she was pleading for Phil, who had done this dreadful thing to her, and suddenly Vail's hatred for Phil became a consuming flame. But she went on pleading. She even tried to take Vail's hand, just as many times he had tried to take hers, and this time it was he who snatched it away. 'I told him I couldn't. I don't know why, but I just couldn't. Something inside stopped me. I know lots of girls do go off for week-ends, nice girls too, and I don't blame them, if that's the only way they can be with the men they love and they're satisfied with that much. But I couldn't. I didn't. You see, I didn't want Phil just for a week-end. I wanted him for always. At least, I wanted to know I had a right to him for always. So I said I was sorry, but I just couldn't. And then Phil made fun of me. He told me I was a sissy. And he told me I needn't be afraid, that he'd take care nothing happened to me. I didn't understand what he meant at first, and then he laughed and explained I needn't be afraid I'd have a baby.'

This can't be Sue who's talking to me; it can't, it can't. I thought she was going to be my son's mother. Hell, that's one of the things that's kept my loving her so! Any man would be proud to have her for the mother of his son, any man except Phil. No one but Phil would have acted as if she was some round heel in heat who mustn't get hooked, because, if she did, it would be awkward for him. . . .

'By and by he stopped making fun of me and explaining things to me because he began to get angry. He said he guessed I didn't love him all that much after all, that I'd just been putting on a good act. And that was the worst of all, Vail. Because, you see, when a girl's in love she wants to do what a man asks her to for two reasons: first because she longs to make him happy and then because she wants to be happy herself. I mean, in belonging to him. I think lots of people forget that. They talk about girls "yielding" as if it were some sort of a sacrifice. It isn't, not when they're really in love. It's what they yearn for more than anything else in the world.'

I can't stand it if you go on talking like this, Sue. I'm going to war. I might be dead a month from now. I can stand the thought of that; the only thing that ever bothered me was, I couldn't get across soon enough. But this is different. This is worse than being wounded; it's worse than being killed, sitting in this place where I meant to make love to you and hearing you say . . .

'But at last he said all right, if I was going to be stubborn about it, we would get married, if I'd promise to keep it a secret. We wouldn't go to a priest because it would take too long to get married that way. You see, I'm an Episcopalian, and he reminded me I'd have to get my baptismal certificate and sign papers about my children's religion and promise all sorts of things before I could marry a Catholic, and Phil would have had to go to Confession and Communion and all that. I asked him if his father and mother hadn't managed to arrange everything very quickly, in spite of those obstacles — someone had told me about their marriage, you see, Vail. And Phil said yes, but that was a very special case, where the priest knew his father well and had great confidence in him and recognized that there was a real emergency. He said he didn't know any such priest, that the chaplain at camp was a tartar, and that it was a Justice of the Peace or nothing.'

Phil didn't know any such priest. Of course he didn't. No priest would feel confidence in Phil, the way Father Navarre felt confidence in Dad, when he said there was an emergency. The chaplain at Fort Bragg would know right away there was something wrong — chaplains wouldn't be any good, to the Church or to the Army either, if they didn't know such things. He would have sent Sue home to wait for the man who'd loved her for years, only to find out just when he was starting off to war that she was married to his brother. No, damn it, Phil isn't my brother. I'm glad of that anyway, even if it makes me a bastard. Thank God I didn't have a scoundrel and a sneak for a brother as well as for a father. . . .

'So we went to the Justice's house. It was a horrid little place. But I didn't mind. At least, I didn't mind much. Of course, I'd always thought I'd be married in church and wear my great-grandmother's wedding dress, like you suggested, and that all my friends would be there, and that afterwards there'd be a reception with lots of flowers and a big frosted cake and champagne and presents. I thought there'd be a wedding trip to some lovely place. So I was a little disappointed because there was just a dingy little parlour with rubber plants in it and the Justice's wife and daughter for witnesses, and then that terrible hotel.'

'A horrid little place.' An unshaven man, in his shirt-sleeves, standing in one corner of a musty room mumbling words which should have been sacred and beautiful and spoken by a priest of God in a sanctuary. 'A terrible hotel.' A lousy dump, a pimp of a clerk, sneering at the soldiers who came in with a bottle under

one arm and a whore on the other – sneering at them but accom-modating them in swift succession. With rooms where the empty bottles the last couples had left still stood on sticky tables, and the soiled towels lay on the floor and the unhallowed bed was still unmade. Where the walls were so thin you had to close your consciousness to the carousal in the alley below and could not close it to the whoring in the next room! ... And I had always planned to take Susannah to a cottage in the St. Tammany woods, where we'd be by ourselves among the clean and fragrant pines, under the friendly stars....

'We had to sit in the lobby, because there wasn't a vacant room. We waited and waited. I'll never forget the soldiers who came in or the girls who were with them – the ones who came in and the ones who went out. They seemed to be coming and going all the time. Just soldiers and girls – girls and soldiers – hardly anyone else. And the girls all looked just alike. They had queer battered hats with drooping feathers and moth-eaten fur collars on their coats. Phil looked at them and said, "My God, even the whores are in uniform now!" '

Phil said this to Susannah, coupling her with those others, just as he had when he told her she needn't be afraid she'd have a baby. Susannah, who's always kept everyone at arm's-length, whom I've loved for just that, more than I've loved her for any-thing else. She sat in that filthy lobby, wearing a trim little tailored suit and watched that drab procession while she waited to go upstairs, and Phil said ...

'Finally a sergeant came through the revolving doors and glanced around. He was alone and he didn't look like any of the men lounging in the lobby with their girls. He was very spick and span and had on white gloves and an initialled arm-band. Phil saw him and muttered, "My God! The M.P.!" I asked him what that would mean and he said to wait a minute, we'd find out fast enough. The M.P. went around stopping in front of all the men in the lobby, one by one. He spoke to them, and after a minute or two some of them left the hotel. He didn't even look at the girls who were with the soldiers. Except when he came to Phil. Then he did look at me for a moment. But presently he turned back to Phil and said, "Let me see your papers." Phil reached into the pocket of his blouse and pulled out his pass. The M.P. inspected it carefully and then said, "Report back to camp immediately." Afterwards he went right on again, speaking to more men, and

Phil looked at me and muttered under his breath, "Well, that seems to be that. We don't get our week-end after all. Not this one, anyway. And it sounds to me as if we wouldn't be getting one for a long while. Unless I'm all upset, my outfit's pushing off ahead of time. Remember, you're not going to say anything about this little fling of ours till the war's over." '

'You mean you haven't seen him since then?'

'No. He went straight back to camp, and I didn't. I'd brought my bags in when I'd left that morning because we'd already decided we were going to be married. So the camp hostess wasn't expecting me, and after he'd made his rounds, the M.P. came back and looked at me again and asked if he could be of any service. Phil said, "Thanks a lot. I'd be ever so glad if you'd take her to the station." Then he said good-bye to me right there, and I didn't hear from him again for a month, and by that time he was overseas. He'd been alerted right away, just as he expected. Of course he writes to me now, once in a while. But he's never said anything about our being married in any of his letters. I'm not surprised at that because I know the censor sees them, and since Phil wanted it all kept a secret . . . They all come addressed to Miss Susannah Prescott.'

'You – you never went upstairs with him at all?'

'That's what I've kept telling you, Vail. We sat in that horrible lobby and waited and waited—'

For the first time her voice broke and she bent her head. So she did not see the swift change that came into his face, any more than she heard the thumping of his heart or sensed the great wave of relief which engulfed him. She was not even conscious of him. For a long time she sat pitifully still. Then she looked up again and went on unflinchingly.

'You know now why I didn't come to your graduation, Vail,' she said. 'And why I made excuses about coming to Belle Heloise and about having you come to Salome. I'd have loved being with you. I've always loved being with you. And I thought, just these last few days, it would be all right. I thought I could do that much for you. I didn't think it would be unfair to Phil—'

'Unfair to Phil! You talk to me about being unfair to Phil, after what he's done to you!'

He seized her hands again, this time holding them so tightly that she could not draw them away from him. 'Look here, Sue,' he commanded. 'If you think I'm going to let what you've told me scare me off, you're making the worst mistake you've ever made in your whole life. You're not married to Phil. You're not married to anybody. That Justice might just as well be a bad dream as far as you're concerned. Forget about him. I'll see to him when I get home. Meanwhile remember you're engaged to me and don't take any more long chances.'

'Vail, you know I can't be engaged to anyone. You know I *am* married to Phil. Everything's going to be all right as soon as he gets back, as soon as I have a chance to talk with him—'

'I'm going to have a talk with Phil myself, maybe sooner than he thinks, and I'll make it mighty clear to him what he's got to do next. I'm not going to spoil the rest of my leave telling you what I think of him. But I will tell you this much: if he ever gets in my way again, I'll know just what to do about that. And don't you ever say again that you love him. If you did, I might choke you. And I'd a lot rather kiss you. What's more, I'm going to.'

CHAPTER TWENTY

HE got his kiss, but afterwards he was sorry he had taken it, for he did not get one in return, and without response there was no reward. Susannah did not struggle against him, but she managed to withdraw her real self so completely that he embraced only its image. When he released her, he instantly knew that the division between them was more than physical. The companionable warmth of her manner, which all the week had given him such a sense of well-being and ease in her presence, had suddenly cooled to one of complete detachment, and when she spoke to him the friendly ring had gone from her voice.

'I'm sorry you did that, Vail. I'm sorry you've said what you have. I thought I could count on you to understand.'

'I do understand. I'm going to make you understand too.'

'You're not going to "make" me do anything, Vail. Please don't ever use that word again in speaking to me. I think we better not try to talk any longer – now, anyway. Goodnight.

Goodbye, rather. You're going back to Belle Heloise in the morning, aren't you?'

'No, not till afternoon. And I thought maybe you'd come with me, Sue. I thought we'd go by the River Road all the way. It's a beautiful drive. You've never taken it, have you? I want to show it to you. I've wanted to for a long while, and this is my last chance.'

'I'm sorry, Vail. If you hadn't said I wasn't married to Phil and talked about being engaged to me yourself—'

'I won't, if you go home with me. I promise.'

'I'm sorry, Vail,' she said again. 'I know you mean that now, but you might forget, if we took a long drive together. You might try to kiss me again.'

'No, I won't, Sue. Look at me. If you'll only look at me, you'll believe me.'

Involuntarily she glanced up at him. His eyes met hers squarely and steadfastly. For a moment she hesitated.

'Do you mean you wouldn't do it tomorrow and the next day, or do you mean you wouldn't ever do it again?'

'It would be easy to lie to you, but I won't do that either, Sue. I mean I won't do it tomorrow or the next day. Of course I'm going to see that Justice of the Peace on my next leave – if I'd only known before what you've told me tonight, I'd have seen him on this one, even if it had meant giving up these days with you. If there were still time, I'd go to North Carolina now. But there isn't. I don't intend for a moment to give you up, though, the only thing I'm promising is that I won't kiss you again against your will, and that I won't talk to you again about marrying me until you're convinced yourself that you're free.'

'But I don't *want* to marry you!'

'You will, some day.'

He was still looking at her squarely and he spoke with complete conviction. Susannah's latent anger flared into sudden flame.

'You're making a great mistake. I'll never marry you, I'll never want to. I made a mistake too. I ought to have known enough not to come here. I ought to have known you'd act this way. I'm not going home with you, Vail. I don't want to see you any more. Don't try to see me again. Don't write to me either. I shan't answer if you do. Goodbye.'

'Aren't you even going to wish me good luck?'

She hesitated again. Her flash of temper was dying down, even more quickly than it had flared up. It was impossible to stay angry with Vail. He was not asking for her sympathy, he did not want that; nevertheless, something about his complete single-heartedness was very moving. She not only wanted to wish him good luck, she wanted to tell him she would be hoping and praying for his safety and for his early return. She did not really mean she did not want to see him or hear from him again. She would have taken great pleasure in motoring up the River Road with him and spending the last day of his leave with him at Belle Heloise. She had always enjoyed his letters, and she knew they would be more interesting than ever from now on, because his experiences would be so much more thrilling than ever before. She would have liked to take back what she had said. She would also have liked to kiss him goodbye, as any well-bred girl would kiss a brother-in-law who was also an old friend and to whom she was genuinely attached. In fact, she had meant to do so. She had thought about it and even looked forward to it. But that was impossible, now that Vail . . . It was too bad.

'Yes, of course I wish you good luck,' she said more gently. 'The best in the world.'

'Then you're wishing that I'll marry you. A safe homecoming in itself wouldn't mean so much to me, Sue. What I want is a safe homecoming to you.'

She made a small deprecatory gesture. 'You see, it's hopeless to try talking. Goodbye again, Vail. And – well, the best of luck to you in everything else.'

She moved away from the wrought-iron railing and crossed the gallery slowly. At the entrance to it she turned, and hesitated a third time. Then, without speaking again, she went into the house.

After he heard her door close, Vail went in himself and turned out the lights which Cresside had left burning for them, pausing a moment between each one. When the friendly drawing-room and the pleasant patio were in complete darkness at last, he went down the curving stone stairway and along the paved entrance hall into the street. Somehow he knew that all the radiance had gone from the Square. But he noticed nothing else. Several late roisterers hailed him tipsily, but he did not hear them; several shadowy figures brushed against him, but he did not see them.

Everything that had passed between himself and Susannah

seemed utterly unreal and fantastic. If Sybelle had secretly married Riccardo, Vail could have understood that; indeed, he knew it was only Rick's firm insistence that he would neither force his way into a family where he was unwelcome, or enter furtively into such a relationship, that had kept her from headstrong action. Joyeuse was also quite capable of taking matters into her own hands; she did not happen to be in love with anyone, but Vail was quite certain that, if she were, she would not let anything stand in her way. Neither of the two, however, would have accepted a reluctant bridegroom, much less besought a lukewarm admirer to take her for his wife. That Susannah had done this was so utterly out of character that the whole procedure was inconceivable to him.

Mingled with his amazement was overwhelming relief. The fact that the opportune arrival of the Military Police had prevented the consummation of her marriage seemed to him nothing less than an act of God. Whatever Susannah said or thought, Vail knew that such a marriage could be annulled, and he was convinced that the time would come when she would be ready and eager to have it annulled. Somehow this must be done before she had a chance to commit another act of folly, this time one which would change her marital status – in other words, before Phil's first leave home. And as soon as she was officially free he himself must persuade her to marry him without further loss of time. He did not question the possibility of this either. He declined to.

The bright expanse of Canal Street, stretching out before him, brought him to an abrupt stop. He had gone past his hotel without realizing it. Turning quickly back, he made a determined effort to come out of his trance, and even stopped to chat agreeably with one or two acquaintances as he passed through the lobby. After he got into bed he tossed about restlessly for an hour or so; but he finally fell into a deep and dreamless sleep, and when he waked the sun was streaming into his room. He fumbled for his wrist watch, then shook it to make sure it had not stopped the night before; the small luminous hands were pointing to half-past ten. He jumped up, shaved, showered and dressed in record time, and went down to the coffee shop, taking a thermos bottle with him. As he was finishing his breakfast he asked the waitress to fill it and put up a couple of sandwiches for him. As soon as these were ready he checked out.

'No use hanging around, with Susannah feeling the way she does now,' he told himself conclusively. 'Better have the extra time at home – I can use it all right. I won't go by the Airline, though – I'd rather see the River Road alone than not see it at all before I leave. And it's a far piece from New Orleans to Belle Heloise when you take it thataway. I might as well get started.'

He had meant to say, at the garage, that he wanted his car washed, but as usual he had forgotten. Cresside often told him, laughingly, that no matter how many cars he had, or what make they were, they always looked and sounded exactly like Leaping Lena, which had long since given up the gasoline ghost. There was a good deal of truth in what she said. The jalopy of the moment had been new when rationing went in, but it had completely lost its original air of jauntiness, and it had developed a series of miscellaneous rattles with which no mechanic had ever successfully coped. Vail climbed in and waved a cheerful good-bye to the attendant who had brought it around. Then he bucked rapidly away towards Claiborne Avenue. It was just one o'clock when he came in sight of the Huey Long Bridge, and, swinging halfway around the traffic circle below it, saw the road home stretching out ahead of him. He actually forgot Susannah for a moment. He remembered only that this was his own countryside, that he loved it beyond any other part of the world, and that he would not see it again for a long time. Therefore, it never occurred to him that at this same moment Susannah, angrier than she had been at any time during the evening before, was engaged in futile argument with a telephone operator at the Monteleone Hotel.

'But Lieutenant d'Alvery can't have checked out. He told me himself he wasn't leaving till afternoon. Yes, I do want you to ring his room again. Yes, I do want you to have him paged in the coffee shop and in the lobby. You better try the garage too; he might have gone down there to see about his car. . . . All right, I will leave a message. Tell him that Miss Susannah Prescott would be very glad to meet him at Antoine's for lunch at one-thirty, and that she'll drive up to Belle Heloise with him this afternoon. B-E-L-L-E H-E— Oh, never mind! Just say up the River Road. At least you must know how to spell that!'

Susannah was very seldom rude to anyone. But then, she seldom had been so upset.

It was a perfect day, and Vail was not in a mood for haste. He wanted to loiter along, looking at every beautiful sight on the way, so that his memory of it would still be fresh and vivid when he was a long way off. Too bad he wouldn't be on hand for the celebration on St. Rosalie's Day; he and Rick had often gone to Kenner for the procession and the fireworks. They had always meant to test the malign powers of the famous tree at Poplar Grove too; but somehow they invariably lingered so long at Kenner that there had never been time for the notorious plantation ruins. There was no time now either; farther on there was so much he wanted even worse to see. Just the same, the story he had meant to track down was curious. Nearly all the old houses along the River Road were supposed to be haunted; their ghosts were as much a part of their tradition as their gardens, and Vail knew that at Belle Heloise the two allegedly went together. But Poplar Grove was the only place he'd ever heard of where a tree, instead of a house, had been linked with the supernatural. According to legend, any animal left beneath it dropped dead. All nonsense, of course. But it would have been fun to take some decrepit old mule there and see what happened. No, not a mule, he thought hastily, remembering Minnie and Betsy Ann, nor a horse either, because of Nostar, and certainly not a dog. But there must be some kind of an animal that didn't matter. And at Destréhan it would be fun to hunt for Jean Lafitte's buried treasure, much the same sort of fun it had been to dig in the Tramontes' back yard, when he and Rick were kids, with Syb there watching them. After the war was over he and Rick might ask if they could dig at Destréhan yet, just for the hell of it. He had meant to tell Sue about the tree and the treasure, if she had only come along. It would have been a relief to talk about nonsensical things like that, for a change. . . .

Still thinking about the legendary treasure and the way he had hoped Sue would take the story about it, he slowed down before the entrance to the old plantation house of Destréhan, admiring the well-ordered verdant lawns and the sloping green roof of the gleaming white house which harmonized with its surroundings in such perfection. Here was one place, at least, which retained its original elegance; and Ormond, a little farther on, was coming back into its own. Its grounds still looked a little bare, but its red brick and white clapboards were glistening with fresh paint, and its wide wings stretched out invitingly beyond its slender col-

onnettes. Yet both Destréhan and Ormond in their prosperity
lacked something which Belle Heloise in its shabbiness still possessed. Was it the love which a family could lavish unin-
terruptedly on a house from one generation to another which was
missing? Destréhan House was now a club for an oil company.
Ormond had recently passed over to new owners. Perhaps that
was the answer.

Just above Norco, the site of another prosperous oil company,
the River Road came to a dead end beside a sign announcing that
trespassers on Government property would be prosecuted. Momentarily Vail, absorbed in other thoughts, had forgotten that
this was the only indication of the approach to the vast Bonnet
Carré spillway. He turned back and took the first side street to
the Airline, remaining on it until he had passed LaPlace. He
might as well drop in at Roussel's, he decided, since he was going
right by it. He did not know a restaurant where the bartender
made better old-fashioneds, or where the trim, white-uniformed
waitresses served turtle soup and shrimp gumbo with more
efficiency and dispatch. A Greyhound bus had drawn up at the
entrance just before him, disgorging its hurried and hungry passengers; the bar, the counter, and the marbleized tables were all
crowded; the jukebox was blaring out 'Oh What a Beautiful
Morning', and every slot machine in the long row flanking the
tables was rattling and ringing. *A fellow ought to have a girl with
him in a place like this,* Vail thought; *if he does, all this racket
and confusion are fun, because he and she are part of it. If he's
alone, he's left out of it and feels a lot lonelier than he does on the
open road. Of course Antoine's is more Susannah's style; we
could have had lunch at Antoine's and our drive too. But, after
all, she used to like Jarreau's; I don't see why she shouldn't like
this too. I believe she would have.* For an instant his sense of
desolation was so great that he thought of going out again without ordering anything. Then one of the trim waitresses came
towards him, smiling confidently, and he said he would have a
double old-fashioned, if she could make it snappy, and she said
sure she could. She did, but while he was waiting he managed to
find a place in front of one of the slot machines, where he
promptly hit the jackpot. Unreasonably elated, he told the waitress he might as well have turtle soup too, and it didn't matter
whether she made it snappy or not. He wasn't in all that much of
a hurry. He could wait until the bus pulled out. As a matter of

fact, he lingered some time after that, savouring the familiar atmosphere. . . .

The Godchaux refinery was going at full blast, he observed, as he came to Reserve after swinging back on the River Road again; the imposing proportions of both factory and field, and the bustling activity which pervaded these, gave irrefutable evidence of the organization's prosperity. If Godchaux could so signally succeed in this region, first as a family, then as an organization, there was no reason that Vail could see why any other closely knit group could not do the same. Yet on the long stretch of road still ahead of him the Colonial Sugar Refinery was the only other large plant of this kind left. Around Lutcher the fields were cultivated for shallots and the unique type of strong tobacco – perique – which was grown nowhere else in the world; but there would be no more sugar, except at the State Penitentiary Farm above St. Gabriel. Oh, sure, small patches here and there, to be sold to the big refineries for a bit of extra cash in the fall; but no real stand of cane till you reached Hackberry, which was run by a Boston Yankee. No, sir, no real stand of cane grown by one of the old families till you got to Belle Heloise. . . .

He was no less puzzled than distressed by this. He knew all the explanations for it without feeling that any of them represented valid reasons. Surely some of the men who had once owned and worked this land could have clung to it and forced it to yield! Surely they could have kept their homes too, granted the same sort of effort and devotion! Only a few of the so-called Big Houses along this road had really been mansions; in most cases their proportions had been suited to families of moderate size and moderate means. The argument that they required armies of servants to maintain them, unlimited fuel to heat them, and vast fortunes to keep them in repair, had no weight with Vail. Trepagnier and Esperance, two of the famous old houses which he had already passed, were 'raised cottages', with their limited living quarters all on one floor; certainly they could not have been hard to run! Vail would have liked to know the unexpurgated story of their abandonment. St. Michael's Convent baffled him in much the same way. Why should this great Gothic building, one of the earliest centres of the Sacred Heart in the Deep South, and for over a century a fashionable school for girls, stand vacantly forsaken amidst rank and straggly growth? Had these signs of disintegration already begun when his mother went to school there? Could they have been at the root of her restlessness and rebellion?

Perhaps when he came back from the war he would find the answers to these questions – especially if someone else was sufficiently interested to help him search them out. But he made a determined effort to dismiss them from his mind now, reminding himself that he had not come up the River Road to fathom its mysteries or brood over its failures. He had come to watch the lovely light on the levee; the undulating effect of the road twisting around this; the peaceful cattle grazing there and the massed clouds overhead. He had come to see the lush vegetation, the clustering cabins, the Negroes loitering along, the old limestones which had once served as filters for the muddy river water. He had come to meet the great sugar trucks, shaped like assault boats, skeletal as they clattered past empty, menacing as they loomed up ahead, overladen, shedding stray stalks of cane in their thunderous progress. Resolutely, as his car swung up to the very doorstep of some house, he tried to close his consciousness to the knowledge that the reason he passed so close to it was because the road had been moved back again and again, when the river, cutting farther and farther to the East, had eaten away the land underneath the wide lawns which had once surrounded it. Several of these houses, more or less intact, were ornate examples of 'Steamboat Gothic'; their cupolas, cornices, belvederes and balustrades still rose in bewildering array. But their shades were drawn and their galleries empty; evidently their owners had felt that without their elaborate grounds and the strutting peacocks, stone deer, fluted urns and latticed gazebos, which had once adorned these, the multiple embellishments on the houses themselves had lost their effectiveness. Doubtless these property-owners had left to dwell in surroundings of more suitable simplicity. Vail could understand such an action and the feeling which prompted it, and the blank look of the more showy places did not affect him as poignantly as the decay of those whose essential beauty was massed on patterns which had survived the centuries. But, after all, the period pieces reflected the mode and the taste of an era which had been not only prodigal but robust; this era was part of American history, and these houses the symbols of it. He could not help hoping they would not eventually go the way of the others. . . .

As he passed one great grove of moss-festooned trees after

another he was still less successful in ignoring their significance; he knew that these groves had once formed the setting for houses long since destroyed by flood or flame, and that, whatever else might still be salvaged, these were gone forever. The bells hanging in separate scaffoldings beside the scattered Negro churches had once been the voices of plantations, just as the one cast by Thiac Maignan for François Estrade still served this animate purpose for Belle Heloise. The bowl-shaped iron kettles used as watering troughs for stock in roadside pastures had once been part of the proud mechanics of sugar-making. The rain-water cisterns, sprawling on short stilts beside houses still more squat, had once been sugar-mill boilers. He could not go a mile without confronting some fresh reminder that this region, once so rich that it was called The Grand Parade of the Deep South, was sinking farther and farther into desuetude; and with each reminder he resolved afresh, almost savagely, that once the war was over he would not rest until he had done his utmost to waken it to new life and new productiveness, and that Susannah should help him to do this. His love for her and his love for the land seemed more and more closely linked the farther he went. . . .

At Burnside even the blacktop ended; from there on he would have only the dusty gravel road until he reached Belle Heloise. It had never been a matter of political expediency to improve this part of the route, though it was listed as a state highway. That was something else again: why should the old d'Alvery place not have blacktop going past it, if the old Bringier and Columb places could? Vail resolved to find out, and, having found out, to take action. He would certainly have his hands full after the war. . . .

Suddenly it occurred to him that he was hungry, that the turtle soup he had eaten at Roussel's was all gone. But he still had the coffee and sandwiches he had brought with him from the Monteleone. As he went past the oilfields at Darrow, he knew he must be near the turn-off to Belle Helène, and decided to go and eat his supper on the steps of this magnificent deserted house. He had ceased trying to fight off his feeling of nostalgia about the vanished glories of the past; probably his mood was allied to the knowledge that without his efforts his own home would soon be a part of it. He watched for his turn-off, followed the dense growth of concealed shrubbery for a few hundred yards, and stopped his car beside the rickety gate where the noble mansion came into view.

It was not approached through an allee at the front, like so many plantation houses; instead the entrance was at the side, through the most beautiful grove of oaks that he had as yet seen. Only the levelled brick foundations remained of the outbuildings which had once stood at the west of the mansion, and these were so obscured by weeds that Vail stumbled over them as he walked along; but on the east the picturesque shell of a narrow, two-story *garçonnière* and a square *pigeonnier* still remained. Above them loomed the Big House. Its upper gallery sagged badly, but otherwise it showed no signs of serious deterioration. Its great square columns were still sturdy, its splendid cornice undamaged. Vail sat down on the crumbling pavement before the front door and looked out toward the river. A long sloping sweep of ground, which must once have been a terraced lawn, framed by magnolias, willows and water oaks, afforded an unobstructed view. The road itself did not show; it was swallowed up in the surrounding greenery. But if the trees on the batture had been cut, passing boats would have been readily visible from the gallery. Vail could picture them as they must have looked in that proud past which had so absorbed him all day, and as they might still look in an even prouder future. Grudgingly he admitted that when it came to location Belle Helène was unsurpassed; there was nothing elsewhere to compare with that splendid grove at the side and this superb open sweep in the front. The approach to Belle Heloise was restricted and confined compared to this.

A rosy sunset, suffusing the portico and the landscape with its radiance, gave added lustre to their beauty. In this lovely light the ravages of neglect were lost and the most exquisite aspects of past perfection intensified. Vail forgot he was hungry, forgot he was tired, forgot he was disappointed and depressed as he continued to sit, looking out towards the river, and trying to remember what he had heard about this place which seemed so tinged with magic. He knew it had once belonged to a man of great prominence named Duncan Kenner, who had been Jefferson Davis's Minister-Plenipotentiary on the Continent during the days of the Confederacy, and who had continued to merit such high esteem that even a 'black Republican' like President Arthur had been impelled to appoint him to the United States Tariff Commission. But who owned it now, or why they did not inhabit

306

it, Vail had no idea. He wondered about its name too. Someone
had told him it was named for the heroine of Offenbach's opera,
based on the faults and foibles of the Empress Eugénie. But that
seemed to him unlikely, for eventually he recalled that its original
name had been Ashland, and the latter designation must have
come long after the trivialities of the Third Empire had lost their
vogue. Now that he thought of it, he did not know how Belle
Heloise had got its name, and he was surprised that it had never
occurred to him before that he should ask. He did not know of
any d'Alvery or Estrade ancestress called Heloise, and if there
had been one he thought he would have. Perhaps some languish-
ing lady, long dead, had read the romance of the scholar Abelard
and his favourite pupil and had been so moved by it that she had
chosen further to immortalize her. He would find out from his
grandmother the next day and write to Sue about it. Of course, it
was all nonsense for her to say he must not write to her. He
would not clutter up the scene with letters, but he would write
whenever he had anything special to say, and this was exactly the
sort of thing that would interest her. She had been ever so
interested in the origin of Salome. The origin of Belle Heloise, or
Belle Helène, for that matter, should be equally intriguing to
her. . . .

Some stray cows, turned out to pasture on the abandoned
pleasure grounds, stopped to stare at him in mild wonder and then
meandered on again. Finally, a Negro, riding past on horseback,
reined in, sweeping off his tattered felt in an elaborate bow, and
wished the visitor a civil good evening. Evidently he was some
sort of a casual or voluntary caretaker. Vail got to his feet.

'Good evening. I hope I'm not trespassing. I was motoring up
the River Road and I just stopped to eat my supper.'

'Yo' doesn't want to buy Belle Helène, does yo', suh?'

'No, I've got a place of my own a little farther up the river. At
least, my folks have – Belle Heloise.'

'Ah done hear of it. An' Ah done hear it wuz a mighty fine
place.'

'We think so. I'm on my way there now. But I've always
admired this one too, every time I've passed it, and I thought no
one would mind if I stopped and ate my supper here.'

'No, suh, no one doesn't mind. Is yo' finished yo' supper
now?'

The Negro was eyeing the untouched package of sandwiches

covetously. It occurred to Vail that he really might be needy, though it was hard to imagine this in such a land of natural plenty. He picked up the package and offered it to the Negro.

'Yes, I've finished. I had this much left over. Would you care for it?'

'Ah thanks yo' kindly, suh. Ah sure does. Ah hopes yo' passes dis way agin, soon an' plenty. Ah lives alone, up dis here road a short piece, and Ah was fresh outen anything to eat dis evening. Now Ah got me a nice supper. Ah's sorry yo' doesn't want to buy Belle Helène. Proud to of met up with yo', suh.'

The Negro rode off, stopping to doff his hat in one more elaborate bow as he rounded the ruins of the *garçonnière*. Vail could not see beyond that. It was not 'good dark' yet, but it was already 'first evening'; dusk was closing in with the astonishing swiftness of regions where no long dim period prevails between the blaze of sunset and the splendour of night. It was logical that there should be no twilight here, Vail thought; the River Road was not a place of shadows, but of either darkness or light. ...

He could, if he chose, take the cut-off between Geismar and Carville, and if he had not lingered so long at Belle Helène he would have done so, for from it branched off, obscurely and remotely, still another road that he loved, one unlike any other that he knew: a ribbon-like white strip, bordered on one side by a quiet bayou and on the other by tiny, tidy farmhouses that somehow seemed even quieter. He had always thought that some day he would find out who lived in those farmhouses, and how; their complete detachment, their almost uncanny tranquillity, had always baffled him. The ribbon-like white strip led to nothing but a peaceful pasture; it had no definite ending any more than it had a logical beginning. Yet for some mysterious reason families had dwelt along it for generations in such contentment that they had never cared to stray. He had thought that Sue might like to see this hidden byway too. He had meant to show it to her this very afternoon. But now it was too dark to see it in any case. He excused himself for not taking it on those grounds, and on the grounds that, as this would be his last ride over the River Road for a long time, he could not afford to stray from it. ...

It went on and on, twisting and turning with the river, and so narrow at many points now that two cars could not possibly have passed each other. But Vail met no other cars and saw almost no signs of life until the huge illuminated plant of the Leprosarium suddenly loomed up ahead of him. Its brilliant lighting, its concrete walks, well-pruned trees and freshly painted buildings gave it the air of an ultra-modern and uniquely prosperous little town, inexplicably located in a region where slackness, poverty, and an agreeably 'do-less' existence were much more characteristic of village life. Only the high wire surrounding it betrayed it as a tragic enclosure, just as the inescapable rays of the searchlight flashing from Monticello Farms, a few miles farther on, marked that as a penitentiary operation. Vail passed them both without slackening speed; he hoped and believed that they were model institutions, and he could not miss them in the dark, as he had missed the picturesque paving stones taken from the old tombs at St. Gabriel. He had meant to show Susannah some of the old inscriptions and quaint names on those; but he had not meant to show her anything that would remind her of misery or crime. He did not wish to be reminded of it himself.

He was almost home now. Hackberry was the only plantation between Monticello Farms and Belle Heloise, and at Hackberry he did slow down, reflecting that it would be courteous as well as pleasant to stop in for a farewell word with Seaver, who would be gratified with his visit, and who would give him the latest news of Charles Boylston while they sipped a nightcap. But the Lodge was in darkness, like all the other houses along the way, though the sugar mill was still lighted and noisy. Besides, now that he was so close to home, he felt as if he could hardly wait to get there. He pressed his foot down on the accelerator and went over the remaining stretch of road at unpatriotic speed.

The cattle gap rattled as the jalopy went over it. *I suppose I ought to have that fixed,* Vail said to himself. *But I don't believe I ever shall. Dad always said the noise it made was the first sound that told him he was home, and that was why he loved it. I do too. I'd miss it if I didn't hear it. Next he used to listen for the pigeons cooing and the dogs barking, and watch for Amen lounging out to take the car. But I don't want anyone. Syb'll be waiting up for me. I've got her to watch for, and all the yard boys in the world aren't worth her little finger. And Maudie makes up for a dozen other dogs.* He was bucking forward through the crêpe myrtles as he thought of this, and as he swung past the iron gate leading to the yucca-bordered path and made the sharp turn that took him up to the right of the house he saw it rising before him in all the loveliness of its lighted windows and galleries, its gracious symmetry, its uncluttered spaciousness, its welcoming warmth. Always it was beautiful in his eyes. But never half so beautiful as when he came upon it at night, after making that sudden turn, and beheld it radiant above its dim lawns, among its dark trees. What did it matter if desolation reigned elsewhere along the River Road as long as this survived? He could not help what happened to other places; but this was his to preserve. He would have it and hold it not only against flood and fire, but against neglect, against sloth, against indifference, against carelessness and all other evils. . . .

Sybelle and Maudie were already in the open space beyond the colonnade. Before he was half out of the car, Sybelle had her arms around his neck and Maudie was leaping around his legs. He disengaged himself, laughing.

'Look, you two, give a fellow a chance. You've got me pinned in between you, and I want to get out of this car. I've been in it nearly all day.' He kissed Sybelle heartily, gave Maudie a quick pat, and in mock desperation managed to slide through to freedom. But Sybelle linked her arm in his, and Maudie continued to leap upon him with joyous barks as they made their way across the gallery.

'I thought Sue was coming home with you, Vail!'

'I thought so too. But she said goodbye to me in New Orleans.'

'Oh . . . I was looking forward to seeing her too. I had the Henry Clay room all ready for her.'

'That was sweet of you, Syb. But maybe it's better this way, after all.'

'Well, if you think so . . . Joyeuse has gone to bed, but *grand'mère*'s still awake, Vail. She thought Sue was coming with you too. She'd planned to give her a slip from the green rose. She's got it in a vase by her bed.'

'That's darn nice of her. She's never given one to anybody before, has she? I'll go and thank her.'

'I think it would please her a lot if you'd have a snack in her room, too. I've got everything ready. We'll have time for our own visit in the morning, won't we?'

'Sure. We'll take time. Come on. Don't let's keep the matriarch waiting. This is pretty late for her, you know.'

They went up the stairs, together, past the Spanish statue, with Maudie close at their heels. Madame d'Alvery was listening for their approach; she turned her head on her great square pillows and looked towards the shutter door leading into the hall. When it opened, and she saw that Susannah was not there, she turned away again, in obvious disappointment, and looked fixedly at the slip from the green rose, rising from a vase on her night table beside the *veilleuse*. She had waited a long time to give this slip to just the right girl. And now it seemed the right girl had not come, after all. Vail saw the movement and understood it. He leaned over and put his hand on his grandmother's shoulder.

'I'm sorry that you're disappointed, *grand'mère*,' he said. 'I'm disappointed too. But you keep that slip where you can take good care of it. Some day Susannah'll be here to get it.'

CHAPTER TWENTY–ONE

IT was still very early when Vail began to stir drowsily, and after half opening his eyes to the restful darkness, he closed them again and burrowed further down between the sheets. Maudie, who had welcomed him with rapture the night before and curled up contentedly at his feet when he went to bed, raised her head alertly for a moment, wriggled along at his side to lick his hand, and then, receiving no response beyond an absent caress, composed herself placidly for further slumbers. But Vail could not go back to sleep again after all. The realization that this was his last day at home had already pierced his semi-consciousness, and though he tried, for a little while, to drown it in dreams, he could not do so. When the first faint streaks of grey light stole into the room he flung aside the bedclothes almost impatiently, lifted the mosquito bar, and slid down from the high four-poster. Maudie immediately sprang up, and after a brief battle with the mosquito bar, which had always baffled and enraged her, freed herself, jumped down and stood expectantly beside him, wagging her short tail in a fresh access of hope and joy.

'Everyone else is still asleep, Maudie,' Vail said, addressing her, according to his habit, as if she had been a human being.

'We might as well start our rounds outdoors. We've got lots of space to cover before night.'

'I'm not asleep. May I come in?' Sybelle called from the next room.

'Just a sec. Wait till I get my pants on. Sorry I waked you, though, Syb.'

'You didn't. I was glad when I heard you speak to Maudie. I'd been awake a long time – that is, more or less.'

'Well, then. I'm sorry about that. . . . All right, come on in now.'

Sybelle swung open the shutter door between their rooms, and he saw, in the slipper chair beside her bed, the doll which had been Riccardo's first present to her. She had persistently treasured this as an ornament since outgrowing it as a plaything, despite the merciless teasing of Phil and Joyeuse; and to Vail, Sybelle's stubbornness in this respect was typical of her tenacity in other ways. No one gauged as accurately as he did the deceptiveness of her apparent docility. She came towards him, digging her fists into her eyes and stumbling a little. Her face was still flushed with sleep and her blonde curls were tumbled around her shoulders; in her quaintly cut, rose-coloured dressing-gown she looked ridiculously young and almost unbelievably lovely. Vail put an arm around her to steady her, and she snuggled her head down on his shoulder and rubbed her face against his neck. He kissed her hair, and then smoothed it gently away from her forehead before kissing it again.

'You're a mighty sweet somebody,' he said with great tenderness. 'I wish Rick could see you, looking like you do now. It's too bad to waste all this on me.'

'Nothing's wasted on you. Nothing's good enough for you. I hope you get the very best there is. Vail, I don't mean to pry, but didn't you get anywhere at all with Sue? What I mean is—'

'Sure I got somewhere with her. Look, what say you and I have breakfast together, as long as we're the early birds? I've got quite a lot I want to say to you, and I didn't have much of a chance last night. It looks as if I wouldn't have another, either. I'll cruise along and start the coffee dripping.'

'I think breakfast's a fine idea. Lethe and Creasy don't get here till eight-thirty.'

'Doesn't *grand'mère* have her coffee before that?'

'Yes, but it's put in a thermos beside her bed at night, to save

Dinah a trip over the stairs the next morning. Dinah's getting mighty old and feeble, Vail. She keeps saying, effin you and I don't hurry up, she won't never have no mo' d'Alvery young 'uns to nuss, afore she gits buried alongside Selah and Lou Ida. She's faithful as they come, but her heart just isn't in taking care of an old lady the way it always was in taking care of a new baby.'

'It wouldn't do to disappoint her in her declining years, would it? We'll have to see what we can do about it. . . . Well, to get off a highly original remark, times do change, don't they? Everyone used to have coffee in bed at Belle Heloise, and there were so many servants to bring it that they practically tumbled over each other on the stairs. Incidentally, I've been meaning to ask you, what became of Dumps? I thought she was shaping up pretty well, for a new house girl, that time I came home from Lake Charles.'

'She was, but she decided to go to California and complete her education, or so she said. That's what Minta said too. I've heard they changed their minds and that they're both getting fantastic wages in a factory – seven dollars a day or something like that. Even allowing for exaggeration, I reckon they're making more than I ever could. I don't know whether you remember Minta, Vail – Phronsie's daughter. She was the prettiest little piccaninny on the River Road when you and I were children, and she's a beauty now. She could easily pass for white.'

'And probably does, where she is now. Well, I don't know as I blame her for trying. . . . Look, we mustn't stay here jabbering like this if we're going to have any time downstairs. You have to be at the office by eight, don't you? I'll make the coffee, Syb. You've got to get into your uniform and I can go along to the kitchen just like I am, this last time.'

He had everything ready when she joined him in the patio half an hour later, looking very trim and efficient in her neat uniform, with her golden hair tucked up smoothly under her stiff cap and collar fastened close around her soft white throat. Vail regarded her appraisingly as she poured the coffee and passed the toast.

'You like this Red Cross work you're doing, don't you, Syb?' he inquired.

She considered the question before answering it. 'Yes, I like it,' she said at last, guardedly. 'I want to do something to help along the war effort, and this seemed the most logical undertaking. I think I'm fairly good at it. Anyhow, I try hard. But I don't love it the way Joyeuse loves the work in the laboratory at the mill. Do you realize how well she's handling that, Vail? There isn't another college graduate left there now, or any men. She's got just high school girls to help her. But I believe Dad would say himself, if he were here, that it's never been better run.'

'I'll bet he would too. And how about her morale? Is she keeping that up? I haven't had a chance to ask her this time, or to see for myself.'

Sybelle laughed. Joyeuse and her 'morale' constituted the pet family joke. On the occasion of his last visit to Belle Heloise before he started to sea, she had given Barry Pereira a somewhat indefinite promise that she would 'try to wait for him'. But she had none of Sybelle's single-hearted fidelity. Several young chemists at the Standard Oil divided her attention among them, and when her pretext of a common interest in laboratory work had worn rather thin, she took refuge in the contention that she had to do something to 'keep up her morale' during Barry's absence, which, according to her, had now been 'unreasonably long'. The reminder that the war itself was dragging out to considerable length, and that Barry would be among the first to regret this, had no visible effect on her; she continued to add to her list of eligible suitors and appeared to derive untroubled enjoyment from their attentions.

'Her morale seems to be getting better and better all the time,' Sybelle said jestingly. 'I don't know why it wouldn't. She has more and more men boosting it. I think it's rather hard on Barry, but, after all, he knew what to expect – she's always been perfectly honest with him. Perhaps you could say something to her before you leave, though – after all, there ought to be some limit.' She glanced down at her wrist watch and gave a startled exclamation. 'I've only got five minutes more, Vail,' she said. 'It's so good having you here, all to myself too, that I didn't realize how fast time was flying. You said there was lots you wanted to say to me. What, besides to ask whether I like my work?'

'I wanted to ask you how much longer you were going to let the family keep you from marrying Rick, hoping you wouldn't say, none of my damn business.'

'I've never said that to you, Vail, have I, about anything? ... I can't very well marry Rick, though, while he's out in the Solomons.'

'Sure that's where he still is? I may be telling tales out of school, but his division's sure been through a terrific campaign and I've heard rumours it was going to be rewarded with a rest on Guadalcanal. You know that's taken shape as one of the large rear area bases now, and has all the comforts of home – pretty near all, anyway – tents and floors and all that.'

He grinned, and Sybelle tried to return the smile. But she shook her head.

'I'd be glad if I thought he was in a tent instead of a foxhole. But I wouldn't be any nearer marrying him.'

'Well, I still don't know whether I'm talking out of turn. But there's another rumour going round that, instead of getting sent to Guadalcanal, a few men are getting sent home. "Secret missions" I believe the usual reason is. Steady there – I didn't say I thought Rick *would* be. I said I thought there was a chance he *might* be.'

Sybelle gripped the table hard. Then she leaned across it and whispered.

'You won't give me away, will you, Vail?'

'You know I won't.'

'If he does get sent back I'll marry him straight off. Even if I have to elope with him. If I have a chance like that, a chance I've hardly dared pray for—'

'Well, you may – and gosh, if I were only going to be here—'

'Yes, I know. You'd help me. You'd stand by. It's one of the reasons why I feel as if I couldn't bear to have you leave, Vail. Daddy's gone and Phil's gone, and even if they'd been here, they wouldn't have helped me. Daddy would have hindered me and Phil would have laughed at me. He wouldn't have understood how much Rick means to me, any more than Joyeuse does. I think maybe Franchot might have, if he'd lived – he was a sensitive little soul. But Phil and Joyeuse don't take love seriously, Vail, the way you and I do.'

'I'll say they don't.'

He spoke so harshly that she looked up at him in surprise. He pressed her hand and rose.

'I reckon we can't stretch those five minutes any longer, Syb,' he said. 'I'm mighty glad you told me what you have, though. You know I'm all for it. And whether I'm here to help you or not, you stick to it. You marry Rick as soon as he gets here, no matter how hard anyone tries to stop you. Don't elope either. Don't – don't do it as if you were ashamed of it. It'll mean a lot to him to have you act as if you're proud of it. I — I happen to know. You can carry it off if you make up your mind to. Have a real wedding, have a big party. Mom will help you when it comes to a showdown. So'll Aunt Cresside and Uncle Fabian. You haven't raised enough hell about it so far, that's all the trouble. *Grand'mère*'s the only one who'll put up a real fight to stop you, when you do, and if you can't get the better of one feeble old lady, you're not half the girl I think you are. Keep your chin up, Syb. Be a fighting lady. Remember I'm betting on you.'

'I will, Vail. Thanks a lot. And there's something I want you to remember too.'

'What's that?'

'That you're my littler brother. That I think more of you than anyone else in the world except Rick.'

For a few minutes after she had left him, he continued to sit at the rustic table, smoking and playing with Maudie's ears. Then he stacked up the dishes and carried them into the kitchen, which was still empty. As a matter of fact, it had always seemed more or less empty to him since Lou Ida left it for the last time, and he was glad to leave it himself and go back into the patio. No other cook ever inhabited it as she had, filling it with husky song and fragrant vapours while she stood indefatigably at the stove preparing the hot cakes and beaten biscuits, the fried chickens and baked hams, the shrimp gumboes and crawfish bisques and turtle soups on which the family feasted. Creassy was skilled in her craft too, and Lethe ploughed through a considerable amount of work during the course of a day; the d'Alverys still were better served than almost anyone else they knew. But there was more grumbling and less gusto than in the old days, less joyous pride in labours well performed, less love and respect for those who directed these. Vail had never laid any of Amen's shortcomings to Creassy's door, and he assumed the reason he did not care for Lethe as he did for Dinah was because Lethe had not been his nurse, and that therefore the same tie did not exist between them. But he did not deceive himself about the general situation at Belle Heloise or blame it all on the war. He knew that something vital and precious was disappearing from the place with its old servants, and that the next generation would never know the fullness of experience which had made his own childhood so rich and warm because of them.

Almost as if he had called her, Dinah came down the outside stairway that led from the rear of the upper gallery to the patio. She still wore the full quaint type of dress which had always been her habit and she had never abandoned her tignon; but instead of moving majestically she now walked slowly and painfully, and he went forward to meet her and to take from her the tray which she carried with such difficulty and with such care. She spoke to him scoldingly, as she had always done, but he was not deceived by that either. He knew that Dinah was not really annoyed with him, that as a matter of fact she adored him, but that she saw no reason why she should not continue to admonish him, exactly as she had done when he was two years old.

'Yo' done wake up Madame with yo' chattering, yo' and Miss Sybelle,' Dinah said reprovingly. 'Don't yo' know dat po' old lady need her rest? Why yo' don't go set in de dinin' room eat yo' breakfuss?'

'Go on, Dinah, quit your fussing. *Grand'mère* couldn't possibly have heard us unless she was awake already.'

'She ain't so well dis mornin', Mr. Vail. She worryin' herself caise yo' goin' away. She say yo' de onlies' one she got left. Po' little Franchot, he daid, an' de Colonell, he gone, an' Mr. Phil gone, an' now—'

Dinah began to rock back and forth, moaning. Vail set the breakfast tray down on the rustic table which he had just cleared and took hold of her arm.

'There's nothing for her to worry about, Dinah. Poor little Franchot's been dead a long time, so there's no use to start grieving about that all over again. And the Colonel isn't in any danger. As for Phil and me, that's just good riddance to bad rubbish. Besides, we'll be back again almost before you know it, bothering the life out of you, the way we always have. I'll go and remind *grand'mère* of all that in a minute. But I want to talk to you first.'

'Yassuh, an' Ah wants to talk to yo' too. All right fo' yo' to say ain't nothin' to worry about, but Ah's tellin' yo' Ah's been hearin' all kinds of queer noises in dis house lately. Madame, she done hear 'em too. She ain't said nothin', but Ah knows. She done hear dat old ghost walkin' aroun', jes lak Ah has.'

'I thought you told me a while back all the ghosts were at Hathaway.'

'No, Mr. Vail, Ah don't never say *all* de ghosts is down to

317

Hathaway. Is ghostes dere all right, but our own ghost, he don't never go away from Belle Heloise.'

'What do you mean, our own ghost? I didn't know we had a ghost of our own.'

'Sure you did, Mr. Vail. Yo' knows dat man what made de gardens and teach de chillun, he's our own ghost.'

'You mean Angus Holt? I know my grandfather used to dress up in a sheet and try to scare everybody pretending he was Angus Holt. I know Phil did too, after Dad told him that story. I don't know anything else.'

'Dey done cober up day face wid de sheet when dey do dat, so no one won't see day ain't no real ghost, an' dey don't say nothin' caise dey knows us can tell 'em by 'em's voices. De real ghost, he show his face an' he speak, too, when he git ready to tell bad news. Yo' po' granddaddy daid long time, Mr. Vail, and Mr. Phil, he gone away 'most two years now. Dey ain't walkin' in no gallery at Belle Heloise. But dat ghost, he walkin' in de gallery 'most every night now. Don't mean nothin' good when he walk dere regular like dat, 'stead ob jes' once in a while lak he generally do. Means he gettin' ready to show his face an' tell his bad news, one ob dese days.'

'I'm sorry you didn't speak to me about him last night just as soon as I got home, Dinah. If you had, I'd have gone out and told him he'd got to stop disturbing my poor old grandmother and my poor old mammy. But it's too late now. I can't do it tonight, because I'll be gone myself. So you tell him for me, will you?'

'Lord sake, Mr. Vail, yo' knows Ah never talks to no ghostes! Ah covers up my head *good* with de bedclothes when Ah hears dat ghost comin'. Ah hears him jes' de same, Ah can't help it, but—'

'Well, if you won't go out and talk to him I don't know what to suggest, but I reckon you better stop talking *about* him and listen to me for a few minutes. . . . What's this I hear about your getting tired waiting for some new babies at Belle Heloise?'

The mournful look faded from Dinah's face, and for the first time a glad light came into her old eyes when she looked at Vail, and a smile twisted her lips.

'Dat's right, Mr. Vail. Here's Miss Sybelle 'most an old maid already, an' yo' 'most an old batch. Ah is worryin' 'bout it, Ah sure is.'

'Well, you won't have to worry much longer. Because I've got a feeling Major Tramonte will be coming home pretty soon, and that when he does you'll be having a wedding here.'

'Yo' don't mean dat pedlar man's boy, does yo', Mr. Vail? Caise Madame she ain't never gwine let my child marry dat boy, an' neither me. My white folks, dey's quality. Ah ain't gwine nuss no babies what ain't quality babies.'

'Now you listen to me, Dinah, and you get this straight. Unless you promise me you'll do everything you can to make Miss Sybelle happy while I'm gone, I'll come back and haunt you myself, dead or alive, worse than any ghost did. And the way to make her happy is to look after her when she gets married. Because she's going to get married and she's going to marry quality. I don't want to hear you saying any more about a pedlar man's boy, you hear? I want you to start saying Major Tramonte right now and keep on saying it till you start saying Mr. Rick.'

For a moment Dinah stood fingering her apron, her expression still mutinous. Vail put both hands on her shoulders.

'That's orders, Dinah,' he said. 'My last ones before I go **away**. I can count on you to carry them out, can't I?'

She looked up at him, the mutinous expression fading from her face and tears welling up in her eyes. She nodded her head slowly several times. Then she broke away from him and turned towards the stairs. He could hear her sobbing as she mounted these, even more painfully and slowly than she had come down. Her wretchedness was so heartfelt that it affected him poignantly. But sitting there, thinking about it, only made it seem the worse. Besides, there was still a great deal to be said and done before he left the plantation. Vail went away from the patio himself and strode out past the stables towards the sugar-house road; then, after a moment's hesitation, he decided to go to the overseer's house first and to the mill itself afterwards. Sance still went home for his dinner whenever he could; though his mother had long since died, his habit of getting back, as often as possible, to the quaint old house was so firmly fixed that he had never even tried to break himself of it. Vail thought that he might find his overseer there alone; in that case, they could talk more privately and peacefully in the picturesque living-room – unchanged, except that it had retained an atmosphere of emptiness ever since Madame Sance left it for the last time – than anywhere else about the place.

Evidently the same idea had struck Sance. At all events, he was standing in the open doorway, smoking his pipe, with an air of expectancy rather than the more characteristic one of haste. He had already finished his dinner, he said; but he hoped Vail would have coffee with him. Thanks, Vail would like to; they could talk while they were drinking; and, forestalling the next questions, he added that he would take it black, not white, and that he would drink it, not eat it. It was pretty near his own dinner time; not that he ever had to worry about spoiling his appetite, but he thought this time it might not be such a bad idea to save up. . . .

He grinned as he spoke, and Sance smiled back at him. But when they had their coffee and were seated opposite each other on either side of the hearth, with the small empty bench between them. Sance could not keep his concern to himself.

'I'll do everything I can to save the crop, Vail. But we're getting behind already, and we haven't been grinding two weeks yet. I've been wanting to ask you how you'd feel about having some of those German prisoners on Belle Heloise. I don't need to tell you that's the way lots of planters are fixing to manage this fall, and with camps opening up at both Donaldsonville and Port Allen—'

'I'll tell you just how I'd feel. They may be good workers, and they may be the only ones you can get. But I'd rather lose the crop than have one of them set foot on Belle Heloise. The reason we're shorthanded is because so many men, white and black both, who belong here, are trying to stamp out everything they stand for. Every time I think of the dirty bastards I can't help saying to myself: "Damn them, they're still alive, and they're still Nazis." I won't have them doing our work on our place.'

'Well, I can see your point. But just the same—'

'Wait a sec, will you? I've got some good news for you. Maybe when you've heard it the picture won't look quite so dark to you. I had a chance to talk with my uncle about our problems here while I was in New Orleans, and he authorized me to order three more Prescott machines.'

'That's mighty generous of Mr. d'Alvery, and I appreciate it. Orders and deliveries are two different things these days, though.'

'I know that. But I've also been in touch with Mr. Prescott. He promised me he'd have one cane-cutting machine here by November first, and the other two soon after that. What's more, he said he could get us four extra carts. With that much surplus equipment you'll be a lot better off than most of the planters who've taken on those damn prisoners.'

'We may be, at that. I don't need to tell you that the best cane-cutting machine ever made doesn't clean cane as well as when it's cut by hand. We may have some pretty serious milling problems as a result of trying to substitute so much machinery for man-power. Besides, it burns me up to think that, though it costs more and more all the time to produce sugar, it's the only basic com-modity that isn't bringing a better price than before the war. But hell! I reckon we can handle all these problems some way.'

'That's the way to talk! Anything else you'd like to get off your chest before I go back to the fields?'

'Two of our boys who've been in the service have come home while you were in New Orleans, Vail. Maybe you'd like to have a word with them, too, before you leave.'

'You bet I would. Which ones are they and what's your latest dope on them? Naturally, I'd rather not let on I don't know.'

'You knew that Cato's boy, Rush, was wounded in the landing at Casablanca last year, didn't you?'

'Yes, I knew that much. Is he one of those who's come back?'

'Uh-Uh. He's quite a hero too. No, I wasn't making a dirty crack. I meant it. He was always proud of his work, even when he was just a kid, starting out as a water boy, and he'd got to be the best derrick operator I had in the yard when he went into the service. Well, the poor devil won't operate a derrick any more — for a long time, anyway. He may have to go back to driving the water cart. I reckon he could do that. I tell you, something turned over inside me when he showed up here one evening and just said he was reporting back to work — still in his uniform, mind you, with the Purple Heart and the African Campaign Ribbon and a Combat Star.'

'Beat all his white folks to it, did he?' Vail asked, with a touch of envy. Then he added, ungrudgingly: 'Well, more power to him! What about the other man? Is he a hero too?'

'I'm afraid not. He was discharged from Camp Rucker for mental derangement — couldn't stand the shock of crawling un-der live ammunition. But he showed up in a uniform too — not a private's, either – a sergeant's. Afterwards he got cold feet because he heard someone on the Draft Board was on to him – cut his chevrons off and hushed his mouth. He's back on the mill floor as an oiler, and as far as I can see he's doing as well as he ever did. That isn't saying so much, and I wouldn't know how serious this "mental derangement" really is.'

Vail laughed. 'I'll give him the once-over and let you know what I think. And of course I want to see Rush. But I mustn't keep you any longer. So long, Sance! You know I'm counting on you. We've never lost a crop at Belle Heloise yet, and we're not going to begin now, either.'

As Vail approached the laboratory he could see Joyeuse standing by the window, gravely inspecting the precipitation of clarified juice in a test tube. The trim white uniforms she now habitually wore were very becoming to her; and the position in which she stood revealed to great advantage the lovely lines of her trim figure. Vail paused for a moment to enjoy the pleasing picture she made. But when she caught sight of him she frowned and called to him impatiently.

'Just look what I'm up against!' she said, indicating the test tube. 'It's all very well to talk about solving labour problems with mechanical harvesters. But everyone who gets off that line neglects to mention how much foreign matter is introduced with the cane. Leaves – grass – root dirt—'

'I know the labour problem can't all be solved by machinery, Joy,' Vail said seriously. He had come into the laboratory, and now he stood beside her, watching her as she went quietly and efficiently on with her work. Her helpers had gone to the boarding-house for their midday meal, but apparently she had no idea of stopping. 'Those problems are eased, though,' he went on. 'At least, for everyone except the chemists. And with a chemist like you the rest of us know that part of the problem's in good hands. I'm ready to leave it right there. I've got lots of confidence in you, Joy. Listen – I've been talking about problems, of one kind or another, all morning. Can't we forget about them for a while and go on up to the Big House? It must be almost dinner time, and I'm hungry.'

'Well, so am I, now that you mention it. There's just one thing I'd like to bring up myself. You know that for years we've been using a line-drawing of the sugar mill on our bags. It's good, in its way, but it's rather static. I've been thinking, if we could have patterns printed on the bags instead—'

'What kind of patterns?'

'Well, centrepieces and doilies. The kind of thing women like to embroider for their dining-room tables. And fancy aprons – the kind they like to slip on over an afternoon dress when they're getting ready to entertain the weekly bridge club and might be caught by the first arrival without time to whisk the apron off. Women like that would feel they're getting a lot for nothing – material and pattern right along with what they'd paid for. They'd ask for Belle Heloise sugar instead of just sugar. The picture of the mill doesn't mean anything to them – they know they can't buy that. But patterns and cloth—'

'I think maybe you've got something there, Joy, certain female weaknesses being what they are – we won't discuss any of the others. Go ahead and try out your patterns. The dies won't cost much and they'd be your only expense.'

'Not just doilies and aprons either,' Joyeuse continued, much encouraged. 'I think we should have dolls too – a pattern for a doll that would have to be cut out and stuffed, and patterns for two or three different dresses she could wear, after they were run up on the machine. I worked them all out to scale. We could label the doll with the name too – Belle Heloise, of course. Little girls would get interested in our sugar as well as their mothers. I've got some sketches all made. I'll show them to you if you like.'

'No; I'm ready to take your word for it that they're good.'

'Just as you say. I didn't mean to unload anything extra on you, Vail. I can look after this part of the job, and I will. You can depend on that, if it'll help any.'

'You know it helps no end. But look, Joy. I wouldn't want you to get a lot of heroic ideas, and give up something that meant a darn sight more to you than chemistry and patterns, just because you promised me you'd stand by.'

'I haven't any heroic ideas. It just so happens that nothing means any more to me than chemistry. The patterns are just a side issue, possibly profitable.'

'Nothing – and no one?'

'Nothing – and no *one*.'

She had disposed of the test tube and was washing up at the small neat sink in the corner. She did not turn around while repeating his question as a statement, lightly emphasizing the last word. But after she had dried her hands on a paper towel, she faced him with her sunny smile.

'Wouldn't two weddings in the family hold you for a while?' she inquired. 'I'll agree to that many. But if you're going to talk about more than that, you and I are going to have a row. Which would seem rather a pity, your last day at home. Come on, let's go eat.'

It was evident to Vail, as he took Gervais' place at the table opposite his grandmother, that a definite effort had been made to give his last meal at home a festive atmosphere. Joyeuse had not taken time to change from the crisp white uniform she habitually wore at the laboratory; but the three elderly ladies were all attired in what even a youthful masculine eye could recognize as 'best dresses'. Though Madame d'Alvery had never worn anything but black since her husband's death, she observed different degrees of elegance in fabrics, and today's costume was made of heavy grosgrain silk which rustled as she walked, and which was adorned with frills or rosepoint lace, fastened at the throat with a diamond and onyx brooch. In a stubborn effort to produce an effect as different as possible from Madame d'Alvery's perennial mourning, Mrs. Randall had long since abandoned her drab greys and wore the brightest colours she could find; today's choice had been a sleazy rayon print with an emerald green background and a pattern of orange curlicues. Miss Mittie wore a genteel lavender silk and her mother's pansy pin.

With gratifying heartiness, Vail complimented them all on their appearance, admired the arrangement of flowers which formed the centrepiece, and praised each dish that Lethe presented to him. He did not think the mirlitons had ever tasted so good to him; he liked them split and stuffed, the way Creassy had fixed them that evening, best of all. The Satsumas were mighty sweet; it must have been an unusually good season for fruit – too bad there wasn't enough sugar to save it all, on a plantation at that!

After he had finished his chocolate ice cream, he continued to sit still, smoking one cigarette after another, and drinking his coffee in slow sips. He was thinking about Sue again, he could not help it; if she had only been there, how much she would have helped him through this hard meal! With her complete *savoir faire* and her natural composure, she would have really eased the inevitable strain, which his forced cheerfulness had only lessened a little. Another man at the table would have helped a lot too; he had never missed Gervais so much, and it was only because he hardened his heart against Phil, on account of Sue, that he did not miss the engaging young devil still more. He thought wistfully about Franchot too. Franchot would have been twenty now; if he had been there he would have helped to counterbalance this ultra-feminine atmosphere. Vail supposed they would always think of Franchot as a frail child. But he might have outgrown the early delicacy, he might have been in one of the services himself by this time, if only . . .

Vail did not want to think about Franchot. He wanted to get off and be on his way in town. He glanced at his grandmother from time to time to see if she would give the signal to rise, but through either accident or design she did not meet his eye, and he knew better than to take the initiative himself at her table. He had heard her say more than once that a man who did not recognize the prerogative of the lady of the house in this respect was in the same class as a man who told his wife, in the hearing of others, that it was high time they left a party – to put it plainly, in the class of social pariahs. But Joyeuse had not inherited a taste for fine points of etiquette. When Vail began pouring out coffee the third time from the delicate porcelain pot which Lethe had put beside him, Joyeuse jumped up, pushing back her chair and turning to him instead of her grandmother.

'I'm sorry, Vail, but I can't hang around any longer. My best helper at the lab is sick today, and I've got all her odd jobs on my hands as well as my own. You know I hope you get the best, and all that.'

'Yes, I know. Well, go on keeping up your morale, but give Barry a break once in a while, if you can, without getting too much of a let-down.'

'I'll think about it. So long, Vail.'

'So long, Joy.'

He rose to kiss her good-bye, and instead of sitting down again walked around to his grandmother's chair.

'I know this isn't in order,' he said. 'Just the same, I'm going to remind you that it's long past your nap time. Dinah's been lurking around in the hall for the last half-hour, looking in at you accusingly. Of course you couldn't see her because your back was turned to her, but I could. I couldn't help it. She made up for your inattention by glaring and signalling at me. Would you like me to give you a hand over the stairs?'

'Not yet. I deplore the lack of manners Joyeuse shows, which is more or less habitual, and also the importunities of Dinah, of which Lucie would never have been guilty. But that is no reason why you should allow your last meal at home to be hurried. Sit down again, Vail.'

'I'm sorry, *grand'mère*, but I'm afraid I can't. Of course I want to stop in at Somerulos Street on my way to the field, and time's getting short. I'll see you upstairs and then I'll walk over to the storehouse with Granny Randall and Miss Mittie. I planned on doing that too, before I left.'

Even Mrs. Randall's congenital pessimism could not prevent her from betraying her gratification at this attention. As she sat down in her small living-room after their short walk from the Big House, she smoothed out the skirt of her hideous green-and-orange print and looked up at Vail with genuine affection.

'I appreciate the way you answered back to Madame d'Alvery just now,' she said. 'It isn't often anyone gets to put her in her place. You've always been mighty polite to me, Vail. I don't believe in flattery to the face, but as long as you're starting off to war and as likely as not won't ever come back, I don't suppose it'll do any harm to say you've always been my favourite grandchild. Far as that goes, I've always set more store by you than I did any of my own children. Your two uncles, the ones you're named after, never gave me a thought once they took up with those flighty girls they married, and neither of my daughters-in-law ever lifted a finger to help me, not even with their pension money coming in and all. I don't see them or hear from them from one year's end to another. Of course, one of them lives in Natchitoches and the other in Harrisonburg, and both these places are a far piece from here. But I'm not excusing them. They could drop me a postcard once in a while, and they could get to Baton Rouge some ways, if they really wanted to. . . . As for your mother, the less said about her the better.'

'I wish you didn't feel that way, Granny Randall – about Mom, anyhow. Of course I don't know about the others. But she's invited you to go and stay with her whenever you felt like it, hasn't she? And doesn't she send you nice presents right along?'

'She knows I don't want to go skylarking around the country at my age,' Mrs. Randall answered, disregarding the second question. 'Besides, I'm not talking about the way she's treated me. I'm talking about the way she's treated your father. If ever a woman deserted her husband, she did. And I don't trust that man she works for; I never have. I wouldn't put it past him to lead her into sin.'

'Now, now, Granny Randall, let's not get out of line. You know that's a lot of nonsense – and not nice nonsense, either.'

He turned conclusively away from Mrs. Randall. Everything that she said had been painful to hear. It hurt him to have her say that he meant more to her than anyone else in the family, when actually he was no kith or kin of hers. It hurt him to have her gloat over his real grandmother's humiliation at his hands, trivial as this had been. It hurt him to have her speak slightingly of her dead sons, whose Christian names he bore, and to slander her daughter, who had been his kind and loving foster-mother. Some women seemed bent on hurting instead of helping as they went through life, he thought bitterly; and, with fleeting horror, he wondered if Sue could possibly develop into one of these, after the inevitable disillusionment which was in store for her. He thought he had seen indications of such a trait in her mother, though in Mrs. Prescott's case this was always meticulously veiled in cool courtesy. . . .

Trying hard to dismiss such a far-fetched fancy from his mind, he looked towards Miss Mittie, whose rabbit-like nose was twitching painfully, and who was clutching a small round object wrapped up in crumpled tissue paper and tied with faded lavender ribbon, which he had an uneasy feeling might be a farewell present. Amen had already waylaid him to give him a charm, guaranteed to protect the wearer against 'disease, death and disaster of every kind'. Meanwhile the Negro recounted in a long, rambling way his feelings of faithfulness and devotion to the d'Alverys in general and Vail in particular. Vail had finally accepted the charm, but cut the sentiments short as civilly as he could. Of course, any offering and any declaration of Miss Mittie's would be very different; still, he knew they might be a source of embarrassment.

'Miss Mittie, would you mind telling me what you've got in your lap?' he asked.

327

'It's something for you, Vail. I know you've always admired it. I want you should have it, to take along with you.'

She stretched out a shaking hand and gave him the small round object. It was unexpectedly heavy. He untied the faded ribbon and parted the crumpled tissue, disclosing the old paperweight with the miniature snow scene.

'Why, Miss Mittie, I can't take this!' he protested. 'It's not like a present that came from some store! You brought it with you when you left Salem for Louisiana. You've treasured it all your life. You've told me your mother did too.'

'I didn't want to give you a boughten present,' Miss Mittie said stubbornly. 'I wanted to give you that paperweight. It'll remind you of me when you're over in Paris, France, or wherever 'tis you're going. I don't want you should forget me while you're gone.'

'Don't worry. I'll never forget you, Miss Mittie. I couldn't. You've been too good to me,' he said gently. He could not tell her there was no possible way in which he could take a heavy, breakable object like a glass paperweight with him. It would hurt her too much. He knew that her offering had been not only loving, but sacrificial. He must find some way to dispose of the snow scene without letting her know about it. He rewrapped and retied the package and put it in his pocket. 'But thanks a lot, Miss Mittie. It was awfully good of you to give it to me. I *have* always admired it ... I'm afraid I've got to be shoving along now. Maybe you'd give me a coke before I start, if you've got any in the house.'

'When I haven't a coke for you, Vail d'Alvery, there won't be any cows left in Texas,' Miss Mittie announced in triumph, scuttling off towards the kitchen.

There had been so many delays that it was late afternoon when Vail reached the little house on Somerulos Street. He whistled as he went up the walk, and Frances Belle came rushing out to meet him, looking pertly pretty in a smart lemon-coloured dress. A young man followed closely behind her and held the door open for her. Vail had forgotten that some young man would almost inevitably be calling on Frances Belle at about this hour. He could not get used to the idea that she was grown up, and it still irritated him.

'Hello, brat!' he said casually. 'What's cooking?'

'Nothing much. . . . You know Punt, don't you, Vail? – Punt, this is my cousin, Vail d'Alvery.'

Punt, a red-headed, freckled young man with a pleasant face, whose surname remained undisclosed, greeted the newcomer with more civility than Vail felt inclined to show towards him at the moment. It was bad enough, in his opinion, to put up with all the young men who were eagerly engaged in helping Joyeuse keep up her morale without running into any equally superfluous callers on Frances Belle, especially at such a time as this. He nodded in the general direction of the inoffensive visitor and asked a couple of curt questions.

'Uncle Fabian here?'

'No, he hasn't come home yet. He telephoned that he'd been unavoidably detained at the office.'

'What about Aunt Cresside?'

'She's in the garden. She said, when you got here, to tell you to come on out there. . . . Look, Vail, Punt and I were just starting to a show. Mind if we go ahead?'

'No. But I hope Punt's got enough cash along to keep you in cokes. I never did.'

'Oh, he saves up to show me a tall time, and you never did that. Will you be here when we get back?'

'I reckon not. I have to report to Harding Field in' – he looked at his watch – 'forty-five minutes.'

'So long, then. Happy landings!'

They kissed each other casually, and she darted off down the walk with her red-headed escort in close pursuit. Vail had always been fond of Frances Belle, but he had never cared for her intensely, or she for him, in the way he and Sybelle cared for each other. Funny, he thought, when she was really his half-sister and Sybelle only his cousin; and, without being exactly offended, he was somewhat surprised that Frances Belle should have taken his departure so nonchalantly. But then you could never tell about girls, especially girls with beaux, he told himself unoriginally, as he walked through the house and went out on the terrace. In the garden the trickling fountain made the only sound; but the chrysanthemums and cosmos were a mass of blooms and some of the early camellias were out too. Here and there the glossy green of their bushes was studded with the dark pink of the Daigaguira, the lighter pink of the Sarah Hasty, and the radiant white of the Neige Dorée. The latter were among Cresside's favourites, and she had a shallow bowl of them on the table beside her. She was lying on a *chaise-longue* with her hands clasped idly in front of her, wearing a white dress. Her face was very white too, and for the first time Vail noticed that she did not look young any more. She was as slender and graceful as ever, and she still had beautiful eyes and soft skin and infinite charm. But somehow the bloom was gone. She looked up at him and smiled.

'Hello, Vail.'

'Hello, Auntie.'

He pulled up a chair and sat down beside her. All day he had been trying to find time for everything he wanted to say – to Sybelle, to Dinah, to Joyeuse, to Sance, even to Miss Mittie. But now, when there were only a few minutes left, and he would have supposed, beforehand, that he would have tried to talk very fast, to make the most of them, he did not say anything at all. He could not think of anything to say, and he knew he could not have talked in any case. He had a lump in his throat and the bones of his breast were too tight. He thought, if they did not loosen, something inside of him would be crushed. It had been hard telling the others good-bye, but it had not been like this. It wasn't hard now. It was impossible.

'Uncle Fabian isn't here?' he said at last. He knew Fabian was not there; Frances Belle had told him that her father was detained at the office. But he had to say something.

'No. He's very sorry. He said to tell you good-bye for him.'

Suddenly Vail knew Fabian had stayed away on purpose, that he had given them this chance to have their last few minutes to themselves, and Vail was deeply touched. Then it occurred to him that Frances Belle had gone out for the same reason, not because she cared more about a date with Punt than a final visit with him, as he had so unjustly assumed. He tried to make amends for his mistake by a show of interest in her caller.

'Who is this fellow the brat's gone out with?'

'Punt O'Malley? He's the Master of the *McDougall*.'

'I don't seem to place either one.'

'He's a nice boy, Vail. His people aren't Baton Rougeans, they're Alexandrians – what your grandmother would call very respectable people.' She paused, and a fleeting smile of understanding passed between them. 'But your Uncle Fabian and I think they're nice too. Punt's had a good education – graduated very young from Loyola and went straight on the river – apparently it was his one love, until he met Frances Belle. He's been here several years now, working for the Standard Oil. The *McDougall*'s one of their boats. She used to tow petroleum products from the refinery here to Avondale and Port Chalmette. Now she's delivering bunker fuels and aviation gasoline to the Army and Navy in New Orleans harbour. Her Captain holds a Pilot's licence as well as a Master's licence and takes a Pilot's watch. Punt was pretty bitter for a long time because he couldn't get into the Army – I believe he has some sort of minor heart ailment that kept him out. He doesn't feel so badly about that any more, though, because he's come to see he's helping indirectly. By the way, he's a great admirer of yours.'

'Why, I never saw him before!'

'Yes, you have, any number of times. But he doesn't stand out in a crowd. You're his hero, though. And now that he and Frances Belle—'

'You don't think it's serious, do you? That baby!'

'She's nineteen. How old was Susannah when you fell in love with her, Vail?'

'That was different.'

'We all think so, about ourselves.'

Silence fell between them. Vail guessed that Cresside was thinking, involuntarily, about her own girlhood and her own suitors, and with a fresh pang he realized that she could not have been more than nineteen when he was born. Probably she was remembering him as a baby, probably she was recalling the first parting between them and telling herself she was thankful she had not known then that a still harder one was ahead. He must say something, he must not let her know he read her mind. Again the words stuck in his throat.

'Miss Mittie insisted on giving me her paperweight when I left. Of course I can't possibly take it overseas, but I don't want to hurt her feelings. So I brought it this far. I thought maybe you'd hide it for me, some place, till I get home, and then I'd take it back to her.'

'You know I'd be glad to. Give it to me and I'll put it away for you.'

He took the paperweight out of his pocket and handed it to her. She turned it over several times, watching the sparkling flakes falling on the miniature village. Then she put it down on the table beside her without speaking again. Vail knew he had to go on.

'I'll write to you as often as I can, Auntie. But you mustn't worry if you don't get lots of letters. I don't suppose I'll have much time to write.'

'No, I don't suppose you will.'

She was not helping him at all. She was trying, but the words were sticking in her throat. He made a desperate effort.

'Auntie, you know I think an awful lot of Susannah. I'd hoped she'd marry me before I left. Well, you know all about that too, because I told you three weeks ago. If there's anything you and Uncle Fabian can do for her while I'm gone—'

'Of course, Vail. We'll keep in touch with her. She's a lovely girl. We're very fond of her ourselves.'

'I'm worried about Syb too. If I only knew she and Rick could get married—'

'They ought to, of course. It's too bad they didn't, long ago. I'll do everything I can to help them, Vail.'

'Thanks a lot. Well ... I reckon I have to be going, Auntie.'

'I know, Vail. I'll walk with you as far as the house.'

He was thankful she was not coming any farther, thankful that since he must say good-bye to her he could do it in this beautiful and secluded spot which she had made so uniquely her own. She put her arm through his, and as he looked down at her, trying to smile, he saw something else he had failed to notice before: her hair was not like a soft black cloud any longer. It was in beautiful order, but it was straighter and flatter than he remembered it, and there were grey threads in it. He had never thought of her as growing old, and he did not want her to realize that he had noticed the first telltale signs of this now, so he was glad that she did not seem to. They went slowly across the terrace together, and she did not pause at all on the way, or fall back, nor did she begin to cry, as he had been afraid she might at the last moment. Her face was whiter than ever, almost as white as her dress now, but it was composed. When they reached the door he looked at her and saw that her eyes were calm, too. They were very bright, as if possibly tears were somewhere behind them, shining through, but these had not come yet, and he knew now they would not until after he had gone. She looked at him with so much love glorifying her face that all the sadness was hidden,

332

and he forgot that it did not look young any longer because something in it was far more beautiful than youth.

'Aunt Cresside,' he said softly.

'Yes, Vail.'

'There's one special thing I want to say to you before I tell you good-bye.'

'You can say anything you want to, Vail. You know that.'

The words did not choke him any more. They came freely at last, just before he bent his head to kiss her.

'I've always wished you were my mother. Ever since I can remember. Ever since I was just a little boy. It's not that I don't love Mom too. But I feel so much closer to you. I feel as if we had always belonged to each other, as if we always would, whatever happens.'

She closed her eyes. The blue-veined, translucent lids veiled them for a moment, the long black lashes fluttered on her white cheeks. But only for a moment. She opened her eyes again and looked at him with the same clear, bright gaze as before.

'Thank you for telling me that before you went, darling.'

'I had to. Good-bye....'

He could not add 'Aunt Cresside' this time. He must not add anything else. But, looking down at her, he knew no more words were needed between them. Everything that counted had been said already.

The loading platform was packed to the last inch of standing-room. The Colonel, gathering more than two hundred young pilots around him, had addressed them informally for the last time. He did not really make a speech. He merely thanked the pilots for their past co-operation, urged them to maintain their high standards of discipline, and wished them good luck. Then he stood watching them with a strange expression on his face as they swarmed aboard a troop train, a solid Pullman with a kitchen in the middle, which was drawn up alongside. The immobility of the train had a sinister quality. It looked like a long steel serpent, momentarily quiescent, but poised to strike when the unwary least expected it. Then, instead of striking, it began to glide slowly away, its evil potentialities still unrealized. As each car slid smoothly past him the Colonel saluted again, the furrows in his face deepening, the lines in his mouth growing tighter and tighter. The train, still moving slowly and portentously, slipped farther and farther away from the quartermaster's warehouses fringing the field. The military band, stationed at the crossroads of the Texas and Pacific, played 'Auld Lang Syne'. Long before its strains died down in the distance everyone on the platform had been lost to sight. Vail turned away from the window where he had been staying and went to locate his B-44 bag, which had been stowed in the ladies' room.

CHAPTER TWENTY–TWO

FOR several weeks after Vail's departure Sybelle waited, with determined hopefulness, for some word which would indicate that he had been right in his 'hunch' about Rick. But when she next received definite word of her sweetheart's whereabouts he was on Bougainville; the Thirty-Seventh Division had joined with the Marines for the invasion of the last island in the Solomons still invested by the Japanese. If any of its officers had been sent to the United States on 'secret missions' after the hard campaign in New Georgia, Rick was not among them. But the 'rest' on Guadalcanal had materialized – so far, at least, Vail had been right; and during this welcome interlude Rick had been promoted again and was now one of the youngest majors in his Division. He had also received the combat Infantryman's Badge, which, judging from the feeling with which he wrote of it, meant almost as much to him as his advancement in rank. Consequently, it meant almost as much to Sybelle, and nothing that Rick wrote, or that she read in the newspapers or heard on the radio, indicated that the Americans were, at the moment, engaged in offensive action. This naturally enhanced her peace of mind; and with the same patience and cheerfulness which had characterized her general attitude from the beginning, she went on with her Red Cross work, dropped in almost every day to see the Tramontes, devoted her evenings to Madame d'Alvery, and every night before she said her rosary and turned out her light wrote a long letter to Rick, recounting the unremarkable events of the day and reiterating her expressions of changeless devotion.

334

As a matter of fact, she did have comparatively little cause for anxiety at the moment, so her serenity was not ill-founded, as she later learned. The first objective of the Americans had been an airfield, so this was built as soon as a narrow strip of land had been conquered. Then the Division had settled down to the defence of this field, with patrols for reconnaissance their only offensive action. But the Japs, though cut off from their main supplies, probed constantly at the American lines, and in March they opened their all-out drive to throw the enemy off the island. They fought with fanatical fierceness, always attacking at night, and the Americans used flares, car lights and fires to illumine the tropical darkness, finally focusing searchlights on the clouds so that radiance would be reflected downwards. In the end their resourcefulness was rewarded: the attack was beaten off, the Japs retreating to the interior, and Rick's Division began to prepare for its next major campaign, clearing a piece of jungle and training in this area to accustom itself to open country once more. But by the time the offensive had reached this stage, and long before Sybelle learned any of these details, the thrilling news had come through that Rick had been awarded the Bronze Star for 'meritorious services during the preparatory training and combat action' both at New Georgia and at Bougainville; and almost immediately after the reception of these soul-stirring tidings Madame d'Alvery had been subjected to one of the most gruelling encounters in her entire experience.

She had wakened from her siesta feeling unusually refreshed and invigorated, and Dinah, after helping her dress and seeing her comfortably settled on her sofa, had gone downstairs to get the customary afternoon coffee. She returned almost immediately, without the coffee, and with an expression of mingled astonishment and dismay on her usually calm countenance.

'Dat pedlar man done come agin, Madame,' she said. 'He ain't brung his boy with him dis time. He done come alone. He ain't come in no cart nor red truck neider. He come in a big shiny Cadillac car, jes' lak de one Mr. Boylston got, only bigger. He ain't gone round to de side neider. He come right up to de front do' and rapped with de knocker.'

'Did you remind him that neither Colonel d'Alvery nor Miss Merry was at Belle Heloise, and tell him that I never receive anyone except members of the family and very old and intimate friends?'

'Yassum, Madame, Ah sho' did. But he say he knew dat all right. He want to see you, anyway – yassum. He come right along in de front hall while he a-sayin' it, too. He standin' dere now. Wasn't no way Ah could stop him.'

'Very well, Dinah. Tell him I will come right away.'

Madame d'Alvery glanced swiftly into the glass to assure herself that her lace cap was set at the most regal angle, picked up her embroidered handkerchief, and descended the stairs with accustomed dignity. She had seldom seen Luigi Tramonte at the outset of his career, because he had usually gone only to the quarters in those days, and, on the rare occasions when he had come to the Big House, only as far as the patio. She had never encountered him since prosperity had put an end to his peddling, nor was she acquainted with any other individuals who might conceivably be classified with him. Therefore she had only the vaguest idea what to expect, and, with considerable surprise, she saw that he was by no means unpresentable. He was dressed in dark, well-tailored clothes, and his snow-white hair, black brows and bronzed skin combined to make his appearance very striking. His figure had the solidity of advancing years, but it was by no means shapeless, and as she came closer to him she saw that his small ears, which lay very close to his head, were slightly pointed at the top, suggesting something faunlike in his nature or heredity. The rest of his features, however, had the fine coinlike quality not unrare among Italians, and his keen eyes met hers with no evasion or abashment. When she bowed, neglecting to hold out her hand, he did the same, and he waited, with no sign of discomfiture, for her to speak first.

'Good evening,' Madame d'Alvery said speaking in a tone of cold civility. To her own discomfiture, of which she was conscious with extreme annoyance, she did not feel certain how she should address him. Obviously she could not call this substantial citizen, who was a total stranger to her, by his Christian name; neither could she quite bring herself to call anyone whom she considered so completely her social inferior Mr. Tramonte; yet the apparently inevitable omission disturbed her. 'Dinah says you wish to see me,' she went on, speaking more rapidly than was her habit in order to escape from her sense of inadequacy. 'I gathered that the matter is very urgent. Will you tell me what it is?'

'Sure I tell you what it is, Madame d'Alvery. That's what I come-a here for. Sure it's verra urgent too. I have-a to talk to you about my Riccardo.'

'Your son?' Madame d'Alvery asked still more coldly. 'Is he in trouble?' she inquired, stubbornly refusing to admit even to herself that she was beginning to realize all too well the purpose of this presumptuous call.

'Riccardo ain't-a never in no trouble,' Luigi retorted proudly. 'You must-a heard about my Riccardo, Madame d'Alvery, whatta fine boy he always been. Not-a jus' now in de war – he lead-a his class atta school, get-a plenty prizes, play-a on alla the teams – baseball, football, basketball, everything. Alla same at University. Get-a Kemper Weliams Sabre, get-a be Cadet Colonel – I getta ready to take-a him into business with me, soon like he finish. I didn't think about any war. Mighty good-a business, too, Madame d'Alvery. Ain't-a no better fancy grocery stores than I gotta – Baton Rouge, Hammond, Covington, Opolousas, Lafayette, Lake Charles, Donaldsonvill, Thibodaux, two in New Orleans. I gotta lot of real estate too – apartment houses, office buildings, country places, alla things like that. I gotta everything to give my Riccardo a good start any time – notta like my poor papa, have-a ten children, live-a in two rooms, work-a in the fields alla his life, earn-a few lire a day. Riccardo alla son I ever got. But he's worth-a ten to me, and everything what I gotta going to be his.'

'I have heard that you have prospered, Mr. Tramonte, and that your son is a great credit to you. But I am still in the dark as to why you felt it was so imperative that you should see me this evening.'

It had proved impossible to continue, indefinitely, to address her importunate visitor merely as you; reluctantly, Madame d'Alvery had succumbed to the indicated form of address. And she was beginning to be afraid that before long she would also be obliged to invite him into the parlour. She could not eject him forcibly from the house. She could not even turn around abruptly and leave him without playing false to her own standards of civility; but neither could she confront him indefinitely, standing in the front hall, partly because she found their relative positions extremely awkward and partly because she had not the physical strength to maintain her own. She was amazingly strong for a woman of her years, despite the legend of fragility which she had managed to maintain with varying degrees of success; but she was not strong enough for that. Neither could she sit down without suggesting that Luigi Tramonte be seated also, for there was nothing in the hall on which she could safely sit. To be sure, an antique settee was located between the stairway and the parlour door, and opposite it, on either side of a long, narrow table, were two chairs which matched the settee. All were exquisitely carved and inlaid with mother-of-pearl. But they were so brittle with age that they could hardly be moved for dusting, and then only with the greatest care. They had been relegated to the front hall for the very reason that no one ever stayed there, and that, while highly ornamental and extremely valuable, they were completely useless. A sudden crash, attended by a precipitate fall, which would land her in an undignified posture, was the last kind of catastrophe that Madame d'Alvery desired. She could visualize no way in which to maintain her attitude of aloofness under such unpropitious circumstances. While she was pondering on her next step, Luigi abruptly jolted her from reflection into action.

'Sure my Riccardo great-a credit to me,' he said, speaking with increasing pride. 'Verra, verra good son. Great-a credit to his mamma too. Good-a sons, they most generally good husbands. Great-a credit to any family.' Luigi paused long enough to let this statement sink in; but as Madame d'Alvery continued to confront him with a masklike expression, he shrewdly decided it was to soon to press this point, and went on to speak of Riccardo's other qualifications. 'Great-a credit to his school and his college. Great-a credit to his country. How many boys you know Majas when they make-a twenty-seven? How many boys you know getta Bronze Star for Meritorious Service?'

'I was aware that your son had won promotions very rapidly, Mr. Tramonte. But I still do not see—'

'Madame d'Alvery, you can't make-a believe you're so dumb like alla that. You know my Riccardo love-a your granddaughter Sybelle. You know he always love-a her, ever since she was a leetla girl. You send-a away to school so she could na see him any more. You think-a my Riccardo not good enough for your granddaughter. Well, I don't-a say anything then, not for a long-a time. I don't want-a my fine boy force his way, any place he ain't welcome – I tella him so, he feela justa the same. I think-a maybe he get over loving Sybelle too; maybe when she ain't a leetla girl any more, she treat-a him different, see, so he say-a to himself: "Don't-a want no stuck-up piece like that for my wife. I want-a real woman for my wife, same-a my mamma a real woman." But Sybelle, she ain't-a no stuck-up piece. She ain't-a no dolly either, like-a she looked when she was a leetla girl. She gotta pink-a cheeks and beega eyes and yellow curls yet, but they don't make-a look like no dolly no more. She's a real woman. She's good enough for my Riccardo just like he's good enough for her.'

'Mr. Tramonte, I must ask you to excuse me. I don't feel I can discuss my granddaughter Sybelle with you. If anyone is going to do that, though I cannot see the necessity, it should be Colonel d'Alvery, after he returns from overseas—'

'There ain't-a time to wait and wait like-a that, Madame d'Alvery. Sybelle and Riccardo, they wait-a too long already, causa the Tramontes they too proud to force-a their way places they ain't-a welcome. We done wrong to be so proud. Now you and me we gotta see Sybelle and my Riccardo getta married before he sent off to more Jap islands. I don't-a know the names of alla those islands, I can't-a pronounce them anyway. But I know they're a long way off, I know when my Riccardo gets way off in too many those places maybe he never comes back.'

'We must not allow ourselves to think about it in that way, Mr. Tramonte. I have a son and two grandsons in the service myself, you know.' Madame d'Alvery glanced from Luigi to the service flag hanging in one of the narrow, many-paned windows flanking the front door, less because she wanted to look at it just then, despite her pride in it, than because she wanted to look away from Luigi. 'I am confidently anticipating their return,' she continued, with sincere conviction. It was really inconceivable to her that Gervais' name or Vail's or Philogene's would ever appear on a casualty list; she visualized calamities of this sort as occurring in other families, but not in hers. Lucien Estrade had come back safely after the War Between the States and Gervais after the First World War; in due time he and her grandsons would come back safely from this war. 'I think you should feel the same way about your son, if you will permit me to say so,' she remarked, for the first time permitting the condescension in her voice to overcome the coldness.

'Well, I don't-a feel the same way about my son. You gotta son and a daughter, Madame d'Alvery, mighty fine son-in-law and daughter-in-law too. You gotta two grandsons and three grand-daughters. If you lose-a one, even two, you gotta lot left. My Riccardo, he's alla I got. When you gotta just one boy, you can't help-a but think what-a it would be like if he didn't never come-a back from those places which I can't-a say. You can't-a help but want-a he should get a bambino of his own before it's too late. You can't-a help but want-a he should be happy while he can. You can't-a help make up your mind he's going to be.'

Luigi spoke with grim purpose and gathering intensity. In the course of each succeeding speech that he had made on the subject of his son Madame d'Alvery had become increasingly aware both of the weakness in her knees and of the futility of her impass-ivity. With the same tardiness and reluctance which she had displayed in finally addressing him as Mr. Tramonte, she now invited him into the parlour.

'If you are determined to talk to me about your son, I think perhaps we had better sit down,' she said. She was aware that never before in her life had she spoken so ungraciously to a guest, but she felt no compunctions on this score. The moment had come when she was obliged to admit the need of fortifying her-self, both figuratively and literally; but she was doing this merely in self-defence. She was by no means ready to admit any of the usual obligations of a hostess in the case of this ex-pedlar who had first forced his way into her house and who now stubbornly pursued his preposterous arguments. She was certain that if Ger-vais had only been at home he would have made short work of such presumption, and she had never longed more eagerly for her son's presence. But since she had been left alone in their aristocratic stronghold, she was determined that somehow she would protect and maintain its traditional inviolability. She led the way into the parlour without a backward glance or a wel-coming gesture, and seated herself on one of the two stiff bro-caded sofas which faced each other on either side of the hearth. A heavy rain was falling outside, and the room was gloomy, damp and abnormally cold; but she did not summon Dinah to kindle the fire or turn on the lights. Holding herself very erect, she faced Luigi, who had seated himself on the opposite sofa, and who also held himself very erect. Dinah had neglected to take his hat when he came in, and as long as he stood in the hall he had held it, somewhat uncomfortably, twirling it from time to time. Now he laid it on the sofa beside him and folded his arms, waiting for Madame d'Alvery to proceed.

'Let me try to make my position clear to you, Mr. Tramonte,' she said with firmness. 'Apparently it is important that I should, and I may say, in passing, that when I speak of position I mean the family position. If my son were here I am sure he would say the same thing to you that I shall. We both have a great regard for the family as a unit.'

'That's a verra fine thing, Madame d'Alvery,' Luigi replied, promptly and disconcertingly. 'My wife, Netta, and my Riccardo and me, alla we feel the same way about our family. That's why I come-a to talk to you about my Riccardo and Sybelle. We alla know, we Tramontes, same all as you d'Alverys, when young folks want-a get married old folks need-a talk about it too.'

'Yes, under normal circumstances. As a general thing, it is a very good plan for fathers and mothers and grandfathers and grandmothers of the two contracting parties to have an understanding about such matters, even before their children and grandchildren do. For instance, if Colonel d'Alvery and I had thought it would be advisable that Sybelle should marry the son of one of our neighbours on the River Road—'

'You ain't-a gotta so many neighbours on the River Road no more, have you, Madame d'Alvery? Just Meesta Boylston way down at Hackberry Lodge, eight, ten miles from here. And he ain't gotta no sons for Sybelle to marry. Faith Estate, those no-count Renos letta it burn to the ground after they bring-a every kind of disgrace to it. Chelmsford and Cedar Grove, they been empty this long while back. Now Hathaway Hall too. I drive-a through the allee at Hathaway to the mansion when I come-a here to Belle Heloise just now. My, my, does that place look-a bad – columns rotting, railings missing, windows broken in, lawns alla growing up in weeds! Factry jus' a shell, and-a machinery alla sold to Mexico, same-a like-a you fine people usta sella your poor slaves donna river. And that was-a fine place, finest on the River Road, when I first come-a here, carrying stage planks and Johnny Crooks and sauerkraut candy in a basket on my back!'

Madame d'Alvery winced. But this was not wholly on account of Luigi's reference to his pedlar's pack, gratingly as this fell on her ears, or even on account of his all too accurate description of the dilapidation of Hathaway Hall, which was an eyesore to her whenever she passed it. Though she shrank from the recollection, she could not now help remembering how she and Mrs. Hathaway had once planned such an alliance as she had just attempted to extol, and how their pride had indeed come before a fall and their haughty spirit before destruction. It was inconceivable that this shrewd self-made man did not know something of that sad and shocking story: indeed, as she swiftly thought over his statement, she was certain that his reference to Hathaway had not been accidental, and she was humiliated that he had scored so quickly and so effectively.

'Suppose we go back a little,' she remarked, a trifle hurriedly. 'I am afraid you did not altogether understand me when I spoke of our family position. Or rather you interrupted me – unconsciously, I am sure. Doubtless you thought I had finished what I started to say. But I had not. What I was leading up to was this: both my son and I have the greatest respect for your industry and initiative, Mr. Tramonte, and I am sure that my dear daughter-in-law has too. We are all aware, likewise, that you have every reason to feel extremely proud of your only son. Far from having anything against him personally, we admire his character and his patriotism. We can even understand why Sybelle as a child and as a young girl should have been so much attracted to him; he is very handsome, he has very good manners, and he inspires confidence. But we cannot help feeling that as she grows older she will be happier with someone whose background is more like her own.'

'What-a you mean-a by that, background, Madame d'Alvery? More money, better moral example, more family happiness than we Tramontes?'

Again Madame d'Alvery winced. It was an incontestable fact that while Gervais was getting deeper and deeper into debt, Luigi had been getting richer and richer; that while the d'Alverys were trying to conceal a corroding scandal the Tramontes had become more and more respected; that while the ancient walls of Belle Heloise had been almost rent asunder by discord, peace and harmony had prevailed in the little house back of the Fancy Grocery Store on Lafayette Street. While she was groping for the right retort, Luigi went on relentlessly.

'You think-a maybe Sybelle don't-a get on with my wife? Never I see no young girl so happy like she is with my Netta.

You think-a she go to better school, travel more, hear more good music, see more nice things?'

'No,' Madame d'Alvery admitted reluctantly. Since she had insisted in sending her own son to Louisiana State University, she could not logically complain because the Tramontes had also done this, or set Grand Coteau on a higher plane; neither could she claim that the aged and unprogressive Miss Mittie, who had been Sybelle's sole mentor until she was sent away, was a better instructor than the energetic and up-to-date young teachers to whom Riccardo's education had been entrusted in his tenderer years. On the subject of travel and general cultural advantages the less said the better. She knew that the Tramontes had given their son a foreign trip nearly every year until the outbreak of the war, and that they had taken infinite pains to familiarize him with all the arts; she had heard Sybelle say, wistfully, a dozen times, that she wished she could go to the opera and the theatre and the museums in New York, like the Tramontes, really meaning with the Tramontes.

'Then it's me, maybe? I don't-a speak much good English, no? Someone told me once, Pascal Tremblet I think, your papa he didn't speak no English at all till that Scotch tramp, what-a you call him, Angus Holt, teach-a him how.'

'That's true, Mr. Tramonte. But it was because my father, and my mother too for that matter, were typical Creoles of the old school. All their people were Creoles too. French was their family language.'

'Well me, I was-a Neapolitan, Italian was-a my family language. What-a the difference, Madame d'Alvery, except that I had-a learn the English myself, alla same time I'm making money to take-a care my wife and bring up my Riccardo, and start my fancy grocery stores? I didn't have no tramp come along to teach-a me, I didn't have no nice house to live in while I was learning. But, mostly, people understand me when I talk to them!'

He paused, but only long enough to take breath. Before the old lady, now thoroughly startled, could form a reply, he leaned forward, resting his strong, stubby hands on his knees as he did so.

'Maybe that-a the trouble, maybe you think-a Riccardo not have nice enough house for Sybelle. I tell-a you something, Madame d'Alvery. I thought of that myself. Sybelle real woman like I

343

said before, verra fine leetla lady too. Me and my Riccardo both knew, ladies like Sybelle, they ought-a have nice houses to live-a in. They oughtn't live back of fancy grocery stores, like me and Netta. So I don't-a go to Hathaway Hall today just to see him. I go to buy him for my Riccardo!'

Suddenly Luigi sprang from his seat, knocking his hat to the floor as he did so. To Madame d'Alvery, recoiling against the hard back of her brocaded sofa, he became an overwhelming, almost a threatening figure. With one hand he thumped his breast pocket, so hard that the result was a loud thudding noise. Raising his other arm, he shook his stubby forefinger in her face. Actually the gesture was only one of emphasis; but to her it had all the elements of a menace. She smothered a slight scream as she braced herself still more firmly against the sofa.

'I gotta the deed right-a here in my pocket!' he shouted. 'The Tremaines, what-a they ever do for it? Leave-a it alla time for that-a skunk Blood to raise-a hell instead of sugar! Get-a themselves killed some way, leave it to a big fool Yankee woman don't know any better than marry Blood. These-a river families! I ain't-a going-a say anything against them, seeing my Riccardo marry into one. But I know what-a I think, just the same. There, I'm saying more than I ought-a. But we Tramontes, we alla know how to take-a care property. Ain't-a no place we ever owned ain't-a been improved. We'll improve Hathaway Hall too, make-a it like it used to be, Madame d'Alvery. It'll be just as nice a home for Sybelle as Belle Heloise was for Adela Ayela when her father gave it to her for a wedding present the time she marry François Estrade. We're going right-a on with the same old family traditions you think-a so much of, giving fine places to our children for their wedding presents! I take-a the agent for that property right out to Hathaway with me today; I pay him cash for it. But the deed, that-a made out to my Riccardo . . .'

While he was talking, Luigi had gradually ceased to beat his breast and shake his fist. Madame d'Alvery, still too startled to speak, drew a deep sigh of relief. Luigi, taking a long breath himself, leaned over and picked up his crushed and fallen hat. Then he brushed this off with his sleeve and deposited it carefully on the marble-topped table that stood near by. Afterwards he sat down on the same sofa as Madame d'Alvery.

'But they can't-a wait until Hathaway Hall's alla fixed up before they get married, Sybelle and my Riccardo,' he said, with no trace of his former ferocity. 'Sybelle, she'll have a nice time doing that, when my Riccardo's gone to one of those queer places I can't-a say the names of. It'll keep-a her busy, give-a her something to think about while he's away. She'll be proud to have-a it ready for him when he comes back for good to go into fancy grocery business with me. She'll need plenty-a room for the bambinos, too, bimeby. But first – my Riccardo, he gonna have a short leave right away, Madame d'Alvery. I gotta telegram in my pocket, too, right alongside the deed. Sybelle, she came-a over to our house from the Red Cross before I starta out here. She gotta telegram too. She say she aint-a gonna to wait any longer, no matter if the Tramontes are proud. It's better don't-a you think so, our children have a nice-a wedding at St. Agnes' and alla their friends coming here for party at Belle Heloise afterwards, than they run off together and get married at Gretna? Tell me quick like anything, because, you and I, we gotta make-a up our minds right now!'

CHAPTER TWENTY-THREE

MEREDITH D'ALVERY had one of the pleasantest and most spacious corner suites at the Hotel Gotham. From her drawing-room window she could look far, far up Fifth Avenue, and there was no hour of the day or night when this was not a thrilling and provocative sight. Her bedroom and bathroom were separated from the drawing-room by an attractive foyer, and a white-tiled pantry led from this, completely equipped with a gleaming refrigerator, porcelain sink, and all the other accessories which made for comfort and convenience in serving everything, from her own solitary but luxurious breakfast to a cocktail party for fifty persons. Not that Merry ever did the serving herself: she had an excellent maid, named Mabel, who took pride in being able to do everything that Mrs. d'Alvery could possibly require in the way of personal service, and when Mrs. d'Alvery wished to entertain, there was always the hotel staff, which was still excellent also, in spite of the war, to supplement Mabel's efforts.

Merry entertained a good deal, and she nearly always did it in this spacious suite because it was so easy and agreeable that way. She did not need to lift a finger herself, and yet she could almost create the illusion of being in a private house.

Of course, she put in an active day at the office, at least from Monday through Friday, but her week-ends were free, and she always took ample time out for luncheon, because many of her most important connections were furthered in this way and through the evening parties at which she entertained so easily and agreeably in her suite. She could nearly always count on leaving the office by five, or five-thirty at the latest, and that gave ample time to be on hand for cocktails, followed by dinner, or for a very elaborate high tea before the theatre and midnight supper afterwards. Mr. Goldenberg had impressed upon her from the beginning that while he expected her office to be run efficiently, he did not consider that her usefulness to the store was limited to office hours. Not by any means. In a sense, she had a twenty-four-hours-a-day job. Some time during the twenty-four hours she must naturally get the requisite amount of sleep, or she would not be fresh for her work; but the hours she was off duty could not possibly be uniform. He expected her to keep them flexible, according to the exigencies of the moment.

In this respect, as in every other, she had more than met his expectations. The New York centre which she herself had organized, after the Paris branch had closed on account of the war, had been of even more value to the store than its predecessor. Merry had given it great prestige and brought great originality to it. Her South American sojourn had proved an extremely sound investment. As a result of it, she had built up a sizeable clientèle among Latin ladies, and wealthy New Yorkers appreciated the same unique touch that intrigued their sisters from the South. Mr. Goldenberg often told Merry that she had done more to further the Good Neighbour Policy than Nelson Rockefeller, and he was not speaking more than half in jest when he said so, either.

The store was only a few blocks from the Gotham, so Merry usually walked back and forth from her office. She had a car, and used it habitually on week-ends. But the walk gave her a chance for exercise, which she needed and enjoyed, and an opportunity to see what other stores were offering. It also permitted the experience, which she had never ceased to find thrilling, of being part of the great crowd which streamed up and down Fifth Avenue. Conscious that her exquisite clothes could bear comparison with those of any woman she met, tingling with perfect health, intoxicated with the success of her career and the richness of her existence, her progress had such a triumphant quality about it that even in their haste passers-by caught its contagion as they glanced at her, and went on their own way reanimated.

In the hotel itself, the doorman, the clerk, the bellboys and the elevator operators were all glad when they saw her coming. She had a pleasant smile and a friendly word for each. And when she approached her own suite, Mabel was always waiting to open the door and to greet her respectfully but warmly. Her mail was laid neatly on the desk, with a list of the telephone calls which had come in during the day meticulously beside it. The flowers that had been sent since she left for the office had been tastefully arranged, and the cards which had accompanied them were placed beside the letters and the list of telephone calls, with a memorandum to indicate whether they had come with the red roses or purple orchids. The clothes appropriate for the next engagement were already laid out in the bedroom. Always the right dress and the right shoes to go with it; if Merry were going out, always the right handbag and the right wrap too; and when the occasion indicated a hat, that was also in readiness. Mabel was very experienced, and she also had a natural flair for suitability in all things and on all occasions.

One evening early in April, the first pleasant warmth of spring, coming with a rush, tempted Merry to take her evening walk at a more leisurely pace than usual. She knew that before the next evening this pleasant warmth might have been blown away by a stiff easterly breeze or engulfed in a cold driving rain, and that there might be no more warm, pleasant days for a month; that was what very often happened in New York. Involuntarily, as she loitered along the Avenue, looking in the shop windows and observing the most arresting details of the novelties worn by smart women, Merry thought of spring as it came to Belle Heloise, in January, with the last camellias and the first paper-white narcissi; then with a veritable burst of bloom in February. Why, it had been spring there for two months already! She wondered whether the purple wisteria and the white Cherokee roses, which between them wreathed one of the oaks so completely that its own foliage was almost hidden, had been allowed to continue climbing over it, or whether they had been wrenched away from it at last. The d'Alverys had been warned, years before, that in time these would ruin the tree if they were not removed. But they presented a beautiful and unique sight every spring, and no one had wanted to forgo the perennial delight. Another beautiful and unique sight was the fruit tree where part of the blossoms were pale pink and part deep crimson. No one had ever explained this phenomenon; no one had ever tried. Spring was not something you analysed, in Lousiana. It was something you enjoyed. . . .

Well, you enjoyed it in New York too, Merry told herself, beginning to walk a little more briskly. The shop windows were full of new things, the women all had on new clothes, fresh asparagus and shad roe were appearing on the menus, Central Park had lost its black, dingy look, and there was a feeling of new life in the air. You were not dependent on a few clinging vines and some multi-coloured blossoms for *joie de vivre*; the city was full of it, even in wartime. Spending had never been more prodigal, prices never more exorbitant, pleasure never more extravagantly pursued. Merry was dining that night with Mr. Goldenberg at the Belle Meunière, and she knew that the bill for the *tête-à-tête* dinner would come to twenty dollars. They were going afterwards to 'The Voice of the Turtle', and the tickets for that would be fifteen. Then, if they went to the Oak Room at the Plaza for a nightcap, the evening's outing would run to fifty at the very least. And this was for a quiet evening's outing; a party for a dozen could easily have cost five hundred. What did it matter? Mr. Goldenberg had more money to spend than he knew what to do with. So, apparently, had everyone else. . . .

As usual, the doorman and the room clerk and the elevator boy all nodded to Merry smilingly; as usual, Mabel was waiting to open the door of the suite for her. It looked very attractive and inviting as she went in. The furnishings and ornaments, which she had picked up in the course of her long foreign sojourns, robbed it of the usual stereotyped hotel atmosphere. The flowers with which, as usual, it was lavishly adorned gave it a festive appearance. It was a little too formal, a little too elegant, to be really homelike, but it revealed scrupulous care, impeccable taste and the domination of a sophisticated personality.

'Good evening, Mabel. Any special news?'

'Good evening, Madam. Mr. Goldenberg called to say he

would come here for cocktails before dinner if that would be agreeable to you. He will assume it is unless I telephone him to the contrary. A telegram came in just a few minutes ago. I called the office, but you had already left. I put it on top of your mail.'

Telegrams, in large numbers, had been part of Merry's everyday existence for a long time now. She accepted their arrival without excitement, though Mabel had standing instructions to advise her immediately of any that came to the hotel during her absence, and, if she could be reached, to open them and read them aloud immediately. However, since she had left the office before this one arrived, it was still unopened. She walked over to the desk and picked up the yellow envelope that lay on top of the neatly slit letters and carefully stacked cards, unsealing the flap. The message was so long that it covered two pages.

RICK ARRIVED SAN FRANCISCO TODAY ON LEAVE REACHING NEW ORLEANS FRIDAY – (Merry read) – HE AND I GETTING MARRIED NOON SATURDAY. HAVE CABLED DADDY WHO HAS CABLED BACK APPROVAL WITH HIS LOVE. MR. TRAMONTE GIVING US HATHAWAY FOR WEDDING PRESENT RESTORATION AT HIS EXPENSE STARTING IMMEDIATELY AND I SHALL LIVE THERE WHILE THIS GOES FORWARD. WEDDING AT ST. AGNES. RECEPTION AT BELLE HELOISE WITH GRAND'MERE'S CONSENT. UNCLE FABIAN GIVING ME AWAY, JOYEUSE MAID OF HONOUR, FRANCES BELLE, NELLIE, SUE AND DRINA BRIDESMAIDS. ARRANGEMENTS NECESSARILY HURRIED BUT GOING FORWARD SMOOTHLY. HOWEVER IT IS BAD ENOUGH TO HAVE DADDY, VAIL AND PHIL ALL OVERSEAS WITHOUT HAVING YOU AWAY TOO. VAIL ALWAYS SAID HE WAS SURE YOU WOULD HELP OUT WHEN IT CAME TO A SHOWDOWN. WON'T YOU SELECT MY TROUSSEAU INCLUDING WEDDING DRESS AND TAKE CRESCENT LIMITED TOMORROW AFTERNOON BRINGING EVERYTHING WITH YOU? WILL TELEPHONE YOU FROM TRAMONTES' HOUSE EIGHT PM EASTERN STANDARD TIME FOR YOUR ANSWER. PLEASE MUMMY BE READY TO SAY YES. NO GIRL FEELS HER WEDDING COMPLETE WITHOUT HER MOTHER. LOVE, SYBELLE.

Merry read the telegram twice, laid it down, picked it up again, and read it once more. Then she turned to Mabel.

'Please telephone Mr. Goldenberg and tell him I'm sorry, but I won't be able to go out with him this evening,' she said. 'I'll be glad to have him come for cocktails and stay for dinner too, if he will. But I'll have to be where I can wait for a telephone call. There's a family emergency.'

'Very good, Madam. . . . Not bad news, I hope? Mr. Goldenberg is sure to ask.'

'No, it isn't exactly bad news. But my elder daughter's fiancé is coming home on leave and she's decided to get married while he's home. She wants me to start South immediately. I haven't been there in a long time. . . . While you're telephoning, Mabel, you'd better call the head porter too, and see if by any miracle there's something to be had on the *Crescent Limited* tomorrow.'

'Very good, Madam. . . . Would you be wishing me to go with you? Shall I ask the porter to get reservations for two persons, if possible?'

Mabel's efficiency had outpaced Merry's planning. She had not yet thought about taking Mabel with her. In her mind's eye she had been swiftly seeing again an exquisite wedding dress she had recently viewed at Jay Thorpe, wishing enviously at the time it had been one of her own designer's creations, and involuntarily thinking that if it had been fashioned on purpose for Sybelle it could not have been more suited to her. It was made of white marquisette with large hand-painted lovers' knots of palest blue scattered over the skirt, matching the clusters of forget-me-nots with which this was embroidered. The low-cut bodice was outlined with forget-me-nots too, the cuffs of the full bishop sleeves and the cap to which the floating white veil was attached were formed of them; the wide girdle was made of pale blue taffeta. Merry realized her mother-in-law would protest that Sybelle should wear old satin and ancestral lace and that any touch of colour was inappropriate for a virginal wedding gown; but she herself knew that this fresh filmy dress was more Sybelle's type than anything they could have dragged out of the attic, that the bows and forget-me-nots and girdle would match the blue of Sybelle's eyes and set off her blonde beauty to perfection. Merry hoped to heaven that this dream of a wedding dress, which was an exclusive model, had not been sold. It was too late for her to find out this evening. But she must have Mabel telephone the minute the stores opened in the morning. . . .

She was tardily aware that Mabel was waiting respectfully for an answer. Now that her attention had been called to the possibility that her maid might accompany her, she realized that such an arrangement would have great advantages. Mabel's efficiency would be a godsend in such an emergency as this; furthermore, her presence would eliminate any dependence on personal service from the Negroes at Belle Heloise. Merry remembered how tenderly Creassy had ministered to her when she went to Belle Heloise as a bride herself, how much the faithful coloured woman had loved her; but she also knew that Creassy had never felt the same towards her after she left her home and her husband, and that she never would again. Quite aside from Mabel's greater efficiency, it would be a relief not to have Creassy's great dark eyes gazing reproachfully at her all the time. . . .

'Yes,' she said at last. 'Yes, I think I'd better take you with me, Mabel. Ask the porter to get reservations for two, if he can. And hurry! I've got to let Mr. Goldenberg know about my change of plan as quickly as possible, so that he can turn in the theatre tickets.'

Neither Mabel's manner nor her tone as she said, 'Very good, Madam,' again gave the slightest indication that the delay which had occurred was due to Mrs. d'Alvery's own preoccupation, and not to any failure on her part to move with alacrity. Merry went on into her bedroom, tossing her hat on the dressing table, and taking off the jacket to her tailored suit. This was Tuesday. If she did get the *Crescent* the next afternoon, she would not reach New Orleans until late Thursday night – only a few hours before Rick got there himself, less than forty-eight before the marriage ceremony. And evidently Sybelle was planning a large and elaborate wedding. How on earth could everything be made ready on such short notice? How could she buy an entire trousseau in one morning? And yet that was all she would have, for the *Crescent* left at two-thirty. Sybelle had given her no idea, either, where the honeymoon was to take place, what kind of clothes she would need for that. Oh yes! And when it came to clothes, Mabel did not have the right kind laid out now. It was the first time this had ever happened. She was not dining in a restaurant and going to the theatre afterwards; she was dining in her own suite, so that she could wait for Sybelle's telephone call.

Mabel came back to the room with an emerald-green hostess dress over her arm and matching slippers in her hand. 'I'm sorry these weren't ready for you, Madame,' she said. 'But I prepared for the Belle Meunière and 'The Voice of the Turtle'. And since you told me you were dining in the suite, I've been on the telephone. Mr. Goldenberg says the change of plan is entirely agreeable to him, but since you are not going out he won't come until seven. I hope that will give you time to take a short rest, Madam. I am sure you must need it. ... The porter is very sorry to say that at the moment the only reservation available on the *Crescent* is one upper. But he hopes to get something better. He has promised to keep right after the Pullman company. Meanwhile he is holding the upper. ... Could you give me some idea, Madam, about how long we will be staying in Louisiana, so that I would have some idea what to pack and how much?'

'You had better pack enough for a week, Mabel – well, perhaps for ten days. I should think we would be back on Monday the nineteenth at the latest.'

She did not take time to rest. She bathed and put on the emerald-green hostess dress, and then she began to make lists of what Sybelle would need and what she herself would need, so that she could save time in the morning. She would not try to do anything about the household linens until after her return. Even though Sybelle was going to start housekeeping immediately – and she did not really see how this was possible in that ramshackle old house – the girl could borrow enough for her immediate needs from Belle Heloise, or probably – the thought was unwelcome but none the less persistent – from the Tramontes. Merry knew that Italians were good providers when it came to linen, as they were about many other things; probably Netta had dozens and dozens of beautiful hand-woven sheets and fringed towels stowed away that had never even been used. So she herself could concentrate on the question of clothes. Besides that dream of a wedding dress – and it simply *must* not be sold! – Sybelle must have quantities of beautiful lingerie, a stunning travelling outfit, at least two evening gowns, the usual basic daytime dresses and tailored suits. She herself must have a costume not only appropriate for the bride's mother, but arresting enough to cause comment. Merry realized it was important to cause comment about clothes, both Sybelle's and her own. It might help to divert comments of other kinds.

She tried not to think about these as she went rapidly on with her lists. She knew that there would inevitably be awkward aspects to her return, no matter how objectively she treated this or how briefly she remained at Belle Heloise. Not that she felt any compunctions about going there. Her conduct during her absence had always been irreproachable; her right to her position there was still incontestable. She herself would have felt hurt if Sybelle had not wanted her at the wedding, and if anyone else, including her mother-in-law, thought it peculiar that she should return for this, after an absence of eight years, they could keep their thoughts to themselves or prepare for crisp rejoinders, just as they preferred. She did not propose to put up with any insolence, and when it came to aloofness, she could be aloof too.

'Mr. Goldenberg has telephoned from downstairs, Madam, to ask if he might come up.'

'You said yes, of course, Mabel.'

'Of course, Madam.'

Even after all these years, Mr. Goldenberg had never shown the slightest familiarity in his association with her. In fact, it sometimes seemed to Merry as if he bent over backwards to avoid this. For instance, he might certainly have called her by her first name by this time, or at least Miss Meredith, as he had before she was married; but he still addressed her as Mrs. d'Alvery. He never came to her suite, or even to her office, unannounced. He had never mentioned Gervais to her since the day of her frantic appeal to him after Franchot's death, when he told her so candidly he thought she was doing wrong to leave her husband, but that if she were determined on such a course he would be glad to facilitate a career for her. The possibility of divorce, so lightly touched upon then, had never again been discussed. Merry knew that if she herself had broached this, Mr. Goldenberg would have assured her that he would make this process as painless and private as possible. She thought it was not inconceivable that if she did seek a divorce, and secure it, Mr. Goldenberg might afterwards ask her to marry him. But she did not feel by any means sure of it, in spite of his years of devotion. She knew he had very fixed ideas on the subject of loyalty in general and family solidarity in particular. . . .

'Good evening. What a lovely spring day this has been, hasn't it? Almost as pretty as a spring day in Louisiana. I don't know, though. I doubt if anything is ever even "almost" as pretty as that, anywhere in the world.'

Mr. Goldenberg had given his hat and gloves to Mabel in the

foyer, and now came into the tasteful, sophisticated drawing-room, which was doubly attractive with the lights on. His remarks about spring in Louisiana constituted his first greeting.

'I thought of the same thing myself, as I was coming up the Avenue tonight. But then I decided I liked spring in New York better after all. I'm sorry I had to ask you to change our plans for the evening. Mabel didn't tell you why?'

'No; I'm sure she knew you'd want to do that yourself, while we had our cocktails.'

Mr. Goldenberg smiled pleasantly at Mabel, who had already entered from the pantry with the silver shaker, glasses of embossed crystal, and caviare canapes on a Sheffield tray. Mabel's expression relaxed sufficiently to indicate that she would be very pleased to return the smile if she had considered that it would be respectful to do so, but that she knew it would not. She set the tray down in front of her mistress and returned to the pantry, where preparations for the service of dinner were already in progress. She knew that Mrs. d'Alvery liked to pour the cocktails herself, unless there were a large party.

'I had a telegram from Sybelle. Perhaps you'd like to see it yourself. At long last she's actually going to marry the one love of her life.'

Merry did not mean to speak satirically, only lightly, but after she had spoken she realized that her tone had not been as tender as a mother's should be, under the circumstances. She handed the telegram to Mr. Goldenberg without further comment. He read it attentively, and handed it back to her.

'Why, I'm very glad to hear about this!' he said with obvious sincerity. 'Those two have certainly been loyal to each other – they deserve all the happiness they can get.' There he went, speaking straight off about loyalty; she was right; it was an almost passionate predilection on his part. But his next remark showed his concern for her. 'It'll rush you a good deal, trying to do everything in one morning,' he said. 'But Miss Shattuck's very efficient. You've done an excellent piece of work training her, and I hope you'll get the benefit of that now, through her help.' Miss Shattuck was Merry's assistant at the office, and Merry was already counting confidently on her. 'If necessary, she could follow you South on Thursday,' Mr. Goldenberg went on. 'She'd still get there before the wedding. She could bring anything you directed her to secure, but that you didn't have time to select yourself. I think you could count on her good judgement and her good taste. You're taking Mabel, of course? And what about reservations?'

'Nothing available but an upper berth so far. But I'm hoping there'll be something better in the morning, through last-minute cancellations.'

'Of course there'll be something better in the morning, whether there are any last-minute cancellations or not.' Mr. Goldenberg took a small pad from his pocket and made a brief notation on it. 'I'll get in touch with you around ten and let you know just what. You'll be shopping by that time, of course. But I'll send you a message. ... Perhaps you'd prefer I didn't stay with you this evening? I know you have a great deal to do.'

'No, I'd like to have you stay, Mabel will attend to the packing, and I've finished making out the lists of what I need to get. There isn't anything more I can do until morning. It won't seem so long to me, waiting for Sybelle's call, if I'm not alone.'

'In that case ...'

They finished their cocktails, and at just the right moment Mabel reappeared to remove the tray. A table covered with a white cloth was wheeled in by a manservant, and immediately afterwards a small metal heater. The leaves of the table were spread out, the silverware arranged, the first dishes removed from the heater: clear turtle soup with sherry, so different from the rich thick turtle stew of Louisiana, but almost as delicious. (Again that tiresome 'almost'!) Mushrooms under glass. Broiled breast of guinea hen. Currant jelly, Broccoli hollandaise. 'Tossed' green salad, about which there was no 'almost' – it could not compare with Antoine's. *Mille feuiles* that were really excellent. All the appropriate vintage wines, and finally a beverage that went by the name of coffee. Mr. Goldenberg drank his without comment or objection. Merry pushed her cup aside. The telephone rang. ...

'Yes, this is Mrs. Gervais d'Alvery. Yes. Hello, Sybelle! How are you, darling? Best wishes and all that! We seem to have a line. I can hear you perfectly. Yes, I found it here when I got in this afternoon. Of course I'm coming. I'll do all the shopping I can tomorrow morning, and Miss Shattuck will do the rest and bring the things South the next day. But it would help me if I knew what you need. I don't mean the wedding dress; I have that

355

lined up already. But for your trip. No, I don't seem to be hearing you quite so well now. ... Why, you can't, Sybelle! ... You can't do that! ... It's absurd, it's impossible! No, I won't try to argue with you over the telephone, but don't you understand? ... Operator, you've cut me off! No, we hadn't talked five minutes!'

For a moment she tried, vainly, to re-establish the connection. Then she gave it up. She turned to Mr. Goldenberg, the expression of her beautiful face distorted.

'They're not going anywhere on their wedding trip!' she exclaimed. 'They're going straight out to Hathaway Hall! Sybelle says Mr. Tramonte has put a lot of people there to work already, and she is sure that by Saturday two or three rooms will be habitable. She doesn't see why they couldn't rough it there just as well as they could at some rented camp, and she insists they'll have a lot more fun doing it there, because it'll be their own home.'

'Why, that's probably true, Mrs. d'Alvery. I should think it was a very wise decision on their part. Certainly Rick wouldn't get any pleasure out of further travel, after coming all the way from the Pacific! And certainly no one ought to do any unnecessary travelling now in any case. Don't you worry about Sybelle's comfort. I know Tramonte. He'll have done miracles by Saturday.'

'Don't talk to me about miracles!' Merry's voice would have been sharp now, if it had not been shaky. 'It seems this coming Sunday's the feast of St. Amico, and that the Tramontes always go to the shrine and march in the procession – you know that little chapel, made of zinc or tin or something, just below Donaldsonville? Some Italian built it as a votive offering because his sick child was cured by a stranger he decided afterwards was St. Amico. I never even heard of St. Amico until Luigi Tramonte told me Netta would never have had a baby if she hadn't gone to that shrine and prayed plenty. Ever since Riccardo was born they've never missed a year celebrating St. Amico's feast. They march all the way from the shrine to the church in Donaldsonville. Luigi's always been one of the men who helped carry the statue of the saint, and Riccardo's done it too since he's been big enough! Luigi and Netta think it's another miracle that Riccardo's getting home safe and well in time for this celebration. He's going to be the main feature of it – at least, unless you count the statue! That's the way Sybelle d'Alvery's planning to spend the day after her marriage – going to a so-called shrine with a lot of ignorant Italians, and afterwards marching with them in a crazy procession and feasting the rest of the day! Can you still say you're glad she and this Dago pedlar's son are getting married, Mr. Goldenberg?'

'Yes,' Mr. Goldenberg answered. 'Yes, I'm very glad. Even gladder than when you told me in the first place. I think you ought to be very proud of your daughter, Mrs d'Alvery. She's willing to prove that she cares enough about her husband to respect the customs that are precious to his family. That means she's also proving that she's worthy of all the other brides in her own family. I believe I'll see if I can't get down to that celebration myself. I believe I'd be glad, all the rest of my life, that I'd seen her and her husband taking part in it.'

CHAPTER TWENTY-FOUR

MERRY did not have to travel in an upper berth, Mr. Goldenberg reached her promptly at ten the next morning by telephone, to tell her that he had a compartment for her, and a lower in the same car for Mabel. He would call at the Hotel Gotham a little before two and see her safely on the train. He would also bring a large lunch hamper, fully stocked. He realized that she probably would not have time to eat lunch before she left, and also that the dining-car service was now very inadequate, owing to war conditions. But she would be well supplied. She was not to worry over anything. Had she been able to get the wedding dress? Good! He was sure everything would shape itself satisfactorily in the end.

By the time she reached the station it required considerable effort to conceal her nervousness and breathlessness. She had not slept the night before, and she had been going at top speed ever since the shops opened, until returning to the Gotham to get into the travelling outfit which, in accordance with custom, was already spread out for her. Mabel was dressed for the trip, and

Merry's baggage was packed, strapped and tagged. She was taking the clothes she had bought for Sybelle in the containers that had been supplied at the stores, and Mabel tagged these also while Merry hastily changed. Then, after ringing for the bell captain, the maid brought a square box from the serving pantry and offered it to her mistress.

'Your corsage, Madam,' she said respectfully. 'Shall I put it on for you?'

The orchids were in a Max Schling box, as usual, exquisitely fresh and perfectly arranged. Mabel pinned them on the lapel of Merry's tailored blue serge and they started for the elevator. Mr. Goldenberg was waiting for them in the lobby and said that the bags and boxes were already in the car. Mabel checked with the bell captain to be sure that nothing was missing, and then they glided smoothly away to the station.

'I've arranged to have the head porter meet us and take us down in the elevator the back way,' he said. 'You can get right on the train, Mrs. d'Alvery, and Mabel can give you your lunch at once in the compartment. I know there's no service outside the diner any more, but you won't need it with what I've supplied. If I may make a suggestion, I'd advise you to go straight to bed and stay there until you reach New Orleans. I don't know when I've seen you look so tired. But there's nothing more for you to think of. Miss Shattuck's told me that you've accomplished wonders, that there's nothing left for her to do. That must mean you've been on the run all the morning, and you certainly will be after you get to Louisiana. Why not have a good rest in the meantime?'

'I think I will,' Merry agreed. Now that at last she had stopped hurrying, she realized how tired she was. 'Thanks for everything, Mr. Goldenberg. I couldn't ever have made it if you hadn't helped, rounding off the rough corners.'

'Oh yes, you could have. You can do anything on which you're really determined. But I'm glad if I've been able to be of some assistance. Good-bye, Mrs. d'Alvery. As I told you, I may try to come to Louisiana myself. I've been away from Baton Rouge a great deal lately, and this is as good a time as any to go back. Unless some unforeseen difficulty arises, I'll see you Saturday; but in the church at Donaldsonville Sunday morning, anyway.'

The lower berth in the compartment had already been made

and the upper one folded back into place. Gratefully, Merry let Mabel help her undress, arrange her toilet articles, and serve lunch from the hamper. When the porter buzzed, Mabel went to the door and told him Madam was very tired and must on no account be disturbed, slipping a generous tip into his hand as she spoke. He brought more towels to supplement the already ample supply, looked about for possible papers to remove, and left with the fervent expression of hope that if the lady wanted anything she would please ring three times, so that he would know it was her and leave whatever he was doing to come. The conductors had not yet been through, so Mabel said she would watch for them outside and forestall their entrance. She had the tickets in her handbag. She did hope Madam would have a good rest. . . .

To her surprise, Merry began to feel drowsy almost immediately. The reaction from the excitement which had kept her awake all night had already set in, and she soon fell fast asleep. When she waked the train was stopping jerkily at some station where lights were burning on the platform. She looked at her watch and realized with astonishment that they must have reached Charlottesville, that she had been sleeping for hours and hours! Charlottesville. . . . That was where Gervais had spent the entire spring of 1943! He had written her briefly when he had entered the School of Military Government, saying that most of the officers' wives were accompanying them there, that he would be glad if she would join him, and that he believed she would enjoy the experience herself. He thought that if they were together at a beautiful place like that, which had no associations whatsoever with Belle Heloise, they might achieve a reunion which would make them both very happy. She had answered the letter briefly and coolly: she appreciated his thought, but the spring trade was keeping her unusually busy; it would not be possible for her to leave New York just then. He had not written her since; when it came to that, he had not written her for a long time before then, either. The solitary letter must have been the result of protracted thought; it must have represented his last desperate appeal. She knew he would never make another. . . .

Why did she have to wake at Charlottesville, of all places? Why could it not have been Philadelphia or Atlanta or any other place that she did not connect with Gervais? She rang for the porter, who appeared as if by magic, and who went to summon Mabel as if on winged feet. Merry ate a light supper, permitted

Mabel to smooth her bed and turn her pillows while she herself prepared for the night, and then tried to sleep again. But she found she could not. She kept thinking about Gervais, who would not be at Belle Heloise to see Sybelle married. Their first baby – their beautiful little blonde girl who had seemed to them, as she soon also seemed to Riccardo, like the little princess in the fairy tale. The night of Sybelle's birth, her own normal and rewarding labour, the beginning of Cresside's secret and terrible travail – these were still vivid and enduring memories. How resourceful and reassuring Gervais had been all through that dreadful period, how co-operative with the doctor and nurses, how authoritative with the servants! The idea of presenting the cousins as twins had been hers, to be sure; but it was he who had carried the idea through to triumphant execution at a moment when she herself had been powerless to do so. And afterwards how delighted they had both been with their own lovely child! How completely they had shared their enjoyment in her! The disappointment Gervais must have felt because his first-born was not a son – so soon assuaged, in any case, by the birth of Philogene – had never been voiced. And now that first-born was about to become a bride herself! Merry knew that while men were proud of their sons, their tenderest feelings were centred in their daughters. Wherever Gervais was tonight, he must be lying awake, thinking of Sybelle, fearful lest some lack of gentleness might mar her bridal rapture, hoping against hope that her happiness with her husband might be lasting and complete. . . .

If Riccardo Tramonte himself could only have been disassociated from those dreadful parents of his! Merry could visualize exactly how they would look and act at the wedding. Netta would be literally strung with diamonds, Luigi would talk in loud, boisterous tones, they would both drink too much champagne. It was bad enough to think of all this, and of having them receive the guests at Belle Heloise, with her mother-in-law and herself. But it was still worse to think about that ridiculous celebration the next day, and she could not help doing it as the train sped along. She was well acquainted with the legend of the miraculous cure. An Italian labourer named Tony Musco, while returning from his day's work, had met a stranger who asked for a meal and a night's lodging, much as Angus Holt had done in coming to Belle Heloise. Tony had hesitated, saying he had but little to offer at best, and adding that his home was a sorrowful one just then. His little boy, Lucien, was critically ill; the distracted father did not even know whether the child might not be dying before he himself reached home. However, the stranger quietly persisted. He was used to humble fare and poor lodgings, he said; and sometimes he had been successful in helping with just such cases as his prospective host described. As soon as he entered the Muscos' kitchen he went to the child, whose crib had been placed there so that his mother could watch over him while she did her other work. Whatever ministrations the stranger performed were brief and seemed simple. But after the family and their unknown guest had gathered around the supper table the little boy roused and asked for food too. The next day he was well on the road to recovery. And as he sat looking at a dog-eared picture book containing the highly coloured prints of saints especially venerated by Italians, he pointed to one of these in great excitement, crying: 'Look, mamma! There is the man who spent the night with us!'

His parents were easily convinced that the child was right – too easily, Merry said to herself as she continued to think involuntarily of the story through the long night. By means of the most rigid economy they saved enough to build a tiny shrine; and as the news of the miraculous cure spread through the Italian settlement where they lived, money was gradually raised to import a realistic statue of the saint. It was given a place of honour in the shrine, which was eventually enlarged to form a small chapel. The local veneration of the saint became more and more general; and, as an increasing number of cures were attributed to him, votive offerings of every description began to pour in – rings, bracelets, earrings, pendants, crucifixes. Their value was such that they could not be left scattered about in the shrine. A velvet stole was made to which they could be attached, and this was kept locked up in the Muscos' house, except on St. Amico's feast day, and shown only to the most honoured visitors. But the Sunday after Easter it was draped around the saint's shoulders, and in all the magnificence of this adornment he was placed on a float, which was carried to the church in Donaldsonville. There he remained during High Mass, while his devotees heaped offerings around him. Then he was restored to his own shrine. But the celebration of the feast continued all the rest of the day, and its character became increasingly hilarious and decreasingly devout as it progressed.

Merry had visited this shrine once, long ago, with Gervais; indeed, now that she thought of it again, she remembered it was just before he had gone to the First World War, when they were not even formally engaged. It was he who had first told her the story of St. Amico, and, half in jest, half in earnest, suggested that they should make an offering to him themselves. She had replied, also speaking lightly, that she did not think Protestant prayers would count for much in such a place; and he had said, all right, he would make the offering by himself. But at any rate she might like to see the stole Tony kept in his house, with all the jewellery sewed on it. He had arranged for that, and secretly she thought that the Italian farmer, as well as the Italian saint, had doubtless benefited financially by the visit. Afterwards she had remembered it only as a pleasant outing which she and Gervais had shared, until, some years later, Gervais told her that Luigi Tramonte, the pedlar who came to Belle Heloise with stage planks and Johnny Crooks, attributed the birth of his son to St. Amico. On this occasion Gervais had made some slightly ribald remarks to the effect that Luigi's own persistent efforts to beget a son could possibly have something to do with it, and they had laughed over the story together. Later still she had heard that some of Netta's most valuable jewellery had gone to adorn the stole, and that additional contributions of this character were frequently made by the Tramontes; also that they made a great point of observing St. Amico's feast day. But she had never given the matter serious thought, even during the period when she had been striving, like her husband and her mother-in-law, to break up the match between Riccardo and Sybelle. Now it forced itself upon her reluctant attention again. Why, in heaven's name, if Riccardo had to come home on leave and Sybelle must revolt against any further postponement of their marriage, did he come at just this time? Why could he not have come a month earlier or a month later? Or why, after waiting all these years to be married, could they not have waited two more days? The marriage in itself was enough of a blow to family pride. But to have the feast of St. Amico added to this! . . .

Merry finally decided that she could not stand thinking of it any longer. She rose, extracted some sleeping pills from her travelling bag, and took a double dose. Then she fell into a heavy drugged slumber, totally unlike her first natural, refreshing sleep, and did not wake again until two o'clock the next afternoon.

They were just leaving Atlanta then, rather late, because they had been held up by a troop train, and Mabel had begun to be worried and had almost decided to go and see if anything were the matter, when Madam finally rang. The coffee in the thermos was still hot, the carefully wrapped rolls still crisp; but Mabel could see that Madam was not especially enjoying her belated breakfast, and that she was further annoyed by the news that the train was late and losing more and more time. They would not be getting into New Orleans until midnight – until two in the morning – until four. . . . Finally the porter appeared with the information that passengers who preferred to remain in the train might do so, staying in the station until seven-thirty. Merry asked for a telegraph blank, and told Mabel to have the porter send a wire from Montgomery.

'I can't have my daughter hanging around that dreadful station, hour after hour, in the middle of the night,' she said. 'There's really no telling now when we'll get in. I don't see anything to do but stay on the train. And that means we won't get to Belle Heloise until nearly noon on Friday! We won't have any time at all to prepare for a Saturday wedding!'

'I imagine the preparations are all very well in hand already, don't you, Madam? And it won't take me any time at all to unpack what you brought with you, once we're there. Mr. Goldenberg said, please don't worry! I'm sure everything will be for the best in the end.'

'Mabel, you said that just like a Baptist minister condoling with a bereaved family. I ought to know. I was brought up a Baptist.'

'I'm very sorry if I annoyed you, Madam. . . . Shall I take the telegram to the porter now?'

Merry was not annoyed with Mabel specifically. But she was very much annoyed with the general situation, and the more she thought about it, the more this annoyance increased. To have the train hours and hours late, on top of everything else! To be obliged to spend another night on it! To be uncertain whether her wire would even get to Sybelle! She had sent it in care of the Estrades on Esplanade Avenue, assuming that was where her daughter would be staying, but she had neglected to inquire during the course of their hurried telephone call, because she had been so upset. She did not dare take any more sleeping pills, for fear she would feel foggy when she had to get up so early, and again she tossed restlessly about. She dozed a little after the train finally pulled into the L. and N. station a little after five, but she had not really slept soundly when Mabel came to call her, and she surveyed herself with great dissatisfaction when she was ready to get off the train.

'I look about a hundred,' she said, half to herself and half to Mabel. 'I don't believe my daughter'll even recognize me.'

'You look beautiful, Madam, as usual. If I may say so, I've never been in service with a lady who had so much style. And when a lady has that, in addition to natural good looks ...' Mabel's unfinished sentence implied that nothing could surpass this combination. 'Here's another corsage for you, Madam,' she added, producing an orchid and a pin. 'The porter's kept it on ice for you. It looks just as fresh as when we left New York. I must say he's been very attentive. I've attended to tipping him, on the scale I thought you would wish. Shall I let him take the bags out now?'

In wiring, Merry had given her car number, and Sybelle was standing by the steps when her mother came out – Sybelle and a dark, extremely handsome young officer whose tunic was decorated with the Combat Infantryman's Badge, the Bronze Star and the Pacific Theatre Ribbon adorned with two battle stars. Rick's train had been on time, so he had reached New Orleans first. Wasn't everything wonderful, Sybelle exclaimed as she threw her arms around her mother, whom she seemed to recognize without any difficulty, in spite of Merry's fears. Now they could all go on to Baton Rouge together. Father and Mother Tramonte were also in New Orleans – of course they'd come down to meet Rick too. But they'd brought two cars, because Father Tramonte had plenty of gas for his business, and there was never enough at Belle Heloise. So no one would be crowded going back. Should they go over to the French Market for coffee first, or would Mummy rather go somewhere else? The Roosevelt, perhaps?

No, Merry answered hastily, she would really prefer the French Market. Besides, it would not take so long to get served there, and she supposed they ought not to waste a minute if they could help it. Actually she was thinking about the Roosevelt when it used to be the Grunewald, of the suite Billy Pereira had engaged for her and Gervais when they came to New Orleans on the *John D. Grace*, of their irritation about the twin beds, of the stalactites and stalagmites in the Cave which later had so practically been transformed into the men's room, of John P. Sullivan and his powerful presence in those bright days of political promise and personal happiness. But her thoughts did not absorb her completely; she was a very competent executive now, she could observe quickly and accurately. She saw that her daughter was even more beautiful than she remembered Sybelle, and she saw how Riccardo Tramonte had managed to retain this radiant girl's love for so many years against such heavy odds. His good looks were different from Vail's, less striking without the strange contrast in colouring, but more classical; the Italian heritage was revealed here in its finest flower. He still spoke and acted with the slightly formal courtesy which had been so carefully instilled in his childhood, and which had so set him apart from his rough-and-tumble American playmates, Vail among them. His smile came rather slowly, but it was still curiously gentle for a man who had been fighting and killing more than two years. He permitted Merry to take the lead in conversation, and Sybelle to make most of the answers, until the first excited greetings and exchange of news were over. But meantime he secured a table on the terrace at the Café au Monde, arranged curb service for Mabel in the shining Cadillac car, and indicated no resentment or embarrassment at being temporarily relegated to the background. After they had finished their coffee and doughnuts, which Merry enjoyed more than she would have liked to confess, he referred almost diffidently to their next plans.

'I'm going to drop off at my cousins', the Montaginos', if you don't mind, Mrs. d'Alvery. It's right on your way, so that won't delay you at all. Then Sybelle will drive this car up, and I'll come along with my father and mother. It'll be about my last chance for a good visit with them before I get married. I'm sure you'll have lots to talk over with Syb too. I'll be out to Belle Heloise this evening to see you both and pick up the car.'

'But—' Merry protested. Surely Sybelle was counting on her fiancé's presence during the drive home! To her surprise, Sybelle seemed to understand and approve the plan.

'Rick and I talked it over together, Mummy, and decided this would be the best arrangement. He and I are going to have all kinds of time together this next month. And I have got lots of things to say to you. It's been even longer since I saw you than

365

since I saw Rick, and we haven't written to each other half so often, either.'

Merry could find no further argument against an arrangement which seemed to have been settled before she was consulted in any case. She sat on the back seat with Mabel, while Rick guided the gleaming car expertly through the traffic, with Sybelle beside him. The girl was neither unduly talkative nor unduly silent; she spoke to him from time to time, naturally and easily, as if they were resuming a pleasant conversation which had been interrupted only the day before. There was nothing strained or anxious in her manner, any more than there was in his. They were obviously completely happy in each other's presence, but they were not snatching greedily at long-delayed rapture, even now. Rick eventually brought the car to a stop before a very imposing residence in Metairie, where another exactly like it was already drawn up, kissed Sybelle without the slightest self-consciousness, and, as she slid over into the driver's seat, asked Merry if she would not like to sit in the front now. He made no suggestion that they should come in to see his parents or his cousins. But after helping Merry into the front seat, he stopped long enough on the curb to speak pleasantly to Mabel.

'I'm so glad you could come with Mrs. d'Alvery. I know how much help you'll be to her and Sybelle – well, and to all of us. And we all need you. There's lots to do.'

'I am sure I am very glad if I can be of service, Major Tramonte.'

Riccardo kissed Sybelle again, reiterated that he would be out that evening, and swung off up the walk. Sybelle started the car and drove away with such smoothness that Merry guessed this was by no means the first time she had handled it. The traffic was not heavy any longer, and presently Sybelle began to chat about wedding arrangements. Everything had gone very easily. They were going to decorate both the house and the church with white azaleas because that was the easiest thing to do right now, and, really, nothing could be lovelier. She hoped Mummy approved the choice. Fortunately there were any number of chickens at Belle Heloise and plenty of shrimp on the market. So they could have two kinds of nice salad. Those would be the mainstay at the wedding breakfast. But Uncle Fabian had given them some champagne and there was still quite a lot in the *cave* too – she felt sure there would be plenty. Mrs. Trosclair in Plaquemine was making the cakes. No one, even in New Orleans, could make more beautiful cakes than Mrs. Trosclair. The Prescotts were going to bring them. Sybelle could hardly wait to see what Mummy had brought for her to wear. She knew everything would be beautiful.

'The wedding dress is a little unusual. I hope you'll be pleased with it, Sybelle.'

'I know I shall. You have such perfect taste, Mummy.'

Merry wished that Mabel had not been sitting on the back seat, where every syllable would inevitably be overheard. She had nothing to say against white azaleas and chicken salad, but she would have liked to take this first possible occasion to protest against participation in the feast of St. Amico. Sybelle went on with her happy chatter.

'We've opened up the *garçonnière*. Of course it's been closed ever since Daddy left, because we didn't need it, and it was just one more place to take care of. But we thought you'd rather be there.'

'I'm sorry you bothered, if it was any trouble.'

'Oh, it wasn't! It was fun. I love seeing it open again. It's had such a blank look ever since Daddy went away. Of course we wouldn't have wanted you to sleep out there all alone. But as long as you have Mabel with you ...'

Sybelle turned around to direct her dazzling smile briefly on Mabel, and again the maid murmured she was only too glad if she could be of service. Merry was sorry she had not thought of saying she would prefer to have the *garçonnière* left unopened, that she would sleep in the Big House for the short time she would be at Belle Heloise. The *garçonnière* would have a blank look now too. Its cosy and homelike atmosphere had been based on its ardent and intimate occupancy by herself and Gervais. When it had been deprived of this, it must indeed have looked blank. And Gervais had lived alone, in that blankness, for nearly six years. ...

'You knew that Daddy had been quite sick, didn't you, Mummy? You didn't? ... Oh, he's much better now,' Sybelle added hastily, seeing Merry's startled look. 'Of course if he weren't, Rick and I'd have planned to be married very quietly, instead of having this big wedding. He wasn't wounded; he caught something in Sicily. Naturally, sanitary conditions are very bad there, and he didn't seem too well even when he left

Belle Heloise. Oh, nothing definite! But Daddy's aged a lot, so much more than you have, Mummy. You'd hardly know him. His hair's almost as white as *grand'mère's*, much whiter than Uncle Fabian's. He was invalided back to Africa for hospitalization. But now he's been sent to England. He's very happy, about that. He thinks he's sure to run into the boys, one of them at least, sooner or later. I've had a cable from Vail, too. I didn't tell you that, either, did I?'

There were unlimited things Sybelle had not told her yet, Merry realized, wishing she did not find this news about Gervais so upsetting. She tried to ask the questions which would give her the greatest amount of information about him and everyone else in the least possible time, as they went speeding up the Airline. But the drive had never seemed so short. They were turning into the River Road almost before she realized it, and Sybelle was changing the subject, eagerly talking of something else.

'Don't you want to go into Hathaway for a moment, Mummy? I do so want to show you what's done already. Then you won't worry about my being comfortable there. And I'm afraid there won't be any time tomorrow—'

'Why, yes, Sybelle, I'm perfectly willing to go there, if you want me to. But I really think I ought to say again—'

'Wait until you've seen it, won't you, Mummy, before you say anything?'

'Very well.'

Merry remained rather pointedly silent until they swung into the alley at Hathaway. At least a dozen men were working on the grounds. Nearly all were elderly, and those who were not either walked with a limp or revealed some other physical disability; but obviously they were accomplishing wonders. The long rank grass had already been mown with a scythe; now it was being cut with a lawn-mower and the edges of the driveway were being clipped. White paint was being applied to the dingy façade in sweeping if unskilled strokes. The centre hall through which they went in had been thoroughly cleaned. Sybelle led the way proudly past the library and the White Ballroom, which were still closed, into the large dining-room, where recent and thorough cleaning was again evident.

'We're going to use this for a general living-room while we're camping out,' she informed her mother. 'And we're going to sleep in the little room off it, that must have been a children's dining-room, or something like that, once. Just for now, I mean. Of course, later on we're going to have one of the beautiful upstairs bedrooms. Look, Mummy, there's a lavatory right here, and Mr. Tramonte's had a shower put in! The plumbing still works and so does the kitchen stove. It's really wonderful, after all these years. Oh, there's the new coolerator! It looks just like an electric refrigerator, doesn't it? And tomorrow morning some more furniture's coming in!'

To Merry everything looked antiquated and barren and taste-less, but she could see that in Sybelle's eyes it was beautiful already, and, as a matter of fact, she knew that it would be in time, and that meanwhile it really was livable. Men and women were both working inside the house, under the capable direction of an enormous Negress with a beaming face, whom the girl presented to her mother as Be-a-trice Washington.

'Be-a-trice is going to be our cook,' she told Merry. 'She's just as good a cook as Carmelite. And she has a niece who's going to be the house girl. Where is Thuger, Be-a-trice?'

'She's hangin' things out on de line, Miss Sybelle, what's she's washed good. Does yo' want Ah should call her fo' you'?'

'No, not just now, thank you, Be-a-trice. My mother'll see her tomorrow. You'll both be over at Belle Heloise then.'

'Us sho' will, Miss Sybelle.'

'Isn't she something right out of a storybook?' Sybelle whis-pered to her mother as they went down the beautiful curving stone steps, which, Merry noticed, had already been cleared of encroaching vines. 'I have to be careful to call her Be-a-trice, though, not Beatrice. She says she'll leave if she's called Beatrice, because that isn't really her name. And Thuger comes from Sugar. That's what her folks called her when she was a little girl; but she couldn't pronounce her S's, so she called herself Thuger, and now that's *her* real name. Father Tramonte got them both for me. He says it's all nonsense to say it's impossible to find servants any more. He says of course you can find them if you know where to look and if you offer them the right wages. He does know where to look, and of course he offers the right wages. You see how it's going to be, Mummy; everything made just as easy and pleasant for me as it was for you.'

'I'll admit that wonders have been done on this place already,

Sybelle. But I'd still be happier if you were going to spend your honeymoon over at the Pass, or some place like that. And I've been wanting to talk to you about—'

'Can't we do it by and by, Mummy? I really think we ought to get home now. *Grand'mère's* been waiting for us a long time, and I want to see all the lovely things you've brought me before Rick gets out, and make sure the wedding dress fits and all that. . . . And you want to get settled in the *garçonnière* . . .'

Merry did not want to get settled in the *garçonnière*. Her dread of going there had been one of the main reasons why she had consented to stopping at Hathaway, and now she asked Sybelle if there were time to stop at the cemetery. Why, they would take time, Sybelle said; but perhaps Mummy would prefer to go there alone. She and Mabel would sit in the car and get a little better acquainted. Merry delayed as long as she could in the family lot, less because she wanted to linger there, once she had assured herself of the beautiful care given to Franchot's grave, than because the nearer she got to Belle Heloise the more she dreaded her arrival. It was far less strained than she had expected, however. Fabian and Cresside and Frances Belle were there already, awaiting her arrival; her mother and Miss Mittie had come over from the storehouse, so she did not have to see her mother-in-law alone. Besides, Madame d'Alvery's greeting left nothing to be desired; it was dignified, it was courteous, it was unreproachful. Again Merry felt, as she had felt in watching Sybelle and Riccardo together earlier in the morning, that conversation was progressing as if it had been taken up where it had been casually left off the day before. Only the underlying reason was different. In the case of Sybelle and Riccardo, their accord was so complete that it eliminated time and distance easily. In the case of her mother-in-law and herself, they had always been so far apart that more separation did not matter. Never, in all the years she lived at Belle Heloise, had Merry been treated with more deliberate courtesy; never, not even when she came there as a bride, had she felt so completely like an outsider.

In spite of this feeling, which increased rather than lessened as the hours went on, the afternoon passed pleasantly and quickly. There were so many people in the *garçonnière* with Merry that she did not have time to brood over its blankness. Everything she brought with her was quickly unpacked and tried on, with repeated exclamations of delight. Sybelle said that the wedding dress with the forget-me-nots was just something out of this world; and how wonderfully the pale blue dress for the maid-of-honour and the dresses of deeper blue for the bridesmaids blended with it! And what lingerie and laces! What hostess gowns and sports suits! Why, there must be just as much as ever to select from in the New York stores! Well, not quite, Merry said; but if you knew how to go about it, you could still manage to keep properly dressed. She was glad everything fitted so well. Mabel could make slight alterations very nicely, if necessary, but none seemed to be indicated. Instead she could start repacking Sybelle's things right away, except for what would be needed the next day. . . .

It was while Mabel was doing this repacking, with her usual skill and dispatch, that Merry noticed an unusual look on the maid's face. Her expression was not exactly mutinous; but somehow it had tightened and hardened. Merry took advantage of a moment when all the others had gone trooping into the little kitchen to get cooling drinks and she could speak to Mabel privately.

'Is anything the matter, Mabel?'

Mabel's expression grew tighter and harder. 'Doubtless I should have expected something of the sort, Madam,' she said, and her voice was tight and hard too. 'But there seems to be no proper provision on this place for a personal maid.'

'I don't think I understand. My mother-in-law's always had a personal maid. Creassy was mine until our old cook, Lou Ida, died, and then Creassy took her place, because I wasn't here any more.'

'I am sorry to be obliged to remind you, Madam, that you are speaking of Negroes. I should not have supposed this would be necessary in the case of a lady like you. Did you expect me to eat in the kitchen with them?'

'I'm afraid I didn't think about it at all, Mabel. I've had so many things to think of at once. But you don't have to if you don't want to.'

'There is no servants' hall, Madam. Only the kitchen and the butler's pantry. I went without my lunch, after that long train trip, too, when I was most uncomfortable, though trying my best to do everything for your comfort—'

'Well, I'm willing to do everything I can, in reason, for your

371

comfort. You could have eaten in the *garçonnière* if you had wanted to. The kitchen here is ready for use. All the family, except myself, is out there now.'

'I am willing to eat in this kitchen, Madam, since there is no servants' hall on the place, and since it is only a matter of a few days. But one of the Negroes must be instructed to bring my meals to me here.'

'We're rather short-handed at Belle Heloise for the moment, and we're getting ready for a big wedding on very short notice. Couldn't you get your own meals, and my morning coffee, the few days we'll be here?'

'I am a personal maid, Madam; not a cook. You knew that when you engaged me. And I am sure you can't say, or any of my other employers either, that as a personal maid I haven't always given satisfaction.'

Merry turned abruptly and walked out of the room, leaving Mabel in front of the open suitcases. Rick had just arrived with Drina Montagino, and the drinks were ready; everyone else had gone into the living-room to enjoy them. But apparently no one had thought of calling her.

'I'm sorry to bring up anything unpleasant at this stage,' she said. She saw that the others had suddenly remembered her, and that they were chagrined at their oversight. They were trying to make immediate amends for it by crowding around her with proffered chairs and glasses. 'No thanks, not right now,' she said, waving them back. 'I just came in to ask if any of you would drive Mabel into town, so that she could catch the next train for New Orleans. I find she doesn't fit in here. She's an outsider. It's so unpleasant for her that she's going to make it unpleasant for everyone else, if she stays. No amount of efficiency could make up for that. We'll be much better off without her.'

Of course they would be glad to remove the disturbing element from the scene, Fabian and Cresside hastened to assure Merry. That is, if she were certain. ... They gathered that she had grown quite dependent on Mabel, and some adjustment ought to be possible. ... She was quite certain, Merry said crisply, and, within an hour Mabel, who had made her life easy for so long, had passed abruptly out of it, and Merry had sought out Creassy, who was already starting the preparations for a big company.

'I've sent my maid away, Creassy,' she began tentatively. Creassy sniffed.

'Does yo' mean dat po' white trash yo' done bring down wif yo' from de East?' she inquired, without pausing in the act of dismembering chickens for frying.

'Yes, if that's what you call her.'

'Ain't nothin' else Ah kin call her. Our own white folks, dey know better dan to treat us lak dat po' white trash done. Anyways, Ah is yo' maid, Miss Merry.'

'I was afraid that I'd been gone so long that perhaps—'

'Shucks, Miss Merry, yo' knows better dan dat. When anyone comes to Belle Heloise, dey belongs here for always, no matter effin dey does go away, once in a while. Doesn't yo' think de Colonel, he's gwine to belong here, after he gits home from de wars?'

'Yes, but—'

'An' Mr. Vail and Mr. Philogene?'

'Yes, but that's different.'

'Ah don't see no difference. Lethe, she can help wid de cookin'. Be-a-trice and Thuger, deys comin' over from Hathaway too. My, my, don't it seem good, Miss Merry, Hathaway open again and quality fixin' to live in it? Us'll manage wid de work. What yo' need I should do fo' yo' right now, Miss Merry?'

'Well, for one thing, there's quite a lot of pressing to be done—'

'Yo' lay yo' dresses out on yo' bed, Miss Merry, lak yo' allus done, an' yo'll find 'em ready soon as yo need 'em. Us is all mighty glad to have yo' back. Only trouble was, dat white trash yo' brung wid yo'.'

Creassy's feeling seemed to be general. Rick and Sybelle had both been very courteous to Mabel, because it was their way to be courteous to everyone. But it appeared that even they had harboured doubts as to whether she would fit in. She seemed more suited to New York than to Belle Heloise. They were glad she had gone. Merry, secretly wondering whether the family did not feel that she too was suited to New York rather than to Belle Heloise, in spite of Creassy's reassuring words, tried hard to feel at home, and failed. Supper was a rather hurried meal because the bridal party had to get into St. Agnes' for the rehearsal. Rick and Sybelle were both going to Confession at the same time, and wondered whether anyone else wanted to go too. Neither of them looked at Merry, specifically, as they said this, but she also did some wondering. Did they realize how long it was since she had gone to Confession? She did not see how they possibly could. But there was a short and slightly awkward silence, which Madame d'Alvery brought to an end by saying that since she was saving her strength for the wedding itself, she would not go to town that evening, and doubtless Merry would like to wait and go to Confession when she did. Perhaps Merry would rather not even go to rehearsal, when it came to that. She must be very tired after her long journey and the trying scene with that impudent English maid. . . .

Merry would not have supposed it could be possible for her to feel as grateful to her mother-in-law as she did at that moment. She would be very glad if they would excuse her, she said. After all, Cresside had told them she would be at the church that evening; she could attend to any last-minute details and as soon as the jubilant bridal party had started into town Merry went wearily back to the *garçonnière* and climbed into the bed which Creassy had already opened after removing the dresses that needed pressing. Merry had never slept in that bed alone before and as she lay down in it now the thoughts of Gervais, which she had been trying to dismiss ever since her train pulled out of Charlottesville, crowded relentlessly in upon her. It had been a shock to her to learn that he had been so ill, that he had aged so much, and that she had not even known of this; it was unexpectedly harder than she had foreseen, not only to occupy alone this room which he and she had shared, but to miss his familiar figure moving about the plantation. Was there, in spite of modern scepticism and modern evasions, a finality about marriage which was inescapable? This had not occurred to her before. But for the last twenty-four hours she had involuntarily dwelt on the thought. She ceased to worry about Sybelle and her daughter's share in the celebration of St. Amico because she was more and more concerned about her husband and her relation to him. . . .

She fell into a deep sleep at last, and did not wake until Creassy touched her on the shoulder and spoke to her. Then she sat up with a start, to see that the shades had already been raised and the mosquito bar lifted, and that sunlight was streaming across her bed.

'Good gracious, Creassy, what time is it?'

'Don't yo' worry about de time, Miss Merry. Yo' was plum

tuckered out. Yo' needed yo' rest. But Ah jes' figured Ah couldn't let yo' sleep no longer, effin yo' was to git to de weddin'. Here is yo' coffee, and Ah's gwine bring yo somethin' else soon as yo's had yo' bath and got dressed. All de others, deys finished a big breakfast and fixin' to go to de church.'

'Why, it can't be all that late! But it looks like a beautiful day, Creassy.'

'Yessum, Miss Merry. Such days is well accepted.'

'That's what you used to say to me when I came here a bride myself. I remember how I loved hearing you. I'd never heard anyone say it before.'

'Us all says it, Miss Merry. Thuger, she gwine be sayin' it to Miss Sybelle mighty soon. Yo' wuz a beautiful bride, Miss Merry, I wuz proud to wait on yo', and Mr. Gervais sure did set his eye teeth by yo'. Now us has got us another beautiful bride and Ah hopes us gets two or three more. Can't be too many d'Alvery brides to suit me or too many d'Alvery babies comin' along to suit Dinah. No, mam!'

Creassy departed, leaving Merry to drink her coffee and to think of the days when her maid had brought not only that first cup which she drank alone, after Gervais had already gone out into the fields, but also of that later mid-morning service, when he returned to their room, and they breakfasted in a leisurely way together. She remembered, too, the skill with which Creassy had kept the shuttered bedroom dark and quiet that first summer, so that she could sleep and sleep, storing up the strength which had made Sybelle such a healthy, happy baby. And now history was about to repeat itself. Yet not exactly. Sybelle's husband would not come in every morning to drink coffee with her, because after his short leave he would be back in the Pacific somewhere, fighting. He would not be safely at her side. Sybelle was not as fortunate as she had been. Her husband had been with her always. It was she who had left. . . .

Well, as if there were any time to be thinking about that! She pushed the bedclothes impatiently aside, made a hasty toilet, and hurried over to the Big House. She met Sybelle coming out of the dining-room, where the last touches had just been given to the table festively prepared for the wedding breakfast.

'Oh, Mummy, I'm so glad to see you! I was afraid you wouldn't be here in time to help me dress, and of course I wanted you to, especially since it was you who brought me all those

375

lovely things. Come on upstairs, quick! Joyeuse and *grand'mère* are dressing already.'

'Then we have a moment to ourselves, Sybelle, and there are one or two things I'd very much—'

'That time-honoured "little talk"? Now, Mummy! You ought to know that went out before the First World War, along with the sort of brides who needed it!'

In spite of herself, Merry smiled. But she spoke seriously.

'No, I didn't mean that sort of a little talk. But I did mean another sort. I want to say—'

'You want to say again you don't think we ought to spend our honeymoon at Hathaway. Well, you spent yours here, didn't you, with *grand'mère* and Aunt Cresside right in the house? And I bet you were happy just the same! I should think the fact that Rick and I would have the house to ourselves, even if it isn't in perfect order, would a good deal more than make up for not having two other women cluttering up the scene.'

'I realize it is too late for me to prevent you from going to Hathaway, Sybelle, and, as I said before, I'm ready to admit that it has been made surprisingly habitable under all the circumstances. But I do want to ask you, for my sake, not to go to that absurd celebration tomorrow.'

'And I was going to ask you, for mine, if you wouldn't go yourself. Joyeuse is coming, so you wouldn't be alone. She realizes how much it would mean to me if my family were represented.'

'*Joyeuse!* That hard-headed young scientist!'

'Yes. But she knows the Tramontes aren't hard-headed scientists. She knows they're very devout Catholics who accept miracles unquestioningly – well, credulously, if you want to put it that way. But she also knows how much it would mean to them, and to me, if some of the d'Alverys were at that celebration. The Tramontes are trying mighty hard to meet our standards. I think we might try to meet some of theirs. Because they've succeeded better than we have, so far. Not just by giving Hathaway to Rick and me, but by everything they've done. It's too bad you didn't go to the rehearsal with us last night, Mummy, because they had a little party for us afterwards that was simply tops. And the loving-kindness they've shown me – well, I couldn't talk about it without crying. We haven't time to talk about anything more now, anyway, and I've said all I can, all

I'm going to. But I'll look for you tomorrow, Mummy. If I don't see you, something's going to be gone between us that we'll never get back.'

Something's going to be gone between us that we'll never get back! Why did Sybelle have to say that, at the end of her strangely assorted remarks, part slangy, part stubborn, part exalted? The words kept ringing through Merry's tired but rebellious head even during the wedding ceremony, all through the reception, in the quiet and empty hours that followed the light-hearted departure of the bride and groom to the adjoining plantation. She was aware, with pride, that Sybelle was the most beautiful bride she had ever seen. Aware, with relief, that the Tramontes were impressive in appearance and dignified in manner. Aware, with satisfaction, that no function at Belle Heloise had ever passed off more smoothly and agreeably than this wedding breakfast. But all the time, through her awareness, she kept hearing those words: *Something's going to be gone between us that we'll never get back.*

She stayed in the Big House until the last jubilant guest had departed, until everything in the deserted rooms had been restored to its accustomed order, until Madame d'Alvery and Mrs. Randall and Miss Mittie were through discussing the details of the wedding and had gone wearily but elatedly to bed. Then she stepped out on the front gallery and looked down the walk towards the iron gate. It was still too early for the full bloom of the yucca which made the traditional bridal arch; but some of the amaryllis was already out, and Sybelle and Rick had followed the time-honoured family custom of newly-married couples by getting out of their car at the gate, instead of taking the sharp right-angle turn and driving all the way to the house. Merry could see her daughter yet, in her exquisite array of blue and white, and Rick in his uniform and his decorations, as they walked up between the scarlet lilies. They had stopped to kiss each other – first just inside the gate, then halfway up the walk, finally at the demilune in front of the house. Meanwhile they had been laughing and talking with each other and with the pretty young girls and the personable young men that followed them. Now they were alone, locked in each other's arms, exultant not only in their present rapture, but in the glad certainty that nothing on earth could prevail to lessen their love for each other.

Merry had felt the same exaltation and the same glad certainty once in her love for her husband, and now . . .

The front door opened, and Joyeuse came out. She had vetoed the suggestion of a tall evening at the Heidelberg with the bridesmaids and ushers, after the departure of the bride and groom. For crying out loud, hadn't they made enough whoopee at the Tramontes' the night before? She had, anyway. She was dead on her feet after all this hullabaloo, and she had to get up early Sunday morning. She did not care any more about frills and furbelows than she did about drinking and dancing. Merry saw that she had taken off her bridesmaid's dress and put on a plain white smock, which she wore with an air of ease and relief. She did not even care greatly about any special person, beyond feeling moderate family affection, though she had the d'Alvery gift of attracting young and old of both sexes to her side. She was much more interested in her work. She would be glad to get back to it, quietly, Monday morning. Meanwhile she must keep her word to Syb and see what she could do with Mom.

'Hello there! Taking a look over the premises, now you can do it in peace?'

'Yes. It's very beautiful here, Joy.'

'Well, it always was, if you remember. I reckon it always will be,' Joyeuse said practically. 'Have you made up your mind about tomorrow, Mom? Because if we're going to that shrine we have to get a pretty early start.'

'What time?'

'Well, the procession leaves the shrine at nine, so we have to be there before that. I reckon it means a six o'clock call.'

'Rick and Sybelle will have to get up at six tomorrow!'

'Yeah. Tomorrow. Not any of the other mornings while Rick's home, though. I reckon they know all about that good old French saying, "*On se leve tard pendant la lune de miel*." They've probably enlarged on that, to suit themselves: "*Et on se couche tot*." However, that's beyond the point. Of course, they could have spent tonight in Donaldsonville instead of getting up at six tomorrow; but if you'd tried that lately you'd realize they were a lot more sensible to stick to Hathaway. The hotel diningroom's closed and the First and Last Chance Cafés fourteen blocks away. Either they wouldn't have had any bridal breakfast or they'd have to go a far piece for it. Well, we should worry, especially as they didn't chance that. But we don't seem to be

378

getting anywhere, talking like this. I'm ready to hit the hay and I should think you would be. Do I call you at six or don't I?'

'I'm afraid I couldn't make it, Joy.'

'Of course, it's up to you. Good night.'

Something's going to be gone between us that we can never get back. Something *more* – Franchot's dead, Gervais overseas, and now Sybelle ... Sybelle who's so loyal and loving, who's never let anything come between herself and Rick and never will, who hasn't spoken reproachfully or acted resentfully because I went away from her father and away from her when they needed me so much, but who says that now – says it and means it. ...

Joyeuse had already gone into the house; she was halfway up the stairs. In another minute she would have disappeared, because she never stopped to salute the Spanish statue. Merry ran after her.

'Joy, I think perhaps I can make it after all. I think you'd better call me at six.'

Joyeuse came back down the stairs. She had been courteous to her mother ever since Merry's arrival; she had made no embarrassing allusions to the past or permitted any awkward silences to come between them. But hitherto she had given no sign of being glad to see her. Now she put her arms around her mother and hugged her.

'That's the spirit, Mom,' she said, her voice joyous, like her name. 'That's the way for a great girl like you to crash through!'

Again it was a perfect spring morning, the kind that Creassy said was 'well accepted'. As Joyeuse and Merry motored down the River Road on the West Side below Donaldsonville, towards the shrine, they could see the sights and hear the sounds that always continued to proclaim spring so buoyantly. The thistle blossoms were pink and cream, and the levee was white with clover; cattle and horses and sheep were all grazing peacefully along it. Merry thought she had never seen so many calves and colts and lambs frolicking beside their mothers. She said so to Joyeuse.

'I wish they didn't have so many cockleburrs on them. Look at the tails on those poor sheep! I'd like to stop and pick the burrs out.'

379

'I noticed that Maudie still gets covered with cockleburrs too, Joy. I tried to get some of them off her the afternoon I came. But she wouldn't let me touch her. She growled at me.'

'She won't after you've been here a few days longer. You don't have to hurry back to New York, do you, Mom?'

'I ought to be back there by the nineteenth. I have a reservation out of New Orleans on Saturday.'

'Oh!'

'But of course I could cancel it.'

'Well, I hope you will. Hang around until after Rick's gone if you can. Syb's going to miss him dreadfully at first. You could be a lot of help to her, fixing up the house. And she's sure she'll have a baby straight off. If she does she'll want you more than ever.'

'I hadn't thought of all that. I'll see what I can arrange.'

Joyeuse was turning from the highway into a narrow dirt road with small dilapidated houses on either side of it and a small zinc chapel at the end of it. Immediately in front of them was an open truck laden with staring white plaster statues of St. Amico, which apparently were intended for sale at the shrine. Ahead of the truck was a bus filled with jolly-looking Negroes wearing uniforms and clasping brass musical instruments to their sturdy breasts. As Joyeuse drew up behind them they jumped out of the bus, ranged themselves on one side of the road, and began to play 'America the Beautiful' with great gusto. A considerable crowd had collected already. The larger part of it was outside the shrine, but the open door revealed an interior, lighted with dozens of candles, where all the stiff little wooden pews were occupied. American flags had been attached crosswise to the wooden supports of the little porch, and at the rear of the nave a toothless old woman was vigorously pulling a bell rope, mumbling as she did so, and occasionally turning towards the occupants of the nearest pews with impatient ejaculations; she was evidently annoyed because the procession was so slow in starting. Most of the congregation was kneeling in prayer and paid no attention to her; but occasionally a pretty, smartly dressed young woman who called her grandma rose and endeavoured to placate her. Occasionally also a worshipper left a pew to slip an offering at the base of St. Amico's statue, which had already been moved from its accustomed position near the high altar and placed on a float in the centre of the aisle. It was adorned with the long velvet stole to which the previous votive offerings were fastened, and among them Merry could see the coral earrings and necklace which Netta Tramonte had worn as a young woman. Netta herself was seated in the front pew on the left with Luigi; Sybelle and Riccardo were beside them. It might have been a family group of long standing. Merry, feeling that all her sophistication was not proof against such a sight and the feelings it had aroused, turned to Joyeuse almost helplessly.

'Do you think we have to go in?' she whispered.

'Yes, I think we do, just for a minute. I can see two vacant seats in that last pew. The procession's bound to start pretty soon, Mom. You won't have to stay there but a minute.'

They went in, making all the proper motions – genuflecting beside the pew, crossing themselves as they knelt beside it, bowing their heads like the others; but it was Joyeuse who led in doing all this and Merry who followed. She did not try to pray; she could not. However, she knelt for a respectful period, and when she rose from her knees she saw that the procession had already started. A cross-bearer was at the head of it. Then came the float on which the image of St. Amico was mounted, with Riccardo at the right of the statue and his father at the left, in front of the other men who were helping to carry it. They had already lifted the float to their shoulders, but Merry could still see the young officer's decorations and his beautifully moulded features above his burden. There was a new look in his eyes, joyous and rewarded and full of thanksgiving, and Merry knew that this look had come there because of Sybelle, not because of the saint. But he did not turn to look at his bride as he went down the aisle, carrying the sacred burden. He held himself very erect, facing straight ahead, and so did all the men with him. Though his exceptional grace and his military uniform made him outstanding among them, they were all good-looking men, Merry noticed, and all remarkably well dressed. A second smaller float, on which statues of the Virgin and St. Joseph were mounted, followed after the first; this smaller one was carried by girls and women in white dresses, Netta and Drina and Sybelle among them. Two of the girls held up the procession long enough to wipe the images with clean cloths before they started. Then they all passed from the shrine, accompanied by some smug-faced little altar boys carrying huge decorated candles, and immediately the sound of the bell was drowned in the music of the brass band. The pretty young woman who, several times before, had tried vainly to placate the indignant old bell-ringer now did so successfully. They hurried out together, in the wake of the altar boys, and the crowd that had filled the chapel and waited outside fell in line too.

'What is our next move?' Merry inquired, turning to Joyeuse. She felt that Joyeuse had taken charge, and she was glad of it; she herself had no sense of initiative at the moment, no sense of anything except unreality.

'Why, we just get back into the car and follow the procession to Donaldsville. Then we sit through High Mass at the Church of the Ascension. There's nothing complicated about that.'

As Joyeuse expressed this, it did not seem as if there were. But Merry still could not rid herself of the sense of unreality caused by the fact that she was following this procession and that her daughter and her son-in-law were taking part in it. She saw some of the cattle on the levee turn to look wonderingly at it as it passed, and stifled a small hysterical laugh; she felt just as she imagined the cows did. She saw clusters of Negroes loitering in front of the cabins along the way, staring like the cows, but smirking too. She felt the same kinship with them. The band had run out of patriotic tunes and had begun to play jazz. Some of the women were dragging small unwilling children after them. One was nursing a baby as she walked. The day was beginning to grow warm, though it was still so early in the morning, and some of the men in the procession were mopping their streaming faces as they went along, panting audibly and giving vent to their feelings in language which could not, by any stretch of the imagination, be considered devout. But Riccardo, carrying more than his share of the heavy burden, was still going quietly and calmly ahead without turning or stopping, his bearing erect and calm. Merry had almost lost sight of him in the distance. But she knew that the sunlight was still playing over the bright ribbons on his tunic and that the joyous, exalted look still shone from his eyes.

By the time Merry and Joyeuse reached the Church of the Ascension Mass was already under way. It had taken them some time to find a parking place, as all the space around the church was already occupied by other cars, except that pre-empted by the Negro band, which stood patiently awaiting the return procession. But an usher conducted them to seats which had apparently been held for them, as these were immediately beside the statue. It now stood in the centre of the nave. The votive offerings on the stole glittered in the light that streamed down from the windows; the pile of crisp bills and printed prayers on the platform surrounding it was growing higher and more unsteady by the minute. Worshippers kept leaving their seats to bring others – a five-dollar bill clipped to an illustrated form, prayer, or merely a humble scribbled petition. Merry watched the pews in front of her, hoping against hope that none of the Tramontes would do this, fearing unutterably that they might. At last, to her horrified amazement, she saw Sybelle slip out of the front pew and come back to the statue, a folded sheet of paper in her hand. She laid the paper on the pile, knelt down for a minute, and then returned to the place where she had been sitting with the Tramontes. She did not look at her mother. But Merry could not help looking at the folded paper. The pile on which it lay was uneven because it had already been heaped so high, and the single sheet was very light. Presently it was caught in the current of one of the large electric fans at the front of the church, as several others had been. It fluttered back and forth for a moment and then fell to the floor of the pew where Merry sat, spreading open as it dropped. To save her life, she could not help looking at it.

'I'm asking for a miracle too, St. Amico,' she read. 'I want my mother. I need her. My father wants her and needs her too. We all do. We've missed her so all these years she's been away. Make her feel in her heart that she need not leave us again. I beg this favour humbly, for Christ's sake.'

An hour later, when Merry went out of the church in the wake of the triumphant procession, she saw Mr. Goldenberg standing in the portal. He immediately started towards her.

'Don't look so surprised,' he said. 'I told you I was going to make it if I could. I didn't get here for the wedding, but I did get here for this service. And it was worth the effort. I don't know when I've been so deeply touched as I was when I saw the procession moving up the aisle of this church, with Riccardo Tramonte and his bride both in it. I congratulate you, Mrs. d'Alvery – on your son-in-law and on your daughter.'

'Mr. Goldenberg,' Merry said, and stopped. People were hurrying past them, but at any moment someone might pause and interrupt them. The band had already resumed its activities. It was playing 'My Country, 'Tis of Thee' in jazz. No time and no place could have been more inappropriate for an important statement. 'Mabel didn't stay,' Merry ended lamely. 'She didn't fit in. So I had to send her back the same day we got here.'

'Yes, I heard. I hope you don't mind too much.'

'No, I don't mind too much. I realized she was an outsider. I realize I am too.'

'Well, that's more serious. You'll have to do something about that, won't you?'

'Yes. I'll have to stay. I'll have to learn how to fit in again. Because I'm' – suddenly the words came with a rush – 'I find I'm wanted and needed here, Mr. Goldenberg. I've got to be with my own people. I can't go back to New York.'

'I knew you never would, Merry,' he said gently.

CHAPTER TWENTY-FIVE

MADAM D'ALVERY herself suggested having the party early in the summer after Sybelle was married.

It was so long since they had given one, she said, that they would forget how if they did not have one presently. Of course, it would not be the kind of party they used to have at Belle Heloise – the service and the food-stuffs were both lacking for that, not to mention the masculine company needed to enliven any festivity. But the *cave* still contained a few fine old wines, and, thank God, coffee rationing at least was a thing of the past – that *had* been a hardship while it lasted, not having it served nine times a day! The supply of festive linen was still adequate too, thanks to the way brides were outfitted in Madame d'Alvery's youth and her mother's and her grandmother's; the less said about present-day trousseaux the better, especially as neither Cresside nor Sybelle had given the family any time for preparation, and this unseemly haste, added to current shortages, naturally complicated a situation which she had been powerless to improve. For the party they would use one of her own damask tablecloths, monogrammed by the nuns. She had always thought that old silver looked especially well on plain damask, and certainly there was plenty of silver; there had been no pilfering Yankees in this war. As for the best porcelain, she had found most of that still unbroken when she last counted the plates, though some of it had been chipped, betraying the carelessness in handling that one must expect now that Selah was no longer on hand to take care of it. But still, enough of the Sèvres service ... She realized that the supply of flowers was low right now, but snow-on-the-mountains and Indian shot made an effective combination, and there were still a few roses. Besides, they might even break off some branches of the luxuriant crêpe myrtle for such an occasion, though usually she was opposed to taking anything from a tree. ...

'Do you think anyone is in the mood for a party these days, Madame Mère?' Merry asked. 'I don't. I know I'm not.'

'No. But perhaps the mood would change. There would be no harm in trying.'

'I don't know just what we'll serve at a party, either.'

'My dear Merry, if you'll forgive me for saying so, you sounded very like your mother at that moment instead of like yourself. I always used to admire your resourcefulness very much. I hope you have not lost it during your protracted sojourn in large cities.' Merry flushed slightly, and Madame d'Alvery continued with assurance. 'I do not think anyone has ever left Belle Heloise hungry yet, and I do not think anyone ever will. We have every sort of fowl on the place and every sort of vegetable. We have butter and cream and eggs. Not that this is any special credit to us. Persons who live on plantations and do not have all that should blame only themselves. On the other hand, I feel that guests who could not be satisfied with what we can offer would be very captious, under all the circumstances.'

'We haven't any sugar,' Merry said rather heatedly. 'At least, we haven't any except the canning sugar, and we haven't any right to use that for a party.'

'I agree with you, my dear Merry, and if the sugar situation were not so tragic it would be humorous. When I think of the acres of over-quota cane Gervais was forced to destroy, when I think of the supplies, even from what we were allowed to produce, that were permitted to spoil in warehouses, because Yankees cannot be taught that sugar is a perishable commodity, it makes my blood boil. But surely we can squeeze enough sugar for the coffee, and, if not, Cresside will come to our rescue. I am afraid the real difficulty lies less with the commodities at our command than with your own disinclination for any kind of a celebration, Merry.'

Madame d'Alvery had hit uncomfortably close to the mark, and for a moment Merry was silent. She was not content to know that from latest official reports Gervais was recuperating satisfactorily from his wounds, that he had been awarded the Purple Heart, that before long he would be sent home, and that when he came he would come to stay. She needed to see him and feel him in the flesh, she needed to pour out her heart to him, bridging all the years of their separation, before she would be appeased. And until appeasement came there could be no rejoicing either. But she tried, after gathering her forces, to answer with renewed spirit; recognizing that the antagonism between her mother-in-law and herself had never before been so great, or with so much reason, she declined to countenance it by bowing before it.

'When do you want to have this celebration, Madame Mère? On the Fourth of July?'

'Certainly not. I do not see any reason why we should celebrate the Fall of Vicksburg merely because professional politicians like to proclaim that there is no longer any North or any South or any East or any West.'

For the first time in many months Merry burst out laughing, heartily and spontaneously. Her mother-in-law regarded her somewhat superciliously until she recognized that Merry's objections to the party had been dissipated by this unforced and unfeigned evidence of gaiety. Then her own expression relaxed and she smiled in her turn.

'Now, not very originally, you will call me the last surviving unreconstructed rebel, I suppose,' she said, still speaking rather loftily. 'And remind me that persons, even in the South, think of the Fourth of July in connection with the Declaration of Independence, and not in connection with the Fall of Vicksburg. However, since we seem to be exchanging reminders, let me recall to you the fact that to this day Vicksburg has never celebrated the so-called Glorious Fourth, and I am not ashamed that I am still in sympathy with my kinsfolk there. Let us have the party on either the third or the fifth, Merry, and let us consider it a celebration of Gervais' wonderful escape and extraordinary progress towards recovery, and of the recognition his bravery has received. Suppose we start making out our guest list immediately.'

It appeared that, after all, the celebration Madame d'Alvery had in mind did not run to large proportions. She wanted to ask Cresside and Frances Belle and Sybelle, all of whom she accused of neglecting her on account of their personal preoccupations, which she admitted was excusable in Sybelle's case, but not in the others'. She also wanted to invite Mrs. Prescott and Susannah, whom she had not seen in a long time. She did not approve of the lengths to which Vail's courtship, which had begun so auspiciously, had now been prolonged. She felt as if there were some mystery about the procrastination, and she thought, if she could see the Prescotts, she might get to the bottom of the matter; she assumed they must have enough gasoline to make at least one trip from New Roads to Belle Heloise. Furthermore, she wished to ask Mrs. Harvey Lawrason, to whom she had taken a great and unexpected liking, and whom she called by her first name, which was Pearl. She had no other suggestions. She would be glad to have some from Merry, if her daughter-in-law had anyone else in mind. Naturally she expected that Miss Mittie and Mr. Randall would join them; and she would be glad to have Fabian and Mr. Prescott also, though, since they would be the only gentlemen, perhaps they would prefer not to come. . . .

'Punt O'Malley might be in town. He is about once in ten days, you know.'

'Punt O'Malley?'

'Yes. The Master of the *McDougall*, Frances Belle's boy friend. And of course Joyeuse always has cohorts she can call in.'

'I am not interested in Punt O'Malley, or in the cohorts, as you call them, around Joyeuse.'

'Well, you weren't interested in Rick either, you know, and now you admit—'

'I really do not care to discuss this any longer at present, Merry. I find I am rather tired. We will have a dove party, and I shall be glad to have you add two or three more ladies, if you would care to. We will have Creole gumbo, and roast duck with pecan dressing and kumquat preserves, and rice and okra, and green corn with peppers, and an aspic salad, and fresh peach ice cream sweetened with saccharine. As I said before, I do not think that anyone will leave the table hungry.'

There was certainly no evidence that anyone had. In fact, as the group moved from the dining-room to the parlour there was considerable murmuring about the folly of having eaten so much, even under great temptation. Mrs. Lawrason asked whether anyone would mind if she went into the garden room and removed her corset, a remark which was surprising to Madame d'Alvery, because she would not have expected a lady to make such a suggestion, and equally so to all the younger persons present, because none of them dreamed that such garments were still in existence outside of museums. By the time Pearl returned to the parlour looking a little sloppy, but greatly relieved, the others were all grouped companionably, some smoking, some knitting, and one or two with tall glasses in easy reach. The effortless, inconsequential conversation, begun at the supper table, was still going on.

'I'd like to hear more about Colonel d'Alvery, Merry, if you'll tell me,' Pearl said, drawing up the only vacant arm-chair and looking about for an ashtray. 'Perhaps all the rest of you know the whole story already, but there was so little in the papers—'

'Well, you do know that he volunteered to go in with the Eighty-second Airborne Division on D-Day.'

'Yes, but I'm not sure why.'

'I'm not sure myself. But Fabian says he thinks the reason so many military government people were sent in with the invasion troops was because there was so much uncertainty about de Gaulle's temperamental marches and countermarches. According to Fabian's theory, Eisenhower wanted the issue of who was running what a *fait accompli* before any fuss could be raised.'

'Sounds sensible to me. And then the plane he was in—'

'It was a glider. The plane that was towing it was shot down and the glider crash-landed behind the German lines. Gervais was hurt in the crash. But of course you knew that too.'

'I know he was wounded, but someone told me it was he who organized the survivors and got them back to the American lines. I mean forward to the American lines. Well, anyway, through to safety. So he wasn't badly hurt, was he? I mean, he couldn't have done that if he had been—'

'He broke his left arm and three ribs. And he had what's called

388

a spinal concussion. I'd never heard about that before, so I had to ask our new family physician, Dr. Jennings, to explain it to me. Of course we'll never feel he's infallible, the way we felt about good old Dr. Champagne; but I suppose he knows what he's talking about in a case like this. It seems that with a spinal concussion several hours elapse between the actual injury and the first signs of it. Then there's bound to be a collapse. However, Gervais didn't give out till everyone in his party was safe.'

'Aren't you terribly proud of him?'

'Of course I'm terribly proud of him,' Merry answered quietly. But her heart was not so quiet. It pounded as she said to herself. *If I only knew how badly hurt he really is. Dr. Jennings says there are no serious after-effects to a spinal concussion, that a patient's usually all right again in a few days, unless there are other complications. Of course we know there were the broken ribs and the broken arm this time, but we don't know that was all. I'm so afraid there may be other complications too. I'm worried on Gervais' account, and I'm worried on my own. I wouldn't be quite so much worried, if I only knew there'd be a chance to make up for these years we've lost through my fault. I'll try to think of all the reasons I have to be proud instead of all the reasons I have to worry. I don't need to think of just what he did on D-Day. That was enough, Lord knows. But he needn't ever have asked for a transfer to Charlottesville, he need never have gone overseas. He could have stayed in New Orleans as well as not. And he wouldn't. I've got that to be proud of, first of all. And I don't suppose he had to go into Sicily with the assault troops either. I'm sure he could have managed to stay in Africa longer, if he'd tried. He needn't have lived in the fields for weeks, camping in olive groves or anywhere he could. I've got that to be proud of too. He wasn't a combat officer; he was a military government officer. He could have played safe – at least, fairly safe. I don't suppose he would have been safe from disease, ever. I suppose he was bound to catch something in the filth of those Sicilian towns where he finally went to do his own job. I suppose he was bound to be sent back to Africa for hospitalization, to be kept there weeks and weeks. And I didn't write to him then. I didn't send him a word that would cheer him through his long illness. I don't see how he can ever forgive me. There's no reason why he should. And now perhaps I'll never have a chance to tell him I'm sorry. Perhaps the next telegram that comes in will say . . .*

'He was attached to the General Staff Corps, in England, before the Normandy invasion, wasn't he?' she heard Pearl Lawrason asking, still eagerly; and Merry answered, again quietly, 'Yes, he went straight to England after he was discharged from the hospital in Oran. He said the English spring was beautiful . . .' *But that wasn't in a letter to me*, she added to herself. *That was in a letter to his mother. It might have been my letter, and it wasn't. I didn't get a letter until he was in a base hospital in France, after I finally wrote him that I was back at Belle Heloise. There were so many things he might have said in that letter – at least if he's been able to write – and he didn't say any of them. He didn't say if a woman stayed away from her husband for eight years she might as well stay away for ever. He didn't remind me that I'd been the one to talk about heartlessness in the first place, and that it was his turn now. He didn't ask if his promotion and his medal were all I cared about. He just said,* I've got something to get well for, honey, now that I know you'll be waiting for me when I get home, that I won't come back to an empty room . . . *Dear Lord, if I only know how much longer the room was going to be empty because he isn't in it.* Her heart was pounding almost insufferably by this time, and it had swelled so that it expanded far beyond its proper place. But somehow she managed to speak quietly once more.

'It's nice of you to be so interested, Pearl. But we mustn't talk about Gervais all the time. Especially since this is an old story to everyone but you, as you said yourself. What did you hear from Harvey last?'

'Oh, he's in Iran. India was just a way-station,' Pearl volunteered, so promptly that Merry knew that she should have asked sooner, that she should not have allowed her own thoughts to absorb her so completely. 'I didn't know for a long time, though. I finally wrote him that I could have sailed half-way around the world since I'd heard from him, and of course that's exactly what he's done himself – *more* than half-way around. On the whole he's pretty good about giving me hints too. In one letter, written after he left Rio, he said, "If it wasn't for hope we'd be pretty well lost," and then I knew he'd been around the Cape. He must be somewhere near Basra now. You know the supply route for munitions and food to Russia runs from the Persian Gulf to the Caspian Sea. When his company got to wherever it is they are, the English were running through three trains a week, on the one railroad. Now they're running through fifteen a day. I'll tell the world that's some difference.'

'I'll say it is!' Cresside exclaimed heartily.

'Yes, and they have an assembly plant for trucks too. Those supplement the railroad. It's terribly interesting work. Harvey's crazy about it. And wouldn't you know, he gets in quite a little hunting on the side too? He says the hunting's wonderful along the river beds in the Persian mountains. There are wolves and jaguars and foxes and boars. Once when he and some other hunters followed their game down to the plains they found the natives trying to drive the wild boar off their fields with sticks. They didn't have anything else to do it with. So they were awfully glad to see the Americans. Harvey and his friends shot any number of wild boar that day. But he says the best sport of all is the gazelle hunting. He's seen as many as two or three thousand gazelles grazing at the same time and—'

She stopped suddenly. Here she had been running on about the hunting in Iran, and she ought to have remembered that the last time Harvey and Colonel d'Alvery went hunting together was the day little Franchot shot the deer by accident. She ought to have talked about something else. But she had thought of the wild boars overrunning the rice fields and the great herds of gazelles grazing freely on the highlands as thrilling and exotic; she had not thought of the tragic memories her stories might evoke. *I'm a damn fool*, she said to herself, thankful that the converation was so general that she did not need to say anything aloud just then. But she continued to reproach herself. *I ought to have told them instead that the thermometer goes up to a hundred and seventy in the shade at Basra, or wherever it is Harvey's stationed, and we think it's hot here when it goes over ninety. We sit in a lovely dim dining-room and still we talk about how hot we are. And Harvey's assembling trucks and loading trains, right out in that desert sun. We have juleps before dinner in silver goblets, coated so thick that you can scrape the frost off with your fingernail, and champagne comes out of a silver cooler so cold that the bubbles sting when they hit your tongue. And Harvey didn't have any ice at all for a long time after he left home, and then only a little, that couldn't be put in anything he drank because it was made from water coming out of infected streams. All he could do was to pack bottles in it, so that the beer inside wouldn't be lukewarm. He doesn't have any water even to wash with, in all that terrible heat; he can't take a bath from one month's end to another. These women who've all had baths before they came here, who drank juleps before dinner and champagne afterwards, don't want to hear about things like that! They've had a wonderful dinner too. How can I tell them the only fresh meat Harvey gets is bought from open shops where the lambs are strung up by their legs as soon as they've been killed, with their wool still on and the blood still pouring out of them? Presently the flies gather on them, so that the wool's covered, and they look black instead of white. How could I talk about things like that? I couldn't! So I tried to tell them something that wouldn't disgust them. Besides, I couldn't tell them Harvey'd been awarded the Purple Heart, and it made me mad to think Merry d'Alvery felt she had so much more to brag about than I did. So I told them the best story I could and now . . .*

'Those gazelles must have been a beautiful sight, Pearl,' Cresside was saying. 'Fabian's always wanted to go to Iran and take me – Persia, he still calls it, of course. You've been there, haven't you, Mrs. Prescott?'

'Oh yes,' Mrs. Prescott replied, in a tone that inferred she had been everywhere. Then she began to talk about the wonderful opportunity she had enjoyed in seeing the ruins of Persepolis, but Pearl did not pay much attention to her. Instead she looked gratefully at Cresside, and Cresside returned the smile. *She wanted to be reassured,* Cresside said to herself. *Poor Pearl! She was afraid she'd blurted out the wrong thing, and she was worrying over that. If she thinks of me at all in connection with this war, she says to herself,* There's a woman whose husband's a cripple, who can't fight and whose only child's a young daughter, right here in the room with her. *She doesn't know about Vail. She doesn't know I have a letter he wrote me on D-Day, tucked inside my dress this minute, but that I haven't heard a word from him since. It was just like Vail to write me a letter on D-Day, and the letter was just like him too.*

DEAR AUNTIE,

Everything is going well and according to plan. Don't worry about me because I'm fine and expect to stay so.

As ever,
VAIL.

He didn't say, If you never hear from me again, this'll show you I was thinking about you right up to the last. *Vail never says things like that. Why, even the day he left, he didn't say,* I know you're my mother. *He knew he mustn't. He only said,* I've always wished you were my mother. *He isn't ashamed, so I don't have to be any longer. I don't know how he found out, and I don't care. I'm not afraid any longer either. I'm too happy because he said what he did to be ashamed or afraid either. He says just the right thing, always, neither too much nor too little. He isn't taciturn, like Gervais claims he is. A boy who is taciturn wouldn't have written at all. A boy would have had a sure enough excuse, not writing on D-Day to anyone. Certainly not to his – Aunt. But Vail did write. He wrote on D-Day and the letter came through very fast. But nothing has come through since. And no one in the family has even thought that was anything to worry about, except, of course, Fabian, who understands, and Sybelle, who doesn't understand, but who loves Vail very much herself. Everyone else is thinking about Gervais and his wounds and his medals. No. I'm wrong; Frances Belle isn't thinking of Gervais and his wounds and medals. She's thinking of that red-headed freckled young pilot who's towing bunker fuels and aviation gasoline for the Army and Navy to the ships in New Orleans Harbour . . .*

The great clock in the hall struck sonorously, and immediately afterwards the silly gilt timepiece under the *silene* on the mantelpiece tinkled out its tune, and for a moment the guests were silent, listening to this. It was only nine o'clock now. Supper had been early, out of consideration for Creassy and Dinah and Lethe, who were not much pleased about the party anyway. But, glancing at her daughter, Cresside knew that Frances Belle, in spite of her surface civility, was already restless, that she was counting the hours until she could see Punt O'Malley again. *Frances Belle doesn't know how fortunate she is, either,* Cresside thought. *She's resentful of every minute that she's separated from Punt, though she knows he's coming back to her, safe and sound, that she'll see him every few days. She isn't thinking of wasted years, like Merry. She isn't self-conscious about saying the wrong thing or jealous of anyone else's fame, like Pearl. She isn't consumed with secret anxiety, like me . . .*

It was true that Frances Belle was not consumed with anxiety. Instead, she was listening to the chugging sound of a boat going down the river, waiting for it to whistle as it rounded the point

393

beyond the batture, and grappling with her first great temptation. She was trying to tell herself that Punt hadn't really *asked* her to join the W.A.V.E.S. or the W.A.C.S. He had only said that perhaps, seeing that he hadn't been able to get into the war, they might be glad some day if she found she could and did; that when their children started asking them what they had done, they might be ashamed if neither of them could say . . . Oh, of course he was delivering high-octane gas for planes, he was in an essential industry. If he'd been forty-eight instead of twenty-eight, he wouldn't have minded – that is, he supposed he wouldn't have. And he knew Frances Belle was giving blood regularly and working at the U.S.O., and that would have been enough, too, if she had been forty instead of twenty. But as it was, he thought maybe some day their kids would think it was queer, and that they themselves would be sort of ashamed, or anyway embarrassed, trying to explain. . . .

I see what he means, Frances Belle was saying to herself, almost petulantly, her ears cocked to catch the boat's whistle, which would sound any moment now. *At first I tried to pretend I didn't, but Punt looked at me, that straight way he has, and I was ashamed right then. Because I did understand. I do. But I don't want to join the W.A.V.E.S. or the W.A.C.S. either. I don't want to be in a camp with hundreds of other girls. I want to be at home with Mummy and Daddy, until I can be with Punt. I'm sure they want me at home – they'd be all alone if I went off and left them. Anyhow, I don't want to go off somewhere on the other side of the world among strangers, I just want to go down the river with my sweetheart, the way he's promised I should some day. I want to stand in the pilot house when he's at the wheel and look down on it. The others may be satisfied to look at the River Road, but I'm not. Even the pedlars don't travel on the River Road any more. Nobody uses it to go between here and New Orleans – everyone takes the Airline. Except for the few cars coming here and to Hathaway and to Hackberry, you never see anything but the school bus and a truck now and then and old rattletraps filled with Negroes, until you get below Burnside. But it's just the opposite with the river. It's crowded with craft of every kind, the way grand'mère said it was when she was a girl, but there are more kinds now: old stern wheelers, pressed back into service; big new ones with huge, powerful engines; long, low cargo boats, fleets of tugs to push the steel barges, tow boats like*

Punt's. Yes, even submarines built up-river, trussed in wooden cradles and floated all the way from Lake Michigan to the Gulf. Cargoes are coming to New Orleans all the way from Minneapolis, from Cincinnati, from Louisville and Memphis: coal and iron, cotton and grain, oil and steel and flour. They're passing right by the house this minute. The railroads can't handle all these and send them on their way to war – the railroads or the old highways. But the river can. It does.' . . .

Frances Belle could tell from the sounds she heard that one boat had now rounded the point and that another was coming. So she went on listening while the others continued to talk. She didn't like sitting in her grandmother's parlour, straining her ears for the chugging and whistling of a boat she couldn't even see. She wanted to be aboard one, looking down on the river which had drowsed for so long, but which had wakened to new life with the war. *I want to see for myself, the way Punt's made me see it at every season in every sort of weather. I want to see it with the sun shining on it, and I want to see it with the fog stealing over it, even though I know fog's its worst enemy, worse than high water or high wind. Because you can still see when there's a flood or a hurricane, but you can't when there's a fog. Punt explained that. When the visibility's zero, kid, there's not a thing you can do but make for shore with your compass and your whistle. The whistle comes echoing back to you from the bank and you can judge the distance by the sound of the echo. It sounds one way when you're near the bank and another way when you're far from it. You don't see how I can tell the difference? Gosh, that's easy! I can't remember when I couldn't. But then I was just a kid when I first went on the river. You have to be a deckhand three years before you're even eligible for a pilot's licence, and some men can't make the grade then. We've got college graduates on the McDougall right now that are still deckhands, that couldn't ever learn to pilot a boat no matter how hard they tried nor how long. Then, again, we've got others who never went beyond the fourth grade, but they're wizards when it comes to handling a wheel. . . . Well, anyway, after you've been a deckhand for three years, if the master and the chief engineer will sign your application, you can take an exam.; and if you pass it you're issued a second-class pilot's licence. You hold that for a year, and then, if you're good enough, you get to be a steersman, you're put in charge of the wheel. Finally, after another year, if you're still doing all right you can* qualify as a full-fledged pilot. So it takes five years at least to do that. Hell, if you couldn't learn to guess how far you were from shore by the sound of an echo in five years, you never could, and I've been doing it for eight.

'I don't want to be a W.A.C. or a W.A.V.E.,' Frances Belle repeated stubbornly to herself. *I want to stand beside Punt listening to that echo, and see if I can learn to tell how far we are from shore. I want to hear a whirlwind coming too. Punt says you can hear it a long way off, that it sounds like a herd of cattle on the run, and that when a pilot hears that sound he puts into shore as fast as he can. I don't know whether I want to see a flood. Punt says it's a terrible sight when you're up twenty feet or more above the land beyond the levee, and look down on the plantations and towns on the other side of it. He says it's a terrible feeling if you think what would happen if you lost control of your boat and went right through the levee and hit all those houses and churches and people and cattle. He says sometimes you can hardly bear to look at it, sometimes you can hardly bear to think of it. But you have to. That's part of being a pilot. So I reckon a pilot's sweetheart could stand it too. I'm sure a pilot's wife could. I could stand anything if I could only have Punt for my husband. But if I have to be a W.A.C. and go off to the other side of the world, away from him then I couldn't bear it, thinking there might be a flood while I was gone and he might lose control of his boat and go through the levee and kill people and knock down houses. If he really loved me he wouldn't ask me to be a W.A.V.E. or a W.A.C. No, that isn't fair. If he didn't really love me he wouldn't care whether our children would be ashamed of us some day. But perhaps we wouldn't ever have any children. I don't think I care much whether we do or not, if I can have Punt. I know I wouldn't want to have one right away, like Syb is going to and like Aunt Merry did. I'd rather be like Mummy. I wasn't born until after she and Daddy had been married a year and a half. And then they never had another. But Punt says our children, so I reckon he wants to have several and he doesn't want them to be ashamed ...*

I wonder if Mr. Reynaud wouldn't let me go on the McDougall *right now, without waiting for the war to be over and all. Punt'll be back tomorrow; I'm going to ask him then. I'm going to say,* Punt, let's get married and go down the river together. You know that room of yours you told me about all nicely furnished up on the Texas, way off from the crew's quarters? Couldn't we have that room for ours, Punt? I'd stay with you in the pilot house while you took your watch. I'm glad you still do that, even though you're the master now. I wouldn't talk to you or bother you, but we'd look at the lights together – the ones beyond the levee and the ones on the river you said looked like stars, and at the real stars too. There wouldn't be any fog that night, I know there wouldn't, or high water or high wind. It would be calm and beautiful, and after your watch was over we'd go to bed. And when we got to New Orleans you'd tell me about the different kinds of lights in the harbour – you'd show me which were the channel lights and which were the lights on the other boats that were navigating and on the boats that were tied up along the shore. They must be a beautiful sight, Punt, all those boats there are in New Orleans Harbour now, more than there ever were before – the men-of-war and the Liberty ships and the big French carrier that's in for repairs, the freighters and tankers, the towboats and harbour tugs and ferries too. I want to see them, moving back and forth across the dark waters, all lighted up, and lying at anchor too, on both sides of the river – our river. I want to hear the sound of the cranes on the ships being loaded, and the men singing and shouting while they work. I could go ashore after we got there, and wait for you, at the Pontalba, while the cargo was being discharged, if I were in the way, and then afterwards we would still have time to go to dinner at Antoine's, or just sit in Jackson Square for a while. Anything, so long as I could do it with you. Please, Punt, don't let's talk any longer about my being a W.A.V.E. or a W.A.C. Let's talk about having a honeymoon on the *McDougall*. I have just as much right to a honeymoon as Syb. And I'm not going to wait as long for mine as she did. I won't. I can't. I want to marry you, Punt; I wish I could marry you this very night. I can't stand it, staying in this stuffy parlour with all these dumb women who don't know how I feel, who just sit here smoking and knitting and jabbering about nothing!

She could hear another boat now, not chugging or whistling, but puffing laboriously, as if it were having hard work to prevail against the current. *I can tell whether boats are coming upstream or going downstream already,* she thought. *If I can do that, I can learn about echoes too.* She pushed back her chair and rose, betraying to everyone the restlessness which Cresside had so long divined. Sybelle, who was not knitting grey socks but a pink baby blanket, looked up at her cousin with a questioning smile.

'Where are you going, Frances Belle?'

'Out on the upper gallery. I want to look at the boats passing by.'

'You can't see anything but the funnels. As a matter of fact, the foliage is so heavy now you can hardly see those.'

'I don't care. I'll see what I can.'

'You want me to come with you?'

'No, I feel like being alone for a while. But thanks, just the same.'

That girl is no better mannered than she ever was, Mrs. Prescott said to herself. But Sybelle understood Frances Belle's mood and was not offended by it. After her cousin had left the room, she looked down again at the wool in her hands, her smile deepening. She was not worrying about Rick just then. He was still on Bougainville, but it had been relatively quiet there since the Japs had failed in the all-out drive which they opened in March, hoping to throw the Americans off the island. After his brief leave, Rick had been transferred from the Infantry to the General Staff Corps. Now the operational officer had returned to the States on longer leave than Rick had been given, and Rick had assumed the full duties of the office, which he was amply qualified to fill. The wording of his citation, announcing that he had been awarded the Bronze Star, was proof positive of this. Sybelle knew every word of this citation by heart, and she repeated it softly to herself now, as she knitted and purled the pink wool:

'Riccardo Tramonte, Major, Infantry, United States Army, for the performance of meritorious services at New Georgia and Bougainville, Solomon Islands. During the preparatory training and combat action of both campaigns, Major Tramonte distinguished himself by a keen knowledge of the training methods required and superior tactical judgment which enabled him to make sound recommendations to the sector commander. His sound advice was based on personal reconnaissance into enemy territory, during which he was exposed to hostile observation and fire. His thorough plan for quickly reorganizing to repel further enemy attacks at Bougainville enabled unit commanders successfully to re-form their units only a few hours after the initial Japanese assault waves had been annihilated.'

I'm so much luckier than Mother, Sybelle said to herself.

She'll never be able to think of Dad's decoration except in connection with his wounds. And Rick never got so much as a scratch all the time he was exposed to hostile observation and fire. I'm sure his mother's right. I'm sure he's under some special protection. She thinks it's Saint Amico and I think it's God's very own. But what does it matter, as long as he has it? If he hadn't, he couldn't have come back here last spring. We couldn't have been married, we couldn't have had that perfect week together. I wouldn't be waiting for my baby now. She continued to look down at the pink blanket, and soon the smile which at first had merely curved her lips wreathed her whole face.

'How's the house getting on, Syb?' Susannah asked. 'We saw the most remarkable change as we went by.' Susannah had noticed the change at Hathaway, from the distance of the River Road, but she didn't seem to notice the pink blanket, though she was sitting within a few feet of it. Sybelle had hard work not to answer contemptuously; after all, the house mattered so little in comparison with the baby.

'Just fine! Of course everyone told me I wouldn't be able to get very far, trying to restore it right now. As a matter of fact, I didn't even try to restore the wing the Tremaines used. It was all falling apart, so I had what was left of it torn down. It was just an addition, anyway, that spoiled the lines of the original building, and we didn't need all that extra space. I'm furnishing that great empty White Ballroom to use as a double drawing-room, and it's going to be lovely. I started out with that, but now I've got all the ground-floor rooms pretty well organized and I've made a good beginning upstairs. I did get discouraged at first, going into store after store, and having one snooty clerk after another ask me didn't I know there was a war on. Seven clerks asked me that, all in one day: I counted. The seventh time it was just too much. I said, "Yes, I do know there's a war on. My father's in it and both my brothers and my husband. How many members of your family are in it?" The clerk stared at me in dumb amazement and mumbled something, and then wandered off. But I walked after her. "I'm going to have our own home ready for my husband when he comes back, too," I said. "I'm going to make it just as attractive as I know how, and I'm not depending on any essential war material to do that, either. I'm going to have it ready for my baby too. You're not carrying a soldier's baby by any chance, are you?" '

The others in the room were all staring at Sybelle in astonishment now. They had always thought she was lovely to look at, and they had always admired her amiable disposition; but they had never credited her with much spirit. The statement that she had so vigorously arraigned an offending sales girl was startling to them. Besides, this was the first that Pearl and the Prescotts had heard of the expected baby, and as Sybelle had proclaimed her condition before it proclaimed her, this revelation was rather startling also.

'The clerk scuttled away like a rabbit after that,' Sybelle continued. 'I think she went to the rest-room and stayed there all afternoon. Anyhow, I didn't see her again, and I was in the store for another hour or so. But I haven't been back there, and I'm not going back. I'm not going to any of the stores where they asked me if I knew there was a war on. I'm going back to the ones that did the best they could for me, pleasantly, and acted as if they were sorry they couldn't do more. I've bought a good many things that way. My father-in-law told me to get everything I wanted and send the bills to him. I knew he meant it, so I've done it. He's been a lot of help to me in other ways too. I believe he knows every carpenter and mason and plumber in the parish. Anyway, he's dug up all kinds of mechanics for me. They're mostly old or disabled and they don't work very fast, but they're getting things done by degrees. I think Rick will see quite a change when he comes back the next time, at least in the house and garden. I'm not trying to do anything with the factory or the fields yet. I'm waiting for Vail to help me with those. It's our idea – Rick's and Vail's and mine – that Hathaway and Belle Heloise ought to be run as one plantation, eventually. It can be done a lot more efficiently that way. I wonder why no one ever thought of it before.'

Someone did think of that before, my dear child. I thought of it, and my neighbour, Mrs. Hathaway, thought of it. We planned an alliance between my son and her daughter; but her daughter stole my daughter's sweetheart, and my son went to St. Napoleon Street for his wife. So all our plans came to nothing, and that was a bitter pill for me to swallow. Now you've married the son of an Italian pedlar, who's the only man we know rich enough to restore Hathaway – except, perhaps, Felix Goldenberg, and it wasn't Hathaway that interested him. And you're planning to run it with the help of Vail d'Alvery, whom you boast about as your litter brother, *and who isn't really your brother at all, though you never found that out and never will. He isn't really the heir to Belle Heloise, either; if it weren't for Fabian, he wouldn't have the right to run it, much less combine another plantation with it. Perhaps you think that wasn't another bitter pill for me.* While Madame d'Alvery was pondering in this way she looked around with an air of satisfaction remarkable for its smooth deceptiveness, and addressed the group at large in an agreeable voice.

'It is very pleasant to be having a party here again, even though it lacks the éclat of some of our previous gatherings,' she said. 'When I was a girl we had a great many balls at Belle Heloise. My father always had the first dance with my mother and the second one with me; after that he danced once with each of the ladies present, beginning with the eldest and going on down to the youngest. Then he retired to the library and stayed there through the remainder of the evening, except for brief interludes when he returned to admonish the coloured musicians. Finally, at one o'clock, he came in with a glass of whisky in his hand. This was recognized as a nightcap and a signal for general departure. I never knew anyone to disregard it. Perhaps after the war we can begin having dances here again. Gervais might revive some of his grandfather's customs in regard to those, as he did in regard to the celebrations at the end of grinding season. I think he would play the part of the old-fashioned host extremely well.' Madame d'Alvery paused to smile comprehensively at the ladies she had been addressing as a group, and then focused her gaze on Susannah. 'We shall count on you to come over from New Roads, my dear, when we inaugurate such a series,' she said. 'You know, I have never yet seen that beautiful dress of your great-grandmother's, which my daughter and grandson have both described to me so enthusiastically. I should like immensely to have you wear it at a ball given here.'

'Thank you, Madame d'Alvery. I'd like that too,' Susannah answered quietly. *My great-grandmother's dress,* she said to herself, *the dress I wore when I went to the sugar festival with Vail, the dress he wanted me to wear when I married him. Phil wouldn't go to the sugar festival. That was the only reason I asked Vail, because I couldn't get Phil. And Phil didn't care what I wore when I married him. It didn't mean anything to him, one way or another. The marriage didn't mean anything to him. Vail's right. It really isn't a marriage. Not just because Phil and I didn't*

401

*go upstairs together in that horrible hotel. But because it wasn't
sanctified, in any sense. A marriage can't be sanctified if a girl
doesn't trust her husband, if she doesn't respect him. And I don't
trust Phil or respect him either. How could I? He's never done
anything to make me. He just attracted me, he just fascinated
me. That doesn't last, if nothing else goes with it. It hasn't lasted—
that is, I don't think it has. I don't think, if I saw Phil this minute,
it would mean anything to me. There'd be that sparkle in his eyes
I've always watched for, there'd be that quirk to his lips that's
always been irresistible. But he wouldn't look me straight in the
face, he wouldn't tell me the truth when he spoke to me. I ought
to feel proud because he's done so well in the Army. He has done
well, almost as well as Rick and Vail and Colonel d'Alvery and
Captain Lawrason. But a girl can't go on feeling proud of a man
in a personal way if he isn't proud of her. If he wants to keep
their marriage a secret, if he doesn't want her to use his name or
live in his home, she ends by thinking about him as if he weren't
her husband at all, as if he were just another man she'd read about
in the paper. I don't want to get any more letters addressed to
Miss Susannah Prescott, New Roads. It doesn't matter what I see
inside, because I've seen the outside first. Not that there's much
to see inside either, or that I've seen anything he's written for a
long time. I'm glad I haven't. . . .*

'How's Barry Pereira and what's he doing right now?' she
asked, turning to Joyeuse. Not that she cared at all. But she didn't
want to think about Phil any more, and she felt it might help if
she talked about someone else.

'Oh, he's fine and he's been on what he calls the banana run
ever since he went to Mobile and took command of the armed
guard on that Liberty ship. He gets back to New Orleans every
three weeks — that's a lot nicer, of course, than if his ship was
in a convoy to Russia, gone for eight or nine months at a time. I
see quite a lot of him this way.' *Too much,* she added to herself. *If he only wouldn't pester me so, teasing me to marry him,
we might have fun together. I'd have time to do some of the
things he wants to do. I'd make time. Now that I'm through
college, now that it's the slack-season on the plantation, I'm not
all that busy. But we no sooner get going than he begins again,*
Joy, look what I've brought you. Joy, I wish you wouldn't act as
if you thought I had leprosy or something – there's nothing fatal
about a little pleasant petting. Joy, I've got the licence right in

my pocket. *I don't want his presents. I don't want his kisses. I
don't want to be married to him. I just want to have fun. I can't
see that Syb's having any fun, with that big tumbledown house
on her hands and a baby coming and Rick over on the other side
of the world. I can't see that Pearl Lawrason's having any fun,
cooped up in that little apartment in the Pentagon, not daring to
play the field any more, like she used to. I don't see that Mom's
ever had any fun on Belle Heloise. She only began to have it after
she went to Paris and Buenos Aires and New York. Maybe Aunt
Cresside's had fun, but she waited a good long time before she
got married. That's what I'm going to do. I'm not going to be
swept off my feet by a snappy uniform, no matter what's inside
it. I'd have to live with that a long while after the war was over.
I'm going to be like Sue and have the sense to stay single. She
doesn't look so well, though, at that. She looks as if she had
something on her mind. Or somebody. Not that I ever thought
Vail got very far. . . .*

'My dear Madame d'Alvery, this has been a most delightful
evening. But Susannah and I have quite a long drive back to New
Roads. So I'm certain you'll excuse us if we're the ones to break
up the party. I assure you we do it most regretfully.'

Mrs. Prescott had risen, and was crossing the room in her
usual poised manner. Everyone else rose too, as she held out her
hand to Madame d'Alvery, who spoke ceremoniously.

'I'm sorry to have you go. But you must come again soon. We
have been seeing too little of each other lately. By the way, your
kinsman, Charles Boylston, has been kind enough to write me
several times. When a lady reaches my age she takes such an
attention as a great compliment. He seems to be enjoying his
stay in Scotland very much. Doubtless he has written you about
it too?'

'Yes, but in very guarded terms. He is in command of the First
Air Intransit Depot operating at some very large air base. I
assume that in such a group as this it is perfectly proper for me
to say that much.'

Mrs. Prescott glanced about her, as if to verify the accuracy of
her statement, and the expression of everyone present seemed to
confirm her right to confidence. Reassured, she continued in
greater detail.

'He says it is an unforgettable sight when a vast number of
planes, circling around in the mist overhead, are waiting for Con-

trol to give the signal which will permit them to land. The region where he is operating is extremely foggy, and often long delays occur on that account. Even officers of the highest rank may be greatly delayed in coming down, and as they have already flown the Atlantic, the problem of fuel becomes acute. Charles has moments of great anxiety.'

Having said this much, Mrs. Prescott shook hands with Madame d'Alvery again and began a tour of the parlour, saying good night to each of the others in turn, her progress still marked by aplomb. She had almost completed her rounds, when a series of piercing shrieks, distant at first, but coming steadily closer, disrupted her ceremonious leave-taking. Cresside, who was nearest the door, moved hastily towards it, only to collide with Lethe, who charged into the room and rushed over to Madame d'Alvery, still screaming.

'Ah done seen him, Madame! Ah done seen him wid mah own eyes!'

'Be quiet, Lethe! What do you mean by this unseemly disturbance? Go back outside at once. I will come and speak to you in a minute.'

'Ah doesn't dare go back outside, Madame. It's outside Ah done see de ghost. Dinah, she done tell me befo' she hear it, but Ah never did believe her till yet. She ain't never seed it anyways.'

The woman was trembling uncontrollably. Her fright was obviously genuine. It had swept into the parlour with her, darting insidiously into every corner of the tranquil room. Madame d'Alvery spoke again, imperiously.

'I will go out with you, Lethe, and so will some of these ladies. Perhaps then we can convince you that you are labouring under a very silly delusion. . . . Was it in the patio that you thought you saw this apparition?'

'Yes, Madame. An' Ah ain't a-gwine back dare, not effen everyone on de River Road was to go wid me.'

'Someone has been playing tricks again, the way Mr. Philogene used to play them.'

'Who be's here to play tricks on us now?'

There was no plausible answer to the question. Madame d'Alvery pressed her lips together.

'Dat wuz de ol' tramp hisself, and yo' knows he don't never come back, lessen—'

'That will do, Lethe.'

Madame d'Alvery walked firmly out of the parlour into the hall and through this to the patio, followed by her family, her guests and her trembling servant. Lethe had left the rear door open when she rushed in, and it still stood ajar. A light puff of wind blew towards them from the garden, making no sound. The patio was dim, silent and empty. Madame d'Alvery touched the switch by the door, and light streamed instantly from the two electrified lanterns suspended on either side of the patio, flooding it with soft radiance. The dimness was dispelled. The silence and the emptiness prevailed.

'You see,' Madame d'Alvery said quietly. 'Go upstairs, Lethe, and wait for me. I want to speak to you alone. . . . Needless to say, I am very sorry for this disturbance,' she added, turning back to her guests. 'I'm afraid it will mar the memories of this evening, which I had hoped would be so pleasant for you. Good night, good night.' Her tone was one of dismissal. Neither the Prescotts nor Pearl Lawrason attempted to prolong their farewells. Cresside hesitated for a moment, but Frances Belle was tugging at her arm, and presently they left too, trailing Sybelle, who was taking Joyeuse back to Hathaway with her. Madame d'Alvery waited until everyone else had gone before she looked at Merry. Even then she did so very briefly, her hand already on the newel post.

'Sometimes we Creoles share our servants' superstitions,' she said. 'But you are not a Creole, my dear Merry. This scene must have been as distasteful to you as to any of our guests. Do not permit your mind to dwell on it. And do not feel that you need to come to my room with me. I can deal with Lethe better alone. Good night, *chère*. I am glad you humoured me about the party. Except for this final diversion, I feel it was a great success.' She went slowly on up the stairs without turning, and pausing merely to salute the Spanish statue. Only the *McDougall*'s whistle sounding on the river broke the engulfing stillness.

CHAPTER TWENTY-SIX

No, I'm not a Creole, Merry kept saying to herself the next few days. *Madame Mère doesn't need to keep reminding me of that. She never used to do it, either. I suppose the reason she does it so much now is that it represents a way of putting me in my place. But there's nothing wrong with my place. I'm glad I could make my own way in the world. I'm glad I haven't any of their silly old superstitions. I don't mind having a nigger act like a nigger, but when it comes to white folks . . .*

She said this defiantly, and then still more defiantly she added, *Cresside needn't gloat, either, because Vail wrote her a letter on D-Day and Gervais didn't write me till the week afterwards. Vail was just going through some ordinary routine and Gervais was performing a great act of heroism. I've already heard that he wasn't seriously injured, and presently I'll hear he's all right again. I know Frances Belle thought, the night of that horrible party, that she was the only person in the room who hadn't the slightest reason to be worried about the man she loves. She was gloating, too, because she sees that snub-nosed pilot of hers every few days, and because he's never any farther away from her than New Orleans. All the others were talking one way and thinking another. Except me. I wasn't worried. I'm not worried now.*

She kept saying this, over and over, but eventually she found she could not go on talking so defiantly, even to herself. Then she whispered, *I am worried. I'm so afraid I'm not going to have another chance. And I must. That couldn't have been the end between us, that night after Franchot's funeral. We've got to have years and years together yet, or the rest of my life won't mean anything to me. I don't see how I could have thought that was really living, in New York. Life doesn't mean anything to a woman unless she can share it with the man she loves. I've always known that, down deep in my heart. I was a fool to pretend I didn't.*

It seemed to Merry that there was no end to the days and nights that she kept saying all this to herself, over and over again.

Actually, it was only a week or so after the party that Cresside came out unusually early, and breathless with haste. 'I'm just a messenger,' she said, still panting. 'If you had a telephone, I wouldn't be here. Gervais landed in New York this morning, and of course the first thing he did was to get right on the wire, the way they all do. He said to tell you he was fine, and not to think of trying to come East. Of course, he's writing you more details. But he expects to be sent to La Garde right away. He'll call again from there. I reckon you'll have him home in a fortnight or so, Merry. I gathered that he was only going to La Garde for a final check-up.'

'But, Cresside, if he wasn't hurt any worse than he let on at first, wouldn't he have been hospitalized in England and then sent back to active duty on the Continent?'

'Well, he might have been hurt a little worse than he let on at first. Of course, he couldn't go into details over the telephone. But he said something about "battle fatigue". Don't forget he'd been through a lot, even before the invasion – the Sicilian campaign, and that long illness and all. He sounded mighty cheerful to me, Merry. You know, I honestly believe, if he had to be bunged up, he'd rather be bunged up enough to justify him in coming home. He'll be so much happier here that he'll get well faster. Can't you imagine how he'd have fretted and fumed if he'd have had to stay in some damn Army hospital, instead of getting to Belle Heloise?'

Merry could imagine. She knew Gervais would rather be at Belle Heloise than anywhere else in the world, and she began to consider carefully where he would be most comfortable. She was afraid the quarters in the *garçonnière* might seem cramped to him. The downstairs bedroom was good-sized, but there was no connecting room where a nurse could sleep, if it should prove advisable to have a nurse and possible to get one. Merry also realized that, whether there was the complication of a nurse or not, it might not be feasible for her and Gervais to share a room, and certainly they could not share a bed, while he was in his present disabled state. Besides, it was in the *garçonnière* that their parting had taken place, in mutual anguish of spirit; if this were the scene of the reunion it might arouse needlessly painful memories of that last time they had been together. After a great deal of reflection, she spoke to her mother-in-law on the subject.

'Madame Mère, I've been thinking that Gervais might like to

407

have his old room back. Of course, the *garçonnière's* in apple-pie order; we could take him there at the last moment if he preferred. But if he were in the Big House, he'd have a lot more space. And with the old nursery – I mean Vail's room – connecting with his, and Cresside's – I mean the Henry Clay room – across the hall, a nurse and I could both be near him, if it were necessary. And you would be too. Naturally, if Sybelle hadn't married, I wouldn't think of turning her out of her own quarters. But since she doesn't need them any more—'

'I had thought of exactly the same thing, Merry. But I hesitated to suggest it. I was afraid you might feel I was trying to deprive you of the privacy you formerly enjoyed in your own small home, because I wanted to have my own son near me.'

Madame d'Alvery spoke with the same cool courtesy which she had maintained ever since Merry's return. She had never once failed in civility towards her daughter-in-law; on the other hand, nothing like a real *rapprochement* had taken place between them. The gulf which had been bridged with such apparent ease in the early days of Merry's marriage to Gervais seemed impassable now. Merry also spoke with cool courtesy in replying.

'Then I'll begin organizing with that arrangement in view. Of course, you'll tell me if anything I do is displeasing to you.'

'I do not anticipate any such contingency.'

The question was not raised between them again, but Merry mentioned her plan to Gervais almost as soon as their first greetings were over. The letter which arrived after the first telephone call revealed that there would not be time for her to get to New York before he was sent out of there himself, even if she disregarded his expressed wishes in the matter, and this was the last thing on earth she wanted to do. But she did go to New Orleans, to await his arrival there, taking a room at one of the smaller hotels, because she knew that the Estrades' attitude would be exactly the same as Madame d'Alvery's and consequently did not want to stay at the old family house on Esplanade. The next telephone call came through direct to her, and, as Cresside had said, Gervais sounded extraordinarily cheerful: he was already at La Garde, the trip down had been very easy, he was feeling fine. Yes honestly. He was only at the hospital for a final check-up. He didn't move around too easily and it tired him to sit up very long. But that didn't amount to anything. There was nothing serious or lasting about battle fatigue. He'd get his strength back in no time at Belle Heloise. And he'd been told he could go there by ambulance in just a few days. Merry could go right along with him if she wanted to. Meanwhile, what about coming down to the hospital? He was in a private room; they could have a good visit together. . . .

She was with him in fifteen minutes, sitting beside the narrow white hospital bed, holding his hand tightly in hers, partly because even this casual touch meant so much to her, and partly because she needed it to assure herself he was really there. His hand was not brown and strong any more; it was white and blue-veined, like his mother's, and so thin that it looked unnaturally long. Her clasp was firmer than his. She realized this, and she knew he did; she also knew that the hand was typical of the whole man and that therefore it would be a long time before he was anything like his old self again. Because of this, and because neither of them could speak easily of his injuries, it seemed better to talk of unimportant things, like the arrangement of rooms.

'Madame Mère and I talked it over, Gervais, and we decided that perhaps you'd like to stay in the Big House – for a while, anyway.'

Again she outlined her reasons, omitting only the one which seemed the most cogent of all, as she had in speaking to her mother-in-law, again she reiterated that the *garçonnière* was ready, if he would prefer to go there. He listened quietly until she paused, looking at him in a questioning way.

'You're right, Merry. I'd better go back to my old room. I'd enjoy it, and it would be more practical all round – easier for the servants too, I suppose, and we've got to think of that, now there are so few left. In fact, perhaps we'd better close up the *garçonnière* until one of the boys needs it. It's on the cards that they'll both be getting married before long. Of course, Phil thought, when he went to college, that he didn't want to settle on the plantation. But he may change his mind. I sure hope he does. In that case we'll let him have the *garçonnière* and turn the storehouse over to Vail, when your mother and Miss Mittie don't need it any more.'

He seemed to consider the matter settled. It was not surprising that he did not care to discuss it long, for it obviously tired him greatly to talk for any length of time. Besides, the constant rumbling of the attic fan was sufficiently noticeable to create a disturbing element, and so were the frequent interruptions to which they were subject. A coco cola machine was just outside Gervais' door, and the officers who were ambulatory cases kept coming up to get drinks, instinctively glancing towards the open door at the same time. Some of them knew Gervais, and came in for a cheery word with him. A pretty girl in civilian dress, wheeling a mobile wagon, approached in a sprightly way: wouldn't the Colonel like some magazines, or some cigarettes or something? No, not right now, Gervais told her, thanks just the same, though. He spoke more cordially than Merry could have, at the moment. She recognized that such incidents were unavoidable, and she realized that to many patients they must constitute a welcome diversion. But when a woman was alone with her husband for the first time in eight years ...! She also wished that before closing the subject of the *garçonnière* Gervais had corrected himself and said 'our room', just as she had corrected herself after saying 'the old nursery' and 'Cresside's room' in talking to Madame d'Alvery. She was further disturbed when the next question he asked stirred anxious thoughts which had lain dormant while her greatest anxiety was for him.

'By the way, when did you last hear from the boys, Merry?'

'I haven't heard from them in quite a long while. I was just going to ask you whether you had.'

'No, I haven't either. What about Cresside? Hasn't she heard from Vail?'

'She had a note written on D-Day, and another about two weeks afterwards. That's all. She hasn't said anything, but of course I know she's terribly worried.'

A nurse entered without knocking or appearing to observe Merry's presence, and thrust a thermometer into Gervais' mouth. He was obliged to wait until she had removed the thermometer and left, which she did as unceremoniously as she had entered, before he could ask the question which was the natural rejoinder to Merry's statement.

'Or Sybelle? He wrote to Sybelle once in a while, too, didn't he?'

'Oh yes! Vail's always been very good about writing letters, until lately. It's Phil who never seemed to have time.'

'Well, that's characteristic. ... Do you see anything of

Susannah Prescott these days? She certainly would have heard from Vail, if anyone did.'

'I've seen very little. She and her mother came to a little party we had on the third of July – it was your mother's idea, Gervais, that we should have one.'

'A very good idea too. . . . And Susannah didn't say she'd heard from Vail, either?'

'No. She didn't refer to him in any way.'

'Some sort of a rift there, do you think?'

'I wouldn't call it a rift, exactly.' She stopped for a moment, another latent fear roused by her own words. There had been a rift between herself and Gervais, whatever they called it or avoided calling it. Dreading to dwell on this, she continued hurriedly, 'Things haven't seemed to come to a head, that's all. Not that Vail hasn't wanted them to. He's never looked at another girl.'

'Possibly he's found another now, more responsive, and that's what's taking up his time. . . . Well, don't worry about him, Merry, or Phil either. If anything were wrong, we'd have heard right away from the War Department.'

'I know. Of course there really isn't any reason why I should worry about the boys. And, anyway, now that I've got you home—'

She did not need to finish the sentence. Now that she had him home every other fear was quiescent. She had her second chance, the chance she had prayed for but had not really dared to hope for. She was immersed in the effort of doing her utmost to deserve this chance. Her devotion to Gervais was selfless and complete. She thought only of what he wanted, of what he needed, of what might expedite his recovery. He stood the trip back to Belle Heloise remarkably well, and after that, though his progress continued to be slow, it was satisfactory, or so the doctors who saw him assured her; there was no real reason for anxiety on his account. By fall he would be able to get around a little again.

'By the time grinding starts?'

'The middle of October? Well, possibly. But certainly by the time it's finished. And why should your husband worry or hurry about taking over? From all we hear, you've got a mighty capable young lady in charge at Belle Heloise.'

It was true that Joyeuse was proving herself more and more efficient all the time. Actually, there was no reason that Gervais

411

should take over, except that Merry felt sure he would be happier when he could. Not that he displayed any discontent or impatience as it was. If the days seemed long to him, he never said so. He read the papers, he listened to the radio, he wrote in his diary. When Cresside and Fabian, or any of his old friends, came to see him, he welcomed them warmly. After he was able to walk about without assistance he went to his office in the old storehouse for a little while every day, and gradually the time he spent there lengthened. He conferred with Sance. His pride in Joyeuse increased obviously as he watched her in action. But his real interest centred in the mail. There was still no delivery at Belle Heloise, and gasoline was so scarce that it was impossible for Merry or Joyeuse to go into town every day. So Cresside brought it out on alternate days and came to the storehouse with it, whistling cheerfully to announce her approach. But weeks went on and still the word for which they were all watching did not come.

At last when the suspense had begun to tell on them all, a form letter came through from the War Department whith the news that Sergeant Philogene d'Alvery, serial number 3892548, had been slightly wounded in action on August tenth on the Danfront-Mortin road and was placed in an evacuation hospital awaiting transfer to a United States hospital in England. A surge of relief engulfed them. Inevitably slightly wounded not only meant that the injury itself could not be serious, but that the removal of the boy to England would take him miles and miles from the danger zone. Their spirits received a further lift a few days later with the arrival of a very brief letter from Phil himself, which indicated he had lost none of his graceless outlook on life, since he claimed his only worry was he would never be able to show the scar even after he got to the point where he could once more sit down in comfort. 'Don't ask me where I'm going to wear that Purple Heart!' he concluded. And shortly after this communication came to Merry and Gervais, Cresside appeared at an unaccustomed hour, her face preternaturally bright. Another letter from Vail had come through at last, and it had wonderful news in it. She'd brought it out to share with them.

' 'Dear Auntie'' (she read aloud),
' "I'm terribly sorry it's been so long between letters, but I'm mighty busy these days. Of course, I can't tell you where

412

we've been or much of what we've been doing, except that our outfit and others like it have the big job of paralysing communications. We've got things so that the Nazis can hardly expect to let a vehicle move on a highway or a train go out of the marshalling yards without some allied plane slamming it. It isn't like in the old days when we had the bombers to protect against fighter opposition. By the way, I got my first confirmed enemy plane the other day, an ME-110. Also I've caught my second oak leaf cluster to the air medal, but think nothing of it. They're as easy to catch as the common cold, even in this climate. But as you'll see by the wording on the left-hand corner of this envelope, you should make a slight change in addressing your next letter." '

She held up the envelope, speaking in a voice that rang with pride. 'Look! "*Captain* Malcolm Vail d'Alvery," and so on, and so on!' she exclaimed. 'It's exactly like Vail to write about it all that way, isn't it? "My *second* oak leaf cluster! *As easy to catch as the common cold!*" '

'Take it easy, Cresside, or you'll bust,' Gervais remarked. 'Not that I blame you much. The boy's done damn well. . . . He doesn't say anything about having heard from Phil, does he?'

'No, he says he hasn't.' Cresside resumed her reading, trying to conceal her feeling that the rest of the letter was a good deal of an anticlimax, as far as she was concerned. ' "I wonder if any of the folks have heard from Phil? I've been trying to locate him, but haven't had any luck so far. When I do I'll let you know straight off. It might be some time, though, because most of our outfits have moved so fast and so far since the break-through at Coutances that I don't suppose even the staff knows from one day to the next exactly where they all are. Two letters about Dad – one from you and one from Mom – have come in this last week. I sure am glad the real hero of the family is staging such a swell comeback. Give him my best and tell him I'd be glad if he'd write me himself, but not to bother if he doesn't feel like it. We'll have lots of time to hash everything over when we're all back at Belle Heloise again." '

CHAPTER TWENTY-SEVEN

EVERY member of the family shared Cresside's feeling of pride and triumph in this letter, and for a few days all thoughts centred on that, rather than on the form letter from the War Department. No further word came through from Phil, after his brief and rather ribald note, so they continued to assure themselves, without forced optimism, that he was all right. Then Cresside, who more than any other person represented the most reliable and frequent source of information from the outside world, appeared with news of an entirely different character.

'It looks as if we'd have to get ready for another wedding,' she remarked casually one afternoon, lighting a cigarette and dropping down in the Turkish chair besides her mother's couch.

'Another wedding!' Madame d'Alvery exclaimed. She had by no means recovered from the shock of Sybelle's, and she did not feel equal to facing another like it. Then she had a brief gleam of hope. 'You mean that Vail's coming home on leave? That at last he and Susannah Prescott—'

'Nothing like that, I'm sorry to say. But—'

'Then, has Joyeuse finally made up her mind to accept Barry Pereira?'

'No, indeed. She's still completely absorbed in keeping up her morale. At least, as far as I know. You might hear about it first if she weren't. Anyhow, Merry'd know before I would. But my one ewe lamb has got her own way at last, like she usually does. I believe she's the stubbornest one of our whole tribe, and that's saying a good deal.'

Cresside made the statement proudly rather than apologetically. Her mother, still preoccupied by the previous one, disregarded it completely.

'Frances Belle? But I did not even know she had a serious suitor, Cresside.'

'Yes, you did, *maman*. At least, I've told you so a dozen times, and Frances Belle has brought him out here once or twice.'

'You're not by any chance referring to that snub-nosed,

freckled young Irishman who pilots some kind of a tug on the river, are you, Cresside?'

'Yes, I am, *maman*. Punt O'Malley. Only it isn't a tug boat he's on, it's a tow boat. And he does hold a pilot's licence and take a pilot's watch, but he's the master. He's doing a very important type of work. I've explained all that to you before – at least, I thought I had.'

'You have explained nothing, Cresside, which would reconcile me to a marriage between Frances Belle and any kind of a river pilot. It seems as if all my grandchildren were on *mésalliances*.'

'I wouldn't say that if I were you, *maman*. I don't think even you can say Vail didn't choose an aristocrat.'

Cresside's voice was level, but its tone was slightly ominous, and the remark itself was too irrefutable for any attempted contradiction. While Madame d'Alvery, feeling that Providence was most unjust in calling upon her to face this fresh trial, sought for some short but divergent rejoinder, Cresside continued her attack along the same lines.

'As far as that goes, the Pereira family isn't exactly poor white trash, either, so you can't even confine your complaints to your grand*daughters*. If I'm not mistaken, there were Pereiras in Louisiana before either the d'Alverys or the Estrades got here, some of them holding pretty important positions, too.'

'You know perfectly well that I was not referring either to the Prescotts or the Pereiras when I spoke, Cresside. But unfortunately there does not seem to be the slightest prospect of consummation in either of those directions. What I meant was—'

'What you meant was that Riccardo Tramonte is a Dago pedlar's son and that Punt O'Malley might be shanty Irish. I got you all right the first time, *maman*. But somewhere along the line you could be fair enough to admit that if ever there was a living embodiment of Prince Charming, it's Rick. I won't go into all his other fine qualities, I won't even dwell on the fact his father's a multi-millionaire. Well, I'll concede Punt isn't in the same class as Rick when it comes to looks. But when it comes to character he's got what it takes.'

'Then I am surprised that he is not overseas, like the other young men we know.'

'He tried desperately hard to get into one of the services. But some kind of a minor heart ailment kept him out.' Cresside spoke with unaffected lightness, as she had in describing Punt's handicap to Vail; she really had no reason to believe it amounted to much. 'So he's been doubly determined to make good where he is, and he's succeeded,' she went on. 'He used to be one of the master's assistants on the *McDougall*. But since the war Punt's been promoted. The former master was getting old and he didn't feel equal to the great responsibility which goes with the job now, so he asked to be relieved. You must realize that Punt wouldn't have been selected if his record hadn't really been outstanding. You don't suppose Fabian sanctioned this marriage without checking up on the boy pretty thoroughly, do you? Frances Belle's the apple of his eye; I don't need to tell you that. He wouldn't stand back and let her make a major mistake. Being Fabian, he'd have found a way to prevent it.'

'And he has sanctioned it?'

'Yes. That's what I came out on purpose to tell you. Punt feels he isn't justified in asking for time off; he takes his job very seriously, and he says he's not having any vacations till the war's over. But Frances Belle'd set her heart on a honeymoon aboard the *McDougall* in any case. Punt's feeling for the river's contagious and she's caught it from him. So Fabian's been to see Mr. Reynaud, the Superintendent of Inland Waterways, and he's consented to let Frances Belle go down to New Orleans with Punt on the *McDougall*'s next trip. It's contrary to the company's policy and all that, but somehow Fabian's persuaded the powers that be to make an exception in this case.'

'And when will this extraordinary honeymoon take place?' Madame d'Alvery inquired, with a sigh which she did not even attempt to suppress.

'Well, we're not sure. Generally the *McDougall* pulls out twelve to eighteen hours after she gets in, but no one ever knows exactly when that will be or how long it will take to load the barges. Sometimes she leaves around ten in the morning. Naturally that would mean a very small early wedding. Other times she doesn't go out till evening. That would give us time for a larger one, with a reception in the garden, if we only had enough notice. But probably we won't have, so we can't plan on it. I'll let you know definitely as soon as I can, *maman*. Anyhow, it will be within the next three or four days.'

Fabian brought the awaited message to his mother-in-law two evenings later. Outwardly she had managed to maintain her usual attitude of detachment and calm but inwardly she had been greatly upset by the unconventionality of the entire proceeding. Frances Belle had been to see her briefly, but the girl had sat on the edge of her chair every minute, her readiness for flight adding to her grandmother's malaise. No, she didn't care at all about a white satin dress and a lace veil. Personally she thought her new tailored Shantung was a knockout, good enough for anyone to be married in, and Punt thought so too. Now, Syb and Rick both went in for things like veils and receptions and all that in a big way, and that was all right by her, if they liked it but she didn't care a hoot about frills like that, and neither did Punt. All they wanted was to get married quick, and get away quick. . . .

Having delivered this uncompromising statement, Frances Belle made good the escape for which she had been prepared all along, and Madame d'Alvery heard nothing further until Fabian appeared and saluted her in his gay fashion.

'Well, the *McDougall*'s in,' he said. 'But, this being Friday, she won't pull out until Monday, probably around eleven in the morning. So the youngsters are going to be married at an eight o'clock Mass and come back to the house for an hour or so afterwards. We'll have a real breakfast for a wedding this time, not champagne and chicken salad and ice cream round one o'clock in the afternoon.'

'Fabian, I simply cannot understand your attitude towards this marriage. When I think that Frances Belle is your only daughter, your only *child* – and the plans you must have had for her—'

'Yes, of course I did. Of course, Cresside did too. We've tried to give her all the so-called advantages. I think we have. She's had a good home, she's been to a good school, she's travelled a lot. If the war hadn't come along she'd have had an old-fashioned début, and she might have been Queen of Comus along with it. She'd have been a golden girl and she'd have met a lot of gilded youths, none of them in the least like Punt O'Malley. As you say, I had my plans all pretty carefully laid. Nothing quite like a war for changing fashions, though, Tante Isabelle. And Frances Belle likes to do things the new way.'

'She likes to do things her *own* way. When I think of how you and Cresside have spoiled that child, Fabian—'

'I'm still betting on her,' Fabian retorted agreeably. 'And it wasn't ever part of my plan, or Cresside's either, to stand in the way of her happiness. Punt O'Malley *is* her happiness. . . . Do you think you can make eight o'clock Mass on Monday all right, Tante Isabelle?'

In a resigned tone Madame d'Alvery said she supposed she could, and she did. The ceremony had more to commend it than she had anticipated. The members of Punt O'Malley's immediate family had come down from Alexandria, and they were really quite presentable. As his four brothers were all overseas, he had asked one of his assistants on the *McDougall*, Rodney Campbell, to be his best man, and this young captain proved to be very personable and well-mannered. Frances Belle looked surprisingly bridal after all, wearing her white Shantung suit and a little white veiled hat. Joyeuse made a bewitching bridesmaid, and Sybelle, who sat with the Tramontes, really seemed to be growing more beautiful every day of her life. Considering the early hour and the short notice, it was amazing how many people were present; St. Joseph's was almost filled. Even the New Orleans relatives and out-of-town friends like the Pereiras and the Prescotts had managed to come. The d'Alverys maintained their prestige in the face of every disadvantage. Madame d'Alvery doubted whether any wedding in Baton Rouge that year had been better attended.

The first upsetting incident did not occur until the merry and informal wedding breakfast was almost over. The telephone rang, and, though no one paid any attention to it at first, Rodney Campbell, who was making himself extremely agreeable to Madame d'Alvery at that point, excused himself and went in to answer it. When he returned to the dining-room, instead of going back to Madame d'Alvery's side, he approached the preoccupied bridegroom, and after several unsuccessful attempts succeeded in attracting his attention. Punt listened to Rodney's whispered communication, looking a little blank, and presently, in turn, whispered to Frances Belle. She edged over to her father, who had taken the vacated seat in the corner beside his mother-in-law, and spoke to him in a voice that was none the less vexed because she managed to keep it low.

'Wouldn't this burn you up, Daddy?' she said. 'You know Punt's orders were to report back to the *McDougall* at eleven o'clock unless instructed to the contrary. Well, he *has* been instructed to the contrary. There's been an unexpected delay in loading the barges. They've been short of space at the S.O. ever since the high water cut the bank right out from under one of the docks. That phone call was to say that Punt and Rodney weren't to report till seven this evening instead of eleven this morning. We can't have this crowd hanging around all that time. Their drinks would die on them, no matter how many you gave them, or else they'd be looping before noon. Can't you get rid of them some way, Daddy?'

'Of course I can. They don't need to know that Punt's orders have been changed. After all, only the immediate family was going to see you off, because of the company's rules against visitors at the plant. Make your get-away in about ten minutes, baby, just as you'd planned to do. But instead of going out to the plant, go to Belle Heloise and stay for a couple of hours or so. Then come back here and we'll have a quiet lunch and a nice afternoon. These things do happen, but they don't add up to much in the long run. You'll still be on the *McDougall* before dark, and there couldn't be a prettier time to start out.'

'But I thought I was going to be on her right away. And the orders might change again. We can't go all that far from the telephone.'

'I'm sure Rodney'll be glad to stick around and listen. If the orders are changed within the next two hours, he can come straight after you. The company's bound to give Punt a reasonable amount of time to get on his boat. Don't worry, honey! Remember, I'll be here too.'

Madame d'Alvery's uneasiness became greater and greater as she listened, with her usual faculty for overhearing whispered conversations, to the proposed changes in programme. She was not troubled because the Standard Oil was grappling with difficulties in loading its barges; her concern centred wholly on Frances Belle and the girl's possible course of conduct during the delay. She was all too well aware that her granddaughter was not the sort of reluctant and unenlightened bride that she herself had been. Far from rushing back to her parents to escape her bridegroom, Frances Belle might insist that there was no reason why an entire day should be wasted when her honeymoon was bound to be so brief at best. Instead of repeating the now historic declaration *'Je ne peux pas me coucher avec ce cochon la! Il veut m'enlever la chemise!'* she was quite capable of saying, in everyone's hearing: 'Come along to my room, Punt – our room, I mean. There's no use hanging around in this crowd all day.'

Again, however, Madame d'Alvery's worst fears proved

groundless. Frances Belle revolted, on general principles, against authority and advice from every source but one – her father's. His she not only accepted but respected. She returned to her bridegroom and whispered to him again. Her vexation was at least partially under control now, her voice softer, and the distance that separated her from her grandmother greater; though Madame d'Alvery strained her alert ears, she could not hear what was said this time. But a few minutes later Frances Belle came over and kissed her, and Punt said good-bye to her very nicely too; then they made the rounds of the room. Frances Belle was not going upstairs to change her dress, because she was travelling in the same one she had worn in church; she was not tossing out a bouquet, because she had carried only a white prayer book. A shower of rice followed her as she went down the walk on Punt's arm, and the car in which they dashed off was decorated with the usual streamers and placards; but they made their escape very quickly and efficiently, and not more than half a dozen persons knew that there had been any change of plan. Neither Cresside nor Fabian gave any impression of wishing to speed their guests; coffee cups were refilled and fresh relays of waffles and sausages appeared. But within an hour or so everyone except Rodney Campbell, Madame d'Alvery, Merry and Joyeuse had left – even Sybelle, who at last had succeeded in getting hold of just the right electrician, and who had no idea of letting him escape her through lack of supervision. When she left she took Mrs. Randall and Miss Mittie with her. The O'Malleys had to get back to Alexandria, the Pereiras and Estrades to New Orleans. After these general departures, Cresside suggested that in view of the early hour at which Madame d'Alvery had risen, not to mention the subsequent effort she had made and the fatigue and excitement she had undergone, she might like to take her siesta earlier than usual, in one of the dormer guest rooms. But Madame d'Alvry was adamant on this point; she did not wish to be absent when Frances Belle and – she pronounced the name with difficulty – Punt returned from Belle Heloise. Her attitude towards the marriage remained unchanged. But no matter how fatigued or displeased she might feel, she hoped she would never be uncivil to a wedding couple on their bridal day.

The corners of Cresside's mouth twitched slightly. She knew what was passing in her mother's mind, and, though herself undisturbed, realized perfectly – since she also had no delusions about Frances Belle – that she must be prepared for almost anything. However, in exactly two hours the bride and groom returned, neither one looking in the least self-conscious, and reported that they had spent the latter part of the morning with Gervais, who had not been able to come to the wedding. He had been mighty glad to see them, for he was all alone in his office, with nothing much to do; in fact, he had urged them to stay and have dinner with him; but they had said they would be back in two hours, so they thought perhaps they'd better. Had there been any further word from the company? No, none at all, Rodney Campbell reported, so he would cruise along now; he'd be seeing them at seven. Merry and Joyeuse also announced that they thought they had better be on their way; the unexpected visit from Frances Belle and Punt must have cheered Gervais immensely: but still he was apt to get very depressed if he were left too long alone, and they had been gone quite a while now. Again the advisability of a siesta, this time in her own room, was urged upon Madame d'Alvery, and again she was adamant. She had never been inside the Standard Oil plant, she reminded her family, and she had always wanted to see it. There was no telling when she would be permitted another pass, the company was so strict about such matters since the war. She would lie down for a little while after dinner, but she would prefer to do so in France Belle's room; it would tire her too much to go out to Belle Heloise and return, and the stairs to the dormers were rather steep. She assumed that the others would spend the afternoon playing bridge. . . .

Again the corners of Cresside's mouth twitched, but she did not fail to sense Punt's wretched embarrassment or to catch the mutinous expression on Frances Belle's face. As usual, Fabian came the rescue, making everything seem easy and natural.

'Very good idea, Tante Isabelle. I've been looking for an excuse to stay away from the office this afternoon. One of the worst old windbags I know is due there for a long recital of his troubles with the levee board. Shall you and I take the youngsters on for a set game, Cresside, and lick the daylights out of them? Or shall we give them a fighting chance by rotating?'

'Give us a fighting chance, won't you please, Daddy?'

She cast one last resentful glance at her grandmother before the old lady took her triumphant departure. Then she and Punt set up the bridge table on the terrace, and the game began. It was by no means one-sided, for they were all good players, and soon their interest in it was unfeigned; though Punt glanced surreptitiously at his wrist watch now and then, the gesture indicated little more than meticulous attention to the passage of time in connection with his duty. When Madame d'Alvery, still obviously triumphant, reappeared, the others were all intent on five hearts, vulnerable, doubled and redoubled, and no one looked up immediately. She had come out softly on purpose, as she had long since learned that much could be gleaned from an unobtrusive entrance; nevertheless, she felt slighted by such complete absorption. Fortunately, Fabian became aware of her presence after a minute or two, nodded to her, and, making a warning gesture to indicate silence, smiled pleasantly. As soon as it was evident that Frances Belle would gather in all the remaining tricks, he rose quietly and went over to his mother-in-law.

'That gives the youngsters game and rubber,' he said. 'Frances Belle's right – all they need is a fighting chance. With that, they can take mighty good care of themselves. Sit down, Tante Isabelle. We'll be having coffee straight off – or maybe it had better be high tea. What time do you generally have supper aboard the *McDougall*, Punt?'

'At six, sir.'

'Then, if you don't report in until seven, isn't there a chance the kitchen will already be closed for the night?'

'I'm afraid there is. I forgot about that.'

Again he looked embarrassed and unhappy. A late and more or less fruitless forage, undertaken to supply his bride with some kind of a sketchy snack so that she would not go to bed hungry, would have been the last straw. Though chagrined at the necessity of his new father-in-law's reminder, he was nevertheless thankful for it. And Cresside acted upon it immediately.

'Of course we'll have supper right away. We've had champagne on ice all day – ever since we found you two were staying. And I know Carmelite has shrimp salad, too. We'll just reinforce those two main items. Let's eat right here, shan't we? We'll pull up another bridge table and put the two together.'

Champagne was Madame d'Alvery's great weakness, and as Fabian had contrived somehow to hoard a dwindling supply of Pommery Sec, she was presently in a much mellower mood. The little supper party progressed pleasantly, and by the time they had finished the *compote* of fresh spiced pears which represented the last of the reinforcements to the shrimp salad, Fabian forestalled Punt in checking on the hour, and announced that it was time they started for the plant. Then, ceremoniously, he helped his mother-in-law into the car drawn up behind the one which had been stripped of its tell-tale bridal adornment. But first he got in a word with Punt.

'You two get along by yourselves. Just park your car at the dock, and I'll drive it back and put it in my garage. Mrs. d'Alvery will take her mother back in ours. By the way, though, I hope you're not going to keep on calling her that! Do you call your own father and mother dad and mom? You don't? – good! Now get along – we'll see you on the boat.'

Punt and Frances Belle had already been on the *McDougall* fifteen minutes when her grandmother and her parents arrived. For a lady in her seventies, who had contrived to maintain an illusion of invalidism for more than half of her life, Madame d'Alvery had shown remarkable agility in getting up the steep gangplank from the pier to the *Slack Barrett*, from that across another gangplank to the *Amos K. Gordon*, and from that across still another to the boiler deck of the *McDougall*. But it was hardly surprising she had not been able to equal Frances Belle's speed in doing all this, quite aside from the fact that the girl had a head start. Before seeking out her granddaughter, Madame d'Alvery investigated the tiny open deck equipped with a few old-fashioned rocking chairs, the oval saloon with small cabins opening from it, and even peered into the kitchen. Cresside and Fabian, though satisfied with a more cursory glance, waited until she had satisfied her curiosity; then they helped her up the steps to the Texas. The door leading into the master's cabin stood open: the wide metal bed, narrow metal clothes closet, small table and straight-backed chairs, which constituted its entire equipment, were all visible. Frances Belle's beautiful little overnight case, its initialled *suède* cover neatly buttoned down around it, and her large square leather hat box stood on the floor beside Punt's battered suitcase. The muslin curtains at the small window, though rather frayed, had been freshly laundered, and the bare little room had the unmistakable atmosphere of recent and thorough cleaning. There was a bunch of flowers on the little table, and on the hooks attached haphazardly to the wall were some coat hangers covered with pink velvet and adorned with ribbon rosettes. Madame d'Alvery was conscious of the cramped conditions and the inadequate furniture; Cresside and Fabian were conscious of the cleanliness, the flowers and the new coat hangers. But before any of them could make any comment, Rodney Campbell, swinging out of the office beyond the bathroom with some printed forms in his hand, nodded to the group hospitably.

'Punt and Frances Belle are up in the pilot house already,' he said. 'Punt's taking the first watch – that'll let him off at midnight. You haven't met Ted Graham, the second mate, yet, have you? Well, he's there with them now and they're all expecting you to go up. Hank Martin, Punt's other assistant who generally alternates with me going down the river, offered to make this trip too, so that Punt could be relieved entirely; but he said no, he'd never been down the river yet without standing his watch, since he got his pilot's licence, and he never would. So instead I'm going to stay aboard all the time the *McDougall*'s in port, and he'll have that time free. Don't you want to see the office while you're on the Texas? Punt won't be down again until long after you've left, and from the look of things I don't believe Frances Belle intends to leave him. But it's all right for you to go in there and poke around by yourselves.'

Rodney grinned, and went off with his forms. Fabian, politely asking Madame d'Alvery if she felt equal to another flight of steps, and having been indignantly assured that she did, led her up the last companionway, after she had taken advantage of Rodney's suggestion that she should inspect the office first. Punt was already standing beside the wheel, his eyes fixed on the barges which a large crew of men were lashing to the tow boat. Another young man, with an equally pleasant face and alert manner, who was standing nearby watching too, turned at once to the d'Alverys and introduced himself before Punt could do it for him.

'I'm Fred Graham, the second mate,' he said pleasantly. 'I was sure mighty sorry I couldn't get to the wedding, but we've got a new baby at our house, and I don't have so much time with him and my wife. I knew you'd understand. We're sure proud to have a bride aboard the *McDougall*. Miss Frances is the first one, as far as I know.'

He looked at Frances Belle with a smile. She was already

perched on the large settee elevated on an iron stand back of the wheel, and had taken off her veiled hat and the jacket of her Shantung suit. Her hair was lightly ruffled and the blouse she had been wearing all day was rather crushed. She looked completely at home and at ease. All the impatience and vexation had vanished from her face.

'Isn't it wonderful up here? Look at that sunset, Daddy. I think it's the most beautiful sunset I ever saw – or perhaps it's just that we can see it better, without a levee or houses or anything like that in the way! And then the flares, and the lights coming on at the plant, and the Missouri-Pacific ferry right behind us! It's all just as I knew it would be, only a hundred times better!'

She slid down from her high seat to fling her arms around her father. The embrace was rapturous, but it was not clinging. She loved him better than anyone in the world except Punt, but she did not need him any longer. Now that she had shown him her proud place in the pilot house, she wanted him to go – her mother and grandmother too. Of course, she had been wishing all day that her grandmother would go, and on their way out to the plant she had made some very cutting remarks about the old lady to Punt. But there was nothing cutting about her manner now, because she was so happy. She did not kiss Madame d'Alvery goodbye with quite the same fondness she showed in embracing her father and mother, but she gave her an affectionate kiss just the same. Madame d'Alvery was so mollified by it that she unbent noticeably on the way home.

'I was not as unfavourably impressed by that boat as I expected to be,' she admitted. 'And I must say all those young men have very nice manners. As you reminded me, Cresside, the war has brought about many social changes. We can hardly expect a girl of independent spirit, like Frances Belle, to accept the same restrictions in her circle of acquaintances that I did. It may be just as well that she should not. Perhaps we were almost too self-sufficient at Belle Heloise in the old days.'

'I'm glad you've come to feel that way, *maman*,' Cresside murmured. 'I'm sure Frances Belle would be very pleased if she could hear you say so.'

At the moment, as Cresside very well knew, nothing Frances Belle's grandmother said would have mattered to her in the least, one way or another. Indeed, it would probably have taken a very strong reminder to make her remember that she had a grandmother. The glass enclosures of the pilot house had all been thrown wide open now, and a cool breeze was blowing through; it swept away the heavy heat of the day, and, with this, the last vestiges of the day's petty irritations and annoyances. The walls presented practically no obstruction, since only a minor part of these was not adjustable to the weather. There was a small wooden space at the right of the wheel, to which a clock, some fluttering forms and a few framed notices were affixed, but that was all. Even the notices were intriguing to Frances Belle, and the wording of one was especially arresting:

'ALERT!' – it said in bold black letters –
'Your Skill and Devotion Will
WIN THE WAR!'

Lettered less conspicuously, on one corner, were the words 'U.S. Dept. of Commerce,' and Frances Belle realized that such signs were probably distributed by the hundred. But she knew there was none taken more literally than this copy, or placed where the man to whom its message was intensely personal and stimulating would have it more constantly before him.

The flame of the sunset was subsiding, but under the darker skies the twinkling lights along the shores seemed all the brighter, and overhead the stars were beginning to come out. A searchlight was playing, too, in a long shaft of silvery radiance from the pilot house to the barges. Punt directed this towards the different places where men were still working below. Every now and then he called to them through a megaphone which he took from the ledge of the wide window before him, where it was conveniently placed, and they called back, cupping their mouths with their hands. But for the most part he seemed to know, instinctively, exactly where the light was needed most. In her fascinated state, Frances Belle watched this phenomenon and all the others about her with such complete absorption that though she heard the *McDougall's* whistle, as she heard other wonderful sounds which had suddenly ceased to be alien, she did not even realize that the boat had started until Punt turned to her, his hands still on the wheel.

'Well, we're off at last, baby,' he said in a tone of relief.

'Really, Punt? Why, yes, I can see we're moving! But very slowly, aren't we?'

'We'll be going faster pretty soon.'

'And nothing can stop us now!'

'No, nothing can stop us now. We go straight through to Chalmette.'

She drew a deep breath. But she did not try to talk. It was enough merely to sit on the high settee, watching Punt at the wheel, and beyond him, framed by the great rectangle of the open window, the river and the shore. They glided quietly past the city, and after that there were fewer and fewer lights as they went along, fewer and fewer sounds too. But somehow the scene became increasingly beautiful in the same measure that it became increasingly dim and tranquil. Frances Belle sat very still, content in the quietude, yet more and more alive to the fact that time was not dragging any longer, that one moment was crowding quickly upon another. Presently Punt's watch would be over. Presently he would leave the wheel and go down to the Texas. Presently he would turn out the last light in the little room and stretch out his arms for her in the dark. Then he would find her quickly and hold her closely and take her for his own. If she had not loved him so much, she would have been a little frightened because that was all so near now, and because strange poignant feelings were forking through her, coming harder and harder all the time. She looked at the clock on the wall beside the sign which said ALERT, and it seemed to her that it was not merely ticking any longer, but whispering too: 'In just a little while now, Frances Belle. In just an hour or two. You've always been a spoiled child, whimpering if you pricked your finger, sulking if you couldn't have your own way. Your father and mother aren't here now. Only your husband. That's very different. He won't stand for any whimpering and sulking. He's going to have his way.' Under her breath she talked back to the clock: 'I'm not a spoiled child any longer. I'm a woman married to the man she loves. I don't need my father and mother here to protect me from my husband. What's his way is my way too. How dare you talk to me about whimpering over a cut finger at the same time you talk to me about becoming Punt's wife?' Suddenly she felt that she wanted to prove what she was saying by going down to the little room on the Texas right away, so that she would be waiting for Punt when he came. If she did that he'd know she wasn't frightened, but ready and eager for his love. She slid down from her seat, and instantly he turned to nod and smile at her.

'You must go down to the boiler deck in the morning and look at the way we're lashed in between the barges,' he said. 'You can't see very well in this light. There are two directly in front and two on either side filled with bunker fuel for the Army and Navy ships. Those are all big barges. Then there are two smaller ones still farther up in front, at the left, filled with aviation gas. Our bow fits right in between the first barge in front and the first two on either side, leaving little open triangles where you can see the muddy water churning around our bow. I think you'd like to do it.'

'Of course I'd like to do it.'

'The best place to stand is right on the open deck where the rocking chairs are. You can go down there as soon as you've had your coffee. I'll send that up to you around nine, when we have ours the second time. I don't want you getting up at five-thirty. That's when the bell rings. Breakfast is at five-forty-five.'

'I'd love to have breakfast with you, Punt. But I won't get up then if you don't want me to.'

'No, I don't want you to. I have to go right back on watch, you know.'

'You don't get off till midnight and have to be back at six?'

'That's right. We have all square watches on the *McDougall*. Some boats have a dog watch, but we never have. We all like it better this way.'

So he won't come down until midnight and he has to be back here at six, she said to herself. *We'll have just five hours and a half together tonight, so we can't waste any of it. I must go down right away, so I'll be ready for him. . . .*

'We're almost to Estrade point,' Punt was saying. 'I'll show it to you when we get a little closer. I thought we might send a telegram to your folks, too, as we go by.'

'Send a telegram?'

'That's what old Don Ferguson, our chief engineer, calls the special blasts we blow just before we get to the Navy Supply Depot, which used to be the public cotton warehouse. You'll hear them tomorrow morning. He lives right near there and his wife listens for them, when she knows the *McDougall*'s coming downstream. Then she gets into their car and starts for Chalmette.

428

I've never known her not to be waiting at the Standard Oil wharf when we pulled in.'

'We have signals something like that on our plantation bell. ... When you and I get settled in our own little house, Punt, you'll have to send "telegrams" to me. I haven't had a chance to tell you yet: Mr. Tramonte said this morning he thinks he has just the right one for us – a four-room bungalow in one of his new developments.'

'Gee, that's swell. And you bet I'll send you telegrams. But right now let's salute your folks at Belle Heloise.'

He reached for the cord dangling above his head and pulled it vigorously three times. 'We mustn't forget to ask them whether they heard that,' he said. 'I've an idea your grandmother will, anyway. She's probably still awake, thinking about you, honey.' He looked as if he would have liked to say more if Ted had not been there too, but he had explained to Frances Belle that a second man always stayed in the pilot house, in case of emergency, and that they would have no chance to talk privately while they were there. She understood the look and she did not resent Ted's presence; she knew Punt would tell her the rest by and by. 'You want to start watching for the dredge below Missouri Bend,' he went on. 'You'll see it any moment now. It's out in the middle of the river, with a pipeline going into shore.'

'What's it doing?'

'Making the ship channel deeper. That fills in every high water.'

'I thought maybe I'd go down and get unpacked. I haven't even taken my toothbrush out of my bag yet.'

Because of Ted, she spoke with elaborate carelessness. But she knew Punt understood her, just as she had understood him, and she thought that probably Ted did too. He seemed to be the right sort.

'Not a bad idea,' Punt answered, also with elaborate carelessness. 'But wait just long enough to see that dredging outfit, baby. The pipeline's lighted, and the quarter boat. Then there are the range lights too, and a big blinking red buoy over at the left of the channel. It's a grand sight, and you wouldn't want to miss it. Look – there it is now!'

There the pipeline was to be sure, glittering like a jewelled chain slung half-way across the river. There was the quarter boat too, drawn up against the left bank, outlined by its network of lights. There were the range lights, silvery as the searchlight had been when it played over the barges, instead of golden like the jewelled chain and the network. There was the ruby-red buoy. Punt had been right in telling her she must wait to see all this; she looked at it with a deepening sense of enchantment. But finally the channel and the dredge were behind them. If there were nothing much to see after that . . .

'Run along, baby. I'll be seeing you.'

Frances Belle went down to the Texas and busied herself by putting her most essential toilet articles in the bathroom, and by laying out her white mules and her white ensemble of satin and chiffon and lace. She had not been entirely truthful in telling her grandmother that she did not care a hoot about bridal regalia. Secretly she would have liked very much to surpass the splendour in which Merry had robed Sybelle, and she could not suppress a slight pang now, because if they had only known beforehand that the *McDougall* would not go out until evening, she might have had the same sort of wedding as her cousin. But at least nothing could have been more exquisite than the filmy nightgown and the shining negligeé that she spread out on the bed now, white as snow, light as feathers, soft as her own delicate skin. After she had arranged them she stood for a moment looking at them raptly. Then she laid her watch and rosary on the little table, after moving this from its position between the windows and placing it beside the bed, and, for a moment, surveyed Punt's battered suitcase with hesitation. She would have loved to unpack it for him, to lay out his pyjamas for the night, his clean shirt and socks for the morning. But after all the suitcase was his, and he might feel she had no right to open it without permission. Besides, he might actually prefer to perform small personal services for himself; she knew her father did, but she had an idea this was because he was unduly sensitive about proving that he was able to do so. She must remember to ask Punt. It was stupid of her not to have done so before; and she must be sure to convince him, when she did so, that she had not hesitated because she was reluctant to perform such services for him. She was eager to do anything she could for him, no matter what.

She unfastened her skirt, hung it neatly over one of the padded hangers, then took off her blouse, stockings and negligible undergarments, extracting others from the ample supply in the square hat box, and putting those she had worn through the day in an

430

embroidered laundry bag. Then she started the water running for a bath. It was unexpectedly murky, and, for the first time, she noticed small enamelled signs over both the tub and the basin, announcing the State Board of Health had pronounced this water unfit for drinking purposes. She was afraid she really would not be much cleaner when she got out of it than she was already, but at least she would feel cleaner. She dumped half a bottle of rosy sweet-smelling salts into the tub, and then she lay in it a long time, forgetting that the water was murky, remembering only that it was cool and soft and scented, and thinking of why she wanted to be so fresh and fragrant.

At last she dried herself with one of the coarse clean towels hanging by the tub, turned out the lights and pulled up the shades. The same fresh breeze that had chased the heat of the day from the pilot house swept in through the windows now, and there was enough light from some unseen source to keep the room from total darkness. Instead it was merely dim and restful, like the river between Baton Rouge and Missouri Bend. Frances Belle was not as faithful or as meticulous about her prayers as Sybelle, and very often she found ready excuses for getting into bed without first getting down on her knees, and merely fingering her rosary while she drifted off to sleep; but tonight she really wanted to pray. However, she hesitated again for a moment. She felt that probably it was not proper to pray – just as she was. On the other hand, she did not want to risk getting the smallest smudge on her nightgown and she might, if she knelt down in it. Then she felt ashamed. The little room had been scrubbed and scoured; it was no mere figure of speech to say she could have eaten off the floor. But in any case, nothing so trivial as the possibility of a little dust should deter her from giving humble and hearty thanks on such a night as this. She put on not only the filmy nightdress but the white satin negligée, so that she was wholly and beautifully covered; then she knelt down and poured out her soul in thanksgiving, as she had never done before in the entire course of her selfish little life. She did not try to follow any formula. She said what came spontaneously from her over-flowing heart.

'Thank you, God, for letting me marry Punt. Thank you for letting me come with him on his boat, down his river, instead of making me go off to be a W.A.C. or a W.A.V.E. Teach me how to be a good wife to him. Because that's all I want, all I want in

431

this world. Just to be with him, just to belong to him. Thank you again for giving me this chance. I'll do the best I can with it. Amen.'

She rose and slipped off the negligeé, placing it across the foot of the bed again. Then she lay down between the cool clean sheets, and again a trivial concern troubled her briefly, as when she considered unpacking Punt's suitcase for him. Perhaps he liked one side of the bed better than the other; some people did. She should have asked him that too, because, of course, he would not tell her without asking, if she happened to guess wrong. He was much more considerate about the comfort of others than she was. But hereafter she would be considerate too. Not just because she had promised, because that was part of being a good wife and an agreeable woman, but because she wanted to, now that Daddy and Mummy and God had let her marry Punt and she had nothing else to wish for. And, after all, there was no present problem; she must get over on the farther side of the bed, because that was so near the wall of the little room that it was impossible to pass easily between the two. She would lie on the farther side, and he would get in on the side where the little table was. . . .

She reached for her rosary and held it firmly, moving the beads resolutely between her fingers, and moving her lips too, in the proper prayers, as she did so. But she could not think about prayers any longer. She had already said the one that really mattered, the one which came straight from her heart. Now she could think only of Punt, who would be coming so soon. She had looked at her watch just before she put out the lights; it had been half-past eleven then. She could not believe that less than half an hour had gone by since, so she switched on the light and looked at her watch again. Only a quarter of twelve? Why, that was impossible – the watch must have stopped! No, it was going, it was ticking away reassuringly and whispering to her, in the same way that the clock in the pilot house had whispered, only this time there was nothing menacing about the murmur. Instead, the little watch was saying, 'In just a quarter of an hour, now, Frances Belle. In just a few minutes. You made Punt very happy, coming down to get ready for him, showing him that you weren't afraid of his love, but instead that you were so eager for it that you could hardly wait. Now you've made yourself very lovely, with your fragrant bath and your exquisite garments. You're a beautiful bride. He'll open the door and look down at the bed, and when he sees you lying there, waiting for him in the dimness, he'll be happier than he's ever been in his whole life. Just as you're happier than you've ever been in your whole life. But presently you'll both be even happier.'

The little watch went on, telling off the moments. But Frances Belle could hear other sounds now besides its prophetic ticking. At first she was hardly conscious of them, because she was listening so intently to the watch; and though she slowly became more aware of them, they did not disturb her. She knew there were bound to be many sounds on the *McDougall* besides the whistle and the bell, and that most of these would be unfamiliar to her. But when she heard startled voices and hurried footsteps, she sat up to listen. Something must be wrong. Then the hurrying footsteps and the startled voices died away in the distance. Whatever had gone wrong must have been almost immediately righted. Of course it would be, with Punt at the wheel. And presently he would tell her what had happened – that is, if he thought it would be worth while, considering all the other important things they had to say to each other . . .

She heard footsteps again, slow ones this time, approaching her room. It was midnight at last. Punt's watch was over. He was coming to her, and she wondered briefly why he was walking slowly like that, instead of hurrying, as she had expected he would. Then she wondered why he knocked instead of coming straight in. It was strange that a bridegroom should stop to do that, a bridegroom who knew his bride had been waiting largely for him a whole hour.

'Come in, Punt. Come in, darling.'

'I'm sorry, Mrs. O'Malley. It isn't Punt. It's Ted. May I speak to you for a moment?'

She reached for the white satin dressing-gown and switched on the light. She was surprised and terribly disappointed. When she spoke again the joyousness had all gone from her voice.

'Yes, of course. Come in, Ted.'

He swung open the screen and entered the room. Then, for the first time, she was frightened. There was something about the expression of his face . . .

'Punt's had a sudden heart attack, Mrs. O'Malley. He slumped right down beside the wheel.'

'Where is he now?'

'He's still in the pilot house. On the settee. Rod's with him.

Of course, I ran for Rod the moment Punt started to slump. But the boat got out of control for a moment.'

'I didn't know what had happened. I'll come right up to the pilot house with you. Is there anything I ought to bring with me?'

'No. You don't need to bring anything.'

'I thought perhaps there was something special he needed when he had one of these attacks. He's never said much to me about them, though. You'll tell me what to do when we get there, won't you, Ted?'

She was already out of bed, knotting the white satin dressing-gown about her slim waist, thrusting her bare feet into the white satin mules. She did not wait for his answer, but ran out of the room and along the deck ahead of him. She could see Rodney at the wheel and several other men clustered around the settee as she went rapidly up the steps to the pilot house. Rodney turned towards her, but the other men fell back at once. Then she saw Punt lying very still, his face white under his freckles. She hurried to him and took his hand, but it fell back on the settee beside him with a little thud. She looked imploringly from him to Rodney.

'He fainted, didn't he, when he had the attack? A faint lasts a long while sometimes, I know. But isn't there something we can do to bring him out of it?'

'No, nothing. . . . A faint does last a long while sometimes,' Rodney said gently. 'Punt hasn't fainted, Frances Belle. I know you'll be a good soldier, for his sake. Because he always was. One of the very best.'

CHAPTER TWENTY-EIGHT

THE nearest place where the *McDougall* could put in was Donaldsonville. When it reached there, Donald Ferguson and Ted Graham went ashore immediately and divided the necessary telephoning between them. Rodney stayed with Frances Belle while they were gone, and at first he tried to talk to her a little. Then he realized it would be better if he did not. She required no soothing, because she was not hysterical; she did not even cry quietly. She simply sat beside Punt, looking down at him in a stunned way. Once or twice she tried to take his hand. Then she folded her own hands, and looked at those. Rodney knew she was not seeing her hands or anything else.

By and by sounds of various kinds began to come from the dock, and the chief engineer and second mate reappeared in the pilot house. Ferguson, who was a kindly-looking, white-haired old man, went over to Frances Belle.

'The ambulance is here,' he said. 'And we've got hold of your father. He and your mother are leaving the house right away – well, of course, they have left it by now. Don't you think perhaps you'd better go down to your room and dress, my dear? Then you can go right along in the ambulance. That's what you want to do, isn't it? You're to meet your father and mother by the station in Plaquemine.'

She rose obediently and returned to the little room on the Texas, dressing in the clean underthings and blouse which she had laid out for morning, and in the white suit and hat which she had worn for her wedding. She had not unpacked anything else, and it did not occur to her to do so now. But she did put the new velvet hangers in her hat box, and she lifted the flowers out of the vase on the table by the bed. When Ferguson came to see if she were ready, she spoke to him about the flowers.

'I thought perhaps I could take these with me, for Punt, until—'

'Yes, of course. You'd like to carry those yourself, wouldn't you? I'll have Charlie, one of the deck hands, come for the bags.'

'Is it all right for me to take Punt's suitcase away too?'

'Yes, of course,' Ferguson said a second time, rather huskily. 'I wish I knew some lady in Donaldsonville, Miss Frances, that I could send with you in the ambulance. But you see I live in New Orleans, so I'm not acquainted much around here, and neither are any of the others. If one of us could go with you it wouldn't seem quite so bad either. But, you see, until the company can send us another pilot—'

'I know. And I'd rather be alone, really. I wouldn't want some lady from Donaldsonville with me. And you are all mighty kind, but . . .'

He could see that she meant it. He went with her to the ambulance, and so did Ted, while Rodney stayed behind on the boat after saying good-bye to her in the pilot house. She sat very still beside the stretcher, just as she had sat very still beside the settee. The driver and his helper told each other afterwards that they had never seen a young widow who took on so little. Fabian's car was already parked beside the platform of the railway station in Plaquemine when the ambulance drew up there. He and Cresside were standing beside it, and hurried over. Frances Belle got out to meet them, but she did not cling to them when they put their arms around her, any longer than she had when she was saying good-bye to them a few hours earlier. Instead she asked questions, in a stunned way.

'What do we have to do next, Daddy?'

'We have to take Punt to a funeral home, darling. I think it had better be one in Baton Rouge. We've made all the necessary arrangements, subject to your approval. In the morning we'll have to go on to Alexandria. Of course, Punt's family will want us to bring him there.'

'Yes. I suppose so. I wish he could stay in Baton Rouge, but I suppose he can't. I can stay with him, though, can't I, until . . .'

'Yes, if you want to, darling. . . . That is, except for just a few minutes. Your mother and I'll stay too.'

'If you don't mind, Daddy, I'd rather not have anyone else stay. Not even you and Mummy.'

'Frances Belle—' Cresside began. But Fabian put a warning hand on his wife's arm.

'We won't stay in the room with you and Punt, darling, if you don't want us to. We'll just stay near, so that you'll know you can get hold of us any time. And perhaps you ought to rest for a little while before we start to Alexandria, so you won't be too tired when we get there. If you'd go home and do that by and by, Mummy and I'd stay with Punt while you were gone.'

'I don't want to go home and rest, Daddy. I want to stay with Punt every moment I can. I won't be too tired.'

Again Fabian quietly warned Cresside against argument, and presently they went on again. Frances Belle accepted without any protest all the arrangements they told her were necessary. It was not until her mother asked her an inevitable question, the next morning, that she spoke obdurately.

'If there's anything you want me to do about clothes, darling, I'm afraid I ought to be getting to it right away. There isn't much time, unfortunately.'

'Clothes?'

'Don't you want a black dress, Frances Belle, and a black veil? To wear to the fun— in Alexandria, I mean?'

'No,' Frances Belle answered abruptly. 'I don't want a black dress or a black veil to wear in Alexandria or anywhere else. I'm going to wear just what I have on to Alexandria.'

'But—'

'Widows wear white, don't they, sometimes?'

'Yes, but not—'

Cresside could hardly say: 'Not the same white they wore to be married in.' So she stopped. But Frances Belle went on.

'I've got enough white dresses in my hat box to wear for the next few days. I don't know what I'll be wearing after that or what I'll be doing. But I do know one thing: I won't be staying in bed for two years, and I won't be going around draped like an undertaker's window all the rest of my life. That's not my idea of the way to show a man you loved him.'

Cresside pressed her lips together. There were so many things that she could not say, or must not say, to Frances Belle. Again her daughter spoke for her.

'And don't worry, Mummy. I won't make that remark in front of *grand'mère* unless she drives me to it. And I don't intend to give her the chance to do that. She isn't coming to Alexandria, is she?'

'No, she isn't equal to the trip. That isn't put on either, darling. She really would have come if she had been.'

'Well, let's be thankful she isn't.'

'So would your Uncle Gervais and Sybelle,' Cresside went on, again feeling it was better to disregard Frances Belle's remark. 'But the doctor advised very strongly against it. However, your Aunt Merry and Joyeuse—'

'That's quite enough. I'd really rather it was only you and Daddy. But I won't say that either, Mummy. I won't say anything that will make you ashamed of me.'

'I'm not ashamed of you, darling. I'm very proud of you. Your father and I keep telling each other how wonderful you've been.'

They had every reason to feel continued pride. Nothing could have been more dignified and controlled than Frances Belle's behaviour throughout the next few days, and after their return to Baton Rouge she went back to her own room in a matter-of-fact way, unpacked, and put her belongings in order. There were no signs of the reaction which her parents had feared would eventually be inevitable. She did not collapse and she did not cry in their presence, neither did she refer, in any way, to Punt. She said she would rather not see any callers, and she did not eat very much, but she spent a great deal of time with Cresside on the terrace, and she went to the table as usual. In the evenings she talked with her father, collectedly, about inconsequential things. Then he came home one afternoon to find that she was not there.

'She went out a couple of hours ago,' Cresside told him reassuringly. 'I was glad when she said she wanted to, Fabian. It'll do her good to get away from the house and have some exercise. She's been shut up here with you and me for a good while now. She's been in her own room alone a good deal, too.'

'Yes, I know. And I know that part of the time she's been crying. But I know that part of the time she's been thinking things through too. She didn't say where she was going, did she?'

'No just that she wanted to take a walk, like I told you.'

He smiled, a little uncertainly, and after that he himself sat with Cresside on the terrace all through the early evening. He was still with her when Frances Belle came back and found them there together. She went to them and stood between them, putting a hand on the shoulders of each.

'Daddy,' she said. 'Mummy.' Then she stopped. Apparently she found it hard to go on, yet they both knew they must not interrupt her, but give her time to say what was on her mind, in her own way. 'I hope you won't feel too badly about what I'm going to tell you,' she said at last. 'I've just done something you may take rather hard, but it was something I had to do. Not just something I wanted to do this time. I've applied for enlistment in the W.A.C.S. If I hadn't been married I'd have had to ask your consent because I'm under twenty-one, but since I am ... Of course, I don't know whether my application will be accepted, or how soon, if it is. But I do think we won't be having many more evenings together. So we ought to make the most of those, don't you think so?'

CHAPTER TWENTY-NINE

NEXT to Frances Belle herself, none of the d'Alverys took Punt's death quite so hard as Gervais. Not that he had seen much of the boy. But he had liked immensely the little he did see, and it had seemed good to him, on general principles, to have a young and healthy male around again, on a family footing. He did not accord this status to any of the young men who so futilely pursued Joyeuse, partly because she herself declined to do so, even in the case of Barry Pereira, and partly because none of them, not even Barry Pereira, went out of their way to show her father any special courtesy or consideration. But Punt had always been very different in this respect; he made a point of dropping in at the storehouse the few times he had been to Belle Heloise, and spending a quarter of an hour or so with the bossman, talking about the war, the crops and the river. Gervais had already begun to feel that the young pilot was really one of them when the bride and groom came out to spend the morning with him after their early wedding. The hours they had been there then strengthened and cemented this feeling. When Gervais was told, early the following day, that the boy was dead, the shock was severe.

He was alone a great deal these days, and possibly this was one of the reasons his mind continued to dwell on the tragedy which had been so startling and which still seemed so futile. But aside from the fact that his loneliness gave him too much time for brooding, he did not especially mind it. The solitude was restful and he was still very tired. He had tried two or three times to go out to the mill, which was running at full blast now, but this had resulted in such devastating fatigue that he had been easily dissuaded from making the effort. Joyeuse and Sance came to give him reports about the progress of grinding, and he took their word that this was satisfactory; he did not even try to see anyone else connected with the work very often. Cresside and Fabian and Sybelle came faithfully to visit him, but this was usually after supper, for they were all busy during the day. It took Merry a good deal of time to do the errands, now that she was obliged to go from store to store in search of the simplest commodity, and Madame d'Alvery spent most of the afternoon taking her indispensable siesta. Gervais also rested after dinner, but not for long; he got up very late and went to bed very early, spending the intervening time in his office and lying down there. Nothing disturbed him. The old familiar quietude of mid-afternoon still descended on Belle Heloise.

It was during this interval that he usually wrote in his diary. There was not much to set down in it these days. 'Nights cool and pleasant. Days warm and fair. No traces here of Florida hurricane, which was, however, very bad. 11 employees of N.O. Port of Embarkation killed while taking tug to East coast, when all hands were lost in storm. This has personal meaning to me as I knew some of these men when stationed at Port of Embarkation. Sybelle naturally concerned over reports about Leyte landings, as Riccardo's division is almost sure to be in re-invasion of the Philippines. Sincerely hope she will get no bad news and somehow feel she will not. She certainly deserves happiness if any girl ever did. Little local interest in national political campaign, as re-election of Roosevelt and Truman seems virtually assured. Most of our people concentrating on defeating unconscionably long list of constitutional amendments without faintest notion of what's in them. Too bad we took all that trouble to write new constitution when Parker was governor, if two-bit politicians are going to tinker with it like this now.'

He had often reflected that diaries were queer things: if you had time to write in them at length, it was because nothing was happening; when you were doing things that were worth recording, you had no chance to set them down. He would not have bothered with the diary any more, except from force of habit; he did not suppose the boys would ever be much interested in a day-by-day account of the familiar happenings at Belle Heloise. Diary-keeping, like letter-writing, had passed out of the picture, probably for good. It had been different during the First World War. He had managed to write his mother regularly once a week then, though there had never been the same sort of demonstrative fondness between them that had always existed between Merry and Phil. It was certainly a long time since they had heard from that boy, and Vail might almost as well have left his infrequent letters unwritten too, for all there was in them, beyond the as-

440

surance that he was safe and well. Of course that meant a great deal. But not as much as if they could have received the assurance that Phil was making a good recovery and would soon be home. . . .

When Phil came home everything would be different. The house would not be sombre and silent any more; it would ring with laughter again. Joyeuse had a naturally happy disposition too; but she took life more seriously since she had become so intent on her work. Her father could not logically blame her for that, nor did he; if she had not stepped into the breach, there was no telling what might have befallen Belle Heloise, with all the male d'Alverys overseas. He had not forgotten the state in which he had found it after returning from the First World War, and it had never been hard for him to visualize Lucien Estrade's mournful homecoming. He himself had Joyeuse to thank that the plantation was more productive than ever; but in order to make it so she had sacrificed much of her light-heartedness and something of her femininity. Gervais could not help regretting that this had happened. In naming her for her mother, he had hoped and believed he was choosing not only well but prophetically. . . .

He thought of her mother, too, a great deal in these days. He and Merry were separated much of the time. The mechanics of running a household, far more complicated than in former years, occupied the larger part of her days, and he had not yet suggested that they should begin to share their old room again. He tried to tell himself – and he felt sure she was doing the same thing – that this was because he was still restless and that he did not want to disturb her; but he knew – and felt sure she knew – that this was not the real reason. He bore no resentment because she had left him when he most needed her, because she had not been wise enough to understand or generous enough to forgive in that great emergency; he knew she had never realized, and never would that Franchot's death had been an even greater blow to him than to her and that his subsequent desolation had been greater too. It was simply not in her power to do this, and a man could not blame a woman for the limits of her power, especially if he had been the one to try them past her endurance. He had rejoiced sincerely over her return, and he was glad to have her at Belle Heloise now; he still loved her dearly and admired her greatly. But some vital element had gone with her the night after Franchot's funeral, when she left the room that they had shared so long and so intimately, and he was afraid that the loss of this element was permanent. Evidently a woman could return to her husband more easily than his yearning for her could revive. At first, after she left him, this yearning had been almost intolerable; he had managed to subdue it, with grim determination and untold suffering; in the end he had been so successful that nothing could rouse it again. He looked at her with grateful eyes when she ministered to his comfort; he thought of her with appreciation as she went efficiently about her many tasks while he sat idly by the fire. But he wanted nothing else that she could do for him, and any pretence that he did would have been an insult to the memory of the sincere and ardent passion through which they had so long been united.

Possibly this estrangement from Merry was the greatest single source of his loneliness and depression, he told himself, as he sat alone in his study one mellow afternoon in late October, alternately scribbling in his diary and staring into the fire. He was not an old man, only a tired and embittered one; when he recovered from his weariness, when he regained a more normal and cheerful outlook, perhaps he would stop feeling the way he did towards his wife. With a fleeting smile, he visualized the probable difference between Harvey Lawrason's homecoming and his own. Harvey's would certainly be boisterous and lusty. That pretty little widow – darn it, he didn't mean that; he meant Harvey's wife, Pearl! – would doubtless shortly present him with a baby, maybe more than one, and Harvey would become a doting father, telling long tedious stories at family parties about his children's cute sayings, instead of enlivening hunt breakfasts with his tall tales and his Which-I-Gods. Gervais had known many a man who had married and begotten his first son – or at least his first acknowledged son – when older than he was himself, and Merry was still a beautiful and desirable woman. Perhaps it was still not too late to begin again as they had first begun. But even as he told himself this he knew it was too late, not because it would be physically impossible, but because it would be spiritually impossible. The cleavage between himself and his wife was too great to be closed by any mere act of union. Perhaps in time he would find some other way to close it, but just now he was too tired to try. He did not want to try. All he wanted to know was that his son was coming home again, safe and well. . .

He must have finally dozed off, in the tedious process of trying to think of something to set down in his diary which would divert his mind from such thoughts as these, for he sat up with a sudden jerk, roused by the furious barking of Maudie in the patio. She had grown up there, like all the puppies, and for a long time that pleasant enclosure and the vine-covered expanse of ground immediately behind it had constituted her world; then this had gradually grown to include the flower beds, the stretches of lawn, the pecan grove and the woods beyond. Now that she was getting old, her world had shrunk again. She seemed content to spend most of her time in the patio, as she had in the beginning, just as he was content to spend most of his time in one room. Men and dogs were a good deal alike, after all, Gervais thought, going to the door of the office to see what could possibly be causing this unwonted commotion on a peaceful afternoon. Then he saw Vail, with Maudie jumping around him as if she had suddenly gone wild, and he too felt a pang of fierce, incredulous joy, followed by a sense of suffocation and rigidity, so that for a moment he could neither speak nor move. After that he managed to hobble painfully towards the open door and to speak huskily.

'Vail d'Alvery! Where on earth did you drop from? Come here and let me see if you're real!'

'I'm real all right. How are you, Dad? Gee, but it's grand to see you. . . . Behave yourself, Maudie! I'm not going to run away.'

He went quickly up to the door and flung both arms around Gervais, half in embrace and half in support. For a moment they clung to each other wordlessly. Then Vail drew back a little, meeting the welcoming amazement in Gervais' eyes with smiling reassurance.

'Why – why – you never wrote us you were due for leave, Vail!' Gervais exclaimed.

'Matter of fact, I didn't know myself I had enough combat hours till I went to ask how soon I'd be able to apply, and found I was already eligible. . . . Let's come in and sit down, shall we? We might just as well get comfortable. I've got quite a lot to say to you.'

'I should think you might have. How did you get here, and when? I didn't hear a car.'

'No, I walked over from Hathaway. Aunt Cresside brought me that far. I burst in on her too. I did try to telephone her from New Orleans, to tell her I'd take the twelve-fifty, but all the circuits were busy, and after I'd waited for them to get clear there wasn't even time to send a wire. But she and I'd had a good visit before we started down the River Road, so she decided not to stick around while I was talking to Syb. She thought she ought to get back to Uncle Fabian as soon as she could. She says he misses Frances Belle terribly. Gee, that poor kid had a tough break, didn't she?'

'Yes, it was pretty tragic. Punt was a mighty fine boy, Vail.'

'That's what Aunt Cresside thinks too. By the way, she said to tell you she and Uncle Fabian will be out right after supper.'

'That's good. But she might have taken time to come over here to tell us the news while you were having your visit with Sybelle, and gone back for you afterwards. Fabian could have done without her that long. And couldn't you have wired when you landed, wherever that was? Then you might at least have had some of your family at the station to meet you, even if you didn't have a brass band.'

'Yes, she could have and I could have. But we both figured maybe you'd like it better this way.'

'I still feel you didn't get much of a welcome, and I'm sorry, because you had it coming to you. I know how dead the place seems at this time of day. You didn't have any more of a homecoming than Lucien Estrade.'

'I'll bet Belle Heloise looked mighty good to him, just the same, when he came in riding Minnie up the driveway, and it looked pretty good to me, too, tramping along. I really didn't want to be bothered with anyone, just at first. And now I've got a chance to talk to you. I'm glad no one's bothering us. I hope they won't for a long while.'

Unobtrusively, without asking whether he would like it done, Vail had helped ease Gervais into one of the big chairs by the hearth. Although the day was sunny and mellow, it was warmer outside than in, and a small fire had already been kindled. Vail poked it expertly, put on another chunk, and, lighting a cigarette, sat down opposite Gervais. Maudie immediately jumped upon his lap and began licking his face and hands. He looked at her, still fondly, but more critically than before.

'Why, you giddy old bitch!' he said. 'You've been having another affair during my absence! When's the new family due, Dad?'

'In about two weeks. I'm afraid it may be the last one, Vail.'

'Yes, it might, at that. I've been hoping to see her through

444

one more accouchement myself, but there's no denying she's already a lady of a certain age, so maybe I won't have the chance. Keep all the puppies, will you, Dad, or at least distribute them in the family? I wouldn't want to lose the strain.'

'All right, Vail. I reckon Sybelle would take at least two and Cresside one. . . . But you weren't thinking of puppies, were you, when you said you had lots to talk about?'

'No, of course not. . . . Be quiet, you wench, or I'll have to kick you out. This is the bossman talking.'

'You didn't hear anything from Phil before you left England, did you?' Gervais inquired. 'We haven't had a word except the letter he wrote a week or so after he was wounded.'

'Yes, I've heard, indirectly. That's what I wanted to talk to you about, Dad.'

Vail tossed his cigarette into the fire and pulled his chair a little closer, speaking with extreme gentleness. Gervais looked up quickly, with sudden fear in his eyes.

'You mean he's worse? You can't mean . . . But we'd have had some word from the War Department!'

'Yes, under normal circumstances. In nine hundred and ninety-nine out of a thousand cases, I suppose. But these weren't normal circumstances. This was the thousandth case. I can't tell you this the way it ought to be told, Dad. I've just got to do the best I can.'

'You can tell me whether Phil's alive or dead, can't you?'

'He's dead. At least, I haven't any proof of it. Nobody has. Nobody ever will have. That's why you haven't heard from the War Department. There wasn't any way you could be notified officially.'

As he spoke, Vail's voice had grown more and more gentle. Gervais continued to stare at him with mounting horror. Vail put Maudie quietly on the floor, drew his chair still closer, and laid his hand on the older man's arm.

'I know how horrible it is for you, hearing this, Dad. I know how much Phil meant to you. It's the hardest thing I've ever had to do, being the one to tell you.'

Gervais made a small, futile gesture. Then he gripped the arms of his chair and turned his head away, his lips moving, as if he were about to say something. At last he managed to speak, in a voice so low that Vail could hardly catch the words.

'I want to hear all you know.'

'Well, it was only by accident I found out even that Phil had been wounded. It's a strange thing too. If I hadn't run into Tony Dalton at the Town Hall that night it might have been a year or two before we ever found out what happened. Tony's one of the Air Transport Command boys that went through primary with me, but never made fighter. He was evacuating wounded from France back to England – I mean those who could sit up in a transport plane and wouldn't have to be sent over by ambulance – so he told me about Phil and how he had brought him to this hospital plant that wasn't more than about one hundred and twenty miles from our base. He said Phil was laughing and cutting up like he always did all the way across. Naturally, if Phil had been seriously wounded I'd have tried to see him right away, but we were due to be briefed for a pretty important mission that night, so I waited till it was my regular turn for a week-end leave before I went. Colonel Jackson lent me his jeep when I told him where I was going and why, and I took off.'

Vail reached down absently to pat Maudie, who had cuddled up beside his chair.

'Well, there really isn't a hell of a lot more to tell you, Dad,' he continued. 'Just what I found out when I got there, which was that one of those God damn rocket bombs had hit the hospital about a week before. You know they weren't like the buzz bombs. Those gave you some warning, but the first anybody ever heard of a rocket was the explosion after it hit. I saw the crater. It looked as though you could have dropped a city block into it. I don't know how many of the boys in that hospital were killed. Matter of fact, nobody knows. The record room was gone along with one entire wing and most of the official personnel, so nobody knew who had been in the hospital and there was no way to check. About all that they could do was to take a list of the names of those who were still alive.'

Gervais attempted to clear his throat. 'Then there is still a possibility—' he began.

'I'm afraid not, Dad,' Vail continued gently. 'Tony Dalton knew Phil. They were at Tulane together, and Tony couldn't have been mistaken. Just to make sure I looked him up afterwards and explained the situation. I asked him if there wasn't any chance that Phil might have gone from the airfield where Tony left him to some other hospital, and he said no, he was positive. In fact, he gave me the names of some of the other boys who had been with Phil, and I got hold of one of them among the survivors

446

and he told me Phil had been with them. I know it's pretty rugged to take, but you want the truth, and that's the way it is.'

Gervais, his whole body bowed forward, stared at the floor. Vail rose and walked towards the fireplace, where he stood with his back towards the grief-stricken figure in the chair.

'I'm afraid there's something else I've got to tell you, Dad,' he continued, without turning around. 'I didn't try to see Phil because I was sorry for him. I wanted to see him because I had an old score to settle. I'd been waiting a long time to do that. I thought perhaps he might be sent home on convalescent leave after he left the hospital, and I had to thrash things out with him before he got back here.' Again Vail waited, giving Gervais time to ask what his score might be, but when at length the latter spoke, he made no mention of it.

'You told Cresside and Sybelle all this before you came here?'

'Not quite so many details. But I told them the main facts. It seemed logical to tell them first, because I saw them first. You don't mind, do you?'

'No. That was natural, as you say. ... Your mother doesn't know yet, though . . .'

It was half a statement, half a question. Vail chose to interpret it as a question.

'No, she doesn't know yet. Syb said she was in town doing the errands. I'll tell her when she gets back, if you want me to. But I thought perhaps you'd rather tell her yourself. But I will if you want me to. *Grand'mère* and Joyeuse too.'

'I'd be very grateful if you'd tell your grandmother and your sister. I don't think I can talk about it much, for a while. But you're right. I'd better try to tell your mother myself. She's going to take this mighty hard, Vail.'

'It won't be any harder for her than it's been for you, Dad. Not as hard, maybe. You'll be able to break it better than I could. I've done a rotten job, I know that.'

'No, Vail, you've done the best you could. There isn't any easy way, or any good way, to tell a man he's lost his son, or a woman the same thing. But she's going to take this mighty hard. You see . . .'

He did not seem to realize that he was repeating himself. He struggled up, and Vail did not try to stop him, or even to help him, this time, as he stumbled towards the door, catching at the furniture to support himself on the way. For a long time he stood looking out into space, and Vail knew it was not the adjacent gardens which he saw, but the invisible cane fields. He was listening, too, not for some sound from the still silent house, but for the clatter of the mill. At last he turned.

'The day Franchot was born,' he said slowly, 'I was in the factory trying out a new set of centrifugals, and Selah came running out to get me. I knew it must be a hurry call, and I didn't even stop to wash the syrup off my hands before I went into your mother's room. She was suffering dreadfully, anyway, of course, and somehow the sight of my hands, dripping like that, was so revolting to her that she couldn't stand it. She'd always been very brave and very patient when she was in labour, before that. But suddenly she began to scream, and between her shrieks she cried out that she hoped to God no son of hers would ever be a sugar planter. Dr. Champagne told me she was hysterical with pain, that she didn't realize what she was saying, but she must have, half-way at least, because she told me afterwards how sorry she was. She may have forgotten all about it by now. I hope she has. But I haven't. It made a great impression on me. I wrote it down in my diary.' He half turned, glancing towards the bookcase containing the neat row of Affleck's Record and Account Books, almost as if he thought of looking for the entry in question. Then he seemed to abandon the idea and went on, 'I felt terribly, not only because I'd carelessly added to her anguish, though that was bad enough; but also because ... Well, maybe we Creoles are a superstitious lot. But when you get to be as old as I am, Vail, I believe you'll feel the way I do: that sometimes its dangerous to hope and pray certain things will happen, because very often the greatest sorrow comes with the answer to such prayers. Just as it has this time.'

He stopped abruptly, recognizing too late the tacit disclosure in his words. Vail put out his hand again.

'It's all right, Dad,' he said. 'I mean, I'm mighty sorry you think Mom may remember what she said, and that you do anyway, whether she does or not. I know how you must feel, and how she will if she happens to remember, because she did get her wish. But of course it wasn't a real wish, just as the doctor told you and as she told you herself. Naturally, I don't know much about such things. I shouldn't suppose, though, that any woman would have an idea what she was saying at a time like that. But on top of everything else, don't start worrying because you think you've given away something you didn't mean to have me know. I've known ever since I was nine years old.'

'But how—'

'We could talk about that some other time, couldn't we? Of course I'll do just as you want. But it seems to me all I need to say right now is that I feel you've always treated me as if I were your son, that no real father could have been any kinder to me or meant any more to me.'

'That means a lot to me, Vail, but—'

'And I'll do my best to carry on here, the way you'd have wanted your own sons to do it if they'd lived. It won't be the same for you, or for Mom, of course. It can't be. But the girls won't ever know. The world won't ever know. And after all, Dad, I love this place.'

'Yes,' Gervais said, still slowly. 'I know you do. And I've every reason to feel proud of you, Vail. Just as proud as I would have been of – of your brothers.' He paused for a moment, but he did not correct himself. 'This place has belonged to us a long time, though,' he went on painfully. 'And this is the end of a dynasty.'

'But it isn't. Don't forget, Dad, my mother's a d'Alvery. So am I.'

For a moment they faced each other silently and steadily. Then Gervais bowed his head before Vail's unflinching gaze and turned without answering, groping his way back to his chair. Vail spoke to him from the door.

'I reckon you'd like to be by yourself for a little while,' he said. 'I'll go along to the Big House and see *grand'mère* – she must be awake by this time. And if Joy isn't ready to lay off for the day, she ought to be. . . . There's a grand girl for you, Dad! And Syb's another – they'll both help us to hang on! I tell you this stretch of the River Road will really be something when Hathaway's going at full blast again, as part of Belle Heloise. And maybe Joy could wheedle Hackberry away from Charles Boylston. He doesn't really want to live there any longer. . . . No; I've got a better plan!'

Gervais still did not answer. Vail knew that he was only half listening, that his thoughts were still sadly centred on his lost son, on the desolate hearthstone.

'If Mom comes in before I leave,' Vail went on, 'I'll tell her you specially want to see her. I reckon she always comes right here anyway, though, after she's been out, doesn't she?'

'Before you *leave* – but, Vail, you're not leaving!'

He was alert again, and alarmed. He knew he should have responded far more wholeheartedly to Vail's grave and moving declaration of gratitude, affection and abiding purpose; he should have given a ready answer to the boy's one touching appeal, instead of turning away from him without a word. Surely, at such a time as this . . .

'Oh, not for good!' Vail was saying now. 'You and I've still got lots to go over before I take off again. But there's someone else I ought to see tonight if I can, and I thought maybe this wouldn't be such a bad time for me to slip away for a few hours. After that I'll be sticking around for nearly a month. . . . The jalopy still runs, doesn't it?'

'Yes, it still runs. Joyeuse uses it all the time – that is, until her gas gives out. I don't know just what the present status of that is.'

'Well, she won't be using it tonight,' Vail announced briefly. 'After all, it's still my car. Joy probably is fresh out of gas – it would be just like her to use all she had and trust to luck to get more – which she would. But I'll get enough coupons somewhere to take me to New Roads. I can pay them back after I get my leave allowance. By the way, I'm going to try to persuade Susannah Prescott to come home with me. I won't bring her here – of course I know you wouldn't want me to do that, right now. But Aunt Cresside said it would be all right to take her to Somerulos Street. You don't mind, do you? I mean, on account of Phil? Because I want to have most of my thirty days at home, but still I want to see as much as I can of Susannah. You must know how that is, Dad.'

He was not hurt, he was not offended, he had not misunderstood. He was only going so that Merry and Gervais could have the evening to themselves, and so that he himself could see his sweetheart. For the first time, Gervais looked back at the boy with something like a smile on his sombre face.

'Yes, I know how it is,' he said. 'And if you'd rather have Susannah stay here, after tonight, we'll do our best to make her feel welcome. She was very fond of Phil herself.'

CHAPTER THIRTY

VAIL started for New Roads assuring himself that of course Sue would come home with him and forcing himself to believe it. But this required considerable will-power. In the first place, he was terribly tired, and his fatigue in itself was depressing. In the second place, though he had done his best to treat the nature of his homecoming as briefly and lightly as he could in talking to Gervais, the only welcoming warmth of which he had been conscious had come from Cresside and Sybelle. It had been a gruelling experience to face both Gervais' hopeless broken-heartedness and the rigid self-control of his grandmother. Moreover, Joyeuse had come in from the factory while he was talking with Madame d'Alvery, and when she heard about Phil she had sunk down in a chair, bursting into unashamed tears. Her face, so bright and alert when she first caught sight of Vail, became suddenly swollen and blurred, and she sat huddled in a little crumpled heap, the trim lines of her figure effaced by her attitude of dejection. Presently she rose and, without speaking again, went off to the little room beyond the boudoir, where she had slept ever since no servant was available for night duty; it was so near that, though she closed the door, Vail could still hear her sobbing. She and Phil had never been quite so devoted as he and Sybelle, but their mutual lightheartedness and kindred tastes had nevertheless formed an extremely close bond between them. It was natural that she should feel his death very keenly and that she should take the tidings of it as she had. It must have been terribly hard for her to hear them. It had also been terribly hard for Vail to bring them.

He did not dwell on the latter fact with self-pity, but with the argument that probably the consciousness of the sorrow his tidings had inevitably evoked had a good deal to do with his own overpowering depression, and that when the various members of his family had been given time to adjust themselves to their loss he would recover from his sense of desolation. He hoped he was not lacking in sensitivity because he was relieved that he had missed Merry; he felt that one more interview like those he had gone through already would have tried him almost past the point of endurance. And yet, he now remembered that he had one more such interview ahead of him. If Susannah were stricken too, the spectacle of her grief would be the worst of all.

He was too essentially honest to pretend to himself that Phil's death was a heavy blow to him. His first feeling, in the aftermath of the rude shock he received in finding the bombed hospital, had been one of personal frustration and defeat. As he had forced himself to tell Gervais, he had not gone to find Phil out of concern, but out of anger, intending to browbeat him into signing a statement which would make it easy for Susannah to secure her freedom; and Phil had been mockingly elusive in death, exactly as he had been mockingly elusive in life. Vail could feel horror over the manner of Phil's death, but he could not feel sustained sorrow for it; he was too conscious of having been defrauded.

And now, at the end of this tortuous road, was he himself on the point of erring almost as grievously as the dead man for whom he had no charity in his heart? In his readiness to accept Phil's heritage as his own and to take Phil's widow for his wife, was he cheating too? Still trying to act and think with complete honesty, he did not evade the ugly question. But, despite his fatigue, despite his depression, the answer which he was finally able to give himself was reassuring and convincing. It was his own heritage he was claiming, not Phil's, he who really loved the land left by their common ancestor, he who was willing to work it, guard it, preserve it, no matter at what sacrifice. Left to Phil, Belle Heloise would have suffered the same fate as Trepanier and Esperance and all the other tragic places that had been abandoned on the River Road. Phil would have wasted his substance in riotous living, he would have sold his birthright for a mess of red pottage, and in the end only desolation and decay would have been left. And what was true of the land was true of a woman. Phil had never loved her either. He had only briefly desired her, and even his desire had been artificially fanned into flame by her declared fascination. What kinship had such a cheap and ephemeral feeling with the devotion of years? How could Vail himself be robbing the dead of a prerogative which had never been either treasured or possessed?

He had already achieved this saner viewpoint before he reached the cemetery, and he stopped there long enough to make a brief survey of the family lot. It was in beautiful condition, and in the care lavished upon it, which he rightly guessed Sybelle and Joyeuse were about equally responsible, he saw an ulterior motive, probably prompted by their grandmother: it must be kept fittingly prepared against possible need at any time. Well, he would do what he could to help in these few days he would spend at home. Gervais and Merry would naturally wish to have a special monument for Phil, and, with All Saints' Day so near, to expedite the erection of at least a temporary memorial. Possibly he could take care of that for them. At all events, he could offer to. He was sorry that he had not stopped long enough to gather some flowers before coming there that evening, but he had not thought of it till now. However, only the gesture was indicated. The tomb where the first Philogene lay with the Estrades and Franchot's small solitary grave were both already adequately adorned.

As a child, Vail had been taken to visit the family lot frequently, according to Creole custom; but he had always hated the Hathaways' prickly lamb and simpering stone mourner, which he was obliged to pass in order to reach the Estrade tombs; and from the time he learned that Sylvestre Tremaine was his father he had never voluntarily done so, until today. Now he stopped and looked resolutely at the two stones which completed the group in the enclosure so long avoided. The Misses Murdock had lavished a large sum of money upon these, doubtless feeling this to be appropriate, considering the handsome legacy, which they represented. But in spite of the elaborate carving with which they were ornamented, the lettering on them was brief; obviously the heirs, with all the eagerness in the world, had found almost nothing to record. Vail looked at this lettering now, realizing the futility and emptiness of the two lives, which had been so much more closely interlocked at the end than ever before:

Regine   Hathaway   Tremaine
daughter of
Roger   and   Emma   Hathaway
and   wife   of
Sylvestre   Tremaine
Borne   April   20,   1900
Died   March   26,   1929

———

Sylvestre Tremaine
son of
Hyacinthe and Jeanne Tremaine
and husband of
Regine Hathaway Tremaine
Borne November 9, 1895
Died March 27, 1929

Nothing else! No record of achievement, because there had been none. No quotations of sentimental or sacred character, because even the Murdocks realized what a travesty these would present. In life Regine Hathaway and Sylvestre Tremaine had been aimless, selfish and sensual; even in death they had not achieved anything that would give them character or stature. Vail wondered now why he had ever shrunk from a sight as meaningless as the graves of such nonentities. He knew that he never would again. He had reminded Gervais earlier that evening that he was a d'Alvery, but he had forborne from adding: 'As much of a d'Alvery as either Franchot or Phil. Their mother doesn't belong to the closed clan, any more than my father did.' The fact that he loved Merry and that she had deserved his love had prevented him from saying this. But it was true. And now the physical fact of Sylvestre's fatherhood lost all its significance in the vast pattern of the lives which it had been powerless to affect with any degree of permanence. . . .

Vail turned in at Hathaway a second time, unable to resist the yearning to see Sybelle again. As if she had been waiting for him, she came running out to meet him, and urged him to stop. No, he said, he was on his way to New Roads, and smiled. She smiled back understandingly; then, with her usual practical thoughtfulness, asked if he was sure he had enough gas; she had some idea how Joyeuse used it up. Well, he could use a couple of coupons. When she came back he told her he thought it would be a good plan if she could get over to Belle Heloise for a little while that evening; everyone there had taken the news about Phil mighty hard. Dad was completely broken up, and so was Joy. Of course, *grand'mère* never flinched; but some time, for that very reason, she would probably break, just as Mom had suddenly broken, in a different way, and this might be the time; there was no way of telling. He still hadn't seen Mom. If Sybelle could manage to be there when she got back from town, he wouldn't feel like quite so much of a shirker timself. Of course she could manage, Sybelle assured him. She had meant to go anyway. Poor Dad! Poor Joyeuse! Poor *Grand'mère*! Poor Mom! But still, as long as they had Vail . . .

'I don't rate as high with the others as I do with you, Syb. There's no reason why I should.'

'Of course there is. You ought to. And you will yet. You wait and see. Don't worry, Vail; I'll go right over.'

It was extraordinary how much better he felt after these few words with Sybelle. He was no longer absorbed by doubt and dread. He could see, and savour, the beauties along the way: the columns and galleries of the Pentagon, snowy and symmetrical beyond the glossy trees which framed them and the soft lights which illumined them; the high tower of the New Capitol, reflected in the still lake which gave the hospital on the opposite bank its name; the tall, twinkling units of the Standard Oil, amazingly imitative, in miniature, of Manhattan's skyline; the mighty arch of the great steel bridge, spanning the Mississippi, which flowed towards the Gulf with deceptive quietude; the level and serene countryside, extending on and on, all the way to False River; then, deep-set in the midst of its verdure yet fronting the glittering stream, one lovely and venerable plantation house after another: Oliva, Parlange, Austerlitz, Pleasant View, North Road, River Lake – at last Salome!

He turned in between the sturdy entrance gates and wound his way quickly through the cedars bordering the drive, towards the hip-roofed house, standing four-square behind its hedge of Cherokee rose. No street sounds penetrated beyond the spacious enclosure shadowed by pecans and oaks, and the privacy of the place was assured by the luxuriant growth of these trees. Yet it lacked the hushed and hidden quality of Belle Héloïse. Lights shone from the windows and from lanterns suspended in the gallery. Household sounds, apparently issuing from the kitchen at the rear, suggested that the evening's work, while progressing smoothly and pleasantly, was not yet finished. In the drawing-room at the front someone was playing the piano and singing an old song. Before he saw her Vail knew it must be Susannah. He had forgotten that she liked to play and sing, or perhaps she had never done so much in the old days. There was nothing remarkable about the performance now. Her voice was pleasing, but it had no great range or volume. Her fingers did not touch false

455

notes as they slipped over the keys, but neither did they bring extraordinary melody and meaning from the instrument. The whole effect was amazingly picturesque and slightly plaintive. But perhaps it was the old song as much as the quaint setting which made it so:

> ' "Love me little, love me long,
>   Is the burden of my song,
>   Love which is too hot and strong
>   Quickly runs to waste.
>   Still I would not have thee cold,
>   Nor too backward, nor too bold,
>   Love which lasteth till 'tis old
>   Fadeth not in haste." '

Vail waited until Susannah had finished the song before he went up on the gallery. He did not want to startle her or interrupt her, and he could see her quite plainly from where he stood beside the hedge. Astral lamps were placed on the small circular shelves at either side of the keyboard; they did not give much light, but it sufficed to reveal Susannah, and, beyond her, the dim lines of her parents' figures. They were listening to her, seated at the rear of the room, beneath some paintings with heavy gilt frames which faintly reflected the lamplight. Vail listened too, while he looked at Susannah with hungry eyes. Her face was lovely and serene, as it always had been, her hair still parted in the middle, as he remembered it, and drawn down on the sides so far that it almost covered her small ears. She had on a very simple blue dress, with a square cut neck and elbow sleeves, and she was not wearing any jewellery. When she finished her song she played a few disconnected chords, and then she rose from the piano and moved towards the front door, which led directly into the drawing-room, for houses of the earlier Spanish type, like Salome, were constructed without hallways. It was almost as if Vail had called her and as if she were answering.

'I was almost sure I heard a car come in,' she said. She seemed to be speaking to herself, rather than to her parents or to any visitor, expected or unexpected. Vail did not find it disillusioning, because there was a logical, instead of a mystic reason, after all, to explain her coming. He was glad this was natural. He had always wanted everything between himself and Susannah to be natural, just as he had always felt that everything between them was inevitable.

'You did,' he said, speaking very gently. He was still afraid that she might be startled. 'It's Vail, Sue. I've come home.'

'I'm glad to see you, Vail,' she answered, just as quietly. 'I've missed you. But not as much as if I hadn't always known you'd come some time.'

She moved across the gallery and gave him her hand. He did not try to take her in his arms. For the moment it was enough to have her come to him like that, freely and without fear, and to speak as if she too recognized the element of inevitability between them.

'I just came in this afternoon. I've got thirty days' leave,' he went on, holding her hand fast. 'I hoped you'd go back with me tonight, so I wouldn't miss any of the time I might have with you. I don't mean to Belle Heloise. I can't take you there just now. I mean to Aunt Cresside's.'

'All right. I'll be glad to go. Come in a minute and say hello to father and mother while I put some things into a suitcase. They'll be glad to see you too.'

'In just a minute. There's something I've got to tell you, Sue, before we go in, before you come home with me.'

His hold on her hand tightened. She waited, silently, for him to go on.

'It's about Phil. I never said those things to him I told you I was going to say. I meant to. I found out where he was and went there on purpose to do it. And I couldn't. Because he was dead.'

This time it was he who waited and she who tightened her handclasp. But she did not make him wait long.

'You can tell me about it on our drive,' she said 'That is, everything you feel like telling. I suppose you've had to tell your family already today. It must have been awful for you, Vail, to be the one to bring such bad news. But you don't need to tell me anything more than you want to. As far as I was concerned, Phil died a long, long time ago.'

Because she did not ask any questions, because she was composed, yet so responsive, he found it easy to talk to her. Indeed, the words came tumbling out with such rapidity that at times they did not form coherent sentences. But Susannah understood even when they did not, and Vail, more and more aware of her understanding, talked on and on. He told her everything there was to say about Phil. He told her about his own work, its dangers and hardships, its delights and rewards. He told her about his feelings for the future, what he wanted to do, and what he felt he must do if Belle Heloise and all it stood for were to survive. This time he did not see anything that he passed on the road; several times Susannah gently called his attention to a turn he had almost missed or a stop light he had failed to observe. He even went past the little house on Somerulos Street and shot along towards Nicholson Drive. As he halted the car, at Susannah's signal, and swung it around to its proper place in front of the old granite block, he laughed a little, half in relief and half in exultation.

'My, but that was a grand ride!' he said. 'Do you remember our first ride, the one when you told me about the wolf that was in love with a dog? I thought that was about tops then, but it was nothing compared to this. What it's meant to get all that off my chest! And to *you*. . . . How early do you think I might come in, Sue, tomorrow morning?'

'Whenever you like. I'll be glad to see you if you come early, but I won't be disappointed or disturbed if you come late. I think you'll find your father'll want to talk to you tomorrow morning. Probably all the others too. They'll be over the first shock by that time; there'll be a reaction. Phil meant a lot to them, but you mean a lot too. Syb's right about that and you're wrong. In a sense he represented their past, their tradition. But you represent their future, their new world. By morning they'll all realize that. I shouldn't be surprised if you didn't get away until late. I'll just sit and wait for you in your aunt's garden. It's a lovely place to wait, anyhow. . . .'

Cresside and Fabian had both stayed up for them. There were highballs made of Irish whiskey, which, by some freak of taste, Vail liked better than any other kind. There were also lamb sandwiches, which were his favourite. He had forgotten until the moment that he had not eaten any supper, but Cresside had not overlooked the possibility. After the others were all settled on the terrace, she excused herself and went back to the kitchen. When she returned, she was bearing one of the light lacquered trays she had bought in Mexico, and on it were milk and salad and a big piece of apple pie. Vail devoured them all with healthy appetite and heartfelt appreciation. While he was eating, conversation continued in an effortless way. They talked mostly about Frances Belle, who was at Fort DesMoines now, and who wrote from there regularly. They thought she was happy there – at least, happier than she would have been anywhere else. For the present, she was hoping for overseas duty; later on. . . . But meanwhile she was finding herself. . . .

'I've put Sue in Frances Belle's room,' Cresside said at last. 'Perhaps she'd like to come and see if I've thought of everything she'll need to make her comfortable. You two male creatures can get along all right without us for a few moments. But why don't you stay too, Vail? The dormer guest rooms are both in order. I opened one of the beds and laid out a pair of Fabian's pyjamas, just in case the idea appealed to you.'

'I think it's a swell idea. You would be the one to have it, Auntie. There's no earthly reason why I should go all the way out to Belle Heloise tonight and then back here the first thing in the morning, using up gas.'

'It was really your uncle's idea,' Cresside remarked. . . . 'Shall we go and have a look at your quarters, Sue?'

'Yes, and I think I'll say good night now, too. Shall we have a breakfast date, Vail? Nineish?'

'Eightish. I couldn't sleep till nine to save my soul. I've been on Army hours too long.'

'You'll shed them easily enough. Carmelite comes later and later, and we don't say anything because it really doesn't matter, the way we live now, and she's still the best cook in Baton Rouge. You surely don't want to get your own breakfast, if you remember the sort she turns out. I'm backing Sue against you this time, Vail.'

'The woman wins. She always does. I reckon. Good night, Sue.'

Again she gave him her hand, and again he realized, with fleeting amazement, that he was not disappointed because she gave him no more. Everything that was happening since he had found her seemed to be forming a pattern, which must be slowly and carefully put together, but which would be perfect when all the parts were in place. He watched her leave with no sense of regret. It was good to see her and Cresside together, friendly and at ease. He liked to think she was going to sleep in Frances Belle's room, next to Fabian and Cresside, and that they had wanted to put her there. . . .

'You ought to be turning in pretty soon yourself.' Fabian was speaking in his usual imperturbable manner. 'You must have had a fairly rugged day. But we might treat ourselves to one more drink first.' He refilled both his glass and Vail's, and settled back in his chair, as if he were in no special hurry to get up or to have his guest do so. 'Incidentally, while we're alone for a few minutes, there's something I might say to you. Not that it's particularly important. I don't want to dwell on it now, and I don't want to bring it up again, unless there's some special reason for it, which I don't anticipate. But it just happens to be one of those things to which we tritely refer as "something you ought to know".'

'All right, then. Shoot.'

'I don't want you to feel as if you were stepping into a dead man's shoes in taking over at Belle Heloise. If Phil had wanted it, which he didn't, you could have stood aside and let him have it, if that was what you felt like doing, for sentiment's sake. But he wasn't the heir to it. I bought Belle Heloise when you were nine years old. It's belonged to me, to all intents and purposes, ever since then. Naturally, I didn't want it for myself. I bought it for you. You're the heir to it.'

'I don't understand—'

'Well, there's no use going into all the details right now. But it would have been lost to the family if I hadn't stepped into the picture. And I did this with two distinct understandings. First, the understanding that Gervais should get out of politics, straight off; he didn't know how to play them, and it wasn't healthy for any of us having him try. Second, that you should always be recognized as his first-born, with all the rights and privileges that went with that. I talked the whole thing over, first with your grandmother and then with Gervais. I made it perfectly clear to them both what I was doing and why. Nothing was ever put on paper – except a few politely mendacious lines to the smart scoundrel who was the Governor of Louisiana just then, to the effect that the plantation required all Captain d'Alvery's time and that therefore he was resigning from the State Senate, the resignation to take effect immediately. We d'Alverys don't need documents among ourselves. We've got our faults, good and plenty. But I'll say this for us: we don't promise anything without knowing what we're doing, and we keep the promises we've made without anyone to tell us we have to. Wasn't it Will Rogers who wouldn't ever sign a contract, because he said a man's writing wasn't any better than his word? Well, that's the way we feel about it too!'

Fabian's tone had grown increasingly light as he talked; he had never lost the touch of whimsicality which had always been one of his greatest charms. His movements had become increasingly clumsy and difficult as he grew older; but somehow no one who was with him ever noticed this, because his face and voice were so attractive and compelling. Vail did not think of it now as Fabian braced himself against the arms of his chair and hoisted himself up by holding heavily to these. He had put his arm around Vail's shoulder before the boy was really aware that he had risen.

'Belle Heloise is yours,' he said with a strange triumphant tenderness. 'I know you'll never do anything to remind Gervais of this as long as he lives. But he's too sick and Sance is too old to carry on much longer without having someone else at the helm. I hope you can start taking over before you go back to France. Of course, Joyeuse has done a swell job. But, after all, running a plantation's a man's work. I want to see a man doing it. Your mother always wanted you to have Belle Heloise, and I have too. I'm glad I could save it for you. Now, you've only got to get the girl to go in it. You picked out the right one a long time ago. And I'm betting on you to do the rest, without any help from me.'

CHAPTER THIRTY-ONE

'LET'S not stay in the garden, Sue. Let's go up on the levee. I've done everything I need to in the fields and factory today, so I'm not on call any longer. And it's a mighty pretty evening.'

'All right. I'll be glad to go.'

She answered so readily that it was evident she welcomed the suggestion as a means of escape. She had been really happy on Somerulos Street with Cresside and Fabian. But here it had been different, as she feared beforehand that it might be. She had not wanted to decline when Vail asked her to spend the latter part of his leave at Belle Heloise; but she knew beforehand that she would feel like an inruder and an impostor in this house of mourning, and it had required all the tact and self-control she possessed to meet the ordeal with dignity and composure. There was so much she might herself have said about Phil and so little she could say, if his family were to keep the bright memory of him untarnished. Vail realized this, but so far there had been no chance to talk to her about it. He had been obliged to give a great deal of time to the plantation. Fabian had been right, as usual. Vail's hand was needed at the helm, and whatever he could do now would ease the burden of the others while he was gone, and prepare the way for the still greater tasks that must be undertaken after he came home for good.

The laboratory was now the acknowledged centre of plantation activities, because it was Joyeuse who directed all of these, while carrying forward her own chosen branch of the work with unflagging zeal. Vail had been tactful enough to visit her promptly in her workshop and so compliment her wholeheartedly both on her ingenuity in getting supposedly unobtainable supplies and on the remarkable administrative qualities she had displayed. Somehow she had improvised an extra clarifier out of scrap material, and performed various feats, scarcely less remarkable. Moreover, all the men working under her respected both her authority and her ability; it had been no small accomplishment for a girl of twenty-one to achieve such excellent results. The new dies had been a tremendous success. Housewives everywhere were asking for the sugar bags from which they could easily fashion centrepieces and aprons with no extra cost, while their small daughters were clamouring for the Belle Heloise dolls. The 'side issue' of which Joyeuse had made so light had already been a sound investment, and with greater production ahead was bound to become an increasingly profitable one. Vail did not overlook mentioning this in speaking of the other contributions she had made. She was pleased with his praise and showed it, but she was not disposed to have him prolong it or take more than her share of the credit. Sance really deserved most of this, she insisted.

'He did wonders with those new three-row flame cultivators, all spring and summer,' she said. 'I didn't know whether I'd better ask Uncle Fabian for them or not, Vail. Of course, last year they were still in the experimental stage and I wasn't so sure they would represent a sound investment. Fortunately we didn't have to do much ditching, anyway. But this year, with drought when we ought to have had rain and rain when we ought to have had drought, not to mention all the labour difficulties, I could see poor Sance was getting desperate. We could have got German prisoners all right. But he remembered what you said to him before you went away. In fact, it had sunk in pretty deep.'

'I am glad it did. Because I meant just what I said, and I feel even more strongly about that now.' He looked at her gravely, and she knew he was thinking, as she was, of Gervais' tragic breakdown, of the wanton destruction which had cost Phil his life, and of Orange and Neely, the two young Negroes from the plantation who had been killed in combat, one shortly before his division left Tunisia, one just after the beginning of the Sicilian campaign. But neither of them said so, and after a moment Joyeuse went on: 'I hated to see poor Sance so whipped down, and finally I decided I'd go and have a talk with Unk. But he beat me to the draw. He showed up here the very evening I figured on going to see him, and asked me, didn't I think we ought to give those new flame cultivators a try, and would three be enough to start out with?'

'Well, that sounds like him. I suppose he didn't even make the suggestion, either, until he had those cultivators parked right in his yard?'

'No. And, Vail, they've taken the place of one hundred and fifty hoe gang! We've cleaned all the cane and burned all the ditches with them . . . but you let Sance tell you about that. After all, that's where he comes in. Besides, he's been hanging around all morning waiting for you, and he won't get anything done today unless you give him a chance to tell you about those cultivators, and the wage and hour control, and the mule-headedness of the Draft Board regarding essential industries, and everything else he's got on his chest.'

'I'm going to look him up as soon as I've asked you one question and given you the chance to tell me it's none of my damn business.'

'I'll save you time and trouble by saying I haven't changed my mind about getting married any more than you've changed yours about German prisoners. Nothing – and *no one* – means any more to me than chemistry. Now clear out, will you, please, Vail, and let me get along with what I was trying to do when you came barging in here! It was fairly important.'

If only everyone on the place had shown the predilection

Joyeuse had for brevity, Vail reflected, rather ruefully, he would have had more time with Susannah. But he must let people talk to him in their own way when they had waited so long for the chance, and when they would not have another chance for so long again. If the men with whom he was to spend his life after the war did not feel they had his considerate understanding as well as his authoritative supervision, he would never make a successful bossman.

With this in mind, he listened patiently while Sance told him that the past year was the hardest he had ever been through, and all the reasons for this feeling. But when the overseer had had his say, Vail had his too.

'I know you've been through a hell of a time, Sance,' he said. 'I don't blame you for worrying over reports from the labour agents that all transient labour has been diverted. I don't blame you for feeling sore at the Government for leaving industries like ours so few essential materials. In fact, I don't blame you for anything. On the contrary, I think you've got a lot of credit coming to you. You've done a swell job in the face of no end of difficulties, just as I knew beforehand you would. But let's talk about some other aspects of the situation for a change. I don't need to tell you that the world's sugar supply is down to an all-time low. You know as well as I do that there's a very short crop in Cuba, due to an unprecedented drought. You know as well as I do that Hawaii's bound to have reduced production because most of the manpower there has been diverted to servicing the Armed Forces. You know as well as I do it's the consensus of opinion that all mills and fields in the Philippines have been destroyed. In fact, you ought to know all this a lot better than I do – details, I mean. You sure have had a better chance to keep informed.'

'That's correct, Vail. I also know that the sugar beet factories in Europe are mostly destroyed, and that the sugar beet production in the United States won't be more than sixty-five per cent of normal. But so what? Except that lots of poor devils are ruined and lots more people are going to be hollering louder than ever for sugar?'

'Well, just add that Java is still in the hands of the Japs, and that therefore every sugar-producing region in the world's been directly affected by the war. It doesn't give me any satisfaction to think about all this disorganization and destruction – I know what it means to the planters and the consumers who are up

464

against it just as well as you do, and I'm darn sorry for them. But I can be practical about the whole thing too. Because I also know what it's bound to mean to us. At least, I think I do.'

He stopped and looked at Sance questioningly, as if giving him a chance to supply the answer. But as Sance only looked at him with curious and respectful interest, Vail went on himself.

'Doesn't it mean that there won't be any more Government restrictions of acreage? Doesn't it mean that there'll be a ready market for all we can grow in Louisiana? Doesn't it mean that as soon as the war's over sugar prices are bound to hit their proper level again?'

'Well, yes, Vail, I reckon it does. And when you put it that way—'

'When you put it that way you can't help realizing we're bound to prosper, these next four or five years, come hell or high water. If we're not going to be in a position to compete with any sugar producers you can name, anywhere in the world, I'd like to know the reason why. You better be getting ready to celebrate, Sance. Happy days aren't here again – not yet. But they're coming mighty fast. We've got to be ready for them.'

After this conversation Vail noticed a gradual but unmistakable change in the overseer's manner. Sance stopped grumbling about the impossibility of securing essential materials and began to talk cheerfully about the elemental law of supply and demand. Vail knew that the time he had put into such talks and into personal supervision at the mills and in the fields was well spent; but this did not alter the fact that he had less for Susannah. It did not keep him from worrying, either, about other aspects of the situation on the home front with which he felt he could not cope so successfully, yet which he knew cried aloud for remedy.

The day after his return he had gone nonchalantly up the stairs, carrying his B-44 bag, and swung open the shutter door to his room. To his amazement and confusion, he walked in on Merry, who was sitting in her slip by the dresser, combing her shining hair. She jumped up with a startled exclamation and reached for a dressing-gown, while he stammered out apologies.

'I'm awfully sorry, Mom. I hadn't the dimmest idea you were using my room. Where shall I put my things?'

'Why . . . you'd like to put them here, wouldn't you, Vail? It was terribly stupid of me not to think of that . . . terribly stupid

465

of all of us. But our minds have been so full of Phil. . . . You see, after your father went overseas the *garçonnière* was closed, and then when he came home again your grandmother and I both thought that perhaps he'd like his old room back again. So I asked him, while he was still at Lagarde, and he said—'

'Yes, of course. Don't worry, Mom. Why don't I just take my stuff down to the Garden Room?'

'But you were born in this room! You've always slept in it! When you and Sybelle were separated, it was she who moved. You can't tell me you haven't any sentiment about it. *I'll* move this time! I'm just mad at myself because I didn't do it before you got here, because I ever let you find out—'

'Of course I've got sentiment about it. But hell, I'm too happy to be home at all to worry about the place I'm going to spend the few hours I'll be dead to the world. What do you mean, "letting me find out," for Pete's sake?'

She looked at him without answering, and then he knew. It was not the mere occupancy of his room which he had inopportunely discovered; it was the degree of estrangement between his foster-parents. Gervais had gone back to his 'old room,' but Merry had not gone back to her bridal chamber; instead she had taken possession of the nursery. If she had not tried to explain, the arrangement might still have seemed natural and convenient to Vail. But it was one of those many unfortunate instances where the lady protested too much.

'You see, your father still sleeps very badly, and it makes him nervous to feel he's disturbing someone else; and since there's only one downstairs bedroom in the *garçonnière* and he still needs someone near him – that is, since he did at first – we both thought . . . But he really doesn't any more. Please don't take your bag to the Garden Room, Vail. I'll just move across the hall to the Henry Clay Room. That's plenty near enough now. We can leave the shutter doors open. And then, with you here, you can call me if your father should want anything and you should happen to hear him first. . . . Unless you'd like to have the *garçonnière* for yours. When he said he'd like to go back to his old room, your father spoke of the fact that some day you and Phil would both be getting married, and that when that happened—'

'He'd offer the *garçonnière* to Phil? Come clean, now; isn't that what he said, now?'

'I'm making things worse every minute instead of making

466

them better. Of course he'd want you to have the *garçonnière* now that Phil—'

'But I don't want it. Not because Dad wouldn't have offered it to me if Phil were still alive. But because I want to keep on in the Big House. Because, when I get married, I want to bring my wife here. Not to one of the outbuildings.'

Vail put an affectionate arm around Merry's shoulder and seated himself on the big bed, drawing her down beside him.

'It was different with you and Dad,' he said gently. 'You wanted a little home of your own, where you'd be by yourselves. I can see how you felt too. *Grand'mère* and Aunt Cresside cramped your style, and in the *garçonnière* you could do things your own way. But it just so happens that *grand'mère* never has cramped my style, and I know she won't cramp Sue's either, when Sue makes up her mind to marry me. They get on like a house afire already. So that's that. But I still don't see, when you understand about my having sentiment for a room, and so on, why you and Dad didn't go back to the *garçonnière* that meant all that much to you. Suppose there wasn't but one downstairs bedroom, etcetera, etcetera? Couldn't you have turned the dining-room into another one, temporarily, for the love o' Mike? You eat most of your meals at the Big House anyway – always have. I should think you and Dad would have liked to have breakfast together again in that one big bedroom, the way you used to, whether you both slept in there or not. And supper in front of the living-room fire sometimes. Supper's mighty cosy eaten thataway.'

'I think your ideas are better than mine were, Vail. I wish I'd thought of all this too. I believe if I had, instead of suggesting the old room, that perhaps your father—'

'Well, you and he could still move into the *garçonnière*, couldn't you, if you feel like that about it? It hasn't tumbled down or anything – at least, it hadn't the last time I looked. Not that I care a hang where I sleep the next few nights, as I just told you. But if you're hunting up an excuse, you can say I do. You can say I barged in on you, taking it for granted I'd have this room – that much is true enough, anyway. And that afterwards I acted so disappointed you really felt—'

'Your father knows how you act just as well as I do, Vail. He knows I'd be telling a tall tale.'

'Well, maybe. But he'd let it pass if he thought you wanted him to. And I'll tell him myself, when I have a good chance, that I'm

467

not moving to the *garçonnière*, married or single, now or ever.'

Vail's attitude, gradually and divergently made known to Madame d'Alvery and Gervais by himself and Merry, gave satisfaction to both, but especially to his grandmother. She regarded him with increasing respect, and her liking for Susannah also continued to increase. Vail took over his own room at once, and though Merry hastily moved some of her belongings across the hall, it was understood from the beginning that Susannah was soon coming out from Somerulos Street to Belle Heloise, that when she did she would occupy the guest room immortalized by Henry Clay, and that therefore Merry's transfer there was only temporary, undertaken to give time for a permanent one to the *garçonnière*. Vail's suggestion about transforming the dining-room into an extra bedroom was accepted, and presently his foster-parents were re-established, apparently to their mutual satisfaction, in their 'own little home'. Watching, with affectionate solicitude, this new adjustment to an old manner of living, Vail was hopefully confident that in time it might prove a happy and harmonious arrangement. With characteristic male reserve on such a subject, Gervais said almost nothing to him about it. But Merry, having once involuntarily betrayed more than she intended to, seemed to find it easy to talk to Vail about the problems which had so far baffled her, and did so frequently and at length. Finally she asked him point-blank whether he had been able to 'see her side' and to understand why she had felt impelled to leave his father.

'Yes, I think so,' he replied, rather hesitantly. 'At least, I suppose men and woman look at things differently, and then, if they belong to different generations, that's another handicap. But I know you are absolutely sincere, Mom. I know you felt you couldn't live with Dad any longer when you left him. And I know that as soon as you felt you could come back you did.'

'But you do feel I was unjust to him?'

'You went away at a time when he needed you very much, Mom; you know that yourself. He must have felt that you were going back on him badly. But I know you felt he'd failed you, lots of times before that, and that finally he'd failed Franchot, which hurt you still more. Of course, I'll never believe he really did fail Franchot – we've been over that before, and you said you'd talked about it to Mr. Goldenberg too; so I hope we don't need to go into all that again. But perhaps, speaking from the viewpoint of an awfully young and inexperienced male, who doesn't even pretend to know anything at all about marriage, I might say I believe one of the reasons you and Dad came to a parting of the ways was because, in so many cases, the same things didn't seem important to you. I read in some darn book that for marriage to be really successful things had to. But I don't see why. Not everything, anyway. I should think there would always be enough basic things that were bound to, so that lesser things wouldn't matter.'

'But how would you divide the basic things from the lesser things, Vail?'

'Well, I've told you already that I really don't know anything about it. But I should think that if two people had the same standards about right and wrong, for instance, just that would help a lot. If they agreed on the way they wanted to live, the way you and Dad agreed about the *garçonnière*, I should think that would help too. And if they both wanted children, and got them, and cared a lot for them. ... Gee, I'm not saying any of this the way it ought to be said. But I don't see why it should make a woman unhappy because her husband wanted to go hunting, and didn't ask her to go with him, when she hated it anyway, if she knew all the time it would mean everything in the world to him to find her waiting for him when he got home.'

'It wasn't just the hunting, Vail. It was—'

'Of course it wasn't just the hunting. I used that as one example of what I'm trying to get across to you, that's all. I shouldn't think money would matter either, which one had it, I mean, or how much or how little, if two people had something else that mattered more, like a common interest or a common purpose. And— Oh, I could go on for ever, I reckon! But doesn't it boil down to the fact that most women set lots of store by things that seem trivial to most men, and the other way round? And that if they both can't recognize this and say, "Well, what the hell! am I going to let that interfere with my being happy about something that counts a lot more?" – why, then they seem to get into trouble, that's all.'

Merry and Vail had been sitting on one of the ornamental iron seats in Angus Holt's garden while they were talking, and as Vail made his final statement the door of Madame d'Alvery's boudoir opened and Susannah came out on to the upper gallery. She had spent a great deal of time with the old lady – indeed, she had felt far more at home with her than she had with Colonel and Mrs. Gervais d'Alvery. But she had learned to tell when her hostess began to feel tired and needed to be alone with her beads and her breviary for a while, and very often this coincided with the time when Susannah herself felt she could not bear to stay shut up in a stuffy room any longer, that she must have air and exercise and freedom, and – she admitted candidly to herself – that she wanted to see Vail. Now she had seized upon an opportunity which seemed to offer itself.

'I think I hear Vail in the garden, Madame d'Alvery, and there was something special I meant to say to him before evening. Do you mind if I run out and call down to him before he gets away?'

'Of course not, my dear. Go, by all means.'

Susannah ran to the railing and looked down, past the old sugar kettle and the brick-bordered flower beds towards the garden seat. The mellow columns of the portico and the moss-festooned oaks framed her lovely face and figure. Vail regarded her with a delight which he made no effort to conceal.

'Hello there! What're you doing indoors a pretty day like this?'

'Oh, I've been sitting on a cushion, sewing a fine seam. But I've finished my stint, and I thought I'd like to do something else for a change. Would I be in the way if I came down to the garden?'

'You might. This is a pretty small seat, and Mom and I are both using it right now, like you see. But if you urged me, I suppose I could draw up another.'

'No, don't, Vail,' Merry said, under her breath. 'It's time I went over to the *garçonnière*. I was just going to tell you so when Susannah came out on the gallery. You and she sit here. I'll see you both later. And . . . I can't tell you how much you've helped, Vail, or how grateful I am to you. But I hope you know. I hope you'll see for yourself, when you come home next time, what a change there's been.'

'I hope so too, Mom. Good luck! Tell Dad I'll be seeing him.'

He had not begrudged the time he had spent with Merry, any more than he had begrudged the time he had spent with Joyeuse and Sance. However, he was glad she was going to the *garçon-nière* now, that he was free at last to be with Sue for the next few hours. He had been able to accept the periods in which he was parted from her philosophically; but the longing for her and the need for her had been there all the time too. Now at last there was nothing more to detain him and fetter him, now at last his longing for her could be assuaged and his need of her could be met. Because this was so, he had spoken to her joyously, in asking her to go up on the levee with him. When she answered with such readiness, saying she would be glad to go, his own sense of happy release was intensified.

'That's good, because I'm mighty glad too. .... What about taking Maudie? Would you mind?'

'No. I'd like to take her.'

At the word 'levee' Maudie had already bounded towards the front door with hopefulness. Now she stood there expectantly, rolling her brown eyes, her beautiful head raised, her short tail wagging, her whole body quivering with excitement. Vail fondled her for a moment, smiling down at her affectionately, and then threw open the door.

'Oh, very well, Maudie, if you really want to . . .'

It was the time-honoured signal which Fabian had always given Belizaire, and to which the descendants of that great sire still joyfully responded. Maudie shot down the walk which was bordered in springtime with the scarlet amaryllis and the white yucca, and waited for Vail to unfasten the iron gate leading into the driveway. Then she was off again, through the crêpe myrtles, past the *pigeonniers*, darting across the road, wriggling under the wire fencing, scrambling up the levee bank. When she reached the ridge she stood still, her distended body silhouetted against the evening sky, awaiting the coming of her master and his other companion. Maudie recognized a rival in this slim, lovely girl, who walked with such quiet assurance beside Vail; but she knew that he wanted the girl to be with him, and his wish was her law and his happiness her aspiration, for her love was sacrificial. If there were twinges of jealousy in her faithful heart as she watched the two young figures ascending the levee, she betrayed this disturbance by no outward sign. Instead, by her immobility, she gave the ultimate touch of tranquillity to the peaceful scene over the west bank of the river. White clouds were lifted, plume-like, against the soft sky; on the farther side of the road, stretching endlessly off into the distance, rose the tall green shoots of sugar cane still unharvested; beyond the levee, the strip of smooth sand widened to form the verdant batture. Above a few birds sailed idly back and forth, and in the distance some ranging lambs cropped the clover. But Maudie was closer than these other creatures; she belonged less to the landscape and more to the lover. He remembered her and rejoiced in her even at this poignant moment.

'Good dog! That's it, stretch out and lie still. We're not going any farther right now. . . . Unless you want to, Sue?'

'No. It's beautiful here. We couldn't find a better place.'

They sat down on the ridge, where they could see the river on one side of them and the road on the other at the same time. Susannah gazed at them both in silence, and Vail, knowing that she was thinking of them too, and in connection with him, did not break in on her reverie. She was the first to speak, and that was only after a long time.

'You love it here, don't you, Vail?'

'Yes. I belong to it. Usually land belongs to a man. Here it's the other way round.'

'I know what you mean. I think you're right, too.'

'But I love you more, Sue. I said I'd never live anywhere else. But if you'd be happier some other place—'

'It's not a case of being happier in some other place. You ought to know that by now. I could have easily loved Belle Heloise too. And the road and the river and everything that goes with them – the groves and the cane fields and the levee and the batture. But, you see—'

'You thought you were going to live here with Phil. You can't get used to the idea of living here with me instead.'

'It sounds terribly bald when you say it that way, Vail. But – yes, I suppose that is the trouble – the root of it, anyway. I loved Phil so much – and then afterwards I despised him so . . .'

Her lips trembled. For a moment she could not go on. Vail put out his hand and took both of hers in his.

'Darling,' he said. He spoke very quietly, and he did not try to draw her closer to him. But there was an inescapable firmness in both his voice and his handclasp. 'I'm going to say something that may hurt you, but if it isn't said now I'm afraid it'll rise up and hit us later on, and I'd rather have it behind us than ahead of us. Phil never loved you. Not even the day he married you. He was flattered, he couldn't help being, because you acted the way you did. I don't mean you were forward or anything like that, whatever you may say yourself. I only mean that you showed how you felt, in the loveliest sort of way. But that you hadn't

472

really found out then what it meant to care for a man. You couldn't have, because love has to be two-sided to be perfect and complete. And Phil never found that out. He got killed before he had time. If he hadn't been, if there had been time, he'd have found out eventually that he loved someone else. He must have had it in him to love someone. But it wouldn't have been you – Nellie Pereira, maybe. And that would have hurt terribly, Sue – a lot more than what I'm saying now, a lot more than it hurt when you humbled your pride before Phil's casual acceptance of your devotion, because you thought you could love enough for two. . . . You're not crying, are you, Sue?'

'No, I'm not crying.'

'Yes, you are. Are you crying because you think I'm unfair, or because you know what I've said is true?'

She did not answer immediately. But when she did, though her voice was low, she spoke clearly and courageously.

'Because I know what you said is true.'

'Well, if you know it, can't you face it? You're made of stronger stuff, Sue – not just fine stuff, but strong stuff. That's one of the reasons I love you so much. Of course, there are lots of others. Shall I tell you what those are too?'

He smiled down at her, adoration in his face. She looked back at him, tears still shining on her long black lashes, but a happier light in her candid grey eyes.

'No – not just now, Vail.'

'All right – just so long as it's only postponed. Because I like telling you. And some day I think you'll like hearing it. I think some day you'll find out you and I are the same sort of people, Sue. Much more the same sort than you and Phil. Not that I'm trying to pay myself compliments. But sometimes people just fit and sometimes they don't. I know you and I do, or will, exactly the way I know you and Phil never would have.'

Again she was silent, reflecting, and again he gave her time to turn her troubled problems over in her heart. But he continued to hold her cool little hands clasped in his, and she was conscious of his strength and his control. However, she made one more protest.

'I shouldn't think you'd want a girl your brother didn't want, a girl who ran after him without getting anywhere.'

'I want the girl I know is mine, the one my brother didn't recognize as his because she wasn't. And you never ran after him.

473

Out of your great bounty, you offered him your love – all the love you could have given him or any man then. But it's nothing compared to the love you could give me now, if you would.'

'Vail, when you talk to me like this—'

'You don't mind listening, do you? You didn't know I could, did you? Well, I didn't either. I never talked to anyone like this before and probably I'll never be able to again. But I can talk to you this way because you really are my girl, and I've got to make you see that.'

The smile that illuminated his face with love when he looked at her was growing brighter and brighter. He pressed the little hands that he was holding so fast. They were not cool any longer; they had grown warm as he held them.

'No,' she said. 'I don't mind listening.' She spoke with a strange new note of shyness and surprise. 'I like to listen to you. I— You're wonderful, Vail, when you talk like this. You make me see things differently. Phil did hurt me, the way you said. I knew he'd have hurt me more and more all the time. And instead of hurting me, you—'

She hesitated, and he waited, giving her time to go on. 'I don't know just how to put it,' she said at last. 'Perhaps you won't be pleased with the only comparison I can think of. We've had an old Negro working for us at Salome, the surly kind – if he hadn't been that kind, we probably wouldn't have had anybody; but even with the labour shortage no one else would take this man on. ... Well, a little while ago he had a sudden illness, and of course we did what we could for him. We got our doctor to take the case, and we bulldozed the nearest hospital into making room for him, and then as soon as he could be moved we brought him to our house in an ambulance. Of course, it's only what anyone would do—'

'It's only what anyone ought to do, but unfortunately everyone doesn't. Not around here, anyway. Go on with your story, darling. I'm interested in it. I've always liked your stories, and this is even better than the one about the wolf.'

'It isn't much of a story, really. I was just telling it to you so that I could make a point. The first time I went to see this man in the hospital he was hardly out of the ether, and no one else was staying with him, so I did, for a little while. And presently he mumbled, "Miss Sue, yo' sure is a post in my life fence. I wouldn't hab stood up without you." I didn't catch his meaning

474

exactly, and I didn't think it mattered much, anyway. After all, he was only half conscious. But when he'd been brought back to Salome, and was all settled in his big clean bed, he said the same thing over again. That time I did pay attention. That time I did figure out what he meant.'

'I can, easily enough. So what?'

'Nothing, except – that's the way I feel about you, Vail. You're a post in my life fence. It wouldn't stand up without you I wouldn't even try to make it, because it wouldn't matter enough. It took me a long time to find out how much you meant to me, but once I did—'

She stopped again, unable to go on. This time Vail put his arm around her. 'There, darling. That's all I needed to have you say. You've told me all I needed to know – now. We can start out together on that. And after we've started we can keep on. It isn't going to be easy travelling, Sue, on the River Road. It never has been. It's been so hard that most people have given it up. Those are the people who made a mistake, because for a while it looked easy, and they were disappointed and angry when they found out it wasn't. They've tried to take short cuts, they've lain down on their jobs, they've been failures and quitters and crooks. But we're not like them. Sybelle and Riccardo aren't either. They're made of fine stuff, and strong stuff too.'

'They'd like to hear you say that. Sybelle thinks you're wonderful, Vail. She's prouder because you're her "litter brother" than she is of anything else in the world.'

'Nonsense! She's prouder because Riccardo's her husband and she is going to have his baby. Just the same I'm glad she thinks she's got something to be proud of as far as I'm concerned. I'm glad she still likes to speak of me as her "litter brother", even if it is an old Negro expression that highbrows look down on. She learned it from mammy, and Dinah's one of the finest persons that ever lived. The words have a special meaning when she uses them, too.'

There was a subtle change in his voice. For a moment Sue thought that something had sobered him, even while he spoke of being happy. But she did not know what it could be, and presently she decided that she had been mistaken after all. Then she forgot about it. For Vail was looking at her again with eyes of love, and suddenly something stirred, deep within her, that she had never felt when she was with Phil. She was hardly aware of the secret fluttering before it had become a swift, strong pang. This was not fascination, it was fate; it was not merely the yearning of the flesh, it was the soul's sincere desire. She caught her breath in amazement and incredible joy.

'What would you think of riding into town with me after supper to tell Aunt Cresside we're really engaged at last?' he asked. 'Aunt Cresside and Uncle Fabian too, of course. We'll tell Mom and Dad before we go, and *grand'mère's* got a present for you that she's waited a long time to give you. Oh, nothing much in itself. But it stands for a lot. But I won't leave you there. I'm going to keep you with me till the last minute this time. Then while I'm gone you can be getting ready for that wedding you always meant to have, seeing if your great-grandmother's dress still fits and all that. Because on my next leave—'

It was his turn to stop. At a magic moment like this, when they were both gazing with such bright expectancy into the future, the very thought of referring to anything connected with a sordid and tragic past was repugnant. But the necessity still remained, and, like the other reference he had known would hurt her, it was better to have it behind them than ahead of them.

'Of course we know you were never really married to Phil,' he said. 'And of course we know he's dead now, too. All the same, there hasn't been time to deal with that Justice of the Peace yet. A marriage can't be annulled in a minute, without any red tape at all. . . . If you don't mind letting just one person in on your secret, I'm going to ask Uncle Fabian to attend to that matter for us. . . . He'll understand. He'll help. There's nothing he can't do. He's always been just like a father to me. I've been mighty lucky that way, having him and Dad both. . . .'

He spoke sincerely and without reservation. He had entirely forgotten the tombstone in the Hathaway lot and its significance in his life.

'Just for added security, I suppose we also ought to wait till the War Department has made an official announcement of Phil's death. I don't know how long that will take, but it might be as much as a year – I mean a year from the time the records were destroyed. But that won't seem so long, will it, Sue, after all the time we've waited already? Of course, if it hadn't been for these complications, I'd have made you marry me the day I got back. Oh! I forgot! You told me I mustn't ever use that word, talking to you!'

'You wouldn't have had to make me, because I'd have wanted to do it. I don't care what words you use, though, any more, Vail. Words don't seem to matter now.'

'They don't, do they? But there's something else that does. I've always understood that when people get this far, if not long before, there's a very pleasant custom . . .'

He bent his head and she lifted hers. Encompassed by the river and its road, they stood, as countless other lovers had stood before them, indefinitely embraced. Maudie continued to crouch, patiently and contentedly, at their feet.

A SELECTION OF FINE READING AVAILABLE IN CORGI BOOKS

War

☐ 552 08410 7	THE DEEP SIX	*Martin Dibner* 6/–
☐ 552 08377 1	AWAY ALL BOATS	*Kenneth Dodson* 7/–
☐ 552 08409 3	THE SEA OUR SHIELD	*Captain W. R. Fell* 7/–
☐ 552 08447 6	COMMAND DECISION	*William Wister Haines* 5/–
☐ 552 08315 1	THE SAVAGES	*Ronald Hardy* 6/–
☐ 552 08168 X	MONTE CASSINO	*Sven Hassel* 6/–
☐ 552 08159 0	THE WILLING FLESH	*Willi Heinrich* 6/–
☐ 552 08221 X	GIMME THE BOATS	*J. E. Macdonnell* 5/–
☐ 552 08314 3	JOURNEY'S END	*R. C. Sherriff and Vernon Bartlett* 5/–
☐ 552 08356 9	THE FIGHTER PILOTS (illustrated)	*Edward H. Sims* 7/–
☐ 552 08396 8	FAITH IS A WINDSOCK	*Miles Tripp* 4/–

Romance

☐ 552 08343 7	FLOWERS FROM THE DOCTOR	*Lucilla Andrews* 4/–
☐ 552 08381 X	THE LONELY ONE	*Sheila Brandon* 4/–
☐ 552 08430 1	RANDOM ISLAND	*Alex Stuart* 4/–

Science Fiction

☐ 552 08350 X	FAHRENHEIT 451	*Ray Bradbury* 4/–
☐ 552 08361 5	NEW WRITINGS IN S.F. 16	*Edited by John Carnell* 4/–
☐ 552 08382 8	THE CITY AND THE STARS	*Arthur C. Clarke* 5/–
☐ 552 08401 8	A CANTICLE FOR LEIBOWITZ	*Walter M. Miller Jr.* 6/–
☐ 552 08431 X	THE MIND TRAP	*Dan Morgan* 4/–

General

☐ 552 07566 3	SEXUAL LIFE IN ENGLAND	*Dr. Ivan Bloch* 9/6
☐ 552 08403 4	LIFE IN THE WORLD UNSEEN	*Anthony Borgia* 5/–
☐ 552 08086 1	ENQUIRE WITHIN UPON EVERYTHING	*Reference* 7/6
☐ 552 08432 8	PUT-OFFS AND COME-ONS	*A. H. Chapman, M.D.* 6/–
☐ 552 07593 0	UNMARRIED LOVE	*Dr. Eustace Chesser* 5/–
☐ 552 07950 2	SEXUAL BEHAVIOUR	*Dr. Eustace Chesser* 5/–
☐ 552 08402 6	SEX AND THE MARRIED WOMAN	*Dr. Eustace Chesser* 7/–
☐ 552 98434 5	GOODBYE BABY AND AMEN	*David Bailey & Peter Evans* 25/–
☐ 552 07400 4	MY LIFE AND LOVES	*Frank Harris* 12/6
☐ 552 98121 4	FIVE GIRLS (illustrated)	*Sam Haskins* 21/–
☐ 552 97745 4	COWBOY KATE (illustrated)	*Sam Haskins* 21/–
☐ 552 98307 1	NOVEMBER GIRL (illustrated)	*Sam Haskins* 21/–
☐ 552 98247 4	THE HISTORY OF THE NUDE IN PHOTOGRAPHY (illustrated)	*Peter Lacey and Anthony La Rotonda* 25/–
☐ 552 98345 4	THE ARTIST AND THE NUDE (illustrated)	21/–
☐ 552 08069 1	THE OTHER VICTORIANS	*Steven Marcus* 10/–
☐ 552 08162 0	THE NAKED APE	*Desmond Morris* 6/–
☐ 552 07965 0	SOHO NIGHT AND DAY (illustrated)	*Norman and Bernard* 7/6
☐ 552 08105 1	BEYOND THE TENTH	*T. Lobsang Rampa* 5/–
☐ 552 08383 6	POSITIVE GOLF (illustrated)	*Gary Player* 8/–
☐ 552 08228 7	WOMAN: a Biological Study	*Philip Rhodes* 5/–
☐ 552 03282 4	50 YEARS A MEDIUM	*Estelle Roberts* 6/–
☐ 552 08323 2	DOVES FOR THE SEVENTIES	*Edited by Peter Robins* 5/–

General (*cont.*)

☐ 552 98178 8   THE YELLOW STAR (illustrated)   *Gerhard Schoenberner* 21/–
☐ 552 08038 1   EROS DENIED (illustrated)   *Wayland Young* 7/6
☐ 552 07918 9   BRUCE TEGNER'S COMPLETE BOOK OF KARATE   6/–

Westerns

☐ 552 07756 9   SUDDEN—TROUBLESHOOTER   *Frederick H. Christian* 4/–
☐ 552 08359 3   KILL DUSTY FOG! No. 58   *J. T. Edson* 4/–
☐ 552 08360 7   SLAUGHTER'S WAY No. 59   *J. T. Edson* 4/–
☐ 552 08400 X   THE RIO HONDO WAR No. 60   *J. T. Edson* 4/–
☐ 552 08399 2   POINT OF CONTACT   *J. T. Edson* 4/–
☐ 552 08262 7   BUTCH CASSIDY AND THE SUNDANCE KID
  William Goldman 4/–
☐ 552 08270 8   MACKENNA'S GOLD   *Will Henry* 4/–
☐ 552 08380 1   THE MAN CALLED NOON   *Louis L'Amour* 4/–
☐ 552 08387 9   MUSTANG MAN   *Louis L'Amour* 4/–
☐ 552 08388 7   KID RODELO   *Louis L'Amour* 4/–

Crime

☐ 552 08272 4   PSYCHO   *Robert Bloch* 4/–
☐ 552 08397 6   DARK OF THE MOON   *John Dickson Carr* 4/–
☐ 552 08316 X   FOUNDER MEMBER   *John Gardner* 5/–
☐ 552 08398 4   TOUCHFEATHER   *Jimmy Sangster* 4/–
☐ 552 08436 0   MY GUN IS QUICK   *Mickey Spillane* 4/–
☐ 552 08223 6   THE DELTA FACTOR   *Mickey Spillane* 4/–
☐ 552 08426 3   THE BELTING INHERITANCE   *Julian Symons* 4/–
☐ 552 08425 5   THE SHADOW GAME   *Michael Underwood* 4/–

*All these books are available at your bookshop or newsagent; or can be ordered direct
from the publisher. Just tick the titles you want and fill in the form below.*

———————————————————————————————————————

CORGI BOOKS. Cash Sales Department, P.O. Box 11, Falmouth, Cornwall.

Please send cheque or postal order. No currency, and allow 6d. per book to cover the
cost of postage and packing in U.K., 9d. per copy overseas.

NAME...

ADDRESS ....

(MAY '70)..